DATE DUE

An Impersonation of Angels

An Impersonation
of Angels A BIOGRAPHY

OF JEAN COCTEAU

Frederick Brown

NEW YORK / THE VIKING PRESS

Copyright © 1968 by Frederick Brown

All rights reserved

First published in 1968 by The Viking Press, Inc.
625 Madison Avenue, New York, N.Y. 10022

Published simultaneously in Canada by
The Macmillan Company of Canada Limited

Library of Congress catalog card number: 68-22873

Printed in U.S.A. by Vail-Ballou Press, Inc.

For Enid

Acknowledgments

Although I have relied chiefly on published sources, this biography is based in part on numerous conversations with people who knew Cocteau, and on letters many of them were kind enough to place at my disposal. For their assistance I should like to thank Nora Auric, Pierre Bertin, Denise Bourdet, Madame Paul Cocteau, Jean Denoël, Edouard Dermit, André Fraigneau, Louis Gautier-Vignal, Françoise Gilot, Valentine Hugo, Élise Jouhandeau, Philippe Jullian, Jean-Jacques Kihm, Raoul Leven, William Liebermann, James Lord, Jean Marais, Claude Mauriac, François Mauriac, Bernard Minoret, Marianne Oswald, Simone Porché, Jacques Porel, Man Ray, M. Riondy of the RTF, Maurice Saillet, Sherban Sidéry, Roger Stéphane, Glenway Wescott, Monroe Wheeler, Jean Wiener, Francine Weisweiller, Jeannine Worms, and Maria Yakovleff.

I owe special debts of gratitude to John Anderson; to François Chapon, librarian of the Bibliothèque Doucet in Paris; to Roger Shattuck; to my editors Catharine Carver and Corlies Smith; and to John H. Field and Enid Harlow, who were helpful to me in more ways than I can enumerate.

F. B.

Contents

Illustrations

[ix]

An Impersonation of Angels

1

L'Enfance Terrible

Rumanians were very much in evidence on the Right Bank of Paris during the *belle époque*, but none more so than the actor Édouard de Max, whose name evoked visions of neurotic ceremonies and dark, Byzantine delights. He had the appearance of a displaced Greek god whose chief employment, now that European society had turned to scientific cults, was the elaboration of his own person. Below a disorderly mass of bluish-black hair, his face advanced along an aquiline nose, collapsing unexpectedly into a mere slit of a mouth, then reaffirming itself at the last moment in a strong chin, which doubled with age. He is described as having had a "glaucous" complexion, owing perhaps to his green eyes, whose feline slant he emphasized with bister. The lids, humid and languorous, remained perpetually half-closed, like an owl's. On his fingers he wore eight rings, in imitation perhaps of Sarah Bernhardt, whose career, briefly, in the early 1900s, coincided with his own, giving rise to legendary quarrels and performances. She played Hermione to his Orestes in Racine's *Andromaque*. De Max had a talent for wild, romantic gyrations and, in mad scenes, hovering somewhere between diction and song, he would purposely revert to the phlegmy, guttural French of a Rumanian. Thus, by looks and native disposition, he was singularly gifted to portray such painted Lords of Sodom, such lunatic princes and monsters of cruelty as Nero and Heliogabalus. Young André Gide dedicated his play *Saul* to him.

De Max behaved with the same panache offstage. His addiction to opium, and to ephebes, was no secret. If he happened to be at the Café Régence, his table swarmed with pretty boys hanging on his every word. "Édouard de Max paid us a visit," wrote Colette, "escorted by adolescents, like a god escorted by nymphs. He flattered them with his eyes, scolded them with his voice; for them he has nothing but tutelary indifference, hauteur, melancholy." Some idea of his flat on the Rue Caumartin may be gained from photographs of Sarah Bernhardt's: velours hangings, deep ottomans, gazelle horns, Persian carpets, canopies, and innumerable cushions forming a kind of Victorian translation of the Thousand and One Nights. De Max lived in fact amidst the bric-a-brac of his roles. Heliogabalus' diadem served as a chandelier, Nero's throne as an armchair. His Spanish Gothic chests had been props for *Hernani*. He bathed in what passed for a Pompeian tub, wrote his letters in purple ink drawn from a porcelain toad, and dried his purple prose with gold powder. At home he dressed in the costume of Hippolytus.

Clothing for this unrepentant narcissist served less to mask than to expose his person, to give it an artificial nudity. Before his performances he would parade through the Bois de Boulogne wearing a velvet suit with pearl-gray homburg, pearl-gray boots, and pearl-gray powder on his chin, and afterward he would drive to the theatre in a pearl-gray "electric." De Max's style was a variation of Bernhardt's: [1] being weirdly eclectic or weirdly uniform, coercing the ordinary stuff of life into a flamboyant monogram, constantly rehearsing one's legend, keeping alive and mysterious with acts, words, masks of calculated exorbitance. Clothing could be understood as the apparatus of freedom; and the free, those *anges maudits* of 1900—actresses and courtesans—set the style. At night the gaslit boulevards, filled with ladies attending the theatre in boas, plumed astrakhans, and leg-o'-mutton sleeves, trailing expanses of silk, looked like a sanctuary for birds of paradise.

If de Max was adored in Paris, in the provinces he was fetishized. When the Maecenas of Béziers, Castelbon de Beauxhostes, invited him to play Prometheus in the town's Roman amphitheatre, de Max had his body shaved for a scene in which he lay, all but naked, on a rock, defiantly gesturing at the heavens. The next day tufts of hair were on sale at the local barber shop.

1. And of the English "esthetes," pearl gray being a fashionable color in their world, as reflected by Jacques-Émile Blanche's portrait of Aubrey Beardsley, "Symphony in Pearl-Grey."

In 1907 Robert d'Humières held a masquerade in his theatre on the Boulevard des Batignolles, the Théâtre des Arts where Oscar Wilde's *Lady Windermere's Fan* was to enjoy a long run. De Max came wearing a Napoleonic eagle on his head and a Bedouin veil. Moreover, he brought his inevitable complement of boys. Two were dressed as Arcadian shepherds. The third appeared as Heliogabalus, his hair teased into dyed red ringlets over his forehead and surmounted by a tiara; he wore a pearl-encrusted cloak, de Max's own rings, and sandals with thongs encircling his thin calves. Even Bernhardt deplored the sight of the group. De Max was asked to leave. His boys were washed of their makeup and put to bed.

Thus Jean Cocteau, as Heliogabalus, made his debut at seventeen, and, fatally, in the persona of a spiritual father. De Max's saturnine face will recur in Cocteau's life, under different names, in the random incarnations of a beauty he wished for himself so desperately as to use its Orphic profile as a signature.

He was born Jean Maurice Eugène Clément Cocteau on July 5, 1889, several months after the Eiffel Tower reached its summit, several months before Joseph Oller founded the Moulin Rouge. Actually, Cocteau was brought up in the vicinity of Pigalle, on the Rue La Bruyère quite near its intersection with the Rue Blanche. The street consisted of elegant town houses, an entire row of them owned by Daniel Osiris, the Jewish financial wizard whose lowly beginnings as a bookmaker's assistant did not prevent him in later life from restoring Napoleon's Malmaison, or endowing the French Academy with the Osiris Prize. Léon Say, Minister of Finance under Thiers, Jules Grévy the President, and before him Hector Berlioz had been previous occupants of the Lecomte house, which lay at the upper reaches of a stolid, bourgeois isle whose main line was the Boulevard Haussmann. From the back windows of his grandfather's town house at number 45, Cocteau could clearly see the Église de la Trinité below, with nothing between but villas and sward. Bohemia was still segregated north of Boulevard Clichy. As late as 1907, when Apollinaire took lodgings on Rue Léonie just around the corner from Rue La Bruyère, it surprised his friends that he should have chosen such a bourgeois neighborhood. Cocteau, who once portrayed himself as a bourgeois chimera (*"fils d'une famille bourgeoise, je suis un monstre bourgeois"*) lived, from the outset, on Montmartre, but not in it.

His father, Georges Cocteau, was a gentle, withdrawn man, so much the soul of discretion that no one can recall him clearly. He worked as an *agent de change* or broker in his father-in-law's firm. His sole passion, however, was painting; in fact, Jean Cocteau as a boy spent hours seated near his father, whom he remembered later chiefly in connection with the odor of oil paints. Photographs of Georges Cocteau show a slightly built figure, nearly shoulderless, possessing a weary, equine face. He died with the century, in 1899, aged forty-nine, having lived very much against his grain. Cocteau confided to friends that his father had committed suicide (though he would often rectify his past, and others', to suit his legend, deferring, for example, his date of birth by three years so as to appear all the more a child prodigy).

His mother, an elegant woman with the bearing of a marquise, was born Eugénie Lecomte. The Lecomtes, according to Cocteau, had been celebrated *ébénistes,* or cabinet makers, under the *ancien régime.* During the nineteenth century their family tree grew well above its artisanal roots, ramifying through the diplomatic corps, the military establishment, and finance. One of Cocteau's maternal uncles, Raymond Lecomte, occupied a series of high diplomatic posts, including one in Berlin, where he enjoyed such favor with Kaiser Wilhelm II and his homosexual camarilla (Count Moltke, Prince Eulenburg, Count Lynar, and Count Hohenau) as narrowly to miss bringing about a Franco-German entente. Exposed by the journalist Maximilian Harden, who saw the Germany of Bismarck degenerating into a government of choir boys, Lecomte was kicked upstairs by the Quai d'Orsay and served for some years as ambassador to Teheran and Cairo. In its loftier altitudes, the Lecomte family could afford the luxury of art. Raymond's passion for Greek and Byzantine statuary derived from his father, Eugène Lecomte, a cultivated bourgeois, authoritarian and at times terrible, whose presence filled his villa at 45 Rue La Bruyère, where Cocteau's parents occupied one floor. What color

Georges Cocteau may have lacked his father-in-law possessed in abundance.

Eugène Lecomte had the money to satisfy his mania for collecting various *objets d'art*. He assembled a library of rare books, a portfolio of Ingres sketches, some Delacroix paintings, Florentine medals, autographs of prime ministers, Cypriote vases, and beautiful antique masks, including one of Antinoüs, the Bithynian slave boy whom Hadrian, his infatuated emperor, brought to Rome in the second century. Cocteau remembers being fascinated by its pale terra-cotta cheeks, its enameled black eyes peering at some indefinite point from inside a red plush casket. When his grandfather's artifacts went up for auction, he kept the mask of Antinoüs: an item that would figure prominently in his future films.

M. Lecomte's outstanding treasure was a collection of Stradivarius violins, kept in the billiard room. They were brought out almost weekly for sessions of chamber music, when Lecomte played cello and Pablo de Sarasate, a celebrated Spanish virtuoso, the violin. Music was the soul of the household, but in the 1890s Paris was virtually a city of *mélomanes*. A musical craze had come over the capital, with *soirées musicales* such as Pierre Véron's on the Rue de Rivoli having to book Melba or Deschamps weeks in advance. Paderewski was lionized when he came to Paris for the Exposition of 1889, playing before thousands on Bastille Day, then privately for the *gratin* (as the French nobility was called) at the Countess d'Ansac's mansion, where the Princess Bibesco joined him in a performance of "Omphale's Spinning-Wheel." Salon ladies found it indispensable to have a house musician on hand. Reynaldo Hahn played at Mlle. Madeleine Lemaire's Tuesdays for nearly two decades. The Henri de Saussines retained young Léon Delafosse, who occupied roughly the same place in Robert de Montesquiou's life that Reynaldo Hahn did in Proust's. "Winnie" de Polignac (heiress to the Singer sewing-machine fortune), whose name will recur in a subsequent chapter, surrounded herself with composers, commissioning works from Fauré as she would in later years from Satie and Stravinsky. Notices such as the following appeared regularly in *Le Figaro*:

There will take place, at the beginning of June, in the home of the Marquise d'Hervey de Saint-Denys, a performance of *Philemon and Baucis*, with the Countess de Guerne singing the role of Baucis.

Beginning in about 1885, the year Victor Hugo died, this floating romanticism fastened on Richard Wagner. Charles Lamoureux conducted Wagner's operas every Sunday during the summer in the Cirque d'été, like a priest conducting mass. When he mounted the podium, his audience turned its eyes inward and observed a sacerdotal trance till the last note sounded. Even Mallarmé, and for that matter all the symbolists, attended these dominical rites. Paul Desjardins founded the *Revue Wagnérienne* on the basis of an idealized affinity between Wagnerian music and symbolist poetry, but, for the most part, Wagner's audience required something other than ideas: the release of dark powers held in thrall by convention, the quickening and mobilization of its unlawful self, complicity in a totemistic universe the reverse of its bourgeois republic, a sense of total being sopped up through the ears. As Léon Daudet put it, "the foggy, uncertain mystique, the penchant for the primordial, the ethnic horizons, the brusque and exorbitant feelings bordering on the miraculous that characterize Wagner's dramas, seemed, in the eyes of French youth, to hold a promise of deliverance."

Cocteau and his grandfather belonged to generations on either side of the philo-Wagnerian. Opera for Eugène Lecomte meant Mozart, Verdi, or, particularly, Rossini (Rossini had been a neighbor of his, years before, on the Chaussée d'Antin; how Lecomte came to possess Rossini's many wigs no one knows, but they represented one of the quainter items in his collection). Conservatory concerts, which he attended unfailingly, did, however, include Wagner along with Beethoven and Berlioz. As for Jean, perhaps his later campaign against Wagner was waged partly in memory of an excruciated child sitting among enraptured cultists. Music for him was theatre: ladies' finery, brooches big as yellow cabbages, velvet chokers, whispered salutations, bearded choristers, and the conductor raising his baton "like the flaming sword of an archangel standing on the threshold of Paradise." Cocteau describes the musical soirées of his childhood when he would secretly await Sarasate behind a halberd-shaped lamp surmounted by a tasseled crimson canopy, as the occasions on which he trespassed the upstairs of his household, those Eleusinian cavities of the adult world: his mother's room hung in flowered chintz, Eugène Lecomte's bathroom containing a large silver tub where, unwatched, the child would conduct obscure and leisurely investigations of his chosen fetish, Rossini's wig. But Cocteau listened more closely than he pretended. He had in fact so expert a knowledge of pre-Wagnerian repertory that musical friends of his, according to one of them, would quiz him by humming little-known arias; usually he could tell them not only the operas but the exact scenes in which they are sung.

Summers and week ends the family gathered in a magnificent house, surmounted by little *tourelles*, in Maisons-Laffitte on the Seine, just north of the Saint-Germain forest. In the late nineteenth century, Maisons-Laffitte was virtually an annex of the Parc Monceau and the Bois de Boulogne. The village possessed, in addition to its lovely château designed by Mansart in the seventeenth century, a race track and stables for those Parisians who might have felt mutilated without their horses.[2]

Incontestably the village's most notable residents were the Lebaudy brothers. Their colossal fortune derived from sugar, which explains Max Lebaudy's nickname, *le petit sucrier*. Like Boni de Castellane, he was, on a scale unthinkable today, a prince of idle pursuits: organizing *corridas* in the village of Maisons-Laffitte, washing his carriages with champagne, diddling the celebrated tarts of Maxim's, adorning their fingers with precious jewels. His antics gave music-hall chanteuses such as Polaire something to sing about. Because he did what they dreamed of doing, because he enacted their wildest fantasies perhaps, the working class, the *populo*, grew exceedingly fond of him. He died young, of tuberculosis while garrisoned in the Pyrenees.

His brother Jacques was very much his foil: stingy, always

---

2. Migrations of the aristocracy within—and without—Paris had, partially, an equine basis: from the Faubourg Saint-Germain to the Parc Monceau to the Bois de Boulogne in quest of bridle paths. In the aristocratic calendar, the days of the week were named (beginning Monday) Saint-Cloud, Enghien, Tremblay, Auteuil, Maisons-Laffitte, Vincennes, and Longchamps. On Fridays, then, the *gratin* converged on Maisons-Laffitte for the races.

dressed in black, a megalomaniac entertaining sick designs upon the world. In 1903 he financed a bloody war against the Bedouins, proclaiming himself "Emperor of the Sahara." Subsequently he settled in America with his mistress Marguerite Dellière on an estate near New York City called Phoenix Lodge. Some years later, in 1919, "perceiving that their daughter was a flowering adolescent," he tried to rape her. Marguerite shot him to death.

Maisons-Laffitte also included benefactors of society: Doctor Gache-Sarrothe, who invented the straight corset, Mme. du Gast, president of the Society for the Prevention of Cruelty to Animals. So that summer residents might not want for entertainment, the Duke de Clermont-Tonnerre had erected a theatre where the great Talma used to vacation.

Sundays Eugène Lecomte, who commuted between his country house and his brokerage firm, would post himself on the Place Sully with a bouquet of primroses, looking beyond the stables for the coach from Paris bearing his virtuoso friends: Grébert, the portly Sarasate, and Camillo Sivori, a veritable dwarf. The children—Marthe, Paul, Jean, and his cousin Marianne ³—did what children immemorially do: dream; scale walls and trees; romp on the lawns among the lindens and begonias of Parc du Château nearby; cycle round the village (the bicycle, imported from England, being something of a novelty); make sketches of their neighbors, who included elegant ladies with *faibles* for pet rabbits which they paraded through Maisons-Laffitte on leashes; or play forbidden games, such as smoking on the sly in the fresh, green promiscuity of the Forêt Saint-Germain.

"Childhood has its odors," wrote Cocteau. "Among others I remember the paste of pictures I'd cut out in my sick room, the lindens of Maisons-Laffitte going berserk at the approach of thunder, the delectable powder of petards whose cartridges we'd harvest from the lawn following a night of fireworks, the arnica of waspbites, the mildewed paper of a collection of the *Revue des Deux Mondes*, the upholstery of the omnibus my family drove to mass on Sundays, the fresh odor of the coach house where shovels, hoses,

---

3. Jean's sister Marthe, later the Countess Henri de la Chapelle, was twelve years older than he; his brother Paul, born in 1881, was eight years older.

games of croquet and lotto lay in a disorderly pile." He was a privileged child unsuspecting any world beyond his German nurse, Fraülein Ebel, his parents, his grandparents who surrounded him in widening gyres of attention. They saw to it that he was clothed by the most elegant children's haberdasher in Paris, and pampered him the more strenuously because he was a delicate boy whose scoliotic backbone, though it never slowed his pace, forced him to make odd lateral movements as he walked, something like a slight listing of one shoulder and compensatory upheaval of the other. In time, he would take dancing lessons with the Minchin family.

France inaugurated the twentieth century with its second Exposition in eleven years. The arched gate on Place de la Concorde, surmounted by a voluptuous statue of Lady Paris welcoming the Universe, and flanked by two columns which Rémy de Gourmont described as "jig-sawed phalli," opened April 14, revealing a huge bazaar of minarets, campaniles, pagodas, Moorish terraces, African huts, and Cambodian temples. While pavilions of every description loomed along the Seine between the Pont d'Alma and the Pont d'Iéna. Industry exhibited its latest marvels round the Esplanade des Invalides. The Rue du Caire had been transformed into a sook. Mme. Yakountichikov, representing Princess Elizabeth of Russia, offered President Loubet of France some simple bread and salt, bread on a silver platter, salt in a gold shaker, while a bearded metropolitan intoned *Te Deums*. Bands regularly blared the Marseillaise. Couturiers on the Rue de la Paix adorned their façades with garlands of electric tulips. Banquets followed banquets.

Of this garish fairyland, which of course he visited, Cocteau could recall only Loïe Fuller, an American whose long, Botticellian figure answered all the canons of beauty "modern style" and who created a new dance by contriving to have projectors throw multicolored light on her as she swirled immense veils round herself, like the swirls Fokine would choreograph for the Ballets Russes a few years later, like the swirls of Lalique's jewelry and of Guimard's subway portals. Artists started spinning webs over the angles of Paris like spiders in a neoclassical necropolis.

The year 1900, however, marked a sinister event in Cocteau's life, for that was when he began his formal education. He studied first in the Petit Condorcet, then for two years in that curious establishment built as a Capuchin monastery under Louis XVI, named the Lycée Condorcet under Napoleon, Lycée Bourbon under the Bourbon restoration, Lycée Napoleon under Napoleon III, and renamed by the Third Republic for Condorcet. The plinth over its entrance might have borne a more Dantean epitaph for all the pain Cocteau suffered therein. "If I close my eyes," he mourned years later, "my memories of school are nil and baleful: roused from sleep for the guillotine, tears, dirty notebooks, texts half-opened in haste, inkspots, a ruler rapping knuckles, chalk squeaking, Sunday *pensums*, gas reeking in empty classrooms, little penitentiary tables on which I'd have to write, a hundred times over, 'eight and eight do not equal fourteen' in a script droopier than the profile of a fish knife . . ."

Cocteau always insisted that he was the prize booby of his class (*le cancre par excellence*) and the recipient of its consolation prizes: in German and in art. But poets (and patricians, for it forms part of the genteel tradition), when they come to describe their school years, often represent themselves as subversive valedictorians who occupied the last seat because they disdained the first. Alas, his records, recently exhumed from the Lycée Condorcet, show that, far from the *cancre*, he was already the Cocteau he would increasingly become. In the fifth form his French professor observed of him: "An intelligent student, but weak and easily distracted; an open, subtle mind, but slightly restive; uneven work." In the fourth form, another professor observed: "Lively mind, develops ideas adroitly, has taste, but he is nervous, highly irregular, carried away by his imagination."

Jean Wiener (whose path would later cross Cocteau's) relates that his older brother, a student at Condorcet, returned from school every day with fresh accounts of Jean's naughty genius. Already the *enfant terrible*, he would disarm his teachers with an insolent charm, yet they were evidently awed by him, to the point of reading his verse aloud and exhibiting his sketches. Somehow he knew operas by heart, spoke German fluently, drew remarkably telling caricatures in the style of Sem (and drew them even on the parchment lampshades at home). Moreover, he could turn pretty Alex-

andrines on the slightest pretext, like pirouettes. He was, in a word,
Cocteau, by spontaneous generation. But apparently he had not yet
learned what he later did, that "the tact of audacity consists in
knowing how far one can afford to go too far," for, in the spring of
1904, he was expelled from Condorcet. "Disciplinary reasons," he
wrote, mysteriously.

More important than these curricular *tours de force* was his
pubic awakening. Years later he described art class at Condorcet as
having been a masturbatory playground where, under cover of
their drawing boards, his friends would test their new-found virility. "Sometimes . . . a cynical teacher would abruptly call on a
pupil about to ejaculate. The pupil, his cheeks aflame, would slouch
to his feet and, mumbling whatever came to his head, endeavor to
transform his dictionary into a fig leaf." In the third form, Cocteau
became infatuated with a certain Pierre Dargelos, whom he followed after class like a puppy. No doubt such sentimental pairings-
off are endemic among thirteen-year-olds, but Dargelos' haunting
reincarnations—in *Opium*, in *Les Enfants Terribles*, in *Le Sang
d'un Poète*, in *Le Livre Blanc*—as the shameless, untutored faun
whose mouth and eyes can kill suggest that Cocteau was already at
odds with the ideal double he would spend his life pursuing. According to his own lights, Cocteau understood intensely, even
morbidly, what is meant by the Fall, for he invented, to explain
himself, an equivalent myth. Dargelos is a real name—it may be
found on yellowing rosters—but it is equally Cocteau's pseudonym for his primal malediction, for the angelic offspring of his
catastrophe. A decade after leaving Condorcet he wrote, "At an age
when gender does not yet influence decisions of the flesh, my desire
was not to reach, not to touch, nor to embrace the elected person,
but *to be* him. . . . What loneliness!" This original forfeiture,
placing the locus of Being outside himself, would make solitude intolerable and anonymity a form of death. He was fated to crave
love in order to be.

A subsidiary but like awakening followed on the heels of this
one. Cocteau was especially intrigued by a boy at Condorcet,
younger than he, who seemed to have a fearful, persecuted look in
his eyes. Being very sickly, he was constantly attended by doctors

wearing sable wraps, but he died of meningitis despite their minis-
trations. His mother summoned Cocteau, because he had befriended
the boy, to her home one Sunday. What he saw left an indelible
impression. Instead of the furnishings common to all bourgeois
households in 1900—ponderous ebony commodes with ivory surfaces, tasseled plush, and coffee-colored upholstery—he discovered
a room such as Beardsley or Wilde would have gladly inhabited, its
walls covered with beige satin, a hammock strung across it, Chinese
ink drawings and a Coromandel screen providing conclusive evidence that its tenant must belong to the so-called *petite classe* of
wealthy bohemians who favored *art nouveau* and things Oriental.
His hostess, wearing purple pajamas buttoned at the shoulder in the
Chinese style, and toasting bread over the fireplace with a gold
fork, resembled young Bacchus more than an aggrieved mother. In
the vestibule another mystifying creature, wearing a priest's hat and
a velvet smoking jacket, crossed his path: a woman to be sure,
young and even beautiful . . . except for her abnormally large
hands and feet.

"Only now," he wrote years later, "can I solve the puzzle of that
visit, that penumbra, that lofty solitude, that bereaved smile, that in-
hibited sweetness, that son smitten by the wrathful goddesses of
Lesbos."

The Church of the Madeleine would always keep Cocteau
nearby, like a magnet holding him within its gravitational field.
Even during his madly vagrant years, flitting from hotel to hotel,
he always lodged on streets converging on it. In his eyes the Place
de la Madeleine had a perpetual aura of 1900, its golden age when
fashion, politics, literature, and journalism milled together with
noisy self-acclaim in surrounding cafés, torn by the Dreyfus affair
but united by a common passion for theatre, on stage and off.
Everybody played a role.

In the courtyard of 45 Rue La Bruyère Cocteau and his young
friend René Rocher (who was to become an actor) improvised a
model stage, complete with prompter's box, using planks and nails
from an abandoned mews next door. "The theatre used to fill my

dreams. . . . When my brother Paul was initiated, with *Samson and Delilah* as I recall, I found it consoling that one of us at least had set sail on the crimson stream, for perhaps it augured my turn to see those vast, forbidden halls of gold."

That crimson stream led to the Opéra in one direction and to the Palais-Royal in another, its tributaries flowing every which way to include palaces such as the Vaudeville or the Renaissance where Guitry, Réjane, Coquelin, Bernhardt, having quit the Comédie-Française, reigned as renegade kings and queens. One tributary followed the Boulevard de Strasbourg where two vast music halls, La Scala and the Eldorado, stood opposite one another, Polaire and Mistinguett vying for the flotilla like vernacular sirens. Another followed Rue de Clichy, carrying revelers to the court of "the guttersnipe swan," Yvette Guilbert. People whose lives revolved about the "boulevard" wanted to be dazzled, not instructed or moved, which may account in part for the extraordinary inflation of stars and the dismal deflation of dramatic art around 1900. Henri Bataille, Henri Bernstein, Georges de Porto-Riche, to name just three of the most celebrated playwrights, created melodramatic vehicles artfully engineered so that actors and audience alike would show to their best advantage. The former, without great personae to inhibit them, might give full reign to their temperaments, while the latter preened before a heroic image of bourgeois mores. Ibsen was ostracized by the boulevard in favor of Rostand, whose polished, antiquarian genius it considered part of France's patrimony, so much so that *Le Figaro*, when Rostand fell gravely ill, published his daily fever chart on page one.

The wealthy had an indiscriminate, almost childlike hunger for spectacles. Opulent livery stood massed before music halls and circuses. When the Nouveau-Cirque opened in 1886, featuring a stage that could be lowered and filled with water for aquatic ballets, *Tout Paris*, including the Duchess d'Uzès (whose love for clowns no doubt inspired her, three years later, to back General Boulanger's abortive *coup d'état*) and Jules Lemaître (the literary academician *par excellence*), sat enraptured. Afterward the management invited them to go underneath the stage. "They visited the machine room as though inspecting stables, and gasped with admiration at the latticed ring sitting on a central piston from which twenty beams radiated."

Raoul Donval, its second owner, had the genius of a Ringling or a Barnum, hiring acrobats and fire-eaters from every part of Europe, pitting death against life, raising the stakes with each new act, pairing clowns such as Footit and Chocolate (a Negro from Bilbao), sponsoring beautiful equestriennes such as the Baroness von Rahden. Donval made a business of bestial fantasies. He introduced a boxing kangaroo (afterward Toulouse-Lautrec invited friends to dine on kangaroo tail), a lady crocodile tamer named Nala Damajante, bears wrestling with men, lions riding unicycles under the direction of their master, Darling. Water ballets in imitation of Loïe Fuller gave way to pantomimes ending with a plunge.

In 1905, when Beketov's Russian circus monopolized the Nouveau-Cirque for a season, the track was filled with snow for an act in which a troika was driven on stage pursued by horsemen who seized the driver and built a fire round him; he would elude the flames, however, executing a plunge into the pool below. Westerns invariably ended with cowboys and mounts tumbling pell-mell into the water. And people, both *gratin* and *crottin*, thronged the circus to see specialists toy with predatory beasts, with gravity, with death, with Sarah Bernhardt's reputation (Bernhardt herself came to see Footit and Chocolate parody her Cleopatra).

Their sense of theatre governed what they saw and what they didn't; poverty and disease came masqueraded, like stock characters in a play that had spilled onto the streets. Alfred Capus, whose plays and articles in *Le Figaro* made him a highly fashionable figure, had "his" beggar on Rue Drouot to whom he gave twenty sous every night, but once, having given him two sous by mistake, the beggar protested: "My prince, what am I to do with two sous?" Distractedly Capus answered, "I don't know, give it to some pauper."

Similarly, the smart set flocked to Saint-Louis hospital every Saturday morning to watch Doctor Péan, a famous surgeon, perform public operations. He would arrive in a gold-embroidered coach drawn by chestnut mares. During the operation this black-bearded giant, who had tilled a farm in the Beauce before taking up medicine, wore a frock coat and a silk cravat, like some stage magician. Even at the gravest moments he played to the gallery, explaining his every gesture and exhorting people to sit down so that those in the back rows might have an unobstructed view of him. "After two hours of this exercise," wrote Léon Daudet, "he would be streaming with blood and sweat, his hands red as an assassin's, his feet dipped in gore, but he would be as brisk as ever. The patients were removed on stretchers, forceps clinking in their open abdomens, like calves." In 1900, genius was expected to wear the trappings of brilliant amateurism, and matters of life or death were viewed through a lorgnette.

Cafés thrived as they could only in a self-infatuated society whose very underpinnings were gossip, dalliance, and food. Maxim's—its walls decorated with a green haze of naiads above the swirls of ebony-framed glass—looked like the place it proved to be: a throne room for grand harlots more concerned with one another than with the men who bore their gorgeous trains. Here they staged their power struggles and fashion shows. Clothing overruled all other considerations. La Belle Otéro had a Mercedes custom-designed so that she need not remove her plumed astrakhan inside. Germaine Gallois, an actress of the period, could not accept roles requiring that she sit down because her corset, extending from armpits to knees and fitted with iron hoops round the back and hips, prevented such a position; this edifice was kept in place by eighteen feet of lacing.

In Maxim's, a Hungarian gypsy orchestra played downstairs in the main dining room. There Georges Feydeau spent all his nights in the company of Cassive, another actress-demimondaine. Sem would sit at the bar drawing caricatures. Prince Troubetzkoy usually arrived at two in the morning. Upstairs, patrons who wished, for reasons of state, to dine incognito could be served in private rooms: the Prince of Wales with Lily Langtry, or Leopold II of Belgium and his beautiful mistress, the dancer Cléo de Mérode. In establishments catering to family groups and to its *saboteuses* alike, the clients partitioned the day so as to avoid awkward confrontations. At the Palais de Glace, where people dined round a skating rink, mothers spirited away their children before seven, when harlotry made its grand entrance.

It was said that on the Rue Royale one lived for love (Maxim's), whereas on the Boulevard des Capucines one lived by one's wits. Le Napolitain, where the wits liked to gather, served as a kind of charnel house for "names" trumped up by influential ladies. A *bon mot* published in *L'Écho de Paris* might suffice to deflate someone's lifetime labor. Not infrequently the author of a *bon mot* was the journalist who publicized it. Catulle Mendès, whose two homes were Le Napolitain and *Le Journal,* owed his huge reputation, in part, to just this kind of public redundancy. Night after night the *beaux parleurs* returned, sharpening their wits at others' expense, performing their latest numbers, condemned to return for lack of self-sustaining genius. The talker cannot retire on one telling repartee. When he ceases to talk he is, like an actor, extinct. Does anyone still read Catulle Mendès' poetry? Or Laurent Tailhade's? Their names depended on their tongues.

Tailhade, an intemperate Gascon who will figure in Cocteau's life, was so much of his age that he did not survive it. He devastated his enemies with bawdy quatrains, using the pseudonym "Tybalt." Whatever the cause, provided it was unpopular, he was apt to promote it. When the anarchist Édouard Vaillant tossed a bomb full of nails into the Chamber of Deputies, Tailhade cried: "Of what importance the demise of colorless populations provided the gesture be beautiful!" When the anarchist Émile Henry, two years later, bombed the restaurant Foyot, Tailhade, who happened to be dining there, lost an eye. Those who expected a palinode failed to understand the simple mechanism of his *beaux gestes.* He stuck a glass eye in the cavity, returning to the fray with redoubled fury, on the anarchist side. "May they impale tyrants," he declaimed, "with Harmodius' laurel-wreathed sword, with Charlotte's dagger or Léauthier's humble paring-knife."

When in 1902 Czar Nicholas came to Paris, Tailhade published an article in *The Libertarian* urging the Czar's bodyguard to kill him. He was brought to trial. Zola defended him, saying, "In France, levying fines on thought and jailing doctrines have become a grand enterprise," but Tailhade, afraid of being absolved, cried,

"Comrades! Long live anarchy!" Zola understood no better than the others that Tailhade had but one doctrine—himself, convinced as he was that "whatever the rabble does it does out of blind imbecility." He spent his two years of confinement in the Santé prison translating Petronius' *Satyricon*.

Shortly before World War I, still impenitently himself, he became a Catholic, to keep his adversaries bewildered. Neither Catholic nor anarchist, Tailhade used all cults to promote his own. His glass eye, for example, was not so much a souvenir of the anarchist struggle as a *louche* adornment. When a group of young writers decided to enlist his support, they found a very surprising *mise en scène:* "We climbed Rue Lepic in Montmartre, then several floors. We found the key in his door. We knocked. Someone bellowed 'Enter!' We walked through an *enfilade* of tiny rooms. The first was empty. So was the second. And the third. But in the fourth, which was all but empty, lay Laurent Tailhade on his bed. Next to him, we noticed a chamber pot, containing his glass eye."

The boulevard, more like a fish bowl than a chamber pot, also had its glass eye. Nothing went unnoticed, as there were forty-two newspapers in Paris at the turn of the century, reflecting all nuances of opinion. *Le Gaulois*, whose holy mission it was to serve *le gratin*, published résumés of its every movement. *Le Figaro*'s society column, "*Tout Paris*," appeared on the first page. Extraordinary liberties were taken with the truth. Literary style counted more than news. Police reporters proved themselves to be masters of the imperfect subjunctive. Literati such as Jules Lemaître, Marcel Prévost, and Georges Rodenbach commented variously on politics, on feminism, on Annamite dancers appearing at the Exposition, on fashion. When Sarah Bernhardt and her playwright Henri Bataille had a dispute, each planted his version in *Le Figaro*, on successive days. The newspaper in 1900 was at once lackey and king.

"Noctambulism was at its height," wrote Gabriel Astruc. "I remember a friend of the composer Rodolphe Berger, who was forced to put on dark lenses when, by chance, he got up in the morning, because for months on end he wouldn't poke his nose outside before eight p.m., and the light of day blinded him."

At the center of this world, where the wings of freedom beat by night, stood La Madeleine, staging Sunday mass at one in the afternoon. Here God rose late, with His prodigal parishioners.

In the third form at the *lycée*, Cocteau's report card showed an ominous and unprecedented word: "docile." This denoted the calm before the storm. By the following Easter, his grades plummeting, his indifference sublime, he was expelled from Lycée Condorcet. In the autumn of 1904 his family remanded him to a *pension* on the Rue Claude Bernard, the Val-André, whose headmaster, Monsieur Dietz, had been André Gide's tutor some years before at the École Alsacienne. As though a composite of his two star pupils, Dietz was by turns the cramped protestant preceptor and a gesticulating Pierrot.[4] It would seem that he did not interfere unduly with Cocteau's education, but those two years under Dietz's government shrank, in retrospect, to their accumulated Thursdays and Sundays, when Cocteau was free for his first adventures in the larger world. The "larger world" was roughly equivalent in his mind to *le boulevard*.

Cocteau had a new friend named Carlito Bouland who, with his pug face and big teeth, looked so uncannily like Coquelin—the first Cyrano—that he learned all his roles. They would combine their allowances and rent a stage-box at the Eldorado, whence they showered Jeanne Reynette and Mistinguett with bouquets of violets. This was not yet the "Miss" of spangles and feathers and gowns. Her stockings rolled halfway down her calves, and, wearing a brief, gauzy frock that mushroomed out in white furry hems, she played the *môme*, the child-vamp, the convulsive gamin beloved for her refrain:

> "*Je suis la femme torpille,*
> *pille, pille*
> *Qui se tortille*
> *tille, tille*"

Twisting, or straddling the prompter's box like a man, she reflected a gutter life the well-born liked to imagine, lyric and crude, where

4. Dietz's son played at the Comédie-Française under the name Garry, and his nephew, Pierre Laudenbach, would make a name for himself on stage as Pierre Fresnay.

suffering or sex borders on epilepsy. She sang *"La Ribouldingue"* (The Spree), *"La Crapulette"* (The Débauchée), and other refrains such as:

> *"Je suis Mam'zelle, sans façon,*
> *Je rigole, je batifole,*
> *Et j'adore le rigodon . . ."*

Poets such as Léon-Paul Fargue and Pierre Mac Orlan regularly attended her performances. Even Oscar Wilde, using Liane de Pougy and Émilienne d'Alençon as supports for his bloated frame, came to pay her homage. But for a whole generation of young boys, including Cocteau and the future surrealists (notably Aragon), Mistinguett coincided with the adolescent froufrou of their senses.

Cocteau, or one of his friends, volunteered to go backstage and pay her tribute on their behalf. From then on they regularly met her at the concierge's booth. She would appear carrying a bouquet of flowers over her heart, with rays of mascara drawn between her lids and eyebrows (called "bicycles"). Together, "Miss" and her young admirers repaired to the Taverne Pschorr or the Café du Globe on the Boulevard de Strasbourg. Mistinguett was nearly twice Cocteau's age.

That she found his company agreeable enough to welcome it twice a week may be both a measure of his charm and her egoism. He was luminously intelligent, and knew it, but he was also what the French call *un joli garçon*, with his long, renard nose, his delicate lips (the upper one immobile while the lower parted slightly to emit an endless stream of conceits), his thickish eyebrows sweeping out from the bridge of his nose like bird's wings, his alert, dark eyes which Mme. de Noailles compared to a nightingale's, and his hair combed young-Hugo style. He had a thin, patrician face and long hands which never ceased gesturing. "Cocteau and his friend Bouland were regular fans of mine," recalled Mistinguett. "I'd spend evenings with them and with Madeleine Carlier in a café near the Eldo. . . . I don't remember what we talked about. Not much, but we were glad just to be together, without playing to the galleries. Often they'd climb onto the back of my coach and sit on the springs, getting their overcoats all dirty." What Mistinguett did not confide in her memoirs she did to friends, that Cocteau lost his virginity to her.

Where had Cocteau met Madeleine Carlier? Possibly at one of those "skatings," the Pôle du Nord and the Palais de Glace (but in either case after seven, when the bourgeois clientele had left), or through the theatrical crowd he had begun to cultivate. The boulevard had its *mômes* as Hollywood had its starlets. Peaches and cream, they would come from the provinces with dreams of success. Some, like Mistinguett, succeeded on stage. Others, who lacked her will and talent, succeeded in bed as demimondaines. Lantelme, for example, was a whore at twelve, working in her mother's brothel. Having fled to Paris, she performed small roles at the Gymnase, where Alfred Edwards, the wealthy and thoroughly dissolute owner of France's largest daily, *Le Matin*, caught sight of her. Deploying his powerful resources, divorcing his wife Misia (formerly Natanson, subsequently Sert), he finally overcame her resistance. Émilienne d'Alençon fled home at sixteen and worked as a rabbit trainer in Franconi's circus before gaining fame and riches as *une horizontale*. But most *mômes* graduated straightaway into devastated old ladies once the blush faded from their cheeks. They lived a few years of sulphurous nights on the boulevard, playing bit parts, sleeping with the smart set (men and women indiscriminately), dressing to kill, figuring in pulp magazines, then, like fireflies, were extinguished.

Madeleine Carlier survived the boulevard. She was born Adèle Martin in 1882. Cocteau relates that she made her debut in the Palais de Glace, a young Montmartrian who entered after nightfall out of curiosity and departed with rich blades in hot pursuit. Actually, she lived with an aunt near the Châtelet and made her real debut somewhat differently. In 1898, having decided to be an actress, she presented herself to the director of the Théâtre du Châtelet, requesting a role. What he saw before him was a fetching young nymph, her blonde hair drawn into a mop which threatened to come undone at any moment. One contemporary described her as a figure "who looks as though she just stepped out of a painting by Helleu." Cocteau, rather more to the point, called her a prefigura-

tion of Brigitte Bardot. She was the perfect "ingénue" on the surface, the director wished to see no deeper, and on December 8,
1898, she appeared as a fairy in a five-act fairy tale by Cogniard,
Blum, and Decourcelle called *Perlimpimpim's Powder.*

This was a modest beginning, but by her next appearance, in
1901, she had evolved from a fairy into a vamp, starring as Madame
Flirt at the Athénée. That part won her a two-year contract at the
Théâtre des Capucines. She subsequently appeared in minor roles
on the stage of the Odéon and the Renaissance and, prophetically,
appeared in a play called *Les Liaisons Dangereuses* by Nozière at
the Duke de Clermont-Tonnerre's theatre in Maisons-Laffitte. By
1904 she had forged a dubious reputation for herself. In January of
that year she sued Monsieur Berny, director of the Théâtre des
Mathurins, for having fired her on the grounds that she refused to
wear a costume offending her "modesty." *Le Gaulois* commented
as follows: "This season, Made Carlier, succeeding Mmes. Émilienne
d'Alençon, Liane de Pougy, Otéro, and Henriette Rogers, has star
billing at the Palace of Justice, in two trials that are smash hits,
authentic ones!"

Cocteau at sixteen lost his heart to a *cocotte* seven years his
senior, and infinitely older than her years. He found ways of escaping Monsieur Dietz's *pension*, meeting her after her performances,
making the rounds of "*Caf' Conç*" such as the Eldorado, staying up
all night, and furtively returning in time for class next morning. At
length what had started as a fashionable escapade threatened to get
out of hand. His family, judging the situation according to their
lights, found her an unmitigated slut and forbade him to see her
again, but they merely commanded a *fait accompli*, for young Cocteau had in the meantime made a galling discovery: his affection
was not rewarded in kind.

If, as Cocteau avers, this adventure lies at the source of his novel
Le Grand Écart (*The Big Split*), then "Made" Carlier's sexual nature may have been no less ambivalent than his own: the young hero,
Jacques Forestier, surprises his beloved in bed with another . . .
woman. It is true that other demimondaines had strongly sapphic
leanings: Lantelme, even Liane de Pougy (who engaged in a tender
correspondence with Natalie Clifford Barney). At the very least,

Madeleine Carlier showed exorbitant interest in the theatre of inversion. Some twenty years later she would in fact campaign for it when the Théâtre Daunou came under her direction: "Life interests me passionately," she announced, "and that is why, without wishing to organize a bizarre program, I shall nonetheless solicit and welcome only works that are truly original, by which I mean works that bring some new idea to the theatre, some psychological case no one has as yet made bold to hint at, let alone discuss openly."

Perhaps, as George D. Painter suggests in his biography of Proust, the future homosexual when still young makes a heterosexual choice that is certain to fail, in order to free himself for his true desire. No choice of woman could have been more doomed than Madeleine Carlier, yet that chosen doom would govern all Cocteau's attachments, male and female alike. It is as if they were unconsciously arranged to leave him detached, like an actor from his audience. By some tragic paradox, Cocteau, whose welfare hinged on love or approval, would seek it from unseduceable adversaries, like a Don Juan who values the one remaining virgin above a world of fallen women. The most just measure of Juan's towering vanity may be his abysmal self-depreciation, just as the goal of his everlasting debauches may be innocence. Cocteau, the boy in love with older women, would become the man in love with younger boys, the apprentice would become a master, but every new ploy to disarm life would open his wounds afresh, every liaison would exacerbate his loneliness, every enthusiasm would take him farther away from himself.

Meanwhile Cocteau had begun orbiting about an actor. Through René Rocher, he found his way into Édouard de Max's circle. De Max admits to having been instantly charmed: "A gamin, a goose, a page, that was how Jean Cocteau appeared, clad in his seventeen years. He was precious, delicate, charming, and his poems were charming, delicate, precious. No, they were better. With all my soul I believed a very great poet had been born, one destined to reign supreme over the most elegant form of French verse. Rostand was now writing exclusively for the theatre. Who would trifle in his place?" Before *Cyrano* and *L'Aiglon* brought him apotheosis, Rostand had in 1893 published a volume of verse called *Musardises*

(*Triflings*). By now Cocteau was trifling as adeptly as had Rostand, writing parlor verse, a virtuoso blend of Parnassus and symbolism wherein the poet, like a magician flushing doves from the hollow of his hand, must derive, from a footfall, a wisp of smoke, a ray of light, a bar of music, as many polished strophes as will prove his stamina inexhaustible. Rostand wrote a poem called "Shadows and Smoke":

> *J'aime les ombres, les fumées,*
> *Ces fugacités et ces riens,*
> *Ces formes vaguement formées*
> *Ces tremblements aériens.*
> *Je t'aime, toi qui ne te poses*
> *Jamais, Fumée, ô soeur du Vent*
> *Et je vous aime, Ombre des choses,*
> *Plus que les choses bien souvent!*

> (I love shadows, wisps of smoke,
> Evanescences and nothings,
> These shapes shaped of vague
> Shimmerings of the air.
> I love thee, who never comes to rest
> Smoke, O sister of the Wind
> And I love you, Shadow of things,
> More often than the things themselves!)

which prefaces an inventory of shadows and smoke, the musings of a lyric meteorologist. Cocteau would keep stride with "Footfalls":

> *Il y a bien des pas dessinés sur la grève,*
> *Pas à peine foulés d'entrevue un peu brève*
> *Solitaires et courts du promeneur qui rêve,*
> *Pas furtifs et fuyants qu'on ne remarque pas . . .*

> (There are many steps outlined on the strand,
> Light footfalls of a hurried tryst,
> Short steps of a solitary dreaming as he walks,
> Steps furtive and fleeing that are barely missed . . .)

Or, where Anna de Noailles's influence eclipses Rostand's, the landscape turns Byzantine, the wind soughs, the air smells of nard, while the poet(ess) is ravaged by some phallic absence. Elegant swoonings, rhapsodies on the color pink, Chopin nocturnes that marry the very form of a formless grievance. Anna de Noailles sang:

> *Ô sanglots de Chopin, ô brisements du coeur!*
> *Ô Chopin, votre voix qui reproche et réclame*
> *Comme un peuple affamé se répand dans nos âmes.*
>
> (O sobbings of Chopin, O breakings of the heart!
> O Chopin, your voice demanding and reproachful
> Like a famished people's oozes through our souls.)

which echoes in Cocteau's "Withered Souvenir":

> *La plainte en mineur des Nocturnes de Chopin*
> *Dans le salon vieillot, délambrissé, dépeint,*
> *Pleurait avec lenteur des douloureuses gammes.*
>
> (The complaint, in minor, of the Nocturnes of Chopin
> In the antiquated room, drab and peeling,
> Slowly sobbed its dolorous scales.)

As though taking on the color of whatever review published him, he waxed d'Annunzian for *Poesia*, writing a satanic-angelic conceit called "Your Eyes" in which the eyes of his inamorata, gouged out, are turned into sapphire rings.

In 1902 or 1903 Catulle Mendès and Gustave Kahn, the symbolist poet, proposed to André Antoine that he lend them his theatre for poetic matinées. He demurred, but Sarah Bernhardt, who fancied this new role, straightaway offered them the Théâtre Sarah Bernhardt where, during several years, distinguished actors and actresses appeared on stage Saturday afternoons, reading whatever poems they chose. These matinées threatened to turn into fashion shows. Berthe Bady would glide out of the wings clad in a chatoyant gown. Bernhardt, wearing a dress whose sleeves reached her fingertips and whose ruff collar impinged on her wild, blonde hair, recited Hugo as she had been doing since youth.

But de Max, whose poetic sensibility was far keener than most actors', succeeded in disturbing his audience. "He would advance toward the public," wrote Béatrix Dussane, the tragedienne, who attended these readings as a school girl, "taking little steps (he wasn't very tall and even off stage wore elevator shoes), with the bearing of a fallen angel, at once icy and explosive. His hand, laden with exotic rings, coming to a beaky point with his index finger, would scan the air, in accordance with the melody more than the action of the verse." Introducing poets either still unknown—the young symbolists—or else still accursed, like Baudelaire (not yet on school syllabi in 1900), doubtless to affirm his heterodoxy no less than his preferences, de Max gave some point to these recitals. He loved allying his name with the new, sponsoring legends that would redound upon his own, launching literary stars. Convinced he had discovered one in Jean Cocteau, de Max rented the Théâtre Fémina, where he happened to be playing that year, and issued the following invitation to *Tout Paris* and to every literary broker of his acquaintance, notably Catulle Mendès:

M. de Max has the honor of informing you that, through his initiative, Laurent Tailhade will, on April 4, 1908, at 3 in the afternoon, at the Théâtre Fémina, 90, Avenue des Champs-Élysées, deliver a lecture on the verse of a very young poet, only 18 years old, Jean Cocteau.
Recitations by:
  Mmes Breval of the Opera
    Segond-Weber, Provost, of the Comédie-Française
    Ventura, Laurent Tailhade, etc.
    Mme Rolland of the Odéon, René Rocher and M. de Max

Tailhade wore a gray cassock for the occasion. Like Huysmans, who in *Against the Grain* has Des Esseintes execute every last Latin poet with the exception of Petronius, Tailhade did as much for French poets, leaving only Cocteau unscathed. It may be more than a pretty coincidence that Cocteau began his literary career under the auspices of Édouard de Max, Nero of the French stage, and Laurent Tailhade, translator of Petronius.[5]

5. The poems recited, and others, formed Cocteau's first published volume, *Aladdin's Lamp* (1908).

Cocteau's vagabondage, from the outset, had the nature of his loves. Wooing another generation, older or younger, amounts to a feigned espousal, the child playing house though still imprisoned in his parents'. Cocteau's flights from home were not Rimbaud's but feints at flight, the fugitive holding tight Ariadne's clew so as not to lose his way in the labyrinthine world. When he ventured into that labyrinth, his steps were tentative, and a prearranged tug from home would save him from himself. His vagabondage proved, if anything, his eternal bondage.

The year he was to enter the Val-André (he was by now living on the Avenue Malakoff quite near the Étoile, where his mother had taken an apartment separate from her parents') Cocteau vanished. For months the family knew nothing of his whereabouts till one day a card arrived postmarked Marseilles. Two policemen hired by his uncle found him working in an Indo-Chinese dock-dive as a dishwasher ("a servant," to use Cocteau's quaint description). He had been taken in, he claimed, by an old Annamite lady who led him to the Rue de la Rose in the ghetto; there he found lodgings in a tenement which he described as a maze of interconnecting rooms used by *voyous* and motley fugitives—whores, junkies, sailors on French leave, thieves—so that when the police entered one door their prey could escape by any number of others. His family was so traumatized that Cocteau never published this adventure, except implicitly: a whiff of it comes in that short monologue called "The Phantom of Marseilles" having to do with a transvestite thug. One close friend of Cocteau's surmises, however, that it was a momentous sojourn: that in Marseilles he may have taken drugs for the first time and had his first homosexual relations. Subsequently he would make annual migrations, if not to Marseilles, to nearby ports of call.

Why had he chosen Marseilles originally? Was it because Wilde, in the eyes of his epigones, had made Venice (which Cocteau had visited with his mother in 1904) and the Midi appear the capitals of forbidden pleasures? Possibly de Max was to blame, for he himself had lived there from time to time reveling in the Levantine carnival of pimps, gyp artists, and fleshpots. Cocteau's and de Max's names are linked, as ambiguously, with still another place, the scene of Cocteau's second evasion.

Cocteau relates that, wandering aimlessly on the Left Bank one day, he happened on an extraordinary site in the Faubourg Saint-Germain: an exquisite mansion, standing in the middle of what must have been a tailored English garden, now overgrown with myosotis. In fact it was the Hôtel Biron, built in the 1720s by Gabriel and named for one of its many tenants, the Maréchal de Biron. Throughout the nineteenth century it had served as a convent school where sisters of the Sacred Heart tutored daughters of Catholic aristocrats. One of their wards had been Eugénie de Montijo, destined to become Napoleon III's Empress. When the Law of Separation took effect in 1904, the Republic seized this property, among others, expelled the nuns, and assigned it to an official "liquidator," who set about letting rooms, not only in the mansion proper, but in its outbuildings, including the chapel. Women, mostly foreigners connected with the arts, swooped in bearing brushes, chisels and pens: among them Mrs. Lounsbury, an English playwright; Isadora Duncan, who offered dancing lessons in a long gallery now destroyed; and Clara Westhoff, a German sculptress. When Clara Westhoff had to leave Paris temporarily, she offered her studio to her estranged husband, a Czech whose German publisher had commissioned him to write a book on Rodin. Rodin, charmed by his commentator, sheltered him in Meudon and, absurdly (for the Czech's French was at best imperfect), made him his secretary, only to dismiss him within a few months during a temper tantrum. Now homeless and unemployed, he accepted his wife's offer and on September 1, 1908, Rainer Maria Rilke moved into the Hôtel Biron. Rodin followed suit, for Rilke, incapable of holding grudges, invited him to see this laicized Eden. Having done so, Rodin could not resist the idea of working in Paris, within sight of the Invalides' golden dome, yet surrounded by fruit trees and a veritable thicket where rabbits still ran wild. Late in 1908 he established his studio on the ground floor.

The concierge informed Cocteau that one room on the second

floor, a large room with bay windows overlooking the grounds—
the nuns had used it for solfeggio and dancing class—could be had
by consent of Monsieur Varenne, the liquidator. Cocteau moved in
that evening. For months he used the Hôtel Biron as a *pied-à-terre*,
unbeknownst to his family: staging parties; promenading through
the garden at night among moon-lacquered statues of nymphs with
Christiane Mancini, his girl friend, in her flowing, black velvet
gown; inviting his new impresario Catulle Mendès (who was so
incredulous that he whipped the furniture with his riding crop);
and living furtively in a world exempted from the disfigurations of
time. That November, however, the state decided to auction the
grounds in forty-five lots and to dispose of the *pavillon* for a
pittance. Cocteau claims it was poetic justice that he, a young poet,
should have saved this charming anachronism.[6] Frantically rallying
writers such as Abel Hermant and Pierre de Nolhac, he started a
press campaign that led to interpellations in the National Assembly,
so embarrassing the government that it deferred the auction indefi-
nitely. Actually, Rodin made personal calls on Clemenceau, Briand,
and Hanotaux, pleading for the Biron; their intercession probably
proved decisive.

Meanwhile the Hôtel Biron had become a *cause célèbre*, and a
group of Right Bank ladies called the Society of Friends of the
Louvre resolved to pay a visit. Their president asked one member,
Mme. Georges Cocteau, to influence her son so that they might
view the estate from his quarters. A woman of great composure,
she did not betray her surprise on learning that Jean maintained a
room there. Friends of the Louvre enjoyed his room for an afternoon, thus bringing an abrupt end to his adventure.

Another celebrated inmate of the Hôtel Biron, whom Cocteau
significantly neglects to mention, was Édouard de Max. Paying a
call on Mrs. Lounsbury (author of *Judith*), de Max found himself
enthralled. "Since I was marveling at this architectural jewel," he
wrote, "she suggested we go downstairs to visit the most illustrious
of her cotenants, Rodin. The sculptor introduced me to the Duchess de Choiseul who, hearing my fresh outbursts of admiration,
replied, 'Come live here then.' 'But isn't the building fully occu-

6. Now the Rodin Museum.

pied?' 'Yes, but the chapel is empty.'" The duchess (an aging though once-beautiful American, remarkable chiefly for her henna hair and lurid make-up, whose influence over Rodin was a measure of his innocence) could not know what she had started. De Max occupied the chapel, which he renovated at great expense, fitting new doors, laying marble floors, and installing, within its sacristy, a bathtub. The Catholic press, spoiling to avenge the Church, found its chance in this blasphemous fixture. It waged a campaign revolving about de Max's bathtub, the altar of heaven knows what black masses. The government, once again embarrassed, issued a general eviction notice. An exemption was eventually made of Rodin, but not, alas, of Mrs. Lounsbury.

The fatal call that de Max paid on Mrs. Lounsbury could not have taken place before 1910, after Cocteau's departure from the Hôtel Biron, for not until that year did the Duchess de Choiseul appear in Rodin's life. Why hadn't Cocteau revealed his secret bower to the actor? No doubt de Max, having given birth to a poet in the Théâtre Fémina, soon thereafter showed signs of wishing to devour him, like an infanticidal cat. Cocteau perhaps exploited de Max, but filial relationships are, by nature, unjust. At eighteen he could be excused. Years later, still smarting from the wound, de Max wrote, rancorously as any overpossessive mother: "After the recitation of his poems, Cocteau, charmed, transported, paid very rare visits to de Max. He had found other sponsors, culled from my acquaintances. He mingled with famous actresses . . . He addressed Catulle Mendès as 'My dear confrère.' He started reciting his pallid verse in salons, supplanting 'My dear confrère' with 'My dear princess.' He is the darling of French nobility."

This gives a bitter résumé of what lay ahead, years of social mongering, of poetical pirouetting, of facile and addictive glory. Cocteau would give an equally baleful résumé: "It must be a dream to live at ease within one's own skin. From birth I've carried an ill-assorted cargo. I've never known a sense of serenity. That, in retrospect, is my balance sheet. And, condemned to this lamentable state of mind, I have, to avoid staying in my room, knocked about everywhere. From the age of fifteen I haven't stopped for a moment." He was an astonishing child, sputtering like a Roman candle, opining brilliantly, marshaling the *jeunesse dorée*—Maurice Rostand, Sacha Guitry, etc.—into masquerades and impromptus. Marie Scheikévitch, a wealthy and literate woman who was one of Proust's close friends, said that watching Cocteau gave her some idea what the young Voltaire must have been like. Like the young Voltaire, but more like Lucien de Rubempré, he was hell-bent on conquering *Tout Paris*, and now he had a strategic base of operation, Mme. Cocteau having lately moved again, this time to 10 Rue d'Anjou where her downstairs neighbor was Laure de Chevigné, Proust's Duchess de Guermantes.

2

A l'Ombre des Jeunes Gens en Fleur

There is a famous caricature of Sem's showing Catulle Mendès as Christ in the Café Napolitain flanked by drunken disciples, one of whom is distributing an armful of halos. Quoting chapter and verse from his own works, Mendès pontificated nightly on poetry, on food, on love, and ate as if every supper were a Last Supper, interlarding his sermons with triumphant cackles. Short and stout, he cut a more commanding figure when seated, for his body was the ruined pedestal of an imperial head; his blue eyes seemed to swim inside their orbits, and a blond moustache sat mounted above his mouth like the trophy horn of an Indian water buffalo. By midnight his beard glistened with fat from his meal, and wine stains showed on the cream-colored surah cravat he always wore loosely tied in a great bow.

"He had something of both the lion and the turbot about him," wrote Cocteau. "His face, around the cheeks, the eyes, the little fishlike half-moon of a mouth, seemed caught in some sort of jelly which kept him at a distance and charged the air, between him and others, with a shimmering, transparent, mysterious density." In the eyes of a young poet, he must have trailed a phosphorescent wake of great names. That "mysterious density" was undoubtedly the aura of his past, for Mendès had known Théophile Gautier as a son-in-law, had exchanged words with Baudelaire, and had spent long evenings with Victor Hugo. Young, he had been the brilliant epigone, writing poems and plays more Hugoesque than Hugo's, more Parnassian than Théodore de Banville's. He never came into his own, but the deaths of his models gave him a kind of originality. He was respected as the great survivor.

After midnight Mendès would saunter through the boulevard

with Courteline and Jean de Bonnefon, colleagues of his at *Le Journal*, whose offices stood only a few blocks away from the Café Napolitain. There he would dash off his theatre review, writing in the presence of men and women who lived for a favorable mention. "Voluble, white, and melting like wax," Colette observed, "Catulle Mendès wrote unrelentingly. Courteline would be shouting recriminations. His batlike voice grated the ears, scraped plaster off the walls. Luminous young women would come to sit in Catulle's shade. Writing all the while, he'd greet them with caressing and complicated names like 'Fledgling who settles on boughs without bending them . . . ,' 'Whiteness humiliating the snow,' 'Cornucopia overflowing with goodies.' " His performance over, he would board the train to Saint-Germain-en-Laye, quite near Maisons-Laffitte, residing at a safe distance from Paris because in the city women, so he complained, made his life unbearable. At least one, the actress Marguerite Moreno, found his reputation as a lover inflated. She confided to Colette that Mendès spent all night declaiming his verse so that by morning he was impotent.

If rhetoric got the better of his art and impaired his sexual prowess, it oddly distorted his vision of himself. A Portuguese Jew by origin, he aligned himself with the anti-Dreyfusards during the Dreyfus Affair. Mendès was a pronounced anti-Semite. "We Semites," he declared in a conversation with Gustave Kahn, a mild-mannered, erudite symbolist poet, "we Semites are marvelous assimilators, but expect nothing original of us." When Kahn cited Spinoza as proof to the contrary, Mendès snorted: "Aha! Aha! I've always suspected that the mother of that optician must have had a crush on some philandering gentile."

This combination of grandeur, fustian, and Jewish self-hatred made him a kind of French Falstaff to the German Wagner, whose cause he embraced when a mere eighteen in the *Revue Fantaisiste*. Mendès' beautiful child-bride, Judith Gautier, proved to be a cultist even more ardent than he. From the age of ten, when her father Théophile took her to the Salle Ventadour for the first Parisian performance of Wagner's music, she consecrated herself to the Messiah. Together, Mendès and Judith (accompanied by that mystic and mystifier, Villiers de l'Isle-Adam) went to Bavaria on a

Wagnerian honeymoon, journeying to Bayreuth by way of Munich, where Ludwig II, at Wagner's urging, commanded for their private pleasure performances of *The Flying Dutchman, Tannhäuser, Lohengrin,* and *Die Meistersinger.* Mendès addressed Judith tenderly as "my brother of the Graal," but the Graal, whose musical emanations sustained their marriage, dissolved it when he appeared in the flesh. Wagner fell in love with Judith Gautier (he was sixty-three and she twenty-six), while Mendès amused himself with the actress Augusta Holmes. During the last ten years of his life, Wagner sent Judith an endless stream of passionate letters, which she answered in kind.

After Wagner's death, Judith Gautier, long since divorced from Mendès, survived as a high priestess of the hallucinated set, living on the Rue de Berri amidst the Oriental bric-a-brac of late-nineteenth-century estheticism, growing stouter in proportion as her fetishes grew smaller until, in the end, she looked like a corpulent goddess devoted to her tiny netsukes and to the puppets in her puppet theatre. Like her friend Bernhardt, Judith Gautier had many imitators (for she had discovered Japan even before Edmond de Goncourt), who appeased their *Weltschmerz* with Wagner and made an issue of their moral exile by collecting Japanese knickknacks.

A dying world is eclectic; it adopts every artifice and foreign ritual, thwarting conventions with the bizarre, the machine world with things triumphantly useless, classical proportions with the disproportionate and mannered. It goes underground. "Let us not be deceived," wrote Rémy de Gourmont in *Décadence,* published at the beginning of the century. "Because man walks, acts, talks, he is not necessarily conscious, nor is he ever completely conscious." And Gustave Moreau, whose paintings made such a strong impact on Marcel Proust, said much the same thing. "The Will never acts unaided in art. The artistic act is a docile submission to the welling subconscious." Spiritism, diabolism, Rosicrucianism all had their devotees and their chapels in Paris before World War I.

As for Catulle Mendès, he lived in an aviary where birds, whom he addressed with the same complicated epithets he used for female admirers, had the run of his house; and he married a Frenchwoman raised in Argentina, Jane, who dressed exotically and wrote Oriental tales. Cocteau caught his first glimpse of her in the lobby of a theatre during an intermission. "[She was] large, painted like an idol, and resembled, behind the aquarium of her veils trailing the foamy scrolls of her pagoda sleeves, a miraculous Japanese fish."

Cocteau became a familiar figure in the Mendès household, having met the Master through Édouard de Max shortly after the Théâtre Fémina affair. Mendès invited him to "come share his omelette." Four days later Cocteau kept his appointment but, after waiting for an hour in the vestibule of Mendès' *pied-à-terre* on Boulevard Malesherbes, realized that the invitation had been forgotten as soon as it was issued. When Mendès finally appeared, he wore a velvet domino mask whose purpose, he hastened to explain, was functional: having bruised his face in a fall, he needed something to steady the nose plaster. They dined among Mendès' canaries and the memorabilia of his past: a portrait of Gautier (who could not stand him), Renoir's pastel of Banville, a framed letter of praise from Victor Hugo, the high-backed Gothic chair draped in red velvet where he had sat manufacturing his forty volumes of verse and theatre. At four o'clock he gargled with Pennès vinegar, washed his eyes in boric solution, powdered his beard, injected a *remède* into his thighs ("through the trousers," according to Cocteau), and made for the Café Napolitain, where, as of five, his table stood waiting for him.

Cocteau gravitated toward Mendès as he had toward Édouard de Max, starstruck and overcome with effeminate awe for the *magister ludi*. Throughout the latter half of 1908 he made Saturday pilgrimages to Saint-Germain-en-Laye, where Catulle would emote, recite, and, all in all, carry on like the literary evangelist he fancied himself, not without cause: a word from him could either make or break, and his enthusiasms often hit the mark. He and Mallarmé were mutual admirers.

On February 8, 1909, at five in the morning a lamplighter employed by the Saint-Germain-en-Laye station discovered, while inspecting the tracks, the horribly mangled body of a man: his brains had spilled over the railroad ties, his cane lay severed, but his top hat was absolutely unmarked. The corpse was carried to the station

and identified by the constable as Catulle Mendès'. He had spent
the previous evening in Paris with friends, who found him less ebul-
lient than usual: he complained of the demands placed on him, but
also reminisced about the journey he once made to Bayreuth with
Villiers de l'Isle-Adam. It was concluded, after an inspection of his
train compartment, the door to which stood partially unhinged,
that Mendès, awakened by a halt in the tunnel just before Saint-
Germain, imagined he had arrived at the station and descended just
as the train started up again. Had he died the death of Elpenor, or
had he committed suicide? Some years later Jane Mendès, reacting
against Cocteau's remark that her husband, having abstained from
drink for an evening, was in an abnormal state of mind, explained
that the head bruises he suffered the previous July became infected,
leaving his mind somewhat impaired. The doctors recommended
trepanation. "In any case," she said, "he sensed that he was doomed.
His distress was immense and chaotic. . . . The day before his
death, he spent long hours weeping in the enforced, wintry solitude
of Saint-Germain." In Saint-Germain his body lay in state, while
mourners crowded in from Paris. "A death mask resumes the angles
of adolescence," wrote Cocteau. "Mendès dead resembled Heinrich
Heine, and I remember his telling this anecdote: as a young man he
paid a visit to Mme. Heine, who fell into a dead faint, believing—
for such was their resemblance—that her husband had regained his
legs and was walking again."

Cocteau continued to see Jane Mendès, and in all likelihood it
was she who encouraged him in his first fugitive venture as a publisher. He and a friend, François Bernouard,[1] decided to create a de
luxe review devoted chiefly to poetry. Their title, *Schéhérazade*,
though it has an unmistakably Mendèsian ring, echoed the fashion
for things Persian: Diaghilev would produce a ballet of that same
name a year later, Doctor Mardrus had brought out his translation
of *The Thousand and One Nights*, and throughout these prewar
years the Right Bank (and even the Left) staged balls to which
guests came dressed as sultans and sultanas.

1. Bernouard also wrote poetry—a slim tome of verse being the passport into literary salons. But he had the good sense to quit, gaining a more durable reputation for
his fine editions, whose ensign is a red rose.

As much to adorn their magazine with an illustrious name as to meet the latest child prodigy toasted by salons and *Le Figaro*, they enlisted the collaboration of Maurice Rostand, who was living with his parents in the Hôtel Meurice on Rue de Rivoli. Cocteau one spring day in 1909 appeared at their hotel as the Rostands were making preparations to leave for Cambo, near Biarritz, where Edmond owned a vast estate called Arnaga. "Cocteau was very different from the person he subsequently became," wrote Maurice Rostand. "A brown, neatly-trimmed moustache shaded his face. His soft hair hadn't yet affected a crest, but he was already possessed of a fascinating intelligence, turbulent and ceaselessly changing."

As for Maurice Rostand, he was at eighteen an egregious dandy, doomed by his oversolicitous mother, by his deified father, and by their pampering friends to form an exaggerated opinion of himself. When he was eight, Sarah Bernhardt, whom he would spend his life imitating, gave him as a Christmas present a small model of the Théâtre Sarah Bernhardt, its Mucha poster and playbill reading "The Red Snail: a verse play in five acts by Maurice Rostand." He never recovered. *Le Figaro*, whose publisher Gaston Calmette was a friend of Edmond Rostand, printed Maurice's poems on the front page and planted rave reviews when Fasquelle brought out his first book of verse in 1909. Delighted with himself, he would visit Charvet's nearly every day to buy a new cravat and minced about with a top hat perched on his mop of orange curls. Canes, red carnations, and silk foulards were the accessories of a poetic *allure*, not to mention Guerlain's gardenia perfume, which he sprinkled on himself perhaps too liberally (as the asthmatic Proust discovered, much to his horror, when young Rostand finally gained admittance to the cork-lined bedroom). But his accessories would become increasingly a woman's, and the poetic pose gave way to outright insanity.

The first issue of *Schéhérazade* appeared on November 10, 1909; it contained pieces by the editors and by boulevard literati such as Abel Bonnard and Francis de Croisset. The lead poem was a feminist panegyric of Scheherazade by Jane Catulle-Mendès. Cocteau contributed a short story, or long prose poem, entitled "How

Monsieur de Trêves Died." A lamentable period piece, it takes place in Venice, where a mysterious nobleman, dying of wounds suffered in a duel, summons his three mistresses—one Russian, one Italian, and one French—whose honor he had defended; they begin fighting with one another, the scene fades, Monsieur de Trêves starts hovering, in his mind's eye, over Venice and expires with the sunset. Pregnant with symbols, it reads like Pater at his worst, a squeamish, falsely poetic style perfectly suited to dying azaleas or to the kind of clever conceit Cocteau published in the second issue, called "Night Leaves a Park" (dedicated to the actress Gilda Darthey), night personified as a woman being driven out by the vulgar sun:

> *Au revoir! il le faut, pour désunir les couples,*
> *Que je longe en glissant sur mes pieds bleus et souples*
> *L'espalier placide où dorment les fruits mûrs . . .*
> *J'ai voulu résister debout contre les mûrs . . .*
> *Mais devant ce vainqueur mon orgueil se dérobe*
> *Regarde: un cri du coq a déchiré ma robe!*

> (Goodbye! gliding along on supple blue feet
> The serene espalier whose fruit are asleep
> I must separate couples lying entwined . . .
> Flat against walls I lagged behind . . .
> But with this assailant my pride will not vie
> Look! my dress has been torn by a rooster's cry!) [2]

The second issue included fourteen previously unpublished poems by Mallarmé, which, presumably, Jane Mendès had entrusted to Cocteau. But with each successive issue (there were only six in all, appearing irregularly between 1909 and March, 1911) *Schéhérazade* became increasingly an organ for the rhyming ladies of Paris, as if its goal were to put words in the mouth of an inscrutable odalisque that Paul Iribe had drawn for the cover. It was prophetic of Cocteau's artistic ties with *haute couture*, especially his close friendship with Christian Bérard, that Iribe (whom Paul Poiret—the Dior of his day—considered a prodigy) should have

2. These poems and others appeared in Cocteau's second book of verse, *Le Prince Frivole*, published by Mercure in 1910.

lent him one of his fashionably pneumatic nudes. He and Cocteau would collaborate on yet another magazine during World War I.

Schéhérazade's table of contents (including poems by Mme. de Rohan and Natalie Barney, Mme. Aurel's maxims, a musical score of Reynaldo Hahn's) gives, if nothing else, a fair indication of Cocteau's strenuous social life. He belonged to that band of wealthy young torchbearers who spent their days paying calls on famous literary figures such as Rostand or Mme. de Noailles and spent their nights adorning salons. Great hostesses of the late nineteenth century such as Mme. Aubernon and Mme. Émile Straus had resigned from the social scene, but Madeleine Lemaire still received on Tuesdays, and Mme. de Loynes, whose "stars" had been Ernest Renan and Hippolyte Taine, preserved the remnants of her salon. Moreover, a whole new generation of hostesses, as yet obscure, had been born, which gave rise to a confused interregnum. Ladies, to avoid conflicts with one another, devised calendars so irregular that even the habitués lost track from one month to another. "Mme. Ganderax receives at 4 o'clock on the first Thursday of every month, and on every Friday save the first." A manual listing Parisian salons by neighborhood and date served as the handbook of young *arrivistes*.

Cocteau, a decade and more after Proust, followed in his footsteps. Hovering about like a gorgeous, spirited dragonfly over parched fields, he managed to glimpse a world on the extreme wane. While Proust, who had retired some years before, was embalming its haughty youth in *Remembrance of Things Past*, Cocteau became acquainted with its irascible old age. Encountering Mme. de Chevigné on the staircase of 10 Rue d'Anjou, where she had moved in 1911 after her husband's death, Cocteau, desperately angling for a pretext to stop and talk, hugged her lapdog, Kiss. "Watch out!" she cried in a voice gravelly from cigarette-smoking. "I don't want him smothered in your face powder." Despite this inauspicious debut they became friends, Mme. de Chevigné, grateful to people who amused her, introducing him all around when they attended the Opéra. "When I first met Aladin," wrote the Princess Bibesco, "he already had free access to Madame de Chevigné's salon. He played the role of page, impertinent, spoiled, doing whatever his fancy dictated. Before long he had been elevated from page to squire, escorting her on her evenings out; they would have themselves announced at the English embassy under the improvised title of Count and Countess d'Anjou, in honor of the street they both inhabited."

Unlike Mme. de Chevigné—who could not read Proust, complaining that her feet got stuck in his long sentences—most of the titled ladies whose salons Cocteau attended had literary pretentions. "Cocteau and I," wrote Maurice Rostand, "often met one another in the salons I began to frequent: Mme. de Pierrebourg's, where more than one election to the Academy was engineered, and the Duchess de Rohan's, where everybody, the best and the worst, Barrès and Théodore Botrel, was received indiscriminately." These ladies, measuring their verse against Mme. de Noailles', belonged to that clan of poetesses so conspicuous and so cruelly mocked before World War I. One entire issue of the satiric weekly *L'Assiette au Beurre*, appearing February 10, 1912, is devoted to such women of letters. The cover shows a gowned lady, astride a winged mule, holding a lyre and singing while her pathetic mount brays beneath her weight. One victim, angered at being called an "amateur," cried, "Just think of it, calling us amateurs: we who no longer even count our feet!" Unquestionably, certain salons could not tell Pegasus from a braying ass. Mme. Aurel—rather like Mme. Aubernon, whose dinner guests were not allowed to wander from whatever topic she announced in advance (adultery, for example)—issued program-invitations reminiscent of a grade school curriculum: one hour of general conversation, one hour of private conversation, then the poet's hour.

Mme. de Rohan's Sundays, however, were the soul of chaos by comparison. Hers was less a salon than a *kermesse* for rhymers who milled about the splendid mansion on Boulevard des Invalides, to the delight of their bountiful hostess. Those whom she particularly liked were favored with invitations to her soirées on Tuesday, when Boni de Castellane and Robert de Montesquiou often appeared. François Mauriac recalls getting an invitation from her as soon as his first book of poems, *Hands in Prayer*, was published in 1909. A gangling youth fresh from Bordeaux, he was dazzled by the company, whose titles the butler announced in a stentorian voice. Mme. de Rohan, part and parcel of a world nearly devoid of sentimentality, prizing wit above heart and manners above everything, in which the actor Le Bargy could in all seriousness give lectures on the art of carrying a cane, was the exception who proved the rule. During the war she converted her villa into a hospital, run by the Dames de France. Maurice Rostand, drafted as a medical auxiliary, spent the war in the very same salon—now filled with wounded soldiers—which he had previously attended wearing formal dress.

Madeleine Lemaire's Tuesdays, featuring Reynaldo Hahn at the piano and enlivened by strange creatures such as Ranavalo, the former queen of Madagascar, had the merit of being ludicrous. Most salons fell short of that, their mirthless egerias finding fulfillment in schemes to elect a writer to the French Academy. Maurice Rostand, arriving thirty minutes late to dinner at Mme. de Rohan's, was snubbed for the evening by her other guests. In bourgeois France, literature was not consonant with social lapses, let alone pranks. It struck poses. Poets wore laurel wreaths, and Muses, the ones to whom young Cocteau paid court, stood on ceremony. At Mme. de Pierrebourg's on the Avenue du Bois, where her lover Paul Hervieu pitted his wit against all comers, Cocteau was occasionally requested to read his verse, which he would do from in front of the fireplace.

Mme. Mühlfeld, the Cinderella of three beautiful Jewish sisters, had literati dispose themselves about her couch, where she showed to her best advantage, for she had crippled legs but was exquisitely formed from the waist up (which explains her cruel nickname, "the beautiful otary"). Her salon, whose protagonists were first Henri de Régnier and later Paul Valéry, waxed bright during the war, while Mme. de Loynes', which had been a light of previous decades, guttered its last reserves of talent. Another monster of punctuality, the Countess de Loynes—born Jeanne Detourbey of a stone mason and a washerwoman in Champagne—did not allow her guests, with the signal exception of François Coppée, to smoke in her presence.

The authority wielded by such women was immense and all-pervasive. They made an art of elections to the Academy and distributed political largesse, especially where the arts were concerned. André Antoine, for example, owed his position as director of the Odéon theatre to Mme. de Loynes, who arranged the appointment with a few strategic dinners in his honor. Prewar France, worshiping as it did the mammaries and buttocks of its women, had the symptoms of a gynecocracy. One of its presidents, Félix Faure, may be said to have died a symbolic death when, making love to his concubine Mme. Steinheil in a secret chamber of the Élysée Palace, he collapsed of a heart seizure.

Cocteau, lacking a sponsor since Mendès' death, began to court Jules Lemaître, whose rise as a critic and Academician had been the artful handiwork of Mme. de Loynes, his titular mistress. Lemaître first met her at a masked ball in the home of Henri Houssaye, a friend from Le Chat Noir, one of the bohemian cafés he frequented. Mme. de Loynes, who had been the mistress of Prince Napoleon, was still sufficiently beautiful to attract a man twenty years her junior; she was, moreover, a cultivated woman and keen enough to perceive from the first that Lemaître, behind his rough-hewn yet oddly feline exterior, had the makings of an Academician. Under her guidance he stopped writing bad verse and came to accept the limits of his scholarly, skeptical turn of mind. Half manicurist, half Muse, Mme. de Loynes took him in hand, much as Mme. Arman de Caillavet had lifted Anatole France from his doldrums, by brute force. She established him on the Rue des Écuries d'Artois, round the corner from her apartment on the Champs-Élysées, and every morning gave (or withheld) her approval to whatever article he had composed the previous evening for the *Journal des Débats*. Appalled by his shoestring ties, she had him outfitted by fashionable haberdashers. Having decided he should write for the stage, she filled her salon with popular playwrights such as Grosclaude and Capus. When the time was ripe for his election to the Academy, she had him elected. A rabid royalist in her advanced years, she ventriloquized her beliefs through him. But Lemaître was not, for all that, a ventriloquist's dummy. Like the wily Odysseus, he looked upon his own transformations with half-cynical bewilderment, allowing Mme. de Loynes to disguise him according to her fancy.

During the 1880s and 1890s a spirit of amateurism had imbued French politics. Clemenceau and Barrès, at daggers drawn in the Chamber of Deputies, had no scruples about frequenting the same salons after dark. This changed radically with the Dreyfus Affair, which, in fusing the political and the social man, split salons right and left. They lost a kind of eclectic grace which had been their chief *raison d'être*. By 1910, when Cocteau made the acquaintance of Mme. de Loynes, whose private fortune helped launch the protofascist newspaper *Action Française*, her only remaining guests were atrabilious monarchists such as Léon Daudet, who amused the company with his ravings and his imitations of Émile Zola. Lemaître, perhaps because he craved some apolitical leavening in his life, welcomed Cocteau, whom he called "my Ariel." He was, like almost everyone else, charmed by this sprite, whose clever verse he could appreciate.

"Had I been a poet," wrote Cocteau in his memoirs (for he later banished his first three volumes of verse from his bibliography), "Lemaître would have feared me. . . . What he liked about me were the petticoats, the harmless trappings of poetry." Lemaître, whose red face and white beard reminded Cocteau of a "hothouse strawberry nestling in January on a bed of cotton wool," reciprocated with vague promises to boost his career, fearing, however, that he would not be understood. "We live in an age of excess," he mourned. "People have lost their equilibrium and the sense of words. My warmest praise would appear faint-hearted." Instead, he allowed Cocteau to read his eight volumes of Athenaeus' *Bouquet of Sophists*. "I shall bequeath them to you," he promised grandly, in the same breath warning Cocteau to beware of wee Anna de Noailles, who coveted the collection and, Lemaître said, would attempt to drag it away "like those insects capable of dragging twigs bulkier than themselves."

It was a prediction uttered half in jest, as Lemaître and Noailles enjoyed being foils, the one large, disheveled, numbering his barbed shafts, the other tiny, blue-blooded, and forever splashing in the flood tide of her own words. Cocteau recalled a July 14th one year before the war when, dining in the Quatre Sergents de La Rochelle with Noailles, Lemaître, and Marie Scheikévitch (a highly intelligent woman, one of Proust's first enthusiasts, at whose salon Cocteau first met Lemaître), a fatal *bon mot* put an end to the festivities. Anna de Noailles, perhaps wishing to add one more petard to the evening's fireworks, secretly invited a fourth guest, Edmond Rostand. In 1897 Lemaître had been the one critic unimpressed by *Cyrano de Bergerac*, and he maintained his aplomb in the face of Rostand's subsequent triumphs. Rostand hoped on this occasion to seduce him. He beamed; he cajoled; but suddenly, at the high point of his brilliant improvisations, his monocle fell out and broke. Perhaps this too was part of the act, for he reached into his pocket and brought out a second monocle, then a third and fourth. Lemaître said nothing, quietly seething. But when Rostand, having burned a hole in the tablecloth, feigned distress and confusion, Lemaître finally spoke. "It's very simple," he suggested. "Sign the hole."

Though Lemaître never did bequeath his eight volumes of Athenaeus to Cocteau, Athenaeus would inspire the title of Cocteau's third book of verse, *The Dance of Sophocles,*[3] whose title page bears the following quotation from *The Bouquet of Sophists:* "In his early youth Sophocles was chosen by Athens to dance at the Salaminian festival." Cocteau, scarcely more than twenty, was dancing nearly everywhere. When Proust late in 1911 visited an exhibition of Chinese painting at Durand-Ruel's gallery, he met Georges Rodier, an elderly dilettante whom he knew from his Madeleine Lemaire days, who started fretting aloud over Cocteau: "What I fear for him is society, he goes into society too much, if he goes into society he's lost!"

Cocteau might have heeded his fears, but never did. He held in his palm the only audience he craved, for the time being. How he appeared in its eyes filters through Romaine Brooks' portrait showing him on a balcony with the Eiffel Tower in the background and white azaleas in the foreground: a bright-eyed adolescent, his body might be a boyish girl's poured into a gray suit, wearing his red rose like a school emblem, and holding a pair of gloves in his lan-

3. *La Danse de Sophocle*, published by Mercure, 1912.

guid right hand as though it were a thin, exquisite *recueil* of his own verse. He looks altogether like a famished, Pre-Raphaelite Byron. The Princess Bibesco recalls Cocteau at age nineteen, when she first laid eyes on him at a dinner party given by Winnaretta ("Winnie") de Polignac, the gruff Singer heiress. "He made a triumphal entry: his head thrown back, his hair twisted into a dark *toupet* above a smooth brow, his face narrow, his nose foxy, his eyes lacquered, slight of build, he walked with the pride of some wild bird fallen into a chicken coop. . . . By way of peroration . . . he declared that he had just come by foot from the Luxembourg gardens where he had awaited spring with whom he had a rendezvous, that he was heralding the Green God who would presently arrive on tiptoe with a cortège of elephants playing the cymbals and blackbirds whistling through their ebony flutes, etc., etc., etc! Having greeted his hostess, he executed a *glissando* across the polished floor and sat beside me at the dinner table."

Cocteau's perfect manners, his velocity, his innocence, his desire to please, his versatile invention, and his ambivalent sexuality made him not only Lemaître's but everybody's Ariel. He was the familiar spirit of a dozen salons. One conquest invariably led to others. The famous Lucien Guitry lived next door, and Cocteau became fast friends with young Sacha, whose passion for theatre answered his own. Through Mme. Chevigné he met *Tout Paris*, including, no doubt, the Greffulhes (the beautiful countess having been another model for Proust's Duchess de Guermantes); through Lucien Daudet, whose name will recur in a later chapter, he met Proust and his acolytes; through the Daudets he met Jules Lemaître; at the Rostands he met Misia Sert (who in turn introduced him to her close friend Diaghilev) and diverse goddesses of the stage such as Bernhardt, Gilda Darthey, and Mme. Simone; through Mme. Simone he met Anna de Noailles.

On spring week ends the *beau monde* forgathered in the countryside, and Cocteau, when not in Maisons-Laffitte with his family, brought his elfin charms to Trie-Châteaux, where Mme. Simone had an estate; to Rostand's Arnaga; to Jacques-Émile Blanche's seventeenth-century mansion in Offranville, near Dieppe; or to the Guitry house in Honfleur where Jean and Sacha would amuse the

guests with their imitations of noted eccentrics such as Lucie Dela-
rue Mardrus, the Sapphic poetess (played by Cocteau), and her
husband, Doctor Mardrus. These week ends were not without their
contretemps. Simone, for example, made the mistake of bringing
together Cocteau and her dour idol Charles Péguy, whose temper
flared whenever someone gossiped about Mme. X's liaison or Monsieur Y's secret vice. "I was imprudent enough," she wrote, "to invite him [Péguy] to the country once with one of our young
friends, full of talent and seductive charm, whose sentimental preferences were not at all a secret. I imagined that his wit would
suffice to certify him. Far from it. The day after their meeting, a
laconic note, drafted in Péguy's Spanish hand, voiced a condemna-
tion allowing no appeal: 'That one, Simone, nevermore!' " She did
not recidivate.

At Jacques Blanche's home, however, Cocteau did not risk meeting the likes of Péguy. Blanche was a painter whose gift had been
stunted by his yearning to cut a figure in high society. He had the
requisite fortune, inheriting millions from his father, Dr. Antoine
Blanche, whose famous lunatic asylum had housed such inmates as
Gérard de Nerval and Maupassant. But this pedigree (his mother
liked to boast that "we have a hundred thousand francs a year, not
counting our dear lunatics") worked to his disadvantage. For a
while, in the 1880s, he and Count Robert de Montesquiou were
close friends, but a brawl ensued—Blanche inviting Robert for a
last tryst on the Île des Cygnes, where he dropped a rosewood box
full of the count's letters into the Seine—and, boycotted by the
gratin, he sought asylum in England. There his exquisite taste,
perhaps more than his art, recommended him to Beardsley, Sickert,
Wilde, and Conder, all of whom lived at one time or another near
Dieppe, where Blanche's parents owned a villa. In his middle years,
when Cocteau came to know him, he remained a *fine mouche* for
celebrities, painting the nobility and famous artists on whom, *in
camera*, he vented his spleen. Stravinsky relates that Blanche came
to do his portrait the morning after *Firebird*. Though Blanche himself had so dismally failed to "arrive," he nonetheless had a flair for
knowing who would.

Cocteau, whose mother had commissioned Blanche to do his portrait, was a frequent house guest. "When I saw Blanche at Dieppe," wrote Élisabeth de Gramont, "he was living, no longer at the Villa du Bas-Fort-Blanc, but in Offranville nearby, where he rented an old Norman farmhouse surrounded by an Elizabethan garden aflame with summer flowers, yellow balsam, hollyhocks, sweet william, bluebells, along with trellised roses. The artist relaxed in the company of his wife and her sisters, painting, playing the piano, reminiscing to Jean Cocteau, whom he was sheltering at the time. Nearly every day he went down to Dieppe, stopping in front of La Case, a promontory crimson with the hundred thousand geraniums belonging to the Count Greffulhe."

Blanche was a connoisseur of talented young exquisites, whose "sentimental preferences," as Simone put it, he secretly shared, but he was a thorough snob as well. That he thought fit to invite Cocteau to Offranville may serve as testimony that Cocteau had indeed arrived. Henri Ghéon, in a review of *The Dance of Sophocles*, leaves no doubt that the Right Bank considered him its future laureate: "When I come to speak about M. Jean Cocteau, I feel slightly cramped. Between his verse and me his face intervenes, or at least the face he has been given by social chroniclers, by theatrical sheets, by all the purveyors of instant glory, who are the first to discern a twenty-year-old genius. M. Cocteau is barely older than that, no doubt. . . . As for his genius, he may believe in it: people have done everything to persuade him of it. Ever since Catulle Mendès ceased to reign over French letters . . . the boulevard has been clamoring for its Poet; the romantic example of Musset, of the poet full of swagger and charm, creating effortlessly, without benefit of study, having only to appear and smile to carry the day—that example was still alive and Monsieur Cocteau appeared just in time to fit the bill. People wouldn't let him go till he agreed to play their child genius."

Having allowed Maurice Rostand a considerable head start, Cocteau soon outdistanced him, for the name Rostand proved a leaden handicap in the long run. Moreover, Cocteau had a variety show of gifts: he was an amusing mimic, an artist, and even, as we shall see, an improviser of ballet scenarios. But Henri Ghéon's caustic, intelligent appraisal in the *Nouvelle Revue Française* was a harbinger of troubles ahead. For the very reasons the Right Bank accorded Cocteau a place on Parnassus, Montparnasse would never quite allow him to scale its superior heights.

His friendship with Maurice Rostand had gradually cooled. To be sure, their names were still linked. They busied themselves with plans for yet another literary review, which never saw the light of day. Having attained their majority, and enjoying the confidence of *Figaro's* Calmette, they sought to promote the fortune of a mere seventeen-year-old, Henri Bouvelet (who never lived long enough to write more than several scattered poems). But Cocteau's circle of acquaintances now embraced more luminous, and more useful, figures than Rostand, whose charm had worn decidedly thin.

Rostand, in turn, had found d'Annunzio and Robert de Montesquiou. Charvet's, dinners with the Count Greffulhe at the Pré Catalan, and masked balls absorbed him completely. His collection of ties included one spangled with silver dust. "I don't know why, but we saw less of Cocteau," he wrote about the 1911–1912 season, sadly unaware of Cocteau's estrangement. In 1912 Cocteau did spend the waning weeks of summer at the Hôtel Colbert in Cambo, he and Maurice swaggering about Biarritz among prodigal Russian grand dukes, gorging themselves on *pâtisserie*, and, with unequal enthusiasm, drafting plans for their new magazine. On his return to Paris, Cocteau, in lieu of a valedictory to Rostand, unburdened himself of the following letter to Mme. Simone:

Dear and marvelous Simone,

Am back, my nose already stuffed again and my cheeks hollow— Paris, unbreathable after the opulence of Basque weather, which must be savoured like colorless honey or a bowl of clear corn broth—The Rs are so nicely matched to Cambo that one's fright is dispelled, all the insane minutiae of their life acquiring a *raison d'être*—The rust and rosy *bouboule*, his monocle, his Lilliputian feet, his red carnation, his weatherproof cape and his cane, the worn blue jeans, his crimson jerseys and his cyclamen scent, the brioche atop a pedestal of sugar and the anarchist . . . divulge their true meaning, and henceforth I shall not be shocked on seeing the Rostands in the lobby of the Majestic, decorated by A. Bit-Phony—Tender chitchat about you with the Countess Anna—Avoiding society, have great projects afoot . . .

Fraternal Embassies [4]

This letter reveals the twofold cattiness of literary and pederastic circles. Like Proust, Cocteau thrived in an atmosphere of intrigue.

Cocteau first met the actress Simone in an elevator. She was on her way to see Edmond Rostand in the Hôtel Meurice, and he to see Maurice, his new literary collaborator, for *Schéhérazade* had just been conceived. Simone was a petite, beautiful, and highly literate Jewess whose acting career took root in the same soil as Colette's writing career: an unhappy marriage. Her Willy had been Le Bargy, sauve and romantic lead of the French stage, whose venality became obvious to her on their wedding night. Seeing that he was more engrossed in his newspaper than in her, she asked why; imperturbably he explained that he had married her for her money. Their marriage survived this admission for several years. She acted her first role on a dare, in 1900. By 1905, the year her marriage dissolved, Simone was no less famous than her husband. If her nervous style of acting and her sharp voice delighted the *aficionado* of Henri Bernstein's melodramas, her qualities of mind endeared her to writers having no connection with the stage, notably Péguy, Alain Fournier (with whom she fell in love), and the Countess Anna de Noailles. Lacking a voice to match her verse, the countess adopted Simone as her official spokeswoman; when invited to read, she would either demur or call upon her proxy.

It was Simone who introduced Cocteau to Anna de Noailles. "She was just leaving some lecture or other," he wrote. "I must admit that on our first encounter she threw me for a loop. Experienced in scintillating, in playing a role, in executing famous somer-

4. This letter has a number of obscure allusions: (a) "the anarchist" may refer to Maurice Rostand's quixotic involvement with a futurist splinter group on the Left Bank; (b) "the Majestic," a pretentious pile on the Avenue Kleber, the favorite hotel of wealthy South Americans, served as the Rostands' home following their departure from the Meurice; its lobby was decorated by two painters given to the floral excesses of *art nouveau*—Hélène Dufau and Gaston Latouche, whose names Cocteau has telescoped into one, La Touche Dufau (A. Bit-Phony).

saults, she accepted Simone's intelligence as sufficient collateral and straightaway, without the least preamble, performed an act her intimates knew by heart, but capable of making any new spectator feel like the village idiot." The countess was not only an accomplished poet but the very soul of a neoromantic renaissance. Cocteau saw in her his spiritual partner and played Seraphitus to her Seraphita. She determined Cocteau's mannerisms, her monologues set him a fatally unforgettable example, she infiltrated his verse and—what may be still more revealing—his very handwriting which, over a period of five years, was absolutely undistinguishable from hers. He came to be known in society as "Anna-*mâle*."

If Anna de Noailles put on the airs of an exiled Levantine princess, she had some title to them, for she was the daughter of a Rumanian prince, Gregory de Brancovan, and of Ralouka Musurus, a Greek beauty whose father had been the Sultan's Ambassador to the Court of St. James's. She was closely allied to another of Rumania's princely clans, the Bibescos, who, like her own family, preferred Paris to their vast domains in Wallachia. Anna spent her youth in two homes, one in Paris, where the Brancovans dined before a Gobelin tapestry representing Ahasuerus and walked down foyers lined with portraits of their crowned and sceptered ancestors, among them Zoë Mavrocordato in whose arms Lord Byron died; the other house, in Amphion, called the Villa Bassaraba, overlooked the Lake of Geneva. In her testament the countess arranged to have her corpse divided accordingly: her heart lies buried beneath a stele in Publier near Amphion, and her body in Père-Lachaise.

If the *beau monde* is more given to music than to literature, this was especially true of the elder Brancovans, Anna's mother being a gifted pianist whose musical companions included Ignace Paderewski. The Brancovan children, however, did not follow suit. Constantin, the eldest son, founded a literary review called *Renaissance Latine* in which Proust published some of his early writing. And Anna, after demonstrating her ineptitude at the clavichord, began from the age of thirteen to write poems, modeling her verse on Musset's. Musset, however, was soon eclipsed by another poet. "Scarcely a day passed," she wrote, "without some friend of my parents reciting a poem of Victor Hugo's." Like the fabled frog who huffs and puffs hoping to inflate himself into an ox, this slight woman filled her lungs and sought the timbre and amplitude of Hugo's voice, making sounds that ring hollow today but coming close enough, in 1900, to satisfy ears keyed for any romantic vibration. With naturalism triumphant in the theatre and the novel, with poetry becoming increasingly hermetic, here was a poet offering accessible sentiments, technical *tours de force*, and a verse line having the sweep of Hugo's. It was pure bravura, but her age loved bravura.

In 1897 she married a wealthy and gloriously titled young nobleman, Count Mathieu de Noailles, bearing him a son three years later, chiefly to get her dynastic obligations out of the way. Matrimony did not suit her; it was a mere hiatus in her headlong plunge toward glory. Even more than her poetry, which suffered the consequences, Anna de Noailles was Anna de Noailles's vocation. "She always had resplendent eyes," wrote Colette, "eyes so big they brimmed onto the temples slightly." And she used her eyes, like a basilisk, to stare down anyone threatening to interrupt her sacred monologues. Anna de Noailles talked as if her life depended on it, nonstop, firing images like buckshot in the hope that one would hit the mark, using her arsenal of conjunctives so skillfully that a single sentence would go on forever. This act of hers was accompanied by a St. Vitus's dance: a crossing and uncrossing of the legs, a sweeping back of copious jet-black hair that fell in long, wild tresses, a clicking of her multistranded pearl necklace, long fingers (of which she was inordinately proud) incessantly at play as if projecting Chinese shadows on the far wall.

Recalling the aftermath of a chamber-music concert at the Princess de Polignac's, Cocteau wrote that suddenly he caught sight of Mme. de Noailles surrounded by a group of ladies. "She was performing singular exercises. The nightingale, before it begins to sing, flexes itself. It croaks and caws, it lows and screeches, and those not acquainted with its customs stand bewildered at the foot of the nocturnal tree. This was merely the countess' prelude. I observed her from afar. She was sniffing, sneezing, bursting into laughter, uttering soulful sighs, letting her shawls and Turkish beads fall to

the floor. Then she made her throat swell, swiftly curled and un-
curled her lips, and began. What was she saying? I don't recall. I
know that she talked, and talked, and talked; people started crowding the room, youngsters at her feet and the older guests seated
around her in a semicircle. I know that the Princesses de Polignac
and Caraman-Chimay (her friend and sister), standing on either
side of her, looked like seconds in a boxing ring. I know that the
servants in black garb and the powdered valets, wearing knee
breeches, peered from behind doors slightly ajar."

Emmanuel Berl, whom she befriended when he was a young
man, suspects that the countess sincerely believed she had no right
to keep quiet, fancying herself the mere transmitter of some divine
message. "I am a great poet," she would openly proclaim. But the
roots of her prolixity come to light in one or two fragmentary
reminiscences. "[As a child] I was entirely dependent on the affection of all other people," she wrote, adding that from the age of six
or seven she sought "to build a private little universe and narrate
myself." Elsewhere she wrote: "A sickly and voracious child, I demanded glory and immortality." This indiscriminate craving for
recognition, for love, consumed her to the end.

No one could have understood this more keenly than Jean Cocteau, a kindred spirit fated to dance within the same circle of fire.
"The countess stuffed her ears to whatever wasn't fanfare," he
wrote, unself-consciously. "Like the charming tree frog, which she
resembled with her starlike hands, her slender form, and her palpitating throat, she could not resist the color red." A Dreyfusard by
profession, she also professed to love the notorious anti-Dreyfusard,
Maurice Barrès—taking no chances with posterity. Privately she
preferred the company of fellow aristocrats, publicly her heart bled
for the people. She received Robert de Montesquiou as well as left-
wing deputies, keeping the latter hidden in her library till the
former departed.

"Mme. de Noailles," wrote Barrès, "is an Oriental princess for
whom the Sultan, whatever his name, be it Waldeck-Rousseau,
Clemenceau, Briand, or Caillaux, always wears an aura of prestige."
Rather, she beheld glory with the eyes of a child admiring it for its
own sake; for her, it was the *summum bonum*, a self-justifying

Essence whose earthly embodiments, however venal, must command respect. Children do not place a premium on modesty, nor did Mme. de Noailles, revealing all of herself in her angry reflexes. Once, discussing love with Colette who said something irritating, she cried: "You, love? Why, you don't even love glory!" Another time, discussing God with Cocteau, who dared cross her, she chased him onto the landing and spat a final assertion down the staircase: "Besides, it's simple. If God exists, I would be notified before anyone else!"

At length this profusion of nerves, words, and white nights took its toll. Toward 1913, the sixth year of silence following the publication of *Éblouissements*, a book that had drawn hyperbolic praise from Barrès, from Péguy, and from Proust, she tucked her head under her wings like a dying bird . . . very slow to die.

An apartment on the sixth floor of 40 Rue Scheffer served as her aerie; there she spent most of the day in bed with the blinds drawn, coming alive only at night. "It would be eleven o'clock or noon outside," wrote Colette, one of the few permitted to see her at that hour, "but in her room it was the dark hour of sleep, of suffering." Like the Countess Greffulhe, who had a house physician all to herself, the Countess de Noailles surrounded herself with medical specialists: Babinski for the nerves, Vaquez for the heart, Henriquez for some other organ.[5] Her illness, like her poetry, was dosed in almost equal parts with theatre and reality. She suffered as it behooved the Countess de Noailles to suffer, with panache. Once, in Munich, after some three and a half uninterrupted hours of Wagner, faint with hunger and enforced silence, she was taken to a restaurant by her companions, among them Emmanuel Berl. "She straightaway gave vent to her phobia of syphilis," he wrote, "convoking the waiters, having them serve witness that the silverware was obviously contaminated: 'Look, just look, the knives are crawling with microphytes.'" Even when it became apparent that life was really slipping out of her, she never let on, husbanding what energy she had so as to set it ablaze for a few hours every night.

5. During her last years Mme. de Noailles formed an intimate friendship with her doctor Mme. Francillon-Lobre, to whom she bequeathed, among other things, her unpublished journal.

In the evening [wrote Colette] she had her whiteness, her transpar-
ence of precious wax, her pale and constricted nostrils, the deep,
serene arch of her eyebrows—in the evening, she had everything we
didn't. Her titled guests and those who governed them listened, awe-
struck. A kind of martial vivacity drove her onward. She spoke, and
night, undoing us with fatigue, passed over her like dew. We knew
that midnight had sounded, that it was one, two, three in the morning. We women felt our faces caving in beneath overheated rouge,
the men began to show a shadowy growth of beard on their chins.
. . . But Mme. de Noailles kept talking, and preserved her floral
pallor. As night waned, her face, just above the cheeks, showed a
faint tinge of pink, like tuberoses.

Half-jestingly, not even half, Anna de Noailles wrote her own
epitaph. It could serve to commemorate a whole society doomed by
World War I: the aristocracy she amused, dazzled, and exasper-
ated, the aristocracy that made her possible. "I shall have been useless," she would often say, adding, "but irreplaceable."

Mme. de Noailles once created a small sensation by saying she
would like to have a child by Jean Cocteau. Unlike Ellen Terry,
who proposed to George Bernard Shaw that they create an ideal
infant endowed with her body and his mind, the countess must
have seen in Cocteau her male self, dreaming, through him, of re-
producing by parthenogenesis. He paid frequent visits to the Rue
Scheffer, "the room of a child 1900 style," its walls covered with
blue and white striped cretonne, its Louis XVI furniture painted
Trianon gray and centering on an enormous bed whose counterpane was invariably stained with ink or paint, depending on the
countess' creative outlet for the day. Beneath water colors of the
Parthenon, of Minerva, of the Birth of Venus, they communed,
two voluble children, one waiting for a breach in the other's
monologue.

Outside her room, in the larger world where she had a gallery to
conquer, he was a redoubtable enemy. One friend of theirs recalls a
dinner at which Mme. de Noailles was, as usual, dazzling the other
guests. Torn between the obligation to begin her meal and the fear
of being upstaged by Cocteau seated beside her, she hit on an inge-
nious solution. Quickly spooning up some soup, she clapped her

free hand over his mouth. "I admit," wrote Cocteau, "that, as soon as I felt springing up between us one of those friendships that endure beyond the grave, I hedged myself with every possible precaution. . . . After several bad experiences, I decided not to meet her in public."

The countess became an integral part of his fantasy world. He described her eyes as being so inordinately large that they seemed simulacra of eyes painted onto white adhesive. Aren't those the eyes (using that very device) that he would give the statue in *Blood of a Poet,* the princess Death in *Orpheus,* the Sphinx *The Testament of Orpheus?* She was unquestionably instrumental in his abandoning the sweetly plaintive mode for classical themes. "I have written this night," she once confessed to her friend Lucien Corpechot, "the only pages I should like to leave behind. They concern my romantic youth and my return to Greece through Homer, through Sophocles. . . . When I was a little girl I wept while reading about prisoners on an enemy galley-ship who obtained their freedom because they knew by heart a song of Euripides. What hope! Those who know a bit of Homer, of Sophocles, of Euripides are guaranteed release from their romantic bondage."

Accordingly, Cocteau hellenized himself, writing a romantic lament on the Trojan War and a long elegy on one of the minor characters in Homer's *Odyssey,* Pirous, whom the Sirens seduced to his death. Not to be outdone by the countess' "Priestesses of the Panathenea" and her "Prayer to Pallas," he wrote an ode to Athena entitled "Homer's Pallas." He coldly echoed her prayers; outside the temple in which she raved, he sculpted a decorative frieze. True, the neoclassical or Parnassian school was still, in its lifeless way, very much alive on the boulevard. Cocteau had steeped himself in Hérédia, Moréas, Banville, and Henri de Régnier. But *The Dance of Sophocles* owes its inspiration chiefly to Anna de Noailles, whose favorite philosopher Nietzsche is partly responsible for the title. "Everything divine is light," wrote Nietzsche. "The only God I could believe in is a god who would dance." The countess delighted in quoting these lines, and Cocteau echoed her enthusiasm. In his memoirs he wrote that the year 1900 signified nothing for him apart from Nietzsche's death.

Cocteau was shaken by Henri Ghéon's article on *The Dance of Sophocles* when it appeared in the September, 1912, issue of the *Nouvelle Revue Française,* for the *NRF,* though still a young publication, already enjoyed prestige beyond its years, the more so that it defended no one esthetic line. Its editorial board—Jacques Copeau, Jean Schlumberger, Ghéon, and Gide, among others—was, to be sure, remarkably intelligent, yet it had no monopoly on intelligence, which in any event does not give rise to a mystique unless accompanied by some singular moral quality (be it virtue or vice). Singular these men were; the Savonarolas of literature, they kept their distance from anyone they thought contaminated by the boulevard. If in time, according to the fatal logic of power, they would fall prey to their own inflexibility, during the teens the *NRF* performed a hygienic function, serving notice on amateurs to beware of literature. Under the circumstances, Cocteau might have taken courage, for Ghéon did at least concede him talent, though emphasizing the deficiencies of his every virtue:

> M. Jean Cocteau seems to me exceptionally gifted: but to tell which of his gifts are authentic and which borrowed would require painstaking analysis. . . . Having to choose a métier, he has chosen the Parnassian and neoclassical: in no time at all he has attained masterful virtuosity. He can, by turns and almost without stirring, be lyric, epic, elegiac. He has a sense of words, when to divide and when to enjamb; he makes good use of rhyme; sometimes he even attains beautiful purity; there isn't a poem in this book that doesn't contain at least one felicitous stanza. . . . But all this, including passages he manages to carry off, lacks the moral fiber to hold it together. It all seems at once discovered by chance and deliberately schemed; this madman is too sure of himself; this artist loses his head too often: he has not yet found his balance.

Cocteau did not take courage, however, nor was it in his nature to find equilibrium. He would fix credulously on one harsh word, discounting a thousand compliments, not so much sensitive as *flayed.* The sensitive person and the *écorché* belong to different orders. The former can modify his voice; the latter, speaking through a voice that is not his own, obeys a dialectic that rules out all possibility of change. Cocteau's affections and suffering derived from his inability to separate himself from others: his self was global, yet phantasmal. Ubiquitous, he was everywhere and nowhere. He was condemned to live on both sides of the fence, but this malediction proved, historically speaking, to be his saving grace. He, better than anyone, could promote a dialogue between the *beau monde* and the avant-garde, a dialogue destined to bear artistic fruit. Moreover, his gift as an impresario declared itself early. By 1912 he was implicated in the worlds of Gide on the one hand and of Proust on the other.

How had he met Gide in the first place? Perhaps at Mme. Mühfeld's salon, or perhaps on his own initiative. Jacques-Émile Blanche says that Cocteau, happening on a copy of Gide's *Paludes* in Offranville one week end, was overwhelmed by the book. This may well be true, for in his first letter to Gide, dated April 20, 1912, he apologizes for his past. It is a revealing palinode:

Sir,

You are about to read a letter dictated by emotion. I have just returned from Algiers, that ever so ugly and ever so captivating city to which I brought your complete works (excepting *André Walter*, difficult to borrow from its prudent owners, and *Amyntas*, which my book dealer will procure for me like balm for a soft, Oriental wound).

Enthusiasm is, it seems to me, one of the highest forms of vanity. The stronger it is, the more it proves what instinctive value we accord our judgment. Hence my discomfiture. For I still find it impossible . . . to admit this vanity without which my transports would be no better than anonymous.

In a way, this is a letter "to be opened later on," inspired by the double voyage I've just made, on boats and in books.—A hasty and feverish childhood, a falling-in with baleful guides, all in all, a terrible detour followed by second thoughts, arising from some atavistic impulse toward the right path: that is what suddenly foists me into your presence; confronting you, I see a face secretive, noble, and *pure.*—You meet in me a Nathaniel who finds that he is "a born prodigal son," but your lamp, shedding light on the steps of a person and on the fence along a road, is also a gentle *beckoning* light. —I offer you my profound gratitude. You have taught me how to spread myself, without spreading myself thin. Isn't that the password to the treasure?

Jean Cocteau

In the face of Gide's quips (like Ghéon, Gide reproached him for his unhomogenized influences), Cocteau flailed about helplessly, alternating between injured self-defense and total self-abdication. He signed his letters "your Nathaniel," thus embodying the hero of Gide's *Fruits of the Earth*, just as he would years later appear before Picasso dressed as a harlequin; at the same time, he defended his poetry on the grounds that it was not for him to choose his style: "Although this dance (*The Dance of Sophocles*) has taken me quite far down the primrose path, and I shall have to attempt a conversion; although it shows my puerile influences and forces me into leaps I find dislocating, it nonetheless represents one phase of my curve, and I have neither the right nor the means to withstand its disorder." Living neither in his own skin nor quite in Gide's, he proudly observed the intricacies of his own design, yet prepared to sign away his name.

Gide, obviously enjoying the role of Luther, and playing, at times wantonly, with someone in whom he sensed not so much the "born prodigal son" as the born victim, took an especially dim view of Cocteau's devotion to Mme. de Noailles. "Your blood," he teased, "reflects a Cretan rose." [6] Cocteau parried by describing himself as a "geranium from the Seine et Oise" (effecting a pun: "Oise" and "*crétoise*" rhyme). But he parried only half-heartedly, half-inclined to side against the countess, half-persuaded of her genius. In a sense, Gide served as his literary conscience whereas Anna de Noailles embodied his manner, his game, his luxury. "Simplify your handwriting," Gide advised, by which he meant the countess' curly script that Cocteau took such pains to imitate,[7] counseling him, in this typically oblique way, to divorce her. Gide, perpetually at

6. Anna de Noailles's own image of herself: her mother's family originally came from Crete.
7. "My works were written with a strange fountain pen. It had been given to me by Madame de Noailles, it disappeared and reappeared in unforeseen circumstances, to assist me no doubt in revising an unjust verdict. A long rubber suction tube syphons up the ink, intriguing everyone who attends the operation. The countess' curly handwriting required very flexible pens unprocurable today."

grips with his own private demons, may have been right for the wrong reasons. It was difficult to know, for Gide's Protestant pact with the simple and unadorned did not reprieve him from fits of jealousy directed against people who indulged themselves without scruple, who could afford flourishes, who, he feared, possessed more charm and levity than he. In all events, Cocteau took his advice: " 'Simplify your handwriting.' This remark," he admitted years later, "served me better than a great deal of literary criticism. Subsequently, my handwriting became quite illegible, but authentic."

What was his truth if not his vulnerability, his exasperating innocence? Because he required love from both sides he was doomed to be a shade floating in between, repeating *Sic et Non* for the rest of his life, like an infernal *pensum*. Fifty years later, only one year before his death, he wrote a tribute to the countess entitled "The Countess de Noailles, Yes and No." The countess and Gide had long since returned to dust, but Cocteau, the eternal youth, hemmed in by his ghosts, still felt called upon to defend himself:

> How many times did I hear myself reproached for being influenced by Anna de Noailles. Our grand inquisitors forget that many poets find their way after living benighted in a milieu in which they must grope about for themselves. The countess, Rostand, Mendès served as guides when I began emerging from a family tainted with eclecticism. It's easy enough to gain one's footing in Literature when the truant path is one's main line, but much less easy for the son of a bourgeoisie from which nearly all our poets have sought to escape. No one scolds Rimbaud for the execrable verse he dedicated to Banville, nor painters for the paintings they did before discovering themselves. It is as if my judges cling to a period in my life when poetry seemed to me a mere game.

But Cocteau was not Rimbaud. While begging his way into the chaste pages of the *NRF* ("Dear Gide, Prince, or Duke, of Imbroglio, HELP! I'M COUNTING ON YOU AND ON GHÉON"), he was also begging his way into the not-so-chaste heart of Robert de Montesquiou. Returning from Algiers, that "ever so ugly and ever so captivating city" where, presumably, he had read the complete works of Gide, he wrote to Montesquiou a few months later: "I have just returned from Algiers, that frightful but captivating city where a flaccid odor of Marseillaise absinthe and Arabic camels floats in the air," turning elaborate compliments on Montesquiou's latest volume, *The Ladies' Gambling Den*, and thanking him "with a respectful and faithful heart for having opened the heavy, resistant door to enthusiasm." Forswearing his "baleful guides" for Gide, who found him too dandified, here he was courting Proust's Baron de Charlus, who found him rather too bourgeois. At the very center of Proust's world, Cocteau encountered, in Montesquiou, a figure no less charismatic than Anna de Noailles.

3

Saints and Maenads

Robert de Montesquiou-Fezensac had all the refinement and awesome consistency of the inhuman. He managed to sustain throughout his life an immaculate pose in defiance of nature, conversing tirelessly with the one person on earth he considered above reproach: himself. Not only did he possess the immense fortune needed to stage his life appropriately but he had, in addition, a veritable genius for narcissism. In his earliest recorded grievance he complained of being addressed in the familiar by his schoolmates: *"Mais je ne tiens pas à être tutoyé!"* A mere child, he already sensed the danger inherent in *tu*, a syllable representing some obscene intrusion, a whole world of touching and feeling, of vulgar exchanges threatening his sublime containment.

It is as if this man, whose name has something improbably ornate about it, had not been born but imagined, by Baudelaire.[1] "Dandyism," observed Baudelaire, "appears especially during periods of transition, when democracy is not yet omnipotent, when the aristocracy is half stumbling and stooping. In the turmoil of such moments, a few men, declassed, disgusted, out of joint but rich in native mettle, conceive the idea of founding a new aristocracy the more difficult to overthrow for having as its foundation the most precious, the most indestructible faculties, which work and money cannot in themselves confer. Dandyism is the last burst of heroism in the midst of decadence." Montesquiou merely paraphrased this, requiring but two sentences to dispose of his antecedents (who included d'Artagnan): "Our ancestors having used up the substance of our line, my father inherited only a sense of grandeur, with the

---

1. Being a ready-made invention, he served as the model for Des Esseintes in Huysmans' *Against the Grain* and the Baron de Charlus in Proust's *Remembrance of Things Past*.

result that nothing was left for my brother, who had grace enough
to disappear early in life. As for me, I shall own the glory of having
added to the ducal hat of the Fezensacs the crown of the poet."

Suffering from a fundamental inaptitude for life, he found his
credo in Balzac's chapter on Swedenborg, the Swedish mystic.
Notwithstanding the vocation he made of appearances, what sustained Montesquiou was his belief in a spiritual Beyond where disembodied doubles address one another in rhymed couplets. On
earth, whenever he found a woman apparently answering his an-
drogynous dreams, she would mistake his compliments for passion
or grow weary of their visual *amour*. For a time he and Sarah Bernhardt, who cannot be told apart in Nadar's photograph of them,
would recite poetry in unison, delighted with their uncanny resemblance. But, alas, Bernhardt was also a voluptuary. One evening she
contrived to have a playlet they were improvising terminate on her
ottoman, with the result that Montesquiou, verging on nervous collapse, returned home and vomited all night and into the next day.

He might have found a seraphic mate in the so-called *petite
classe:* ladies such as the Baroness Deslandes or Jeanne de la Vaudière, who served as the Muses of *art nouveau*. But the baroness,
whose tiny hands and feet delighted Sir Edward Burne-Jones, preferred muscular lion-tamers,[2] while Jeanne de la Vaudière, author of
The Mortal Embrace, The Half-Sexes, and *The Androgynes,* lived
a withdrawn life in the family château of Parigné-l'Évêque,
where it was rumored that she communed by torchlight with her
parents, whose glass coffins lay in the cellar.

Robert de Montesquiou never for a moment lost his reason, being
himself *reasoned*, here again answering Baudelaire's conception of
the perfect dandy: "[Dandyism] is above all the ardent need to
make of oneself something original, contained within the outward
limits of convention. It is a kind of cult of the self which can survive the quest of whatever happiness may be found in others, in
woman, for example. . . . It is the pleasure of astounding and the
proud satisfaction of never being astounded. A dandy may be

2. Enamored of a lion-tamer at the Neuilly fair who seemed indifferent to her
advances, the baroness attired herself as a kind of priestess and contrived to enter
the lion's cage, where she recited a poem by Jean Richepin. Her boudoir, prefiguring Mae West's, was lined on all sides with white bearskin.

blasé, he may even suffer, but if he does he will smile like the Spartan being gnawed by the fox." Finding no human answer to his ideal of measured sublimity, appalled equally by the excesses of a communicant like Jane de la Vaudière and by passionate women, Montesquiou found lifelong consolation in *things*.

No less obsessed with the "pure" than Mallarmé or Whistler, he unfortunately lacked their imagination; his poetry, cluttered with the names of flowers and jewels, merely bears witness to his rarefied taste. "I am the king of transitory things," he proclaimed. Compulsively designing and dismantling household after household, like stage sets enhancing his own exquisite person, Montesquiou had no peer as an interior decorator.

The villa he called Pavilion of the Muses, opposite the Bois de Boulogne, stood as the consummate expression of his career. Its courtyard, planted with sycamores and boxed rosebays, introduced what Montesquiou described as "the vaulted protuberance of an ample rotunda supporting a semicircular terrace." The marble vestibule housed two statuary groups by Augustin Pajou, and a Cyprian Venus, her face the image of Marie Antoinette's, being towed by a pair of dolphins. The vestibule opened onto a salon whose blond oak wainscoting was adorned with gold thread; a dozen crimson plush chairs, silver-edged, surrounded a large divan covered in tapestry bearing a motif of garlands and birds. Adjoining the salon was the dining room, its fireplace flanked by four Herculeses whose uplifted hands supported the mantel; above it, Whistler's portrait of Montesquiou, looking diabolic and disapproving, glowered over the guests. Beyond, a staircase led to more intimate quarters: the Empire room where Léon Delafosse, a gifted, fey young pianist whom the count favored for a time before cruelly dismissing him, would often perform beneath Ingres's sketch of Franz Liszt; and the rose room, so called on account of its brocade hangings figured with an immense rose vine. The house was, moreover, littered with the countless mementos of Montesquiou's Japanese period when, guided by Jacques-Émile Blanche and Whistler, he had pillaged Paris and London for rare netsukes, Tanagra figurines, Coromandel screens, and every variety of lacquered box.

His library clearly betrayed the weird twist of Montesquiou's mind, for there, interspersed among the volumes (including a whole set that the Goncourt brothers had bound in Japanese silk) lay assorted oddments such as Michelet's bird-cage, Marceline Desbordes-Valmore's guitar, a lock of Byron's hair, Beau Brummell's cane, Henry Becque's spectacles, Baudelaire's drawing of Jeanne Duval's eyes, a plaster cast of Countess Greffulhe's chin, and another of La Castiglione's foot.[3] He seemed to take cynical pleasure in reducing the nineteenth century to a few symbolic droppings. The count's *pièce de résistance* he owed to his beloved major-domo, Gabriel d'Yturri, who unearthed the object in the courtyard of a Versailles convent: the pink marble basin, weighing some twelve tons, which Louis XV had given Mme. de Pompadour for her hermitage. So proud of it was Montesquiou that he hired a photographer to record each episode of its laborious journey from Versailles to the Pavilion in Neuilly.

Montesquiou's poems and novels fill twenty volumes, and, as might be expected, he was no less concerned with the material appearance of a work than with the work itself. His first volume of poems, *The Bats*, appeared in a limited edition which he donated to the few people whose beauty or genius (Mallarmé, the Countess Greffulhe, etc.) made them worthy of the gift. It came in a silk-covered box figured with bats; the volume, printed on rice-paper and protected by yellow silk end-leaves, included original drawings by Whistler and Forain. Like an actor who will play only for a known audience, Montesquiou, fearful of losing his most valued possession—face—surrounded himself with the happy few on whom he could rely not to mishandle him, embedding his words in precious matter beyond the means of vulgarians. He did not produce books so much as *objets d'art*, upholstering the void he was lucid enough to sense in himself. His closest literary associate was Émile Gallé, the celebrated glassmaker, who adorned his vases with quotations from *The Bats;* such was their mutual vanity that they corresponded on little plaques of veneer.

But Whistler, more than anyone, gave the count a spiritual example he would never afterward forget. The Great Esthete invaded

3. La Castiglione was the most famous courtesan in Paris under the Second Empire, and Napoleon III's mistress.

his every mannerism; Montesquiou affected a drawl, like Whistler's, that accelerated toward the middle of a sentence, ending in barks and strident volleys of laughter, all of which he scanned, like a maestro, with one or another of his jewel-encrusted canes. And Whistler's *The Gentle Art of Making Enemies* served as his manual of comportment, his breviary.

The count's insolence was renowned, and nothing was more apt to provoke him than the pretensions of the *nouveaux riches*. Thus, when he and Yturri received an invitation to dine one Sunday in Versailles with Monsieur Bardac, a wealthy financier, they appeared with their faces smeared with sun-tan lotion and wearing white shoes and trousers to signify how lightly they regarded the event. Waving his Panama hat and cane, Montesquiou greeted Bardac by saying: "Unimpeachable sources tell me you have only fourteen million but, judging from the humble proportions of this abode, a very pleasant one but still not Chenonceaux nor the Marais, I see that you are worth ten times that." Turning to Mme. Bardac, he feigned contrition at disturbing her, "because I know what Sundays in the country mean for housewives" (a dozen servants listened aghast). Addressing their young son, whom Proust later befriended, he delivered a lecture on patricidal children, beginning with the House of Atreus.

Montesquiou placed his honor above every other consideration, even when it was ruinous to do so. Having squandered much of his fortune, he asked Bernard Berenson to send acquisitive American millionaires his way. The latter answered, "I shall be delighted to visit your wondrous house. . . . Although I am still in a position to guide the stumbling rich so that they will recognize and purchase true works of art, I have no one on hand for the moment." When clients did finally appear, his pride overriding his need, Robert could not forbear ridiculing them. Reckoning honor more precious than material success, he was Maecenas in his own auction house.

Appalled by the foibles of his contemporaries, frightened by their aging faces, and lonely since Yturri's death, Montesquiou abandoned the Pavilion of the Muses for a pink palace in Vésinet whose previous tenant had been a Parsee millionaire named Mr. Tata. At least forty women, whose lives he had poisoned in verse epigrams called *The Forty Shepherdesses*, breathed a sigh of relief at seeing him some ten miles removed, though he attended dinner parties and the ballet often enough to make them mind their tongues. His speech, his mannerisms, his apparel survived, however, in young esthetes who (as Marcel Proust once had) considered him a paragon. Finding one pretext or another, Proust would decline Montesquiou's repeated invitations, but Maurice Rostand, Albert Flament, and Jean Cocteau paid him court. "Cocteau was imitating everyone," wrote Élisabeth de Gramont, who first met him in 1911, "even people whom he hadn't met, or the deceased. At that time Montesquiou's sounds still reverberated in the air, and Cocteau, like a hertzian wave, had captured them. Acting like a network of telegraph wires, he would relay all the various currents flowing into Paris."

Cocteau laid siege to Montesquiou's all-but-impregnable heart. In August, 1909, he sent him a copy of *Aladdin's Lamp* with the following dedication: "For Count Robert de Montesquiou-Fezensac, in admiring memory of a man who inquires with his heart and not his nose." The same summer, Cocteau sent him a poem in condolence for the death of Yturri and celebrating Montesquiou's new residence in Vésinet:

> Gloved in white, coiffed in gray, dressed in parma
> Garlanded with hydrangeas, faithful to number nine
> You barter your villa for a new abode
> Which you've imbued with still greater charm,
>
> The memory of a heart of which your own is bereft
> Places in your eyes the solemn beauty of a tear
> And your sharp voice is the tireless weapon
> Impaling fools, from the frog to the ox.[4]

A precious poem indeed, accompanied by the following letter:

Sir,

I should be hard pressed not to apprise you of my fresh and respectful enthusiasm. The joy compelling me to this leaf of paper,

4. *Ganté de blanc, coiffé de gris, vêtu de parme, / Fleuri d'hortensias, fidèle au chiffre neuf / Vous troquez votre hôtel contre un refuge neuf, / Que vous avez encore empreint d'un plus grand charme, / Le souvenir d'un cœur dont votre cœur est veuf / Pose à vos yeux la beauté grave d'une larme / Et votre voix aigue est l'infatigable arme / Qui transperce les sots, de la grenouille au bœuf.*

now that I have acquired your book (having to acknowledge most gifts, even from people dear to my heart, usually weighs upon me onerously) is my other excuse for importuning you. Owing to the "deafness" of youth and my silly petulance I once misjudged you; *your* eye, however, discerns, weeds out and chooses instantaneously. I hope one day to find the bridge that will allow me to arch the distance between us, for if I stir, become deformed and reformed like the bank of a river, at least the river no longer carries me away.

Cocteau blamed his failure to win the count on certain rivals. Montesquiou was greatly diverted by these foppish youths defaming one another on his account and remained deaf to Cocteau's repeated entreaties. "I have such respect, such admiration for your work and person," wrote Cocteau, "that I must speak out. . . . I love my friends with courage, bravura, pride, tenderness, deference, and gratitude. Though the honor of possessing your affection has not been my lot, I have the deeply felt pleasure of having secretly offered you mine, unwaveringly." He then curses unnamed gossips "who have run swiftly as Phidippides, without, alas! dropping dead once they've cried their news."

Every such letter persuaded Montesquiou afresh of Cocteau's masochism, and he was not one to spare a masochist the pain he craved. Whenever the two met, at the theatre or at Mme. Daudet's, he would pretend to mistake Cocteau for Anna Pavlova, saying "I know the woman well." Undaunted, Cocteau renewed his struggle for Montesquiou's approbation; unmoved, the count repulsed him. Faux pas followed one another in swift succession, each drawing a new apology from Cocteau:

Dear Count,

I owe you some serious apologies. . . . Last night I had Saint Veronica's fever. Afire with the ecstasy of it, I threw off the sheets of my sickbed to attend this spectacle of affection and enthusiasm. The empty theatre seemed a nave, the scene of a large bosom exhaling a cry of love heavenward; it was at that moment, whose beauty increased when you suddenly made your presence known, I heard you reproach me for bringing my unworthy self to the theatre. That made "my heart so heavy" as to give my sorrow the appearance of being feigned. I could have answered by saying one does not forbid a believer from entering a holy place. But my pain transmitted to my tongue I forget what inept and inapt words. I humbly beg your pardon.

The incident to which he alludes must have taken place in 1911 in the Châtelet theatre, during a rehearsal by the Ballets Russes of Gabriele d'Annunzio's *The Martyrdom of Saint Sebastian*. If so, Cocteau had stumbled into the count's private psychodrama. Together Montesquiou and d'Annunzio staged a Byzantine drama in which Saint Sebastian possesses the equivocal charm of Beardsley's boys and in which Diocletian, the emperor who loved and martyred him, displays the clumsy sadism of a heathen lording it over the here-below. To play Saint Sebastian, Montesquiou recruited Ida Rubinstein, a beautiful Russian Jewess who had recently joined the Ballets Russes. Nude beneath Saint Sebastian's armor, here was the ephebus of Montesquiou's dreams, the last incarnation of Seraphita. In love with both d'Annunzio and Rubinstein, Zeus and Ganymede, the count derived tragic joy from promoting their liaison, off stage and on. Cocteau had crashed a party of archetypes in which he seemed unpardonably *de trop*.

Some palpable signs of Montesquiou would rub off on Cocteau, such as the pink satin cuffs he wore turned up and the ivory-knobbed cane he carried for many years, but his influence was more than met the eye. Montesquiou, living on his own terms, forging his person into a work of art, stood foremost among those "powers of artifice" whom Cocteau admired, the more fervently because he himself could never master their aplomb. Vulnerable, exerting himself to amuse his audience, Cocteau knew whereof he spoke in saying "nothing is more difficult to sustain than a bad reputation." Of two minds, requiring both approval and disapproval, wanting to shock yet hoping to please, he was too erratic for a career of insolence. His scandals would never be as scandalous as he believed; his outbursts would be so disproportionate as to show his underlying innocence. He was the mischievous child who fancies himself a demiurge, the *voyou* imitating Satan. In later years, living in a room adorned with Delacroix's engravings for Goethe's *Faust*, he had before his eyes day and night an image of the greatest "power of artifice," a romantic Lucifer in mid-flight, leering disdainfully over his shoulder.

Cocteau had probably first met Montesquiou at the Daudets' on Rue de Bellechasse. Mme. Daudet, Alphonse's widow, did her utmost to make Montesquiou a "regular" at her salon, reckoning one such aristocrat more valuable than all the writers inherited from her famous husband. He did come, reciprocating with *bons mots* [5] and a verse portrait showing her as the venal, self-seeking "bourgeoise" she was. Lucien, her younger son, fared no better. Set on becoming the count's *mignon*, he wrote a novel called *The Prince of Cravats* whose inspiration was obvious. Montesquiou, unimpressed, administered a verbal hazing which began: "Young Lucien Daudet / Round Princes liked to play." Evidently Lucien's physical beauty did not, for once, prevail.

By 1910 Cocteau had become a familiar face on Rue de Bellechasse. He and Lucien, eleven years his senior, were boon companions. "I owe him many treasures," wrote Cocteau. "Apart from his friendship, and the second family I found in his, it was through him I came to know the Empress Eugénie, Jules Lemaître, and Marcel Proust." Death claimed Alphonse Daudet and Edmond de Goncourt in 1897; Jean Charcot had disappeared some four years earlier, and Zola would barely survive the century. The Daudet salon remained intact, its thick drapes and immovable furniture keeping time at bay; the air smelled the same, hidden braziers perfuming the room with lavender; Renoir's portrait of Mme. Daudet, Albert Besnard's of Lucien, and Eugène Carrière's of Alphonse leading his young daughter Edmée, arrested the family at full bloom. But its tenants had changed. The older son Léon, whose fascism his father would have deplored, swaggered about town. Madame, having thoroughly undone Lucien, queened it over the exquisites who

5. For example, on hearing that Mme. Daudet had arranged a match between her only daughter, an unusually plain girl named Edmée, and André Germain, scion of a colossally wealthy banking family, whose homosexuality was no secret, Montesquiou exclaimed, "*Ce sera un mariage blanc et or!*" ("It will be a marriage white and gold"—a white marriage being an unconsummated one).

comprised his world. The bearded naturalists of yore had been succeeded by young men given to unmanly artifices.

Lucien was bound to spend life as a pet. Burdened with his
father's name and upstaged by a brother whose vocabulary and
expertise at alley-fight tactics made him the most redoubtable
journalist of his day, Lucien lived in the wings. Hoping to fashion a
career, he tried painting, but his chief accomplishment was in
having been Whistler's only French pupil. His gifts could not crys-
tallize, with the result that he turned into a sumptuary creature
whose beauty and amiable hysteria made perfect sense nowhere but
in the drawing room. He was, according to Jules Renard, "a handsome boy, curled and pomaded, painted and powdered, with a little
squeaky voice which he takes out of his waistcoat pocket." Given
alternately to self-abasing liaisons and illusions of grandeur, he
prowled about for young men of the working class, but lived two
seasons of the year in Cap Martin or in Farnborough Hill where,
nearly half a century after her husband Napoleon III had lost his
Empire at Sedan, Eugénie, now an octogenarian, still held court.

Lucien and the empress abetted one another's dreams; he, hanging on her every word, restored her the throne while she, reminiscing minutely and preserving every detail of court etiquette,
granted him membership in an honorary society in which attending
one's empress sufficed to justify one's life. Writing home every day,
Lucien kept his mother abreast of the ghostly routine making up
life at Cyrnos.[6] Occasionally he would allow friends to trespass this
hallowed ground of his (provided they understood their privilege).
In the spring of 1911, Mme. Cocteau and Jean took rooms at the
Hôtel du Cap Martin. Lucien noted, "It is understood that Jean
will be presented to Her Majesty, not here but in Teba, for during
Holy Week only people previously presented are received at Cyrnos. I was explaining this to him when whom should we hear but
the Empress arriving with Solange to select material for her Teba
wardrobe! Jean looked at her from my window; the sight of her in-

6. Cyrnos was the name of Eugénie de Montijo's villa in Cap Martin. Lucien's
collected letters to Mme. Daudet appeared under the title *Dans l'Ombre de l'Impératrice Eugénie*.

timidated him and he fled without being seen." Cocteau did meet
her the following day, and has described the moment:

> I was beginning to lose my nerve, to fear the apparition which could
> no longer be deferred, to conjure up Winterhalter's Decameron
> showing the Empress seated amidst her maids of honor . . . when
> the encounter took place, quickly, unexpectedly, small and black like
> an accident. And, as in the case of accidents, I had time to see the
> obstacle approaching in slow motion, to master my nerves, to anes-
> thetize my emotions. . . . Lucien presented me. "I can no longer
> decorate poets," she said; "here, I shall give you this," brusquely tear-
> ing off a bunch of white daphnes, offering it to me, and watching as
> I placed one in my lapel. . . . [Together we strolled about the
> garden.] She stops and several times bursts into laughter. That voice,
> that laugh breaking off and throwing her backward, where have I
> heard them before? It's a memory of arenas—it is the laugh and
> cackle of young Eugénie de Montijo, the laugh and cackle which
> must have scared, fascinated the timid Napoleon III, the laugh and
> cackle of all young Spanish women stamping their hooflike feet and
> slapping their fans to applaud the matador who was killed.[7]

"Lucien Daudet, Mauriac, and I," wrote Cocteau, "formed a
little band and we were nearly inseparable. What especially amused
us were the parties given by poetical society matrons." Together
they would spend weekends in Offranville at Jacques Blanche's
invitation, the three looking like birds of a feather—jaunty and
favoring pencil mustaches beneath their variously prominent noses.

François Mauriac's adventure among the catamites was not nearly
so long as its unpleasant consequences; fifty years later he would
find himself the victim of his own juvenilia when a journalist of
doubtful repute saw fit to publish a letter in which he had exclaimed to Cocteau, "I kiss your chapped lips!" His liaison coincided with a momentary default of faith; Mauriac's real circle consisted of Bordelais friends whose common idol was the Catholic
poet Francis Jammes.

Cocteau and Daudet tricycled about town with other third

7. This succession of images brings to mind an apocryphal story connected with
Cocteau's ballet *Parade*, which Diaghilev would produce in 1917. The performance
over, one balletomane, incensed, according to Cocteau, by the hoax perpetrated
on her, suddenly appeared backstage and pursued him with a hatpin.

wheels, notably Count Étienne de Beaumont. This immensely tall, elegant, rich young aristocrat, whose eyes had a way of lounging about their sockets or suddenly boggling as if mounted on peduncles, appears to have exercised considerable influence on Cocteau. He had very little education but professed to love the arts. What Beaumont lacked in depth, however, he made up in scandalous hauteur, in extravaganzas, in decoration, staging—at his mansion on Boulevard des Invalides—masquerades for which he became famous in the twenties. Though worshiped by his pious, self-effacing wife, and worshiping her in turn, he made no effort to conceal his sexual preferences. Under Edith's eye, he, Cocteau, and Daudet would cavort about the garden of the Hôtel de Beaumont in black tights, doing exercises prescribed by a painter and dancer named Paulet Thevenaz who devoutly believed in rhythmic calisthenics.

Another of the "thirds" was Reynaldo Hahn, a composer of Lucien's age. He, Cocteau, and Daudet were not profoundly congenial to one another, but they did possess some cohesion owing to the star round whom they revolved in common, a star not as yet quite fixed in the heavens, materializing unpredictably, and known only to the privileged few: Marcel Proust.

Proust's friendship with Hahn and Lucien Daudet dated to the mid-nineties. Hahn, a Venezuelan Jew possessed of a lovely tenor voice, often sang for Alphonse Daudet, but Proust first met him during a musical soirée arranged by Madeleine Lemaire. They soon became fast friends, spending afternoons at the Louvre, discussing Sainte-Beuve, and trading anecdotes on the *gratin*. Presently Proust would begin signing his letters to Hahn "Burnibuls." Hahn was the kind of dilettante Proust loved: introspective yet socially adept, wryly observing people from behind a polite mask, and kind because, knowing his limits, he could afford to be. "I, who am not and shall doubtless never be a master," Hahn wrote, "derive pleasure doing what masters can't be bothered with, carefully constructing a dumb page of arpeggios." Even after Hahn found himself eclipsed in Proust's heart by Lucien Daudet, he remained a staunch friend. Proust's relationship with Daudet was somewhat different. The latter, because he had no firm identity, could conspire the more fully in Proust's. Not only did he try talking like Proust, he ratified his keen sense of the absurd. "Their joint appreciation of people's absurdity brought on a distressing affliction: sooner or later, whenever they went out together, they lapsed into a paroxysm of hysterical laughter." Proust described it as "blind, agonizing, irresistible *fou rire*."

When it was he first met Proust, Cocteau could not recall, but he observes that his "band," notwithstanding Proust's reputation as a social butterfly, always treated him as a great man. Cocteau, who met Proust through Lucien Daudet, proved to be an acolyte jealous of his position and bent on keeping the "happy few" few. He would not, for example, share Proust with Maurice Rostand. "Among Cocteau's letters," wrote Rostand, "which he littered everywhere, disorder being something we considered an attribute of poetry, I happened to notice my name in a letter from Marcel Proust, who, mentioning that he had seen me and my brother one evening at the Opéra, wanted to make my acquaintance. . . . Because Cocteau had not introduced me I decided straightaway to meet him."

If Proust visited his rituals on Cocteau, friendship with Proust could not be otherwise than ritualistic. It involved verbal spoofs, labyrinthine excuses, nocturnal happenings, dinners at the Ritz, and whipped chocolate at Larue, recitations from *Swann* in the cork-lined bedroom, cab rides observing the fixed, hermetic itinerary of a drunk. Proust's rare outings by day usually had some specific object: a building, a painting, a faintly remembered meadow. Cocteau once accompanied him on a visit to Mme. Ayen, who owned a large collection of Moreau's paintings; afterward the two stopped by the Louvre to see Mantegna's *Saint Sebastian*. But his cab rides by night had no such object; they were madly intransitive, "like a telephone ring in an empty house," having all the symptoms of a fit. When he received at home, Proust proved cordially schizoid. Anxious yet afraid to test his manuscript on friends, he would read it aloud but, suddenly hearing himself read, would accuse himself of being a bore. "When we had coaxed him into continuing," wrote Cocteau, "he'd extend his arm, snap up any lead from his jumbled papers, and unexpectedly plop us among the Guermantes or the Verdurins. . . . He'd moan, guffaw, excuse himself for reading so badly." During one such hiatus he visited the bathroom without troubling to close the door; Cocteau could see him "in shirt sleeves, a purple waistcoat over his mechanical toy torso," wolfing down a plate of cold noodles.

Playing a favorite game of Proust's (invented by Mallarmé in *Loisirs de la Poste*), Cocteau would address his letters in rhyme:

> Postman, convey these words without further ado
> To Marcel Proust, on Boulevard Haussmann 102.[8]

These words often announced his own imminent arrival. For hours he would sit with Proust. By 1910 the cork-lined room had become a veritable warehouse for *Remembrance of Things Past*, whose episodes cluttered every surface. A visitor found himself sitting among signs, imbecile fetishes mirroring an unseen universe—such as the photographs of duchesses and footmen, or the copy of *Gladys Harvey* bound in a courtesan's petticoat. Cocteau compared Proust's room to Captain Nemo's *Nautilus*, submerged but equipped with precision instruments plotting an ideogram of the world above.

Did Cocteau fancy his own room on Rue d'Anjou a kindred jumble? It was, rather, the stage setting, a parody of Proust's. The more Proust enclosed himself the more brilliantly his imaginary universe fanned out, while Cocteau, forever dispersing himself, would create an art of enclosures. Proust's room was nothing if not a vehicle of expression; Cocteau wrote best writing about rooms, whose adolescent inmates fail to flesh their dreams, to animate their dolls, to *substantiate* themselves. The clutter on Boulevard Haussmann dissolves like a sign into significance; the one on Rue d'Anjou reflects itself. "This room which kills me," Cocteau would write, "which is a small replica of my drama."

Proust visited Cocteau at 10 Rue d'Anjou, aware that this was also the residence of Laure de Chevigné, whom he had loved forlornly twenty years before. Once, as Proust would rarely commit himself to an announced hour, Cocteau resolved to spend the evening downstairs with the countess, leaving word for Proust to join

---

8. "*Facteur, porte ces mots, te débarrassant d'eux / Au boulevard Haussmann chez Marcel Proust, 102.*" Another rhymed address was: "*102, boulevard Haussmann, oust! / Courez, facteur, chez Marcel Proust.*"

him. At midnight, returning to his flat, Cocteau discovered his quixotic friend on a bench outside the door. "Marcel," he exclaimed, "why at least didn't you wait for me inside? You know that my door remains unlocked." Proust, muffling his voice with his hand, answered, "Dear Jean, Napoleon killed a man whom he found waiting for him inside. Obviously, I wouldn't have read anything except your Larousse, but what if open letters had been straggling about?"

Proust, Lucien Daudet, and Cocteau could claim one defeat in common: Montesquiou. Each had in successive decades courted him, none arousing his unqualified enthusiasm. Proust came closest but, like the others, suffered a congenital defect that Montesquiou could pardon but not quite overlook: the absence of "de" from his patronymic. Moreover, these three had the scruples, the complicated manners, the epicene grace abhorrent to Montesquiou, who liked his men callous. "He's the virile pederast," wrote Proust of Charlus, alias Montesquiou, "in love with virility, loathing effeminate young men, in fact loathing all young men, just as a man who has suffered through women becomes a misogynist." Making a virtue of necessity, Proust, Daudet, and Cocteau found intimacy through their stigmata. Rejected, they avenged themselves on their social superiors by observing them from afar, through caricatural lenses. If they lacked an aristocratic particle, they possessed an abundance of miscreant humor.

But, *en famille*, their humor often gave way to a kind of visceral stuffiness which found release in lightning quarrels and thunderclaps of fealty. Cocteau and Proust staged elaborate scenes over a fur-lined coat, a *pelisse*, for example. Visiting Proust one winter evening, Cocteau announced that he did not own a greatcoat and was freezing. Proust, whose sympathy nothing could awaken more quickly than the mere mention of chill, offered him an emerald with which to buy one. Cocteau refused, but Proust would not be denied; the following day a tailor, his tape-measure in hand, appeared at 10 Rue d'Anjou, only to be summarily dismissed. Proust now took offense. "He supplemented his epistle of grievances," wrote Cocteau, "with other grievances covering some twelve pages which he asked me to convey to the Comte de B—[Étienne de Beaumont]. . . . This interminable indictment ended with a postscript: 'On second thought, say nothing.' " Another time, at Larue, where he and Cocteau often had a midnight collation with the Ballets Russes, Proust in turn complained of being cold. Cocteau straightaway fetched his *pelisse* from the cloakroom, leaped onto the ledge running behind the red plush bench on which patrons sat side by side, and dropped the coat over Proust's shoulders. His gesture was recorded by Proust in doggerel verse:

> To cover my shoulders with satin-lined mink,
> Without spilling one drop from his huge eyes' black ink,
> Like a sylph to the ceiling, or on snow a thin ski,
> Jean leaped on the table and dropped by Nijinsky.

Like other original scenes Cocteau would stage, this was not original—Bertrand de Fénelon (Proust's beloved friend) having executed the same leap, with the selfsame coat no doubt, at Larue, some years before. It would have a third performance, this one definitive, in *Remembrance of Things Past*, where Robert de Saint-Loup is the acrobat. "It is you, dear Jean, at Larue," Proust wrote in a copy he dedicated to Cocteau.

In September, 1913, Proust sent advance proofs of *Swann's Way* to Lucien Daudet and Jean Cocteau. Hitherto they had heard only brief passages delivered by Proust himself. Now, reading it from cover to cover, both realized why they had always treated him as "a famous man"; he returned their excited compliments by asking them to review the book. Daudet's article appeared in *Le Figaro*, and Cocteau's in *Excelsior*. "*Swann* is a gigantic miniature, full of mirages, superimpositions of gardens, plays on space and time, broad cool touches in the style of Manet," wrote Cocteau, whose own style, when he achieved it, would be the elliptical reverse of Proust's. Whereas *Remembrance of Things Past* vouchsafes people and things their *bulk* (an "ideal" bulk, so to speak) by throwing them out of conventional focus, blurring their lines, giving double and triple images, Cocteau will stage a world reduced to its telling features, where *personnages* move like vectors and wear heraldic masks.

That Proust, even in 1912, considered Cocteau more than a

"boulevard" poet cannot be doubted; he protested against Ghéon's harsh review of *The Dance of Sophocles*. But Proust, at once too close and too removed, could not properly advise Cocteau. Only after the latter had attained himself would Proust appreciate the path which had brought him there. Thus, seeing Cocteau's ballets *Parade* and *Les Mariés de la Tour Eiffel* some years later, Proust acknowledged their originality by saying of his character Octave, who mates features of Cocteau and Picasso: "This young man staged sketches, designing sets and costumes that worked on contemporary art a revolution rivaling that accomplished by the Ballets Russes. In short, people well qualified to judge considered his works highly important, almost works of genius, and I, moreover, agree with them. . . . Those who had known him at Balbec . . . aware that he had been the dumbbell of his class, having even been expelled from the *lycée*, surmised that Andrée had created the works he signed. . . . But all this was false." [9]

Cocteau's wrench from his facile posturing would be administered not by a creator but by a great impresario, Sergei Diaghilev, whose spiral livelihood depended on new talent, and whose keenest pleasure he derived from defying the artistic conventions of his age.

In 1909 anyone proposing that the Opéra (officially The National Academy of Music and Dance) offer its patrons a whole evening of ballet would have been dismissed as a fool. The *corps de ballet* did perform, but its role corresponded to that of clowns. Every long opera had a dance number amounting to an interlude, a pleasant "divertimento" which allowed the audience to catch its breath. The routine never varied, nor did the steps; all the roués could safely doze through most of *Faust, The Prophet*, or *William Tell* knowing by an inner alarm precisely when to wake for a close look at the tutu-clad girls. In fact, Wagner's operas, because impossible to interlard with ballet, fell quite flat at first. But dance understood as something more than acrobatic *tours de force* had died in

9. George D. Painter in his biography of Proust notes that Andrée may have been modeled after Jeanne Iribe, Paul Iribe's sister, to whom Cocteau was vaguely engaged for a brief period during the war.

France a century before. Now its exponents came from abroad, first single spy from America, then in battalion force from Russia. By the 1890s Loïe Fuller had reminded the French public (doing it, moreover, from the stage of Les Folies-Bergères) that the dance can *express*. Untrained, quite incapable of performing an *entrechat* or a *plissée*, she swirled her iridescent veils like some ethereal body enveloping her own. When she danced, "sculptured by the air, the clothes rose and fell, swelled and contracted . . . recalling the fluid, tenuous lines of *art nouveau* designers with their predilection for goblets shaped like tulips, grilles like ramblers, and frames of desks and screens like espaliered trees." Unlike the plumpish ballerinas of the Opéra (Julia Sabra, for example, whose bosom taxed all the containing powers of her corset, and whose bloomers came down to the knees), Loïe Fuller created an illusion of slender, deliquescent forms such as "The Orchid," "The Fire," "The Lily." Her performance translated spectacularly the painted dreams of Gustave Moreau, Edvard Munch, Gustav Klimt, and Adolphe Appia.

But it remained for Isadora Duncan to fulfill the prophecy of Loïe Fuller's veils, creating all her effects with nothing but her body. "She gave promise of being someone—a promise kept," wrote Loïe Fuller on meeting young Miss Duncan. Her first Parisian appearance on May 30, 1903, made little impact. French critics seemed more impressed by her precepts than by her dancing. A year later she returned, performing now at the vast Trocadéro rather than the Sarah Bernhardt Theatre. Barefoot, her body visible beneath a gauzy veil, she executed an all-Beethoven program, wreathing, spiraling, recreating all the poses of an Attic frieze. "Unending acclamations hailed these dances unique in the world by their grace, their harmony, their ingenuous nobility, and their expressive power," wrote the music critic Louis Laloy. After ten curtain calls, she addressed the six hundred people remaining, "Isadorables" as they would be known. What she did not say, but had said the year before was this:

The school of the ballet today vainly striving against the natural laws of gravitation or the natural will of the individual, and working in discord in its form and movement with the form and movement of nature, produces a sterile movement which gives no birth to future movements, but dies as it is made.

The expression of the modern school of ballet, wherein each action is an end, and no movement, pose, or rhythm is successive or can be made to evolve from a succeeding action, is an expression of degeneration, of living death. All the movements of our modern ballet school are sterile movements because they are unnatural; their purpose is to create the delusion that the law of gravitation does not exist for them. . . .

To those who nevertheless still enjoy the movements, for historical or choreographic or whatever other reasons, to these I answer: they see no farther than the skirts and tricots. But look—under the skirts farther—underneath the muscles and deformed bones. A deformed skeleton is dancing before you. . . .

It is the mission of all art to express the highest and the most beautiful ideals of man. What ideal does the ballet express?

No, the dance was once the most noble of all arts; and it shall be again. From the great depth to which it has fallen it shall be raised. The dancer of the future shall attain so great a height that all other arts shall be helped thereby.

This lecture was entitled "The Dance of the Future;" its prophecies were soon borne out. What Isadora could not suspect, however, is that her vision would be made fully incarnate by her *bête noire*, a ballet company. Gradually dance re-emerged in France, Fuller's veils adumbrating Duncan's body, and Duncan's body foreshadowing the Ballets Russes. Moreover, they formed an evolutionary continuum. When Duncan toured Russia in 1905 she gained at least one convert in a young dancer from the Mariinsky theatre named Michel Fokine. And when, in April, 1909, Diaghilev brought his newly formed Ballets Russes to Paris for their first season, Fokine accompanied him as the choreographer.

On the evening of May 17, 1909, aristocratic Paris, beautifully attired and bejeweled, turned out *en masse* for Diaghilev's opening. Rodin, Ravel, and Robert de Montesquiou looked on from their stalls. Jean Cocteau was among the few writers present. The Countess Greffulhe, whose patronage assured Diaghilev a *succès de snobisme*, feared the worst, for some weeks before, when Diaghilev introduced her to his dancers at a dinner party in the Crillon Hôtel, she discovered not the sylphs she anticipated but robust, unlettered provincials. How could they hope to embody the dream figures of *Le Pavillon d'Armide*, their first scheduled ballet? As soon as the red curtain parted, the countess' fears were dispelled. An audience used to blear sets and twilit stages found before them Alexandre Benois's gorgeously colored pavilion; eyes hemmed in by chocolate-box pictures of the rococo opened wide and started from their heads at seeing Nijinsky dance a *pas de trois* amid the gold, the Sèvres, the Gobelin tapestries, the Versailles these Russians had brought to Paris. One miracle succeeded another. Roza performed "The Jester's Dance." And in the Polovetz Camp scene from *Prince Igor*, following *Le Pavillon d'Armide*, wave upon wave of wild Polovetzi women rushed toward the footlights. The audience broke into thunderous applause.

"When I entered the loge to which I had been invited," wrote Anna de Noailles, "I didn't quite believe in the revelation I had been promised by certain initiates; but straightaway I realized that something miraculous was happening, that I was witnessing something absolutely unique. Everything capable of striking the imagination, of inebriating, of enchanting and conquering would seem to have been brought together on that stage."

Some nights later Pavlova danced in *Cleopatra* but for once found herself eclipsed—by Ida Rubinstein, doing what came naturally to her, allowing her angular body to assume the poses of an Egyptian bas-relief. Léon Bakst provided a sybaritic setting. Slaves attired in topaz and emerald tossed garlands of roses onto a huge lapis lazuli rug.

The Russian Ballet immediately revolutionized fashion. Ladies, descending on their couturiers with a water color of Bakst's in hand, would emerge as sultanas. Paul Poiret, recognizing the importance of this new travesty, began to design turbans modeled on those worn by rajahs in Indian miniatures at the Victoria and Albert Museum. In 1911 he would give a costume ball, "The Thousand and Second Night," inviting some three hundred members of the *gratin*. They gathered at the entrance, where a half-naked Negro, wearing Bukhara silks and armed with a torch and yataghan, officially welcomed them. Crossing the garden, in which illuminated fountains played beneath blue and gold awnings, they entered the villa itself. In one room, Mme. Poiret sat among maids of honor singing authentic Persian airs. In another, Édouard de Max, standing on a pyramid of cushions, attired in a black silk gandurah and his neck garlanded with strands of pearls, recited tales from *The Thousand and One Nights*.

Interior decoration followed suit. Bakst's pistachio greens and lapis lazuli, or Benois's severe variations on black and white reached epidemic proportions. In lieu of a New Year's card, Cocteau would send Henri Bernstein a black slate with *Bonne Année* scribbled in chalk, so as not to violate the playwright's new color scheme (which, moreover, he adopted for his own room at 10 Rue d'Anjou). Before long "there was not a middle-class home without its green and orange cushions on a black carpet. Women dressed in the loudest colors, and the *bibelots* were all striped . . . Soon shops, brasseries, and cafés followed suit, postwar dance halls were directly inspired by them, and the 1923 exhibition showed many traces of their influence."

At first only those artists whose lives revolved about the boulevard acknowledged the Ballets Russes: Jacques Blanche, Reynaldo Hahn, Montesquiou, Jean-Louis Vaudoyer, and Cocteau. The Left Bank paid Diaghilev little heed, assuming that his was merely another extravagance invented for high society. They could scarcely be blamed, for Diaghilev made his first pitch to the larger gallery, expecting that snobbism would seal his enterprise with gold. In all events, Robert de Flers and Gaston de Caillavet, in their play *Le Bois Sacré*, neatly summarized the popular opinion (shared by most serious artists) of the Ballets Russes: "We're starting to become very elegant gents," says one character, "to make very chic acquaintances, very rotten, very Ballets Russes."

It took a season for the young pontiffs of serious literature, notably Henri Ghéon, to appreciate the revolution Diaghilev had wrought. *Firebird*, Stravinsky's first contribution to the Diaghilevian repertoire, allayed his suspicions: "*Firebird*," he wrote in the *Nouvelle Revue Française*, "being the fruit of a corporate intimacy among choreographer, composer, and painter, shows us the most exquisite miracle of sound, form, and movement working together in ineffable harmony. . . . When the bird appears it is truly the music which has conjured it forth. For me Stravinsky, Fokine, and Golovine are but one name." Thus by 1910 history already showed signs of observing Isadora's prophecy that "the dancer of the future would attain such heights that all the other arts would benefit." When, three years later, the Théâtre du Vieux-Colombier mushroomed from the *NRF*, its director Jacques Copeau would enforce principles already adopted by Diaghilev.[10] And presently Diaghilev would collect young composers and painters within his magic circle, showing France what genius had been incubating on the sly in Montparnasse, half-starved for recognition.

But the global effect produced by the Ballets Russes was greater than the sum of its component revelations: Bakst's splash of color, Stravinsky's music, Fokine's choreography *expressing sound as movement*, Nijinsky's powers of levitation, Karsavina's extraordinary grace. The Ballets Russes staged an art form disclosing, however clothed and controlled, its primitive sources. Theatre evolved from dance and dance from the Dionysian festival. "The red curtain," wrote Cocteau, "rose on spectacles giving such joy that they will revolutionize France and ecstatic crowds will follow Dionysus' chariot." Benois put it more explicitly: "The success of the ballets is based on the fact that Russians are still capable of believing in their creations, that they still retain enough spontaneity to become absorbed, just as children are completely absorbed in their play, in the Godlike play which is art. This secret has been lost on the Western stage, where everything is technique, everything is consciousness, everything is artificiality, and from which have gradually disappeared the mysterious charm of self-oblivion, the great Dionysiac intoxication, the driving force of art."

Sergei Diaghilev, who created the Ballets Russes and, against all odds, held it together for twenty years, was a man possessed. He had a singular birthmark: a mutant lock of white hair (on account

10. In France, Lugné-Poë, director of the Théâtre de l'Œuvre, had contended, fifteen years before Diaghilev, that all elements of a theatrical production must work together as reciprocal dimensions of a single form, engaging the so-called "Nabis" (Bonnard, Vuillard, Maurice Denis) to paint sets for him. His productions of Ibsen, Jarry, and Maeterlinck proved revolutionary, influencing, among others, Stanislavsky. Diaghilev enlarged the esoteric circle of Poë's principles.

of which his dancers nicknamed him "Chinchilla") lending interest to his otherwise porcine face. Firmly believing in signs and omens, he wore this lock like one, parting his hair down the middle so as to segregate white and black.

If Diaghilev's life followed an unwaveringly straight line, it was the vector shooting out of opposing forces. His dualism gave him his vocation, and his demoniac energy. In 1895, at twenty-three, he wrote to his stepmother:

> I am:
> 1. A charlatan full of brio
> 2. A great charmer
> 3. An insolent man
> 4. One who possesses much logic and few scruples
> 5. A being afflicted with a total absence of talent. But I believe I've found my true vocation: "Maecenasship!" I have everything I need except money, but that will come.

His appearance (and it would serve him to good effect) belied his poverty. He was huge, with a head that hatters had trouble fitting. His eyes, always humid and curved "like Portuguese oysters," rarely betrayed any emotion. On entering Larue, his bulk magnificently clothed in an opossum-collared coat and silk scarf, he looked as if he had been borne there on the backs of a thousand serfs assuring him a princely revenue. Descended from an unbroken line of Russian lords who, wrote Stravinsky, "did not know the meaning of economy and nonchalantly . . . buried themselves in debt for the sheer pleasure of satisfying their least whim," Diaghilev upheld his ancestors' tradition. As Stravinsky observed, "he loved to 'produce' his life in the grandest possible manner," but the grand manner took the perverted form of self-sacrifice amounting to prodigality. Diaghilev lived *through* the Ballets Russes, spending huge sums of money on every production, while having to dismiss his own valet when, at one point, he lacked the money to pay him his wages. In proportion as Bakst's stage costumes grew more lavish, Diaghilev's opossum coat grew increasingly threadbare. He had the makings of a passionate monk, but, unwilling to deny his appetite for splendid decor and for young men, he placed his apostolic energies at the service of art. He considered each of his ballets a sacramental event.

"If he signed no work," wrote Jacques Blanche, an early devotee of the Ballets Russes, "he was the *deus ex machina,* the professor of energy, the will that gave body to others' conceptions. He draws out the best in everyone, he knows how to extract gold from the earth covering it."

This quality asserted itself as soon as he came to Saint Petersburg from Perm in the Urals, a sturdy provincial laughing so heartily "one could see the back of his mouth," but anxious to cut a figure among artistic celebrities. Through a cousin of his, Dima Filosofov, Diaghilev began to frequent a group of young artists, casually associated under the name "Nevsky Pickwickians," who shared in common an antipathy for bourgeois realism. Their paintings, Bakst's and Benois's in particular, clearly show the influence of *art nouveau,* the development of which they followed in Western European art reviews. At first they paid Diaghilev, known to them only as "Dima's cousin," little attention. He seemed an inconsequential lad, foppish and Oblomovian, who neither read nor visited museums. But a visit to Florence had the most striking effect upon him. Within one month he had visited twenty-four museums and fourteen studios. The slothful giant, inexplicably awakened, became a veritable dynamo. On returning to Russia, he drafted plans for a lavish review to be called *Mir Iskusstva,* "The World of Art." Abruptly, Dima's satellite, at twice remove from the Nevsky Pickwickians, found himself at their center, providing them a tribune, converting their ideas into a movement.

"Diaghilev was not a creative genius," wrote Benois; "he was perhaps rather lacking in creative imagination. But he had one characteristic, one ability, which none of us had and which made of him what he later became: he knew how to *will* a thing, and knew how to carry his will into practice. Many a time Bakst, Filosofov, Serov, and I tried our hardest to infect with an idea of ours the inert and indifferent Diaghilev. How his lethargy annoyed us! It is strange to think that this tireless worker was actually upbraided by his friends for his laziness. And then suddenly the position would be reversed. Once *convinced*, Sergei, his eyes alight with the love of action, began to dash about busying himself with all the details necessary for the realization of the plan. Once having taken a matter in hand, he adopted it as his own."

Projects followed one another in swift succession. In 1899 Prince Volkonsky, newly appointed director of the Imperial theatres, made Diaghilev his assistant. Immediately Diaghilev seized the opportunity to mobilize his friends; having won permission to produce Delibes's ballet *Sylvia*, he entrusted Bakst with the costumes and decor, while Benois served as general director. At the last moment, however, the project collapsed owing to protests from the Imperial theatres' directorate, who were outraged that young men be allowed such privileges. The cabal, threatened by this young energumen, arranged to have Diaghilev dismissed under "paragraph three" (usually invoked for embezzlers), which meant that Diaghilev could never again serve the Crown. Eight years would elapse before he produced another ballet, this time abroad. Meanwhile Diaghilev served his apprenticeship as an impresario. In 1905, traveling the length and breadth of Russia, often by sledge, he collected enough Russian portraits to fill the vast Taurida Palace. Brought to Paris in 1906, the collection took up twelve halls of the Salon d'Automne. This exposition was highly important in Diaghilev's life for it gave him a wedge into Western Europe.

Paris provided him a ready-made audience. Politically, France and Russia were locked in a loving embrace. Tolstoy was all the rage, and high society had numerous Russophiles, including the Countess Greffulhe, whose patronage allowed Diaghilev to return the following year with a mixed bag of musical offerings. In 1908, leading a caravan of singers and musicians westward, Diaghilev introduced Feodor Chaliapin in *Boris Godunov*. Eight Paris performances of Moussorgsky's opera decided his future: hamstrung by Russian officialdom, he would found abroad a Russia which Russia denied herself. "What did he desire?" asked Robert Brussel, a music critic close to Diaghilev. "These three things: to disclose Russia to herself; to disclose Russia to the world; to disclose the new world to itself—accomplishing all this by the simplest, the most direct, the easiest of means available, through painting and music and, only somewhat later, through dance."

Benois had reawakened Diaghilev's interest in the dance. Employing his uncanny gift for spying potential genius in embryonic form, Diaghilev recruited his company on repeated return trips to Russia. In 1909 his Ballets Russes company was ready to invade the West.

On the Parisian Right Bank no such venture as Diaghilev's could survive without a Muse—the wealthy, well-connected, fund-raising kind—as his troupe, lacking Crown support, danced on the brink of insolvency. One such Muse materialized in 1908: a voluptuous Pole whom Cocteau would describe as a "beribboned tiger." *Boris Godunov* had so impressed her that she bought all unsold seats for the eight performances, a gesture subsidized by her husband, Alfred Edwards (the Hearst of his day). A few years later she would marry the Spanish painter José Sert, thus acquiring the name by which she became widely known: Misia Sert. Diaghilev found in her not only a patron saint but the link he sought with French art and letters. If Edwards gave Misia millions, her first husband, Thadée Natanson, founder of *La Revue Blanche*, had given her friends. At seventeen, she was entertaining artists such as Bonnard, Vuillard, Mallarmé, Debussy, and Valéry, among others. Now, living in a penthouse on Quai Voltaire, she would place her various alimonies at Diaghilev's disposal. It was here that Cocteau made Diaghilev's acquaintance.

Before long Cocteau, always quick to master the latest society game, made himself thoroughly at home backstage at the Ballets Russes, amusing the dancers and Diaghilev alike. Babbling brilliantly, darting about the set during rehearsals, he became the court jester whose importunities, being part of his stock and trade, made him all the more lovable. "Like a mischievous fox terrier," wrote Karsavina of Cocteau, "he bounded about the stage, and had often to be called away: 'Cocteau, come away, don't make them laugh.' Nothing could stop his exuberant wit; funny remarks spluttered from under his voluble tongue—Roman candles, vertiginous Catherine wheels of humour. That sudden appearance of Cocteau in the studio would bring a boisterous note. As if he had vowed never to

locate himself anywhere, his voice now spoke from behind canvases, now called from the garden, unexpectedly addressed us from
the top of the gallery." Karsavina recalls seeing him still only once,
when, at his request, she told him the Russian fairy tale of the Firebird. "He sat attentive as a child."

The Russians, earthy and fanciful playmates, proved to be an an-
tidote to the stuffy atmosphere of literary salons. After premier performances the company would foregather at Larue, where Cocteau
was known to dance on the tables. By 1910 he had become so much
the house pixy that Diaghilev took amusing liberties with him. Once,
returning from some celebration together, Diaghilev, descending at
the Hôtel Mirabeau, gave their driver whispered instructions to continue as far as the Hôtel des Réservoirs in Versailles. Cocteau, either
asleep or entranced, suddenly found himself jogging along country
roads. Returning tit for tat, he made a drawing of Diaghilev attired
as the Young Girl in *Spectre of the Rose*, a bonnet on his head and
a rose stuck in his corsage. Their divertissements were not always
quite so innocent, however. Cocteau and the Russians frequently
sallied together into "Sodom and Gomorrah," as the Madeleine quarter was known, and at least once visited a famous hotel brothel
called the Chambannais whose entrance—a grotto encrusted with
seashells—appealed to their baroque sensibilities. Bakst found the
women "superb," but the women set upon Nijinsky, crying, "I want
the virgin!"

Cocteau's diaspora of friends included a resident of the Hôtel des
Réservoirs, Reynaldo Hahn, with whom, the year of Diaghilev's
jest, he would contrive a new ballet, *The Blue God*. Not content to
watch from the wings, Cocteau wanted a hand in the spectacle itself. Thus, by October, 1910, the company mascot had declared his
intentions of writing a libretto. Originally *The Blue God* was to be
performed in 1911 in London, during the festivities celebrating
George V's coronation. Diaghilev, Bakst, and Nijinsky deferred
their return voyage to Saint Petersburg for the autumn ballet season long enough to clarify their ideas with Cocteau and Hahn. The
group, meeting at the Grand Vatel restaurant on Rue Saint Hon-
oré, dispatched a conspiratorial note to Gabriel Astruc, Diaghilev's
impresario:

Dear Friend,

In the name of everything you hold dear, not a word to *anyone at all* about the ballet we are planning, and especially about the possibility of including it in the Coronation festivities.

Yours ever,
Reynaldo Hahn
Sergei Diaghilev
Léon Bakst
Jean Cocteau
Nijinsky

In fact Diaghilev did not stage the ballet until 1912. It proved to be a fiasco, Diaghilev consigning it to oblivion after his London season of 1913. Apart from its innate deficiencies, *The Blue God*, performed alternately with Balakirev's *Thamar*, overtaxed the public's appetite for exotic stories. "Diaghilev," wrote Grigoriev, his stage manager, "was doubtful in particular about Hahn's music, which he had been obliged to accept for reasons of policy." In view of Hahn's social connections, Diaghilev perhaps hoped to appease the *gratin* in accepting his score; it was a beggar's compromise, "policy" signifying impecuniousness. Hahn's music, scaled for a drawing room, soughed pitifully from the orchestra, while Nijinsky and Karsavina together could not bring alive the Oriental hocus-pocus of Cocteau's scenario.[11] Bakst surpassed himself, but the ballet clung for dear life to its beautiful trappings.

Cocteau's argument reads as if written by a haberdasher: "There was once a young man who wished to be a priest. After seven days of prayer and solitude he was led to the temple amidst crowds performing ritual dances and dressed in the saffron robe of those who serve the Lotus. But, as he was preparing to divest himself of his beautiful crimson jacket and his tall white plume . . ." In Act II the scene switches to a dungeon, where the temple beasts (fed on honey, lambs, and nightingales) prepare to devour a young woman; a Goddess, springing from the pistil of a Giant Lotus, saves her. As Cocteau needed some pretext for Nijinsky, the Goddess conjures forth a Blue God from the depths of a pool.

11. The scenario was jointly written by Cocteau and Frédéric de Madrazo, a painter-dilettante rather in the manner of Jacques Blanche.

Dance, like poetry, struck Cocteau as a game, not "the Godlike play which is art" but its fashionable forgery. His views had not matured beyond the mock-theatre he and René Rocher constructed when children in the courtyard of Eugène Lecomte's house on Rue La Bruyère. At twenty-three, without childhood to excuse him, he was a dilettante puttering about a real theatre. At Bakst's suggestion, Gabriel Astruc commissioned him to draw a poster of Nijinsky for *The Spectre of the Rose*, the result being a variation on Bakst's design. He wrote elegant program notes. Together with Paul Iribe he published a handsome brochure on Japanese paper entitled *Vaslav Nijinsky*. It included a six-line poem by Cocteau and six drawings (one for each line) by Iribe. Posters, program notes, exotic fairy tales, Nijinsky's musk, the chance for self-advertisement, and that huge social whirligig set in motion by Diaghilev summed up, for the time being, his dance appreciation. "The Russians," he wrote to Gide in June, 1912, "don't matter much to me. I like their Vestris [12] because he reminds me of Menalque and the aeroplane, I like him for what his person suggests and proposes. You can have the rest."

Perhaps Cocteau, feeling certain that Gide deplored the Ballets Russes, wished to exonerate himself. It is equally possible that he was still smarting from a wound inflicted by Diaghilev the previous spring, soon after *The Blue God* had its first performance. Aware that his attempts to win Diaghilev's admiration had failed, he unburdened himself one night on Place de la Concorde while accompanying Diaghilev and Nijinsky home from dinner. "Nijinsky was brooding, as usual. He walked ahead of us. Diaghilev was amused by my simperings. When I questioned him about his reserve (I was used to praise), he stopped, adjusted his monocle, and said: 'Astonish me.' The idea of surprising anyone had not occurred to me before." Riding the coat tails of fashion, Cocteau had achieved his goal. Having achieved it, he suddenly found himself nowhere, ostracized variously by those whose attention he sought. Diaghilev's challenge, coming as it did from a foreigner with no ax to grind, proved more telling than Ghéon's outright slap. It coincided, more-

12. Vestris was a great French dancer of the eighteenth century. Cocteau here refers to Nijinsky.

over, with the lesson he was being taught, less succinctly, by Montesquiou. But it needed time to register. Self-pity would forestall regeneration.

Cocteau, mobilizing his defenses, fancied himself a misappreciated phantom, overlooked because naked. "I've pitched my hammock," he wrote to Gide, "far from Slavic or Hellenic dangers, for I am not certain Sophocles isn't exerting himself in an Athens . . . of closed façades behind which everyone gorges himself on Mlle. Silve-Mirepoix's packaged bread as if it were the Host." "Others" lived behind façades whereas he freely gave of himself. Only later would he admit his collusion with the packaged-bread eaters: "Beginning around 1912 a phony audacity, tempting some, misconstrued by others, both groups unanimously hating true audacity, invaded a populous category of worldly esthetes. Dilettantes and *précieux* fancied themselves the cat's whiskers, and there was born a declassed class midway between the solid bad taste for which it was intended and the new tabernacle, beyond its reach, fortunately." Diaghilev's naked challenge would not affect him until bolstered by some *mise en scène*. As always, Cocteau's imagination wanted a proven model. It was furnished by Igor Stravinsky.

The première of *The Rite of Spring* took place on May 29, 1913, at the Théâtre des Champs-Élysées. It literally unseated the spectators. As soon as the prelude began, its opening flute line suddenly invaded by dissonant horns and running amok, derisive laughter rose from the audience. Several people sitting in front came to blows. The tumult spread. Demonstrations provoked counter demonstrations. Titled ladies started to scream like fishwives. Stravinsky took refuge backstage, where Nijinsky, the choreographer, stood on a chair shouting the beat for the dancers because Pierre Monteux could not make his orchestra heard above the roar. Diaghilev, hoping that the glare of publicity would restore order among the crazed *gratin*, instructed his electrician to keep switching the house lights on and off. The commotion was such that enthusiasts and protesters could not be told apart. "The orchestra played unheard," wrote Carl Van Vechten, "except occasionally when a slight lull occurred. The young man seated behind me in the box stood up during the course of the ballet to enable himself to see more clearly. The intense excitement under which he was laboring betrayed itself presently when he began to beat rhythmically on the top of my head with his fists. My emotion was so great that I did not feel the blows for some time." The aged Countess de Pourtalès, her diadem askew, brandishing her fan, was heard to scream, "This is the first time in sixty years anyone has dared make fun of me!"

At two in the morning, Stravinsky, Nijinsky, and Diaghilev, accompanied by Cocteau, had themselves driven to the Bois de Boulogne, observing absolute silence. As their coach jogged along the acacia-lined paths and round the lakes, Diaghilev began to sob, muttering a line of Pushkin through his tears, "Would you like to tour the islands?" In Russia, Stravinsky explained for Cocteau's benefit, one tours the islands as in Paris one visits the Bois de Boulogne, and it had been on such a night as this that they had conceived *The Rite of Spring*. "My true friendship with Stravinsky dated from that coach ride," wrote Cocteau. "He was returning to Switzerland. We corresponded." [13]

They had met three years earlier during a rehearsal of *Firebird*. Their next meeting occurred on the street. Stravinsky, hearing a voice hail him from behind, "*C'est vous Igor?*" recognized Cocteau, who used first names (and often the familiar *tu*) on the slightest acquaintance. Each provided the other a supplementary organ. Stravinsky, looking very much the provincial dandy, needed a hand to guide him round Paris, while the ever voluble Cocteau could always use another ear. "His conversation was a highly diverting performance," wrote Stravinsky, "though at times it was rather like that of a *feuilletoniste* out to make a 'career.'" When Stravinsky in the spring of 1912 installed himself at the Hôtel Crillon on Place de la Concorde, Cocteau, living nearby, became his constant dinner companion.

The Rite gave their friendship a curious, almost venal twist, however. Seeing Stravinsky suddenly raised aloft by this *succès de scandale*, Cocteau, hoping to gain some altitude by hitching himself

13. It should be noted, however, that Stravinsky, on several occasions, has denied that any such coach ride through the Bois de Boulogne took place after the performance of *The Rite of Spring*.

to a star plainly in the ascendant, proposed that they collaborate on
a new ballet. Stravinsky, recovering from typhoid and caring for
his ailing wife, had moved from Paris to Switzerland. In January,
1914, Cocteau, accompanied by Paulet Thevenaz (the young Swiss
artist who prescribed calisthenics to Cocteau, Beaumont, and
Daudet), followed him, the two taking rooms at the Grand Hôtel
in Leysin. While Thevenaz painted portraits of the Stravinskys,
Cocteau expounded *David*, a ballet destined to die unborn. Clearly
inspired by *Petrouchka*, its setting would have been a traveling circus, outside the tent in which "David," the real show, unfolds. An
acrobat would come on stage doing stunts to draw a crowd; then a
clown, transmogrified into a box intended to symbolize the carnival
phonograph (Cocteau's coefficient of the antique mask), would
bark a publicity harangue vaunting David's exploits. "It was in a
way the first draft of *Parade*," Cocteau later wrote, "though un-
necessarily fraught with scriptural quotations and a text." In the
throes of creation, Cocteau dashed off the following note to Gide
in Paris: "Intense work—Igor Stravinsky is a dynamo. He amazes
us—*David* will become, I believe, something extraordinary, like
nothing you can imagine."

David never progressed beyond costume drawings and a ragged
argument. Its Nemesis was Diaghilev, who descended on Leysin
expressly to sabotage the project. Doubly incensed—by Cocteau's
"excessive fondness" for Nijinsky and his autonomous collaboration
with Stravinsky—the great impresario further felt cut to his proprietary quick because he was aware that plans were afoot to stage
David under auspices other than his own. Preposterously, Cocteau
had in mind Jacques Copeau, editorial chief of the *NRF*, whose
theatre, the Vieux-Colombier, was now halfway through its first
season. Copeau never strayed from literary drama, but presumably
his policy had not yet been established. "If Copeau stages it," Cocteau wrote to Gide, Copeau's close friend, "I promise him he will
have 'packed houses.'" In his memoirs, Cocteau offered altruistic
motives:

> It was for me a period of transformations. I was moulting, I was in
> full growth. Quite naturally, an excessive need for sobriety, order,
> and silence supplanted my frivolity, dispersion, and chit-chat. More-

over . . . I sensed how repugnant Igor's genius must have found the querulous atmosphere of the Ballets Russes, and the difficulty an artist had concentrating in such a vast and formidably equipped setting.

Even if we allow him his altruism, self-interest nonetheless played some role in dictating his choice of Stravinsky. For two years Cocteau had sought unavailingly to infiltrate the *NRF*, his many oaths, wheedlings, and retractions outweighed by his past. Now, wearing Stravinsky like a cassock, he hoped to gain admittance. "It was for me a period of transformations." But all his periods were. It is as if Cocteau had been condemned to play life on a checkerboard, his opponent the Spectre of Anonymity, perpetually scheming to reach the end squares so that, crowned, he might continue moving, in any direction he pleased, for the sake of moving. De Max had crowned him with Mendès, Diaghilev with Stravinsky. Had *David* materialized, Stravinsky would have crowned him with the Left Bank. Diaghilev in persuading the composer to finish the score of *The Nightingale*, forestalled that move by three years.

"Cocteau was very brilliant when I saw him last," T. S. Eliot told Stravinsky in 1951, "but he made me feel it was a rehearsal for a more important occasion."

David's miscarriage did not prevent the birth of *Potomak*. In Leysin Cocteau finally completed a work he would not afterward abjure. He dedicated the book to Igor Stravinsky, and in it he writes, obviously alluding to *The Rite* "One night at the theatre a new masterwork was performed. People hissed, laughed, caterwauled, barked. Oh, how I envied that martyrdom! I envied, I feared that martyrdom. I was ashamed, feeling unworthy of it."

The book was begun the previous year at Offranville (in André Gide's presence), where Cocteau, to amuse one of Jacques Blanche's young nephews, invented fantastic tales about a monster he called the "Potomak." When the child tired of the Potomak, Cocteau made drawings of another monster whom he named Eugène. "The Eugène, the first Eugène, the Eugènes' envoy, fascinated me. He had features of the armadillo, of the water caltrop, of larvae, of Aor's curve (the scimitar), of the orb, of the gyroscope adorned with murmurs." Presently Eugène, his head resembling nothing so much as a gun turret, acquired a mate whose face is featureless except for googly-goo eyes and a mouth seemingly inspired by the suctorial organ of a lamprey. Cocteau amassed a whole album of drawings in which schools of carnivorous Eugènes set upon a plump, bouregois couple named the Mortimers.

As one hallucination led to another, Potomak began to stir its larval self, with the result that Cocteau, initiated by a child, found himself behind the mirror, at grips with his own private beast. *Potomak* reads like a cinematic *Season in Hell*. Straight dialogue abruptly shifts into hermetic images, prose discovering that it cannot contain itself any longer breaks into riots of free verse, discourse alternates with macabre "pop" refrains and metaphysical lullabies, words perform freewheeling puns, while the whole dream sequence pivots on the narrator's three visits to Potomak. What is Potomak? A "megoptera coelenterata" fished from the Potomac and now, imported from America, on display in a fish bowl within a cellar on Place de la Madeleine, its eye "drowned in prisms," its great pink ears shaped like conches, its diet consisting of oil, gloves, misspelled words, Wagernian music, Ballets Russes programs, mandragora, and fire balloons. Since Potomak has more or less Cocteau's address, we may surmise that it also has his mind, that it *is* his mind. Isn't he observing it, polyplike and fetal, while it digests its own contents?

But the monster also bears a distinct resemblance to a movie projector, storing dreams and spewing them forth in reels. "The arc lamps and the mercury tubes had just been turned on. The Potomak became saturated with phosphorescence." Cocteau had by 1913 become an avid movie-goer, frequently descending into those "caves," dark and stuffy like Potomak's, to see "Rio Jim, New York, Fantômas, Captain Scott, the aquarium of boxers moving in slow motion, the eye of a fly, and the instantaneous flowering of a rose."

In the postface to *Potomak*, Cocteau recalls a film by Alfred Collins, *The Pickpocket* (1903), during which he became intrigued with the camera, "that grinder of silences," projecting cones of light containing unseen images. "I tried to surprise the unpublished dimension wherein the drama unfolds during the trajectory from lamp to wall." Raising the film to a metaphysical plane, he imagined the pickpocket materializing on a wall outside the cinema and, exposed, fleeing from the police. The camera, embroiling dream and reality, stands as a replica of his own predicament. "The Potomak distresses me," says the narrator. "By what wavy bonds do its sleep and waking life weave together? My confused life and the coherence of my dreams give me kinship to this Potomak. A single fluid courses through both of us. . . . I continue living in my dreams and dreaming in my diurnal mechanism. . . . the life of dreams opens the box of human dimensions." Viewing Potomak and the narrator in this light—Potomak a combination fetus and camera elaborating its placental dream life, the narrator its spectator reliving his own childhood—a passage such as the following becomes clearer: "Potomak's role is to be the Potomak, mine is to travel, to learn, to fly in an airplane, to invent dynamite. You get angry [he is speaking to his literal-minded girl friend, Argémone] because I question you on my mysteries of your childhood and recount my own."

Having extroverted himself completely, Cocteau let it be known that his sole preoccupation now would be the inner life. "I had swiftly ascended the ladder of official values; I perceived how short, narrow, and crowded that ladder was. I discovered the ladder of secret values. There one plunges into oneself, toward the diamond and the pit gas." Stravinsky had been one source of inspiration. Gertrude Stein was a second. "One evening I heard some friends laughing over a poem by an American woman. Her telegraphic message went straight to my heart. 'Dinner is west,' Gertrude Stein decided quite simply in the middle of a white page." [14]

But it was Rimbaud, he claimed, who exercised the decisive influence upon him. *Potomak* opens with a letter describing a certain "Pygamon" and his wife Jézabel (or Queen Pretty), pseudonyms for Catulle Mendès and Jane. Cocteau, alias "Persicaire," assaults them wantonly, as if his future would stand in abeyance till he fully execrated his past. Pygamon promises the narrator that he will bequeath him his yacht. "I didn't inherit a ship, but I did inherit

14. On account of this reference Gertrude Stein could never quite bring herself to dislike Cocteau.

something quite different. The queen handed me a volume. Bound
between ugly covers, it was a copy of the *Illuminations*. Reading it,
I understood everything." Even as he was proclaiming his literary
virginity, Cocteau had lost it anew. Liberated from conventions and
models, spurning them in favor of artless images and commonplaces, salvaging only his dictionary from this colossal auto-da-fé,
he copied his very "tabula rasa" from a *Season in Hell*. "The
greatest literary masterpiece is but a scrambled dictionary," he
wrote in *Potomak*, adding in the postface, "My poets were: Larousse, Chaix, Joanne, Vidal de la Blache.[15] My painters: poster
artists." This comes directly from Rimbaud's *Délire II:* "For a
long time, I used to boast that I possessed all possible landscapes and
found the celebrities of painting and modern poetry contemptible. I
used to love idiotic paintings, lintel sculpture, circus backdrops, inn
signs, Épinal images, unfashionable literature, Church Latin, purple
prose misspelled, our ancestors' novels, fairy tales, little children's
books, old operas, silly refrains, naïve verse rhythms."

Potomak contains the germ of Cocteau's future *œuvre*. Its oddly
transparent characters,[16] revisiting their childhood, discoursing on
death, behaving like fast-motion non sequiturs, prefigure Cocteau's
as yet unborn dreamers. The monster's fishbowl, serving as the cen-
terpiece of *Potomak*, will become those rooms in *Les Enfants Terribles*, *Les Parents Terribles*, and *Le Grand Écart* confining death-
bound adolescents. Oedipus had begun his inward voyage home.

Yet Cocteau's revolt did not confer freedom upon him; however
boldly hermetic this new attitude proclaimed itself, it relied on an
audience. "Discover what the public reproaches you for, and cultivate it," wrote Cocteau. "Therein you will have discovered yourself." The rebel, defining himself from the outside, will ultimately
come meekly home. His negation cannot sustain itself; it predicates
and, in its own way, reinforces an Establishment. Apart from its
scandalous repercussions, it is nothing. What Cocteau admired in
The Rite of Spring was not its primitiveness but the illustrious mar-

15. Vidal de la Blache wrote a geography text commonly used in French schools;
Joanne, like Baedeker, was noted for his guides. "Chaix" is a French travel and
timetable guide.
16. "Persicaire," "Argémone," "Bourdaine," etc.—names he lifted from herb jars
in the Offranville pharmacy.

tyrdom it brought Stravinsky. Having written *Potomak*, he observed and queried: "I saw that it was not a book, but a preface. A preface to what?" He had written a preface to a preface to (acknowledging Gertrude Stein's inspiration) a preface, a brilliant manifesto bound to reiterate itself endlessly.

Cocteau, however, was satisfied that he had produced something worthy of Gide and Stravinsky, a pagan hymn answering *Fruits of the Earth* and *The Rite of Spring*. In March, watching the snow fall over Leysin, he dedicated his book to Stravinsky: "Igor, I planned to offer you a book and I am offering you instead my old skin." Back in Paris several months later, he wrote Gide, staying at Cuverville, the following note:

My dear Gide,

Last evening, weary of risking nothing, of mobilizing the Russians and of judging Joffre—I read *Fruits* aloud to my host [17] who was lucky enough to be hearing it for the first time. How far removed we felt from the war, in this climate of poetry which no shrapnel could penetrate. I admire and embrace you.

Jean

Nathaniel, having now come into his own, could address himself hereafter as plain Jean. But five years would elapse before *Potomak* saw its way into print. On August 1, war was declared. Within six weeks the Kaiser's armies had overrun Belgium. Cocteau was, much to his dismay, found unfit for military service; this catastrophe nicely coincided with his own drama. It promised him untold opportunities to risk his new skin, so while others were doing their utmost to avoid the draft, he called on his acquaintances to help him play war. An impresario soon came forward, in the person of Misia Edwards.

17. Louis Gautier-Vignal, a young Provençal count, who had recently come to Paris from Nice.

4

War Theatre

Cocteau was not the only one spoiling for war. The whole civilian population succumbed to military fever. On August 2, 1914, with mobilization in full swing, Parisians ran amok. Misia, having joined the tide of humanity then deliriously flooding the boulevards, suddenly found her buxom self hoisted onto a white stallion whose cuirassier she adorned with a wreath of flowers. Gyp artists, circulating through the crowd, sold pictures of the Manneken-Pis urinating on Kaiser Wilhelm's head. Anyone wearing a French uniform became, *ipso facto*, a hero. Women besieged military convoys on Rue de Dunkerque, planting roses in the barrel of every rifle. Theatres were ordered shut down, but the Pied Piper found free play outside; during the first twenty days of August he led more than half a million men eastward to Champagne and northward to Flanders. That grim fairy tale would hold true. The soldiers found themselves swallowed, if not in the Venusberg, in muddy earth, the majority never surviving to see Paris again.

The capital became a war city overnight. Cafés and restaurants now closed at eight. With artisans away at the front, shopping became a tactical problem, as if Paris were hamstrung by a chronic *congé national*. Public transportation came to a virtual halt. At night the city observed a blackout, searchlights scanning the sky for *Taube* planes and for Zeppelins; the latter would, that autumn, make devastating raids on the outskirts. Along the Quai de Billy mile upon mile of lorries belonging to Galeries Lafayette, Bon Marché, the fashion houses, and professional movers stood immobilized, awaiting conscription. Cours-la-Reine looked like a Magritte collage, with herds of unruly livestock crowding the street and pavement; two thousand cows pastured on the racetracks of Auteuil and Longchamp while five times that many sheep grazed in the Parc de Bagatelle.

As soon as news returned that French armies had fallen back to the Marne, the government removed to Bordeaux, the *beau monde* following suit. As August wore on, Parisians started an exodus, one million strong abandoning their homes within a month. The rest could not afford to move, but they were rewarded with the pyrotechnics of war. Looting stores whose proprietors had foreign names (the Maggi milk company, for example) became a municipal pastime. When enemy planes appeared overhead, Parisians would rush agog into the streets. Cocteau turned from mimicking literati to mimicking war. His back hunched, his arms outstretched, tiptoeing, he played a Zeppelin. His antics, appreciated by society, shocked Gide who was working as a nurse at the Foyer Franco-Belge. The two met in a tea parlor shortly after the fall of Mulhouse, on August 20, Gide recording his indignation as follows:

> I took no pleasure seeing him again, despite his extreme courtesy; but he is incapable of being serious and all his thoughts, his witticisms, his sensations, the extraordinary *brio* characterizing his everyday speech appalled me like a luxury article on display during famine and mourning. He was wearing something like a soldier's uniform, and the whiplash of events ruddied his face; he has forfeited nothing of his old self, merely converting his petulance into a martial attitude. Speaking of the massacres in Mulhouse, he finds amusing epithets; he imitates the sound of sirens, the whistling of shrapnel. Then, changing the subject (for he notices I'm not amused), he says he's sad. He pretends to be sad for the same reasons you are, and abruptly weds your thought. . . . Oddly, I think he'd make a good soldier. He agrees, saying that he would be courageous.

Cocteau, though declared physically unfit, wore a blue officer's uniform far spiffier than ordinary military issue. It should be said, as an extenuating circumstance, that life was made miserable for any grown male walking about Paris in civilian clothing. People dropped venomous asides; their reproving glances arraigned him as an *embusqué* (a draft dodger) or, still worse, a spy. Paul Morand in his war journal relates a characteristic imbroglio, whose victim was his friend Francis de Miomandre. The latter, taking a tram to work, was verbally set upon by the lady ticket collector. "There are some people who prefer the Right Bank to the trenches. . . . A pen isn't quite so heavy as a rifle, is it?" When he attempted to defend himself, she delivered a blow to his head with her iron ticket punch. He ran to a pharmacist and had the wound bandaged. Later that day, returning from work, he boarded the same tram. The same ticket collector, not recognizing him bandaged up, gave him patriotic priority: "The glorious wounded first," she cried. "Come along, my officer."

Spy-mania reached epidemic proportions. In 1915 alone, the government would receive some thirty thousand letters from anonymous authors denouncing so and so. Theatres having reopened, one group of actresses protested before Dalimier, the Radical minister, that their male costars should be dragooned from the stage. The distemper afflicting Frenchmen vented itself in psychotic name games. Thus, Rue Richard Wagner in Passy was rebaptized, Eau de Cologne became known as Eau de Louvain, and the florist association gave French names to all flowers which had previously had German designations. Louis Aragon recalls seeing people kick dachshunds on the street.

All in all, this febrile patriotism boiled down to political apathy. According to military manuals, one salutes not the man but the uniform. Civilian France tacitly adopted that regulation, forfeiting its mind for fetishes. This most cautious of peoples inducted itself wholesale. Having outlawed questions, it wallowed in sinister consensus. The expression "war theatre" assumed literal meaning behind the front lines, in Paris.

Cocteau had various reasons for contriving what resembled a pilot's uniform. He did so partly from sibling jealousy, for Paul, his older brother, had become a pilot as soon as war broke out. Moreover, aviation carried enormous prestige, its goggled adepts inheriting the mystique formerly bestowed on mounted cuirassiers. After 1910 airports had sprung up near Paris, swiftly attracting people from all walks, particularly the idle rich, whose appetite for speed had surpassed first the horse, subsequently the automobile. Issy and Buc became focal points of their new cult.

During July and August, Cocteau—like Agostinelli, Proust's be-

loved chauffeur—started to frequent Buc, at first in the company
of Louis Gautier-Vignal, through whom he met Roland Garros,
the daring young aviator who had won instant fame in 1913 with a
solo flight across the Mediterranean. A dreamy, obliging South-
erner, Garros took Cocteau aloft at irregular intervals throughout
the latter part of 1914, even when they risked some danger of encountering German aircraft. In her diary for January, 1915, the
Princess Bibesco noted:

> Rendezvous with Jean Cocteau at Larue where we have our special
> table. Jean has changed "affects," as he likes to put it. The poet has
> adopted a star as his emblem and has become a tourist in the celestial
> vault: he accompanies Garros on reconnaissance missions behind the
> enemy lines. . . . Jean describes what happens in the land of per-
> petual morning. Above the clouds covering France and Germany like
> the shadow of some assassin, it is spring in the Alps. . . . Jean of the
> Star asked his friend Garros whether he might descend from the
> cockpit to collect some anemones, and he places them, Persephone's
> bouquet, on the luncheon table. The next day, he comes accompa-
> nied by Roland Garros.

To be seen with a national hero—and they often visited Larue
and Misia's salon together—increased Cocteau's stature tenfold,
for Garros had something of the charisma that Lindbergh would
later enjoy, especially in the eyes of European youth. Thus, young
poets such as Tristan Tzara and André Breton voiced admiration
for "swashbuckling adventurers;" indeed, all the surrealists-to-be
reveled in the *Perils of Pauline* and the protean mischief of Fantômas, partly because adventurism seemed the gratuitous reverse of
all values promulgated by bourgeois society. Cocteau's obsession
with "angels" dates from the period of his loopings above France:
he dedicated a book-length poem, *The Cape of Good Hope*, to
Roland Garros. It would seem, however, that they felt their glory
mutually redounded upon one another. Cocteau publicly fretted
over the aviator, and Garros, writing from a Silesian prison camp
where he spent many longer months after being shot down over
Germany in 1915, exulted in *The Cape*. When Garros died in 1917,
the cockpit of his plane, according to Cocteau, was found papered
with manuscript leaves from the poem.

The outbreak of war seriously compromised Paris's social season. Small teas supplanted the salon. Largely bereft of men, Right Bank ladies employed their energies caring for the wounded. Even Anna de Noailles would visit hospitals, doing her act before wounded *poilus*, whom she left more confounded than consoled (most of them impatient for her to finish her interminable sentences so that they'd get their ration of tobacco).

But Misia's imagination ranged farther afield. Mincing about sick wards did not suit her style; moreover, the sick and maimed had not yet been delivered in great numbers, and it was prevalently believed that Marshal Joffre would rout the Germans by Christmas. Feeling pent up and disadvantaged by her foreign name (in turn Godebska, Natanson, Edwards, and Sert), Misia wanted a scheme whose flamboyant execution would at one stroke prove her patriotism, confirm her logistical talent, permit her to join battle, and help France. With the Red Cross lacking sufficient resources, she decided to create an ambulance corps of her own. What diplomatic red tape this entailed, her friend Philippe Berthelot (nonchalantly running Quai d'Orsay, specifically its propaganda and censorship wing) cut through. Exerting her copious charms on General Galliéni, hero of the Madagascar campaign and now military governor of Paris, she procured his official blessings.

By the simple expedient of raiding several German-owned hotels in Paris, she amassed quantities of linen. A glance at Quai de Billy, cluttered with derelict lorries, told her whom to address for ambulances. Whatever her name, it meant gold for couturiers. Hadn't her first trousseau cost fifty thousand dollars? As Mme. Edwards she had spent a fortune on her celebrated pastel gowns. The fashion industry, at once grateful and hankering for future credit, gave her fourteen delivery vans which Saoutchik, a coachwright, transformed into ambulances. Mustering people proved more difficult than linen and vehicles. Understandably, her friends quailed at placing their fate in her hands. Of those who joined her, José Sert, her lover, had to; Saoutchik came for the ride (on his own wheels); Paul Iribe, the dress designer, and Jean Cocteau had Épinal images on the brain. Their corporate derring-do reflected the most complete naïveté. Presently, they would witness a sobering spectacle.

When it finally departed, their convoy looked altogether unfit for a mission of mercy. Misia's immense Mercedes carried the avant-garde. Iribe wore a costume that looked like a deep-sea diving suit. Cocteau's nursing outfit had been designed by Paul Poiret. Sert, sporting pale gray knickerbockers, sat in the back seat next to his large camera. It was late August. Fruit orchards stood untended. The Île de France looked peaceful, its coppices intact, its baked white roads transecting fields green with beets and alfalfa. Could this motley group possibly suspect that on the chalky moorlands of Champagne Joffre was just then ordering a general retreat?

On the Varèdes highroad, they noticed something amiss. Carcasses of cattle, blasted skyward by artillery, dangled from the trees. Near l'Hay-les-Roses a still more horrible spectacle greeted them. "From afar," wrote Misia, "I saw a group of Negroes in dreadful condition. When we came nearer they turned out to be German prisoners wounded in the face. Their wounds, as yet undressed, were crawling with flies." At Rheims they finally saw the full fury of modern warfare. The convoy, arriving from the west as German missiles started falling from the east, found Rheims almost reduced to rubble. Men were having their limbs amputated without benefit of chloroform. A priest, shuffling from litter to litter, administered extreme unction to the dead and dying; with a knife he pried open mouths locked by tetanus, in order to insert the holy wafer. Meanwhile German shells exploded nearer and nearer the gasoline depot, "like a blind man groping for the doorknob." Misia's convoy, having delivered its medicine, turned about, wending homeward via Meaux, where General Manoury's troops already stood aligned opposite von Kluck's. The first battle of the Marne had gotten underway.

Gide's hunch was right. Cocteau acquitted himself well during the grim days in Rheims. Mortar exploding ten steps away could not arrest his tongue. With unfailing wit, he held forth as though in a literary salon, and angels seemed to guarantee him safe conduct; when a bomb hit his refuge, he emerged from the cellar safe and sound. Only after returning to Paris did the company find occasion to bicker. Misia, anxious to show General Février, head of the "sanitary" corps, that her charges had survived intact, summoned everyone to her flat. Cocteau came on crutches. Sert called him a fraud, while Cocteau protested that he was suffering from a dislocated thigh. "I am undergoing," he wrote, "the reaction, the trauma of an accident in Rheims—quite a bad one. When one is in a frenzy, one goes on, one cannot stop. Now the army doctor begins to give me cause for anxiety and my limp is quite genuine. . . . Sert made a scene, thinking probably that I had bluffed. . . . How little he knows me!"

Misia, celebrating one *beau geste* with another, donated her ambulances to the Empress of Russia. The ceremony was held in the vast courtyard of the Invalides.

Late in August the *beau monde* had taken flight, migrating southward. Bordeaux suddenly looked like a world capital. Cafés such as the Gazeaux swarmed with Parisian dandies who substituted the Chapon Fin for Larue. By night the quais of the Gironde came alive: bankers, ministers, courtesans all awaiting the latest communiqués. After France's victory on the Marne, the city relapsed into provinciality. Evacuating their hotels overnight, the *septembrisards*, as they came to be known, rushed home.

Theatres reopened, but their repertoire reflected the jingoism at large. Every night Marthe Chenal, her undulant body draped in a tricolor flag, sang the *Marseillaise* at the Opéra. Corneille eclipsed Racine at the Comédie-Française. Music halls seemed to have lost their sense of humor. In his *Revue 1915* Vilbert introduced the song *"On les aura"* (We'll get them); by 1918 he had sung it two hundred and forty-seven times. The war had imposed a moratorium on young talent so that playwrights such as Porto-Riche and Bernstein unhappily survived themselves for another few years. When Italy declared war on Germany, the Opéra-Comique halted its performance, cast and audience alike singing the Italian National Anthem. How apt was Stendhal's image about politics affecting literature like "a pistol shot in the concert hall!" On the whole, France, seeing the *grande armée* of Napoleon revived from its hundred years' sleep, took an imperial, swashbuckling view of itself, which events would not be long in tarnishing.

If France regressed a century, newspapers conformed to her infantilism. Promoting or cashiering the truth at their convenience, they now misplaced it altogether. Sentimentality and prurient war-mongering went uncensored. A review such as *Le Divan* printed any scrap of paper submitted from the trenches. Cocteau himself got into the act. Following their return from the Front, he and Paul Iribe founded a tabloid-size magazine called *Le Mot*. The first issue appeared on November 28, 1914.

Cocteau turned red, white, and blue. Self-advertisement and fashion reporting had trained him for propaganda. Making esthetic pronouncements, writing patriotic verse, drawing cartoons under the name "Jim," he monopolized *Le Mot*. His Eugènes quite unexpectedly came into their own. Distended to look like Zeppelins or propped on horses like malignant humpty-dumpties, they embodied every form of hatred directed against *le boche*. But Cocteau, always one to cover his bets, poked fun at xenophobes as well, for from the intellectual's vantage point, Mortimers at home posed a livelier threat than Eugènes from abroad; indeed, they were the two faces of a single monster. The French conservative has a way of arming himself with Germany to justify the suppression of his French adversaries. Thus, cubism in 1914 found itself prosecuted on the grounds that it derived from "Munich." Cocteau, while inveighing against the *boches*, prudently kept an eye cocked on the home front. "An artist friend," he wrote (referring, no doubt, to Albert Gleizes) "has sent me a letter in which he says the following, 'I'm sure this war will produce a backlash. Lucid minds will be thought egotistical, the work of art will be judged from a sentimental angle. . . . They will speak about French art, referring to the eighteenth century when they should be drawing from primitive sources.' "

Cocteau engaged in a polemic with Saint-Saëns, whose hatred of "the foreigner" extended even to Shakespeare. But he himself proved to be only several degrees less intolerant than the senile composer, for, ironically, the letter from his artist friend was prophetic of the attitude Cocteau would adopt after the war when, as leader of *Les Six*, he hailed a return to "the French tradition." Cocteau, for all his enlightenment, could not conceal his limits. "Schönberg," he wrote in *Le Mot*, "is knocking his head against old notes; while Stravinsky's lucid coldness helps to deliver him from Oriental poetry, Schönberg calculates, dislocates, hems himself in, won't forgive himself his love of *Tristan and Isolde,* composes by machine, adjusts his Herr Professorial spectacles." Similarly, a few years later, when he became editor of Éditions de la Sirène, Cocteau would propose that his friend Gautier-Vignal make a compendium of Nietzsche's Germanophobic remarks.

A rift appeared in French society. Soldiers, returning home from their campaigns, discovered a patriotic mockery of war. One restaurateur remodeled his establishment to look like a trench. Salons moved underground: momentarily dispersed, they reconvoked in shelters ("chic" shelters, literary shelters, etc.). Even gastronomy survived behind the trappings of austerity. Society, though altered, was still itself while the veterans, to whom war gave the irresponsibility of children and the catatonic wisdom of old men, often returned home as honored pariahs. It is as if death had founded a manic-depressive fraternity allying *boches* and *poilus* against their common enemy, the civilian. France thus was divided into two nations. Patriotism was the luxury of noncombatants. By 1916 generals, trying to rouse their troops, brandished music-hall slogans and civilian cant. The following document, hitherto unpublished, requires no comment. Dated October 18, 1916, its author was General Brissaud, commanding the 12th Infantry Division:

> The Commanding General noted that military salute was awkwardly executed by the troops and incompetently returned by the officers, Hence, the salute will be executed by the 12th Infantry Division according to the prescriptions listed below:

> ### *The Salute of the True Poilu*
> ### Three motions

> FIRST MOTION—Like a true Gallic cock, stand on your spurs and vigorously snap together your heels: quickly bring your right hand into the position of the regimental salute, strain all your muscles, chest inflated, shoulders drawn back, stomach drawn in, your left hand open, your pinkie touching the seam of your trousers, plant your eyes squarely in your officer's, raise your chin, and say inwardly: I AM PROUD TO BE A POILU.

SECOND MOTION—Lower your chin imperceptibly, make your eyes laugh, and inwardly address your officer as follows: YOU'RE ONE OF US, YOU TOO. YOU SQUAWK SOMETIMES BUT SO WHAT. YOU CAN COUNT ON ME.

THIRD MOTION—Raise your chin, make yourself bigger by extending your trunk, think about the *boches* and yell inwardly: WE'LL GET THEM, THE BASTARDS!

The Officer's Salute
Two Motions

FIRST MOTION—Wrap the soldier in an affectionate look, return his salute, your eyes fixed on his, smile at him discreetly, and say to him inwardly: YOU'RE FILTHY, BUT YOU'RE BEAUTIFUL!

SECOND MOTION—Raise your chin, think about the *boches,* and say inwardly: THANKS TO YOU, WE'LL GET THEM, THE PIGS!

This text must be learned by heart.

As Parisian social life began to rekindle, Cocteau gravitated toward its small flame. He frequently attended dinner parties given by Philippe Berthelot and Étienne de Beaumont, by Misia Edwards in her penthouse overlooking the Seine, and by the Princess Soutzo in her room at the Ritz. Accompanied by friends who shared his enthusiasm for clowns such as the Fratellini brothers, he haunted the Medrano circus in Montmartre. So did Breton and Aragon, serving their dada apprenticeship, which carried them from the flea market to the circus to the Electric-Palace cinema, but somehow their conscientious naïveté could not match Cocteau's fervor. Temperamentally the jester, his hectic virtuosity akin to an acrobat's, he thrived at the Medrano.

Movies also began playing a large role in his life. Nights were long, and nothing could better dispel the lenten atmosphere of wartime (pre-1917) Paris than *The Mysteries of New York,* starring Pearl White, whose fast-motion exploits made her a kind of deity: the Artemis of her age. Writing to Albert Gleizes, who had gone to New York after being "reformed" out of the army, Cocteau gave a preview of coming attractions: "Tomorrow *The Mysteries of New York* opens, a magnificent tetralogy for concierges, the poor man's Bayreuth, a combined novel-cinema to which I shall rush with

Varèse and Valentine Gross, making ourselves believe 'that we are all together on the shores of the Hudson.' " This parenthetical cuteness was an enduring quirk of Cocteau's: uttering a phrase yet quoting it, as if, uncertain of his reader's mind, he were both himself and his own neutral commentator. It was also his habit to write explanatory prefaces to his own works. In all events, seeing *The Mysteries of New York,* based on the pulp serial novel by Pierre Decourcelle, had "camp" appeal in 1915, like the Louis Philippe furniture cluttering every *petit-bourgeois* flat. The arty set adopted what they liked to call *le goût concierge.*

Meanwhile the Front occupied his dreams. Mme. Cocteau was actively fretting over Jean's bachelorhood. Discreetly, she tried to promote matches, but, apart from a minor flirtation with Jeanne Iribe, Paul's sister, he resisted. Had she stooped to reading his correspondence, Madame might have surprised her son's misogyny. "Paris is detestable," he wrote to Gleizes; "a hyenalike joy, lacking grandeur and the excuse of being a riposte, holds sway—Women, fierce and beautiful, wear crinolines and sport their Spartan thighs. 'We're killing them! We're killing them!' scream old ladies." Swaying wildly between hatred of war and infatuation with it, writing an "Ode to Joffre" one minute and decrying generals the next, he seemed, in the opinion of friends, on the verge of nervous collapse. It was his customary therapy to get drunk on his own words. "One night," wrote Bernard Faÿ, "on leaving Étienne de Beaumont's, where we had dined, Cocteau held us rooted for an hour or two on Place de la Concorde with his imitation of General de Clapiers, whose platitudes he parodied so masterfully that our sides were splitting with laughter, and we left him exhausted and annoyed at the lateness of the hour. The next morning I avoided all conversation."

His therapy did not work, however. Polarized between Rue d'Anjou and the playground, Cocteau resided beneath his mother's roof (as he would for some years to come) yet longed for the saps, the trenches, the lunar desolation not far distant. Some people find their souls amid disorder, the saying goes. It certainly applies to children, who thrive on ruins; a bomb will abet their dreams, giving them the more crannies for hide-and-seek. This was Cocteau's fa-

vorite landscape. In *Orphée*, a film he made years later, the titular
hero, piloted underground by an angel, encounters there a bombed
city whence his real self had been transmitting him telegraphic illuminations.

Cocteau's war poem, *Discours du Grand Sommeil*, begins thus:

> Well the angel
> not the messenger of Bethlehem springing
> from the crèche
> like a first tongue of fire,
> nor that other, the sailor,
> entering through the window
> and touching her,
> the Holy Virgin,
> with his feathery hump.
> Not those charming monsters
> but the unformed angel,
> lying inside, asleep
> who, sometimes, gently
> stretches from head to toes:
> he's waking up!
>
> This angel says to me:
>   Leave.

In December, 1915, Cocteau's angel materialized in the person of
Étienne de Beaumont, who after endless negotiations won official
consent to form an ambulance corps. He had no difficulty recruit-
ing a motley group of literati, including Bernard Faÿ, Pierre de
Lacretelle (Jacques' brother), Cocteau, and François Le Grix. They
set out one winter dawn in a state of high exaltation, wearing uniforms so various that they resembled a circus family. The expedition began as it would end some four months later: calamitously.

Beset with flat tires and waylaid by their own fanciful notions of
the route to Flanders, Beaumont and company had covered fewer
than two hundred kilometers when night caught them in open
country. They maneuvered for hours through sleet and thick fog
before stumbling upon a village, whose inn they straightaway invaded, against the protestations of its keeper, billeting themselves in
empty rooms while Faÿ, the benjamin of their group, reserved a

table in the dining hall. As soon as Faÿ began to sip his Dubonnet, one, then two, then a score of British officers wearing monocles and fancy braid marched in. Faÿ recognized the last to enter as Sir Douglas Haig, Supreme Commander of the British Expeditionary Force. Faÿ now understood why the innkeeper had been reluctant to admit Beaumont's bedraggled cortège; moreover, he felt sick with apprehension that his fellows upstairs were plotting some reprisal against the surly innkeeper. His fears proved justified. Oblivious of the audience awaiting him, Beaumont came walking majestically down the staircase, attired in black silk pajamas. Behind him minced Cocteau, wearing pink pajamas. Both had bangles about their ankles, and the clicking, according to Faÿ, sounded thunderous in the appalled silence maintained by Haig's staff. On the morrow, Beaumont's convoy resumed its journey north, having paid the innkeeper as much for his discretion as for his rooms, and having torn from the guest book a page on which their names were recorded.

Their ultimate destination was Nieuport on the Belgian coast, where a combined British-French encampment impinged on the northernmost flank of the German lines. The great battles had all but flickered out with winter approaching. But as trench warfare abated, artillery pieces answered one another with redoubled fury. Day and night, along the entire Belgian coast, British monitors anchored some few miles out to sea lobbed shells over the quiescent troops, making the sky look like "the ceiling of a candle-lit room, as the flame gutters." Here Cocteau spent the winter of 1915–1916.

The ambulance unit pitched camp on the seaboard of "Sector 131," including Nieuport-Ville, Nieuport-Bains, Coxyde-Ville, and Coxyde-Bains: formerly elegant resorts which enjambed one another like the Long Island Hamptons and, in balmier days, had made an issue of their social differences. Now reduced to bombed-out shells, the villas served as safety-posts for various corps stationed round about. Zouaves, Légionnaires (*Les Joyeux*), kilted Scots, French marines, and English infantry sought refuge here, like crustaceans billeting themselves in the tiaras of dead mollusks. Beneath the Coxydes and the Nieuports a vast network of interconnecting tunnels, each exit and entrance named after a Parisian

Métro station, led directly to the river Yser, so that it was possible to disappear through a hole in Coxyde and emerge on the Front where enemy trenches serpentined confusedly in all directions, like a Moebius strip, sometimes north, sometimes south of one another. At two points where no man's land had been pared down to the merest sliver, *boches* and *poilus* could hear one another sneeze. On the margin of this sector, separating land from sea, stretched Sahara-like dunes, "a feminine landscape, smooth, arched, wiggly" whose troughs naturally camouflaged the Allies' artillery.

Cocteau had his work cut out for him. Sniping took its daily toll, which meant slogging back and forth through a vast labyrinth of trenches, bearing soldiers who weighed like lead. It was an exceptionally mild, wet winter. The rains proved more redoubtable than the enemy. Soldiers sat steeped and miserable in a quagmire, which might have been worse except that a martinet of a French colonel in Sector 131 had ordered his trenches to be lined with planks of fir. Cocteau quickly endeared himself. "Here," wrote Pierre de Lacretelle from the Front, "the sun is Jean, thanks to whom one forgets the mud, the boredom, the sadness and horror of sufferings witnessed."

Cocteau's critics, Gide for example, taxed him for being glib about war, but his feeling went deeper. Hungering for savage delights, he tasted them at the Front. "We loved the war like a Negress," wrote Louis Aragon. Correcting genders, this probably had more than metaphorical truth for Cocteau, whose nights and beds proved totally haphazard: Bessoneau tents, marine hammocks, a plank provided him by the Zouaves, his own stretcher along some path where night and weariness took him unawares. The trenches offered the same exhilaration he once knew in Marseilles (and would know again), living incognito among pimps, trulls, and cutthroats. Wasn't this, from a bourgeois child's vantage, *la vraie vie?* Cocteau loved the Highlanders and the bisexual Senegalese, implying as much to Gide, whom he could not but irritate: "You would like it very much here—Venetiany Arabic trenches, like Luna Park—the sharpshooters belly dance and the Zouaves offer me prehistoric rings. Serenity is not found in neutral country; it's here 'mixed in with the game,' like singing Whitman, and one sleeps peacefully beneath shells, bombs, mortar. I shall tell you about my Christmas night, only ten meters from the *boches,* with Magi and fat stars overhead."

At the same time, he wrote to Gleizes of feeling inconsolably alone among madmen bent on "destroying the old fables while trodding the new ones underfoot," and to Mme. Simone the following: "The moon is jumping and the sky crumbling. One stops one's ears and thinks about the Far West—a spectacle of destruction that dashes one's belief that one has the old instinct to create." Partly he winnowed his different sensations according to his correspondent, but this duplicity about war seems to have been genuine. It crushed and exalted him. Few poems of Cocteau's ring so true as *"Tour du Secteur Calme"* in *Discours du Grand Sommeil,* about a soldier dying as the medics carry him through the trenches. He uttered *boche* freely, but the word turned to ashes on his tongue one night when he heard "Tannenbaum," which he and his brother had sung as children, echo from the enemy trenches.

Pieced together from various memoirs, Cocteau's own narrative describing his adventures at the Front would sound like an Arthurian allegory filled with little white lies and intriguing reticences. Newly arrived at the Front, he was assigned a post among the North African Sidis, replacing some youth discharged by his superior officers for "card-sharping." The Sidis, who had been "enchanted" by the young man, vented their anger upon his substitute, sending Cocteau on perilous missions through "the triangular Wood" from which he always returned, to their repeated dismay, alive. When the Arab battalion was shifted to the Somme, its officers left Cocteau behind, in charge of matériel. Two days later an angel wearing the chevron of a marine captain discovered him adrift in the flooded trenches. "Listen," he said, "you're not about to stay here superintending a water closet! I'm taking you along." Thereupon Cocteau became the mascot of marines billeted in a ruined villa at Coxyde-Bains where the chief enemy was boredom. In this war they were abetted by their Parisian elf, who romped about like a tourist at large in Herculaneum, inventing games and exploring culverts.

This mosaic of fact and fantasy portraying Cocteau's life at the

Front ends like the tale of his expulsion from the Hôtel Biron years before. The moral of the ending could be "Avoid exposing yourself to publicity," but it proves how like a moth he gravitated toward its glare. Undone at the Hôtel Biron by a newspaper campaign which he had initiated, so here too he suffered the penalty of his courage. An admiral having recommended him for the *croix de guerre*, his hoax was thus brought to light. Two military policemen escorted him from Coxyde-Bains to Coxyde-Ville, where, on the pretext of collecting some personal effects from a cellar, he escaped through the grating. Walking aimlessly about Coxyde, whom should he encounter but his friend Louis Gillet, General Élie Boissel's aide-de-camp, en route to Dunkerque in the general's automobile. They went off together, passing by Coxyde-Bains, where the marines beheld Cocteau, stripped of his epaulettes a few hours before, now hobnobbing with the brass. The following day, nearly all his comrades perished in a trench at Saint-Georges.

What foul odors he smelled, what grime and blood and misery he saw day in and day out, are filtered through a myth machine from which they emerge deodorized, decorative, and smiling. According to Cocteau's fantasy, war possesses all the attributes of the aristocratic life: money is not an issue, conventions do not apply, and uniforms amount to the sacred apparatus of invisibility (doubly so as his own was fraudulent). Many of Cocteau's tales, those bearing on his own life no less than those offered as fiction, pivot about some hoax. This one was no exception. "Had he been an authentic marine," wrote Cocteau of Guillaume, hero of his war novel *Thomas the Impostor*, "he would have found the going rough. Having become a marine without being one, he could fully savor his happiness."

Governed by the sense of his own fraudulence, Cocteau made a virtue of necessity, declaring, "I am a lie who tells the truth." Fastened to his lie, he cultivated it for its own sake. *As if*, born of some primitive rebuff, became for Cocteau an etiquette requiring preface upon preface, costume upon costume, lies dovetailed in lies, and exacting—for whatever freedom it afforded him—an exorbitant fee in loneliness. On a more literal level, however, that formula, *as if*, takes its departure from some inadmissible point. Cocteau was not offered the *croix de guerre*. Lavishing his favors rather too indiscriminately, he aroused the jealousy of an Arab sergeant who threatened to disembowel him and might well have made good his threat had Beaumont not intervened with gifts. The ambulance corps was rotated to another sector, and Cocteau swiftly packed off to Paris.

Cocteau returned to Paris in March, but left for the Front once again in May, with a mobile unit containing a library and X-ray apparatus. For several months he shuttled unpredictably between Paris and Flanders. By July 29 he was back for good. Philippe Berthelot secured him a post in the propaganda and censorship bureau of the Ministry of Foreign Affairs, the so-called *Maison de la Presse* whose employees, many of them artists and writers, officially belonged to the "22nd Division," a ploy by which France gave its more talented citizens a sinecure without shame, thus excusing them from military action (Milhaud was one such employee). Moreover, his new post brought Cocteau into the entourage of Philippe Berthelot, one of the outstanding diplomats of his age.

Following in the footsteps of his father, Marcellin Berthelot—a scientist of genius, an educator, and France's Minister of Foreign Affairs in the 1890s—Philippe was, in the truest sense, an *uomo universale*. As a diplomat he had no peer. Contemptuous of politicians, he stood behind successive premiers and foreign ministers like a gray eminence, putting immortal aphorisms in their mouths. "War is too serious an affair to be confided to generals," was his *bon mot*, not Clemenceau's.

His whole person bespoke the cynical aristocrat. Immensely tall, often sporting an astrakhan, his face shaped like a parallelogram starred with two limpid, blue-green, unforgiving eyes, he left people, Gide for example, dumb-struck. "I am distressed by the narrowness of his forehead," wrote Gide. "Since, in spite of it, he has a prodigious memory, his ideas must have lost their thickness to stay within the warehouse of his brain." Even Gide, mocking because frightened of Berthelot's exterminating intelligence, paid tribute to his memory, which stored not only the diplomatic history of France but half its verse. The few people whom he exempted from disdain were poets, notably Paul Claudel and Apollinaire, whose

genius he was among the first to recognize. A group of young dip-
lomat-writers working under his protection—Jean Giraudoux, Paul
Morand, and Saint-Jean Perse—quoted him scripturally.

This small world of high catholicism included a short, cherubic,
extraordinarily keen-witted prelate named l'abbé Mugnier, whose
combined suaveness and purity gave him great prestige on the
Right Bank . . . and elsewhere. He was the confessor-elect of all
the suffering half-believers among the *gratin*, his own faith being
far more ecumenical than Claudel's. Jacques Porel, the actress
Réjane's son, relates the following anecdote. Mugnier, trying to lift
Porel's faltering spirits one day, said, "Oh, my child, one must love
life. We must passionately contemplate all its beauties. Take romantic literature, which lies close to my heart. Well, what I love about
it is, it shivers with life." Seeing that Porel was only half-persuaded,
he continued, "And then, my child, one must love life because
. . . it's all we have!" Moreover, Mugnier, a formidably well-read
priest, was instrumental in several clamorous conversions: above all,
Huysmans'. His memory rivaling Berthelot's, they staged verse recitals in which one would begin a line of verse at random and stop
at the caesura, challenging the other to recall the second hemistich.
United by poetry, the skeptical diplomat and the worldly prelate
sustained the spirit of the eighteenth-century France during a reign
of complete barbarism.

Their presence gave a kind of spiritual armature to the salons—more intimate now but just as active—where aristocrats and
fellow-travelers foregathered. The Berthelots, the Countess de
Chevigné, the Beaumonts, Misia Edwards, Princess Eugène Murat,
and Hélène Soutzo (a beautiful Rumanian princess living at the
Ritz who later became Paul Morand's wife) received, if not
weekly, fortnightly. Proust, more pallid than ever, would sometimes emerge from his reclusion. The abbot invariably accepted
their invitations, which meant a considerable journey for he lived in
the far reaches of Montparnasse, on Rue Méchain, where the sisters
of Saint-Joseph de Cluny—whose chaplain he was—provided him a
small apartment.

Cocteau, his conversation like the carbonated bubbles in soda
pop—exhilarating and short-lived—attended unfailingly. "It is im-

possible," wrote Morand, "to relate one of Cocteau's stories. . . . After Cocteau, his eyes like gimlets, his hands which speak, his mimicry, other people's gestures seem ponderous; the next day one remembers nothing. The Grand Duchess Anastasia used to say, 'He's a card, young Monsieur Cocteau; unfortunately I forget everything he says; I'm going to buy a little notebook.' " Cocteau played much the same role in this society that Voiture had in seventeenth-century salons. By turns petted and petting, whiny and consoling, he availed himself of a child's prerogatives, titillating the grownups with his fancy, with his pranks, with his grievances. At Mme. de Chevigné's he would fold the fire screen around his hostess' beloved poodle Kiss and place sugar cubes outside. Who else but he could do that with impunity? Only five years before she had forbidden him to pet Kiss lest his face powder set her sneezing, and it was a measure of Cocteau's rise in society that now his hay fever took precedence over the dog's. "To think, all my Julys for the next fifty years botched, my favorite month, too," he exclaimed one July evening. "His colds, the way he describes them," Morand wryly commented "are as catastrophic as railway disasters." He was indispensable to society, the buffoon without whom it could not take itself seriously, a pet in which it indulged itself for fear of growing bored. Society was not concerned with his private disasters, nor he with society's. He was more likely to confide in Gide, as he did in the following letter, written during the winter of 1917.

A period of imbroglio! What pain! and now what bitterness—my distress grows from day to day—Seeing you did me some good—I'm not feeling well. I'm suffering. *I'm groping about in a sullen penumbra.* One tries to reach a loved one, and succeeds only to find oneself jilted. Asphyxiating from disappointment, failure, weariness, loneliness, etc., etc. The indifference of an eye that now inspects you whereas once it drank you up. The limpness of a hand that once sought none but yours—It's abominable.

Considering Gide's arch attitude toward him, it may seem odd that Cocteau should have unburdened himself so freely; the intimate tone of his letters, however, was often not a sign of intimacy but an appeal for intimacy, entailing telegraphic, noncommittal reports about some vague physical or emotional excruciation. His correspondence and his life were almost unrelated, which allowed him to write as many as twenty letters a day following, almost invariably, the same formula: a massive compliment, the subject at hand, and a physical complaint which may have been one part true, another part habit, and third part the commonplace maneuver of a child pleading innocent before adults, guilty not of this or that, but guilty. That formula served him for the better part of his life. There is no correspondence more imperturbably identical with itself, more monotonous than Cocteau's. His handwriting changed according to his models, but the substance of his letters never.

His civilian life swayed between the Medrano and the Ritz. In wartime the latter had become a keep in which the embattled *beau monde* sought refuge in the evenings (Proust, entering a new phase, began to dine there so regularly that he was known as "Proust of the Ritz"). When the lights were turned off in observance of the 9:30 curfew, many of its aristocratic diners, having evacuated their town houses in favor of hotel suites where life proved more convenient, simply retired aloft.

How they amused themselves may be gathered from the July 28, 1917, entry in Paul Morand's journal. The previous evening had been a particularly dramatic one. He spent it with Hélène Soutzo, Étienne de Beaumont, Jacques Porel, Joseph Reinach, Cocteau, and Proust. Their conversation revolved about hypnotism. Beaumont was singing the praises of a medium named Monsieur Delagarde whose "fluid" (his stupidity notwithstanding) "was terrific." The company lost no time in summoning Monsieur Delagarde, who, instantly put Beaumont to sleep. He was on the verge of perforating the entranced count with scissors and pins ("an experiment in insensibility") when Edith de Beaumont began to scream, and he reluctantly desisted.

As soon as this feature ended, another began. The lights went out, and sirens mounted atop the Eiffel Tower began to wail, announcing the first all-out Gotha air raid of the war. "Somebody must have stepped on the foot of the Eiffel Tower; it's complaining," yelled Cocteau, craning his head out the window. Proust, unperturbed, was still musing about hypnotism. Sleepers, he concluded, want their futures told so as to avoid admitting their pasts.[1]

Cocteau ventured into Montmartre at every opportunity, bringing younger members of the smart set who, at the Medrano, found themselves shy and speechless among the "hypertrophied and chlorophyllic clowns." Cocteau, on the other hand, knew them by first name. "I much prefer clowns to actors," he told Morand. "They are far more intelligent. Mme. Errazuriz claims that that's because clowns sleep with their poodles." After watching the trapeze artists and geese dancing the tango (the latest craze to sweep Paris), his appetite whetted for gamier delights, he would visit the Tabarin "skating" where, under cover of tricolor bunting and phony uniforms, pimps, black marketeers, cocaine pushers, hoods or "Incas" from the outlying boulevards, and whores mingled indiscriminately. In this remote suburb, transvestites, according to Morand, walked about openly: women dressed as men, and aviators "in widow's weeds."

By 1917 fashion had begun to acknowledge the existence of cubism. Mme. Errazuriz, a wealthy and brilliant Chilean whose aristocratic bearing sanctified her weird costumes, appeared at Misia Edwards' salon in sailor cloth figured with little black and white squares: material witness of her admiration for Picasso. On New Year's Day, again at Misia's, Cocteau and André Saglio-Dresa, Director of Fine Arts in charge of French exhibitions abroad, nearly came to blows on the subject of cubism, Cocteau vehemently defending what a few years before (in *Le Mot*) he had all but dismissed. Picasso's price at auctions was rising dramatically, and poor Jacques Blanche's falling in exact ratio. The latter took Cocteau to task by lashing out at his new idol, Picasso, whom he considered an opportunistic will-o'-the-wisp: "Cocteau has periods," he was heard to whisper, his lips pursed and resentful. "He's cyclical. Six years ago I lived through his Anna de Noailles phase; Jean spoke about her so relentlessly that we, who all admired her very much, couldn't stand to hear her name! Nowadays it's the Picasso phase. I know

1. Communicating with spirits over a "turning table" became so epidemic a pastime during the war that the rector of the Madeleine delivered a series of fire-and-brimstone sermons condemning the practice. Self-proclaimed witches abounded, selling mole paws and wolves' teeth.

friends of Picasso in Barcelona and I have his number! He's a crafty fellow who uses people, despite the impression he gives of being a blunt, paint-slinging Montmartrian. He's using Cocteau."

Although Blanche's indictment was partly right on all counts, he hit the mark a glancing blow, for if Picasso used Cocteau, Cocteau equally used Picasso. Moreover, he was not cyclical but simultaneist. Misia came nearer the truth when she declared, in Cocteau's absence, that he felt compelled to seduce everyone at the same time—Picasso, Mme. de Chevigné, and the marine corps—adding, in a nonchalant air, one of her patented *aperçus* whose malice would beg its own pardon: "Imagine, wasting his best years pleasing, instead of striving to displease." Thanks to certain people, notably Mme. Errazuriz and young Valentine Gross, Cocteau pried open doors hitherto closed to him.

Paris consists of a plain, the Marais, and two bluffs enclosing it. A plain-dweller, Cocteau always affiliated his destiny with the heights. Perfectly at home among the nobility of the Marais, he lived dangerously on Montmartre, which, since artistic bohemia made its exodus to Montparnasse toward 1910, was becoming more and more vulgar, all but a few sections of its former self overrun by hectic pleasure-seekers and *apaches* (Picasso had taken to carrying a pistol for protection). Having met the Medrano harlequins, who liked him, Cocteau now longed to meet their painters on Montparnasse, who regarded him warily. As soon as the opportunity presented itself, he began enrolling them in schemes by which to promote their fortune and his own. In 1916, the war playing no small part in lowering social inhibitions, the plain and the bluffs started, at first shyly, then avidly, to crossbreed. Mongrel dinner lists appeared, including illustrious names such as Beaumont, Chevigné, and Murat, but also humbler ones variously foreign, semi-foreign, Jewish, and invented: Pablo Picasso, Erik Satie, Darius Milhaud, and Guillaume Apollinaire. If war provided a favorable climate for miscegenation, Cocteau acted as one of the presiding priests. His desire to cut a figure among artistic revolutionaries bore fruit in *Parade*, which represents a pivotal moment not only in his career, but in that of the avant-garde.

Between tours of the Front, he had been cultivating an entirely new set of acquaintances in Paris.

Soon after his return from Leysin in 1914 Cocteau attended a rehearsal of the Ballets Russes at the Théâtre des Champs-Élysées. It proved to be the company's last full season for several years. The war flung its dancers over three continents, but even before September, 1914, it had begun to disintegrate. The previous summer Diaghilev dismissed Nijinsky outright when he learned of his marriage to Romola in Buenos Aires, a self-spiteful gesture he could scarcely afford. He recruited young Vladimir Miassine from the Moscow Grand Theatre, but the latter was not a dancer of Nijinsky's stature, nor yet the choreographer he would become under the name Léonide Massine. Moreover, the repertoire showed fatal signs of rootlessness. The night Cocteau attended, Ballets Russes was rehearsing *La Légende de Joseph*, an extravanganza compiled by Richard Strauss, Hugo von Hofmannsthal, and José Sert. Cocteau's attention, however, was focused not on the ballet nor on Count Kessler, whose money was behind it, but on a young woman sitting next to the count, Valentine Gross. He hovered about her all evening, seeking some pretext to alight. When at length the count introduced them, she offered a limp hand which seemed to forbid any conversation. Why his anxiety to meet her at all?

He was partly intrigued by her incuriosity. Normally women oohed and aahed when Cocteau, a *joli garçon* whose angular prettiness was of 1900 vintage, executed his pirouettes. Mlle. Gross glowered with emphatic selfhood. More to the point, she associated with people whom he wanted desperately to know. Cocteau, possessing the keenest nose of his generation, caught on her the scent of young talent, musical and literary, which had just begun to assert itself.

Born of Alsatian parents living in Boulogne-sur-Mer, Valentine Gross came to Paris during Diaghilev's first season, 1909, with the intention of studying at the École des Beaux Arts. She faithfully attended every performance of the Ballets Russes, bringing along a score which, owing to a musical education, she could follow with ease. In the dim light of the Châtelet or of the Opéra, she would swiftly sketch the dancers' movements above the appropriate bars, thus leaving her small mark on the margin of musical history. These sketches, along with wax-on-wood paintings and pastel drawings, brought her to Diaghilev's attention. He allowed her to attend rehearsals, where she might draw undisturbed, and when in 1913 the Ballets Russes opened at its new residence, Astruc's Théâtre des Champs-Élysées, the lobby contained an exhibit of her art. Jacques Copeau, at work organizing the first session of his Théâtre du Vieux-Colombier, took notice and employed her on the costumes and sets of Henry Becque's *La Navette*, which he produced the following year. Thus, she became acquainted with his entourage, including Gide, Gaston Gallimard, Valery Larbaud, and Léon-Paul Fargue. All the while attending the École des Beaux Arts, she moved in avant-garde circles. A combination of high seriousness and little-girlishness set her apart. Statuesque, she nonetheless had the wide-open eyes, the brightly rouged cheeks and white bandeaux of an infanta. This incongruity—a full-blown beauty who mistook herself for a Kewpie doll—was not without charm. Moreover, there lay—beneath the artifices, the loquacity, the exasperating sing-song, the little missy airs—a sensibility.

By 1915 she had a salon, meeting Wednesdays, whose habitués could be found Sunday evenings at the home of Cipa and Ida Godebski, Misia Edwards' stepbrother and sister-in-law. Her salon attracted various literati from the *NRF*, but its personality was decidedly musical. Edgard Varèse, back from Berlin with a collection of atonal scores, frequently came. Ricardo Viñes, the great painist, would play Spanish music while two composers, the one just beginning his career and the other experiencing a second birth, sat in the audience. Georges Auric, a mere fifteen, had already made his precocity known throughout musical circles, while Erik Satie, who had lapsed into silence for twelve years, was now, at forty-eight, being rediscovered.

Satie, who lived in a poor suburb of Paris, made a weekly habit of conveying his quizzical self to Valentine Gross's apartment on the Île Saint-Louis. They had met earlier in 1914 at the apartment of a composer named Roland Manuel, whose enthusiasm for Satie's early "Rosicrucian" pieces influenced his furnishings and apparel. Dressed in a gandurah, he would—by the light of a single taper—play *La Porte héroïque du ciel* or, alternatively, read the poems of that mystical fop from Lyon, Sar Péladan. The fact that Manuel and Satie had been classmates at the Schola Cantorum, studying counterpoint with Albert Roussel and analysis with Vincent d'Indy, may not seem odd, but one was twenty-five years older than the other.

Satie, having earned an esoteric reputation in the 1880s and 1890s for his *Gymnopédies* and *Gnossiennes*, mysteriously decided to revolutionize his life in 1898. A minor pillar of Montmartre's bohemia, he left Paris for a dingy room in Arcueil-Cachan, carting his few possessions the six miles in a wheelbarrow. While his best friend Debussy (whom he had freed from the spell of Wagner's music) and his former protégé Maurice Ravel were being acclaimed, Satie, whose immaculate pride matched his sense of humor, buried himself in Arcueil. Willful anonymity was his reply to a public that failed to give him what he considered his due. He earned a living by writing songs for Montmartrian music-hall singers such as Vincent Hyspa, walking those six miles every day to save the bus fare. Flouting Debussy's advice ("At our age you don't shed your skin again"), he enrolled at the Schola Cantorum for reasons he understood perfectly well, the study of counterpoint (which flatly opposed the harmonic devices in vogue) forming a segment of that unwavering musical line that Satie had begun to trace for himself as early as 1903 with *Three Pieces in the Shape of a Pear*. History, lagging behind his esthetics, would shortly catch up. After the war young French composers rejected the harmonic flux of impressionism in favor of clarity, humor, economy, polytonal construction: all features of Satie's music.

But even before that, Debussy and Ravel, whom success had made philanthropic (though not toward one another), used their prestige on his behalf. In January, 1911, the Société Indépendante Musicale, at Ravel's suggestion, performed three pieces that Satie had written twenty years before; a few months later Debussy conducted two *Gymnopédies* at the *Cercle musical*.

In 1911, at the age of forty-five, Satie laid aside his clay pipe and his corduroy suits (twelve, all identical) in favor of cigars and a bank clerk's suit whose correctitude was as extreme as his previous garb had been bohemian. His pince-nez perpetually askew, his faun-like face prolonged by a naughty goatee, his hands immaculately clean (because, in accordance with his strict and highly eccentric standards of hygiene, he used pumice stone instead of soap), Satie wore his professorial self like armor to protect a gleeful, timid, and no doubt profoundly hurt child. His withering humor served, at least in part, the same purpose. To Valentine Gross, whose tenderness and solicitude overcame the child's defenses, the man could impart his real self freely. Calling her "my dear big girl," he would confide his woes and enthusiasms, as in the following letter:

Dear Valentine,

I'm suffering too much. It seems to me I'm accursed. This cadger's life disgusts me.

I'm looking for, and would like to find, a niche—a job—however trivial it may be. *Screw art:* it's put me in too many "binds." It's an asshole's trade, I daresay, the artist's.

Dear friend, forgive these lovely turns of phrase—lovely indeed.

I'm writing to everyone. Nobody answers, not even a friendly word. Damn it!

You, dear Friend, who have always been good toward your old friend, I beg of you, see if it wouldn't be possible to place him somewhere so he can earn his bread and butter.

Anywhere. The most menial task would not repel me, I guarantee you.

Do it quickly: I'm at the end of my rope and can't wait any longer.

Art? For a month and more I haven't written a note.

I don't have any more ideas, and don't *want* any. What now?

Your old comrade

Erik Satie

This letter, dated 1918, was written during a post-partum depression. Satie had recently completed two major works, the music for *Parade* and his symphonic drama *Socrate*. Being down and out again proved the more difficult because of his brief interlude of glory, when commissions from Misia (through Diaghilev) and from Winnie de

Polignac allowed him to buy a new umbrella every week. The *beau monde* observes nothing so faithfully as its whims. In 1913, according to Auric, it considered Satie an aging buffoon. By 1916 he was all the rage. Valentine Gross was certainly instrumental in this shift of opinion, having introduced Satie early in 1914 to Vogel, the wealthy patron and publisher who commissioned *Sports et Divertissements*: twenty incredibly brief pieces illustrated by Charles Martin. Moreover, she introduced him to Étienne de Beaumont and Jean Cocteau. Cocteau, forever echoing *le dernier cri*, announced Satie's Second Coming throughout the salons of Paris.

Cocteau's interest in Satie pivoted on a specific purpose. In the spring of 1915 another idea for a ballet seized his imagination, this one based not on the Bible but on the closest thing to it, Shakespeare. Like *David*, Cocteau's adaptation of *A Midsummer Night's Dream* would involve a circus scene, but instead of simulating one in some theatre, he proposed using the Medrano itself, with the three Fratellini clowns playing Bottom, Flute, and Starveling. Edgard Varèse was to conduct the Medrano orchestra, and Cocteau had persuaded Albert Gleizes, residing in New York, to design the props, which he imagined vaguely cubistic. In a letter to Gleizes, Cocteau spewed forth his half-digested ideas:

> The *Dream* can and must be a marvel. Medrano orchestra a potpourri of everything we like directed by Varèse—Clowns, etc. . . . you're my savior. My translation [of Shakespeare] is literal—big excisions (the whole "charm and dalliance" bit—untranslatable and boring)—what remains is a kind of cinema of the sublime. I ask of you, hands joined in prayer, urgently: a red for the first rug—a canary yellow for the second—apple green for the third. . . . I want to project onto the rugs the attributes of a magic lantern—shadows of tree patches, doves . . .

No sooner had Cocteau mentioned the idea to Gabriel Astruc than the impresario's enthusiasm was kindled; having sponsored a circus review at the outset of his career, he never revisited the Medrano without recalling nostalgically those vagabond years. Arrangements were swiftly made: the circus rented, a philanthropic cause found, and a patriotic overture adopted. All proceeds would go to the Theatre Directors' charity, and the orchestra, when

Oberon made his entrance, would strike up "Tipperary." But some more incidental music was needed. "We borrowed it from Erik Satie's *Gymnopédies*" wrote Astruc, whose memory probably deceived him, for the *Gymnopédies* were as ill-suited to a *Midsummer Night's Dream* as Gregorian chants to a Punch-and-Judy show.[2]

In fact, various composers, including Debussy, Stravinsky, Roussel, Ravel, and Florent Schmitt were approached, but Cocteau, delighted with *Three Pieces in the Shape of a Pear*, which he had heard Viñes perform with Satie, probably at the Godebskis', in April, 1915, angled for Satie's collaboration. "We were simultaneously inspired" wrote Cocteau, "as though by telepathy, with a desire to collaborate"—an exaggeration, no doubt, for Satie, a loner to his core, was not visited by overpowering urges to collaborate with anyone. In all events, he did write some music (published posthumously as *Cinq Grimaces*) but for some reason which even Astruc cannot recall, the project, after several rehearsals, collapsed.[3]

As soon as it did, Cocteau decided to use the ruins to cement his friendship with the shy, prickly composer. Another idea had meanwhile occurred to him. For one of two reasons—because he was on distant terms with Satie, or else sufficiently close to have quarreled—he asked Valentine Gross to intercede. The icy façade she had presented Cocteau in 1914 was by now thawing (so swiftly, in fact, that the following summer, on leave from the Front, he would spend a week with her in Boulogne-sur-Mer). He had actually been made privy to her apartment, but never on Wednesdays, since Mlle. Gross—out of inverse snobbism and mindless partisanship with the avant-garde—wished to segregate Cocteau from her "regulars." Moreover, Satie did not straightaway embrace the idea, understandably, as Cocteau seemed fertile in stillbirths. Behaving like a reluctant bride, he finally agreed, however, to meet his suitor

2. Unless this was indeed Cocteau's original idea. Much later he would use such incongruity to good effect in his film *Les Enfants Terribles*, in which the background music is Bach-Vivaldi. Moreover, the first draft of *Parade*, as we shall see, called for a responsive litany, almost Gregorian, between two voices, a contralto and a child's.
3. In his own memoirs Cocteau telescoped these two collaborations, on the *Dream* and *Parade*, into one—evidently preferring to forget the former. But the idea for *Parade* was not born until the *Dream* failed to jell.

at the home of his duenna. What came of their meeting at the Quai de Bourbon, on the afternoon of October 18, 1915, was the first idea for *Parade*, an original construction spackled with elements of *Potomak* (as yet unpublished) and the debris of *David* and *A Midsummer Night's Dream* (the *guignols*, the cubistic decor, the phonographic voice, etc.). Before leaving for the Front in May, 1916, Cocteau gave Satie a sheaf of notes to serve as a fillip.

From the Front, Cocteau, already foreseeing Diaghilev's role, kept Misia Edwards abreast of his collaboration with Satie, for she held almost absolute sway over Diaghilev. He wrote to Misia:

Satie is an angel (well disguised), an angel from Arcueil-se-Cachan.[4] My lot in all this is not lending him a farcical hand—on the contrary. May our collaboration move you as it did me the day I told him what he should write. An Anjou evening unforgettably rich and charged with mutual electricity. I gather from his post cards that the thing is progressing along the lines I hoped it would. It is *his* drama and the eternal drama played between the public and the stage—taking a form as simple as Épinal. You know my *love*, my cult for Igor—my distress at leaving a spot on the beautiful snow of Leysin and perhaps my project for a book on him. Above all, he must never get the notion that I am "grafting" a slip of *David*—*David* there was a clean portion and a confused one: a portion of me and a portion of circumstances, so to speak. I bumped into Igor while advancing, unbeknownst to myself, toward Satie, and perhaps Satie is at the angle of a path that will lead me back to Igor. All in all, the Stravinsky-Cocteau adventure was *pregnant* with misunderstanding —our meeting with Satie contains nothing but lighthearted happiness. . . .[5]

4. "Arcueil-se-Cachant" literally means Arcueil hiding itself, a lame pun on Satie's suburb.
5. Misia, despite her lovable airs, made a hobby of sowing discord. She had been instrumental in breaking up the Stravinsky-Cocteau collaboration on *David*, and Cocteau feared she would recidivate. Her patronage was essential, as no one but Diaghilev, her bosom friend, was producing ballets. When Rolf de Maré founded his Ballet Suédois in 1920, Cocteau transferred himself to him. "Blind Misia is balling up everybody with everybody else," he wrote to Gleizes. Misia wanted her investments to bring her the dividend of fame. Like Doucet, the couturier, she paid promising but impecunious poets to write letters to her. On deciding to support *Parade*, Misia obliged Valentine Gross to write her a letter "admitting" that the ballet was conceived in her (Misia's) presence at the Quai Voltaire.
Stravinsky, who had always known on which side his bread was buttered, remained faithful to Diaghilev and Misia until other patrons made them dispensable.

Misia held the purse strings, and she was not about to loosen them till assured of a good run for her money. The idea seemed too abstract. "Think of the public," she cautioned Cocteau, who found this an odd caveat coming from someone who fancied herself a *Dreyfusarde de Pelléas*, in other words, a musical nonconformist. Her reservations were not, however, completely unjustified.

From the outset, *Parade* proposed flying in the face of its audience, showing the public its eternal incomprehension. It was a kind of sequel to *The Rite of Spring*, taking the furor of that performance and making a ballet of it. Cocteau conceived a ready-made scandal. The ballet takes place *outside* the theatre (a *parade* being the farce performed by circus people in front of the tent to draw a crowd), where the headliners try unavailingly to trump up business. "They emerge from a void and return to a void." What greater insult to an audience than telling it that the theatre is empty? In its most primitive version, *Parade* already had three stock characters who survived all subsequent recastings: a "Chinese Prestidigitator," an "Acrobat," and a "little American girl." Cocteau gave Satie three sheets of onionskin on which he had delivered himself of ideas about each. It is a curious document charting his mind's zigzag course as it foraged for associations. Of "the little American girl," for example, he wrote:

The Titanic—"Nearer My God to Thee"—elevators—the sirens of Boulogne—submarine cables—ship-to-shore cables—Brest—tar—varnish—steamship apparatus—*The New York Herald*—dynamos—airplanes—short circuits—palatial cinemas—the sheriff's daughter—Walt Whitman—the silence of stampedes—cowboys with leather and goatskin chaps—the telegraph operator from Los Angeles who marries the detective at the end—the 144 express—the Sioux—the cordillera of the Andes—Negroes picking maize—jail—the reverberation—beautiful Madame Astor—the declarations of President Wilson—torpedo boats—mines—the tango—Vidal Lablache—mercury globes—projectors—arc lamps—gramophones—typewriters—the Eiffel Tower—the Brooklyn Bridge—huge automobiles of enamel and nickel—Pullman cars which cross the virgin forest—bars—saloons—ice-cream parlors—roadside taverns—Nick Carter—Helene

Boodge—the Hudson and its docks—the Carolinas—my room on the seventeenth floor—panhandlers—posters—advertising—Charlie Chaplin—Christopher Columbus—metal landscapes—the list of the victims of the Lusitania—women wearing evening gowns in the morning—the isle of Mauritius—*Paul et Virginie*

Similar images pertain to the Chinese Prestidigitator and the Acrobat: things submarine and stratospheric, heights and depths, the Far West and Far East, the silence of thunderous events in silent films, the inaudible transmission of messages by telegraph. Somewhat later, he gave Satie a libretto scored for two voices in which the above images—in somewhat chastened form—serpentine down the page, curving this way and that as if to elude some suddenly pervading silence, or else to draw, by inference, their blank underside. Physically, it is imitation Mallarmé but its jablike lines bring to mind Cendrars, whose verse had just come to Cocteau's attention. The "score" arrived with a covering note:

Dear and admirable Satie,

I'm at the height of emotion—Here are some pages. You're free to use them all or one for each—don't even consult me—The notes in green are just new ideas for the use of song . . . [their] freshness and warmth may come across, above the noises of your orchestra. They refer to the mystery of the interior—breaths of the world—dreams of dreams and of *exactitude* without which the dream is worthless.

Try to include as much of it as possible, in whatever order you wish—but these pages *belong* to you. . . . They come from *Le Cap de Bonne Espérance*, a bulky poem which *we* shall like. How much I like you, and how I like our work, *already completed!*

Let's go, frigate!

In fact, their work, far from being already completed, had scarcely begun. Ultimately Cocteau's libretto was scotched; though lines survive in his poem *Le Cap de Bonne Espérance*, it was supplanted in the final version by noise-makers. But the idea inspired Satie, whose own style, combining the music hall and counterpoint, coincided very nicely with Cocteau's. It called for that subtle mixture of humor and pathos—*guignol* gestures versus the human inner

voice, the tragicomedy inherent in any Punch-and-Judy show—
which Satie managed so succinctly in such works as *Sports et Divertissements*. His music is imbued with tender irony. An idea first
announced in the plaintive mood will, shifting to another key, regard itself from a slight distance, from another angle. It is music
which, like Cocteau, simultaneously speaks and quotes itself. Two
kindred minds discovered a common pretext to lay their masks on
the line, but in other respects their ways differed. They advanced
like the tortoise and the hare, Cocteau leaping ahead, then waiting
while Satie plodded forward. The one would perform all kinds of
pirouettes while the other applauded from far behind.

"Dear Friend," wrote Satie on April 25, 1916, "Excuse me, sick,
with the grippe. Only way to notify you would have been telepathy. Tomorrow, agreed. Valentine Gross tells me wondrous
tales. You are the man *with ideas*. Bravo! Your old, Erik Satie." A
week later he wrote again, saying "Dear Friend, I received the
manuscript. Very astonishing! I'm putting my ideas in order. Write
me, won't you? There's a dray horse's work ahead. I'm resuming
the whole of it."

The combined goadings of Cocteau and Misia (who, having decided to sponsor the work though still dubious about Satie, proved
to be a most exacting patroness) could not make Satie move more
swiftly. "Dear Friend," he wrote on June 8, slightly peeved, ever
puckish, and perfectly adamant, "Don't be anxious or nervous: I'm
working. Let me go at it, good old chap. Know that I shall not
present you the work until *October*. You will not learn *a note* of it
beforehand. That I can promise you!—Will you allow me to say
that you are the author of the subject? I need to. Madame Edwards
is backing this project. I told her she'd have to wait until *October*. I
want to do well, *very*; *you must* give me credit—If you come to
Paris, send word—Best wishes to Valentine Gross and yourself."

Cocteau at the Front since early May, was biting his nails to the
quick for fear that Satie might lose interest in their collaboration.
He tortured every word in Satie's letter, and asked Valentine,
"Does 'it's astonishing' mean warm or chilly in his faun language?"
He had no recourse but to wait, with Valentine Gross's presence
for consolation. She was in Boulogne visiting her mother and he in

a hotel down the block, his ambulance corps having been rotated to Boulogne in June.

Meanwhile another figure had entered Cocteau's life, one who changed the course of *Parade* and made Cocteau his lifelong evangelist: Pablo Picasso.

5

Arts and Craft

Picasso had moved to Montparnasse shortly before the war. By the winter of 1911–1912, when he was sufficiently recognized to have epigones, and when cubism was old enough to have warring factions, his personal life reflected the decadence of Montmartre itself. The tenants of that ramshackle building on Rue Ravignan called *le bateau lavoir* or "laundry boat"—himself, Juan Gris, André Salmon, Max Jacob—and their constant visitor Apollinaire, had dispersed; the heroic age had brought Picasso a measure of affluence, and this affluence, together with sheer ennui no doubt, relaxed his bond with Fernande Olivier. What divertissements Cocteau found on the Butte in 1915, Picasso had exhausted by 1912: the Medrano, white nights in a café perversely called The Hermitage, and in another on Place Blanche, the Grelot.

But in that year he fell in love with a delicate young woman named Marcelle Humbert, née Gouel. He dubbed her Eve, symbolically, as she represented for him a fresh start, a beginning. Picasso's "Periods" correspond very closely to his women (and along with them his dogs and his poet laureates). So it was with Eve, "small and perfect" as Gertrude Stein described her—a kind of mandarin doll, whose former lover had been Marcoussis. Her advent marked the end of Picasso's long sojourn on Montmartre. Together they headed south, moving to and fro according to circumstances and fancy: from Avignon to Céret in the Pyrenees, from Céret (where Fernande Olivier's presence proved discomfiting) back to Avignon, from Avignon to a tiny hamlet six miles north called Sorgues, where Braque and his wife joined them. Picasso, his soul now reinstated, worked like a demon, painting every surface in sight. The whitewashed walls of their hired villa in

Sorgues were irresistible. On one he painted a cubist oval still life to which he became so attached that Kahnweiler, to keep him happy, ordered the wall demolished and the appropriate fragment brought to his gallery in Paris. When Picasso himself returned, it was to a studio on Boulevard Raspail in Montparnasse, where thanks to his friend, dealer, and factotum Kahnweiler, the oddments from his various Montmartre studios lay congregated.

Around 1912 Montparnasse started to acquire the artistic eminence once associated with its rival hill. True, the literary group responsible for Paul Fort's *Vers et Prose* had, a decade before, adopted the Closerie des Lilas, a small café down the street from Picasso's new atelier, as their meeting place, but it was a largely proletarian quarter whose main thoroughfare, Boulevard Montparnasse, looked like a street in the present-day outskirts of Paris, the so-called "Zone": a congeries of neighborhood cafés, coal yards, sawmills, rubble-strewn lots, and low tenements. Suddenly little cliques of artists began to settle here. The "laundry boat" and its Ashkenazic counterpart on the Rue de Dantzig, *la ruche*,[1] or "beehive," lost many of their tenants to ateliers within earshot of the Carrefour Vavin.

Two magnetic figures whose apartment on Boulevard Raspail served as the cortical center of the avant-garde were Serge Ferat, a Polish painter, and his sister, the Baroness d'Oettingen. The former helped organize a cubist exhibition called the *Section d'Or* while the latter, writing under the name Roch Grey and painting under a variety of pseudonyms, launched a review dedicated to the modern movement, *Les Soirées de Paris*. Actually, the *Soirées* had been founded by André Billy, but as it was threatening to fold after the seventeenth issue, Hélène d'Oettingen purchased it for a pittance—some two hundred francs—appointing Apollinaire its co-director. With their first issue, which contained five cubist still lifes, they lost the forty remaining subscribers. Adding impertinence to

1. The *ruche* was founded by an obscure sculptor named Alfred Boucher, who, possessing private means, bought what had been the wine pavilion at the 1900 World's Fair, transported it to a lot he owned on Rue de Dantzig, converted the rooms into one hundred and twenty studios, and let them to poor artists for very little money. His phalanstery looked like a combination music kiosk and Chinese pagoda. Most of the eastern Europeans flocked there—Chagall, Soutine, Zadkine, Kremegne, etc.—while Spaniards preferred the *bateau lavoir*.

paradox, their second issue was devoted to Henri (Le Douanier) Rousseau, whose genius the baroness appreciated from the first. Egeria of the avant-garde, this extraordinary woman loved putting matches to volatile compounds. A few futurists mixed with a few cubists sufficed to set the house afire by midnight, whereupon the principals would douse their arsonous tempers at the Rotonde nearby. Thus Severini, Soffici, Chirico, Picasso, Léger, Modigliani, Kisling, Max Jacob, Blaise Cendrars, and the whole *Section d'Or* group, including Gleizes and of course Ferat, staged Homeric battles in the baroness's home.

The Rotonde café helped enhance the new Montparnasse. It opened in 1911 and soon proved more attractive than the Dôme, its older rival across the Carrefour Vavin: more attractive to Mediterraneans at any rate because, facing south, its terrace caught the sun (Germans and Scandinavians preferred the Dôme), more attractive to poor artists because its proprietor, "le père Libion," let them eat croissants for free.[2] In 1913 its back room was a veritable caucus chamber for political and artistic revolutionaries; in addition to Vlaminck, the cubists, their impresario Apollinaire, Diego Rivera, and Jewish artists from eastern Europe mingling among the local pimps and workers and whores and clerks and models, there was a group of Russians generally absorbed in foreign newspapers and in chess games; their number included Lenin, Trotsky, Ehrenburg, and Lunacharski. Only Trotsky, whose great friend was Diego Rivera, displayed any interest in art (heatedly defending "socialist realism" against Vlaminck) though Lenin did play a minor role in the artistic *comédie*. Down and out, he tried to earn a living as a model, but his tiny stature disqualified him; instead, he would cadge meals from "Aicha the Negress," a Creole model whose generosity was never, in later years, recognized by the Soviet state.

It is remarkable how unerringly these Russians, in whatever city

2. Libion was, moreover, an *amateur d'art*, particularly fond of Modigliani, with whom he shot craps. When Modigliani lost, Libion would exact a painting, thus acquiring a whole gallery of them. Another unexpected art lover and habitué of the Rotonde was Zamaron, commissioner of police, whose office walls were lined with Utrillos, Modiglianis, Soutines, and Chagalls, which he bought for negligible sums, exploiting, some said, the fear that foreign artists lived in of being deported to their native countries.

they spent their exile, chose the most significant cafés. In 1914:
Paris, the Rotonde. In 1916: Zurich, the Café Voltaire, where dada
originated. It is as though the Great Event which lay ahead, at the
end of their trek eastward, were announced by successive petards.

As for Picasso, he did not like mingling in back rooms. The new
era meant happy domesticity and work for which he economized
his energy, while others squandered themselves in talk. "He was a
handsome little guy at the time," wrote one habitué of the Rotonde,
"a handsome scamp with gleaming teeth and fine, enameled black
eyes." Wearing a shabby raincoat and checkered jockey's cap, he
would stay at the Rotonde long enough for a *café-crême*, eavesdrop-
ping on conversations but keeping aloof. Before the outbreak of
war, he abandoned his studio on Boulevard Raspail for another
on Rue Schoelcher, its windows looking out upon the gravestones
of Montparnasse cemetery. One of his biographers has written that
Picasso liked to wander through the streets at night, as it gave
him the pleasure of being conscious while others slept: "it felt like
a triumph over death." So much the more reason to live and work
opposite a sea of tombs, like a Spanish heresiarch braving and
mocking the death's-head he holds in constant view.

Being Spanish saved him from the war, at any rate, which he
considered a stupid embroilment absolutely no concern of his.
While almost all his friends were drafted or volunteered—including
Braque, Derain, Léger, Kisling, and Apollinaire—Picasso continued
working, insulated from the world. He had no gallery for the time
being as Kahnweiler, a German subject, had moved from France to
Italy (where the war caught him) to Switzerland rather then face
internment; and it was prudent for foreign aliens, even Spaniards,
to keep off the streets with spy madness afoot; the police periodically raided the Rotonde, arresting deserters or anybody suspi-
ciously swart. His company consisted, then, of Eve, Max Jacob,
and various compatriots such as Pablo Gargallo and Ortiz de Zarrate. If Picasso's paintings during this period seem somewhat austere, this was not attributable to events, which remained outside his
ken, but rather to his own style whose internal development re-
sulted in the questioning of style itself, in the creation of a world of
flatness and pictorial puns.

War did strike home, however. Eve, her health always fragile, was badly affected by the lack of food and especially the appalling cold which, afterward, remained the keenest wartime memory of most Parisians. During the winter of 1915–1916 she took sick and, after a short, painful illness, died. "My poor Eva is dead," Picasso wrote to Gertrude Stein on January 8, 1916; "a great sorrow to me . . . she has always been so good to me." That rocklike sense of self which her presence had given him now helped Picasso survive her absence. Gertrude Stein recalls that on leaving Montmartre he lost his "high, whinnying Spanish giggle." A photograph from this period shows him in his studio wearing boxer's trunks, his fists clenched, his legs planted far apart like the branches of an inverted Y, his virile, chunky frame issuing a dare to the world. It signified a stand in the fullest sense. He is flanked by a group of cubist canvases.

Cocteau met Picasso during the fall of 1915 between expeditions to the Front. There was no lack of painters within Cocteau's circle of acquaintances, most of them connected with the *Section d'Or*, a group of minor cubists whose gallery on Rue La Boëtie lay in the middle of Cocteau's stamping ground. Albert Gleizes, married to Juliette Roche, daughter of a prominent political personality, thus moved in Cocteau's world. Indeed, Cocteau had been a witness at their wedding. André Lhote, whom he apparently met through Gleizes, used Cocteau as his errand boy in the *beau monde*. Roger de la Fresnaye, a somewhat more original artist than those two academics of cubism, frequently appeared at Valentine Gross's flat.

As it happened Cocteau was introduced to the Master not by his imitators but by Edgard Varèse. According to Cocteau, Varèse conducted him to Picasso's studio on the Rue Schoelcher in the spring of 1916. "The plaster frieze of the Parthenon cavalry," wrote Cocteau, "mounted the staircase to my left. Your windows beetled over the Montparnasse cemetery. How can I ever forget that visit? A mere glance at the disorder of a room in which the least detail argued against silliness—you became my guide—told me that never again would I incur the guilt of wrenching my ethics without fearing the black arrow of your eye." It was, he added, "a meeting written in the stars."

Their meeting, however, took place not during the spring of 1916—for at the end of the previous year Varèse had set sail for America—but in the autumn of 1915 at 10 Rue d'Anjou where Cocteau lay in bed with a heavy cold; Varèse brought Picasso. Why did Cocteau thus alter the date and setting if not because he couldn't very well allow posterity to imagine him attired in pajamas and sniffling during "a meeting written in the stars"? Rather than something absolutely unique, it was the most recent in a series of just such astral encounters, each accompanied by *mea culpas* and Oedipal eye-gougings. If Picasso's periods were marked by his women, Cocteau's corresponded to his men. But that distinction of genders enrolls the whole of existence. Women, by loving different aspects of him, allowed Picasso to come into his own; they set him rebounding against his own multifarious ego. Cocteau's love for other men involved a capitulation of being, a forfeiture of self and manhood. As he himself recognized, it was never a matter of wanting to possess, but of wanting to *be* some other.

This sense of loss, this existential leeching, expressed itself frequently in visual terms. He speaks fearfully of Picasso's eyes releasing arrows. When in the first throes of infatuation with Montesquiou he had praised the count's eye, which "discerns, weeds out." Somewhat later, after *Parade*, he would claim that a woman, aiming for his eyes, chased him backstage armed with a hatpin. The eye (and its paraphernalia: mirrors, glaziers, and so on), seeing without being seen, or sightless like a statue's, pervades his poetry, his theatre, his films. Eyeless, one is unsexed. Cocteau's celebrated "meetings" come to resemble so many glorious castrations, each commemorating afresh the original. Eyes rolled in, he *was* by being the beloved's creation. For de Max he played Heliogabalus, for Mendès the *boulevardier*, for Montesquiou the esthete, and for Gide Nathaniel.

Little wonder, then, that on his second visit to Picasso, whose virility quite surpassed anything he had ever encountered, he wore beneath his trench coat the costume of a harlequin. True, Picasso, who was just then doing a number of cubistic (and noncubistic) harlequins, dictated the role. But Cocteau assumed it willingly and played it, with Picasso, to the end. It was as if the very problems obsessing the painter—the interplay between *trompe-l'œil* and pictorial fact or, as in his collages, between those newspaper clippings, bits of linoleum, and the painted surface embedding them—had sprung from the canvas and become a three-dimensional drama. As a harlequin, Cocteau embodied a pun akin to the collage, though its tragic reverse, for Picasso had grafted onto him not a token of reality—the newspaper or the square of cloth—but a painted surface, Picasso's own reality. Cocteau described Picasso's tergiversations as "the twists of a matador"; but he wasn't, in Cocteau's eyes, so much the matador as the bull, whose movements are far more unpredictable.

What need of Picasso's Cocteau filled is somewhat more mysterious, but Picasso adopted him during Apollinaire's absence, just as he would readopt him in the fifties after Paul Éluard's death. Picasso wanted poets near at hand to serve him as lightning rods and, like his women, they rotated in accordance with his cyclical self. Cocteau first appeared shortly before Olga Kohklova, and reappeared with Jacqueline Roche, like an epiphenomenon of the bourgeois phases in Picasso's life.

Shortly after they met, Cocteau invited Picasso to collaborate with him and Satie on *Parade*. Picasso, who had hitherto never done work for the stage, accepted the challenge. By September, 1916, the three, trying to bring their different perspectives into focus, assembled at Picasso's on Rue Schoelcher or at Cocteau's on Rue d'Anjou, where Cocteau's mother treated her son's odd friends with unquestioning consideration.[3] Picasso, making the rounds of studios and cafés, (in 1916 Montparnasse began to revive: the Rotonde, closed by the police, reopened, and Kisling held perpetual open house in his atelier on Rue Joseph Bara), would drag in tow one or another of his collaborators. Together, they were as weird a trio as the Marx brothers.

3. She was particularly fond of Satie, closer to her age than to her son's, and during his frequent quarrels with Cocteau she would attempt to reconcile the two. In later years she would invite Satie to dinner even when Jean was absent from Paris.

"In Montparnasse," wrote Cocteau, "I kept my Right Bank costume or my uniform. . . . If I make an issue of costume, it's because costumes were an issue in Montparnasse, and some became
legendary." Cocteau rivaled Granowsky, the "phony cowboy"
who appeared at the Dôme in chaps, a ten-gallon hat, spurs, and a
checkered shirt. Cocteau's composite uniform consisted of high
laced boots, like an aviator's only yellow, madder-red jodhpurs, a
black field-service tunic, and the familiar *bourguignotte* or steel
helmet, which an artist named Marcel Mouillot painted purple for
him. Whatever impression this made on the rope-sandaled bohemians of Montparnasse was magnified tenfold when Cocteau
showed up at the Rotonde with Paquerette, Poiret's star model,
wearing green slippers and a shocking pink gown. In any case, the
impression he really made did not quite tally with the romanticized
accounts he gave to Gleizes abroad and to posterity. "The Rotonde," wrote Cocteau in 1950, "was our mall, our haven, our
domain. I disembarked from the far shore. I was adopted. For in
those days it was still necessary to be adopted by the natives."
Keeping Gleizes abreast of all his movements, he wrote in 1916:
"Picasso is a sentimental mandolinist and a cruel picador. He drags
me by force to the Rotonde but I balk, although his young clique
welcomes me with open arms. Besides blaming the cubists for
'forming a circle' at the Rotonde and the Dôme, I'm persuaded that
one sterilizes oneself around the cups and saucers."

As a rule, Cocteau criticized only those circles in which he did
not move. It is doubtful that Montparnasse welcomed him with
open arms; protestations of that sort merely bore witness to his extreme insecurity. "The way Picasso contemplates me with a moist
eye," he went on to say, "the 'circle' speaks to me with a kind of
thrilled respect. You'd get a kick seeing the stupor of artists in shirt
sleeves who observe the scene from afar and who had always believed that good taste, a cane, and a collar were the emblems of
fatuity." This observation is not quite consonant with the previous
one, for "thrilled respect" will not make people open their arms.
Some of the artists who "had always believed that a cane and collar were emblems of fatuity" still did; in the same letter Cocteau
converts the pluperfect into a present, saving his reputation by the

impersonal *il y . a*: "there are gifted young men who know nothing of society and judge it according to a ready-made image." Cocteau's exercises in mythomania call for an *explication de texte* of lines between lines; the written text amounts to an elaborate writhing about some unwritten, unmentionable sore point. The artists accepted him at best reluctantly, on Picasso's say-so, and perhaps that is the way Kisling's portrait of Cocteau should be read, for in the background, working at a table, is Picasso, like the patron whom Renaissance artists used to incorporate into group scenes. Montparnasse regarded Cocteau the way the Right Bank regarded Picasso. Just as Blanche indicted the latter for using Cocteau, Picasso's friends thought Cocteau was leading him astray, and when they saw the two leave for Rome in 1917 to rehearse with Diaghilev, they clicked their tongues apprehensively.

Modigliani, whose elegance shone through his rags, proved an exception. He had not only a cultivated background in common with Cocteau, but a reputation for dilettantism. He painted Cocteau in Kisling's studio, and drank the gin and Seltzer water Cocteau brought with him like beads to appease the natives. "If I close my eyes what do I see?" Cocteau reminisced. "Our *place d'armes*, Modigliani standing up, shuffling about like a dancing bear. Kisling is repeating to him again and again, 'Home, let's go home, let's go.' He refuses. He shakes his black, curly locks 'no, no.' We try to convince him. Kisling resorts to force. He grabs hold of his red belt and pulls, whereupon Modigliani changes his dance, raising his arms like a Spaniard, clicking his fingers and revolving about himself. The interminable red belt unwinds. Kisling walks away. Modigliani bursts into terrible laughter and prances the more wildly."

Satie, impenitently himself, or his mask, felt quite at home in Montparnasse which was tame by comparison with the Montmartre he once inhabited. He would hold forth at the Rotonde, his little bowler placed discreetly beside him, smoking his inevitable cigar and admiring the volutes of smoke whose design he could seemingly organize at will. But his favorite café, because it stood on the periphery of Montparnasse quite near the Gare de Sceaux where he would catch the train home, was the *café-tabac* on Place Denfert-Rochereau. There, when not engaged, over potent mixtures such as beer-and-calvados, in endless discussions with Kisling or others, he wrote much of the music for *Parade*. Pierre de Massot, a young Lyonnais who became involved with Picabia and dada, recalls that Satie had a discriminating palate. During the early 1920s, the two had dinner together nearly every night, at the Grill-Room Médicis, at the Nègre de Toulouse on Boulevard de Montparnasse, at the Pied de Mouton near the Gare d'Austerlitz, or at the Stryx on Rue Huyghens, Satie embroidering their walks with all manner of quaint details culled from his encyclopedic knowledge of Old Paris. By 1917 Satie was quite as popular among the ladies of the Left Bank as among those of the Right. He frequently visited Sybil Harris, an American whose flat on the Rue Delambre served as a kind of lounge for Montparnasse artists; and, on a half dozen occasions, Gertrude Stein when she resumed residence at 27 Rue de Fleurus after a brief wartime absence from Paris. As for *Parade*, its basic conception had by the fall of 1916 undergone major changes, each one rocking the tub in which Cocteau, Satie, and Picasso had set themselves adrift. Incorporating three such people was not the string trick whose devious but sure-fire formula Cocteau revealed some years later.[4] It was, rather, a difficult birth attended by three midwives whose flaring tempers threatened periodically to throw the baby out with the bath water. Everybody's ego was at stake. Paranoia alternated with loving acquiescence. The three divided into two against one, with Cocteau the one defending his baby against face liftings and amputations proposed by the other two.

Cocteau was inclined to treat Satie condescendingly. For example, he, Diaghilev, and Stravinsky would take Satie for walks through "Sodom and Gomorrah," the Madeleine area where homosexuals on the make lingered about in droves. Twitting Satie, whom he imagined utterly naïve, Cocteau would feign surprise at the great number of beautiful young men. Being considered nothing more than a brilliant primitive, a kind of musical Douanier Rousseau, so

4. "Take some string, knot it by making two circles lengthwise. Pass the loop thus obtained around Diaghilev's finger. Insert my finger into the space and turn following the direction of the first turn. Attach this second loop to Picasso's finger. Take a pair of scissors. Ask Erik Satie to hold firmly a third loop between the thumb and the index finger. Cut the left side of the string. Tie the cut end to the other after having slipped it through the first loop. Give a sharp tug. All the fingers are free and I have in hand two rings made of string, one inside the other."

upset this highly sophisticated, proud composer that once, in the lobby of the Hôtel Édouard VII, he interrupted Cocteau to yell, "I am not a caterer!" decanting his spleen on the public at large, whom he called corporately a "prick." Their disputes were so bitter and the name-calling so uninhibited ("One can be a skunk," wrote Satie, referring to Cocteau, "but not as skunkish as he") that it is a wonder they could ever address one another again, yet wounds healed overnight. Picasso reduced Cocteau to puppylike adoration, so much so that the painter, sure of his own position in the heavens, described Cocteau as "a spark in the comet's tail—I am the comet." At one dark juncture, Satie refused to write another note, while Cocteau, moping at home and threatening suicide, accused the whole world of betraying him, his mother included. In a letter to Valentine Gross, he delivered himself of all his fantasies, insisting that Apollinaire wanted to knife him in the back, that Montparnasse, like the *NRF*, was involved in a conspiracy against him, that he did not know how "to cut the Gordian knot." To the extent that his paranoia had some basis in reality, Cocteau enforced that reality. One can create enemies by wanting to be liked at all costs.

Trouble announced itself very early in the collaboration when Picasso, unwilling to add a mere patch of his own, threatened to write a whole new version of *Parade*, abetted by Satie. "If only you knew how sad I am," wrote Satie to Valentine Gross. "*Parade* is changing, for the better, *behind* Cocteau! Picasso has ideas that please me more than those of our Jean! And Cocteau doesn't know it! What can be done! Picasso tells me to continue with Jean's text, and he, Picasso, will work on another text, *his own*—which is astounding! Prodigious! I am getting frantic and sad! What can be done? Knowing the wonderful ideas of Picasso, I am heartbroken to be obliged to compose according to those of the good Jean, less wonderful—oh! Yes! less wonderful! What can be done! What can be done! Write and advise me. I am frantic." Needless to say, he was not so frantic as Cocteau when the latter got wind of this dastardly plot but, incapable of resisting Picasso and wishing to save *Parade*, he acquiesced. His policy throughout can be summed up in a line Cocteau gave, a few years later, to the narrator of his ballet

Les Mariés de la Tour Eiffel: "Since these mysteries escape me, I shall pretend to be their organizer." Only a week after his frantic letter, Satie was able to tell Valentine Gross that "it's settled. Cocteau knows all. He and Picasso have come to an understanding. What luck!"

It was Picasso's idea to embody the voices (which were to announce through a hole in the backdrop the virtues of each performer) in larger than life-size figures called "Managers." The Managers would appear in large hunks of cubist scenery completely disguising the actors they encased, as if portions had been jigsawed out of the backdrop and set in motion downstage. Picasso thus introduced a dimension whose significance ultimately made good sense to Cocteau, for it sharpened his original notion of pitting illusion against reality—the very subject of *Parade*. "When Picasso showed us his sketches," he wrote, "we realized that it would be interesting to put in relief three poster figures [meaning the Acrobat, the Little American Girl, and the Chinese Prestidigitator] with superhuman, inhuman characters . . . so closely identified with the false scenic reality as to reduce the real dancers to puppet stature."

It is uncanny how Picasso, ignorant of all theatre except the circus, cut straight to the heart of the modern stage where puppets and hieratic masks from the symbolists and Alfred Jarry to Jean Genet break down the cracker-box illusionism, the psychological make-believe of nineteenth-century drama. What he did was simply translate his feelings about *trompe l'œil* from the canvas to the stage, much as Braque would in 1923 when working on Diaghilev's *Les Fâcheux*. So aware was Braque of the stage as a framed box, in which the dancers, located *behind* the frame, had no other reality than that of silhouettes, that he wished to treat them as silhouettes. "I shall make them into silhouettes," he told Kahnweiler, "and they will only be seen full face; as for their backs, I shall choose a color which will blend with the decor. Thus, when they turn round, they will disappear and won't be seen."

Diaghilev had not allowed it, but Picasso in *Parade* used a variation of this same device. The Managers *are* decor; that is their very role. Attired in scenery, they become emblems of illusion, thus acquiring the kind of reality they would not have if portrayed realistically (which brings to mind Hegel's dictum that "nothing is truer than appearance as appearance"). The backdrop moves forward to the proscenium, cramping the "image" into an imaginary surface. The ballet, like cubist painting, achieves a different order of reality. It tells you what it is—a *parade* "representing" the real drama which unfolds behind or in front of the *guignols*: behind them, for they appear onstage as their own proxies enticing the audience to go "inside" and see them, in front, for with the backdrop telescoped into the proscenium where does the stage lie if not in the audience proper? The concluding bill, flashed before the spectators just as the red curtain fell, promoted this ambiguity:

The drama

which

didn't

take place

for those people

who stayed outside

was

by

Jean Cocteau   Erik Satie   Pablo Picasso

Conceptually, the three created a theatre in the round where the drama's focal point, for those spectators who troubled to go inside, lies in the audience. It was, in this farfetched sense, a cubist spectacle, but cubism probably had less to do with it than theatrical experiments elsewhere. The notion of the theatre in the round had enormous currency in Europe, and if France lagged behind, Jacques Rouché's book on Stanislavsky, Reinhardt, and Gordon Craig, which appeared one year before the war, helped bring her up to date. In a 1915 issue of *Le Mot*, Cocteau made reference to Reinhardt's production of Shakespeare on an Elizabethan stage. This, plus Craig's "super-marionettes," lurked in the background of *Parade*.

Satie kept his promise to deliver some music by October and not before. "Dear Friend," he wrote to Cocteau on October 19, "I have worked at our 'thing,' *very hard*. The 'little American' is going well. The 'rag' is in good health; it's well placed. I won't, however, be able to show it to you tomorrow, as I can't work on it this afternoon. You'll be 'flabbergasted' by it at the audition. . . . I have written *a lot* for our 'thing.' Lots. Believe you me, dear Friend. Until tomorrow and my best wishes to Madame Cocteau." On December 12 he cheerfully informed Valentine Gross that his work was done. In characteristically circular fashion, he had written the beginning last, *Parade*'s prelude being a musical apostrophe to the red curtain. Meanwhile Picasso had made a portfolio of sketches. It remained now to fuse the whole into a ballet, which meant traveling to Rome where Diaghilev's company was in the midst of a season's engagement at the Teatro Constanzi.

At first Satie was enthusiastic about going. He had even purchased valises. But at the last moment he changed his mind. Trudging the six-mile axis between Paris and Arcueil, those two fixed poles of his universe, was one thing, but a train ride to Rome quite another. It would have been a revolutionary orbit beyond the confines of civilization. "Do you know Rome?" Satie was asked by an Italian diplomat in Paris. "Only by name, sir, only by name," he replied. Moreover, he had already begun work on his major opus, *Socrate*. Cocteau's entreaties failed to move him. Picasso also hesitated, for crossing frontiers as a foreign national in time of war involved a risk possibly greater than the gains he envisaged. His mind was, at length, swayed by Diaghilev, who visited Paris in January 1917 partly to make penultimate arrangements with the creators of *Parade*, partly to buy contemporary paintings. The point at which his two missions coincided was Picasso. Not only did Picasso and Diaghilev get on famously, but the prices Diaghilev paid for Picasso's work persuaded the artist that a trip to Rome might bring further advantages. On a flying tour of Montparnasse studios reminiscent of the one he had made in Rome some twenty-five years before when first sprung from Russia, Diaghilev purchased dozens of paintings by Picasso, Gris, Rivera, Metzinger, Lhote, Léger, and Braque. Cocteau, playing dealer, sold one canvas among several which Gleizes had entrusted to him and proudly informed the artist of his deft hagglings.

The Ballets Russes, orphaned of France and England after August, 1914, had performed on the fringes of Europe and wandered as far afield as South America and the United States. The war trapped Karsavina in Saint Petersburg for five years, until 1919, and the Austrian authorities had interned Nijinsky in a camp, from which Diaghilev, desperately needing the dancer for his New York season, arranged to free him.[5] The Atlantic crossing aged Diaghilev. Mortally afraid of German submarines, he refused to leave his cabin, where throughout the trip he sat huddled in his overcoat and three life preservers, keening like an Irish widow. New York audiences reimbursed him, however, for his trials. After five wildly successful months at the Metropolitan Opera, Diaghilev and the company returned to Europe for a summer's engagement at the Royal Theatre in Madrid, the Ballets Russes having found an ardent admirer in King Alfonso XIII. In September, 1916, the company returned to America for a second five-month tour, traveling the length and breadth of the United States under Nijinsky's dubious charge, while Diaghilev, with a small nucleus of eight dancers including Massine and Wozikovski, established himself in Rome. There, in February, 1917, they were joined by Cocteau and Picasso. Satie, preferring Paris even during this coldest winter of the war to Rome, had remained behind.

Rehearsals of *Parade* did not begin in earnest for some weeks after Picasso and Cocteau arrived. Picasso set up shop opposite the Villa Medici, where he constructed models of the Managers' *carcasses*, or casings.[6] Sporting white ducks and a straw derby, he proved popular with everyone: with the stagehands, with Diaghilev, and with the dancers who lived in the Hotel Minerva and rehearsed in a grotto called the Taglioni Cellar. "We walked by moonlight with the dancers, we visited Pompeii and Naples," wrote Cocteau. So romantic was the setting, it swayed Picasso's mind to thoughts of matrimony, the object of his suit a Diaghilev dancer, Olga Kohklova, whom he would indeed marry the following year. Moreover, he became friends with Stravinsky, a giant as short as he.

5. King Alfonso XIII of Spain was instrumental in bringing about his release.
6. A well-known photograph showing Picasso seated on his huge drop curtain "with Italian workers" was taken, not in Rome, as captions to it generally announce, but in a studio near the Butte-Chaumont in Paris; moreover, the Italians were Russians (except for Carlos Socrate). Most of Picasso's work for *Parade* appears to have been done in Paris after his return from Rome, where he spent much of his time touring and wenching.

Unlike other such highly touted encounters, this one eventually bore fruit, in *Pulcinella*. Stravinsky had come to Rome at Diaghilev's behest to conduct *Firebird* and *Feu d'Artifice* for which an Italian futurist, Balla, prepared a special decor. Having thus obliged the impressario, Stravinsky went south to Naples with Diaghilev, Cocteau, and Picasso, in hopes of recovering his health, which had been impaired by attacks of neuralgia. "Instead of the sunshine and azure blue I had expected at Naples," he wrote, "I found a leaden sky, the summit of Vesuvius being shrouded in immovable and ominous mist. Still, I retain happy memories of my fortnight in this town, half Spanish and half reminiscent of the Near East." Together, he and Picasso explored Naples, spending hours at the aquarium and combing antique shops and dealers' establishments in search of old Neapolitan water colors.

Meanwhile, Picasso and Cocteau were jockeying for position with Diaghilev, who favored the painter's choreographic schemes, or so it would appear from the account given by Serge Lifar, Diaghilev's last protégé: "Their rivalry centered on the fact that Picasso, in his exaltation, saw each dancer as a bit of mobile scenery, or a vehicle of that scenery, as well as a dancing dancer . . . whereas Cocteau had recourse to imitative means deriving from the daily facts of life, means in which, it must be said, the dance's sole purpose was to present something having nothing to do with dance."

By the time the kinks had been ironed from *Parade*, it contained little that was Cocteau's. His very words disappeared in favor of noisemakers and a metronome ticking to and fro as the Managers shuffled about portentously. Though later, in *Le Coq et l'Arlequin*, Cocteau ascribed these changes to himself, he was, it should be remembered, a past master at recommending *faits accomplis*. Seeing the libretto frittered away before his very eyes distressed him at first, just as it would, somewhat later, Satie, whose music was all but drowned by the cacophony of whistles, typewriters, and sirens.[7] "I composed," he wrote peevishly (and mistakenly), "a

---

7. The noisemakers were probably inspired by the futurists in Rome, who, infatuated with machinery, were staging spectacles with sound effects. Diaghilev was on rather good terms with the futurist group.

background to noises that Cocteau considered indispensable for the creation of a certain atmosphere around his characters." Otherwise, Cocteau stood in panting admiration of Picasso. He ransacked his mind for appropriate epithets: "An anarchist and a king," "a legislator who listens to the call of the Muses and bows beneath a code severe but absolutely personal," "the Bird of Benin" (which is how Apollinaire designated him in *Le Poète Assassiné*).

If Picasso courted a dancer, so did Cocteau, to keep up appearances. Maria Chabelska (who danced the Little American Girl), twenty years old and fresh from Russia, could not quite understand the cryptic episodes of her suitor's courtship, not even when, together in Picasso's atelier—Picasso having discreetly absented himself—Cocteau rumpled the bedsheets while she observed him primly from a chair. Obviously he wanted virility in his idol's eyes; the girl was but a stage prop. "In Rome," wrote Cocteau, "I saw nothing of Rome. I had eyes only for my collaborator."

Though Cocteau preferred Naples to Rome, in general Italy made him homesick for Paris. At the beginning of April he returned, some few weeks before the others, with the intention of warming up his one-man publicity machine. A flurry of letters fell from 10 Rue d'Anjou. To Gide (who didn't attend), he wrote, "Won't you come see our *Parade?* It's a good slice of Eugènism, processed through Picasso." Apollinaire was invited to contribute not only his presence but the program manifesto. How natural that he, the "impresario of the avant-garde," should sponsor a spectacle amounting to its coming-of-age, its baptism in fire (literally, as Big Bertha was lofting shells into Paris from ninety miles away). Yet how odd, too, that he should be asked for his blessings, like the sympathetic parent the younger generation elects from the older; for Apollinaire was about Picasso's age. The war had seemingly accelerated the normal course of events, aging men prematurely, like a historical syncopation. When Apollinaire returned from the Front in 1916, his physical and spiritual person altered by a head wound, his confreres welcomed him like the grand old man of the avant-garde. In fact, that December 31, they threw a banquet in his honor, attended by ninety guests, reminiscent of the one thrown some years before in honor of the Douanier Rousseau.

During his absence the spirit underlying Apollinaire's prosodic experiments and the new art forms it had been his mission to explain infiltrated a consciousness extending beyond Montparnasse. The war broke down social barriers, but it also made almost every manifestation of human thought, including poetry, music, and painting, a political act. This merger of art and action, whose effects were both brilliant and devastating, would obsess French letters and, to a lesser extent, music and art for the next generation.

It would not be too much to say that the creators of *Parade* anticipated, albeit half-wittingly, the future—for with their ballet the "new spirit" visited itself upon the larger world, and suffered the consequences. In Montparnasse, art had enjoyed immunity from distinctions such as "right" and "left," but that era was now drawing to a close. Having entitled *Parade* a "realistic ballet," Cocteau was outdone by Apollinaire, who coined the word "surrealist" in his program note: "From this new alliance—for up to now decor and costumes on the one hand and choreography on the other were only artificially allied—the result has been, in *Parade,* a kind of surrealism wherein I see the jumping-off point for a series of manifestations of this New Spirit which, finding today an opportunity to exhibit itself, will not fail to seduce the elite and promises to renovate, from stem to stern, the arts and mores."

Did the performance, however, live up to this text, written beforehand, and to the retrospective hullabaloo it unfailingly draws in histories of the avant-garde?

Parade opened on May 18, 1917, at the Théâtre du Châtelet, to a heterogeneous audience coming from both banks. After a short chorale, the curtains parted, revealing Picasso's monumental drop, which depicted a family of harlequins inside a tent with their menagerie: a white-winged horse, a monkey, and a dog. There followed Satie's fugue for string quartet, the "Prelude to the Red Curtain," whereupon the drop rose on a stage showing the curtained entrance to a circus booth. The First Manager, a Frenchman (danced by Wozikovski), is stamping to and fro, his heavy steps accompanied by music "neither major nor minor, neither tonal nor atonal" which simply marks time; it is monotonous and compulsive, like the word patter of a barker trying to draw attention, his act rendered the more comic by his accessories: a property clay pipe, a walking cane, a top hat, and himself (encased in appropriate scenery). A whistle sounds and the familiar vaudeville placard looms from within the booth, reading "1," which summons onstage the Chinese Prestidigitator danced by Massine bowing and nodding like a mandarin doll to Satie's *ostinato* accompaniment, breathing fire, making an egg disappear, and finally removing his vermilion, black, and yellow self as a tom-tom starts to pulsate in the orchestra pit. This gives the American Manager his cue. Wearing cowboy boots, chaps, an Uncle Sam top hat, encased in skyscrapers, his property arm holding a megaphone and his real arm a placard reading PA/RA/DE (in descending order), he alternately stamps disgust at the audience for confusing the parade with the real show, and pitter-patters in silence.

The curtains of the booth part once again, announcing the second act while violins vie with the clacking of an Underwood typewriter. In bounds the Little American Girl, wearing a sailor coat, a white skirt, white knee stockings, and black shoes. As the orchestra plays a jazz passage entitled "The Steamship Rag" (*Ragtime du Paquebot*), she cavorts like Charlie Chaplin and Pearl White combined [8]: swimming a river, driving a car, brandishing a revolver, and surviving a storm at sea. The "public within the play" fails to respond, and she departs, succeeded by the third Manager, a horse whose forelegs were Novak and hindlegs Oumansky, or vice-versa (the horse was supposed to be mounted by a dummy Negro, but for lack of time Picasso could not make the dummy costume). After a few capers he rides off and the placard reads "3," introducing a pair of Acrobats, Zverev and Lopokova, who leap from between the curtains of the booth, the one a blind man and the other a dark girl, both dressed in sky-blue tights patterned with white cometlike shapes. Their tumbling, accompanied by a waltz, proves unavailing. They go off stage, the girl carried by her partner. In a last-ditch effort to persuade the audience, all three Managers collapse together, to music recapitulating the three main themes, while

8. It is as though the little American girl were racing through a stylized summary of *The Perils of Pauline*, though Massine claims Cocteau had Mary Pickford in mind.

Edouard de Max in one of his daintier roles. (*Photo: G. Sirot*)

Above, left: Maurice Rostand (at right) in 1931 with his brother Jean. (*Photo: Keystone*)

Above: Catulle Mendès shortly before his death in 1909. (*Photo: G. Sirot*)

Left: Robert de Montesquiou as painted by Boldini in 1897. (*Photo: Giraudon*)

Below: Georges Auric. (*Photo: Lipnitzki*)

Right: Stravinsky and
Nijinsky (in the costume of
Petrouchka), 1912. (*Photo:*
Bib. Opéra)

Below: At the Paris Opéra in
1929. Diaghilev, who was to
die a few months later, had
arranged for Nijinsky to see
a performance of *Petrouchka*
in hopes that the shock of
recognition would restore his
sanity. Left to right: Benois,
Grigoriev, Karsavina,
Diaghilev, Nijinsky, Lifar.
(*Photo: Lipnitzki*)

The Six with Cocteau in 1921; left to right: Darius Milhaud, Auric (a profile drawing by Cocteau), Cocteau, Honegger, Germaine Tailleferre, Poulenc, and Louis Durey. (*Photo: Lipnitzki*)

The Six reunited in middle age. (*Photo: Lipnitzki*)

Left: Picasso in 1917, wearing the sober apparel he adopted during his courtship of Olga Koklova.
Right: Cocteau in May, 1916, dressed as a Marine, on the beach near Nieuport. The inscription reads: "the sea, cold and oyster-colored, jostling its sheepfolds (sector 131)." (*Photo: Segalab*)

Cocteau in 1920, among the implements of his literary factory at 10 rue d'Anjou. (*Photo courtesy Élise Jouhandeau*)

Cocteau in 1921. (*Photo: Segalab*)

Left: Cocteau posing as young Bacchus crowned by a fruit tree on Madame Francis de Croisset's estate near Grasse, 1918.
Right: Cocteau working at the seaside resort of Piquey in the twenties. (*Photo: Segalab*)

Left to right: Cocteau, Jean Hugo, Radiguet, and Pierre de Lacretelle in Lavandou, 1922. (*Photo: Segalab*)

Left: Lavandou, 1922; left to right: Pierre de Lacretelle, Jean Hugo, Radiguet, and Cocteau. (*Photo: Segalab*)

Below: Piquey, 1923; behind the boatman, left to right: B. Nathanson, Cocteau, Auric, and Radiguet. It was during this summer that Radiguet contracted the typhoid to which he succumbed in December. (*Photo: Segalab*)

Bottom: Piquey, 1923; left to right: François de Gouy, Auric, Radiguet, B. Nathanson, Cocteau, Russell Greeley, Jean Hugo. (*Photo: Segalab*)

Jean Desbordes.

Coco Chanel making alterations, 1926.
(*Photo: Rapho-Guillumette*)

Above, left: "Panama" Al Brown in 1932, several years before he met Cocteau. (*Photo: Keystone*)

Above: André Breton, the pope of surrealism, 1935. (*Photo: Segalab*)

Left: Jean Hugo and Marie-Laure de Noailles in the garden of the Noailles' palace on Place des États-Unis, 1939. (*Photo: Segalab*)

Jean Marais in 1937, the year he met Cocteau.

Marais as Xiphares in Racine's *Mithridate*, performed in November, 1952. This was his valedictory to the *Comédie Française*. (*Photo: Keystone*)

Above: Cocteau and Picasso in 1943 at the home of the Anchorenas on Avenue Foch. The Anchorenas, a vastly rich Argentinian couple, commissioned artists to paint the fixtures of their apartment. Matisse did several doors and Cocteau the piano cover. Picasso proposed doing their bathroom door, which was delivered to his studio and never returned. (*Photo: Segalab*)

Left: Cocteau and Picasso in the Midi.

Above: From left to right: Picasso, Francine Weisweiller, Jacqueline Roque, and Cocteau disposed around Picasso's goat. (*Photo: Birnback Publishing Service*)

Right: Edouard Dermit ("Doudou") and Madame Weisweiller on the Weisweiller yacht, *Orphée II*, near Cap Ferrat.

Left: Cocteau at Santo-Sospir, recuperating from his first heart attack in 1954. (*Photo: Sanford H. Roth from Rapho-Guillumette*)

Below, left: Stravinsky and Cocteau in the early fifties. (*Photo: Rapho-Guillumette*)

Below: Cocteau standing in front of the blackboard on which he inscribed his social calendar and telephone numbers. (*Photo: European*)

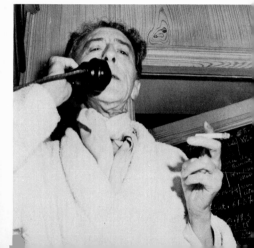

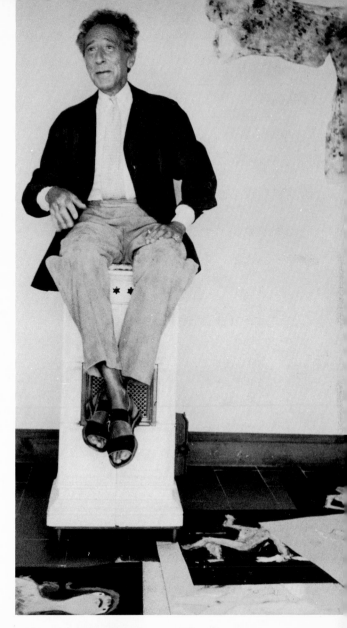

Right: Cocteau propped on a coal stove in his studio. Nailed to the wall is a suit of woolen underwear which he had used to wipe his brushes until finding it sufficiently interesting for exhibition. (*Photo: Sanford H. Roth from Rapho-Guillumette*)

Below: Cocteau in his studio at Santo-Sospir; in the background, an Aubusson tapestry he designed. (*Photo: Sanford H. Roth from Rapho-Guillumette*)

Cocteau in 1963. (*Photo: AGIP—Robert Cohen*)

the little American girl sobs and the Chinese Prestidigitator stands inscrutably by. *Parade*, coming full circle, ends with seven measures drawn from the opening theme.

We have already alluded to the cubistlike conception of the theatre in *Parade*. The play within the play is a side show enacted in front of a play-crowd which refuses to enter the play-theatre, yet as the side show unfolds it becomes a real play enacted for a real audience sitting visibly in front and invisibly behind. But Cocteau felt that the three (or four, counting two acrobats) music-hall performers were the most cubistic feature of the spectacle. "It was a matter of taking a series of real gestures and transforming them into pure painting without losing sight of the power of their volume, material composition, colors, and shadows." What *Parade* did was take its raw material from the music hall and circus, mating their naïve popular routines with the ballet, somewhat the way Picasso and Braque had embedded oilcloth grained like wood, *clichés* if you will, in their paintings.

This is analogous to surrealism's favorite game of drawing dream sequences out of a commonplace, showing language at work *inside* words, where "significance" gives way to direct sensation and unconscious ellipses. Just as the word thus conceived exists on its own terms, opaque rather than a mere sign, so Punch and Judy, because they do not merely imitate reality, possess a kind of theatrical reality which brings them near the root meaning of *"personnage"*—persona, or mask. Punchinello *is* all the more us because he does not look, talk, and move "like" us. Spastic and soprano, he has the purity, the inviolability of an archetype, a minor one to be sure, whose conventional grimaces, physical etiquette, simple pathos, and humor are his essence. He is what he is, an illusion reflecting itself, and that raw equation Satie reinforced by a score that runs circularly, ending where it began. One critic reviewing *Parade* actually referred to the *guignols* as "super-marionettes," using Gordon Craig's term, and it is altogether possible that Cocteau, though claiming absolute originality, was inspired by Craig's ideas, filtered through Rouché.

From Cocteau's viewpoint, *Parade* was especially significant. The *guignol*, midway between tragedy and pathos, his appearance the ideogram of his soul, himself his mask, would provide the model for many of Cocteau's theatrical and fictional adolescents. The performance itself, however, proved disappointing. For one thing, Picasso's *carcasses* threw the Managers' step-dance out of kilter. Wozikovski and Stetkovich had rehearsed without them, so they had some trouble maneuvering and their cardboard exoskeletons prevented them from hearing the music clearly. Because of hurried rehearsals, many of the sound effects, what Cocteau called the ballet's "main tack," were suppressed. *"Parade,"* he wrote, "was so far from being what I could have wished that I didn't want to see it from the front, confining myself to the wings where I adjusted the notice-boards bearing the number of each turn."

Above all, *Parade* was not the scandal Cocteau later made it out to be. True, there were cries of *sales boches* (dirty Krauts), but the audience did not produce anything near the uproar accompanying *The Rite of Spring.* For one thing, the ballet public had matured since then; for another, this audience was in large measure hand picked.[9] Moreover, recent events upstaged the performance. On March 16, news of the Russian Revolution first reached the West, and in April the Germans wheeled their new cannon, Big Bertha, toward Paris, bombarding the capital from ninety miles away. Verdun was being contested at the loss of a million lives. The audience lacked spunk for violent demonstrations, Cocteau's subsequent reports to the contrary. Those scattered catcalls may have been aroused as much by the inept choreography (one dancer, Chabelska, describing it as much too literary) as by the novelty.

Perhaps the most accurate account of the reception it got lies in Morand's diary: "Full house yesterday at the Châtelet, for *Parade.* Canvas scenery by Picasso, circusy, gracile music by Satie, half Rimsky, half dance-hall. The Managers . . . produced a ripple of surprise . . . Cocteau's pivotal idea—freeing dance from its conventions in favor of lifelike gestures—and his modern themes (the gunning of an automobile, photography, etc.), stylized in movement, seemed a little blurred. Lots of applause and a few jeers."

Parade ended not with a bang but a half-amusing, half-pathetic

9. The "patronesses" included the Countess de Chevigné, the Countess Étienne de Beaumont, and Mme. Cipa Godebska.

whimper. The music critic of *Carnet de la Semaine*, Jean Poueigh, having written a particularly nasty review, Satie sent him a post card which read:

Sir and dear friend,
    You are nothing but an asshole, and an unmusical asshole at that.
                                                            Erik Satie

Poueigh pressed suit, and Satie was arraigned at civil court before a gallery including Cocteau, Léon-Paul Fargue, Lhote, Jacques Rivière, and Ricardo Viñes. Satie, his inevitable umbrella hooked over one arm and holding his little bowler over his breast as he answered questions, found himself described, along with all other modern artists, as a *boche*. The claque jeered. Satie's lawyer protested that Dunoyer de Segonzac, Roger de la Fresnaye, Derain, and Apollinaire—all of whom had acquitted themselves well at the Front—could scarcely be taxed with unpatriotism. The claque cheered. In the end Satie was condemned to eight days in prison. As the prosecutor left the courtroom, Cocteau, leaping from his seat screaming, "I'm going to smash his face in, the prick!" administered a resounding slap, for which he was ushered downstairs to police headquarters and roughed up. Satie, distressed by the violent legal tirades inspired by a scatological postcard one line long, begged the authorities to release Cocteau, assuming the blame.

But Cocteau wanted the blame himself, on the grounds perhaps that he who assumes all of it gets all the credit as well. His outbursts always had a calculated air; he inevitably managed to lose control of himself in the presence of a reporter, thus manipulating the public record so as to make his own role central. Cocteau played for the press box which, for lack of time and space, craves facile résumés and a prime mover. He was, in other words, a master at making news, and making news calls for a suppression of history. A collaborative event, a "movement" is, in a sense, born the instant it becomes public: it has no influences, or genesis. Its progenitor is its publicity agent. *Parade* is an outstanding case in point. True, the original idea was Cocteau's, but little more. Each "I" in his résumé of the collaboration is a "they" transposed, each invention a necessity imposed upon him and justified after the fact. Thus,

a letter he wrote to Léonide Massine in April, 1917, having returned to Paris before the others, becomes especially revealing, and
pathetic:

My dear Massine,

Why doesn't Diaghilev . . . ever write to me directly? I would
tell him to suppress me completely, even on the playbill of *Parade*
—my aspirations go beyond journalism, just as yours do. I dictated
the score to Satie note by note. I brought along Picasso, against his
scruples, no matter what he says to the contrary. I collaborated with
you amicably, joyously, loyally, seeing to it that ideas dear to me
were imprinted on your superb work—I ask *nothing more.*

If I am astonished, it's out of justice, not niggardliness.

I regret only one thing, that these "scenes" will probably prevent
future collaborations as effective as *Parade.*

Jean Cocteau

P.S. If I didn't push my taste for theatrical perfection to the point of
effacing myself, I would have kept the words.

Having told Massine that he dictated every note in Satie's score,
he told Satie, in turn, that he had dictated every step in Massine's
choreography. Summing up these separate confidences, one would
think he had created *Parade* single-handedly. That sum he reserved
for the public at large, but apparently he believed his own publicity. Gide, who had not attended the first performance of *Parade* in
1917, visited Cocteau backstage during the December, 1920, revival. "One doesn't know," he wrote, "whether to admire most
Parade's pretention or its poverty. Cocteau is pacing in the wings,
where I go to see him; aging, contracted, miserable. He knows perfectly well that the costumes are by Picasso, that the music is by
Satie, but he wonders if Picasso and Satie are not by Cocteau!"
Resentful of Cocteau's identification with *Parade,* Satie and Picasso boycotted the revival. "I shall have nothing more to do with
Cocteau's humbug!" wrote the composer.

The repercussions of *Parade* were enormous. It brought Picasso
out of bohemia and marked the beginning of his world conquest.
It established Satie. It launched Diaghilev on a second phase during
which he relied more on French painters and composers than on

Russian. And it represents a datable point in Cocteau's career when obscurity started waxing into fame.

Parade was only the first step. Between its performance and its revival three and a half years later, Cocteau appropriated not merely a ballet but a whole musical movement. By 1919 he had become the spokesman and *ex post facto* organizer of a group of young composers eventually dubbed the Six.

World War I brought the avant-garde a blessing in disguise. Theatres closed down in 1914 and one year later only the largest could afford to reopen. The Pasdeloup and Colonne concerts resumed in 1915, but their programs, like the theatres', rehashed proven favorites. Many art galleries folded for lack of clients, and bookstores, their proprietors having been drafted, thinned out. Moreover, the *beau monde* severely curtailed its patronage. Young artists were thrown as never before upon their own meager resources, which they pooled in order to survive, physically and creatively, with the result that some few home-grown salons sprang up on the Left Bank, attracting distinguished artists from all of Paris. Young Adrienne Monnier opened her book store *Aux Amis des Livres*, on the Rue de l'Odéon in 1915. Her first famous visitor was Paul Fort, the aged "Prince of Poets," from whom she bought a complete run of *Vers et Prose*. Early in 1916 another poet, Léon-Paul Fargue, dropped by with a stack of his books. Before long, writers as diverse as Gide, Cendrars, Paul Valéry, Cocteau, and the future surrealists Breton and Aragon, regularly visited her shop, mainly to pass the time of day. Her nunlike devotion to writers and to literature had no equivalent on either Bank. She established an atmosphere at once human, sacerdotal, and workaday in which artists breathed freely. At her poetry readings they congregated as professionals rather than pampered and subsidized geniuses. It is revealing that Satie, whose symphonic drama *Socrate* had been commissioned by the Princess de Polignac, gave a preview of it in the back room of Adrienne Monnier's book store, for even music, hitherto associated far more closely than the other arts with aristoratic sponsors, now shifted its center of gravity to the Left Bank.

Here, too, the avant-garde began sponsoring itself, and one

Jeanne Bathori played Terpsichore to Adrienne Monnier's Euterpe. A gifted singer, Bathori proved an equally gifted impresario, arranging a series of concerts in the Théâtre du Vieux-Colombier (vacant since Copeau's departure for America in the fall of 1917) which provided an audience to young composers such as Arthur Honegger, Francis Poulenc, Darius Milhaud, and Georges Auric.

But of these several self-service forums, the most extraordinary was a painter's atelier on Rue Huyghens in Montparnasse where all the avant-gardes held forth simultaneously. It was here that the Six crystallized as a movement. Six Rue Huyghens is an address often thought consubstantial with Cocteau, who neglected to correct that view in newspaper articles he wrote for *Paris-Midi* in 1919, propagandizing an entity that was very much alive before he so much as stepped foot in Montparnasse.

The studio at 6 Rue Huyghens belonged to an artist named Émile Lejeune who arrived in Paris from Switzerland in 1910. As it was originally intended to be an art school, its proportions were vast, some fifty feet by twenty, and high enough to have a gallery or loft where the painter slept. Mornings Lejeune let his studio to a certain Devallières, who conducted art classes there. By the outbreak of war, however, Devallières' "academy" had gone out of existence and Lejeune, in financial straits, found some well-heeled Americans to rent the atelier, he himself moving into a garret. Times were exceedingly grim on Montparnasse. Painters who later became famous sold their works for the price of a meal, or else survived thanks to soup kitchens. The Russian artist Marie Wassilieff [10] operated a canteen where Modigliani, Soutine, Lenin, and Trotsky among others, could eat for a dime. The chief instructor in sculpture at the Académie Colarossi, a large art school where Lejeune was studying, followed Wassilieff's example, but the gruel at his canteen was watery and inedible. To improve it, Lejeune hit upon the idea of raising funds through a concert series, which would help unemployed musicians and artists alike. He was abetted

10. Marie Wassilieff was reputed to have been Trotsky's mistress. On those grounds she was imprisoned by the French authorities when the Russian Revolution broke out, and brought to trial. Trotsky's legend was such that hordes of people packed the courtroom to see what his mistress looked like. They were disappointed to find a tiny woman not quite five feet tall.

by Arthur Dandelot, the music impresario, and in due course the concerts took place late in 1914. The next spring, however, Lejeune and Kaelin, the instructor in sculpture, had a falling out, which might have ruined their enterprise if the Americans to whom Lejeune let his atelier had not, conveniently, decided to go home.

The concerts were resumed, then, during the summer of 1915, at 6 Rue Huyghens. A previous tenant who studied acting as well as painting had constructed a podium, and Lejeune borrowed chairs from a park attendant at the Luxembourg gardens; so, on Saturday evenings, the atelier was transformed into a concert hall. Performances proved so successful that it was decided to form a society, with Paul Morisse of *Mercure de France* the president, Édouard Vidondez treasurer, and Dandelot music director. Only members and their guests were permitted to attend. Lejeune took tickets at the door, and all receipts went to *L'Appui aux Artistes,* a charity for indigent artists. Meanwhile that other soup kitchen, Marie Wassilieff's, had also evolved into a concert hall, where a Swede named Melchers held recitals. The two groups merged, Melchers replacing Dandelot as music director.

Lyre et Palette, [11] as they called themselves, thus had an organizational history by 1916. The lyre was very much in evidence: a recital of Debussy's music was held in April (Picasso contributing a sketch to the program) and a fortnight later a combined Satie-Ravel festival. But the palette did not become conspicuous until the autumn of 1916, when a neighbor of Lejeune's, Ortiz de Zarrate, one of Picasso's hangers-on, suggested that he and other artists be allowed to exhibit their paintings in Salle Huyghens. The previous summer they had held open air exhibitions near the Rotond, but chilly weather had driven them indoors. Ortiz introduced Lejeune to Picasso and Kisling, the latter—a very energetic and gregarious

11. The name was changed in 1917 to *Peinture et Musique,* for complicated reasons. One concert was interrupted by a Zeppelin raid. The audience, threatening to run amok, was finally calmed by the pianist, who continued to play in the dark. The incident was fully reported in a German newspaper, and the German article reprinted in a Swiss paper which came to the attention of French authorities, who insisted, largely because Morisse was an outspoken pacifist (therefore a *boche*), that *Lyre et Palette* be shut down. Lejeune remonstrated with Alfred Cortot, Minister of Fine Arts and a musicologist in his own right, who allowed the society to continue provided it assumed a different name.

member of the bohemian community—availing himself of this opportunity to help down-and-out Modigliani.

The result was a kind of pan-arts festival, lasting from November 19 to December 5, 1916: a pivotal event in the history of the avant-garde, for it brought on stage figures whose stars would rise meteorically between the two wars and collected an audience heralding Montparnasse of the 1920s. The painting exhibition, consisting largely of Modigliani's work, included Kisling's, Matisse's, and Picasso's as well. Paul Guillaume, the art dealer, contributed twenty-five African masks and sculptures from his collection. The program featured poems by Cendrars and Cocteau, Cocteau's dedicated to Erik Satie. Two days later, there was a Satie festival, *Instant Musical,* to which Cocteau brought Diaghilev and Ernest Ansermet. And on November 26 the Salle Huyghens staged a poetry reading which Paul Morand described as follows in his Journal:

> I dined on this rainy Sunday in Saint-Germain. Returned to Paris toward four in the afternoon. Went to a Montparnasse atelier, among the cubists, in Rue Huyghens. Three hundred people in a small hall; cubist paintings on the wall; Jean Cocteau, Madame Errasuriz, Erik Satie, Godebski, Sert, wearing large automobile capes, their velvet lapels drawn over their noses, as though muffling themselves in a place of ill repute. I see Apollinaire for the first time, in uniform, his head bandaged. The only really funny thing is the poetry of little Durand-Viel, who is five years old, recited by Jean Cocteau with a straight face and complete self-assurance. He is completely at ease in this milieu quite new to me. Verse by Cendrars, Leroy, Max Jacob. At last I've seen Apollinaire.

Thus, Cocteau, a late-comer to Salle Huyghens, had by December, 1916, elbowed his way to the front row and stage, reading not only his own poems, but those of his niece Françoise Durand-Viel and of his close friend, Jean Leroy (who was killed in action early in 1918). He had very quickly "gotten the idea" and played deft variations on it, for the poems of a five-year-old served, or so he fancied, the same esthetic as Guillaume's Negro sculptures and Satie's furniture music: the sublimity of the naïve. Admonished by Apollinaire and Reverdy, who resented his facile mimicries, he would apologize to them. Meanwhile he occupied, briefly, the center of the Montparnasse stage, importing his own numerous claque from the Right Bank. Eyes boggled at the long, shiny limousines drawing up at 6 Rue Huyghens, at the elegant ladies who descended and pushed their way into an atelier inadequately heated by its pot-bellied stove, where a motley group had assembled.

It was the same group that would fill the Châtelet in May for *Parade*. A combination of music and Cocteau had brought the *beau monde* to Montparnasse. The pan-arts festival of November-December gave rise to larger poetry readings, to concerts and to painting exhibitions, and "Going to Rue Huyghens Saturday evening?" became a byword on the Right Bank, according to Cocteau. "Many things that grew up quickly were born in this cradle during the war," he wrote. "People exposed, declaimed, sang, played. Artists from the Rotonde, located at the angle of Boulevards Raspail and Montparnasse, smoked their pipes, wearing sweaters and caps, next to opulent ladies. What didn't we do (by dint of bad organizing) to discourage the public? Programs were too brief, chairs were lacking, and feet froze, etc., etc. But Salle Huyghens was constructed under a lucky star."

In January Max Jacob read poems by Pierre Reverdy, as yet known only to the very few. On another occasion, Apollinaire, Cendrars, Cocteau, Max Jacob, and Reverdy read together. On January 26, 1917, a second painting exhibition was held, including works by Othon Friesz, Vlaminck, Severini, and Lhote, which led to a dozen more during 1917. Poor Lejeune, hoisted on his own petard, was now confined to the loft, where Kisling's dog Kouski, surveying the room below, accompanied poetry readings with strange canine sobs. Cocteau brought his fancy friends *en masse* for the Saturday night concerts to hear the work of a group of young composers, drawn there by Satie. They included Georges Auric, Louis Durey, Germaine Tailleferre, and Arthur Honegger.

The Six, a title invented in 1920 by Henri Collet, music critic of *Comœdia*, conveys the image of a perfect six-pointed star whose identical points radiate from a common center. In reality their differences—temperamental and esthetic—were more striking than their kinship. United by the accidents of age, place, and concert repertory, by Cocteau's social exertions, by a body of vague likes and pet peeves, by Collet's insignia, they stuck together for only a short while, until the accidents (and advantages) which inspired their association disappeared, and maturity emboldened their separate musical personalities. Between 1916 and 1924, most artistic movements were in the nature of a *cri de guerre*. They found strength in numbers. They adopted a Manichean stance. They checked their own internal differences in order to make some common point. They restrained larger natures within the movement from expressing themselves fully, and gave a firm personality to people lacking one. Thus Honegger, Milhaud, and Poulenc did not really come into their own till later, while Durey and Tailleferre all but vanished. The same applies to dada and surrealism. Gone was the relatively serene atmosphere in which cubism evolved. Scandal became a preeminent virtue of art, and the bigger the scandal the better.

Several members of the future Six were known to one another long before Satie, after a concert arranged by Cendrars in June, 1917, at Salle Huyghens, proposed calling them *Les Nouveaux Jeunes* (The New Young). Milhaud had met Honegger and Auric when all three were studying counterpoint with Gedalge at the Paris Conservatory, between 1911 and 1914. Honegger would commute thrice weekly from Le Havre, and during his visits they regularly congregated at Auric's flat to play their compositions for one another. Auric was a child prodigy, inordinately well-read, witty, and opinionated. When war broke out he was only fifteen, but his age did not disqualify him from hobnobbing with older musicians, some of them celebrated, like Ricardo Viñes through whom he met Satie, Varèse, *et al*. Next to this brilliant brat, Honegger appeared all the more solemn, inward, and Swiss, while Milhaud, born to a family of wealthy, cultivated Provençal Jews, resembled neither man.

Displaying a kind of thoroughbred benignity and self-assurance, Milhaud proved popular in the salon world. By the time he left for Rio de Janeiro in 1916 as Paul Claudel's diplomatic secretary, he had become a regular visitor at the homes of Mme. Daudet, the

Princess de Polignac, and Philippe Berthelot. During the years he spent abroad, 1917 and 1918, his music often figured in concerts performed by the *Nouveaux Jeunes,* now including Francis Poulenc, who met Satie through Ricardo Viñes.

Actually, Milhaud was known to both Poulenc and Satie before his diplomatic hiatus. He had met the former at the country estate of mutual friends when Poulenc was a boy of sixteen composing his first pieces. As for Satie, "I came across him," wrote Milhaud, referring to the winter of 1918–1919, "during a reception in honor of the Queen of Rumania. . . . The first thing he told me was that he had often heard me studying during the summer of 1916. Whenever he paid a visit to friends living across the street, he would hear me (as my windows were wide open) indefatigably repeat the same motifs on the piano, which greatly intrigued him as he didn't know who was living in that apartment." Thus, when Milhaud returned, he found his own predestined pew in the musical chapel whose unwitting architect was Jeanne Bathori. Her programs at the Théâtre du Vieux-Colombier, in November, 1917, incorporated for the first time those six names: Honegger, Durey, Poulenc, Tailleferre, Auric, and Milhaud. Building on Bathori's foundation, Cocteau added the upper stories and the façade.

Throughout the fall and winter following *Parade,* Cocteau flitted between the south of France and Paris, an itinerary he would observe for the rest of his life as a means of preserving his emotional equilibrium. The seashore was at once a cure for his arthritic ailments, a place of enforced writing, and an escape from personal imbroglios in Paris, imbroglios he hated yet fostered. He would boycott the capital, then, fearful that life was slipping away from him, return, like the little boy who suddenly rushes out of the garden and tiptoes furtively back to see what the garden does when he's not playing there. When not fulminating against Paris, "which becomes increasingly impossible to live in," Cocteau wanted his friends to keep him abreast of everything. That people somehow ate, grew, and created without him he interpreted as a conspiracy of silence. "Incredible silence on the part of Georges [Auric] and Satie," he complained to a friend. "They won't acknowledge my

texts and letters and telegrams. Astonished by their complete indifference. Tell them so if you see them. Am feeling better except
for physical prostration and stomach trouble."

Feeling unmissed, he would notify everyone of his illness and his
depression. In October, 1917, writing from the Hôtel Chantecler in
Piquey-par-Arès (a tiny resort north of Bordeaux to which he
would return year after year), he unburdened himself to Count
Louis Gautier-Vignal: "Very sad and taking sunbaths, black inside
and out on the negro coast, bassin d'Arcachon, too sick for lakes,
the doctors prescribing this semi-sea where I miss your petrol-
powered canoes—Without Félix [Cocteau's barber] my hair is
sprouting long—am living in Uncle Tom's cabin. . . . Not
working—strange landscape of mimosas, pines and pulpy plants."
He added in another letter: "With my heavy beard, red shirt, and
carbine, I look like a hero straight out of some dime novel 'in the
land of scalp.' The Lhotes have a cabin nearby." The following
January he stayed with the Francis de Croissets in Grasse, where
olive trees and sloping terraces supplanted the pines and flat, sandy
Landes of Piquey, but his inner landscape had not changed.[12] "Yes,
of course, Renoir," he wrote to Gleizes in America, "but I say
'down with Renoir like down with Wagner.' What a scandal it
makes in the monkey cage whose monkeys have just gotten to the
stage of tuning their nerves to impressionism. . . . Bring me back
as many Negro ragtimes and as much great Russo-Jewish-American
music as you can."

Cocteau had become a fan of Gaby Deslys, the glamorous
chanteuse who, between 1917 and 1921 (when she committed suicide), eclipsed even Mistinguett. She spent part of the war in New
York, where American millionaires had lavished jewels upon her
and where one king, Manuel of Portugal, offered to share his
throne with her. On returning to the Casino de Paris in 1917, she
brought with her the first jazz band Paris had ever heard. It became
all the rage. People soon had Negroes on the brain. Cendrars wrote
an *Anthologie Nègre*. Poulenc composed a *Rhapsodie Nègre*. The

12. Mme. Francis de Croisset was Mme. de Chevigné's daughter. By a first marriage, to Bischoffsheim the banker, she bore Marie-Laure, who later married Charles
de Noailles and played a considerable role in Cocteau's life.

city convulsed and even the *beaux quartiers* shivered somewhat, for that same year, 1917, Étienne de Beaumont, who loved sponsoring avant-garde spectacles, hired the whole American Army band to play on the sward behind his town house, awakening staid and elegant Saint-Germain with percussive sounds of the new era. Milhaud, en route from Brazil to France, visited jazz cabarets in Harlem. Cocteau, keeping abreast and even slightly ahead of the new wave, had correspondents such as Gleizes transmit him the latest ragtimes. Jean Wiener, the pianist at a cabaret called the Bar Gaya, would drop by 10 Rue d'Anjou in the morning with a music ledger, note tunes as fast as Cocteau could hum them while taking his bath, and play them that same evening.

By way of compensation for the hard knocks of Parisian literary life, Cocteau sought to prevail upon the Six and their foster father, Satie. Together with Blaise Cendrars, he directed a small press called Éditions de la Sirène,[13] which published, among other things, Satie's *Socrate*. Though *Socrate* was brought out with Satie's blessings, the composer, afraid that Cocteau had begun to consider him his private property, invited René Chalupt, the poet and musicologist, to write a preface. "I was flattered," Chalupt recalled, "though fairly certain his choice had been dictated by unwillingness to let Cocteau monopolize him, Cocteau being the natural choice under the circumstances. . . . The very day Satie came to see me about a preface for *Socrate*, he had no sooner sat down than the doorbell rang. It was Jean Cocteau! We immediately changed the subject of conversation. I cannot but think that this sudden visit, without precedent and without sequel, was not a pure coincidence."

Satie's paranoia exceeded even Cocteau's. If his relations with Cocteau blew hot and cold, so did they with everyone. Though cherished by the Six, he kept his distance from them, fearing any contractual bond whatever. Moreover, Auric seemed rather suspect. Once, the young composer, while putting his umbrella in a

13. Éditions de la Sirène had been founded by Cendrars and Cocteau in collaboration with a printer named Laffitte on Rue de Glacière. According to Cocteau, the success of *Cap de Bonne Espérance* turned M. Laffitte's head; he rented a sumptuous flat and hired a number of secretaries, but went bankrupt when Cocteau withdrew from their venture.

stand, had accidentally punched a hole in Satie's. Satie, seeing malicious intent behind this, never quite forgave him.[14] By 1923 Auric was calling Satie "a Norman notary" (Satie came from Honfleurs), "a suburban pharmacist," and, in reference to Satie's affiliation with the communists, "citizen Satie." Satie administered, as only he could, an accurate and devastating blow to Auric's swollen ego: "Those who tell me that my lamented friend is a mere 'flatfoot' exaggerate; he is, quite simply, nothing but an Auric (Georges), which is already more than sufficient for one man (?) alone."

The Six harbored no such resentment toward Cocteau, however, and his brief reign as esthetician, publicity agent, part-time cymbalist, and rabble rouser, proved to be one of the less neurotic episodes in his career. By early 1919 he had so firmly entrenched himself as spokesman for the Six that when Mme. Vandervelde, wife of the Belgian Minister of Fine Arts, invited the group to Brussels for a concert, it was he who delivered the introductory speech. His devotion went even beyond words. During a large concert organized by Delgrange on June 19, 1919, the première of Milhaud's *Libation-Bearers*, whom did the audience see perched behind the percussives but Cocteau, clapping cymbals and tapping the triangle alongside Honegger, Auric, Poulenc, and . . . Lucien Daudet, Cocteau's elegant and frail shadow.

Gradually these musical high jinks grew into a movement. The Saturday-night concerts in Montparnasse gave way to Saturday-night carousals in Montmartre. The group would meet at Milhaud's flat near Rue Chaptal, a few blocks from Cocteau's birthplace. Paul Morand ritually mixed the cocktails (another recent importation from America) while everyone got high and Poulenc played, as he did every week, his *Cocardes*, based on poems by Cocteau. By mid-evening, this intimate group had invariably snowballed into a numerous crowd including musicians, friends, and friends of

14. The brassiness and irony associated with the Six found their perfect expression in Auric's music, which prompted Satie to remark, in the early 1920s, after Durey's resignation: "Of Six there are only five, of five there are only three, of three there is but one"—excluding in the first instance Durey, in the second Honegger and Tailleferre (the former attached to Wagner, Strauss, Schönberg, the latter to Debussy), and in the third Milhaud and Poulenc.

friends. *En masse*, they would mill up the Rue Blanche to a little restaurant called the Petit-Bessonneau.

After satisfying its appetite, this multitongued monster, craving noise and thrills, found its heart's delight at the Montmartre Fair. The men, with muses such as Marie Laurencin, Valentine Gross, and Irène Lagut tagging along, reveled in the cockeyed, mechanical concert of player organs, steam calliopes, and phonographic barkers "which seemed," wrote Milhaud, "to grind up, implacably and simultaneously, all the folderol of music halls and reviews." Alternatively, there was the Medrano circus, whose Fratellini clowns Milhaud and Cocteau would, somewhat later, persuade to act in their farce *Le Bœuf sur le Toit*. By early morning a few limp members of the original body returned to Milhaud's flat, thus bringing the festivities full circle.

But the Six could not remain itinerant, cramping themselves into the Petit-Bessonneau and into another restaurant, Chez Delmas, on Place de la Madeleine.[15] At length they were reprieved from their gypsylike existence by a tall, gangling youth named Louis Moysès, who had recently emigrated to Paris from Charleville. He had rented an empty shop on Rue Duphot, in a building owned, as it happened, by Jean Wiener's father. Wiener, a fine pianist who earned his living playing in cabarets, suggested to Moysès that he open a restaurant-cabaret, guaranteeing him a ready-made clientele. Moysès responded to the idea and it was thus that the Bar Gaya—a white-tiled grotto not much larger than a lavatory—came into being.

Cocteau had only to lift his telephone receiver to trigger a devious circuit extending throughout Paris; on opening night more people appeared than the Bar Gaya could accommodate, a happy predicament repeated every week end of its existence. Moysès had found a windfall, Wiener a jazz cabaret very much to his liking, the Six a home, and Cocteau such local preeminence that his given name, in a room usually crowded with Jeans, sufficed to identify him. The Six were transplanted to Cocteau's native soil. Within a

15. These Saturday dinners at Chez Delmas did continue, intermittently, through the early 1920s.

few blocks of 10 Rue d'Anjou there now stood Salle Huyghens' successor, and in its hothouse atmosphere of jazz and Right-Bank intrigue Cocteau flourished. Meanwhile, he had published a thin pamphlet entitled *Le Coq et l'Arlequin*, which further reinforced his reputation as the Six's spokesman; the public, not unreasonably, read it as a manifesto. It is dedicated to Georges Auric, and its philosophy stems from the aphorisms of Erik Satie.

"The music hall, the circus, American Negro orchestras all fecundate the artist just as life itself does," he wrote. "Using the emotions that such spectacles awaken doesn't amount to making art from art. These spectacles are not art. They excite like machines, animals, landscapes, danger." It was a favorite device of the Six to adopt popular tunes and write them into their own compositions; striving for the canned effects of the phonograph, of the steam calliope, of the player piano, of the hurdy-gurdy. What they produced was a sharp-edged instrument, music whose diatonic figures, set in different keys, grate against one another like flint-stones and set one's teeth on edge. Milhaud wrote a "shimmy" and "romance and rag caprice," Auric a fox trot called "Adieu, New York," and Poulenc any number of fanfares for fife and drums scaled to a parade of toy soldiers.

The mood does vary but within a narrow range from the gay to the impish, from the impish to the brutal, from tongue-in-cheek to the bitter tongue. There are innocent airs, strutting along rapidly in C Major like eighteenth-century symphonies until tripped by a jazz note or diverted into another key, when their initial zeal turns colicky. There are violent scores such as Milhaud's *Libation-Bearers* whose polytonal chords (as in "The Exhortation") convey the throbbing and shrieking of a blood bath. There are songs commensurate with Apollinaire's Bestiary and Cocteau's brief poems. There are musical quotations from *Louise*, Schubert's *Military March*, the last measures of Stravinsky's *Apollon Musagètes*, each given a scurrilous twist. There are tunes that call forth carousels, hurdy-gurdies, gingerbread fairs, and sonatas that execute a pirouette in three swift movements, like Haydn's. It is music intensely modern yet willfully atavistic. It will pluck clichés from the air, like Maurice Chevalier's refrains, but also coquette in the style of

Couperin or Rameau. What it would not abide was music that loses its edge in grandiloquence or cloudy sensation: Wagner's continuous melody and Debussy's deliquescent epics.

In *Le Coq et l'Arlequin* Cocteau turned Verlaine's symbolist prescriptions inside out. "Music above all," he wrote, "and in composing it, choose the even: heavier and less soluble in air." The cock is the Gallic cock, and his antagonist is Harlequin, whom Cocteau defines, quoting Larousse, as "a ragout composed of various leftovers." The Russians and especially the Germans having contaminated French music, Cocteau called upon his countrymen to find themselves. In finding themselves, they would hear Cocteau: "I admire the harlequins of Cézanne and Picasso, but I don't like Harlequin. He wears a mask and a multicolored costume. After disavowing the cock's cry he hides. He is a night cock. On the other hand I like the true cock. . . . He says Cocteau twice and inhabits *his* farm." Eclecticism and paradox, he goes on to say, are hateful to the modern generation, which "despises their smile, their faded elegance. It fears the enormous. That's what I call escaping from Germany."

Smallness, rapidity, and humor became integral elements of a style. The Six often scored pastorales, suites, and serenades for fewer than ten players. Milhaud composed a symphony for seven reeds. It was Satie who gave them their cue. They imitated his pastiches of musical titles and instructions ("Unappetizing Chorale," "To be sung like a nightingale with a toothache"). From him they also learned that brevity is the essence of wit. Their compositions often have the time span and limited development of one *bon mot*, the flashy reticence of "furniture music" which loudly begs to go unheard, the playfulness that keeps aloof from its own gestures.

Obviously this music reflects something larger than itself, the doom of absolute truths and of their theatrical appurtenances. It is content with the precision of a detail, of a harmonic pun, crude, stripped, and gay; its attention to balance and to classical form has something of the tiny skiff gracefully riding storm waves. If it openly plagiarized, it thus accomplished the double purpose of seizing the fugitive day and stating its own limits. This renascence of interest in form for its own sake came as a reaction against

Wagnerian systems, against the amorphous baggage of German music, against the sentimentality they sensed even in Stravinsky. "Theatre corrupts everyone and even Stravinsky," wrote Cocteau. "I consider *The Rite of Spring* a masterpiece, but I discover in the atmosphere created by its performance a religious complicity among adepts, the hypnotism of Bayreuth. Wagner wanted theatre; Stravinsky finds himself dragged into it by force of circumstance. . . . Wagner cooks us slowly; Stravinsky doesn't give us time to say 'Ouch!' but both act upon our nerves. It is visceral music: octopi you must flee lest they devour you. That's the fault of theatre."

But the Six, or five of them, were French, and disdaining the gut in favor of the clear head was perhaps not altogether an esthetic choice: a Mozart, with greater economy than theirs, produced works more vital. Urbanity cannot be considered the crowning achievement of classicism. By choice or not, they often, at the beginning, stood outside their subjects, never quite losing their heads. By choice or not, they made a virtue of poverty, which falls very much within the French tradition. One contemporary critic describes Milhaud's work as "a perpetual glancing off from states of incandescence."

Cocteau suffered the short-windedness of the composers he defended, and it shows in the staccato *pensées* of *Le Coq et l'Arlequin*. "The eloquence I was allotted," he once wrote to Gleizes, "doesn't have much stamina." Cocteau never spoke so truly. There was a curious relationship between his writing and his conversation, the two explaining one another. His brilliant prattle was an act of consumption, not creation: like chain-smoking, it waged war against neutrality and boredom, it gave a scent to odorless time, it camouflaged his person. If his auditors always complained of forgetting what he had said the evening before, what he said was meant to be unrepeatable and forgotten; it amounted to an *objet de luxe* set ablaze night after night. Paper, on the other hand, summoned forth all his ghosts: schoolboy precepts, bourgeois inhibitions, the judgment of an unknowable posterity, the awful definitiveness of the written word.

White paper, ink, the pen frighten me. I know that they are in
cahoots against my will to write. If I succeed in conquering them,
work ignites me, the machine heats up, and the mind goes full speed
ahead. But it's important that I stay out of it as far as possible, that I
doze. The least awareness of this mechanism interrupts it. And if I
wish to start it up again, I must wait until it decides to, without trying to convince it by some snare. That's why I don't use tables,
which intimidate me. . . . I write at any hour, on my knees.

The mere physical presence of another person he interpreted as
an act of faith, but, correspondingly, the absence of people represented a threat. Yet Cocteau's spoken anecdotes (repeated again and
again) proved no more telling than his written aphorisms. Along
with the instantaneous use of *tu* and his exquisite manners, they
formed the theatrical apparatus of intimacy, which excused him
from being intimate. Eruptions of the innermost being frightened
him. He neither solicited nor gave confidences, except from and to
the great (but then, on Olympus exceptions are the rule). On the
level of acts, names, masks, career, "shop," his altruism was quickly
kindled. Thus, he might, though personally indifferent to some
younger writer, gladly help him find a publisher. The same applies
to his writing, which veers away from self (most especially in his
autobiographical works) rather as Milhaud's work glances off from
states of incandescence. It tends toward the universal, toward the
aphoristic in the tradition of eighteenth-century picaresque, and the
"emblematic psychology," as he will call it, of his fiction and plays,
the very speed with which they elapse, the glittering images which
reflect mainly themselves, amount to an evasion of depth, a kind of
scared inaptitude which Cocteau dressed in all the regalia of an
esthetic.

"Picasso," he wrote, "taught me how to run faster than beauty,"
but Cocteau's canons of beauty were not those of the avant-garde.
He was a cultivated bourgeois masquerading as a literary Jacobin.
Waving the banner of experimentation, he really felt more at home
among proven models. Years later, in *La Difficulté d'Être*, he admitted as much. "When I read a book, I marvel at the number of
words I encounter and dream of using them. I make note of them.

When getting down to work, it's impossible for me. I restrict myself to my own vocabulary. I can't manage to escape from it, and it
is so limited that work becomes brain-wracking." Then, after stating his preference for frugal styles, "those of Montaigne, Racine,
Chateaubriand, and Stendhal," he argues his way into this arbitrary
constellation made of stars lumped together from opposite points in
heaven: "Wealth lies in a certain penury."

While backing into his classical niche, he repeatedly assured the
public that he did so out of artistic defiance. Making flourishes with
his hands and his hind-quarters, he thus wiggled insecurely through
life, unable to own up to his own self. In the 1920s it was avant-
garde to be "classical," and the proof he adduced was a poet
younger than the surrealists, Radiguet. When, in 1930, the
Comédie-Française produced his *La Voix Humaine*, a touching
melodrama very much in the tradition of Henry Bernstein (from
whom he borrowed the idea), Cocteau disavowed both literary
right and literary left, as if to say, "I'm standing as far right as
Bernstein, in his very place, but it is an optical illusion: the avant-
garde is spheroid and I've gone farther left than anyone else."
What he did say was:

> I congratulate myself that an instinct of revolt—the spirit of contra-
> diction inhabiting the poet—has whispered into my ear a unified and
> static play, a complete contradiction to the seizures of jazz and mod-
> ern cinema.

When finally elected to the French Academy, he would accept, but
only in the name of its illustrious nonmembers, of the *poètes
maudits*, alluding to black wings tucked inside his official uniform.

Cocteau's role as musical impresario was a kind of consolation
trophy he offered himself for a series of literary setbacks. Trying,
from 1917 on, to cut a figure in the poetic avant-garde, he was
brought low by André Breton.

6

The Angels Come of Age

In 1916 André Breton, twenty years old, walked into Adrienne Monnier's book store for the first time. It was an apparition she would not afterward forget, for he already had the face and the bearing of a pontiff. "He was handsome," she wrote, "but his beauty was archangelic rather than angelic. . . . The face was massive, well-drawn. He wore his hair rather long and tossed straight back with nobility; his gaze remained foreign to the world and even to himself. He seemed scarcely alive, the color of jade. Breton didn't smile, but he did laugh sometimes, with a clipped, sardonic laugh punctuating his speech without disarranging his features, as with women fastidious about their looks. But perhaps the most remarkable thing about Breton's face was its heavy and excessively fleshy mouth whose lower lip was abnormally well-developed." With age and authority, those features became increasingly salient. André Masson's portrait of Breton, done twenty-five years later, shows him more aquiline than ever, his face seemingly cut into sharp facets, with a scroll-like growth of Gorgon hair and an eye absent-looking and unforgiving. It was a face that refused to collapse, as though sustained by its crystalline ego.

Appropriately, crystal was Breton's favorite substance: at once a personal emblem and an object lesson in art. "The house I live in, my life, what I write: it is my dream that these should appear from a distance the way cubes of rock salt appear from close up." This dream he translated into a persona whose startling integrity borders on the inhuman. In fifty years, from the time he was a *lycée* student writing poems in imitation of Mallarmé until his death, Breton's scrupulously neat, classical script scarcely changed. His prose style was likewise remarkable for its high-flown recititude, full of internal tangents and subordinate embroilments but always conscious of its structure. He spoke slowly, deliberately, isolating each word as though even the most common were chiseled from some occult intention: a style later adopted by other members of the surrealist group. In this respect he differed radically from his first literary friend and mentor, Valéry, whose rapidity of speech was legendary. Yet that difference was perhaps only superficial. In the writing of both men one finds a common fascination less with literature *per se* than with the wellsprings of thought and of creation. Valéry's influence upon Breton was incalculable. They shared the same vocation but, more than that, honored in their lives a kind of schizoid equilibrium between the respectable and the subversive, between the public self and the occult. Even as he was being inaugurated into the French Academy, whose mainstay he became, Valéry nostalgically recalled the secret society of his youth, the symbolist chapel in which he cut his poetic teeth: "All schools and even the world's great religions have always begun as tiny coteries, cells long closed and impenetrable, proud to be flouted and hoarding their private visions."

Behind the official Valéry there lurked that other who rose every morning at five and for five hours committed his innermost self to notebooks, thus writing twenty-two thousand pages never suspected by the countesses and duchesses who listened to his every public address with bated breath. There was, similarly, an official Breton, the *chef d'école* and esthete who wore the horn-rimmed spectacles (fitted with window-glass) of an Oxford don, who displayed super-refined manners, who abhorred Nietzsche and deplored sodomy. The other Breton made a pilgrimage to Freud, used his heavy cane to deadly effect in literary quarrels, and made a cult of someone in many respects his opposite: a hysterical, dandified youth named Jacques Vaché.

Adrienne Monnier notes that Breton, when she first saw him, was wearing the sky-blue uniform of a medical auxiliary. Having studied medicine before the war, he was assigned to an army hospital in Nantes where he first met Vaché, suffering from a leg wound. Vaché, a year older than Breton, spent days drawing picture post cards for which he invented weird captions or obsessively arranging the few objects on his night table. As soon as his leg mended, he got a job unloading barges in Nantes, otherwise amusing himself bar-hopping and movie-hopping at night. Clothing particularly fascinated him; attired by turn as a British army officer, an aviator, and a doctor, he would parade through Nantes pretending not to recognize his friends. At home, Louise, his odd companion, sat silent and motionless for hours on end, stirring only to prepare tea for her master, a gesture rewarded, according to Breton, with a hand kiss; Vaché boasted that he had never made love to her. Afterward, in Paris, Breton saw him only four or five times, once during the intermission of Apollinaire's play *Les Mamelles de Tirésias* when suddenly Vaché appeared in the aisle waving a pistol which he threatened to fire into the audience. Returning to Nantes, he died from an overdose of opium, apparently a suicide although his death, reflecting his life, remains a matter of conjecture.

As for Vaché's literary views, he liked Jarry, whose incendiary humor, deriving "from a sensation of the theatrical (and joyless) futility of everything," answered his own. Otherwise Vaché professed total indifference to art and artists, considering them play-actors who mistake their stage for life. "I concede a little affection for *Lafcadio* because he doesn't read and produces only by amusing experiments, like the murder—and then without any satanic lyricism—my old rotten Baudelaire!—what he needed was a little of our dry air: machinery—presses with stinking oil—throb—throb —throb—whistle! Reverdy—the POHET amusing, and boredom in prose; Max Jacob my old fraud—PUPPETS—PUPPETS—PUPPETS."

It little matters that Vaché may have been a foppish Anglophile and frustrated painter. His alibis became, to Breton's mind, archetypal virtues. "Vaché was the first to insist on the importance of acts," wrote Breton. Jerking convulsively from "act" to "act" like some human non sequitur, he enacted his instincts, whose only law was their absolute lack of one. In other words, Vaché, supremely the actor, became apotheosized as a nature god, a *force de la nature* whose manifold guises and apparent illogic ultimately signify his glorious self-confidence. According to the myth that Breton created, Vaché's mind resembled nothing so much as a blind mechanism which, revved up beyond consciousness of itself, indifferently creates and destroys, as if creation and destruction were coefficients of instantaneousness.

Vaché's mythical speed goes hand in hand with his mythical status as a destroyer. Breton spoke of "Jacques Vaché's swift journey across the sky of war, his appearing in every way extraordinarily rushed, this catastrophic haste which makes him obliterate himself. . . ." Magnifying Vaché's mock massacre during *Les Mamelles de Tirésias*, Breton saw in it a metaphysical gesture: the simplest surrealist act, he would proclaim, is emptying a revolver aimlessly into a crowd. And when he compiled his roster of surrealist precursors, Breton included himself as a spiritual avatar of Vaché: "Vaché is a surrealist in me."

The surrealist in Breton lay dormant for some years. From 1916 to 1920 he was busy fashioning a literary career—hobnobbing with leaders of the poetic avant-garde and getting published in the two major literary reviews founded during the war: Albert Birot's *Sic* and Pierre Reverdy's *Nord-Sud*. The former was an indiscriminate miscellany dedicated to the cause of futurism and its by-products: bruitism (literally "noise-ism") and nunism (from the Greek *nyn* meaning "now"). *Nord-Sud*, on the other hand, proved as single-minded as *Sic* was eclectic, its contributors—invariably Reverdy, Max Jacob, and Apollinaire—belonging to that select poetic group known as cubist. Despite all that separated the two, Breton paid homage to Apollinaire, whose return from the Front was responsible for a sudden quickening of literary life in Paris and whose sponsorship no young poet ambitious to make his mark could do without. Breton visited him at his sickbed on May 10, 1916, the day after Apollinaire had undergone trepanation. When the latter recovered sufficiently to leave the hospital, Breton would, along with everyone else in the *Nord-Sud* circle, meet him at the Café de Flore where Apollinaire, his head bandaged and his bloated body attired in artillery blue, presided on Tuesday afternoons.

Such was Apollinaire's regard for Breton that when *Calligrammes* appeared early in 1918, he invited the twenty-two-year-old poet to review his complete works for *Mercure de France*. "I have thought of asking a favor of you," he wrote to Breton. "I don't know anyone who could speak as well about what I've done as you." Whatever Breton's private confusion, people immediately sensed that he was hewn of one piece and possessed a poetic destiny. Perhaps this is what Reverdy meant by pure. "You and Aragon," he wrote in 1918, "are undoubtedly my purest friends."

Breton had met Louis Aragon, another medical student, in Adrienne Monnier's bookstore in the fall of 1917. Their meeting proved to be a *coup de foudre*, uniting them for the next thirteen years. "Aragon's heart beats in Breton's chest," wrote one of their friends. It was as if Breton wore Aragon like a set of claws, though in 1917 Aragon had not yet become the polemicist that his tour of the Alsatian Front would make of him. "He adored poetry," wrote Adrienne Monnier, "without demanding that it be too off-beat. When I met him he was doing his first year of medical studies. He had copies of Verlaine and Laforgue in his pockets and was deeply shocked by the crudity of his classmates. I remember one of our first conversations in which he confided to me that the coarseness of asides he heard in the medical amphitheatre brought him to the verge of tears."

It would be difficult, or else perfectly logical, to deduce from this the future author of *Irene's Cunt*, the Ariosto of surrealism, the Communist convert whom the French state would bring to trial for writing a poem "inciting insurrection." At twenty Aragon had the manners and exquisite dress becoming a young man brought up in elegant Neuilly where his father, during their strolls in the Bois de Boulogne, would familiarly greet Maurice Barrès.[1] What set him apart, however, was his prodigious memory for verse, his sheer power of verbal invention. If Breton measured words, Aragon squandered them riotously. They were two young men drawn to each other as much by their radical differences as by their kindred backgrounds. In Aragon, Breton saw his Byronic self. In Breton, Aragon saw the magistrate who would lay down his law. A French Marxist named Victor Crastre, who first met Aragon in the mid-

1. Aragon is reputed to be the natural son of the Parisian prefect of police who, in 1889, after General Boulanger's abortive *coup d'état*, persuaded the general to exile himself from France.

twenties, observed that throughout their conversation, which took place in an ornate café lined with mirrors, Aragon was judging his own performance from every angle; he concluded that Aragon, had he so chosen, might have become the greatest actor of his age.

He did. Bashful, he became the most strident of the surrealists. Quixotic, he has to this day maintained a façade of undying love for his matriarch Elsa Triolet and of unwavering fidelity to his patriarch, the Communist party. A snob, a cultivated bourgeois to his fingertips, he is now poet laureate of the proletariat. A human reversible, he has followed a career carrying him full circle from the bourgeois establishment to the Communist, by way of scandal, libertinage, a sustained plunge into the Unconscious.

By 1918 Breton and Aragon had made friends with another young poet, Philippe Soupault, who was allied to the Renault automobile fortune. The three became inseparable. They would meet nearly every morning at the Val de Grâce military hospital (to which Aragon was assigned) and breakfast together on Boulevard Saint-Germain. During the darkest days of World War I a new literary chapel was born, with clandestine gods in Rimbaud, Lautréamont, Jarry, and Jacques Vaché. Its members had no café for their *lares*. so they walked, and it was during one such walk that Breton, Aragon, and Soupault decided to launch a literary review.

> I remember the first time we entertained the idea [wrote Aragon]. . . . It was during the winter of 1917–1918, along the Boulevard Flandrin as André Breton had just finished showing Philippe the letters of Jacques Vaché and we were dragging our soiled uniforms through the railway smoke on the outskirts, forgetting to salute officers, forgetting every kind of deportment, forgetting the hour and ourselves and the bitter cold. Awareness of a really new spirit and one so close to us, awareness also of the hostility this spirit would encounter, of the impossibility of demonstrating it anywhere. In those days there was only one live review, *Nord-Sud*, and we were quite certain, despite our liking for Reverdy, that *Nord-Sud* would never admit this new *fact*.

Their initial name for the review was *Le Nègre*, which they quickly discarded. Reverdy suggested *Carte Blanche*, which they found too naïve. At length they decided, after consulting Valéry, to call it *Littérature*, presumably in the ironic sense intended by Verlaine: "and all the rest [meaning rhetoric] is literature."

The first issue appeared in March, 1919, and its table of contents scared no one. It included such established avant-garde figures as Gide, delighted to have found favor (very short-lived) with the younger generation, and Valéry, who, though well-known, was just beginning to publish in earnest at fifty and therefore felt an affinity with the young belying his age. As issue succeeded issue, the impression took root that *Littérature* was at once a successor to *Nord-Sud* and a surrogate of the *NRF*, many of whose authors it published. Rather than revolutionary, it was broadly modern, interlarding the really new—such as Lautréamont's *Poésies* (which Breton had unearthed in the Bibliothèque Nationale where he spent afternoons copying it out)—with the tepid contributions of André Salmon and Paul Morand, or with Raymond Radiguet's dubious juvenilia. Not till late 1919 did some specimens of automatic writing appear, but even these, as Breton's manuscript notes show, were carefully revised to read like Mallarmé.

Littérature and its editors were in danger: the magazine of becoming literary and the young men of becoming *Wunderkinder* of the literary establishment. They appeared wherever it was proper they should, at *NRF* parties, at Paul Guillaume's art gallery for recitals of poetry and music, at Léonce Rosenberg's gallery, in Valentine Gross's flat (just above Paul Morand's in the Palais-Royal, where she had taken up residence in 1917), at Adrienne Monnier's bookstore, where Valéry reigned supreme. Apart from the obvious and novel thrill of power, however, they felt, in their role as scions of Apollinaire's *Esprit Nouveau*, like impostors. Breton, in his tiny hotel room on the Place du Panthéon, chafed with boredom and self-disappointment, indicting himself with Jacques Vaché's penultimate letter:

> Agreed, we have resolved to leave the WORLD in a state of startled ignorance, until some satisfying and perhaps scandalous demonstration. However . . . I depend on you to prepare the way for this God deceiving, slightly sneering, and withal terrible—How funny it will be, don't you see, if this true *Esprit Nouveau* should unleash itself! . . . Apollinaire has done a lot for us and is certainly not

dead; moreover, he did well to die in time. It's been said, but it's worth repeating: HE MARKS AN EPOCH. The marvelous thing we shall be able to do—NOW.[2]

Soupault amused himself as best he could by offering his umbrella to pretty women on sunny days, stopping a bus to inquire of its passengers whether they knew the address of Philippe Soupault, asking a florist for a swift-growing vine as he had an assignation that same afternoon with a lady waiting on the balcony above. Only Aragon, not yet discharged from the army and shuttling between Alsace and Paris, seemed to have encountered something new, for as medical officer his main duty in Saarbrücken was to inspect the city's two bordellos. But Vaché's imperative, the NOW, was receding into an unlived past and puzzling future, seemingly bargained away for *Littérature*.

To understand their haste one need only consider their heroes and heroines. Bourgeois by upbringing, the surrealists came of age between 1914 and 1918. The war, exercising a twofold effect, at once declassed them and offered them *its* perspective. It is as if they identified destruction with nature, inventing heroes whose heroism consisted in their magical metamorphism, their violence, their dark powers, their uncanny science. Vaché (the mythological figure he became) is indistinguishable from Fantômas the film villain—wildly admired by Breton and Aragon—whose knowledge of society's sham psyche allowed him to foil his pursuers, but Fantômas in turn descended from the romantic Lucifer. Exalted as "Master of Fright," "The Torturer," "The Emperor of Crime," Fantômas emerged as a latter-day avatar of Balzac's Vautrin, Maturin's Melmoth, Byron's Manfred, Ponson du Terrail's Rocambole, and, above all, Isidore Ducasse's alter ego (and pen name) Lautréamont. At war with bourgeois mores, the surrealists-to-be thus inhabited an Underworld even before taking up residence in the Unconscious. Crime prefigured Nature: one apocalyptic, *necessary* act sufficing to undermine the shaky foundations of Cartesian logic.

Their heroes had suitable molls. "An entire generation's idea of

2. Vaché appears to have tempered his remarks in view perhaps of Breton's affection for Apollinaire. In another letter, to Breton's friend Théodore Fraenkel, he dismissed Apollinaire outright as an artful confectioner of verse, "like Cocteau."

the world was formed in the movies," wrote Aragon, "and one film
especially summed it up, a serial. The Young fell head over heels in
love with Musidora, in *The Vampires*." At the center of its sleep,
surrealism enthroned the Adventuress, by turns man-eating and
man-creating, ambiguously virginal and sluttish. Vaché had a female counterpart in Pearl White, whose fast-motion exploits if anything surpassed his own. As Pauline in *The Perils of Pauline*, she
defied gravity, death, walls, leaping about with imbecile haste. The
romantic sensibility—its inward infinite, its penchant for the bizarre
and surprising, its black humor, its revolutionary fervor, its depraved virgins, its explorations of the erotic at the boundary of
death, and of cruelty—took root in fields loamy with the humus of
the dead, as it had a hundred years before during the aftermath of
revolution and Napoleon.

What, then, was Breton's excitement to read in a letter from
Tristan Tzara, one of the co-founders of dada, with whom he had
been corresponding since February, 1919: "I would have become a
sweeping adventurer playing some subtle hand in world affairs if I
had the physical strength and nervous constitution to perform this
one exploit: not getting bored." Breton immediately responded:

> I've just been strongly moved by the avowal of your weakness in the
> face of boredom—Just as you say: I would have become a sweeping
> adventurer playing some subtle hand if. . . . ,—that's what I would
> become (so I tell myself every moment, thinking of you) if . . . A
> possibility that tempts and repulses me by turns. All my efforts are
> for the moment directed along that one line: conquer boredom. I
> think of nothing else day and night. Is it an impossible task for
> someone who gives himself to it wholeheartedly? Do understand that
> I insist on seeing what lies on the other side of boredom. . . . I am
> even making some small progress.

Tzara, a born organizer, ever since 1917 had been peppering the
capitals of Europe with copies of his reviews *Dada* and *Dadaphone*.
He was known throughout avant-garde circles, to whom he offered
his reviews in exchange for theirs, but Breton did not seem to take
serious notice of him until January, 1919, when *Dada Manifesto
1918* came to his attention. In it he read the following:

I tell you: there is no beginning and we do not tremble, we aren't sentimental. An angry wind, we tear the laundry of clouds and of prayers and prepare the great spectacle of disaster, fire, decomposition.

Vaché died in January, 1919, and Tzara straightaway took his place in Breton's life. The two corresponded throughout the year, Breton trying to persuade Tzara to live in Paris, Tzara hesitating to leave Zurich. When Tzara was finally prevailed upon, the news of his coming electrified the French avant-garde. In January, 1920, Breton, Aragon, and Soupault gathered in the apartment of Francis Picabia (where Tzara had pitched his few belongings—mainly a typewriter). They expected to see in Tzara some luminous faun or Michelangelo's Moses. Instead they beheld a wee man, bespectacled and intensely nervous, who spoke broken French. A Rumanian Jew and a philosopher by training, Tzara felt ill at ease in the glare of Breton's expectations. It did not take long, however, for the one to overcome his shyness and the other his initial disappointment. Tzara and Picabia, old hands at scandalous high jinks, set about organizing dada's debut in Paris, while the *Littérature* group, awed by Tzara's and Picabia's revolutionary sophistication, cheerfully did the footwork. Breton and Aragon rented a hall called the Palais des Fêtes (more modest than its name would imply) and engaged several actor-friends to read dada texts. Picabia and Tzara took care of the agenda.

The Palais des Fêtes on Rue Saint-Denis was as far removed from the Boulevard as from Left Bank literary circles. The hall, sandwiched between two cinemas where Breton and Aragon used to watch Fantômas, *Les Vampires*, and Chaplin films, was chosen then, for symbolic and sentimental reasons. It stood in a neighborhood densely populated by jewelers, watchmakers, wig merchants, and cosmetic dealers, many of whom attended the demonstration expecting to hear about France's financial crisis, for the main bill had been announced in *L'Intransigeant* as a lecture by André Salmon on *"La Crise du Change:"* a title no less ambiguous than *Littérature, change* meaning currency as well as alteration. The merchants filed out one by one as Salmon made it clear that his subject was Apollinaire, not inflation. Those who remained, the intellectuals and the literary gossip mongers alerted to Tzara's presence in Paris, waited for the Joker to show his hand.[3] They did not have long to wait, for the program was designed so as to progress from serious avant-garde poetry to a series of antics one more impertinent than the next, with an intermission of music by *Les Six*. Thus, the two young actors Pierre Bertin and Marcel Herrand, along with Jean Cocteau and Pierre Drieu la Rochelle, began by reading poems by Jacob, Reverdy, and Cendrars, whereupon Breton appeared on stage with a Picabia painting which looked like a wilderness of black striations embellished with the letters L.H.O.O.Q. Read aloud, these letters form the sentence *Elle a chaud au cul* meaning "She has a hot ass." When this finally dawned on the audience, it responded uproariously, shouting and stamping till appeased by the music of Satie.

After intermission the protagonists started to goad their audience anew. Part II was a reprise of Part I, though pitched at an eerier level. The same people who read at the outset, including Cocteau, read again, but the poems of Ribemont-Dessaignes, Soupault, and Paul Dermée made no sense. They served as a kind of masher reducing the spectacle to soft pulp in which Tzara would sprinkle some final grains of imbecility. On he came, like Batman's Penguin, preceded by a fanfare of rattles, reading "one of his latest works." What he recited was a speech recently delivered by Léon Daudet, a royalist and proto-fascist, before the National Assembly, but his voice was drowned out by Aragon and Breton who stood in the wings ringing bells. Tumult reigned. The audience hurled bawdy insults at Tzara, and one spectator, Florent Fels, director of the literary review *Action*, screamed "Back to Zurich! To the gallows with him!" Even certain participants, such as Juan Gris and André Salmon, feeling they had been enrolled under false pretenses, turned against the organizers.

As for Cocteau, he was delighted to participate in any first, but alas, his dada première proved to be his valedictory. As soon as party lines were firmly drawn, he found himself on the outside. It

3. One of the chief gossip mongers of Paris, Jacques-Émile Blanche, suffered a heart attack on his way to the meeting, which prompted Aragon to say: "Dada has just appointed its first victim."

took some doing, however, for Breton to impose his view of Cocteau upon Picabia and Tzara, neither of whom fully shared Breton's home-grown animus.

Breton's grudges were awesome things; time only hardened them into geological strata of his mind. The one he held against Cocteau was monolithic. It came into being very early and outlived its object. In one of his first letters to Tzara, Breton drew up a roster of writers whom he planned to exclude from the pages of *Littérature*. Cocteau figured prominently. Some months later, in December, 1919, Breton wrote to Tzara as follows:

> In Paris, nothing afoot (which mustn't discourage you from coming, on the contrary). The Ballets Russes awful, from what I hear. We've long since resigned ourselves to that, and the rest. People aren't stirring much, except Cocteau who is giving "artistic" lectures in Brussels. What do you know, he's boasting that he received your best wishes and cards of good hope.[4] That's possible; but then you don't know him very well. My own feeling, completely impartial I assure you, is that he is the most hateful being of our time. I repeat, he has done me no wrong and, besides, hatred is not my strong point.

On the contrary, hatred *was* Breton's strong point. What he hated was not a person, but a thing, or a person transformed into a thing. He and Cocteau were absolutely star-crossed. The former could not forgive the latter his homosexuality, his studied flamboyance, his literary politicking, his well-born intimates, his financial cushion, and the sheen of modernity he wore so becomingly. All that was Cocteau clashed with his own ponderous and deliberate self. Cocteau's attitude offended Breton, as it did Reverdy—for the same reason: he made brilliant pastiches of styles they had reared for themselves out of nothingness; what for them represented a law governing their lives was for him a momentary flare. Furthermore, Breton, who saw himself as nothing if not a *chef d'école*, wanted no rivals. He was Apollinaire's legitimate heir and Cocteau, he felt, a fraud threatening to snatch the crown and scepter.

What precisely was Cocteau's claim to the throne? Apollinaire

4. A reference to Cocteau's latest collection of poems, *The Cape of Good Hope*.

seemed to respect him chiefly as a kind of satellite of Picasso and in his program note for *Parade* altogether slights Cocteau while singing the praises of Satie, Picasso, and Massine. Yet it was on the basis of this note, in which Apollinaire coined the phrase *Esprit Nouveau*, that Cocteau fancied himself the New Spirit incarnate. Here, as in many other instances, there is an imponderable discrepancy between the public record and the private. The former pictures Apollinaire and Cocteau walking side by side, Apollinaire addressing Cocteau in a tone of tutelary *bonhomie*. Cocteau wrote:

> I see him browsing through the streets of Montparnasse, strewn with hopscotch squares, carrying round about himself an arsenal of fragile things, avoiding breakage, and proffering learned remarks to the effect that Bretons were formerly Negroes, that the Gauls didn't wear mustaches, that "groom" was a corruption of *gros homme*, which the English picked up from Swiss porters in London. . . . Sometimes he stopped, lifted his pinky, and said (for example): "I have just reread *Maldoror*. The youth of today owe much more to Lautréamont than to Rimbaud."

Privately, Cocteau grieved, during the winter before *Parade*, about some dirty trick Apollinaire and Misia Sert had played against him. Publicly, Apollinaire came to his defense when Théodore Fraenkel, a member of Breton's circle, embarrassed Cocteau by signing the latter's name to the poem published in Albert Birot's review *Sic*, a poem that turned out to be an acrostic: the first letters of each verse spelled PAUVRES BIROTS. As soon as he got wind of it Cocteau denounced the anonymous author in the June 15, 1917, edition of *L'Intransigeant*:

> The story behind the hoax in *Sic* is an ugly one. Alas, it sums up certain modern literary mores and doesn't deserve to be peddled publicly. *Sic* gave, above my signature, half a page to something that wasn't mine. The acrostic proves the director's innocence; I accuse him, therefore, of mere carelessness. If this letter will put an end to misunderstandings that serve the anonymous prankster I should be grateful to you for publishing it.

Apollinaire, according to Cocteau, took it as a personal foul, a gross violation of literary protocol, and visited one café after another to ferret out the culprit. Yet, assuming that this campaign took place, that Apollinaire did mobilize himself on Cocteau's behalf, why shouldn't he have arranged to publish Cocteau in *Nord-Sud*? The benediction would have required only two fingers of his right hand, but he apparently never lifted them; Cocteau, yearning to appear in Reverdy's review, succeeded only once, with a capsule summary of the *Parade* collaboration.

The discrepancy between the public and the private vanished only when Apollinaire died on November 9, 1918. Cocteau was present to claim his mantle. "The morning of Armistice, Picasso and Max Jacob came to 10 Rue d'Anjou," wrote Cocteau. "They told me that they were worried about Guillaume, that fat was enveloping his heart, and that we should call Capmas, my friends' doctor. We called him but it was too late." At five that evening, Apollinaire breathed his last. When Picasso learned of it, he continued the self-portrait he was in the midst of drawing (a very Picassoesque tribute), and shifted the publicity work to Cocteau who, in turn, shifted it to Salmon, one of Apollinaire's oldest friends. At midnight Cocteau wrote the following:

My dear André,

Poor Apollinaire is dead—Picasso is too sad to write—He has asked me to do it and to take care of obituaries. That's not my line. Would you be so good as to assume the obligation? Apollinaire didn't see himself die—my doctor had hopes of saving him, but both his lungs were infected—It's a great sorrow. By a miracle of energy he held out until five.

His face was serene and quite young.

Cocteau had spent part of the evening in Apollinaire's room, memorizing every feature of his dead face: "His little room was full of shadow and shades: those of his wife, of his mother, of us, of others who were shuffling about or meditating. . . . His dead face illuminated the linen encircling it. When he was alive, his obesity wasn't obese. So his stilled breath didn't seem still. It was as if he were moving amidst very delicate things, on soil mined with some unnamably precious explosive. Singular appearance, almost subaqueous."

Cocteau also left a deathbed portrait of Proust. He seems to have hovered over more fresh cadavers, attended more wakes, walked in more funeral processions than any of his contemporaries. Not that he was a ghoul, for he also seized every opportunity to be a witness at weddings (Picasso's, Gleizes', Valentine Gross's, Georges Auric's). Partially this reflected a love of ritual. Partially it reflected his desire to associate himself, for the record, with great men at capital moments in their lives. Sitting vigil over a corpse sometimes betokens a greater intimacy than existed in life. Indeed it was Breton's contention that Apollinaire had no use for Cocteau, whom he ridiculed as "*Fapoite Paponnat*" (Falsepoet Paponnat) in *Le Poète Assassiné*.

If Cocteau used *Parade* as cubist credentials to enter otherwise closed circles, *Le Cap de Bonne Espérance*, a book-length series of poems published in 1919 by the Éditions de la Sirène, served the same purpose. Obviously influenced by Apollinaire's *Calligrammes*, it reads like an accumulation of poetic telegrams delivered to the author from the far reaches of his self (at the Front or in the cockpit of Garros' airplane). It is a kind of free associative flight in which words are adroitly gambled onto the pages so that irregular spaces appear between them and syllables come undone as if to give the impression that the poems have a silent paradigm:

> I elaborate
> In the prairies of interior
> silence
>
> the work of the mission
> the poem of the work
> the strophe of the poem
> the grouping within the strophe
> the words of the grouping
> the letters of the words
> and   the least
> curlicue of each letter

Images, on the verge of freewheeling, are held in place by a system of tensions: between language and silence, gravity and weightlessness, dreams and a kind of hyperlucidity which Cocteau com-

pares to the uncanny surefootedness of a tightrope walker. But the
fundamental tension lies between Cocteau and himself. This appears
to be the significance of the "angel," here portrayed as an aviator,
as Cocteau's liberated double flying through a middle-distance between life and death. The angel is Garros, Cocteau's inamorato. It is
also, however, a Self exonerated from weight and complete, a Cocteau endowed with eyes to perceive his existence full round from a
celestial remove. Thus the pivotal event of *Le Cap* is Jacob's struggle with the angel, but where in the Bible Jacob emerges a whole
man distinct from his twin and changes his name from Jacob
(meaning follower) to Israel (meaning prince), Cocteau attaches a
reverse significance to the struggle. "I have difficulty being a man,"
he writes. His angelicism amounts to the fantasies of a paralytic, to
the free flight obsessing a prisoner. *Le Cap* is a form enveloping a
hollow, a telegraphic epic alluding to the *Inconnu*, but the Unknown turns out to be Cocteau himself. The poet gallivants all over
creation in search of his absence, leaving behind an iridescent wake
of words that point glamorously but never signify. All this would
seem to predicate a God; for lack of one, the poem has its locus in
vacancy:

> Listen to me behind silence
> Listen to me above silence
>
> My bone jars against
> the frame of alpha
> and of omega
>
> I am sliding
> along the intervals
> incalculable
>   oiled
> down sonorous slopes
>
> . . . . .
>
> I am waiting   in ambush
>   a hunter of angels
>
> . . . . .
>
> I am teasing eternity.

Throughout the poem Cocteau leaves such clues as this to his nagging dream: seeing without being seen, which may have been his translation of being or not being. He coveted the immaculate existence, the Oneness, the lyric self-coincidence of an Image. Isn't this what he implies by "teasing eternity"? He will imply it again, more directly, in a novella published some years later, *The White Book*, in which two men stand on either side of a sheet of trick glass transparent for one viewer and mirroring for the other. As the man standing on the mirror side presses his lips against his own image, the narrator, standing on the transparent side, kisses him. In *Orphée*, the angel Heurtebise will be a vendor of glass, as if to signify that one achieves the privileges of invisibility, that one gets a tragic warranty of selfhood only beyond the glass, beyond life.

Telegrams should be brief. *Le Cap* goes on for a hundred pages, utterly mistaking its own prosodic assumptions. It falls on either side of itself, at once long-winded and short of breath. Cocteau would need a few more years to find himself. By 1923 he was writing what he wrote very well indeed, *concetti* more appropriate to his gifts.

Cocteau's society friends could not make head or tail of his poem, which pleased him immensely. At last he had declassed himself and written something genuinely hermetic. "*Tout Paris* is working on the Cape" he wrote to Gautier-Vignal. "Madame de Chevigné is taking Cape lessons from Frédéric." [5] Not trusting the poem to fend for itself, and suspecting conspiracies of silence afoot, Cocteau arranged readings throughout Paris; he met with disaster in various forms, including silence. At Étienne de Beaumont's mansion, "Jean," according to one of his auditors, "began to declaim, not like an actor coming to the forestage, but like an aviator taking wing. He lurched forward, hurled his voice heavenward, and let it soar. He skimmed the ground, his words piling on top of one another and shattering, then soaring anew. He put all his verve, talent, fire, passion into this lyric declamation which transported him beyond himself and made him seem a kind of prophet uttering

5. Frédéric de Madrazo—a society painter with whom Cocteau had written the scenario of *The Blue God* eight years before.

sibylline words. But, however clearly he spoke, we could barely follow him, more aware as we were of his fervor than of his literary creation. With the initial cry, 'Peninsula of altitude,' we lost him, and when he came back to earth, exhausted, we remained silent."

Étienne de Beaumont, his mind turning frantically to formulate some egregious compliment before the silence should prolong itself any further, came up, typically enough, with a brutal insult instead. "My little Jean," he cried rushing to embrace him, "you are Voltaire." Cocteau, having thus inspired a comparison from which *Le Cap* was intended to liberate him, burst into tears. This augured ill. At Valentine Gross's flat his reading was attended by none other than André Breton whose basilisk stare so unhinged Cocteau he complained of feeling faint half-way through his performance. But the classical imbroglio occurred at Adrienne Monnier's book store, in February, 1919.

Cocteau had used all his ingenuity to foist *Le Cap* upon the proprietress of *Aux Amis des Livres*. She was not fond of him for the same reason that other people found him intolerable. "Personally," she wrote, "he gives me a migraine." His voice, nasal and resonantly metallic, rapping away without reprieve, found her deaf to its boyish charm. "He was such a spoiled child," she continues, and prosecutes him as an adult poet: "He is unquestionably a poet, more in prose than in verse as I see it. He has a style all his own, with a falsely sensuous virginity, whereas in verse his artifices, reinforced by those inherent in verse, are carried to a mulish extreme. . . . At the time of *Le Cap*, he had just discovered modern poetry. . . . He is never the first to leap over the barricades, but he is always the one to plant the flag."

Inviting him to read his poetry in her back room never occurred to Adrienne Monnier. When *Le Cap* appeared, various society matrons telephoned her, voicing their hopes that she would prevail upon Paul Valéry to give Cocteau's book a gentle blurb. In fact, their overtures hardened her resolve to avoid Cocteau, until he cornered her one Sunday afternoon following a concert of Satie's music at Léonce Rosenberg's gallery. "Gide," he announced, "would like me to read *Le Cap* at Rue de l'Odéon." That name proved to be the open-sesame, for Gide's merest wish had the

power of fiat in Adrienne Monnier's mind. As soon as she acquiesced, Cocteau reported to Gide: "Adrienne Monnier would very
much like me to read *Le Cap* at Rue de l'Odéon in your presence. You'll come, won't you?" Taken in by this simple stratagem,
she avenged herself by refusing to supply cakes and port. Cocteau
therefore ordered the mushiest confection that ever oozed from
Rebattet's brain, something called a "bridge," which, for lack of
silverware at the bookstore, left evidence of itself all over the thirty
guests.

Respecting Cocteau's wishes, Adrienne Monnier had snubbed the
Right Bank—all but three ladies devoted to her establishment—while
inviting every young person of her acquaintance. But the young,
excepting Breton and Soupault who, "aglow with hostility," followed Cocteau like omens of catastrophe, turned out to be a group
of girls. His reading fell on deaf ears. Only the society ladies, like
three Fates, acclaimed him a genius. Thus, even in this sanctum
sanctorum of serious literature, Cocteau could not escape the fatuity and wrongheaded admiration of his native claque.

Fearful of finding himself outflanked on the left, Cocteau attempted the impossible, to crash the pages of *Littérature*. What is
more, he nearly succeeded, using a maneuver not unlike the one
that duped Adrienne Monnier. If Gide was Adrienne Monnier's
weak spot, Louis Aragon was Breton's. Cocteau and Aragon had
much in common: products of the Right Bank, both of them theatrical, dandyesque, talking as though their lives depended on it,
nurtured on the decadent romanticism of Wilde and Barrès, bent
on seducing the world, waylaid by self-spite or self-proof into
underground careerism. The two, unbeknownst to Breton, corresponded regularly in 1919 when Aragon was stationed on the
Rhine. Finally Cocteau prevailed upon Breton to accept *Le Coq et
l'Arlequin* for publication in the first issue of *Littérature*. His name
does appear in the table of contents, but he advanced no further. At
the last moment his text was scratched at Erik Satie's behest.

In March, 1918, when Adrienne Monnier arranged a preview of
Socrate at Rue de l'Odéon, it was Cocteau who delivered the introductory remarks, but several months later a pall settled over his
friendship with Satie, as we have already seen in that letter

of grievance sent to Gautier-Vignal from Grasse: "Incredible silence on the part of Auric and Satie who acknowledge neither the texts I've sent them, nor my letters, nor my telegrams. I'm astonished by their complete indifference. If you see them tell them as much. Feeling better except for fits of weariness and stomach trouble." No single incident caused Satie's estrangement. He was appalled by Cocteau's tentacular intimacy. It seemed to him that the writer had been riding his coat tails, and *Le Coq et l'Arlequin* confirmed his dark suspicions. Hence the veto in *Littérature*.

Satie's affection for Mme. Cocteau was not impaired, however. He wrote her on December 31, 1919: "Dear Madame, Happy New Year, very happy! Long live the NEW YEAR! The Old One wasn't very droll, was it? The less said about it the better: it was vile beyond words. What will become of it? . . . Where are the old years? In the Past? Really? . . . It's beyond belief! Good day, dear Madame; accept my sincere wishes. Your ever respectful Erik Satie." Mme. Cocteau, bringing to bear her dry wit, her hospitality, and her calm, helped Jean mend his ragged relations more than once. The pall lifted in 1920 long enough for Satie and Cocteau to collaborate on a short ballet, *La Belle Excentrique*, danced by Caryathis. The following year it settled in once more.

When Aragon returned to Paris late in 1919, Breton overruled Louis's friendship with Cocteau. Instead of protesting, Aragon placed his wit at Breton's disposal and ridiculed Cocteau as "Miracle" in *Anicet*, a dada novella-scenario-allegory published in 1920. It would take sixteen years and Aragon's excommunication from the surrealist movement before wounds healed. They were not only deep but wide, for Breton never stopped at plunging the knife: he insisted on turning it. Cocteau found himself barrred from *Littérature;* lest he construe this as a general verdict against his circle, Breton made a point of publishing Auric, Milhaud, Paul Morand, and, worst of all, Raymond Radiguet, Cocteau's young protégé.

Perhaps Cocteau invited the lashes liberally administered him throughout his life, but the whipping boy is no more pathetic than the whipper. Cocteau was so open, so compulsive in his self-promotion and self-abasement as to have a kind of innocence; that much cannot be granted the people who abused him. To be sure, his "fidelity," warmth, and expenditure of self were never so free of some self-seeking purpose that people could not sense the corruption in those qualities, yet all too often they emerged more compromised than he for having answered him with the one or two extra blows that turn justice into brutality. Nothing illustrates this better than Cocteau's courtship of the dada diarchs, Francis Picabia and Tristan Tzara.

Picabia was fully ten years older than Cocteau. His father, a wealthy industrialist, descended from Spanish nobility transplanted in Cuba and held some vague diplomatic post in the Cuban embassy. Francis, though born and raised in Paris, showed evidence of his Latin lineage very early. At eighteen he eloped to Switzerland with a woman some eight years his senior and the wife of a newspaper director. His father, though secretly proud of him, cut off his allowance, and the couple, holding out in Lausanne till winter approached, finally had to return to Paris. This represented the first major conquest in a life that rivaled Casanova's. Picabia could not deny himself any possibility, and the range of possibilities increased in ratio to his fortune. "I need to live sprawled on perfumed rice powder," he wrote some years later to his friend Pierre de Massot, "to eat the pulp of fruit, and to see buttocks corseted in sable and mink. The women I behold playing baccarat have eyes and nipples encircled with fatigue and pleasure. I like things that wear and wear out quickly."

It was this viewpoint that decided the course of Picabia's painting career. Art, like life, existed for him only at its extremes, where it verges on suicide. What distinguished Picabia, more than his average gift as a painter, was his adventurism, his singular aptitude for guessing the next form that the subjective must take in art. At twenty-nine, a prosperous young painter influenced by Sisley and Pissarro, he suddenly severed relations with his dealer, Danthon, who was content that he should turn out one neo-impressionist canvas after another. The next five or six years saw him slide along a nonfigurative continuum which started with cubism, evolved into geometrical abstractions akin to Kandinsky's, and ended with mechanomorphic designs mysteriously related to their titles, such as the internal combustion engine he called *Portrait of Marie Laurencin.*

Picabia's meeting in 1910 with Marcel Duchamp proved to be a paramount event for both artists. Temperamentally foils, Picabia explosive, Duchamp a pursed and exacting Norman, they had one overriding feature in common: humor. In 1911 and 1912 they saw one another every Sunday at the home of Duchamp's brother Jacques Villon in Puteaux, where the *Section d'Or* group—including Gleizes, Metzinger, Roger de la Fresnaye, and Fernand Léger—gathered; but the two were as far removed, artistically, from that group as the *esprit de finesse* from the *esprit de géométrie*. Pascal's categories apply perfectly. Gleizes and Metzinger were finicky to a fault, delighting in theory perhaps more than in painting. Duchamp and Picabia vaulted gracefully to their artistic deaths in two great arcs. "In my work," wrote Picabia for Alfred Stieglitz' review *291*, "the title is the subjective expression, the painting is the object."

Picabia came into his own during the war. To avoid action at the Front he persuaded General de Boisson, a friend of his father's, to make him his chauffeur, but even this seemed too much like work. In 1915 he was sent abroad on behalf of the Quartermaster to purchase a cargo of molasses from Cuba. The boat docked in New York, and Picabia went no further. In addition to such war-time expatriates as Gleizes, Duchamp, and Edgard Varèse, Picabia knew a number of Americans in New York including a wealthy collector named Walter Arensberg and Alfred Stieglitz, whose "Photo-Secession Gallery" at 291 Fifth Avenue exhibited works decidedly beyond the fringe. Furnishing a remarkable example of simultaneous evolution, the Stieglitz-Arensberg circle in New York and the dadaists in Zurich were, during the same year, cracking the same jokes, destroying the same icons, and exhibiting the same "readymades." Picabia produced scores of mechanical drawings, but when the effects of alcohol and opium made it impossible for him to handle his brushes, he turned to poetry. Meanwhile a board of French military examiners sitting in New York discharged him (honorably) from the army.

To restore his health, Picabia moved to Barcelona, where he and still another group of like-minded expatriates—Arthur Cravan, Marie Laurencin, and her husband, Otto von Watgen—founded a successor to Stieglitz's magazine *291: 391*. But scarcely eight months later he reembarked for New York and one year after that, in February, 1918, committed himself to a psychiatric clinic in Switzerland. Incapable of painting, he published, at his own expense, a second book of verse, *Poems and Sketches of the Daughter Born Motherless*, which, as soon as it came to Tzara's attention, inspired a correspondence. Evidently Picabia found hysteria with Tzara more to his liking than serenity within a clinic. In February, 1919, he moved to Paris and urged Tzara to join him there:

> Jean Cocteau is in everybody's bad graces. Erik Satie declares that he's an idiot and others call him a brat; anyway you see what a delightful life can be led here—For me they're a bunch of cooks doing up their dishes with Boulevard des Italiens sauce—Juliette Roche is also in Paris, she wants to return as quickly as possible to America, finding life in Paris unliveable—Nevertheless you must come as soon as you can.

Picabia had no patience with literary cliques. If the pretentiousness of *Tout Paris* sickened him, so did the ethic of poverty, the conscientious drabness prevalent among serious literati. What was a fortune good for if not to indulge his fantasies? Like Derain, Picabia had a passion for sports cars, and bought a new one almost every year. The car he purchased in 1913 led to an adventure characteristic of Picabia's mode of life.

One day Picabia met Apollinaire at the Bar de la Paix an hour before the latter was to deliver a lecture to some art club. They decided to take a brief spin through the Bois de Boulogne in Picabia's new automobile. This proved so delightful that Picabia suggested they continue driving as far as Boulogne-sur-Mer some one hundred and fifty miles distant for a fish dinner. Fish reminded them of the English Channel, so they boarded a steamer for Folkestone and spent the next week on a beach.

Picabia was in fact the adventurer that Breton and Tzara dreamed of being. He had a genius for manic gestures, for immersing himself in his own serial novel, each installment of which was a self-contained de-cerebralized Happening. Thus, his wife, Gabrielle Buffet-Picabia, gave birth to one of his children in the fall of 1919, and his mistress, Germaine Everling, gave birth to another in early January; the same midwife presided at both events. "Picabia, who is the most cerebral man I know," wrote his friend, Pierre de Massot, "lives in a state of continual paradox."

A virtuoso conversationalist, Picabia would hold forth in Germaine Everling's sumptuous salon, pontificating on art and telling anecdotes while Tzara sat opposite him, his eyes glazed, in a catatonic stupor from which nothing could awaken him more swiftly than the word dada. Between them a wide variety of people might be present, for Picabia welcomed his society friends and his co-dadaists alike. If Marthe Chenal, the opera singer, sought his company so did Erik Satie. Collaborating with Breton did not prevent Picabia from seeing Cocteau, whom he accepted on ambiguous terms. "Cocteau enters, refined, delicate, fragile, a showy silk cravat knotted about his neck, and straightaway seduces everyone present," wrote de Massot. "Standing, it's as though he were performing a dance. With incomparable wit and verve, he mimics by turn Marinetti, Breton, Tzara, Madame Lara, Crommelynck, Picabia, Madame Rachilde, himself, etc., and makes everyone smile, even laugh. Who could describe the seduced smile Picabia wears as he listens to Cocteau!"

It was a smile such as kings award their jesters. Cocteau was there to amuse him, and to be abused in turn. Picabia brought out all of Cocteau's schoolboy prurience. Cocteau seems to have considered the painter a red-hot daddy who simply would not tolerate a namby-pamby son. Once, for example, he arrived at Everling's rather too early for aperitifs. Picabia continued drawing while Cocteau flitted about the salon. Suddenly the telephone rang. Cocteau answered it. An arch voice on the other end asked for Picabia. "Cocteau's face," Everling recalls, "lit up with mischief and, mimicking with extraordinary truth the voice of an old man, he said: 'My grandson is not at home, sir. . . . He's gone out in his automobile.' When the party on the other end inquired as to when he would return, Cocteau continued: 'My grandson did write down the hour of his return on a piece of paper. . . . Unfortunately I

am very old, I don't see very clearly. . . . In fact I can see only
through my asshole, and I've kept my pants on.' " Picabia learned
subsequently that his caller had been the representative of some
foreign museum anxious to buy one of his works. This was not an
isolated incident. When Picabia and Everling vacationed in the
Midi, Cocteau periodically sent them tidings embellished with his
own masterfully drawn phallic cartoons. One, called "The Philandering Fireman," shows a woman screaming from a second story
window while a fireman below directs a stream of water into her
mouth from his phallic hydrant.

If Cocteau had some thoughts of joining the dada movement,
Picabia and Tzara seemed more amenable to his ambitions than
Breton and company. While the latter jealously guarded their virginity at the Café Certâ in Montmartre, the former frequently
mixed with Cocteau's smart set at the Gaya and, somewhat later, at
Le Boeuf sur le Toit. Tzara, when down and out, was not averse to
accepting a gold cigarette holder from Cocteau, yet Cocteau soon
discovered that the true dadaist would, on principle, always bite the
hand that fed him. Snubbed by every major avant-garde review,
Cocteau at last prevailed upon Picabia, or so he thought, to publish
three poems in his *391*. When the proofs arrived, he corrected them
in the presence of the editors, treating them both to dinner afterward
at Prunier's. As soon as he left, Tzara and Picabia tore up the
poems. In March or April, 1920, Cocteau wrote Picabia an official
valedictory:

My dear Francis,
    You know my candor and the scruples constantly besetting me.
You also know how precious I consider your friendship. NO ONE CAN
WRITE IN ANY STYLE AT WILL. What you do expresses you, amuses
me, interests me. What Tzara does often moves me profoundly. I can
even say that Tzara, though his work lies at the antipode of my own,
is the only poet who moves me that way. Ribemont is pure, I am
sure of it. But Dada, Dadaism makes me unbearably uncomfortable.
    I used to think that they (Dada and Dadaism) might do some good
by airing the cubist cell—but the meeting you held the other evening
was horrible, sad, timid, anything but audacious or inventive. Picabia
creates, wants to create a "drama," a "predicament," a "no," a blas-

phemy, an atmosphere of refurbished romanticism. Tzara disorganizes. I, a Parisian, find myself confronted with the first successful attempt at foreign propaganda. That's your right, and you have seen with what alacrity I have supported your attempt, actively in fact, out of repugnance for misguided patriotism.

Now I have a physical obligation to act (never against you, or against Tzara, or against the others—friendship or the memory of one being sacred in my eyes) against Dada, the Dada spirit which, in the hands of several collegians, has become as outmoded, as boring as Jarry, Duparc, Sacha Guitry, Bruant, Madame Lara, Ibsen.

Return my three poems for *391* and don't see me again if this letter disgusts you. I have written it because I hold you in such high esteem and remain, as ever, your friend.

Poor Cocteau was given cause to rue that modest postscript, for Picabia lost no time publishing it in his other magazine, *Cannibale*, and the young wooly-woolies of *Littérature* turned it to good account: "Jean Cocteau has made it known that he stands at the extreme right," they smirked. "That's all very well, but at the extreme right of what? Music perhaps?"

The postscript has an epilogue. After several years had undone old alliances and created new ones, Picabia sponsored a New Year's Eve party in the home of Marthe Chenal. No dadaists were present, as Picabia had severed relations with the movement some months before. The guests included Léonce Rosenberg, Satie, Jean Hugo, Picasso, Ambroise Vollard, Brancusi, Poulenc, Auric, Radiguet, and Cocteau. The statuesque Chenal, dressed in white and standing at the head of a marble staircase, welcomed them as they arrived. Picabia stood beside her, for the hostess knew few of her guests by name. He seized the opportunity to introduce Auric as Cocteau, and Cocteau as Auric, sensing that the opera singer, who disliked modern music, would infallibly put her foot in her mouth. She did, complimenting Cocteau (Auric) on his ballet *The Newlyweds of the Eiffel Tower* but lamenting that the score—to which all Six contributed—did its text a profound injustice. As the New Year approached, she gave full reign to her daffiness. Picabia, a pill addict, had named the ball "*Réveillon Cacodylate*" in honor of a patent medicine reputed for its regenerating powers. Chenal, with

Picabia to her right and Cocteau to her left, delivered a speech which stands as one of the purest examples of natural dada:

> The word "cacodylate" has not been used today to symbolize the strength you will derive this evening, I hope, from contact with one another. In each of your hearts you desire a change for 1922, a purely external change naturally, for the sun is external, the moon external, and the stars of our brain are visible only to ourselves. All of you here are stars of the first magnitude, although from different heavens; the heaven of chance, the heaven of art nouveau, the Parisian heaven and the conservative heaven. To my right I have Francis Picabia who represents the extreme left. When asked to what he stands extremely left of, he answers that he has no idea! To my left here is Jean Cocteau, the extreme right of the left. And myself, between the two, I am neither right nor left, but I'm happy to have united in this little villa a group of militant individualities who will give the world and France of 1922 the vitality and youth we desire for it.

In 1922 the dada movement utterly collapsed.

When the *NRF* resumed publishing its monthly review in June, 1919, the editorial board made it clear that its attitude toward Cocteau had not altered since Ghéon's review of *The Dance of Sophocles* seven years before. Following his hyenalike instincts, Gide prepared to devour a victim already disabled by other predators. Cocteau's cadaver served several purposes. It would relaunch the *NRF* on a clamorous note. It would seal Gide's newly formed friendship with Breton.[6] Above all, it would rejuvenate Gide, ever fearful, like Cocteau himself, of growing older than another generation. Moreover, there was a personal vendetta involved, for Gide suspected Cocteau of wanting to seduce Marc Allégret, his young protégé. Preliminary skirmishes took place in early May when Gide announced his intention of publishing an open letter to Cocteau.

The announcement was made by Jacques Rivière, editor-in-chief of the *NRF* (who visited Cocteau on Gide's behalf). "As I

6. In 1919 Breton wrote, rather naïvely, to Tzara: "You have no idea how alert André Gide is. I have seen him prodigiously interested in modern experiments in literature and painting and if you could only hear him talk about Negroes!" Gide secured Breton a small editorial position with *NRF;* he held it for barely a year.

told you," Rivière wrote, "I plan to see Cocteau on Thursday. I shall strive to make him listen to reason and explain to him the impression your letter makes on a neutral (I shall present myself, somewhat hypocritically alas, as such, since I must)." Cocteau, incensed, asked to read the letter beforehand. Gide, taking cover behind his editorial board, refused, whereupon Cocteau, taking cover behind illness, asked for the right of rejoinder. "My dear Gide," he wrote on May 6, "it was for you to choose between the public and me—You made your choice, but since my mother is ill, I cannot attach as much importance to your 'controversy' as it deserves. All I ask is space in which to reply." Gide, with the bogus sincerity of a parent persuaded that the whipping he is about to administer will hurt him more than his child, answered the same day that he had no choice. "The only way I can give friendship is sincerely." On June 1, his letter appeared. Its pretext was Cocteau's pamphlet, *The Cock and the Harlequin:*

My dear Cocteau,
    I have already told you what pleasure I derived reading *The Cape of Good Hope*, what still livelier pleasure I derived hearing you read it, for you read with enormous talent.
    I awaited *The Cock and the Harlequin*, with great impatience mixed, I must confess, with apprehension. I suspected that I was going to find the key, not to your talent, because that is part and parcel of "the man himself," but to your esthetic, and an explanation of that in you which disconcerts me precisely because I feel that it is concerted. Not that I do not recognize and have for a long time the astuteness of your maxims, but some of them, I fear, have less to do with you than with the person you would like others to believe you are. . . . And I am not contending that your aphorisms are insincere, far from it; but I *am* contending that, with all the sincerity in the world, you deceive yourself about yourself.
    I believe, for example, that you have nothing to gain by seeking to paint with few colors. Your most agreeable lines are, on the contrary, those in which you abandon yourself to the charming demon of analogies, which seems to me the essence of your poetic gift.
    Likewise, when you say that an artist mustn't "skip steps," what do you mean by that, and what else have you been doing all your

life? I've often said it to you personally: each time I speak with you I think of the dialogue between the bear and the squirrel. When I'm shuffling along you bound ahead. I'm certainly not reprimanding you for bounding, but for wanting to persuade us and yourself that you are a logician. . . .

Lastly, I must confess the discomfort I experienced reading your "defense" of *Parade*. As a rule it doesn't seem to me fitting or politic of an artist to explain his work; first, because he thereby limits it, and when a work is profoundly sincere it grows larger than the meaning its author gives it; secondly, I hold that the best explanation of a work must be its sequel. In the case of *Parade* my discomfort is increased because the reader of your explanations has no way of referring to the play, so the most courteous thing to do would be to acquit him by default.

But if the public and the critics gave *Parade* the kind of reception you are protesting against, I would need better proof before ascribing the blame to their fatuity; your commentaries justify your play less than your audience's incomprehension. Could you reasonably hope that the spectators would understand that the *true spectacle* was not at all the one you were presenting? For if mystics would share your opinion about the apparent world and about the whole human comedy, a work of art on the other hand has no other *raison d'être*, no other goal than to parade the secret reality. . . .

But my discomfort only makes the pleasure I have gotten from your little book the keener, and since as you say "the worst fate a book can receive is not being reproached for anything" I am sure you will accept these few observations in the amicable spirit with which they are written.

Cocteau answered Gide's didactic spanking with libelous squawks, which Gide, knowing that Rivière would veto him, offered to publish in the *NRF*. On June 11, after Cocteau had submitted his rejoinder, Rivière wrote to Gide: "Let's be sincere [an obsessive word in the Protestant-ridden *NRF* circle]: both of us were intimidated by Monsieur's colossal moxy—it is moxy that enables him to succeed everywhere. But, reflecting more closely on the matter, we must confess that nothing authorizes him to answer your measured, deliberate letter by this volley of perfidies having

no psychological point." Accordingly, Cocteau was invited to ex-
purgate all personal references from his reply. Instead of doing so
he threatened to sue. It never developed into a legal suit, but Cocteau consoled himself by publishing his piece in *Les Écrits Nouveaux*. The following is the nub of that reply in its original version,
including (in brackets) a paragraph he finally decided to cross out:

. . . I wonder if your silhouette doesn't hide a throng of others, if
the *NRF* hasn't at last uttered the "Let's go, Gentlemen" of a fray
that has been years in the making and if your letters won't confer
upon me the honor of being spokesman for a whole clan. . . . You
have, Gide, a system of mysteries, silences, alibis, and imbroglios. It's
my turn, now that I think of it, to admit feeling like a flat-footed
bear striving to follow, in the tree, your squirrel-like games of hide-
and-seek. [Where is Gide? Is he in the country? in Paris? A letter
arrives from Cuverville . . . but X has seen him slinking through
Auteuil beneath a wall-colored cape. Gide cultivates the esthetic of
unsuccess, the edition limited to four copies. He despises official
rewards . . . yet he submits his novels to the *Revue des Deux
Mondes* and dedicates a preface to Bourget.] Does Gide like Z? Does
he admire Y? When one questions him he sniffs, he tilts his body, he
shrugs his shoulders. His knee says Yes, his elbow No—and wasn't I
the first, Gide, to ascribe this ambiguous attitude to your sensibility?
The latter obliges you not to commit your fragile preferences to the
grindstone of discussions. . . .

You even purchased a canvas of Braque's, and when I asked you
what it represented—if it wasn't a bunch of grapes—you impatiently
answered that you didn't know and didn't care. That's it in a nut-
shell. If Braque hadn't begun by painting a bunch of grapes which he
then disfigured according to his fancy, you wouldn't find this canvas
the less pleasurable. Apelles' grape was an "eye decoy for birds,"
Braque's is a mind decoy for men, not a bit of decoration. What
attracts you is a certain decor, a certain racket, a certain Jazz-
bandism or Jazz-bandifism—all of which are the froth of the modern
movement.

In every revolution there is a screeching period of savagery, a
"terror" when the exotic influence presents itself in the shape of
human sacrifices, bonfires, gaud. . . . A need to react against such
excess dictates the new order. It is this new order which matters. . . .

And then, leaving the door to some future reconciliation slightly ajar, Cocteau concluded with a compliment whose polemical effect was to give still sharper edge to his libel:

> Because, when still a child, I was reproached for skipping steps, I set about ascending an absurd flight of stairs—you are one of several who made me understand that there was another flight. Bounding from one flight to another, at the risk of breaking one's neck, is not what I call skipping steps. . . . Now, allow me—since you would dissuade me from logic while vouchsafing me some lyricism—to profess unreserved love for your *Paludes*.

The toll this quarrel took on Cocteau's nerves Gide recognized a month later when they chanced to meet in public. Shaken by the sight of Cocteau's drawn, melancholy face, he exonerated himself by telling his victim of his remorse. Cocteau, unable to hold a grudge, instantly forgave him. But they ceased corresponding for some two years, and Gide's June campaign had done Cocteau permanent injury. By 1920 the little review *Le Petit Bleu*, rehearsing the spirit of Gide's letter, dismissed Cocteau as a plagiarist.[7] That label stuck.

The entire quarrel may also be viewed in the light of a letter Proust wrote to Cocteau after the reading *The Cock and the Harlequin*, which he admired, and admired for the very quality Gide abhorred: Cocteau's gift of concision. What drew Proust to Cocteau drew Gide to Dostoevski, for the writer who is condemned, out of creative asphyxia, out of some ingrained *goût de perfection*, or by virtue of a French classical education to produce aphoristic statements is often found worshiping the prolific artist capable of apprehending, of describing process. And vice versa. Gide was jealous of Cocteau, to be sure, but he also saw in him his own style caricatured. Proust did not have to make any such effort of disassociation; he wrote in February, 1919:

> My dear Jean,
>   I have read, I have reread *The Cock and the Harlequin*, with rapt wonder. There is not a thought in it which is not profound, not an expression which is not incredibly felicitous. I can hear you

7. Gide laid claim to some of the unacknowledged aphorisms in *The Cock*.

speaking when you write: "The source nearly always disapproves of the river's course." . . . I envy you your captivating formulae. The story you tell about the history of *Parade* interests me more than I can say! Your description of Nijinsky's exit is astonishing. There are contradictions between some of your thoughts (for example, how can you say down with Wagner and Saint-Saëns in the bargain without defending Strauss against Puccini lovers?) but that delights me for I like the different faces of things. I'm always contradicting myself . . .

Alas, Cocteau's tantrums, especially his verbal assaults on Jacques Rivière of the *NRF*, ultimately estranged Proust as well. In August, 1922, three months before Proust's death, Rivière wrote to him: "I am profoundly grateful to you for the vivacity with which you have taken my side against Cocteau. You may be sure, dear Marcel, that if I have often been lukewarm toward his courteous advances, I know that the latter are always dictated by the hope or expectation of some public compliment."

It must not be imagined that the larger public had the least inkling of Cocteau's disgrace. On the contrary, it considered him the avant-garde incarnate and Cocteau did nothing to discourage that notion. Even as he was exchanging blows with Gide and smarting from Breton's latest rebuff, he serenely quoted the former and enthusiastically back-slapped the latter in a series of articles for the newspaper *Paris-Midi*.[8] The title of that series is particularly revealing, *Carte Blanche:* the very title, as Cocteau informed his readers, that Reverdy first proposed for the review eventually named *Littérature*. Scavenging is also a form of intimacy. Cocteau, in admitting his sources, thus suggested that he was in deep connivance with the very people who despised him, that he spoke on their behalf as a kind of plenipotentiary delegate of the avant-garde. "Beneath this rubric" (i.e., *Carte Blanche*), he wrote, "I propose to keep my readers abreast of the new values. The public has no idea

8. Cocteau often did this, quoting luminaries who disliked him: a generous gesture but one intended to convey an idea of camaraderie. In 1923, when delivering a speech before the Collège de France, he quoted Jacques Rivière, whose feelings about Cocteau have already been made clear.

what lies between the Academy and the Boulevard. That void is responsible for grave divorces."

Every week for four and a half months, he played his latest number, delivered himself of immortal apothegms, called attention to the Salle Huyghens, gave profiles of each member of the Six, announced the publications of Éditions de la Sirène, congratulated *Littérature* on discovering a poem of Rimbaud's (*Les Mains de Jeanne-Marie*), covered the first 14th of July celebration since the Armistice and, all in all, embodied Young France. It was a breathless performance, like his conversation, omniscient talk-of-the-town which reinforced his reputation as a Fantômas of the liberal arts, ubiquitous and prophetic. He even scooped *Littérature* on Tzara's imminent arrival in Paris. "Tristan Tzara will come to Paris to publish two issues of the review *Dada*, which he directs in Switzerland and has caused scandals there. I find in it the exciting atmosphere of an intermission at the Casino de Paris where a cosmopolitan crowd jostles itself listening to the Jazz-Band. If one accepts the Jazz-Band, one must welcome a literature which the mind savors like a cocktail." [9] That Breton should hear of the Coming from Cocteau was almost enough to make him seek some other messiah. As it turned out, Tzara decided to remain in Zurich for another nine months.

Cocteau shadowed, and sometimes foreshadowed, the activities of his rivals. Did *Littérature* plan to publish for the first time some quatrains of Mallarmé? Cocteau announced that Éditions de la Sirène would bring out a whole book of them, illustrated by Raoul Dufy.[10] Cocteau sewed confusion between his group, the Six, and dada after their official rupture in April, 1920. A month later he started a broadsheet called *Le Coq*, whose format was the twin of Éluard's *Proverbes*, which first appeared the previous February: a single sheet folded twice and covered from edge to edge with manifestos in mixed type or with signed proverbs. The spirit underlying *Proverbes* and *Le Coq* was, however, only superficially

9. One well-known *bon mot* of the period was the following declension of cocktail: "*Un cocktail, des Cocteau.*"
10. Without permission from Mallarmé's literary executor, Doctor Bonniot, who promptly asked Gide for the name of a lawyer.

alike. Éluard, along with Jean Paulhan, viewed the word as "a thing in itself, a resistant matter to be reduced," not the mere hieroglyph of its conventional meaning; in proverbs they saw a triumphant example of the word-object, the concrete abstraction, the essence of poetry. *Le Coq* addressed itself chiefly to music, the Six reiterating *ad nauseam* their dislike of Wagner, of Debussy, of the "sublime." "I'd like to make money with my music," wrote Durey down one margin. And Auric called for a return to popular French art forms, declaring that jazz, which served to dissipate the vapors of impressionism, had outlived its purpose. Between the willful naïveté of a Cocteau or an Auric and Éluard's linguistic experiments lay a world, but the public did not make nice distinctions. It was all dada to them, and Cocteau turned their ignorance to good account just before the revival of *Parade*. "The horse in *Parade* will reappear on the stage of the Théâtre des Champs-Élysées," he wrote in the December 21, 1920, issue of *Comœdia*. "When we first put on *Parade*, Dadaism was unknown. We had never heard of it. Now, there can be no doubt that the public recognizes Dada in our inoffensive horse. I like my friends Picabia and Tzara, to be sure. When they need it, I lend them a hand, but I am not a dadaist, which is undoubtedly the best way of being one." [11] His ambiguous protestations only served to pack the house, as the mere mention of dada sufficed to attract smart ladies from the Right Bank who loved the elementary tit-for-tat of being insulted by the demonstrators and answering them with eggs.

Was it sheer coincidence that Cocteau decided to release, in 1921, the year dada staged a mock trial of Maurice Barrès, a snide text

---

11. By "lending a hand" Cocteau meant an exhibition of Picabia's paintings December 9 at the Povolozsky gallery on Rue Bonaparte. Staging a parody of the usual *vernissage*, Picabia invited not only his fellow dadaists, but the lunatic fringe of *Tout Paris:* the Princess Marie Murat, Étienne de Beaumont, the Baroness Deslandes, and Mme. de la Hire (at whose estate the dada group hypnotized itself *en masse* one night, Crevel nearly persuading six sleepwalkers to hang themselves from a coat rack). Also in attendance were Satie, Picasso, Valentine and Jean Hugo, the minister of Cuba, and Raymond Duncan. Tzara declaimed sixteen dada "songs." Between songs Cocteau, wearing a stovepipe hat, "performed" various tunes with drums, cymbals, castanets, and an automobile horn while Auric and Poulenc accompanied him on the piano. Breton found the miscegenation of Tzara and Cocteau's jazz-band intolerable. Several months after this event, Picabia, afraid that Breton was turning dada into a metaphysical discipline, divorced himself from the movement.

called *Visits to Maurice Barrès* which he had written some years
before? Cocteau and dada appeared to share the same peeves, and
they both had a liking for cynical antics.[12] Were they not therefore identical? A reporter present at Marinetti's lecture on his latest
art form, tactilism, noted that Cocteau was seated "among other
Dadaists." Evidently the reporter had not attended a dada demonstration at Salle Gaveau in May, 1920, when Soupault savagely
knifed a balloon bearing the name Jean Cocteau. Any possible
misunderstanding was, however, dispelled the night of June 18,
1921, at the Théâtre des Champs-Élysées, where a new ballet
company, Rolf de Maré's Ballets Suédois, performed Cocteau's
Newlyweds of the Eiffel Tower.

There was no question of Diaghilev's staging it, for he and Cocteau did not see eye to eye. Furthermore, Misia's musical opinion
carried more weight than ever with the impresario, and she made
no secret of her dislike for the Six. Thus, Rolf de Maré— a Swedish
millionaire passionately fond of ballet and of Jean Borlin, his star
dancer—arrived at an opportune moment. He overruled Ingel-
brecht, his conductor, who shared Misia's feelings, and agreed to
produce the *Newlyweds*, a group effort for which all six of the Six
composed something.

Cocteau unloaded his bag of tricks. The *Newlyweds* was to represent a cross between Greek tragedy and vaudeville, the dancers
wearing grotesque masks and two "recorded" voices fulfilling the
role of choir. With admirable economy, Cocteau thus salvaged the
phonograph from *David* and the idea of a liturgical text, explaining
the dances, which Diaghilev had jettisoned from *Parade*. He placed
this all-purpose apparatus at the service of a fantasy in some ways
the reverse of *Parade*. Had Gide's criticism hit home? Cocteau presented a dream inherent in its surface: the scenario, far from string-
ing together private associations, takes off on a series of clichés.
Had he been influenced by Jean Paulhan's precepts? In the first
issue of *Proverbes*, Paulhan wrote: "Words wear out by virtue
of being used, and once they've reached common speech they no

12. Such as the farce he and Radiguet staged in 1921, *Le Gendarme Incompris*,
which the critics treated as a piece of sheer hypermodern nonsense. Cocteau afterward revealed that the text, delivered by a stock-comedy policeman, had been
lifted verbatim from Mallarmé's *Divagations* ("*Ecclésiastique*").

longer reveal much about themselves." Cocteau justified *The Newlyweds* as follows:

> Poets must bring objects and feelings out from behind their veils and their fogs, must show them suddenly, so quickly that a man will have trouble recognizing them. They will then strike him with their entire youth. . . . That is the case with commonplaces, old, powerful, and universally accepted, like masterworks, but whose beauty and originality no longer surprise us because they've been worn out. In our spectacle, I reinstate the proverb.

Cocteau staged a spectacle which gives a full measure of his wit. Like much of Ionesco's theatre, *The Newlyweds* is organized around blurbs which, taken literally in a rapid-fire sequence of skits, lead to utter madness. The ballet opens, after Auric's overture, on the first platform of the Eiffel Tower, with an ostrich striding across the stage followed by a hunter. The latter takes aim and fires, releasing a telegram which invites the "Director of the Eiffel Tower" to a nuptial feast. The director, awoken by the blast, arrives and points an admonishing finger at the hunter, who explains that he meant to rescue an ostrich caught in the tower's webbing. His tale is borne out by a photographer who suddenly arrives looking for an ostrich which leapt from his camera the last time he said "Look at the birdy." Throughout the ballet, odd creatures will leap from his camera whenever he attempts to photograph the newlyweds. At this point, the orchestra strikes up Milhaud's Wedding March, the celebrants appear, the photographer has them pose and the two phonographs (Pierre Bertin and Marcel Herrand), whose commentaries accompany every dance, describe them thus:

PHONO ONE: The bride, sweet as a lamb
PHONO TWO: The father-in-law, rich as Croesus
PHONO ONE: The groom, pretty as a heart
PHONO TWO: The mother-in-law, phoney as a slug
PHONO ONE: The general, stupid as a goose
PHONO TWO: Look at him, he thinks he's riding his mare, Mirabelle
PHONO ONE: The ushers, strong as Turks
PHONO TWO: The bridesmaids, fresh as roses

The general, accompanied by Poulenc's music, reminisces about mirages he saw in Africa, whereupon a mirage in the shape of a lady bicyclist heading for Chatou appears, gets proper directions, and disappears. When the photographer finally snaps the shutter, a bathing beauty from Trouville emerges. After she is enticed back into the camera, he snaps the shutter again and a child appears. He is the newlyweds' future child and everybody tries to guess what he will become: a captain, an architect, a boxer, a poet, president of the Republic, or a cadaver in the next war. But he is also the "Child to Come" of village fairs who symbolically massacres the older generation. This he promptly does, stoning the wedding guests with macaroons, to Milhaud's fugue (the original title of the play was *The Massacred Wedding*). But they revive. In swift succession, the photographer—a magician *malgré lui*—produces a lion who devours all but one boot of the general, the general is borne into the camera to Honegger's Funeral March, and the photographer converses with his camera, which, finding the general indigestible, vomits him up. Meanwhile, the whole group, celebrants and photographers alike, freeze long enough to be purchased, as *The Wedding*, by a wealthy art collector. As soon as the collector leaves they thaw; the photographer calms the apparatus and, as he counts slowly from one to five, absorbs everyone present into his negative.

The whole play pivots around a pun, for the word *cliché* in French means both banality and snapshot. The camera, instead of recording the deadly pomp of a bourgeois wedding, brings alive its "negative," the underside of its poseurs (the French word for lens is *objectif*): a bathing beauty, a patricidal infant, a lion. Isn't this a reincarnation of Potomak, the motion-picture camera that has an inner life of its own? And the photographer becomes its custodian. "Since these mysteries escape me," he says, "let us pretend to be their organizer." In every possible way, Cocteau inverts inside and outside, allowing stock phrases to take their zany course and stock characters (wearing grotesque masks designed by Jean Hugo) to put their feet in their mouths. The cliché—a bourgeois wedding on the Eiffel Tower—does not become a cliché till at last the photographer succeeds in taking a snapshot.

"The secret of theatre, which calls for rapid success," wrote Cocteau in his introduction, "consists in laying a trap, thanks to which one-half the audience will rollick at the door so that the other half can take seats inside. Shakespeare, Molière, the profound Chaplin, know this very well." He goes beyond that, laying a trap for his own characters, who bear a likeness to the Cocteau between quotation marks, quoting himself as a form of defense and of humor. The newlyweds are bourgeois yet not bourgeois, puns on commonplaces, just as his Antigone, his Romeo and Juliet, his Oedipus, his Orpheus will live borrowed lives, their dramatic reality being parody. They are nothing if not style, their author's signature. They *are* masks. "In his Funeral March," wrote Cocteau, "Honegger amuses himself parodying what our musicologists solemnly call: MUSIC . . . Not one of these musicologists understood that his march was as beautiful as sarcasm." This implied connivance with the happy few, the bittersweet confrontation between the thing and its quoted, ridiculed self, an art form content to pun on art, doing so with the utmost rapidity: all this broaches the spirit of High Camp which determined the artistic personalities of both Cocteau and Auric. High Camp never loses its head, and what, indeed, did Cocteau call *The Newlyweds* but "a construction of the mind"?

Unhappily, few people in the audience heard Cocteau's text, for it was sabotaged by dada. The previous day the dadaists, led by Tzara, had infiltrated the Théâtre des Champs-Élysées for a "noisist" concert, which they planned to interrupt as they had interrupted Marinetti's lecture on tactilism in January. Marinetti, afraid they would recidivate, alerted Jacques Hébertot, director of the theatre, whose make-up, beringed fingers, and train of ephebes were strongly reminiscent of de Max's. As soon as the dadaists began throwing leaflets from their balcony into the orchestra below, Hébertot strode forward. They ignored his warning. A policeman was therefore summoned and stood guard over the dadaists during the remainder of the concert. When, the following day, Tzara and company arrived at the theatre for a scheduled lecture, they found all the doors locked. That same evening *The Newlyweds* was to be performed, furnishing the dadaists a ready instrument of vengeance. They planted themselves in the orchestra; throughout the performance one or another would rise and shout, "Long live dada!" overwhelming the "phonograph" voices on stage. Critics were thus obliged to devote their reviews to Jean Hugo's costumes and to Irène Lagut's decor. Cocteau had now been twice undone: first by Diaghilev, who disallowed the text of *Parade*, and then by the vociferous Tzara.

His adversaries' tactics only increased Cocteau's fame. By 1921 he was as fêted on the Right Bank as he was ostracized on the Left. When not improvising jazz with the Six he would stage public showdowns with their archenemy, a man twice Cocteau's size named Henri Béraud.[13] Insults only recharged his dynamo, lighting up one scheme after another. *The Newlyweds* was the most brilliant of these. The first had been a short farce with music by Milhaud called *Le Bœuf sur le Toit*, produced in February, 1920.

Milhaud returned from Brazil in 1919 with a large collection of South American tunes: popular refrains, tangos, maxixes, sambas which he wove together in a spirited rondo called *Le Bœuf sur le Toit* (the name of a Brazilian folk air), hoping that Chaplin might use it for a film. Cocteau proposed instead that he rather than Chaplin be allowed to write a short scenario. He and Milhaud collaborated during the summer of 1919 at Milhaud's home in Aix-en-Provence, amusing themselves in a variety of musical ways. Milhaud having composed a score for Cocteau's poem "Hymn to the Sun," they somehow collected enough brass and battery to play it. "I got assistance from the brass section of the municipal band, I rented a bass drum and some percussion instruments. We all installed ourselves on the terrace. Jean read the text, several friends including Hélène Hoppenot and Louis Durey played the percus-

---

13. To give an idea of Béraud's style, he wrote in *Mercure:* "The young Cocbin, son of a well-heeled father . . . Jean Cocbin has nothing but money and in this respect his group resembles him. . . . When one thinks that Mallarmé, Chabrier, and Cézanne used every expedient just to scrape along, one cannot but feel that the septet of little millionaires had chosen the right moment for its fatuous pleasantries. . . . They defile a profession into which they have introduced themselves like parvenus, oiling their paws and feeding parasites. . . . There is more talent, awareness, and originality in the least review of Rip's and Gignoux's than in all the work past and future of M. Jean Cocbin."

sion instruments, the Marquis de Grimaldi Régusse, arriving unexpectedly was given the triangle. The cacophony was appalling."

By September Cocteau had created a scenario whose amalgam of Damon Runyon and biblical antiquity places it midway between *David* and *The Newlyweds*. The setting is a speakeasy whose patrons include a Boxer, a Negro Dwarf, an Elegant Woman, a masculine Redhead, a Gentleman in tuxedo, and the Barkeeper. The Barkeeper wears a mask of Antinoüs. Smoke is represented by five large hoops suspended in midair. The dice are enormous cardboard cubes. When suddenly a policeman arrives the speak-easy becomes a dairy bar where everyone is sipping milk. Taken unawares, the policeman is decapitated by a ceiling fan and the Redhead, as Salome, dances with his head on a platter—a dance ending in headstands (the two women were played by the Fratellini clowns). The policeman comes back to life and is given a bill a yard long. Everyone moves slowly, in contradiction to the hectic score: a device Cocteau learned from a film by James Williamson in which actors perform an aquatic ballet under water as the orchestra plays a polka.

The name Cocteau was collateral enough for members of the *gratin* who fancied modern art. He presented Étienne de Beaumont a seating plan of the Comédie Champs-Élysées; the count agreed to buy the front rows and stage boxes at exorbitant prices, getting part of his investment back from the Shah of Persia, who paid the equivalent of one thousand dollars for a stage box. Every last seat was sold, but Cocteau, fearing an empty house, had previously asked Lucien Daudet to send *Tout Paris* three hundred chits, each good for one admission. Tumult reigned at the box office, where Lucien Daudet, enjoying one of his finest hours, finally quelled the wrathful mob.

If Lucien had transferred his elegant person from the superannuated splendor of Eugénie's Cyrnos to a ticket booth on the Champs-Élysées, his mother did her utmost to keep stride. Milhaud and Cocteau were frequent guests at Rue de Bellechasse. The former recalls dining there one evening with a certain Prince Firouze who had so pronounced a liking for Hawaiian music that he never attended restaurants without his own guitarists. Mme. Alphonse, ever solicitous of her guests, hired two Hawaiians for the occasion, and served her son's friends dessert in the shape of a caramel house surmounted by a candy ox, the whole structure buttressed with vanilla ice cream.

Not all parents attempted to keep up with their offspring. The younger set of aristocrats, those who had come of age during the war, went modern, and their emancipation proved to be as drastic as the etiquette of prewar life had been severe. If they shared their parents' obsession with fashion, fashion was no longer dictated by the aristocracy. Couturiers saw beauty not in the shape of a statuesque, amply proportioned matron but as the Baudelairian nymphet, vamping and angelic. Art nouveau had come into its own, and the singular predilections of Montesquiou, the Marchesa de Casati, Sarah Bernhardt, and the Baroness Deslandes now constituted "chic." That ghastly word became epidemic. It was chic to be dressed by Coco Chanel. It was chic to dance the tango. It was chic to like Barbette, the American transvestite. It was chic to smoke opium, to howl at dada demonstrations, to attend Beaumont's costume balls, to admire whatever Jean Cocteau wrote and, better yet, to have him as a dinner guest. Maurice Martin du Gard, the literary gossip monger *par excellence*, made the following collage of conversations he claimed to have overheard at the Comédie des Champs-Élysées a few months after *The Newlyweds*, the first main event of the fall season:

"I'll arrange dinner for you with Jean." "Oh, Princess, how grateful I'd be." "Yes, call me tomorrow, no, the day after, I shall have arranged everything. A small dinner, as he doesn't care for extravaganzas. And besides, he doesn't dine, he talks, he pecks, and lunch really suits him better. Why, he goes to bed at ten!" "Jean was sidesplitting, he was at my place yesterday. Sublime!" . . . Hélène de F. mentioned in passing, "I still chuckle just thinking about it." "How lucky you are, dear," replied the ravishing creature at her side, "he's inaccessible, always with his painters when he isn't with his musicians!" "You forget, my dear, that he works and must even live his life," said Marie, intervening: Marie who had a name, a title,

. . . and who, waiting for the crowd to thin out at the exit, had turned around: "I was his neighbor in the Midi. Impossible to have my little Jean. Always writing."

It was rare indeed for Cocteau to go to bed at ten. That was the hour when he made a postprandial appearance at the cabaret named after his farce, *Le Bœuf sur le Toit*, the cabaret where all the tiny threads of Parisian high life were wound into one umbilical cord. This was the successor to the Bar Gaya, whose clientele had become so numerous it could no longer squeeze into that grotto on the Rue Duphot. In January, 1922, Louis Moysès found a larger location on the Rue Boissy d'Anglas, midway between Place de la Madeleine and Cocteau's own Rue d'Anjou. In gratitude to the men who had launched him on his career as restaurateur, he gave it a name unequivocally theirs.[14]

The phenomenal success of Le Bœuf sur le Toit was owing partially to Moysès himself. He had all the virtues of Olivier Dabescat, the headwaiter at the Ritz, whose minute familiarity with aristocratic clans, their webbing of marriages and liaisons, made a lasting impression on Marcel Proust. But Moysès had few of Olivier's vices. Whereas the one was a stickler for protocol, a classic case of the domestic more snobbish than his master, the other understood that his fortune depended on his tolerance. Whereas Olivier dressed impeccably, Moysès was large and floppy, with a cigarette perpetually dangling from his mouth. Each was the perfect major-domo of his aristocratic generation. Moysès knew whom to seat together and whom to keep apart. Moreover, artists and writers he liked were allowed to drink on the house, or, like the peripatetic Fargue, to use Le Bœuf as a *poste restante*.

Another memorable fixture of Le Bœuf was its co-pianist, Clément Doucet, whom Wiener found as he had found Moysès: through his father. One of the elder Wiener's friends owned the patent to a bizarre musical instrument called the Orphéal which resembled a harmonium, though fitted with a keyboard. Depending

14. Naming his restaurants after Cocteau's works became something of a habit with Moysès. He later opened two more cabarets, naming them Le Grand Écart and Les Enfants Terribles. Cocteau had no ownership in them, as people often supposed.

on what stop knob one pulled, the Orphéal would sound like a violin, a cello, a piano, an organ, or a flute. Of the eighty Orphéals its proprietor sold, all eighty prompted lawsuits, for only one person alive could operate the poly-hymnal monstrosity: its demonstrator, a fat, sleepy, amiable lad who drank quantities of beer. The meeting of Wiener and Doucet at the Orphéal's showroom marked the beginning of their long association inside Le Bœuf and on the concert stage. With his customary nonchalance, Doucet would read books while performing at Le Bœuf. By the time he finished "Ain't She Sweet," "Black Bottom," "Breezin' Along with the Breeze," "The Man I Love," "Sometimes I'm Happy," he had simultaneously read one detective novel from cover to cover.

Le Bœuf was a snob cabaret, an "in" spot where the smart set met for drinks after dinner and stayed until the early morning. It occupied the center of a world less interested in art, in writing, and in music than in the sheer celebrity of artists, writers, and musicians. Here "chic," talent, renown, beauty, and vice had the market value of a landed title. Chic enthroned Chanel where Poiret had never been accepted as a social equal by the ladies he dressed. Talent and renown sanctified Derain, Picasso, Artur Rubinstein, Fargue, Satie. Beauty admitted names which did not outlive their faces. But vice threw the doors wide open. Not that people were more licentious than before, but in many instances the fulfillment of desires, accounted legitimate or otherwise, became a *raison d'être*. Just as love matches superseded marriages of convenience (leading to a much higher divorce rate), opium and homosexuality became ways of life, topics of self-advertisement, social identities, prisons. The impoverished Boni de Castellane at least had his prejudices, which sustained him to the end. The impoverished nobleman driven to represent a champagne company knew the baldness of economic necessity. But the young who inherited fortunes without inheriting the social prejudices of the prewar *gratin* had no other frame of reference than their exasperation, their unlimited hopes, and their gender. The war utterly destroyed a certain past and they were cast into the modern world no better equipped for it than Hottentots. Thus, opium and inversion, because they served to fill a void, often became everything. A Proust compartmentalized his life, deriving one kind of pleasure from salons or from Larue, or from the Ritz, and another from male bordellos. The postwar generations wallowed in incongruity. Le Bœuf was at once Larue and a bordello (chiefly male) where "high tone" consisted of sexual ambiguity, campy spoofing, brashness, and qui pro quos.

Veterans of prewar France rarely got the hang of it. They arrived like shades from the nether world, making certain assumptions, drawing comparisons, and left befuddled. Thus, King Ferdinand of Rumania expected to find· a reincarnation of the Café Anglais or Maxim's. He came, incognito, escorted by Étienne de Beaumont and his ever voluble compatriot, Anna de Noailles. Spying the beautiful chanteuse Louise Balthy, who had once toured Rumania, he dispatched Beaumont to her table. Beaumont asked the singer to join the king's entourage for champagne, and to respect his incognito. Such arrangements had often been made in Maxim's or in the Café Anglais between royalty and harlotry (though normally in a *salon particulier* on the second floor); the king presently learned that prewar protocol no longer held sway, that the magnificent tarts of yesteryear were a vanishing breed, that Le Bœuf was not Maxim's. Balthy had all the tables in the middle of the cabaret pushed to either side, she walked down the aisle making three elaborate curtsies, and when she reached King Ferdinand's table, inquired at the top of her voice, "Well, Your Majesty, how's tricks?"

Marcel Proust also visited Le Bœuf, not long before his death. On July 15, 1922, he was taken there for dinner by two friends, Edmond Jaloux and Paul Brach. Immediately comparisons started flying. He found the chicken excellent but the service inferior to that of the Ritz. This was no doubt Proustian courtesy, for the meal had been hurled at him by a "hideous" waiter on whom he avenged himself by awarding someone else an enormous tip. As the evening wore on, Jaloux left for a soirée and Brach was joined by drunken friends "who engaged in hostile banter with a band of unbelievable pimps and queers at the other end of the bar." Proust had entered a world whose individual elements he recognized but whose incongruous ensemble escaped him. Homosexuality had become "chic," and Le Bœuf its stronghold. Like the value given money for its own sake, it proved a great leveler, lumping together opposites, compromising pedigrees, altering manners and conversations. The Princess Marie Murat openly dallied with other women. And the Countess de Chevigné, the inaccessible idol of Proust's youth, one of two models for his Duchess de Guermantes, married Monsieur Noilly, a wealthy manufacturer of vermouth.

"Those New Year's Eve galas at the Bœuf," recalled Cendrars, "during Moysès' heyday, when Clément Doucet and Jean Wiener would play endlessly on back-to-back pianos, on entering I knew whom I would meet there. There was that seaworthy dowager, the old Duchess d'Uzès, with her straight talk, her clay pipe, her bottle of Bordeaux. There was Coco Chanel, a loner. When the jazz warmed up, Jean Cocteau, like a jack-o'-lantern, his wick smelling of heresy, would perch himself behind the drums. There was Marthe Chenal trying once again to get her grappling hooks into Ambroise Vollard, that white Negro, by making him dance. There was the publisher Peignot, who, one Christmas night, after leaving Le Bœuf drove his car down the steps of the Madeleine Métro station, then came back up in reverse. There was Madame Leygues, with her famous necklace of I don't remember how many, many meters of pearls, Misia Sert, young Auric, old Fargue . . ."

Above the bar hung Picabia's *Œil Cacodylate*, an eye signed by dozens of habitués, supervising the high life with the inert gaze of an octopus. This was an age exhausted from running in every direction at once. The new-found freedom of postwar Europe was a fantastic source of energy. Directed one way, it ran the wheels of utopianism; directed another way, it blew up the whole works. At Le Bœuf the wheels were turning in both directions, unpredictably manic and depressive, all the time. Ultimately this freedom may have built its own prison, one far more exiguous and anguishing than a neatly ordered society. It may have produced Hottentots, but Hottentots more concerned with their humanity than their civilized elders had been. If they read at all, they read Sade, the romantics, Baudelaire, Rimbaud, Lautréamont, and whoever else endorsed their binges of fantasy, their self-squander.

The heart of Cocteau's world, however, was still his mother's flat at 10 Rue d'Anjou, an elegant building whose staircase spiraled around an immense chandelier six stories long, its copper stem producing a spray of light bulbs at every landing. The vestibule of the Cocteau residence gave the visitor idealized glimpses of Mme. Georges and her son. To one side hung Wencker's portrait of Cocteau's mother as a young woman in 1880, done up in a cakelike bonnet with a veil, her left hand grasping the knob of a parasol. To the other side hung Frédéric de Madrazo's portrait of Cocteau himself, looking silky, dark, and Byronic. Another view of Cocteau, Jacques Lipchitz' granite bust showing all his angularity, like one of Fouquet's Flemish courtiers, stood on a pedestal head-high. The portal between this vestibule and the apartment itself was guarded by the valet Cyprien, an old family retainer whose wife, Aimée, did the cooking and, perhaps infected by the spirit of the house, devoted her leisure hours to writing (no one knew quite what).

Mme. Cocteau was usually to be found in a small salon to the left of the vestibule. A plaid blanket spread over her knees, she spent much of her time reading. As often as not her guests were Jean's adolescent protégés, in whose eyes she had the prestige of a Madonna. "When she stood up," wrote Maurice Sachs, "her brow crowned with white hair, thin and straight in a black dress, her bearing made it clear that she represented an aloof but very humane bourgeois aristocracy." That she could reconcile her own way of life with her son's bears witness to exceptional strength of mind, or to willful, maternal *bêtise*. It may be presumed that he gave her enough to pray about at mass, which she attended each morning. Mme. Cocteau was the spine of Jean's life: she withstood his paranoid onslaughts, she consoled him, she gave him an allowance, she entertained his friends, she provided him the order he needed in which to be disorderly. Her influence over him was such that for many years after he had left her, his own residences were never more than pads, opium parlors, curiosity shops which he exchanged for one another, gladly abandoning them altogether to live in villas as someone's pampered child.

Cocteau's room stood opposite the entrance. It was furnished with a narrow, iron-framed bed, a large architect's table of white wood, rattan chairs, and a free-standing armoire, but this was the least of it, for manuscripts, letters, dozens of copies of Cocteau's own works, drawing implements, bottles of every description formed a kind of shifting bog in which items submerged never to be seen again. The walls were covered with images tacked there at random: photographs of Rimbaud, of Verlaine, of Carpentier the heavyweight boxer, of the Fratellini brothers, sketches of Cocteau by Marie Laurencin, Roger de la Fresnaye, Picasso, Picabia, and Irène Lagut. On the mantel lay a large paper die, three crystal polyhedrons soaking in a saucer full of water, a clay pigeon, a cardboard box serving as the frame for a piece of black cloth pasted onto its inside wall. From the ceiling there dangled two straw horses Milhaud had brought back from Mexico and a cage wrought of pipe cleaners. "It was the warehouse of gay and frothy accessories which heralded the true fashion of the period: objects of chance, of fun, solemn curiosities, poetic baubles."

But if it set one fashion, it equally commemorated another, for Cocteau's room displayed the kind of prominently mysterious fetishes which had filled Montesquiou's library. This clutter, usually seen as the rich, organic secretion of its tenant, reflected a vacuum. Cocteau papered his prison with *trompe-l'œil* dimensions, but the eye they intended to deceive was less his own than his visitors'.[15] They formed a cubed backdrop in the midst of which Cocteau moved so familiarly as to strike his young audience dumb with awe. "Cocteau had me sit down," recalled André Fraigneau, his lifelong friend, "but he remained standing. And, walking round the room, he embarked on that monologue of which I never tired. . . . What was its point? To give his new guest the impression that there he was at home, that the dreams and the labors of the celebrated poet were his guest's as well. It was a way of ennobling the young visitor by having him participate in the lofty games of art and thought."

The purpose of that monologue may have been to put his visitor at ease but it equally served to give him possession of his own ostensible dreams, labors, friends, and past, to make them his *own*. Moving from object to object, he would describe their provenience: this

15. Cocteau once described the writer as a prison from which his works escape, only to be pursued by police the world over.

sketch was done under such and such circumstances, that black piece of cloth was the Chinese silhouette of Isadora Duncan, the paper die had been painted by Picasso. This tour, rehearsed for each new visitor, was a kind of verbal appropriation akin to his superb mimicries. Fraigneau having mentioned Barrès in his letter of self-introduction to Cocteau, Cocteau did an imitation of Barrès, as if to demonstrate thereby his intimacy with the *maître*.

Caricature and imitation go beyond description; they *digest* their object. Cocteau's tours amounted to a mock show altogether reminiscent of Picasso's. Just as the latter, when guiding visitors through his studio, would always pronounce a set speech over the same artifacts in order to husband his energy, Cocteau hid behind the Poet-at-Perfect-Ease, intimate yet on stage. Unlike Picasso, Cocteau devoted more of his energy to the persona than to the self. He conducted his *petites levées* at eleven in the morning with the ceremonial flourish of Louis XIV rising and bathing in the presence of his chamberlains. While young men milled about his room, Cocteau, wearing black pajamas and a terry-cloth robe, addressed them from the adjoining bathroom. "Cocteau, wearing a hat which served to hold in place a towel knotted at the forehead," poised his face over a casserole of steaming water until, beet red, he considered his beard soft enough for the razor. Throughout these rituals, he would continue to speak and to gesture, sometimes parting the shower curtains to make certain that his audience had not disappeared. Afterward, having combed his hair, tightly knotted his pink tie, attired himself in an elegant jacket pinched at the waist and upturned at the cuffs so as to show swatches of its pink silk lining, having put on his felt hat, grasped his ivory-knobbed cane, and collected his white gloves, he would sally into the street with a flying phalanx of Cocteauroons, like some praying mantis accompanied by a swarm of adoring beetles. He was in his early thirties and famous. He was de Max "escorted by adolescents like a God escorted by nymphs."

Adolescents haunted 10 Rue d'Anjou in hopes that Cocteau might grant them an audience. They loitered on the sidewalk and were known to fall asleep on the staircase. Ten or fifteen strong, they would visit the cinema with him. What he liked they loved, what he disliked they abominated. His jumbled room had dozens of replicas in Paris. Chez Millat, where he had his hair cut, was patronized by these young dandies, all demanding the same *coiffure*. And those who felt rebuffed would carry their smarting sensibilities to Gide, Cocteau's rival archangel. "My relations with Gide," wrote Cocteau, "were from start to finish a game of blindman's buff, a groping sequence of reconciliations, spats, open letters, grievances whose source may well have been that incredible band of young mythomaniacs who circulated between us an amused themselves by jumbling the deck."

This band of effete acolytes became an invariable feature of Cocteau's life in the twenties. Their prototype, whose legend was known to them in all its details, entered Cocteau's life in 1918 and departed from the world six years later. Raymond Radiguet.

7

An Illusion of Paradise

octeau first met Radiguet in an art gallery during a *vernissage* to which the fifteen-year-old boy had come with Max Jacob. It was 1918. Several days later, at 10 Rue d'Anjou, Aimée informed him that "a child carrying a cane" was seated in the vestibule. Slightly built, bashful, lost in his overcoat, with hair so long he appeared to be wearing side-whiskers, Radiguet presented himself on the strength of Max Jacob's recommendation. From his pocket he fetched a crumpled leaf of note paper on which two of his poems were scribbled; he proceeded to read them, squinting, for he was decidedly myopic. "From the first," wrote Cocteau, "I can say that I guessed Raymond Radiguet's star. By what sign? I wonder."

This is the public record. André Breton gave a different version of the circumstances under which Cocteau first met Radiguet. Walking with Radiguet one day in the neighborhood of the Madeleine, he encountered Cocteau. Breton instantly sensed a current of electricity passing between Radiguet and Cocteau, and knew with absolute certainty that lives had been altered. Indeed, when the three parted Breton walked off alone, furious at Cocteau for having robbed him of a disciple: further reason for them to live at swords' points.

One thing may not be doubted. Radiguet at fifteen was being vied for by his elders who pushed him into precipitate fame and contributed to his early death. He lived only twenty years, but they were Saturnian years the length of a human era. Like the romantic period, the twenties glorified the genius of youth. It speeded up the life span of human beings as it speeded up everything else. It accredited only the flash fire which burns bright and briefly. It created legends around some few who had the good sense to die or to disappear at full bloom. The surrealists created Rimbaud's legend and Lautréamont's. Cocteau created Radiguet's.

Radiguet was one of several children born to Maurice Radiguet, a well-known cartoonist whose work appeared in many of the Parisian dailies. He spent his early youth in Parc Saint-Maur, a village on the Marne near enough to Paris for many of its inhabitants to commute daily. The order and conventionality of Radiguet's upbringing ended with the outbreak of war, which shifted attention from schoolwork to the street, where bombs were falling and soldiers of every description milled about. A student at the Lycée Charlemagne, Radiguet attended classes irregularly, spending his truant hours on the Marne, in his father's boat where he read Mme. de La Fayette, Stendhal, and Proust. Presently a woman named Martha stumbled into the midst of this literary company. The wife of a soldier at the front, she met Radiguet during one of his long walks along the river bank. They engaged in that short-lived, feverish affair described in Radiguet's novel *Devil in the Flesh*.

By May, 1918, Radiguet had already published a little poem in the satiric weekly called *Le Canard Enchaîné*, but the decisive event of his young life was his meeting with André Salmon, the poet and friend of Apollinaire who had taken up journalism some years before. At *L'Intransigeant* it was one of Salmon's duties to choose the daily cartoon, which brought to his desk "an agreeable little fellow some fifteen years old, his cheeks blushing, his large collar starched, wearing knee-breeches" who had carried Maurice Radiguet's portfolio all the way from Parc Saint-Maur. After several such interviews, Radiguet summoned the courage to show Salmon his verse, which he signed "Rajki." Salmon found the verse better than its *nom de plume*. He helped the boy procure odd jobs with weekly papers such as *L'Éveil*, *L'Heure*, and *Rire*. Moreover, he encouraged Radiguet to show his verse to Apollinaire. The latter found it so like his own *Alcools* that he suspected the author of wishing to engineer another of those *mystifications* which periodically played havoc with the Parisian literary world.

When Radiguet presented himself in person, Apollinaire scolded him severely.

His first meeting with Max Jacob proved to be far more delightful. Like Cocteau, and for many of the same reasons, Jacob found the gifted, beautiful, unbalanced boys who occasionally reeled into his orbit irresistible. He would mother them, educate them, grow weary of them, reject them, and repent. A Breton Jew from Quimper, Jacob converted to the Catholic Church in 1909. A mystic and a voluptuary, a Celtic gnome who split hairs like a Talmudist, a remarkable poet who preferred to be taken seriously for his water colors, an erudite man who elected to learn catechism from the most simple-minded ecclesiastic in Paris, an invert given to tormented flirtations with married women, a friend by turns tender and viperish, Jacob had been one of the most prominent figures in Montmartre of the Laundry Boat years. In the Laundry Boat he shared an atelier with Picasso and earned his living by giving piano lessons, writing children's books, and casting the horoscopes of local concierges. When baptized, following a mystical vision, he named Picasso his godfather.

"Max was marvelous," Picasso reminisced to Françoise Gilot. "He always knew how to touch the sore spot. He loved gossip, of course, and any hint of scandal. He heard once that Apollinaire had arranged for Marie Laurencin to have an abortion. One night a little while after that, at one of our poets' dinners, Max announced he had composed a song in honor of Apollinaire. He stood up and, facing toward Marie Laurencin, he sang:

> *Ah, l'envie me démange*
> *de te faire un ange*
> *de te faire un ange*
> *en farfouillant ton sein*
> *Marie Laurencin*
> *Marie Laurencin.*[1]

Marie Laurencin turned red, Apollinaire grew purple, but Max stayed very calm and angelic-looking."

1. Ah, you arouse my desire / an angel to sire / an angel to sire / by fingering your breast / Marie Laurencin / Marie Laurencin.

By 1918 he was living on Rue Gabrielle near the Madeleine, but was apt to bob up anywhere, a bald elf who wore shoestring ties, a black, sleeveless raincoat, and white linen gloves. It is as if he met all the winds of the world standing on one toe, like a weather vane in the shape of a jester whom any chance breeze could turn this way to God or that way to the devil. Wherever he pointed, his young friends went. Before long Radiguet, through Jacob, had met Reverdy, Juan Gris, Picasso, Modigliani, and Breton. He would stay in Paris until late at night with poets and painters, then catch the "theatre special" back to Parc Saint-Maur. If he missed the train, he would walk home through the Bois de Vincennes or, more often, sleep on the floor of someone's atelier. At sixteen he had one foot in Paris and one still at home, leading an incredibly dissolute life yet maturing with equally incredible rapidity.

"He liked above all the idea of growing old," wrote Cocteau. "He detested youth, in the Wildean sense of the word. He was afraid of charm and brilliance. Just as others are wont to say 'When I was young,' he used to say 'When I grow old.' " This ambition to be old fascinated everyone who met Radiguet. It was impossible to guess his true age. He wore sobriety like an oversized suit which he hoped fit him; at times it seemed to, at other times it made him look like a young mummer even younger than his years. This was the equivocal creature who appeared before Cocteau carrying a short cane and wearing the haphazard outfit he wore in those days: a resin-colored jacket so large he had to turn up its sleeves, striped black trousers which fell in accordion folds over his shoes, shoes down-at-heel, and a straw derby.

Cocteau was immediately struck by Radiguet's physical beauty. It was the kind of sculpted, Greek face that never failed to quicken his senses. He was seduced by his dark, angelic looks, his self-evident genius, by his mute plea to be brought out, by his reticence. Perhaps, too, Cocteau had some notion of playing Verlaine to Radiguet's Rimbaud. Keenly aware of literary precedents, Cocteau might have found an equally good one in Pygmalion.

Before long Radiguet was wearing a monocle and dressing like a dandy. Cocteau recommended him to Jacques Doucet, the vastly rich couturier whose hobby it was to collect those avant-garde reviews, manuscripts, and first editions which now form the library of twentieth-century literature bearing his name. Doucet paid young writers to correspond with him and to send him lengthy commentaries on one another. It was thus that Breton, Aragon, and Tzara, among others, earned a living. The couturier paid in kind as well as cash. "Dear Monsieur Doucet," Radiguet wrote in November, 1919, "I shall come next Tuesday at 3 p.m. I am glad that my first chronicle did not displease you. I am busy working at the moment and hope that soon I shall have other 'articles' to show you. I received my gloves last Monday, and thank you for them." A month later he sent Doucet a sheaf of poems and solicited alms for the New Year: "I should like to offer flowers or bonbons to some of my lady friends."

Cocteau sought to find him regular employment, and pulled strings with Philippe Berthelot: "I am sending you Raymond Radiguet," he wrote in 1921. "He's a miracle (not a prodigy)—The adopted son of our group. THE POET. He has just written a novel which I consider ONE OF THE FOUR OR FIVE MASTERPIECES OF FRENCH LITERATURE. . . . If you could find him a propaganda post which wouldn't absorb him and would give him enough to live on, you would help us furnish him the serenity he deserves."

He was now the mascot of *Les Six* and led about on a leash by Cocteau. He attended their Saturday-night dinners. He wrote for *Le Coq*. He collaborated with Satie and Cocteau on a comic operetta called *Paul et Virginie*. He wrote a *bouffe* play of his own, *The Pelican*, which was staged at the Théâtre Michel on May 23, 1921. By 1921 he had moved into a hotel near Cocteau's home; his room was littered with the poetry of Ronsard, Chénier, Malherbe, and La Fontaine—unexpectedly conservative reading for someone whose life was nothing if not a series of uproarious experiments.

Yet Radiguet managed somehow to occupy the still center of his wild revolutions. Even as he was dissipating himself, his talent began to solidify and to take definite shape. The few opinions he voiced were invariably pithy and unalterable. "How many times I sat next to him," wrote Joseph Kessel, "to hear his brief, heavy, and rich aphorisms. They were full of disconcerting reflection and terrible maturity. While his eyes concentrated on a wall which he didn't see, his mouth, with that slight contortion of the lips characterizing it, sculpted, one by one, the most original and apt opinions." However it came to be, Radiguet did possess a kind of superinduced wisdom terrible beyond his years. His demoniacal mode of life cost him his middle age; his sobriety cost him his youth.

Cocteau found in Radiguet a justification for his own literary conservatism. Against Breton he pitted this young anti-Rimbaud who refuted the bohemian establishment. Until 1920 Radiguet served as a pawn in the Breton-Cocteau power struggle. Breton published him in *Littérature*, partially to wound Cocteau. By the spring of 1920, however, when *Le Coq* was founded, Radiguet had plighted his troth. "Radiguet," wrote Cocteau, "used to read our works in the hold of his father's boat on the Marne. . . . We became his classics and he dreamed of contradicting us. That is why I quickly guessed that this student would become my master and would teach me a new order." To the extent that Radiguet reminded Cocteau of the existence of French poetry before Baudelaire he may be considered his master. Cocteau read at most little and at best vagrantly, but in any case nothing that was not "modern." Under Radiguet's tutelage, he acquired a taste for the classics.

It is difficult, however, to know who was influencing whom. The Radiguet whose poem "*À Plusieurs Voix*" Tzara published in the *Anthologie Dada* (May, 1919) had not yet jelled. He wrote dada for Tzara and Mallarmé for Breton, dreaming chiefly, one may suppose, of seeing himself in print. Possibly Cocteau did, as he claims to have done, repeat day in and day out, "Raymond, be banal; Raymond, write like everyone else," for Cocteau's conscientious preciosity was merely the inner face of his traditionalism. But that is doubtful, and even so, no amount of repetition could have written Radiguet's novels for him. Cocteau wanted a suit of emblematic armor, and he was prepared to cut it according to the material Radiguet provided him. The summer of 1921 saw the gestation of *Devil in the Flesh;* on that small masterpiece Cocteau would, forever after, ground his own pretentions to genius. "Originality," he would say with evidence in hand, "consists in trying to write like everyone else and not succeeding."

Actually, the novel was begun in February at the Hôtel Gilly et Jules in Carqueiranne, a small port midway between Marseilles and Saint-Tropez. Radiguet had gone there by himself because, according to Valentine Hugo,[2] he was tired of Cocteau's polyandrous attentions. Yet Cocteau's arrival in March, along with Roger de la Fresnaye, seemed to give him pleasure and reassurance. "Solitude suits me so well! and Paris so badly, from the viewpoint of work, which is really what interests me most," he wrote to Doucet on April 2. "Furthermore, I haven't been alone all the time. Juan Gris, la Fresnaye, and Jean Cocteau have come to see me. The awful moment in solitude is the one when a writer loses his footing, when he's no longer certain of what he's doing. At such moments a visit from friends is highly useful."

Cocteau returned to Paris in June to supervise *The Newlyweds;* then, along with Pierre Bertin and his wife, the pianist Marcelle Meyer, he rejoined Radiguet in the Auvergne, at Besse. By September they had moved to the Hôtel Chantecler in Piquey. There, in a room whose three windows looked out on the Bay of Arcachon and on a wilderness of pines, Radiguet continued to write. "This is paradise on earth," wrote Cocteau to Doucet, "but there are neither apples nor serpents. We eat fish, we live naked in the sun, we bathe and meet nary a soul. . . . I had sworn to myself not to write a line—yet I'm working. Radiguet is midway through a novel which will help hoist him in the public mind to a level where I have always held him in my esteem. You'll see."

Whenever Radiguet's flame guttered out, Cocteau would revive it with a breath of ozone. On one occasion early in 1922 Radiguet despairingly hurled part of his manuscript into the fire; Cocteau locked him in his room until he had rewritten the destroyed chapters. When the book was done, Cocteau took it to La Sirène, which agreed to publish it, offering terms, however, that Cocteau found inadequate. He thereupon gave the manuscript to Bernard Grasset, who had been astute enough to pick up *Remembrance of*

2. Valentine Gross had married the painter Jean Hugo in 1919. Cocteau and Satie served as witnesses at the wedding.

Things Past when Gallimard rejected it. Once again he gave evidence of his astuteness.[3]

Devil in the Flesh, when it appeared early in 1923, caused a scandal. Grasset felt no allegiance to the gentlemanly protocol which had hitherto governed the publishing world of Paris. Moreover, Flammarion had proved, the previous year, how profitable modern advertising campaigns can be. Its two literary directors, Max and Alex Fischer, published Victor Margueritte's feminist novel, *La Garçonne,* amid such lurid publicity that within months 750,000 copies had been sold. Margueritte, trading specious glory for real gold, made a fortune and was expelled from the Legion of Honor. Radiguet did not, like Margueritte, stump the provinces to see that bookstores remained well stocked. On the contrary, he spent most of his time in Grasset's office while Cocteau looked after his interests. Red flyers declared that Radiguet had written his novel at seventeen. Advertisements such as the following appeared in the daily press:

Sensational!!!!

DEVIL IN THE FLESH

by

Raymond Radiguet

Around this astonishing work, written by an extraordinarily young author, controversies have wracked the literary world; sides have been taken, disputes rage. It's a success almost without precedent and no one can afford to ignore a book which exhales a breath of remarkable intensity.

Sale price: fr. 3.40

Newsreels showed Radiguet in Grasset's office signing a contract for ten novels at a monthly retainer of fifteen hundred francs, which Cocteau called "A bridge of gold!"[4] Frédéric Lefèvre, the literary chronicler, interviewed him. *Débats* devoted a special insert to Radiguet. Even Paul Valéry praised the novel, though cautiously.

---

3. According to Cocteau, Radiguet accepted a considerable advance from Grasset. This money was intended for M. Laffitte with whom Radiguet had previously signed a contract. Instead, he bought a magnificent camel's hair coat and an expensive valise and departed to Fontainebleau for a holiday with a group of American friends.

4. *Un pont d'or,* which literally means a monthly compensation or retainer.

Radiguet won the "New World Prize," worth seven thousand francs (or about five hundred dollars) subsidized by an American millionaire but awarded by a French committee consisting of Bernard Faÿ, Jean Giraudoux, Jacques de Lacretelle, Paul Morand, Valéry Larbaud, Max Jacob, and . . . Jean Cocteau.[5] The Association of French War Veteran Writers immediately cabled the American Legion protesting that the novel "deeply wounds the feelings of war veterans" and "presents the French family and wartime France in a false and odious light." Aragon discounted the relevance of Radiguet's age: "We are given a book to judge," he wrote in *Paris-Journal*, "and not an extract from the bureau of public records."

The fire raged, with Cocteau fanning it behind the scenes. Maurice Martin du Gard, editor of *Les Écrits Nouveaux*, recalls being visited at his printer by Cocteau, who wanted to see the galleys of an article Radiguet had written about *Devil in the Flesh*. It contained a highly flattering reference to Cocteau, which did not prevent the latter from observing, "You've set Raymond in excessively small type." Cocteau thus adjusted every little cog and flywheel of his immortality machine.

Cocteau did most of his writing during the summers, in a series of concentrated efforts which left him free to spend the other three seasons talking. Not that he forswore conversation in Lavandou, Carqueiranne, and Piquey. Radiguet, Auric, and he (among others) lived in close quarters, and Cocteau could not resist rooting for Parisian truffles buried in the neighboring villages. "I've learned," he wrote from Pramousquier to one Pierre de Lanux, "that you are on that isle facing us, with the charming Lady of the Manor. . . . Couldn't all of you come dine here [Auric, François de Gouy, and an American friend of Madame B. V.'s named Russell Greeley]? You will come upon savages anxious to have you visit them. Notify me one day in advance." The postcard was embroidered with afterthoughts such as "I burned down a whole forest to catch your eye" and "Gide is vacationing in Porquerolles." But his summers in the Midi during 1921 and 1922 were remarkable for the number of manuscripts produced, as if Cocteau and Radiguet had found in one

5. Morand, Larbaud, and Giraudox voted for Philippe Soupault's *The Good Apostle*. The other four voted for Radiguet.

another sources of mutual inspiration. While Radiguet labored at *Devil in the Flesh*, Cocteau wrote quantities of poems, plays, and novels. They beheld themselves as the twin stars of a new movement devoted to old virtues such as rhyme in poetry and simplicity in prose.

Cocteau's manifesto of their literary position, "Professional Secret," is contained in a book of essays entitled *A Call to Order*. "The accursed-angel attitude," he declared, "has made of the accursed a protégé, a privileged person; it is adopted nowadays like a status symbol. Few people attain that position. The young don't realize that the public possesses no judgment, that one must be accursed not only by the larger public but by the avant-garde." Having thus discredited Breton, he proceeds to say the very things Breton was saying: that style is neither a natural resource nor a manufactured thing but a by-product, that poetry is visceral or nothing, that its chief goal should be to depict in a new light the ordinary things our eyes record without even seeing.[6] Apart from these commendable platitudes, Cocteau does provide a key to his writing, to the literary self which had begun crystallizing some ten years before in *Potomak* and which reinforced its identity successively in *Parade*, *The Cape*, and *The Newlyweds*. That key lies in the following passage:

> Poetry in its raw state enlivens the reader who experiences it with a fit of nausea. This ethical nausea arises from death. Death is the underside of life, which is why we can't visualize it, but the idea that it forms the weft of our human being keeps obsessing us. We come to feel our deaths pressing against us, yet doing so in such a way that any contact with it is impossible. Imagine a text whose sequel we cannot know because it is printed on the back of a page only one side of which we can read. Well, the outer face and the inner—a convenient expression on the human level though probably nonsense

6. He likened writing to perspiring, bleeding, and defecating, as circumstances and mood dictated. In "Professional Secret" it is perspiring. To the young writers who were forever sending him packets of unpublished verse, his stock reply was "A poem is blood." In intimacy, or to scandalize, he would say, "I am shitting poetry."
    Even as he was denouncing dada in "Professional Secret" because of its "exoticism," of its cultivated "tics," he contributed two distinctly dadaistic texts to a Picabia issue of *The Little Review* in spring, 1922, for the benefit of American expatriates: "Cocteau Hailing Picabia," and "Cocteau Hailing Tzara."

on the superhuman—this vague reverse side creates around our acts, our words, our least gestures a hollow which dizzies our soul as certain parapets cause the heart to flip over.

With Cocteau the visible half succumbs to its underside, it surrenders its flesh to the gnawing emptiness all around. His novels and plays have the simplicity of skeletons dancing their *danse macabre* on an ice floe. They form a hideously smooth surface where local color and psychological incidents cannot gain purchase. They force characters to move precipitously, nonsensically, like human vectors whose point and existence lie in their direction.

The two novels Cocteau wrote in the early twenties, *The Big Split* and especially *Thomas the Impostor*, illustrate this perfectly. The characters owe their existence to flight and to pursuit. They are nothing if not a series of Terry Tune imbroglios, mad crisscrossings, embraces and ruptures in mid-flight, gratuitous gestures, missiles impelled hither and thither by some exterior design that makes them hit or miss one another with the mindless inconsequences of rocks flashing through space. His novels are like picaresque tales inverted; the hero does not rise haphazardly, he falls haphazardly, and comes into his own with a last nonsensical *quid pro quo:* death. Death governs the action from the outset in *Thomas the Impostor* and the mask worn by its hero, and the giddy performance he gives, constantly imply the unnamable. Unmasked, Thomas dies. In *The Cape* Cocteau spoke of the poet as a tightrope walker performing above the void. In his novels he marshals paper masks against death; they have nothing in their defense but style.

From one vantage point, then, Cocteau's is an art of tragic implication. The absolute surface of his writings has a corollary in absolute depth; style as a way of life beckons the vacuum beyond life. From another vantage point, it is an art of tragic evasion. Cocteau is the poet of adolescent alibis and *Thomas* a garbled, accelerated epic of youth avoiding its murky depths with a fragile persona, begging the question of personality with an impersonal, angelic Self. In either case Cocteau allows for nothing between oblivion and naked style, between the unfathomable depths and the futile arabesques skated on its icy surface. He is telling his own predicament, by indirection, like a cartographer, who gives the shape of a sea by drawing the land masses around it. Cocteau appeared, at least, to understand the haste which ultimately left him a lifetime of accumulated *tours de force* pierced by glimpses of his own velocity, a stack of prefaces to prefaces, the imprisoning outlines of his sorrow: *Thomas, Les Enfants Terribles, Opium, La Difficulté d'Être.* "Living," he would write in *Opium,* "is a horizontal fall."

By 1923 the relationship between Radiguet and Cocteau had altered. In one way they drifted apart; in another they beheld one another in a more equable and comradely light than before. Radiguet was no longer a fledgling; having tried his wings and found them air-worthy, he took flight. It is revealing that in 1922 he should have moved from the Madeleine quarter, away from Cocteau, to a hotel facing the Luxembourg gardens, the Hôtel Foyot, whose restaurant was a favorite gathering place for senators after their sessions in the Palais du Luxembourg.

Not that he ceased to attend Le Bœuf. He often spent evenings with Cocteau and Barbette, an American who looked altogether like an English martinet except on stage, where, transformed into a sexy blonde, he flew the trapeze wearing a set of wings. But Radiguet started to dally with the opposite sex. His constant companion at Le Bœuf was a young woman named Bronja Perlmutter who, along with her sister, had become floating fixtures of the place, like rootless water lilies.[7] While Radiguet sat with her at one table, Cocteau, seated at another, would send him note after note. It is almost as if Radiguet, angelic appearances notwithstanding, took pleasure in taunting his erstwhile lover, but dalliance and taunts seemed at least to rejuvenate him.

He had outgrown his custodian and earned enough money to indulge his appetites, which proved, on occasion, Rabelaisian. The records of the Hôtel Foyot show that at one sitting he consumed cocktails, one bottle of champagne and another of Chambertin old vintage, two varieties of sole, stuffed pheasant, cheese, ice cream, meringue, coffee, and liqueurs. He bought elegant clothing and expensive luggage. He was the constant guest of Étienne de Beau-

7. Soon after Radiguet's death Bronja married René Clair.

mont, who would figure as the titular hero of his second novel, *The Count d'Orgel's Ball*, and of the brilliant, bull-like Princess Marie Murat. In the window of every other bookstore *Devil in the Flesh*, piled twenty copies high, formed the pedestal of his photographic portrait. The manageress of his hotel would probably whisper to clients, "For a long time I sheltered Pierre Benoît; now I have Raymond Radiguet," and senators brought to dinner copies of his novel for autographing.

Clinging to some shreds of bourgeois custom, he would send an allowance to his brothers and sisters and take out insurance before long trips. What trips he made on the spur of the moment were prompted by older companions. Thus, one night as he was staggering home drunk from Le Bœuf with Brancusi, the latter suddenly proposed, in front of the Dôme, that they board a train for Marseilles. Within a few hours they had done so. En route it occurred to them that they might as well continue to Corsica. In Marseilles Radiguet, still wearing his dinner jacket, bought more appropriate clothing in an army-navy store. For two weeks they lived in a Corsican fishing village consuming brandy and returned, much against their will, when their money threatened to give out.

Cocteau, who had been irked by this impromptu, resolved to stage one of his own. In February, 1923, he and Radiguet crossed the Channel to England. Did they see themselves as shades of Rimbaud and Verlaine? No doubt some such comparison lurked in Cocteau's mind, but in all events he was not about to adopt his predecessors' shabby style, and take dirty lodgings in Whitechapel. From the Carlton in London he wrote to Gautier-Vignal: "We are in London. That seems to me prodigious enough. Your Jean." Impelled by sheer curiosity (Cocteau, like Proust, had a particular foible for blond, ethereal young Englishmen), the two pushed northward to Harrow and Oxford, as to Cythera.[8] Cocteau em-

---

8. Cocteau ascribed their journey to a dream he had had in which he saw an old-fashioned beaked cane in a shop near Harrow, a shop with a crocodile in the window. Since he had a passion for such canes and could find them nowhere, he decided to observe his dream. "The next day I related my dream to Radiguet and proposed we leave for Harrow. He liked larks and believed me. We leave. . . . At Victoria station I find myself facing Reginald Bridgeman, a friend of mine who lives in the English countryside and whom I didn't notify of my visit. He takes

ployed his leisure time writing a speech which he would deliver in March before the Collège de France. That speech, "On an Order Considered as an Anarchy," laid the basis for Radiguet's legend.

If their friendship maintained a precarious equilibrium, it apparently teetered from one extreme to another. Wasn't the nature of their liaison such that each could not but find the other cloying yet indispensable, affirming one another's loneliness? They were by turns master and slave. Despite his nymphomaniacal craving for company, despite the difficulty he had *being* by himself, Cocteau did his utmost to forbid any sane intimacy. He wanted at all costs to be unique, and Radiguet's uniqueness redounded upon him. The generation separating them protected Cocteau from odious comparisons, and if he openly admitted his debt to Erik Satie and to Pablo Picasso—"my masters," he calls them in "On an Order Considered as an Anarchy"—the one was a composer, the other a painter. His masters' nonliterary mediums, Radiguet's youth, and his own monologue kept Cocteau apart, and being apart was the crux of being Cocteau. Hence the paradox that his works, so clamorously "personal," all refer to an impostor, to a legend, the paradox that his legend was a form of discretion. In other words, creation for Cocteau amounted to self-creation. His literature gave him the name he craved, only rarely betraying the self he was. "I am a lie who tells the truth," he said, justifying his invention. But whose truth?

"Raymond Radiguet appeared," he wrote in "On an Order," echoing Boileau's *Art Poétique* where Malherbe's appearance put to flight all the mannered popinjays poaching on pre-classical France. "I staked my fortune on the Radiguet number, as in the dedication of *The Cock and the Harlequin* I wagered on the Georges Auric number. Shall I confess that in so doing I risked no more than the player who cheats? Antennae point out to me beforehand the numbers that will win."

us home and puts us up. I relate my dream and ask how I go about finding Harrow. It's the next station after mine, he says; we shall go there tomorrow. It was my alma mater. Your shop doesn't exist. Besides, tomorrow is Sunday and you won't find any stores open. At Harrow we lunch at a hotel called The King's Head. After lunch we walk up the main street, its ruins not yet reconstructed. I spy an open shop in whose window hangs a golf bag made of crocodile skin. I enter. I find my canes in a vase, exactly as in my dream."

By the end of 1923 he was left empty-handed, with nothing but a winning number. Radiguet would disappear, bequeathing Cocteau his legend like a moulted skin.

A harbinger of death spooked into the flat of Jean and Valentine Hugo the night of April 21, 1923, as Cocteau, Radiguet, and Auric sat around an end table on which they rapped questions, receiving—Mme. Hugo avers—rapped replies from some unseen Presence. The séance lasted until two in the morning and so intrigued the participants that they reassembled four nights later at the same table. While Radiguet recorded the dialogue, Cocteau and Auric took turns conversing with the spirit: "J.C.: Is it the person who was here the other day in this table? NO. J.C.: Is it the same person? YES. J.C.: Who are you? DEAD. J.C.: Are you a dead person? NO. J.C.: 'Dead,' why that doesn't make sense. YES IT DOES. J.C.: Can you reveal your name? NO. J.C.: Is that forbidden you? I AM DEATH. J.C.: Is it death speaking? THINK ABOUT ME." Five nights later they gathered a third time. Now Auric, trying to fetch a little poem from the rapping table, was told: I AM NOT A POET. I AM DESTINY. ONLY I CAN LAUGH ABOUT IT. YOU, CRY."

In July Cocteau and Radiguet returned to Piquey. They were soon joined by the Hugos and somewhat later by Auric. In one hectic year Cocteau had written two novels, two books of verse, and adaptations of two plays by Sophocles (*Oedipus* and *Antigone*). With Radiguet he had written the libretto of an opera based on *Paul et Virginie*, with a score which Erik Satie would leave unfinished at his death in 1925. Now he rested, which meant that his correspondence slackened to a mere downpour. Radiguet was nearing the end of his second novel, *The Count d'Orgel's Ball*, and relaxed by taking long walks along the beach, through pine woods alive with owls and around a swamp where he showed Valentine Hugo how to catch razor-fish, tormenting them in ways that struck her as cruel. Early in September the Hugos decided to spend some weeks in the Camargue, further east. Cocteau and Radiguet accompanied them to Bordeaux where the four dined at Le Chapon Fin. The Hugos would never see Radiguet again.

"A disorderly man who is about to die but doesn't yet suspect it," wrote Radiguet at the end of *Devil in the Flesh* with astounding prescience, "often tidies the world around him. His life changes. He files his papers. He gets up early, he goes to bed at a reasonable hour. He gives up his vices. His friends congratulate him. Therefore his brutal death seems all the more unjust. HE WAS ABOUT TO LIVE HAPPILY." During the summer of 1923 Radiguet was seized by a passion for order and hygiene. He neatly classified all the file cards on which he scribbled ideas for his characters. He started drinking more milk than alcohol. In Paris he spoke to Grasset as to his literary executor, giving instructions as if from beyond the grave.

"My last memory of Radiguet," wrote Grasset, "dates back to the month preceding his death. He had to go to the Saint-Maur town hall . . . for some formality and asked me to accompany him. We left Rue des Saint-Pères in my automobile. I was driving. That day he was more open than usual, expatiating at length on the language of *Count d'Orgel's Ball*. He spoke, in this connection, of certain 'provisional' words which appeared in the text he had recently showed me, as though leaving to my discretion the definitive form of his work. This distressed me. . . . He spoke of the imperfect state of his novel, in a worried way that struck me as odd. On our return, as we were crossing the Bois de Vincennes, he unknotted his scarf and handed it to me, 'for you to keep,' he said, 'as a souvenir.' "

One night in his room at the Hôtel Foyot he began to shiver uncontrollably. These shivering fits recurred. Cocteau and others urged him to see a doctor but, obsessed with the desire to finish his novel and resentful of being treated like a boy, he refused. In December, gravely ill with typhoid, Radiguet entered a clinic on the Rue Piccini. On December 9 he told Cocteau: "Listen to something awful. In three days—in three days I shall be shot down by the soldiers of God." When Cocteau remonstrated, he said, "Your intelligence is less accurate than my own. The order has been given. I heard it." On December 12, his body undermined by alcohol and offering no resistance to the fever, he succumbed, late at night, alone.

Several days later his parents and a huge throng from Le Bœuf including Picasso, Brancusi, and the Negro band attended obsequies for him at the Church of Saint-Honoré d'Eylau. Then his coffin, covered with a white pall and adorned with a single bouquet of red roses, was placed within a white hearse drawn by two white horses. In pouring rain everyone walked across Paris to the Père-Lachaise cemetery. Coco Chanel was there; she had arranged the funeral, paid the hospital bill and medical expenses. Russell Greeley and François de Gouy, Radiguet's summertime friends from Pramousquier, were there; they paid his debts at the Hôtel Foyot. Moysès was there; all of his young client's unpaid-for drinks were now on the house.

The best measure of Cocteau's despair is that he could not bring himself to attend Radiguet's funeral. "I am trying, for my mother's sake, not to die, that's all," he wrote to Valentine Hugo, herself recovering in Montpellier from an attack of peritonitis. Although he did not commit suicide, he never came closer. His letters to Max Jacob were such that the poet, living in part-time retreat as the jolly friar of Saint-Benoît-sur-Loire, quit clowning for once and replied:

> I appeal to your reason, don't alloy your sorrow with demoniac mischief and be careful with your poetic turn of mind. I should like to see you leave your room, and go confess if there is something preventing you from communing. . . . We shall mourn him all our lives. I have others to mourn as well, and no longer feel the urge to laugh—but no nerves, Jean. The bereaving soul is wary of nerves. My Jean, I beg of you, don't fall ill: I tell you, you are a man, but you are also a great spirit, why then don't you use your spirit to master your nerves? . . . Don't stay by yourself, speak about other things to people, and read one or two pages of the Gospel every day. "Let the dead bury their dead," says God, who knows what sorrow there is in death, to show that one mustn't allow oneself to crumble in coffins with a poor heart.

Cocteau's dreams collapsed. Two suffice to make a movement, but not one. With Radiguet's death, Cocteau sensed that he, too, was increasingly *a past*. Satie's death in 1925 would bring that sensation home the more poignantly. The Six had by now dispersed. Cendrars had gone to South America and would not return for years. Picasso, tiring of the smart set, sought company among the surrealists, Paul Éluard in particular. The war had embalmed the world of Cocteau's teens, cutting him off from it; now the death of his masters and of his protégé embalmed his twenties. He created a legend, a Golden Age which he would try to preserve, although feeling dead within it. Golden Ages were not meant to be lived, but regretted: by definition, they belong to the past. "This epoch," he wrote to Élise Jouhandeau in 1950, speaking of the early twenties, "this epoch which clings to my skin like a shirt of Nessus, as if I had done nothing but *Le Bœuf sur le Toit*, and jazz . . ."

He was now in his mid-thirties yet still saw himself as a young luminary. Insulted by time, Cocteau sought asylum in dead, timeless things: in his effigy, and in the euphoria of opium. "I wanted to attain white whiter than snow and I saw how my instruments were smudged with nicotine," he wrote in 1925. "So I formed Radiguet to bring about, through him, what I could not do myself. I obtained *Count d'Orgel's Ball*. Now I am alone, stupefied with sorrow, standing amid the ruins of a crystal factory."

8

The Versatile Inferno

Radiguet's untimely death left Cocteau staring at himself, cruelly deprived of an intermediary, a legendary shadow, a proxy existence. Nothing captures his state of mind better than a sheaf of thirty drawings he sent the publisher Champion in October, 1924, from Villefranche; it is entitled *The Mystery of Jean the Bird-Catcher: Monologues.*[1] Each drawing represents a different Cocteau: the aging dandy, the young sailor, the pontiff, the angel, the poet by turns serious, inspired, asphyxiated, the geomancer, the drug addict. They are embroidered with conversations between Cocteau and his past or possible selves. It is as if he were groping in the midst of multiple non-being for a means of life, for a single Image, like a bird-catcher deceived by his own decoys, his elusive quarry being himself. He explains in the introduction:

> By virtue of exercising senses deeply slumbering within me, I have seesawed in a world that provided me a key to the meaning of ours. Falsehoods distress me, and my only means now of behaving with a natural air would be to play a role. . . . The things that permit men to act, to form allegiances, to engage their gears have sunk into my vague depths and there taken the place of whatever directs my life, condemning me to solitude. I'm not proud of it. I am living the predicament of people who, curious about poison, take some without understanding the danger. Impossible to backtrack. I am inhabiting death. It usually seeks out people in their homes. It will find me ensconced in *its* home.

1. "Oiseleur," or bird-catcher has a homosexual meaning inasmuch as "bird" in French argot means phallus.

Cocteau makes the startling assertion that during the previous twelve years, since 1912, a malady whose symptoms may be detected in the above portraits had made his life a matter of sheer will power. His appetites, then, were the more exorbitant because he lacked them. His self-interest drove him relentlessly, on account of his frightening indifference. His craving for fame sprang from the fear that without fame he would be nothing, that anonymity amounted to death. His protesting too much in every conceivable way was owing to a deep-seated sense of fraudulence: the challenge once made by Diaghilev, "Astonish me!" was a traumatic issue which must have nagged him every day of his life. He lived in vain hopes of amazing, of seducing some few people gifted, in his eyes, with divine powers. Their unanimous refusal to take him seriously was warranty enough, he felt (despite himself), that they possessed *la part de Dieu*.

Being unique was a style in its own right, one which Cocteau both cultivated and damned, like the romantics, whose monstrous egotism was equally the sign of their selflessness; whose affection for utopian revolution and nostalgia for Golden Ages translated their subservience to a God, or to a Father against whom they measured themselves; whose penchant for suicide revealed their self-anger (suicide being a first and last assertion, a taking of one's life into one's own hands). Cocteau merely did more conspicuously what everybody is prone to do: create a legend of his life with an ideal beginning, middle, and end. If in 1912 he exploded into self-consciousness, writing *Potomak* soon thereafter, the origins of that trauma surely lay in his childhood. The legend thus served as a kind of self-decoy. It posted a glittering marker, 1912, which excused him from backtracking further, with the result that he would remain a child half-fleeing, half-pursuing his self. The year 1912 and its appositive legends—Diaghilev's "Astonish me" and the discovery of Gide's *Paludes*—demonstrate the personal impersonality so characteristic of Cocteau; he advertised, he glorified his trauma in order to avoid it. He turned even the unconscious into a façade, choosing death sooner than selfhood. Not even real death at that. Had he brought himself to the point of suicide, he might have grasped his life. In opium, Cocteau chose a death mirroring his life: death by proxy.

According to Cocteau's legend, Louis Laloy, a musicologist whose philo-Orientalism extended to drugs, gave him his first dose of opium in January, 1924, when the two were residing in Monte Carlo for the Ballets Russes' winter season. Cocteau had gone there, at Diaghilev's behest he claimed, totally inconsolable after Radiguet's death. A host of friends—Auric, Poulenc, Satie, Marie Laurencin, Juan Gris—were in Monte Carlo at work on various ballets. Sharing his sorrow did not, however, banish it, and the euphoria Laloy offered him proved irresistible.

But Cocteau, far from being inconsolable, was sufficiently himself to engage in intrigues with Auric, upsetting Satie so violently that he returned to Paris prematurely, and depressing Gris, who wrote to Kahnweiler, "As for the inseparable friends, Cocteau and the composers have been remarkably distant, and so has Braque. Not that it is of any importance, but still it has helped to make life here unpleasant." Moreover, Cocteau had been smoking opium for years, possibly since his childhood flight to Marseilles and certainly in de Max's entourage. It would appear, however, that Cocteau, at loose ends, began to smoke far more than he had before. Opium became a way of life. From 1924 until his death, with an intermission for World War II, drugs governed Cocteau, influencing his loves and disaffections, the company he chose, his voyages, his writings, his finances.

At least twice he committed himself to "disintoxication" clinics in Paris, first during the spring of 1925 and again, for a period of five months, in December, 1928. Neither treatment cured him, but the second failure produced a hodgepodge called *Opium*, which contains more penetrating glimpses into Cocteau than his other autobiographical writings. How grimly logical that Proust, after leaving the psychiatric clinic to which he had committed himself on account of his asthma, should have written *Remembrance of Things Past*, whereas Cocteau, on leaving his clinic, wrote of his sickness. George Painter suggests that Proust wanted, though inadmissibly, to prove himself his physician's intellectual superior, that he *chose* illness so as to embark on his voyage of self-discovery. Opium was a substitute for the epic Cocteau never wrote, for the project which forever eluded him.² His massive self-abuse amounted to the *Remembrance* he did not, and could not write.

Avoiding himself at every turn, wanting to be what he could not be, Cocteau discovered in drugs his bogus medium. Opium gave him a Self akin to some angelic stillbirth: beautiful but devoid of fluid, intact but living a life as artificial as the drug sustaining it. Opium condemned Cocteau to brilliant smatterings. "My dear Marcel," he would write to Marcel Jouhandeau early in 1929, "your book reaches me in a clinic where I am trying to understand why I cannot live without recourse to deadly remedies." In 1959, approaching his seventieth year, he would write to Élise Jouhandeau: "Being and living are two different things. By virtue of trying to be, I forgot to live."

Such categories as Being and Living, with capital letters, are fundamental to the romantic mind. The quest for Being at the expense of life runs through nineteenth-century French literature: Stendhal, Flaubert, Baudelaire, Rimbaud, Mallarmé. It did not by any means stop with the century, however. In ways more similar than each would have admitted, Breton and Cocteau perpetuated that quest. "Everything leads one to believe," wrote Breton, "that there exists a certain vantage-point in the mind whence life and death, the real and the imaginary, the past and the future, the communicable and the incommunicable, the high and the low cease to be perceived as opposites. One searches in vain for any other motive to surrealist activity than the hope of determining this point."

Cocteau was similarly obsessed with the One which, for him as for Breton, gave palpable signs of itself in a substance they both held in fetishistic awe: crystal. "The house I live in," declared Breton, "my life, what I write: it is my dream that these should appear from a distance the way cubes of rock salt appear from close up," thus implying that from a distance the crystalline life— reflecting itself, its core an appearance, not superficial but pellucid —would be subject and object in one. For Cocteau, who made a

2. In his *Letter to Jacques Maritain,* Cocteau appears to have recognized that opium was not an attempt to live life but his ultimate evasion: "My flight into opium is Freud's Flight into Sickness."

collection of crystal paperweights, "the crystal paperweight came to represent art and comfort," he wrote in his 1916 introduction to *Potomak*. "I was amazed at myself for having preferred cloth, furniture, vases wherein dust and satiety settle. It ceased to be crystal . . . a cube . . . six faces . . . a paperweight, but an intersection of infinites, a carousel of silences. Like those who press their ears against seashells to hear the roar of the sea, I brought my eye near this cube and believed that in it I had discovered God."

Cocteau's "intersection of infinites" and Breton's supreme "vantage-point in the mind" can be translated to mean an absolute present. Organizing his career in view of glorious occasions when he would *possess himself definitively*, the romantic discovers that every such occasion, when at last it comes to pass, elapses instantaneously, squeezing the victim out of himself anew, like a vise whose jaws are past and future. This absolute present, which amounts to a view from beyond the grave, Breton sought in hyperinduced dreams and Cocteau in opium.

> There is in man a kind of fixative [Cocteau wrote in *Opium*], that is, a kind of absurd feeling stronger than reason. . . . Without this fixative, a life perfectly and continuously aware of its speed would become intolerable. It allows the condemned man to get a night's sleep in his death cell. It is this fixative I lack. Perhaps it comes from a sick gland. Medicine considers this infirmity an excess of awareness, an intellectual strong point. I have every reason to believe that this ridiculous fixative, which is as indispensable as the habit masking from us the daily horror of having to get up, to shave, to get dressed, to eat, functions in others.

Opium furnished Cocteau a fraudulent self. It plunged him into time by taking him out of it. It plunged him into his senses by removing his sex. "In opium," he wrote, "euphoria leads the organism to death. Its tortures stem from a backing into life. A wild Spring infiltrates the veins, washing along ice floes and molten lava." But the addict pays for his euphoria with all the life fluid in his body. Cocteau understood, partially, the mechanism of his catastrophe, or so the paradoxes in his introduction to *The Mystery of Jean the Bird-Catcher* suggest: to appear natural he would have to play a role, and when death came to claim him, it would find him living in *its* home. Incapable of life, Cocteau was equally incapable of death. Opium, inventing a simulacrum of both, rooted him in a kind of no man's land, an angelic middle distance which he described well, as in the following passage from *Opium:*

> One memory strikes me. When, after the Satie trial, I gave vent to "threats of taking the law into his own hands with a barrister performing his duties," I did not for an instant consider the consequences of my act. It was a passionate act. The present absorbs us utterly. Our psychic life contracts so much as to become a mere point. No more past, no more future.
>
> The past, the future torment me, and passionate acts are few. Well, opium mixes the past and the future, making of them *a present One*. It amounts to the photographic negative of passion.
>
> Alcohol produces fits of madness.
>
> Opium produces fits of wisdom.

But whose wisdom? Opium served to hold intact the bits and pieces of Cocteau's persona. For half a century he would repeat again and again the same catch phrases, aphorisms, puns, names, symbols, turning his dialectic of paradoxes to every whim and purpose, proving things and their opposites until he was nothing but his own compendium of memorable quotations, his own quotation, a virtual madman who thought, except at rare moments, that he was Jean Cocteau.

His *Letter to Jacques Maritain*, written in 1925, provides—under the guise of public confession—another variant of his lifelong monologue. It amounts to a proof of God by Cocteau, resulting in a proof of Cocteau by God.

Raïssa and Jacques Maritain, the one a Jew, the other a Protestant, had the proselytic fervor of many Catholic converts. They specialized in the artistic avant-garde. Sunday was open house at their cottage in Meudon, half-way up a hilly street which led to the town's observatory. Writers, attracted by Maritain's known sympathy for modern art and poetry, made pilgrimages to the Rue du Parc, where the Maritains served tea in a salon which seemed organized around a portrait of Léon Bloy. Maritain, rather Christlike with his beard and luminous blue eyes, might, for the novices

present, diagram the Holy Trinity on a small blackboard he kept
for didactic occasions, but as often his conversation turned to the
same profane subjects discussed at literary salons and in Le Bœuf.
His regular visitors, apart from intellectual priests such as Father
Charles Henrion and Father Garrigou-Lagrange, included Claudel,
Cingria, Jean Hugo, Chagall, Rouault, Ghéon, and Max Jacob. Unlike Claudel, who favored a return to the primitive church, Maritain sought a philosophical reconciliation between Christianity and
the twentieth century, falling prey to his own superb intelligence,
which read its prejudices into works great and minor alike. Like
many a philosopher who strays into letters unable to tell a good
poem from a bad, he was an easy mark for fads.

Cocteau met Maritain in December, 1924, through Georges
Auric, whose circles of acquaintance extended throughout the
planetary system of Parisian arts and letters.[3] Maritain was already
familiar with his works, particularly *The Cock and the Harlequin*
and *The Cape of Good Hope*, which contained the few references
to Eternity that Maritain's dialectic needed to gain purchase. It was
almost inevitable that he and Cocteau should meet. Radiguet's
death, Max Jacob's proddings, Cocteau's nostalgia for a Father, his
need for an order in which to be disorderly, and perhaps the example of Gide's dalliance with Claudel brought Cocteau to Meudon,
just as the bankruptcy of surrealism would, some five years later,
send Aragon to Moscow. "Yes, my dear Jacques," Cocteau reminisced in his *Letter*, "dining for the first time in your house . . . I
recaptured the odor of Maisons-Laffitte where I was born, the same
chairs, *the same plates* which I used to turn, compulsively, so that
their blue motifs would coincide with the bottom of the glass. We
met beneath the sign of childhood."

3. Many years later Cocteau asserted that it was through Reverdy he made Maritain's acquaintance. Although Reverdy had indeed grown increasingly devout
and would in 1926 retire to a little house in Solesmes situated near the abbey, it is
implausible that he would have exerted himself for the sake of Cocteau's salvation,
even to the modest extent of introducing him to Maritain. The two poets were
never on friendly terms, Cocteau's assertions notwithstanding. Thus, in 1924, after
their apocryphal reconciliation, Reverdy, having consented to dine with Cocteau
in a Montmartre bistro, proceeded to denounce him in such violent language that
Cocteau burst into tears.

Soon afterward, Cocteau entered the Thermes Urbains, a clinic on Rue de Chateaubriand opposite the flat of Jean and Valentine Hugo. He remained there for some two months, taking needle showers and diathermic baths. On leaving the Thermes Urbains, he convalesced in Meudon, where Jacques Maritain cared for him according to ancient prescriptions of the faith and surrounded him with models of probity such as Father Charles, a bronzed, angular priest who lived in the African desert ten months of the year and recuperated, during the other two, in the Vosges. "Confronted with this man's ease," Cocteau sighed, "what did my own look like? —a ham-actor's charm. He smiled, told stories, exchanged memories with Henri Massis. Myself, stupid, *groggy* as boxers say, I was observing from behind a thick sheet of glass the white thing stirring in the depths of heaven." The morning of the Feast of the Sacred Heart Cocteau was given communion by Father Charles in Maritain's chapel. The following October, in Villefranche where he had spent the entire summer, Cocteau wrote the pamphlet called *Letter to Jacques Maritain*, rehearsing, in the light of God, his biography from 1912 on, deforming it where necessary as Christians will deform the Old Testament so that it prefigures the New.

"If He counts us, if He counts our hairs, He counts the syllables of verse. Everything is His, everything derives from Him. He is the model of audacity. He has borne the worst insults. He requires neither religious art nor catholic art. We are His poets, His painters, His photographers, His musicians." Having thus posited his consanguinity with God, Cocteau gave himself a scriptural career. His wanderings had been those of John the Baptist. He juggles his past into sainthood and his stage devices into theology. "Paris tears me apart. . . . For the past thirteen years I have been avoiding society; I am a man of solitude and of savage pleasures."

If he cut a scandalous figure, didn't Christ? If he fell afoul of the Establishment, wasn't Christ an undesirable among the Pharisees? Therefore, Cocteau proposed to found a "school of undesirables" whose undisputed leader he would be, and an "art for God's sake" whose canons may be found in everything he had written since *Potomak*. Picasso had taught him "to run faster than beauty"; now the esthetics of slow and fast motion became a theological consideration. God, like opium, had revised his metabolism, slowing him down, giving him the time to be human: "Nothing fascinates me more than the angel which a slow-motion camera forces out of everything like a chestnut from its shell. What? Since, in relation to God, our centuries elapse in a twinkling, we are being shot in slow-motion. A bit less speed, then, would unravel souls and anodynize human relations." In other words, God was a nameless intuition he had been harboring since the age of twenty-three. At the root of his careerism, of his addiction, of his pastiches, of his pederasty lay, misconstrued, love for love. All his vices had been the deficiencies of a Virtue.

God was "in." The young esthetes who knew by heart Cocteau's latest book of verse, *Opéra,* who bought their ties at Charvet's and had their hair cut by Millat, now attended mass. Maurice Sachs, a chubby Jewish boy who traipsed after Cocteau for years, had himself converted in Maritain's chapel on August 29, a few months after Cocteau. Le Bœuf suddenly abounded with penitents while seminaries abounded with clerics reading Cocteau's verse. The hypervirile, protofascist, militant Catholic *camelots* who gravitated round Charles Maurras at *L'Action Française* joined forces with the young homosexuals who hung in locust clusters around Rue d'Anjou, an alliance less singular than one might suppose, as the behavior of both parties under the Nazi occupation later demonstrated. Meanwhile Cocteau had fallen in and out of love again. Even as he was recording his public confession in Villefranche at the Hôtel Welcome, freed of quack remedies, the sweet odor of opium lingered in his room from a night spent smoking.

Whatever Cocteau's reasons for cultivating Maritain in the first place, he never derived from him the faith trumpeted in his *Letter.* He exploited the Church for his own ends like a husband who provides the spouse he no longer loves a consolatory substitute, the solution to a bad marriage being a divine triangle. When Glenway Wescott, the American writer who was living at close quarters with Cocteau in the Midi, wondered at the discrepancy between the latter's pious representations to Maritain and the impious sum-

mer he had just led, Cocteau confessed that his conversion was a
hoax engineered to save not himself but a lovelorn youngster
named Jean Bourgoint who was threatening suicide. Five or six
boys had already killed themselves over him, he claimed; this seventh he would beguile into surviving.

Cocteau was a veritable Pied Piper whose flute brought into the
magic circle any number of nubile youths spoiling for liberation, or
adrift and wanting a dark angel to reassure them that their homosexuality was, in his eyes, a nimbus. They streamed in from the
provinces, their culture consisting chiefly of Cocteau's latest work,
with little else than their puberty to recommend them. A few years
sufficed to tarnish their physical charm. If they did not kill themselves they mutilated themselves. If they did not mutilate themselves they forged some passing fancy of Cocteau's into a full-
blown career. Cocteau was perpetually involved in a tragicomic
routine with the Fates, ducking the pies they hurled at him; some
boy in back was always getting splattered. He thus left behind him
a succession of bewildered scapegoats.

A brother and sister, children of a wealthy Protestant family
from the provinces, are a startling example. They sent Cocteau, by
way of introducing themselves, a copy of his own verse wrapped in
flowered silk with thousand-franc notes sandwiched between the
leaves. Soon afterward they visited him. The boy lost no time falling in love with Jean Desbordes, Cocteau's protégé at the time.
Rebuffed, he hired a butcher to cut off his finger which, legend has
it, Cocteau received the following day by post, though the boy
later claimed to have buried it in the sand of some beach.

Maurice Sachs, who contrived to live off Cocteau for some years,
died a parasite's death, starving by slow degrees once he had been
expelled from his victim. Born of a wealthy Jewish family given to
frequent marriages and divorces, he had an upbringing by turns
genteel and shabby. At the age of twelve he happened on a copy of
Sade's *Hundred Days in Sodom*, which left a lasting imprint on his
mind. Effusive yet crafty, Sachs was a kind of literary con man,
unpredictably loving and thieving. At eighteen he discovered Coc-

teau; before long he had adopted his dress, was forging his signature, and worshiping his idols.[4] When Cocteau converted, he, too, converted, doing Cocteau one better by entering a seminary. Jealous of Cocteau's very being, he aped his manners, he free-loaded on his friends, he fawned upon his mother, and absconded with precious books such as an autographed copy of *Swann's Way* (which turned up soon afterward at the Hôtel Drouot auction house). It was suicide by identification. Some years later—after trying to start life afresh in the United States, where he represented himself as a connoisseur of art and married, disastrously of course, the unbalanced daughter of a Protestant minister from Seattle—Sachs wrote *Sabbat*, denouncing Cocteau as violently as he had once praised him:

> When I think about it calmly and sincerely, I must say that rarely have I met a man with less heart than Jean Cocteau. It is true that that word has no very precise meaning, but if heart is defined as a sum of pure, generous, disinterested enthusiasms, a fervor which gives of itself without expecting to be remunerated, admiration for its own sake, tenderness for everything alive . . . if this *humidity* which bathes the soul and renders it more comprehensive and superior, if this is what we mean by heart, then Cocteau did not have any. Furthermore, he used to speak of heart with the kind of obstinacy people display when determined to pass themselves off as something they are not. There was in him a dryness verging on the monstrous, but what he misconstrued to be movements of the heart was his nagging, anguished desire, febrile and feminine, to possess everything: secrets, allegiances, beings, things. The price he paid for his possessions made him think he loved them: he burned the way ice burns, without warming.

Yet a few years before his death, Sachs pleaded with Cocteau to forgive him his defamations.

Jean Bourgoint was a more beautiful victim. He not only entered a seminary but stayed inside and observed a lifelong vow of silence. One brush with Cocteau sufficed to turn this young Apollo into a Trappist monk. He and his equally ill-fated sister Jeanne

4. His thefts are said to have included a packet of letters written by Mauriac to Cocteau before World War I; after Sachs' death the packet fell into unscrupulous hands and was used in an unsuccessful attempt at blackmail against Mauriac.

appeared in Cocteau's life in 1925; when they left him, they left the
world. As soon as he had graduated from high school in Meaux, he
followed a friend of his named Fouquet to Paris. Fouquet having
formed friendships with Henri Sauguet and "Bébé" Bérard, Bourgoint immediately fell into a circle—that of the Hôtel Nollet—
which overlapped Cocteau's.

Tall, blond, and blue-eyed, Bourgoint was the Alcibiades of Cocteau's dreams. Glenway Wescott, who also fell under his spell, described him in the guise of a Wisconsin farmboy, Timothy Davis:
"He was a boy of great stature and almost perfect beauty. He was
indebted to his mother's family for his eyes blue as a plum, his
pointed lips and small nostrils; he inherited from Jesse Davis the
burned pink of his skin, his very large hands with rounded nails,
and a certain rudeness of bone and ripeness of muscle." Bourgoint
slept with Cocteau, smoked opium with him, and vacationed in
Villefranche during the summer of 1925.

Rendered impotent by opium and imbibing quantities of mineral
oil to keep himself alive, Cocteau entered the Thermes Urbains not
for Maritain's sake but, if anything, for Bourgoint's. The latter
would post himself in a park within view of Cocteau's window and
after nightfall, for several months in succession, wave farewells
with a white handkerchief. When at length Cocteau emerged from
the clinic, he found himself indifferent to Bourgoint, as if his love
for the boy had been a figment of his addiction; cured, temporarily,
of the latter, so was he of his feelings.

It was then, apparently, that he launched the scheme of conversion, knowing full well how futile it would be to appeal to Bourgoint's reason. By now a veteran at jilting and being jilted, Cocteau,
to spare the boy and his own conscience alike, supplanted one
addiction with another. If Cocteau educated his young lovers, it
was by way of possessing them. He was, to be sure, immensely
kind, but the dangerous pleasures he knew how to take (and survive) in tolerable doses proved fatal to youths who lacked his re-
straint. He killed them or created them, consigning them to an
oblivion they found unbearable or amalgamating them into his own
legend. In either case, his world prevailed over theirs, enveloping
them in a kind of limbo whose hectic, drugged luxury made any

return to the past unthinkable and placed their future in his hands. He became their fate, randomly providential or catastrophic, but declassing. Bourgoint leapt from obscurity into oblivion by way of Rue d'Anjou. Following his break with Cocteau, he was cared for by Jean Hugo at Hugo's country house in Mas-la-Fourques. Then he forfeited his name and all title to his passions, entering the monastery where he would spend the rest of his life.

Jeanne Bourgoint was equally ill-starred. Having married, she alighted from her nuptial bed with gonorrhea and had to have half her insides removed. The night of a ball given by Violette Murat and attended by all of arty-fashionable society, she committed suicide.

It is implausible that any one set of circumstances, let alone the pretext of wanting to "save" Bourgoint, inspired Cocteau's religious seizure. His affections for certain people led him along the most curious by-paths, and possibly Étienne de Beaumont was right in asserting that Cocteau's sudden religiosity stemmed from his enthusiasm for Jacques Maritain. Troubled and sick, he was drawn to the Church just as, troubled and sick, he would gravitate toward the French Academy thirty years later. The Establishment gave him self-confidence, for which he apologized by contending that "conformism is the new anticonformism of the 20th century." In other words, embracing one's Father had become avant-garde. Above all, what could have been more likely to vouchsafe Cocteau a reputation for poetic "depth" than mystical transports? Villefranche was alive with rumors that he had been seen by fisherboys in an ecstatic trance before a statue of the Virgin.

Cocteau's summer life reflected his Parisian life in various ways. He always gravitated toward the densest body of luminaries. And he lived in little hotels the equivalent of his delinquent pads near the Place de la Madeleine. Until 1924 he described a far-flung triangle with points in the Auvergne, at Piquey on the Atlantic, and at Pramousquier on the Mediterranean. After Radiguet's death he restricted his movement to the Riviera, whose tiny ports had just begun to eclipse the northern resorts of Trouville and Deauville. Between 1924 and 1929 his summertime address was the Hôtel

Welcome in Villefranche, a town lying adjacent to Nice and Monte Carlo. Glenway Wescott, another of the Hôtel Welcome's habitués, describes Villefranche as it looked to him in the mid-twenties:

A little half-moon of stone-and-plaster town in a narrow-necked harbor, all the buildings facing the sea, flesh-pink and yellow like a faded canary-bird and different shades of white with blue shutters; all one cliff of tenements, a street which was a staircase crossing at right angles another which was a filthy tunnel; around little squares the walls painted with false windows and false half-open or closed shutters and ornaments in false relief, like opera settings of canvas seeming to hang diagonally overhead, seeming to sway because of the brightness of the air; with a constant festivity of washing on strings from window to window, worn-out banners and ragged flags of underwear, with glimpses of disheveled beds, and shapeless females leaning out of the upper stories with their dresses slipping off their shoulders; and all the ground floors breathing forth an odor of the saliva of a vast beast.

The vast beast, in the shape of America's seventh fleet, lay anchored offshore and the odor it exuded onto Villefranche came less from its saliva than from its sperm. The bar of the Hôtel Welcome, where girls of every complexion and sailors of every nationality mingled, was the scene of several memorable uproars staged the night before the fleet put out to sea, with everybody running amok, throwing hard-boiled eggs, imbibing entire bottles of whisky without pausing for breath, and singing to guitar music. Atoning for the relative propriety of his life in Paris, Cocteau lived summers in the eye of a hurricane.

I'm living in a weird place [he wrote to Marcel Jouhandeau]. It's a box suspended in the upper branches of a flaming Christmas tree. On the first floor of this hotel-bordello sailors beat one another up and perform belly dances. I hear the bass drum throbbing jazz; it's as if they were printing a newspaper in the basement. The noise of the machine, the tarts throwing nervous fits, choirs of sailors (they imitate their movie brethren), etc. . . . The departure of the *Pittsburgh* was a dream, with a band playing the Marseillaise in slow tempo and twelve projectors lighting up the girls sobbing at win-

dows of the hotel [sic]. . . . God and the devil scorn me. Dear
Marcel, write, encourage me. The Church turns its head the other
way as I pass by and the sailors' bar vomits me up. My asylum is this
blue room which leads into yours and this sleep in which I die.

Elsewhere he describes the Hôtel Welcome as a kind of boarding
school governed by its inmates, like the "pension" in *Le Grand
Ecart*. He and his friends—Christian Bérard, Georges Hugnet,
Glenway Wescott, Mary Butts, Monroe Wheeler, Phillip Lassell—
were constantly wandering into one another's rooms. Cocteau occupied a corner room surrounded by a balcony from which he could
view the motley throng two stories below: gully-gully men, sailors
walking into and stumbling out of the Welcome Bar, and crowds
of young prostitutes brought from Marseilles by *Tante Fifi*, a
benevolent old madame who supervised them from the vantage
point of a nearby café, her stockings rolled down so as to expose
the hearts tattooed on her knees. Cocteau's room, redolent of
opium, featured, in addition to the pipe cleaners which hung from a
light bulb and swayed in the breeze, little objects he called "mys-
teria," each one representing a scene from some Greek tragedy.
Opposite him lived Lady Rose, an English eccentric who wore sail-
cloth dresses figured with roses painted by her son Francis and
who, fancying herself endowed with prophetic powers, set upon
perfect strangers to tell them their fortunes. The floor above was
occupied chiefly by friends visiting the long-term residents, by
sailors, and by fey boys who materialized, hung around for a time,
and evaporated like the sea mist. Poor Maurice Sachs sat on the
beach in his cassock lobbying for Cocteau's attention while an
American named Tom Pinkerton made advances to him.

The Hôtel Welcome became an international focal point, a *point
de repère* drawing Diaghilevians from Monte Carlo, Anglo-
American millionaire bohemia from Nice, stray French counts, and
consorts from all about. Behind its pink façade and *trompe-l'œil*
shutters lay all the ingredients of an Alexandrian potpourri. The
hotel formed part of a world half-drowned in its own fantasies. A
world had been exploded by World War I and the *disjecta membra*
of the wreck washed up all along the Riviera, like elegant fixtures
of some luxury liner. Prince Yusupov (Rasputin's assassin) and

other exiles paraded their dandified selves through the halls of Palace Hotels ringing the Mediterranean. Courtesans papered their walls with worthless Russian debentures given them before the Revolution, and one was reduced to selling the gold taps, designed as replicas of Saint Basil's cathedral, from which water used to pour into her solid silver bathtub. Edwardian relics, cut off from the past, had migrated south with no other purpose in life than to preserve it a while longer. Lily Langtry, now Lady de Bathe, arranged to sit in the darkest corner of parlors where only the straight lines of her profile emerged; but unavailingly, as Mrs. Patrick Campbell, sitting in another corner, summed up the ravages of her face. Victims and beneficiaries of time, of chaos, and of inflation mingled with one another: impoverished nobles surviving on credit and war profiteers gambling away millions at the casino, stately matrons and young English noblewomen who would not let their titles interfere with their pleasure, opium addicts and opium purveyors, the spiritually disinherited and spiritual confidence men such as Gurdjieff, whose devotees did not seem to mind his habit of munching raw garlic.

But perhaps the most striking figure in this Neronian festival was Isadora Duncan, now quite plump and living on doles from an American millionairess named Miss McMillan. Her studio stood at the far end of the Promenade des Anglais, outside Nice proper: a pink, windowless shack on a vacant lot strewn with empty tin cans and discarded bicycles. The door bore graffiti etched by lovers and friends; among them, next to the handle, was a heart with "Jean" in Cocteau's signature across it. Cocteau must have felt very much at home in Isadora's flat where she lived, as he always imagined his *monstres sacrés*, amid the cluttered mementos of a wild and peripatetic life. It was, according to one young admirer, "furnished with fake Louis XV furniture from the Galeries Lafayette, aspidistras in pots from Oriental bazaars, and dyed bulrushes in fake Sèvres vases. There were crocheted antimacassars, curtains, and tablecloths in all the rooms. The walls of her untidy boudoir were covered with photographs of her innumerable lovers: famous writers, Negro boxers, millionaires, sailors in uniform, and a few royal princes. Her bed was festooned with grubby mosquito nets, and the old-fashioned bathtub in her dressing room was filled with odd-ments which had to be moved constantly by the "pigeons."

Isadora, followed by two young American homosexuals whom she called her pigeons, was a familiar sight in Villefranche. Bare-foot, surmounted by a mop of magenta hair and trailing the folds of an orange-scarlet negligee, she carried her ruined majesty along the jetty in quest of sailors, and, quite often, to the Hôtel Wel-come. Though nearly fifty, Isadora was still, indeed more than ever, responsive to the appeal of young, sandy-haired men, and not infrequently they repaid her maternal lust with adulation.

Cocteau in *The Difficulty of Being* tells one anecdote which conveys the flavor of life in Villefranche, to which Isadora grandly contributed her incense and nard. It was decided to celebrate Francis Rose's seventeenth birthday in the dining room of the Hôtel Welcome. As the role of master of ceremonies fell to Coc-teau, he had his chair covered (*à la* Catulle Mendès) in red velvet and a bust of Dante placed before him. He wore a beige suit lined with black satin for the occasion, but his was a comparatively modest costume. Some priest, a large Greek cross suspended from his neck, saw fit to wear purple socks and bronze-colored shoes with his soutane. Maurice Sachs, still playing the seminarian, sported a scroll-shaped clerical hat in the Spanish style and carried a gramophone with a tortoise-shell trumpet. One of the great eccen-trics of her time, Lady MacCarthy of Monte Carlo—a fat, aged lady with Hindulike features—arrived in a frilly green dress so preposterously inappropriate to her bulk that she looked like "a cabbage reeling on tiny feet." A friend of Lady Rose's, known only as "the captain," was dissuaded from leading his donkey into the reception room but balked at facetious suggestions that he re-move the Basque beret he was never seen without. The atmosphere there was so disorienting that Cocteau and a group of surrealists, including Robert Desnos, could not even bring themselves to quarrel.

Last to appear was Isadora Duncan, attired in her diaphanous Greek tunic. As Cocteau described it, she came wending through the streets with Francis Rose, wreathed in flowers, at her side and spent part of the evening on a window embrasure, enveloping the

young man like a placenta. Possibly it was this which enraged the
captain, for suddenly his large silver watch (it ordinarily swung
from a length of cord he wore about his waist in lieu of a belt)
came flying through the air. Cocteau claims that he roared "Old
Lady, unhand that child!" and enforced his command with a cane.
At any rate, Isadora's toga had been torn and her eye blackened.
When one of her pigeons sought to calm her, she seized a lobster
covered with mayonnaise and hurled it at him. It landed instead on
Lady MacCarthy's lap. The latter leapt, as best she could, from her
chair and would have been at Isadora's throat had Cocteau not intervened. The incident started a general affray among the French
and American sailors on hand. "Mother," wrote Francis Rose, "remained indifferent and behaved as if nothing out of the ordinary
was happening." When peace was finally restored the guests sat
down to dinner, all but the captain, whom they found spread-
eagled on the balcony, knocked unconscious, apparently by the
whisky bottle at his side, and covered with blood. "I am geographi-
cally centered," wrote Cocteau to Jouhandeau, "in a place inhabited by those who suffer, who love, and who play a mysterious
game of chess. Do you understand me?"

Suffering because of opium. Suffering because it was an episto-
lary habit of his to suffer. Suffering because he liked to figure as a
melancholy knight. Suffering because his need for love—like the
form of love he practiced—left his appetite perpetually unappeased.
"My inhuman, unreal condition is killing me," Cocteau wrote to a
friend from Villefranche in January, 1926. "I fled . . . the change
of scenery has proved trying. After the water of Paris clean water
is too clean, too limpid—my mug frightens me and I'm sick: rheu-
matism, miseries—hideous fits of loneliness—unmentionable dreams."

Working on the economic principle that the scarcer a product is,
the higher its market value goes, Cocteau arranged extensive ab-
sences from Paris, but, once in Villefranche, he never ceased to fret
over conspiracies afoot or to lament the "vitiated" taste of the
times, doing battle from afar with his favorite windmills—the *NRF*
and the surrealists—promoting intrigues *in absentia*, and sometimes
persuading himself of fanciful reconciliations. "When some day
you come to understand the glacial injustice at work against me,"

he wrote in November, 1926, to Jouhandeau, with whom he had quarreled, "and when your eyes see me in clearer focus, like Reverdy's (after nine years!), you will find my friendship waiting for you intact." Jouhandeau remained unmoved, and Cocteau, making as he often did a mental erasure of all his other friends and conquests, saw his well-being threatened by this one: "I am stupefied, cast down by your letter. . . . Think of the *hideous pain* you are causing me. You who can understand and explain everything, tell me why I am fated to hatred. I am nothing but love, and want only love."

Meanwhile he found occasion to blame the surrealists for provoking the suicide of a young poet named Paul Sabon. As for the *NRF*, any mention of it enraged him. "Imagine," he wrote to Jouhandeau, "I was about to throw away unread, as I usually do, the latest issue of the *NRF*—it gives me a pain in the ass with its exegeses of an exegesis of the Anabasis of the treatise of the Nigger of the Narcissus—when whom should I discover in it but Marcel, your wonderful fairy tale, your admirable 'Prudence.' What a joy! Admiring anything in a review, in *that* review!" Yet apparently he subscribed to it, or took pains to have it forwarded to Villefranche. Furthermore, he did not disdain to publish in it. The July, 1926, issue contains an article of Cocteau's on Barbette, the stage hermaphrodite, an important article as it outlines a viewpoint peculiar to Cocteau's theatre:

> The reason for Barbette's success stems from the fact that he addresses himself to the plural audiences sitting within one, and mysteriously wins contradictory votes. For he appeals to those who guess in him the man, and to others whose soul is moved by the supernatural sex of beauty. Barbette performs in silence. Despite the orchestra accompanying his movements, his graceful turns and perilous acrobatics, his number seems to transpire at some distant remove, in the streets of dreams.

Everything is an act, Barbette's womanhood, and his manhood. Like Cocteau's own heroes, he is *in his very essence an actor*, standing beside himself, enacting himself, going through motions he is not at liberty to change: ambiguously theatrical and fated.

Between 1923 and 1926, in Piquey and in Villefranche, Cocteau wrote a series of variations on classical themes, culminating in his play *Orphée*, which kept him very much in the public eye. Their incongruous window-dressing—oracular horses, temperamental waifs, mirrors, angels, narrators in morning suits cast among the Greek mannequins—served Cocteau for the remainder of his life, on stage and in films. He invented a style which enjoyed enormous vogue in café society of the late 1920s: a style melodramatic yet spoofing, wise and wisecracking, irreverent but somehow sadly aware that it lacks the confidence or the energy to make a statement of its own, touting and mourning its own sterility. It provided a theatrical counterpart to the music of *Les Six*. Its kindred spirit in art informs the paintings of Christian Bérard and Pavel Tchelitchew: sleek and invertebrate, given to cumulous landscapes, ghosts, clowns, pierrots, and pale, pale children.

Appropriately, the idea of fashioning his own legend and theatre within the framework of Greek mythology first suggested itself to Cocteau through his favorite fetishes, a cane and a goat's horn, as if it were by contemplating his phallus that he discovered Greece:

> I was living, together with Radiguet and Auric, in a boarding house run by the Bessy family in Pramousquier where a childhood friend of mine, Philippe Legrand, paid me a visit. He was just returning from Greece and brought with him one of those shepherd staffs whose handle is a goat's horn arched like Minerva's eyebrow. He presented me this cane as a gift and during my long walks round the Cap Nègre, it gave me the notion of restitching the hide of classical Greek tragedy, and setting it to the rhythm of our age. I began with *Antigone*.

The result was an accelerated version of Sophocles' tragedy. Written the same year that he was working on *Thomas the Impostor*, it has the same essential theatricality, its characters going through their motions perfunctorily, performing their *tours de force* almost like puppets, as if the play were being staged to get itself over with as quickly as possible. A single voice represents the chorus, speaking (in a monotone like somebody reading a newspaper article aloud) through a hole in the backdrop. Antigone and Creon, Creon and Hemon engage in verbal fencing which sounds less like the tragic stichomythia it was trying to emulate than the vicious give-and-take of Parisian literati in a salon. It becomes apparent that Cocteau created a dramatic form out of quotation, the tragedy of his characters inhering in the game they play: their names are namesakes, their faces are replicas, their lives observe a known script. Cocteau used Sophocles' *Antigone* to give his own the status of a play within the play. The drama derives from Antigone's very inaptitude for being. She goes through the motions, theatrical and doomed, not only as Antigone, but as a play on Antigone, acting at a literary remove from herself.

Cocteau supervised every detail of its production. Charles Dullin, usually chary of authors who overstepped their bounds, made an exception here. He had, several months before, in October, 1922, installed himself and his troupe in the Théâtre Montmartre on Place Dancourt, a charming shell of a playhouse surviving from the nineteenth century: behind the theatre stood an Elizabethanlike courtyard with a mews where Dullin housed his she-ass Gypsy, and a hayloft which served as his acting school. The first play he staged drew all of eleven spectators, who huddled near the potbellied stove. Before long, however, his theatre was, like the Salle Huyghens, discovered by the *gratin*. One day the Queen of Belgium attended. Cocteau brought other titles of nobility, taking advantage of the freedom Dullin allowed him. "Cocteau mimed the roles to perfection and, had he wished to perform them all, he would have done so very well," wrote one of the actors. "Furthermore, he would have replaced the electrician, the handymen, the decorators. But though he had a hand in the adaptation, the masks, the painting, and the choice of costumes, he was content to perform the invisible role of the chorus. Standing on a ladder behind the backdrop, he projected his lines through a megaphone."

Raymond Duncan, attired, as always, in a peplum, was appalled by the spectacle. If Cocteau's text was not sufficiently impure, Picasso's backdrop added the finishing touch; it consisted of one huge swatch of blue-violet jute larger than the walls it covered so that the surface appeared to be cracked and wavy, playing optical tricks beneath the lights. Throughout the performance, Duncan and his Duncanians hooted "tu . . . tu . . . tu . . .", amplifying their hoots by means of trumpets not unlike the ones used by Métro conductors. Cocteau, speaking as the choir through a hole in the backdrop, laced his script with insults aimed at the demonstrators. When, some months later, *Antigone* was revived, the Duncanians demonstrated anew. This time, not content to hoot, they besieged the stage itself, but were held at bay by Creon's guards, using their wooden staves to good—if unexpectedly nontheatrical—effect. Cocteau hurled taunts from behind the backdrop while a number of impartial spectators did their utmost to reconcile the warring factions.

Cocteau's next move in his campaign to refurbish the classics took place during the summer of 1924, in a more genteel setting. Étienne de Beaumont, whose love for the spectacular had hitherto exercised itself in private, at masked balls staged within his eighteenth-century mansion on the Boulevard des Invalides ("The Temple of Uppercrust Muses") now decided to pit himself against Diaghilev. The count exemplified the mutation which had taken place within the *corps d'élite* of French aristocracy. Nothing could have been more classically patrician than his grooming, his carriage, and his manners. Indeed, he was so obviously *formed* that even his more egregious tics—a peculiarly high-pitched voice and a whinnying laugh executed with intakes of air—seemed part and parcel of an orthodoxy. Yet he was given to public ventures such as his forebears would almost certainly have deplored.

Circumstances abetted his début as an impresario, for Massine and Diaghilev had recently parted ways. The choreographer, along with Diaghilevian refugees, promptly offered his services to Beaumont. Beaumont rented the Théâtre de la Cigale and sponsored a series of spectacles called *Les Soirées de Paris,* incorporating the talents of Jean Hugo, Gabrielle Chanel, Cocteau, Tzara, Picasso, Satie, and Roger Désormière (a member of that loose confederation of young musicians devoted to Satie and thus called the School of Arcueil).

It stands to reason that Cocteau should have lit on *Romeo and Juliet;* the theme of children foredoomed, their purity unable to survive outside its own playground, was eternally attractive to him. In 1915 he had already attempted a scenario of *A Midsummer*

Night's Dream. Just as then he had written to Gleizes explaining that he planned to cut out the *côté fleurette*—Shakespeare's "frippery"—so now he spoke of "paring *Romeo and Juliet* to the bone." The result was a spectacle half play, half ballet whose chief merit lay in its frippery, for Cocteau, ignorant of the English language, merely refurbished a nineteenth-century prose translation. In any case, the words were only a pretext for Jean Hugo's costumes, which had the merit of being original. They were entirely black except for white gouache stripes outlining the Elizabethan millinery, doublets, and bodices. On a dark stage, against a black backdrop, the characters moved like white tracery.

It is revealing that Cocteau should have used the word *joli* (which he pronounced with a lisp) obsessively. Beauty intimidated him. On the other hand, prettiness—an original twist, a decorative signature looped around a classic or around a platitude—was something which he could manipulate like no one else. Cocteau's theatre has the toy dimensions and the speed of a pun. It seems to say, we are only children, but how heroic our mischief. It does not move the audience to fear or to pity; it connives with it, as children connive against the adult world, and the adult world sits, implicitly, on the stage in the sturdy persons of Shakespeare and Sophocles. The trick consists in being ornately original, in taking a classic, for example, and frittering it away until all that remains is a feathery silhouette, or else taking an inanity (*The Newlyweds*) and making some bulky issue of it.

The same year that he adapted *Romeo and Juliet* for Beaumont's *Soirées* he wrote the scenario of a ballet, or "danced operetta," *The Blue Train,* for Diaghilev. What is *The Blue Train* about? Nothing, and that is its point. The dancers merely imitate picture postcards showing swimmers on the beach, golfers, tennis players. Milhaud's score is unremittingly plain. "Give me music," Cocteau commanded, "like the kind one hears at the movies when a newsreel shows the prime minister's wife visiting a charitable institution." Art becomes the surrogate of taste, but taste consists in the mere inversion of established values so that, by his tics, his sarcasm, his unmitigated perversity, by the *tours de force* he executes on the shoulders of an elephantine subject, the naughty child will signal his own presence. In *The Cock and the Harlequin* Cocteau inveighed against music which demands to be heard head in hands (and so the Six composed mocking variations on great themes). Likewise, he justified his manipulations of Sophocles and Shakespeare as a campaign to remove the patina from classics.

Gide, after attending *Antigone*, accused Cocteau of being flippant. "It is for me of great importance," Cocteau rejoined, "to know whether a man like you can believe that a man like me is trying to provoke laughter with *Antigone*. If the answer is yes, which I refuse to believe—then at last I have the key to our endless misunderstandings, the proof of an optical angle which distorts *everything*. Your faithful J.C.—P.S. Removing a patina and showing fresh colors persuades the public that one is showing them an absurd poster. That is the real meaning of this laugh." Gide's reply ran as follows:

> But of course not, there is no misunderstanding, and there never has been one. Let's simply say . . . that there are in *Antigone* several awkward spots which lend themselves to misunderstanding. The question is, do you place yourself at Sophocles' vantage point or at Cocteau's. I know that you like Sophocles, but I fear you like him especially for his dance. "Patina." Only good wines age well. A patina is the recompense of masterworks.

If Gide found Cocteau's vantage point mystifying, Cocteau's vantage point *was* mystification. He eluded logic, he subscribed to no fixed canon of beauty, he arranged to peep over the horizon where least expected. Just as the tragic destiny of his characters consists in their having none, so Cocteau made a veritable career of ambiguity and surprise. For the same reason that he played with classics, he promoted *le goût concierge*, deeming fashionable the sodden Louis Philippe furniture found in every middle-class home or praising *The Mysteries of New York* as an epic tetralogy the equal of Wagner's Ring, much as today "campy" circles set store by Victoriana and Batman. His was an esthetic content to be the fulcrum of a seesaw, raising the low aloft and bringing low the lofty: a still center lying nowhere, unidentifiable, creating and undoing fads.

The spirit of the Cocteau circle was one of catty irreverence, and xenophobia. Its whole *raison d'être* lay in being "in," and "in" was a floating locus which fastened like will-o'-the-wisps on unlikely fetishes which may have had no adhesive virtue the previous month or year. It lived on exclusivity and battened on innuendo. Anyone not sharing Cocteau's opinions had to be disarmed, tricked into pretense, and judged pretentious. Cocteau was a master of one-upmanship, practicing his craft not only on the petty-bourgeois English who invaded the Côte d'Azur for their holiday, but on monuments such as Bernard Berenson, who stood his hallowed ground with pomp and ceremony. The following letter, which Berenson addressed to his secretary Nicky Mariano from Hyères, is strongly reminiscent of King Ferdinand's humiliating misadventure with Louise Balthy in Le Bœuf sur le Toit:

Dearest Nick,

I feel bruised and tattered in much the way that I was after having been all but killed by a mob at Aquila a few days after Italy went to war with Austria.

It happened like this. I was lunching with the Noailles. She sat between me and Cocteau and Rivière sat a little further away. We fell into a discussion about art over a creation of Picasso's that had just arrived and hung in the sitting room. This masterpiece consisted of a surface about the size and shape of the London *Times*. Not far from the top was a circle of sepia about five inches in diameter. Under it to the left was a column of small print looking as if it had been photographed from a newspaper. To balance this there was fixed with thin headless nails a piece of bran sacking.

Cocteau insisted that this was as complete and satisfactory a work of art as any Raphael and with every logical right to be so considered. I tried to make him consider the matter in detail and with the least possible irony. It infuriated him but he kept up a certain appearance of calm while pouring out a lava torrent of sheer verbiage that physically overwhelmed me. My hostess trembled with rage and her eyes flashed fire and to relieve herself she kept powdering her cheeks and painting her lips. Rivière agreed entirely with Cocteau. The company behaved toward me as if I were Edith's Mr. Blandhorne and had in a Zaouiah insulted the Prophet and blasphemed the Koran.

I had never been treated as such an outsider, never made to feel so helplessly, hopelessly in the presence of a world which knew me not.

When later I described the scene and the occasion thereof, the Picasso, Norton swore that it was all a *burla* from beginning to end. I wonder . . ."

Norton was quite right to suspect a *burla*, for the Picasso was not a Picasso but a pastiche of one by Cocteau.

The underlying poverty of this self-admiring milieu comes clear in a play like *Orphée*, which the Pitoëffs produced at the Théâtre des Arts in June, 1926. The play advertises itself as a refurbishing of the Greek myth, yet the myth hangs like mistletoe over a domestic melodrama which might be entirely vapid if not for Cocteau's verbal razzle-dazzle; it does not revive the myth, it puns on it but remains coyly outside. Ever since *Parade* Cocteau had been harping on the theme of illusion and reality, impeaching the audience for having eyes that boggle at shiny surfaces, yet himself staging only the shape of some drama, as if unable to give it the breath of life. True, Gordon Craig and Pirandello before him belabored the esthetic of theatricality, but theatricality for Cocteau was less an esthetic than a ploy (as chastity is not a virtue in the impotent man). Magic, that word Cocteau used so freely, grows from the inside out: it is nothing if not creation, yet Cocteau treated it as another "thing," not an incantation but a name dropped, not poetry but a prop.[5]

5. Similarly, the chapter in *Opium* entitled "Coincidences surrounding a name and a play" gives a magical aura, stuck on like a brass halo, to *Orphée* with the following account: "Marcel Herrand having decided to rehearse the play on the eve of its first performance, we all assembled at my place on Rue d'Anjou. We were rehearsing in the vestibule and Herrand had just spoken the line 'With these gloves you will cross through mirrors like water' when a frightening crash was heard at the other end of the apartment. All that remained of the bathroom mirror was its frame; shards of glass lay strewn about the floor. Glenway Wescott and Monroe Wheeler having come to Paris for the première of *Orphée*, they were stopped on the way to the theatre by a collision on Boulevard Raspail: one of their car windows was broken and a horse poked its head through. One year later I was dining with them in Villefranche, where they shared a very isolated house on a hill. They were translating *Orphée* and told me how incomprehensible a glazier would be in America. I countered by recalling that Chaplin played the role of a glazier in *The Kid:* 'It's rare in New York and rare in Paris,' I said; 'one rarely comes across them nowadays.' They asked me to describe a glazier and accompanied me across the garden toward the gate when we heard and saw a glazier who, against all expectations and defying all likelihood, wended his way along the deserted road and vanished."

Thus he gives the following set directions for *Orphée:* "A living room in Orpheus' villa. It is a curious room, rather like the room of a prestidigitator. Despite the April sky and its stark light, there is a hint of mysterious forces surrounding this room. Even the ordinary objects have a sinister look about them." And, fearful that this upholstered mystery might not appear sufficiently obvious to his audience, Cocteau arranged to have the protagonist come on stage before the curtain rises and deliver the following caveat:

Ladies and Gentlemen, this prologue is not the author's. I am certain he will be surprised to hear me. The tragedy whose roles he has confided us is a precision maneuver. I should like to request that you wait until we have finished our performance before expressing your feelings. The reason why is this: we are performing at a very high altitude and without benefit of a safety net. The least, untoward noise may cause us to lose our balance and result in the death of myself and my comrades.

This stands as another in his long line of prefaces to prefaces, each quoting the former and their sum amounting to illustrious silence. The play itself is a preface, to its author, for in the last act, when Orpheus' disembodied head is questioned by the police inspector, it answers to the name Jean Cocteau, born in Maisons-Laffite. Excusing himself from the prologue by one stunt, and introducing himself into the plot by another, Cocteau remained, however, conspicuously absent. If he identified himself with Orphée, the play does not authorize his name-dropping; it is so much more a synopsis than a world in itself that it seems almost impertinent of him to have obtruded himself, as if his signature were enough to give some artistic bulk to a mere innuendo.

But neither can the significance of the Orphic myth in Cocteau's life be denied. What he meant and signally failed to reveal about himself in the play he succeeded in doing some twenty-five years later when he made a film version. The difference between the play and the film hinges chiefly on the altered character of Death. In the former she is cast as "a very pretty young woman wearing a bright pink gown and a fur wrap;" in the film, however, she is older, severe yet maternally competent. It becomes apparent, as the film unfolds, that she is a mother, embodying the mother's double role of death-dealer and life-giver. Cocteau makes that collusion obvious when he defines Death, at the outset, as Orpheus' death: "Each of us possesses his death and it governs us from the moment of birth." She removes people from the world with the instruments, and in the costume, of an obstetrician delivering a child from the womb.

Orpheus' amorous craving for her has a corollary in the angel Heurtebise's desire for Eurydice, the live woman. An otiose and chichi figure in the play (in which he figures as a glazier), Heurtebise becomes significant in the film as an alter ego of the hero. Taken together, Orpheus and the angel form a dialectic of impotence, the one incapable of death, the other of life: death and life cast as Woman. Placing both under the dominion of womankind, Cocteau respects the Greek view, according to which goddesses hold sway over the earth and the underworld. "What does the marble in which a masterpeice is being sculpted think?" cries Orpheus as the Maenads begin stoning him to death. "It thinks: they are striking me! ruining me! insulting me! I am lost. . . . Life sculpts me, Heurtebise, let it finish its work." Thus murdered by life, he is resurrected as a statue by death, the Maenads and the Black Princess operating in harmony with one another, lobbing him back and forth.

Even the double-take at the end of the film, when Orpheus, dispelling both Death and the Maenads and returning to earth, rescues his selfhood from the vicious cycle of femininity, even this does not really mark a departure from the myth, which, like many another Greek myth (that of Pentheus, for example) swings irresolutely between the feminine principle and the masculine. In Cocteau's film, Orpheus' victorious resumption of life with Eurydice—Death the Mother and Heurtebise her emissary son having been arrested —amounts to an avowal and a defense of homosexuality. Having awoken from his bad dream, what is it Orpheus resumes? Not so much life with Eurydice as his work. A namby-pamby figure, Eurydice merely answers Cocteau's need for a feminine element in his homosexual theory of creation. That theory he enunciated in *Opium*.

Art is born of coitus between the female and male elements which constitute us all: the two are better balanced in artists than in other men. It stems from a kind of incest, from love of self with self, from parthenogenesis. That is what makes marriage so dangerous for artists, marriage being a pleonasm, a monstrous striving toward the norm. The sign of the "melancholy lord" which stars so many geniuses comes from the fact that the creative instinct, satisfied in other ways, leaves sexual pleasure free to exert itself in the pure domain of the esthetical and also directs it toward sterile forms.

So, the ménage of Orpheus, Eurydice, and their son consists of only one person, Cocteau, whose creation renders woman superfluous. How much more convincing, however, the bulk of the film than its conclusion, the tale of Orpheus' twofold impotence than his claim to creation, his Dionysian defeat than his Apollonian victory. Cocteau himself seems to have recognized this. The angel's last words to Death are: "We had to put them back in their mire," referring to Orpheus and Eurydice. Incapable of life as Heurtebise, the Mother's angelic surrogate, and incapable of death as Orpheus, Cocteau went very far indeed toward summing up his own predicament. "I saw the first copy of *Orphée* and am satisfied with it," wrote Cocteau to a friend in 1950. "It isn't really a film, it is myself, a sort of projection of what really concerns me." What really concerned him was the presence of the primitive, endogamous matriarch lurking in every *bourgeoise*, but he did not really do her justice until his later years, in this film but especially in *Les Parents Terribles* where she is divested of her Greek trappings.

In the 1927 revival of *Orphée* Cocteau himself played the angel. The profile of Orpheus and the star of the "melancholy lord" embedded themselves in his signature and remained with him until the last.

In 1927 Cocteau realized a dream he had been nursing ever since *The Rite of Spring:* associating his name with Stravinsky's. *Oedipus Rex* was, however, the offspring not of a love match but of a marriage consummated somewhat out of desperation. Like two hollow men, they had only enough spunk left to etch their names into a gravestone, and to recriminate one another while so doing. This gravestone they offered as a gift to Sergei Diaghilev.

Stravinsky had come to an impasse not unlike Cocteau's. He had always suffered a lack of melodic inspiration, but this did not plague him so long as there was Russian music and folklore to orchestrate, with Diaghilev providing him a stage. The war and the Revolution forced him into permanent exile, with the result that he became a suckling of foreign traditions and innovations. Like Diaghilev, he relied on the composers and music at hand, Russian (specifically the "Five") before the Revolution, and Occidental afterward, but, beginning with *A Soldier's Tale*—composed in Switzerland shortly after the Revolution—that reliance became unabashed.

It could be argued that artists grow tropistically, away from their blind spot. Thus the discovery of cubism may be owing to Picasso's insensitivity to color. Stravinsky's lack of melodic gift, set in bold relief by his exile, brought about a similarly resourceful inversion. In *Pulcinella* he applied his genius for rhythm and orchestration to themes of Pergolesi. *Mavra*, which Diaghilev produced in 1922, amounts to a musical spoof of nineteenth-century comic opera, jumbling together and dislocating by various contrapuntal devices the stock musical figures of *bel canto*. The orchestral music of his neoclassical period, such as the "Concerto for piano and chamber orchestra" and his "Serenade" of 1925 owe their inspiration directly to Bach, Handel, and eighteenth-century Italian composers.

As in many of Picasso's paintings, the external armature of Stravinsky's music, the object in other words, is somebody else's work. "Supplanting the object directly observed, lived, or simply imagined, but in all events *extracted from a universe outside music*, are *forms already congealed in sonorous matter*." Means become an end, and every composition serves as a kind of prism through which composition *per se* may be viewed. Adopting musical things, Stravinsky used them to deliver a commentary on the nature of thingness in music, which brings to mind an observation Breton made in 1930: "It was already true a century ago, as Hegel demonstrates in his *Esthetics*, that in the more advanced forms of poetry the subject must inevitably appear as something irrelevant; since then it has even become impossible to state the subject in advance."

Cocteau's adaptations of Greek theatre, which sprang from the same intellectual source, clearly point out the dangers of universalism: all that remains of the mythical issue is a decorative blip. Likewise, Stravinsky was never more truly universal than during his Russian period: the neoclassicist he became reduced himself to his musical signature. How revealing, in view of this, the spiritual crisis he experienced in 1923, which brought into his household a priest named Father Nicolas. Undoing himself as a Russian musically, and living in Nice, that *cul-de-sac* of exiled intellectuals who, for want of native soil, bathed their uprooted persons in the Mediterranean, Stravinsky turned so piously Russian Orthodox as to condemn the ballet for being "the anathema of Christ." Compensating for the hyperintellectuality of his art, Stravinsky resurrected his motherland in its least intellectual form.

Stravinsky and Cocteau had never lost touch over the years. If they did not always see eye to eye, they sat side by side in Le Bœuf and in various salons, notably the Princess de Polignac's, where many of Stravinsky's works were first performed privately. The composer was irked by the aspersions Cocteau cast upon him in *The Cock and the Harlequin* but, anxious to keep astride with the modern movement and reproving his Russian self as exotic, he started to compose, in earnest, "rags" which bear comparison with music of the Six; Cocteau, in turn, made amends in a postscript to *The Cock*, and arranged to have the piano score of Stravinsky's "Ragtime" published by Éditions de la Sirène.

Both artists were at the height of their fame, and both fell under the influence of clerics who held sway like black offspring of their impoverished sensibilities. Their collaboration did not therefore come about by accident. Its symbolic prologue took place the summer preceding Radiguet's death and Stravinsky's religious seizure, at a party given after the première of *The Wedding* by two Americans, Gerald and Sara Murphy, aboard a barge moored near the Chambre des Députés. "The first person to arrive was Stravinsky, who dashed into the *salle à manger* to inspect, and even rearrange, the distribution of place cards. He was apparently satisfied with his own seating—on the right hand of the Princess Edmond de Polignac." At length the other guests arrived, including Picasso, Milhaud, Ansermet, Diaghilev, Kochno, Larionov, Germaine Tailleferre, Blaise Cendrars, Tristan Tzara, and Cocteau. Afterward everyone danced while Ansermet and Marcelle Meyer played the piano. When the hilarity was at its height, Kochno and Ansermet took down a huge laurel wreath bearing the inscription *Les Noces* (*The Wedding*) and held it like a hoop. Stravinsky, no doubt fortified by drink and by that sensation of freedom which allows people to do at sea what they will not dare do on land, ran the length of the room and leapt through. Meanwhile Cocteau, attired in the barge captain's uniform and bearing a lantern, walked along the deck, shouting through each porthole, "We're sinking." For once he was prophetic.

Stravinsky's first inkling of the opera-oratorio *Oedipus Rex* came to him as a vaguely felt desire to create some large-scale dramatic work, but the impossibility—now that he considered himself an expatriate—of composing in Russian, and his imperfect knowledge of any other language, discouraged him until, in a Genoese book stall, he happened upon a life of Saint Francis. One passage, in which the biographer observes that Saint Francis had recourse to French whenever he wished to express some strong emotion religious or poetic, disdaining his native Italian as an inept and debased language, impressed Stravinsky who, even before he chose a theme, decided it must be sung in Latin, "a medium not dead but turned to stone and so monumentalized as to have become immune from all risk of vulgarization." On his return to Mont Boron near Nice, where he was living with his family, Stravinsky began to hover about the Greek myths and finally lighted on Oedipus. "I wished to leave the play, as play, behind," he wrote. "I thought to distill the dramatic essence by this, and to free myself for a greater degree of focus on a purely musical dramatization." Needing a librettist, Stravinsky turned to Cocteau, who was residing nearby, at the Hôtel Welcome:

I thought that I could not do better for my libretto than to appeal to my old friend Jean Cocteau, of whom I saw a great deal as he was then living not far from Nice. I had been frequently attracted by the idea of collaborating with him. I recall that at one time or another we had sketched out various plans but something had always arisen to prevent their materialization. I had just seen his *Antigone* and had been much struck by the manner in which he had handled the ancient myth and presented it in modern guise. Cocteau's stagecraft is excellent. He has a sense of values and an eye and feeling for detail which always become of primary importance with him. This applies alike to the movements of the actors, the setting, the costumes, and, indeed, all the accessories. . . . For two months I was in constant touch with Cocteau.

According to Cocteau, they took a trip together in March, 1926, through the mountainous country to the north of Nice, stopping at inns and "counting the several melodies from *Faust* where Gounod surpasses himself," but it was far from being an Arcadian collaboration, and Cocteau's unusual reticence about it may serve as the most telling indication of what pain he experienced.[6] Stravinsky was wont to run roughshod over the prima donnas with whom he collaborated. His musical imperatives always prevailed over the literary, but it cost him a few friends, such as Gide, who felt that in *Persephone* his text had been cruelly mistreated. Cocteau was similarly distressed at finding himself upstaged. Stravinsky required a "still life," a libretto so unobtrusively conventional as to heighten the musical drama. Instead Cocteau submitted a lively text "told," Stravinsky felt, "in horribly meretricious prose." It took two more versions before the composer at last gave the text his imprimatur and even then he insisted on a final shearing.

"What is purely Cocteau's in the libretto?" he said later. "I am no longer able to say, but I should think less the shape of it than the gesticulation of the phrasing." Cocteau, however, was a master at husbanding his resources. Just as he had retrieved the text which Diaghilev jettisoned from *Parade* to build *Le Cap de Bonne Espérance*, so now he salvaged the original text of *Oedipus Rex* and would eventually use it in *La Machine Infernale*.

With his *Oedipus* rendered totally unrecognizable in Latin trans-

6. Elsewhere, Cocteau dates the excursion in February and refers to a "guide who spoke in oracles. We called him Tiresias."

lation, Cocteau hoped at least to play the part he had created with himself in mind, that of the Narrator. Here, too, he was foiled, by none other than Diaghilev, who was staging the work, written in honor of his twentieth anniversary as a theatrical impresario, despite the fact that *Oedipus* displeased him ("a very macabre present," he grumbled). The Narrator's lines were read by a handsome young man chosen by Diaghilev for the express purpose of spiting Cocteau. The homosexual arcana of their quarrel made the staging of *Oedipus,* as of all their collaborative ventures, a last-minute slapdash affair, aggravated here by Diaghilev's distaste for the music and by Stravinsky's tardiness in finishing the score. Diaghilev had worked with Cocteau at regular intervals during a generation; on *Le Dieu Bleu* in 1912, on *Parade* in 1917, on *Le Train Bleu* in 1924, and on *Oedipus* in 1927, but the sum of these collaborations never quite amounted to a close friendship. If Cocteau succeeded in "astonishing" Diaghilev, it was, each time anew, by virtue of his stagehoggishness.

Oedipus was, at any rate, their last imbroglio. Toward the end of his life Diaghilev strove to deliver himself from his semibondage to French composers (notably Auric), dismissing them as writers of *musiquette* and promoting the more muscular compositions of Prokofiev.[7] "Constructivism," in music if not in painting, became his dying slogan; although a mere shadow of his former self, dying of diabetes, he was sufficiently the great impresario to sponsor another controversial refugee of genius from Soviet Russia, George Balanchine. In 1929, the year Diaghilev died, he was still alive to threats of competition within the ballet world, enough to explode on hearing of Ida Rubinstein's newly formed company, "I ask myself only one question: what's the use of all that? No, we need somebody, a Napoleon or the Bolsheviks, to come and blow up their shanties, with their public and their tarts who fancy themselves artists, and do away with the millions they spend buying musicians."

But this amounted to a death twitch. During the last four years of his life, Diaghilev became less and less a man of theatre and in-

7. The young composers whom he backed—Markevitch, Rieti, and Nicolas Nabokov—all subsequently lost their edge and defaulted to the School of Paris.

creasingly the Russian nobleman, the *barine* he had never really ceased to be. The impresario was all but eclipsed by the bibliophile. Everything Diaghilev earned from the Ballets Russes he spent on rare Russian editions, including three books from the press of Ivan Feodorov, the Gutenberg of Russia. Lying on his bed he would, for hours on end, comb through catalogues and bibliographies and dream of establishing a library of Russian incunabula in Western Europe. On August 19, 1929, he died, in that spiritual home of great esthetes, Venice, where thirty-five years before he had first awoken to the World of Art. His remains were ferried across the bay to the cemetery of Saint Michael in a funerary gondola flanked at prow and stern with winged angels.

In its last years under Diaghilev's administration the Ballets Russes served as a kind of litmus paper distinguishing the blue bloods from the red. Diaghilev's collaborators were, *ipso facto*, antirevolutionary, or so the surrealists would have it. When Max Ernst and Joan Miró executed the sets for Diaghilev's production of *Romeo and Juliet* in 1926, Breton and Aragon issued the following protest:

> It may have seemed to Ernst and Miró that their collaboration with Monsieur de Diaghilev, sanctified by Picasso's example, would not have grave consequences. That collaboration obliges us, however—as we consider it of paramount importance to keep the advanced posts of the intellect clear of all slave-traders, whatever their ilk—to denounce out of hand an attitude which abets the worst partisans of moral ambiguity.
>
> It is by now obvious that we attach little importance to our artistic affinities with this person or that. We should like to make it known that in May, 1926, we are more than ever incapable of sacrificing to those affinities our image of revolutionary reality.

The party lines were clearly drawn, then, by 1926, surrealists standing to the left and Diaghilevians to the right. This arrangement of forces would be brought into still sharper focus during the 1930s, when Aragon, Sadoul, Éluard, and others defected to the Communist party while those artists and composers who had stood

within or on the fringes of Diaghilev's circle became the Establishment, administering the state theatres and running the major orchestras. René Crevel, a gifted poet and the fair-haired boy of
surrealism, shuttled between the two worlds, now observing
Breton's edicts, now frequenting Marie-Laure de Noailles's circle,
but this was an exceptional feat, requiring not so much balance as
imbalance. Crevel killed himself in 1935.

Cocteau and Max Jacob were the literary peacocks of the smart
set, which, spurning the intelligentsia and standing aloof from
politics, called itself neoromantic. There is no precise way of defining neoromanticism, but it specialized in pierrots and angels and
children, it made an issue of "sentiment" and occultism, it preened
over its own decorative naïveté. It was a movement composed of
the half-talented, the half-called, and the half-committed: painters
who proved far more original at dress or set designing, composers who ultimately made their mark, if at all, as conductors or
critics. The soul of neoromanticism stares coyly out of the paintings of Christian (Bébé) Bérard. Bérard—whose father was the
last in a dynasty of distinguished architects and whose mother came
of nobility minor but wealthy thanks to their string of fashionable
funeral parlors [8]—gave up painting angels and wraiths to become a
set designer of great distinction, Dior's gray eminence, and an arbi-
ter of taste whose drawing pen set and undid fashion for two
decades.

Gravitating around Cocteau and Bérard (but each an epicycle in
his own right) were Henri Sauguet the composer, Roger Désormière, Vittorio Rieti, a sprinkling of Americans and of White Russians such as Boris Kochno, Nicolas Nabokov, Igor Markevitch,
and, more remotely, Pavel Tchelitchew, whose career in Paris did
not survive an unfavorable remark dropped by Cocteau after his
first exhibition. Their favorite gathering places in Paris were the
Villa Spontini, where Bérard lived with his parents until setting up
house with Kochno in the early 1930s, and the Hôtel Nollet,
whose tenants included Sauguet, Max Jacob, and Vittorio Rieti.
Summers, they flocked south to Villefranche, to Toulon, or to
Hyères, where Marie-Laure de Noailles, one of their eccentric

8. The Borgniols.

Muses, made them welcome at her large estate. It was she who prevailed upon her husband to subsidize the filming of *The Golden Age*, *The Andalusian Dog*, and *Blood of a Poet*.

Cocteau gave *élan* to this milieu, doing what he liked to do best, running the wheels of his celebrity machine, promoting the kind of intrigues that made every group he influenced a reticle of sexual bonds knotted unhappily with open secrets and mutual praise, organizing claques for concerts or for *vernissages*, and collaborating whenever the occasion arose. Like everyone else, though perhaps more energetically, he lavished himself on Igor Markevitch, that faun-like youth born the year Diaghilev challenged Cocteau to astonish him, and launched at sixteen by Diaghilev himself. When the seventeen-year-old Markevitch composed an ambitious cantata for soloists, choir, and orchestra, Cocteau wrote the words.

Working with him was highly complicated [wrote Markevitch], for Jean, the most exquisite person alive, was also the most difficult to pin down. At the last moment, before a scheduled work session, I would receive a special delivery letter, or else some mysterious messenger—always a different one and always referring to himself as a secretary—announcing that Monsieur Cocteau wanted it known that he was dying but could see me the following week. Jean's health at that time was indestructible, but he had a whole arsenal of imaginary illnesses to put off the importunate, to postpone his rendezvous or defer his work until later, with infantile excuses and all the ruses of an eternal truant. At length he would arrive at our little apartment on the Square des Batignolles, but don't imagine that getting down to work was all that easy! Jean would take off his shoes, amble about the apartment, rumple the covers, ask to drink and eat extraordinary fare which my mother would have my sister fetch from the corner grocery. This was still another pretext to defer work, for when my sister returned Jean would summon her and tell stories, illustrating them with sketches he made with such facility that we stared wide-eyed.

Working on the theory that there is no better way of reinforcing an Establishment than advertising it as avant-garde, and no better way of advertising the avant-garde than staging a *beau geste* at the expense of some minor opponent, Cocteau embroiled himself publicly with Vladimir Dukelsky, doing so in a way reminiscent of his outburst during Satie's trial and of his cat fights with Henri Béraud on behalf of *Les Six*.[9] Imitating the surrealists, who had denounced Diaghilev in 1926 for his anti-Bolshevism, Cocteau in 1927 launched a campaign against Diaghilev, though for the opposite reasons. The impresario, though appalled by the Soviet regime, was apt to endorse it now and again out of bravado, and Lenin was even reputed to have offered him the post of People's Commissar for Soviet Stage Production. More to the point, his taste for French music diminished in proportion as he fell under the sway of Prokofiev, whose pro-Soviet ballet *Steel Steps* aroused the ire of Russian *émigrés* sitting in the audience. After the performance Dukelsky, who had had the privilege of sharing Diaghilev's box with Prokofiev, assured the latter that his music would prove the undoing of "the decadent Parisian *musiquette*." Cocteau, standing nearby, seized this one French word, easily deduced its Russian context, and shouted, "Dima, we Parisians send you a load of shit" (addressing him in the familiar, as always), whereupon he slapped the young composer and vanished before his blow could be answered.

Diaghilev, eternally fearful that a scandal would lead to his deportation, begged Dukelsky not to retaliate, but his entreaties fell on deaf ears. When at last he caught up with Cocteau, Dukelsky found him surrounded by acolytes whose presence gave him the courage to scream, "Return my slap, Dima, return my slap! Let's fight!" Considering prudence the better part of valor, Dukelsky challenged him to a duel, a challenge he renewed later in the evening backstage, where Cocteau, "in his light tan gabardine suit, with shocking pink lining displayed by artfully unbuttoned sleeves, leaning on Desbordes, his newest 'literary' discovery," was delivering an anti-Russian harangue before an attentive crowd.

When, the next morning, Dukelsky's seconds—two former officers in the Wrangel army—called upon Cocteau at 10 Rue d'Anjou they were turned away by Cocteau's valet Cyprien, whereupon Dukelsky, donning his best morning coat, decided to pay Cocteau an

9. Dukelsky's ballet *Zephyr and Flora* was produced by Diaghilev in 1925. Somewhat later he took up residence in the United States, changed his name to Vernon Duke, and won fame and riches as the composer of "April in Paris."

impromptu visit. Cyprien, seeing his elegant apparel, made the mistake of letting him enter, and Cocteau had no recourse but to appear, and be slapped. "The effect of my action was most unexpected," wrote Dukelsky. "Cocteau grabbed me in his arms, embraced me and sang out: 'Let us embrace, Dima, let us embrace.' "

The following day Cocteau wrote Diaghilev a letter of self-explanation, describing Dukelsky as an unmitigated coward.

The legend Cocteau had created of Radiguet compelled him to find replicas, to legendize other young men so as to sustain his belief in the original and, above all, in himself. Radiguet's death punched a hole in Cocteau's life, a hole he could never repair for it became a mythical point of reference, and the legendary stuff with which he filled it was apt to seep out through the bottom, into the real world. The gnawing sense of his futility thus sponsored Épinal images, great blow-ups which by their very nature came in serial form. Radiguet's successor was Jean Desbordes, on whom Cocteau is described as leaning, in the Dukelsky anecdote, to deliver his anti-Russian harangue. Their liaison lasted some five years.

Cocteau was corresponding with Desbordes before he met him. This was not in itself exceptional, as Cocteau received dozens of letters from aspiring young writers in the hinterlands who by chance fell on his poems or novels and, jubilant at finding an author concerned with adolescence, made bold to share their lonely ruminations with him. Moreover, Cocteau had a far-flung reputation for not being able to resist answering letters, particularly if they came illustrated with photographs boding well. Desbordes had not troubed to send Cocteau a photograph of himself, and when he announced intentions of visiting Villefranche, Cocteau feared that he would be "bespectacled and beak-nosed." He had nothing to fear. Desbordes proved to be a slight, feline youth of twenty with high cheekbones and sensual looks reminiscent of Radiguet's. Being attached for the time being to the Naval Ministry in Paris, he wore a sailor suit, which only enhanced his appearance in Cocteau's eyes.

Twenty or even ten years before, a youth such as Desbordes would unfailingly have addressed himself to Gide, but Cocteau had so far eclipsed Gide as to capture a boy suffering the Gidean syndrome; Desbordes, brought up in Rupt, a small village on the Moselle, was a homosexual and a Protestant given to writing pagan georgics weakly descending from *Fruits of the Earth*. His few prose poems, suffused with a spirit of barnyard pantheism confusedly Oedipal and mystical, rising at their best to a kind of suave eloquence, might have served Tartuffe in good stead, as a manual to alleviate the scruples of prospective bedmates. Cocteau lay hold of them as if they were the New Testament; he wrote in his preface to *J'Adore* (as these poems, once put in order, were eventually entitled):

> He brought me a typed packet of unformed cries. Suddenly he was falling asleep, he was talking about another world, he was flying, he was walking on water. My mind was quickly made up: I would devote myself to the task of teaching him how to induce this chance sleep, how to become aware of himself without losing his freshness. . . . Radiguet's genius had all the outward attributes of the highest talent; that is how he hoodwinked the world. Jean Desbordes' genius has only the looks of genius. Our age, rotten with talent . . . calls for this lover's clumsiness.

Cocteau was more than half-persuaded, then, that he had discovered another Radiguet, and said as much: "Yes, Bernard!" he wrote to Bernard Faÿ from the Midi in 1927, "it's a miracle from heaven; Raymond has returned in another incarnation, and often unmasks himself." But his lingering doubts over Desbordes' genius gave his hyperboles a slightly demented froth. Only half aware of it, he used Desbordes as a plausible wedge out of the Catholic Church. Having an odor of sanctity was not, he well knew, likely to guarantee him the youthful audience whose approbation he wanted, yet renouncing the Church outright would have revealed the frivolity of his recent conversion. "It furnished me," Cocteau later admitted, "a pretext to get out of an equivocal situation." *J'Adore*, a "Christian" monologue certain to outrage Maritain, served Cocteau as a *deus ex machina*. He had only to convince himself and the public at large that Desbordes and his writing were worth the repeal of his sanctity. Like a medieval physician, Cocteau cured one predicament by creating another.

Cocteau conducted his campaign with the slatternly evangelism of an American politician, prevailing on every Catholic homosexual whose word carried some weight in the world of letters, on every literary journalist of his acquaintance, on every influenceable critic. Hearing, for example, that Bernard Faÿ had expressed some mild interest in *J'Adore*, he seized the opportunity to write him as follows: "My very dear Bernard, Poupet reports that you are very interested in the book which I love above all others and which is raising a storm of controversy. I would like to see you, to embrace you, to thank you, and to ask you to write a little critical essay which, in view of your position, would have a decisive impact on the United States. Jean Desbordes would love you and you know how rare it is to meet a pure being without the shadow of a shadow." Faÿ remained unpersuaded. So did Edmond Jaloux, the critic and novelist, whose favor Cocteau curried uninhibitedly:

> Don't think that I would allow myself to "ask" you for anything in a realm where your liberty must remain intact, but in reading Desbordes' book with your heart's eye, you would reimburse me with a little of that joy which has been stolen from me by the ungrateful attitude of our age—for I know that you will see, as I do, the wonders of these Brontës of France, these terrible and adorable loves, these frantic fairy tales, these swift characters—and see them with a primitive's joyous ejaculations. It would lift a weight from my heart to have you speak about this book as we have spoken together in the past about other matters; it would be a preface to the joy of living.

When Jaloux favored *J'Adore* with only moderate praise, Cocteau wrote: "You know very well that this book is higher, more perfect in its contours and fullness than you admit. If not, then I wouldn't love you as I do—Must you adopt such reserve, and be so unjust for the sake of newspaper readers? (It is I speaking, not Desbordes who lives in Chablis and will be moved by your compliments) . . . I embrace you from the depths of this distress which is with me to stay."

Desbordes' arrival called for a new retrospective of Cocteau's *œuvre* (which, depending on the angle and the light, proved a wonderfully various instrument, by turns cubist, neoclassical, neoromantic, and Catholic). In view of his latest love, Cocteau shifted another degree and beheld himself as a Christian primitive, bringing to bear *The Cape of Good Hope:*

Be assured that primitive man saw the moon with his eyes the way we see it today with telescopes. It is probable that one day men will outfit themselves with a diving suit which will permit them, not to explore the forbidden zone, but to rediscover a zone of the senses atrophied with age.

I have an intuition of that zone. That is why my poem *The Cape* remains a dead letter, why my work is understood perversely, why I am so often considered a heretic, because, by means of fragments, I bring alive a kind of abstract reality, a dead region of the primitive human body. . . . Science does not trespass God's realm. It corrects the human infirmity. God begins after all possible discoveries; ethics change according to those discoveries, and the ethics of God begin after all our ethics.

The Middle Ages would have burned a Maritain.

In this same statement, Cocteau delivered himself of certain images worth underlining, for they would later form the basis of his first film, *Blood of a Poet:* "I am a poet: a bundle of irreconcilable contradictions, baneful solitude. . . . The poet is a brilliant and profound plant. He embodies the spirit of humus, of individualism, of the monster, of the millionaire. When revolutions cease paying heed to their poets, they founder. Christ is an active poem. When He dies, He signs His work with a cross, in blood."

Cocteau's star, hanging pendantlike from his signature, was the appropriate symbol for a man who whirled so fast as to have lost his center of gravity somewhere among his radial points. It was also a badge of martyrdom, for Cocteau never ceased to complain of being unappreciated by the public. But if he made such an issue of the "inside" versus the façade and of the evils of journalism, he knew better than anyone how much talent he had squandered on his façade and what credit he solicited from journalists to recoup his losses. "I am an example of the limitations of the power of criticism," he protested. "I ask for a lot: admiration, praise, remuneration leave me cold." On the contrary, an unfavorable review sufficed to unhinge him for days on end and bring alive his rheumatic miseries (this remained so throughout his life). The least of literary journalists was worth an elaborate courtesy, for Cocteau relied on public opinion to vouchsafe his works what they only mimicked: depth. He wanted to be known as "deep" and he actively lobbied for the title of genius.

Thus, when his friend Faÿ was putting the finishing touches on *Panorama of Contemporary French Literature*, Cocteau paid him a visit and cavalierly made the following request: "Bernard, say whatever you like about me in your book: it little matters. I insist on only one thing, the word GENIUS, that's all, you understand me." Faÿ, tallying Cocteau's multiple talents, decided that no one of them nor their sum amounted to genius but gave Cocteau what he considered his due, and perhaps slightly more. Cocteau disagreed. "You perceive nothing of my role," he protested in writing, "of my immense work. . . . To have omitted mentioning *Le Grand Écart*, to have put *Thomas the Impostor*—first of those light-footed, *gay scienza*, halcyon books anticipated by Nietzsche—on the same level as Aragon's rococo and Lacretelle's pleasant platitude . . . after Morand and Giraudoux, those great fabricators. No, it's scarcely believable. YOU?"

The "You?" may well have been an "I?" disguised, for the saving grace of Cocteau's legend was his awareness of its flaw. Awareness *was* its flaw, so painful, so inadmissibly human that, whenever it threatened to grow wider, he would mask it with opium. Hence his binges and his cures following the death of Radiguet and the collapse of his straw man Desbordes. Cocteau, Desbordes, and Bérard, all three of them drug addicts, migrated to Villefranche several summers in succession before moving slightly westward to Toulon, around 1930, nearer the Noailles and the Bourdets, at whose "White House" Paul Morand and Jean Giraudoux often vacationed. Desbordes would gradually fade from the scene. Oddly enough, he seems to have had a protector in Mme. Georges Cocteau, aware of her son's loving depredations and fearful perhaps that young Desbordes might go the way of Raymond Radiguet. Desbordes wrote to her from Villefranche:

Jean has received the *Revue Européenne* and I thank you from the bottom of my heart for the kind words you had for me. But put your mind at ease. Jean is not dragging me where I cannot go. His life is quiet and free and the people most intimate with him are not wicked. Anyway, I am very retiring and don't care to have company. Without Jean I really don't know how I would have muddled through. He taught me the necessary things which I would never have learned on my own. It is he who built my future, and did so for the simple, divine reason that he likes what I write.

That future of his, lacking a foundation, collapsed utterly. When Cocteau saw Desbordes at the première of *The Infernal Machine* in 1934, it was after a separation of some two years, and he was appalled by his emaciated appearance. Somewhat later, Desbordes married a woman considerably older than he. He died in 1944, a Resistance hero, tortured by the Nazis.

If Cocteau had made himself preposterous on Desbordes' behalf, that was the token fee he paid to get out of his Catholic imposture. The genius he attributed first to Radiguet, then to Desbordes, sanctified his about-faces, which were not really about-faces but a return in each case to some more comfortable, natural footing he had lost along the way. Just as he issued *Thomas the Impostor* on the occasion of Radiguet, his *Livre Blanc* appeared in 1928 as a kind of companion volume to *J'Adore*.

The novella *Le Livre Blanc* was published in a limited edition of twenty-one copies by the Éditions des Quatres-Chemins, whose director, Maurice Sachs, had predictably thrown off the cassock only to resume his career of literary Tartuffism. It appeared in a larger edition two years later, with sketches by Cocteau. In the swift, clean prose of *Thomas*, it tells the story of a homosexual, bringing on stage for the first time in Cocteau's work his childhood idol Dargelos, and recounting his flirtation with the Church. It is thinly disguised autobiography, yet does not bear Cocteau's name. In fact, Cocteau resorted to the coy and preeminently Cocteauian device of signing his preface to an *anonymous* book whose authorship he would neither admit nor deny, thus taking up position in that ambiguous no man's land of his where, quoting himself, he speaks from behind a mask, and where, undressing himself, he turns out to be *wearing* his body. It reflects the same point of view which totally escaped Gide after *Antigone:* mystification. Thus the following masterpiece of *sic et non:*

Too many and too limiting are the circumstances which clearly disqualify *The White Book* from appearing under my signature. However, I am—and admit it—still tempted to lay my name thereto, theft tempting our fingers to seize an object gilded by the peril and gratuity of the act. . . . But let us smile upon these sumptuary scruples which more befit a dear old fool dreaming of the good old lawless days. We reject them; but tell me now if we have not often dreamt of falling asleep, of writing while in sleep, and of waking on the morrow to find the work written and with no other thought than to have to attend to the job of correcting proofs?

If Gide did not receive one of the twenty-one copies, *The White Book* nonetheless owed, in part, its existence to him, for beyond a doubt it was Cocteau's answer to Gide's defense of homosexuality, *Corydon*. The books are to one another as the invocation and response of a litany. That Cocteau oriented himself with a view to Gide is obvious in their correspondence. Outwardly rivals, in private they were still master and protégé, Cocteau bending backwards to please Gide, to avoid his recriminations.[10] In the 1930s they walked more their separate ways but even then followed one another indirectly. Thus, the year after Gide resigned from the Communist party Cocteau would seize the opportunity to write for Aragon's *Ce Soir*, a Communist party organ. And when, in the late thirties, François Mauriac's son Claude made his literary debut, he became a bone of contention which Gide and Cocteau worried, as in previous years they had contended for the discipleship of Maurice Sachs. Gide recorded their rivalry in *The Counterfeiters* where Cocteau appears in the guise of Robert de Passavant (Passavant meaning "unknowledgeable"), a sinister popinjay whom Gide takes obvious pleasure in thrashing:

> For Passavant, the work of art is not so much an end as a means. The artistic convictions he displays are the more vehement for their lack of depth; no secret necessity of temperament dictates them; they answer the dictates of the period; their battle cry is: opportunity.

10. After reading *The White Book* Gide wrote in his journal: "What futile fluster in the dramas he relates! What affectation in his style! How he plays to the gallery! . . . What artifice! Certain obscenities are described quite charmingly, however. The really shocking part of it is his pseudoreligious sophistry."

The Horizontal Bar. What will soon seem oldest will have seemed at first most modern. Every accommodation, every affectation is the promise of a wrinkle. But it is thus Passavant wins the young. Little does he care about the future. He addresses himself to the present generation (which is certainly better than addressing oneself to the past)—but since he addresses only the present, his works run the risk of disappearing along with it. He knows this and does not promise himself survival; and that is why he defends himself so bitterly, not only when he is attacked, but when critics show any reserve. If he felt that his works would endure, he would allow them to fend for themselves without justifying them at every turn. More than that, he would consider misreadings and injustices good reason to congratulate himself. So much string to retwist for the critics of tomorrow.

Cocteau's coy abstentionism offered several advantages. Neither denying nor admitting the authorship of *The White Book,* he could thereby afford scandal yet claim modesty, call himself a genius (as he does in the preface) without depending on the independent judgments of a Faÿ, make himself a perpetually intriguing object by exposing just enough of himself to create an aura of mystery about his person. Above all, he could earn the liberty of fashioning his own legend in the image of himself. This schizoid posture was fast becoming a natural one for Cocteau. In art he stood beside himself as from opium he derived a spurious sensation of "being." Yet all that unhappily prevented Cocteau from committing himself to his art, happily reprieved him from the "rapture of the deep" of opium. In December, 1928, he entered a clinic on Rue Pozzo di Borgo in Saint-Cloud for a second attempt at curing himself of his addiction. "Again I've weaned myself away from a remedy which always turns into a despot," he wrote to Gide in February, 1929.

Even a clinic could not seriously crimp Cocteau's sociability. He wrote letters at his usual rate, received friends almost daily, and, consulting the roster of inmates, discovered that he had a neighbor in Raymond Roussel, the wealthy hermit whose extraordinary dream travelogues *Locus Solus* and *Impressions of Africa* had already earned him a place in Breton's surrealist genealogy. Cocteau made out of the Saint-Cloud clinic what he made of every place he inhabited—of the Hôtel Biron, of the ruined villa in Flanders, of the Hôtel Welcome, of the flats he would take in Paris on the Rue Vignon and in the Palais Royal, and of the villa Santo-Sospir where he spent his last years: a mysterious inpost, a privileged hiding-place—known, advertised, celebrated—where a group of children are landlords, the initiates of a secret society founded on talismans, myths, whisperings, innuendos. The work of Cocteau's which best conveys this dream of life in a tree house suspended above time and space was written, at a feverish pace, during his incarceration at the Saint-Cloud clinic. "Your visit," he assured Gide, "was very sweet for me, and enriching. I owe you so much; there was a time when, had you not intervened, I would have gotten lost following the example of my counterfeit handwriting. Now I want to announce the true benefit of my cure: work is working me. I am disgorging the book I have meant to write (but couldn't) since 1912. This book is coming without my forcing it—it orders me around, mistreats me, and I have done several months' work in nineteen days." That book was eventually titled *Les Enfants Terribles*.

"A hundred and fifty years ago," wrote Albert Camus in *The Fall*, "people used to grow dreamy over lakes and forests. Today, we are infected with cellular lyricism." That remark, though aimed at the prison literature inspired by World War II, fits Cocteau very well. His stories rarely wander outside rooms, rooms in which some couple elaborates its doom: mother and son in *Les Parents Terribles*, in *La Machine Infernale*, and in the film *Orphée*, the queen and the anarchist in *The Two-Headed Eagle*, Tristan and Isolde in *The Eternal Return*, beauty and the beast.

In *Les Enfants Terribles* the doomed couple are brother and sister. Their lives elapse, chiefly at night, in a room not unlike Cocteau's, cluttered with the hundred fetishes through which they communicate beneath their cranky banter. "Singular beings and their asocial acts are the charm of a pluralistic world which expels them," Cocteau explains. "It is anguishing to see the cyclonic speed at which these light and tragic souls move. It all begins with childhood things; at first all one can see of it are its games." Games, a drawer filled with talismans, objects stolen from the outside world, washed of their patina and inserted into the private mythology of Paul and Élisabeth: all furnish a room, like a stage, bathed in red light, which comes alive at night. Brother and sister, Cocteau repeatedly tells us, are actors enacting "their own masterpiece," observing a rhythm akin to the internal rhythm of art, torpid yet swift like the hallucinations of the opium smoker. They are at the same curious remove from themselves as Cocteau's Greek characters, going through the motions of Sophocles' tragedies. "Servants of an inflexible law, they would bring that law back to their room as to a honeycomb."

More than that, however, they are the figurations of Cocteau's recurrent dream, the several variations of which have in common this: some liaison so necessary it is as if the partners were only one person Janus-faced, so natural as to dissolve in the "outside" world, so tabooed it can sustain itself only in a room insulated from time and space. If Cocteau on several occasions in *Les Enfants Terribles* invokes Racine, his novel, like Racine's plays, unfolds like a game played parenthetically within history, broken up the instant the parenthesis opens.

The image, prevalent in some form throughout Cocteau's works —the dual One torn apart by a world intolerant of such perfection —is the core of a short dramatic masterpiece Cocteau wrote the same year he wrote *Les Enfants Terribles: La Voix Humaine*. It has only one character, a woman engaged in a telephone conversation with her lover to whom she is bidding farewell. The play consists of that farewell. It opens with the telephone ringing and closes with a click of the receiver. Wrong numbers, an exasperating partyline, and a disconnection provide the tragic peripeties in a conversation rigorously banal yet dramatic, filled with tender courtesies whose purpose is to avoid the word love, temporizing, wheeling round about itself even as it moves ineluctably toward silence. All that holds the two together is a thread, a cord looped through the dark world where it is at the mercy of interfering parties and unseen manipulations. "*Coupe, coupe*," she cries at the end, meaning not only hang up, but stab, stab.

In *Opium* Cocteau, forever defending himself, defended *La Voix Humaine* as follows:

An unesthetic act, an act of presence perpetrated against the esthetes, against the snobs, against the young (the worst snobs), capable of moving only those who await nothing and don't prejudge. . . . I mean to link up with the true public which is to be found only at the Comédie-Française and at the Bobino. Big receipts. Full house. Encores. It isn't the public which needs shocking but the elite. Bring off a scandal of banality, get into the official repertory, figure on the main bill.

La Voix Humaine represented Cocteau's longest step toward true popular success. It was performed by Berthe Bovy at the Comédie-Française on February 17, 1930. Cocteau had thus made, not a new departure—as he let it be known—but a return, via the most devious of routes, to what he had never spiritually left: the Boulevard of Holy Monsters such as Bernhardt and de Max, and the music hall of Mistinguett, Damia, and Fréhel. During the thirties, he would surround himself increasingly with actors and *artistes*, some of them well known, some of them stray cats picked up in the *bas-fonds* of the entertainment world. Withdrawing altogether from literary circles, he would find company in his interpreters, launching stars the way he had made literary geniuses. He would write lyrics for Marianne Oswald and for Edith Piaf. He would associate with Suzy Solidor and Panama Al Brown. He would revive forgotten boulevard plays such as Bataille's *Love Child* and, giving them a clever twist, endear himself to a café society which, unnerved by the collapse of banks and nation states, clamored the more wildly for his neurotic fairy tales.

When Cocteau emerged from the clinic in Saint-Cloud he settled in a small flat on Rue Vignon (number 9), just behind the Église de la Madeleine. It had taken him some forty years to leave his mother's home, but having done so, he devised elsewhere the exact clutter he had left: canes, Greek decanters, his blackboard, the head of Antinoüs, crystal baubles, a large canvas by Christian Bérard showing an angel behind a lectern, a case made of pipe cleaners projecting eerie shadows onto the wall. "I couldn't describe it," he wrote of his flat. "Its fullness was its vacuity. Furniture and objects came there of their own accord. One didn't see them. What one did see was this vacuum, a loft of emptiness, a trash can of emptiness, a vacuum full to overflowing. Ghosts filed through in serried ranks. . . . The visitor liked this room, observing in it nothing unusual except the ensemble. This ensemble comforted him, sat him down, relaxed him, cut him off from the outside. The invisible people were at my beck and call. They did the serving and warmed the drama to the proper degree."

When Jean Wiener paid Cocteau an impromptu visit at Rue Vignon in 1930 the mystery escaped him. He was met first by a sweet odor unmistakably that of opium. At Cocteau's side stood Maurice Sachs, rotund as ever, wearing a pearl gray suit and a white carnation in his lapel. Cocteau himself was scarcely recognizable. Deathly pale and enveloped in a black dressing gown, his features pinched and his hair teased into a frizzy crest, he bore a striking resemblance to some old, formerly elegant lady, an impression reinforced by the ribbon he was wearing round his neck. It was as if Cocteau had translated from Rue d'Anjou not only his room, but his mother as well.

9

Self-Impersonations

The experimental film in France could afford its impetus in the 1920s thanks to the endorsement of the *beau monde*. Although chary of dada and of surrealist literature, a few restless aristocrats would subsidize any form of highjinks provided they got an immediate return for their money, a show accessible and spectacular. The avant-garde cinema appealed to them much as the Ballets Russes had appealed to their parents. Indeed, *Entr'acte*, made in 1924 by Picabia and René Clair, formed part of a ballet staged under the auspices of Diaghilev's chief rival, Rolf de Maré. Étienne de Beaumont, perhaps anxious to outdo Maré, commissioned René Clair's brother, Henri Chomette, to produce a film for his *Soirées de Paris*, but the result—a reel showing the effects of light catching crystal surfaces—proved eminently forgettable. Most of the experimental films produced during the early and mid-twenties bore a family resemblance to Chomette's *Reflections of Light and Speed:* photographic antics in which analogous forms are placed against one another, or futuristic machine ballets prefiguring today's arty short. None of them, however, had the scale or cinematic purpose of *Entr'acte*. It took two Spaniards to bring French cinema out of the doldrums. In 1928 Luis Buñuel and Salvador Dali produced *The Andalusian Dog,* which struck Breton, when he saw a preview of it, as irreproachably surrealist. The "official" scenario appeared in a subsequent issue of *La Révolution Surréaliste*.

Buñuel produced the film with a considerable sum his mother had given him for that purpose, or what remained of it after he had had his fill of Parisian night life. He and Dali prepared a series of "gags," strung together in a way calculated to discourage rational analysis. These gags feature their authors' favorite fetishes, sadistic fantasies, mule dung, and priests: all the humus one might expect to find in the head of Spanish *révoltés*. The film opens with the now famous telescoping of two images: a thin cloud sectioning the moon and a razor sectioning a woman's eyeball. It comes to a climax, of sorts, in the attempted rape scene:

> She withdraws step by step into a corner where she protects herself behind a little table.
>
> He takes on the attitude of the villain in a melodrama; he looks about everywhere, searching for something. At his feet he sees the end of a rope and picks it up with his right hand. His left hand searches the floor and grabs an identical piece of rope.
>
> The young woman, flattened against the wall, follows the actions of her assailant with terror.
>
> He advances on her, hauling with great difficulty whatever is attached to the two ropes.
>
> We see first a cork, then a melon, then two brothers of a teaching order, and finally two magnificent grand pianos. The pianos are filled with the carcasses of two donkeys, whose hoofs, tails, croups, and excrements overflow the body of the instrument.

Buñuel and Dali wanted to contrive a dream sequence so repellent that the snobs could not call it beautiful, so painstakingly illogical that critics could not bring order out of chaos. For its first scheduled projection at the Ursulines theatre, Buñuel filled his pockets with little stones, anticipating that the audience would wrathfully hurl itself at him. What, then, was his surprise to hear (from behind the screen where he had been playing records of Wagner's *Tristan and Isolde* and an Argentine tango) thunderous applause. The four hundred artists and aristocrats present found *The Andalusian Dog*, against all odds, beautiful.

Buñuel's official response appeared at the head of his official scenario in *La Révolution Surréaliste:* " 'A successful film' is what the majority of people who saw it thought. But what can I do about people who go crazy over anything new (even if the novelty outrages their inmost convictions) or about a venal, insincere press, or about the pack of imbeciles who found beauty or poetry in what is, essentially, nothing less than a desperate, passionate appeal to murder." While Buñuel, like Breton and Aragon, was sincerely distressed to find his poison turned into culture food by the smart parasites who like nibbling at art, he could not but feel elated. It takes far more money to produce a film than to put out a small literary magazine. Buñuel needed a rich sponsor, and one, who had seen *The Andalusian Dog,* soon materialized in the person of Charles de Noailles.

Photography had become all the rage in the *beau monde.* Étienne de Beaumont never gave a ball without inviting some photographer to mingle with the guests. Even the Countess Greffulhe had become a shutter-bug, converting a little room adjoining the chapel of her country villa into a photographic studio where she communed with professionals such as Man Ray. For Charles de Noailles it was more a passion than a hobbyhorse, and he indulged it with all the revenue at his disposal. The grand ballroom of his mansion in Paris served as a movie theatre where he gave previews of films produced at his expense. His château in the south of France—a construction of severe gray cubes built inside the ruins of an ancient Saracen fortress overlooking Hyères and the sea—provided the setting for a short film of Man Ray's, inspired by Mallarmé—"The Mystery of the Château of Dice"—in which the Noailles' guests (including Étienne de Beaumont) wore nylon stockings pulled over their faces so as to give themselves a ghostly air. Not content to sponsor home movies, however, the viscount invited Buñuel to produce another film, handsomely offering him one million francs (the equivalent of a quarter million dollars). He got not only a film but something he had not bargained for: a scandal.

L'Âge d'Or, as the film was eventually entitled, had its first showing on November 28, 1930, in a Montmartrian movie house called Studio 28. The following is a synopsis that was offered to members of the Film Society when *L'Âge d'Or* finally made its way across the Atlantic to New York in 1933:

> The early scenes, which constitute a prologue, are of such ordinary and indescribable monotony that they begin to engender an almost morbid fascination, proving a valuable contrast of mood when the main action develops. In a dreary landscape of arid rocks, scorpions are living. A discouraged and ineffectual bandit, who is climbing about the rocks, notices a group of archbishops who have arrived to

hold mass in this mineral setting. Running back to inform his comrades of the presence of the Church, the bandit finds his comrades in
a strange state of weakness and depression, but they seize their
weapons and advance, excepting the youngest of them all who cannot even rise. They stumble across the rocks. One after another, they
fall exhausted. Their leader falls too, just within sight of the group of
archbishops who, as the pall of desolation falls over the entire island,
are now mere skeletons disposed with their vestments among the
stones.

A great maritime expedition comes in sight of this coast. The expedition consists of priests, nuns, the military, statesmen, and several
civilians. They are assembled for the founding of Imperial Rome.
Suddenly piercing cries attract the attention of all. In the mud
nearby a man and a woman are engaged in an amorous struggle. The
man, so oblivious of the spectacle which he makes, represents the individual in revolt against an established world with which there can
be no compromise. The pair is separated by force, the man arrested
by the police.

Dragged through the streets of a modern city, this man, who is the
protagonist of the film, struggles to escape, as each object he sees
transforms itself into reminders of his beloved. Finally he is released,
when his identity is revealed by a document describing his high position and the importance of a patriotic and humanitarian mission confided to him by the Government. Meanwhile the woman has been
invited to a party given by the Marquis de X. It should be noted that
this modern party offers a parallel with the era of the *ancien régime*
just preceding the French Revolution. The guests, solely concerned
with the incidents of the party, are completely blind to nearby
events not of their own world. A serving girl is thrown into the
flames from the kitchen, a tumbril is driven across the ballroom floor,
a boy is shot by his father for not much reason, whereas the one
event to profoundly disturb the guests is the upsetting of a teacup.

The protagonist arrives at the party and perceives his beloved
across the room. From this moment all his activity is directed
towards love. The body of the film is concerned with successive love
scenes, dominated by acts of violence and frustration.

In the course of a final ineffectual episode the protagonist is summoned by the authorities and accused of having failed in his mission;
that in consequence thousands of old people and innocent children
have perished. He answers with foul insults and returns determinedly

to the woman he loves. At this very moment an inexplicable accident separates them forever, and the man is last seen throwing a burning tree out of the window, a large agricultural implement, an archbishop, a giraffe, feathers.

As an epilogue, the survivors of the Château de Selligny are seen, after the criminal orgies of the Marquis de Sade, crossing the drawbridge covered with snow. The last incident is accompanied by a *paso doble*.

Under Chiappe, the Corsican prefect of police who ruled Paris with an iron hand in the twenties and thirties, French fascists were at liberty to grind their axes, knowing that the *gendarmerie* would unfailingly appear too late, if at all. Their chief *bêtes noires* were Jews, Bolsheviks, and that vipers' nest of everything they considered un-French: surrealism. Such was Chiappe's intolerance of modern art that he considered even Brancusi pornographic and on these grounds closed an exhibition of his sculpture. A surrealist exhibit was wrecked by toughs who were seemingly at liberty to do what they pleased. Sergei Eisenstein's *The General Line* was banned in February, 1930.

The bombs Buñuel had anticipated after *The Andalusian Dog* detonated belatedly on December 3, 1930, during a public screening of *L'Âge d'Or*. In attendance were delegates from two clubs which would play a conspicuous role in Parisian street life throughout the 1930s: the Patriots' League and the Anti-Jewish League. One sequence in the film appears to have been previously agreed upon by fascists present as the moment to revolt. Stink bombs exploded all over the cinema, preluding a general brawl in which spectators were injured, seats torn up, the screen splashed with purple ink, and surrealist paintings on display slashed to ribbons. *L'Âge d'Or* became a pivotal issue in the battle between right-wing and left-wing newspapers. Buñuel was prevailed upon by the censors to remove two brief sequences denigrating the Church, but *Le Figaro*, for one, would not rest until the film had been eradicated. Defending family, country, and religion, it waged an all-out campaign which soon achieved its goal. On December 11, 1930, *L'Âge d'Or* was banned and all available copies of the film confiscated by the police.

As for the Noailles, Buñuel's film placed them in disrepute among the fellow aristocrats whom they had invited to a private showing the previous July; although it is reported they were "crimson with embarrassment," the grotesque incongruity of having a liveried major-domo loudly report the names and titles of guests as they arrived to watch this Ur-drama would suggest that the Noailles, barring some fit of naïveté, knew what they were about. At any rate, *L'Âge d'Or* succeeded in offending equally the *gratin* and the *crottin*. Charles de Noailles was expelled from that *sanctum sanctorum* of social snobbery, the Jockey Club.

Cocteau had been an avid movie-goer since his early teens, but the idea of making a film did not seriously occur to him until an example had been set by his avant-garde adversaries. In later years he contended perhaps too vehemently that he had not seen *The Andalusian Dog* before shooting his *Blood of a Poet:* a highly improbable lapse for someone as professionally ubiquitous as Cocteau. In any case, he must have heard it discussed in art circles and no doubt read the scenario when it appeared in the December 15, 1929, issue of *La Révolution Surréaliste*. That he made *Blood of a Poet* with Buñuel's film in mind seems obvious from the first sequence, involving a macabre image apt to startle the audience: if not a razor sectioning an eyeball, a hand growing a mouth. Moreover, Cocteau admitted his jealousy, presenting himself as the underdog in a political contest for the suffrage of Youth. When asked in a 1951 interview how he happened to venture into film making, he replied: "At that time everything was political, including the Arts and Letters. That is the essential difference between this era and that. *Blood of a Poet* derived from a political situation and was aimed against the surrealists who, despite their declarations to the contrary, were all-powerful." Thus, when Charles de Noailles invited Cocteau to produce an animated cartoon, Cocteau proposed instead that he be given a million francs to make a full-length film.

Cocteau was hard pressed to distinguish his vantage point from the surrealists'. In a preface written years later to the published scenario of *Blood of a Poet*, he contends that the subject occurred to him before surrealism even existed. "The interest it provokes to this day comes no doubt from its isolated position among works with which it is classified. . . . At the time of *Blood of a Poet* I was the only member of a minority group capable of avoiding voluntary demonstrations of the Unconscious in favor of a kind of half-sleep in which I treaded through my own labyrinth." On other occasions, he liked to gaze upon 1930 as from a great height whence his work and Buñuel's could not be distinguished from one another. "We admired the same values and fought on the same level, whereas nowadays the confusion of levels would make these battles incomprehensible. It has already done so; witness what takes place in South America, where my films are attributed to Buñuel and his to me."

Cocteau's film and Buñuel's have little more in common than their oneiric trappings. *Blood of a Poet* was not so much a labyrinth through which Cocteau walked half asleep as a treasure hunt in which he feigned surprise at finding objects he himself had planted. In *Blood of a Poet* he rehearses, using a new medium, stock themes which had begun to congeal into his legend. *Orphée*, shot twenty years later, would observe exactly the same shape and arrive at the same conclusion. As in *Orphée*, there are two episodes on earth and two, rather more sustained, in the dream world beyond the mirror. Like *Orphée*, *Blood of a Poet* ends with an apotheosis of the artist as homosexual.

Not surprisingly, Cocteau found the means of prefacing his own work. Toward the beginning of *Blood of a Poet* he appears amid the cameras and lighting equipment, draped in cloth from which a plaster hand extrudes, to inform us that—like Orpheus, Oedipus, and the *enfants terribles*—he will be enacting his own masterpiece. To make this abundantly clear, he will recall at crucial moments this plaster hand representing the poet petrified in destiny.

Episode I, "The Wounded Hand or the Scars of the Poet," shows a young man bared to the waist and wearing a courtier's wig, standing before a canvas on which he has freshly painted a self-portrait. Suddenly the portrait's mouth begins to move. When the young man erases it with his hand, it embeds itself in the palm. The mouth, or wound (for Cocteau meant by it the poet's stigma), will not close. Under water it bubbles; out of water it pouts obscenely. At length the poet presses it to his mouth and writhes with ecstasy. The following day a statue—in the shape of a woman wearing Greek drapery—materializes. Hoping to rid himself of his otiose mouth, he smears it onto the statue, which by that stroke comes alive and reproaches him: "Do you think it's all that simple to get rid of a wound, to close the mouth of a wound?" As Destiny, or Glory, or Death, the statue confronts the poet with himself. Trying to flee, he discovers that his room has overnight turned into a kind of *cul-de-sac* lacking windows and doors. When he cringes before a mirror, he finds himself mocked by his own literary pronouncements. "Congratulations," the statue cries. "You have written that one can enter mirrors yet you yourself didn't believe it."

After leaping through the mirror, he finds himself in the corridor of a dreary hotel called "The Hôtel des Folies Dramatiques," [1] where Episode II takes place. Like a voyeur in a brothel, the poet moves (with great difficulty, taking laborious steps like Orpheus on the *zone* between this world and the other) from door to door, looking through successive keyholes at the acts in progress. The first involves a Mexican closely resembling the young man; he is shot twice, and rises twice. The second act, entitled "Lessons in Flight," shows a sinister schoolmarm brandishing a whip, and a little girl wearing the costume of a circus performer. The girl is being taught how to fly and learns her lesson so well that from the ceiling she sneers at the floor-bound mistress. Room three features a play called "The Mysteries of China," which unfolds in shadow-form on a wall, projected there by an opium lamp; we see the hand of a smoker inserting a cone of opium into his pipe with a needle while smoke rises (the absence of players, or their presence as mere shadows, presumably symbolizes the "photographic negative of life," as Cocteau put it in *Opium*, created by the drug). When the poet-voyeur, having looked away, brings his eye to the keyhole again, what does he behold but another eye zooming toward him. He then moves on.

Outside room four lies a pair of shoes, one a woman's and the

1. "Folies Dramatiques" was the name of a popular movie house in Paris.

other a man's, announcing the hermaphroditic spectacle within. From behind an enormous sofa, the white, masked face of a woman appears, her torso limned in chalk on a blackboard transecting the sofa lengthwise. Male limbs suddenly start to grow out of the chalk drawing. After a dance of jumbled genders, the hermaphrodite, lifting its dress, reveals a placard over its groin. It reads "Danger of Death." Again the poet finds himself staring at eyes, this pair belonging to a mask surmounted by a Louis XIV wig. Now at the end of his odyssey, he is handed a pistol and told how to use it by a voice belonging to an unseen woman who delivers her instructions in the monotone of a cookware demonstrator. The poet having done as instructed, his blood becomes a peplum and a laurel wreath sprouts round his forehead. "Glory even now!" the author interjects. At this, the poet's heart begins to beat again, the beat grows deafeningly loud, it rises above the grinding noise of a bulldozer and the peal of a children's choir. The poet backs out of the mirror into his room, staying only long enough to destroy the statue with a mallet. "Breaking statues," the author declaims, "one runs the risk of becoming a statue oneself." The next shot bears him out. We see, standing amid ruined tenements, a statue which at closer view proves to be an effigy of the poet.

Episode III now begins, and the statue is transplanted to the Cité Monthiers, that courtyard where, at the beginning of *Les Enfants Terribles*, a snowball fight erupts among students of the Lycée Condorcet, resulting in the confrontation of Paul and his beloved, Dargelos. That episode is reenacted, but here the snowball hurled by Dargelos hits Paul. A close-up shows the boy lying in the snow, blood trickling from his mouth. Without further ado, the Cité Monthiers becomes a theatre fitted with a gallery where smartly dressed spectators are taking seats. They witness below a game of cards contested by the poet and Dame Destiny, who is no longer a statue but a live woman. At one point the poet contrives to improve his hand with an ace of hearts spirited from the cloak of the dead boy lying at his feet but, tricks unavailing against fate, a black angel appears, gathers up the child, and absconds with the ace of hearts, whereupon the poet's adversary warns him that "without the ace of hearts, my dear, you are lost." He takes a pistol from his pocket and shoots himself, this time definitively. The camera, zooming in, shows his bloody head lying, like the dead child's, in the snow. Above, the spectators applaud.

"Her mission accomplished," the author explains, "the woman became a statue once again—an inhuman thing, wearing black gloves, betrayed by the snow on which her steps would thereafter leave no more traces." Departing from the courtyard, she glides along a trellised wall. The camera focuses on a large, sculpted door flanked on either side by identical busts of Diderot. When the door flies open, the statue is revealed within. She descends four steps; at the bottom of the perron a bull appears. The statue wraps him in a cloak stained with random blots which assemble themselves into a map of Europe. The bull's horns are transmogrified into a lyre. The film ends with an aerial view of the statue lying inside a swell of veils, the lyre and a planisphere at its side. Woman having become a statue, the statue then becomes undifferentiated matter, its features blurring into hard, shiny facets of marble. The author says, "The fatal boredom of immortality," whereupon the large chimney stack which had begun to crumble in the first frames of the film falls completely apart. And the film ends.

Blood of a Poet has never been considered from a biographical viewpoint, which is all the more surprising since Cocteau was infatuated with his own past, taking a lover's liberties with it, making, undoing, revising it at every turn. The film's original title was in fact *The Life of a Poet*, and *Blood of a Poet* amounts to another *vita* pivoting about *Parade*, *Les Enfants Terribles*, and *Thomas the Impostor*. It begins with his "awakening," sponsored by Diaghilev and Gide: the wig belongs to a young courtier, that is, to the "frivolous prince," to young Cocteau who heard himself constantly compared to young Voltaire. The stigma may be viewed as a sign of his "election"; attempting to avoid himself by shifting the wound onto an easy image of immortality, he merely gives voice to his fate. The statue prods him into that "underworld" he had been celebrating since *Potomak*.

What is the first sequence beyond the mirror if not a recapitulation of *Parade?* It is a film within the film, which is clearly brought home by the name he gives the "hotel." The poet witnesses a music-hall review whose routines, excepting the first, parallel those of the ballet, though freighted with subsequent associations.[2] Thus, the little girl flying recalls "the Little American Girl" (like her, she is wearing the accessories of a circus performer), but also *The Cape of Good Hope*. The "Mysteries of China" corresponds to "the Chinese Prestidigitator," whose image blends with that of Louis Laloy, the Orientalist who allegedly gave Cocteau his first opium pipe; the room is a den inhabited by shadows (for the addict lives an "inverted" existence akin to a photographic negative). The hermaphrodite's number recalls the two Acrobats in *Parade*, with a further allusion to Barbette (playing a small part in this film), whose act combined hermaphroditism and acrobatics.

Moreover, the three acts—*The Cape* and Garros, opium and Laloy, *Orphée* and Barbette—fall into chronological order. It is as if the poet were at once moving from station to station of his Cross and narrating his progress, like Christ and the evangelists in one. Having completed this music-hall Passion, he shoots himself and bleeds profusely, calling to mind the host in a painting mentioned at the outset of *Blood of a Poet*: Uccello's altarpiece *The Profanation of the Host*. The poet is that spectator of *Parade* who witnesses the "interior drama," who enters the tent. In other words, the armature of *Blood of a Poet* during this sequence is *Parade*, just as it will be *Les Enfants Terribles* in the following sequence. We have here, not Cocteau within Sophocles, but Cocteau within Cocteau, enacting "his own masterpiece," moving within himself yet at some remove from himself, like the opium smoker, the dreamer, the myth maker. Twice the poet peering through the keyhole beholds his own eyes peering back. Why then the fraudulent death, the laurel wreath, the cry of frustration at the end of this sequence? Because the dreamer, having plunged so deep, will go no further. He reverts to the role of censor, that placard "danger of Death" over the hermaphrodite's sex spelling out his fear. At this point he wakes up.

The next plunge will take him deeper, into the childhood of *Les*

---

2. The Mexican twice shot, twice revived, and bearing the voyeur's features may well refer to Radiguet and Desbordes, both of them swart and both embodying Cocteau's "ideal" face. Radiguet's prophecy was "The soldiers of God will shoot me dead in three days." Cocteau all but persuaded himself that Radiguet had come to earth again in the person of Desbordes.

Enfants Terribles. It is worth recalling the letter Cocteau wrote to Gide in 1930 from Saint-Cloud: "I owe you so much; there was a time when, had you not intervened, I would have gotten lost following the example of my counterfeit handwriting. Now I want to announce the true benefit of my cure: work is working me. I am disgorging the book I have meant to write (but couldn't) since 1912." What remains concealed at the end of the poet's first dream sequence will come to light at the end of his second. He loses the game of cards to a woman, having lost his trump card, his "heart" to an angel. Is this an avowal of his homosexuality? In the next scene Zeus mates Europa, symbolizing Cocteau's theory of art as hermaphroditic self-fertilization. The woman becomes a statue, but our last view of the statue shows Cocteau's Orphic drawing superimposed on the statue's face. The second and real suicide sanctifies the poet. He has fulfilled his artistic destiny, signing his work in blood, and beholding himself transformed into marble.[3] Cocteau's exalted identification of himself with Christ is borne out not only by his reference to Uccello's *Profanation of the Host*, which pictures the host shedding blood onto the floor, but that remark he made three years before the shooting of *Blood of a Poet* in his interview with Maurice Rouzaud: "Christ is an active poem. When He dies, He signs His work with a cross, in blood." The film amounts to Cocteau's self-apotheosis, rigged out in avant-garde trappings.

But there is another aspect to *Blood of a Poet* which discloses the lucid and perhaps tragic underside of Cocteau's legend. Each dream sequence is a play within a play. The first unfolds within a movie house and the second within a theatre, suggesting that even here, in the deepest core of his being, Cocteau viewed himself as an actor whose masks conceal other masks: hence the mortal blood and hard marble pitted against the wigs, masks, and theatrical frippery of his anterior life. The film ends with a block of marble standing on a rise like some as yet unveiled tombstone. What indeed was Cocteau's intention in creating another self, a legend, an ideal biogra-

3. Blood and marble are closely associated images in Cocteau's world. The blood is the poet's and marble is the poet's fate, always in the guise of a *belle dame sans merci*.

phy, if not to make himself beautiful? "Striving to be," he would write years later, "I neglected to live." His art is thus predicated on death; only after dying would Cocteau cease to contradict, by his life, his literary persona. Only after becoming a name would he fulfill himself.

The one interpretation of *Blood of a Poet* which Cocteau endorsed wholeheartedly was one reputed to be Freud's, that the film is like watching a man through a keyhole as he applies his make-up.[4] Unfolding partially within the theatrical setting of *Parade* and *Les Enfants Terribles*, it unfolds wholly within a single allusion to *Thomas the Impostor*, whose hero comes from Fontenoy and dies there after his brief career under a noble alias. The first shot shows a gigantic chimney beginning to crumble as the author says: "While the cannons of Fontenoy were thundering in the distance, in a modest room a young man . . ." The last shot shows the chimney crumbling to bits. *Blood of a Poet* means to observe the ambiguous time of dreams, filming in slow-motion the history of a traumatic instant and reviewing in fast-motion, like the mind of a drowning man, the legendized sequences of an entire lifetime.

Like *The Testament of Orpheus* made in 1959, *Blood of a Poet* is a crazy quilt of Cocteau's previous works. But if each of these works involves writing about writing, the mask we see of a face we don't, the "parade" staged of a drama backstage, the visible shadow of an invisible form, they amount to a sum of boxes inside boxes, of signposts pointing to other signposts staked in the desert. Cocteau's *Blood of a Poet* bears comparison with *The Perils of Pauline*, whose titular heroine tumbles from one misadventure into another, always, somehow, rescuing her virginity.

Though *Blood of a Poet* was completed in the fall of 1930 after some five months of shooting, various circumstances deferred its public première until January, 1932. The scene in which an elegant group watches the game of cards from their gallery had to be redone. In the original version, Charles and Marie-Laure de Noailles, the Princess de Faucigny-Lucinge, and Lady Abdy played the spec-

4. Cocteau quotes Freud's article on several occasions but apparently no such article exists, since Freud, suffering from cancer, never went to the films after 1931 or so. Either Cocteau was quoting a spoof or he had put his own words in Freud's mouth so as to give them more weight.

tators but, according to Cocteau, they insisted that that sequence be refilmed without them, in deference to their relatives who took offense at seeing them applaud a suicide. Above all, the Noailles wanted the storm which had been raised by *L'Âge d'Or* to abate before releasing yet another film repugnant to Family, Church, and State. "At the Vieux-Colombier theatre," wrote Cocteau, "my film, which was badly printed, badly edited, and badly projected, raised scandals and provoked battles, without being able to defend itself with polish." After *Parade* Cocteau had voiced the identical grievance. In reality, *Blood of a Poet*, like *Parade*, provoked no scandal of any measurable magnitude. On the contrary, it reduced the public to good behavior. "The mystery," wrote Cocteau in his preface to *The Newlyweds*, "inspires a kind of fear in the public." *Figaro*'s reviewer began by quoting that observation, and continued:

> That sentiment seems to have dominated the public during the first showing of the film, although it would have been so simple to have abandoned oneself to the poetry of parables, to attach a face to each of the abstract figures, to concretize them according to one's dream or one's fantasy. . . .
>
> It is deplorable that this important work was presented in form of a working copy, improperly focused, and presented at 11:15 p.m., hours after the scheduled time. The uncomfortable seats aggravated our impatience.

Just as the public of 1917 had been tempered by events far more calamitous than *Parade*, the prudes and patriots of 1932 had already exhausted their reserves of outrage over Buñuel's *L'Âge d'Or*, by comparison with which *Blood of a Poet* seemed "poetic." On the Right Bank, Cocteau, whatever his excesses, could do no wrong. He had mastered the tact of audacity, and it unmanned him. Such was the credit he enjoyed that a woman passing herself off as Mme. Jean Cocteau managed to embezzle some thirty-two million francs. Having always coveted what he called "the supernatural sex of beauty," all he got from the larger public was the dubious virility of fame.

Cocteau had spent the summer of 1918 in Grasse as the guest of Mme. Francis de Croisset. In 1930, and intermittently throughout the thirties, he stayed in Hyères with Mme. de Croisset's daughter, Marie-Laure de Noailles. Generations were flowing by, but Cocteau breasted the current, pausing to rest at one landed estate after another. The Lady of the Manor thus remained eternally young and Cocteau the eternal pierrot. His act never changed: the audience revolved. In the midst of the Great Depression, the Noailles and their guests romped about Hyères like Boccaccian refugees from the Plague. Gide, whose conversion to communism in 1932 would make such elegant holidays unthinkable, described the Noailles estate, where he spent the early days of 1930, as follows:

At Hyères, with the Noailles, where I rejoined Marc, who is with Cocteau and Auric. I was going to stay for lunch only; but I gladly allow myself to be coaxed into staying for dinner, then overnight. The extreme and charming amiability of our hosts; the prodigious ingenuity of the comfort they furnish; the whole apparatus of luxury is so nicely calibrated that this morning when, after my bath, the English valet brought me breakfast, I buttered my toast with a spoon for fear that the knife missing from a platter laden with delicacies and fruits might attain the proportions of a catastrophe.

Gymnastics, swimming in a vast pool, new games whose names I don't know, played with shuttlecocks, balls, balloons of every description—one in particular played by four of us (the very congenial professor of gymnastics, Noailles, Marc, and myself) with a medium-sized ball which each team tried to keep from hitting the ground on its side of the high-strung net. We were playing more or less in the nude, then, all sweaty, we'd plunge into the tepid water of the pool. This game amused me more than I thought it possible, amused me like a child or like a god, and all the more so that I didn't feel myself awkward. The absurd things Pascal said about games! The struggle, the effort seems beautiful to me precisely because it is gratuitous.

Cocteau lived more at ease with gratuity. Indeed, luxury was a necessity of life for him. Having Chanel, Marie-Laure, and other wealthy ladies nearby in case he should fall reassured him. The scruples besetting Gide scarcely occurred to Cocteau. He would spend the thirties, that political decade *par excellence*, in an opium cloud: the sumptuary poet, the anarchist de luxe writing masques for a formal garden and memoirs about his Golden Age.

"I was very moved by your letter," wrote Cocteau to Élise Jouhandeau, who had seen a private showing of *Blood of a Poet.* "That film was made not with a camera but a lancet. I am staying at home, my nerves shot." To repair his worn nerves he spent nearly half of 1931 with Christian Bérard and Jean Desbordes in the Midi, just outside Toulon: a vacation prompted by the Parisian ague but prolonged by a disease which had already struck close to Cocteau: typhoid.

Bérard and Cocteau adopted different hotels, a measure by which they hoped, apparently, to get some work done. Cocteau lived in the Hôtel de la Rade overlooking the old *darse*, or wet-dock, of Toulon. Before long, friends of his had colonized every floor, as in the Hôtel Welcome, and they conversed from balcony to balcony with proprietary unconcern for their neighbors, whose dreams of a quiet summer on an isolated promontory were soon dashed. Bérard had found quarters in an unused wing of the Hôtel de Tamaris not far away. The domestics had strict orders not to bother him. Amid the most unsightly disorder, Bérard painted or read detective novels, American movie magazines, and Rimbaud. He arranged to keep out of the sun all summer, lounging about his private annex of the hotel in a bathrobe woven of sky-blue flannel and decorated with tiny cat heads. Only when the sun showed signs of setting would he emerge, an obese man whose wild red beard gave him—despite his baby face—the appearance of a river god.

Evenings the arty crowd would assemble at Édouard Bourdet's: Bérard with his little white Maltese perched on one shoulder, and Cocteau with a Malagasy monkey he had adopted. Georges Auric, who had recently gotten married and was living in a house which belonged to Marie-Laure de Noailles, would come over from Hyères. It was a crowd preoccupied with theatre. Édouard Bourdet, their host, wrote well-constructed plays reminiscent of Bataille's or Porto-Riche's (the latter had been his mentor), a talent which, combined with his gentlemanly bearing, predestined him for the directorship of the Comédie-Française. Far more than his close friend Jean Giraudoux, with whom he dined almost every Sunday for twenty years, Bourdet had the correctitude and measured speech of a diplomat, yet lived at ease among people nothing if not flamboyant. When not talking theatre, playing poker, or absorbing himself in his game of *bilboquet*, he would complaisantly watch them perform their antics.

He was, in other words, a perfect foil for Cocteau, who dropped by almost nightly with Desbordes and his Annamite "boy" in tow, waving a freshly written poem or ready to devise party games for his host and hostess. Cocteau loved costume skits. Indeed, this love of costumes was an invariable in Cocteau's life. The youth who had played Heliogabalus to de Max's Emperor became the young man playing a pink-clad nymph, with bangles round his legs, to Beaumont's black Majesty. And this young man became the Celebrated Poet staging transvestite skits with Christian Bérard in the "Villa Blanche." Denise Bourdet remembers one which appears to have been a variation of *The Newlyweds of the Eiffel Tower*. Cocteau, mincing about as a "fiancée from Toulon, 1900," wore a fish net from head to toes and a little white cap with holes for the eyes, ears, and mouth. In his arms he bore a large bouquet of tuberoses.

Summer nights were given to such divertissements, and to others calling for no dress at all. Cocteau formed a *liaison* with a sailor known as Pas-de-Chance (No Luck) with whom he was often seen frolicking about Toulon, the sailor in a sweater unbuttoned so as to demonstrate his tattooed chest and Cocteau in a white bicyclist's costume which he combined, to very odd effect, with a black collar and tie. Pas-de-Chance figures prominently in *The White Book*, but their affair ended when the young man lived up to his name. *L'Intransigeant* reported in 1931:

> At the Gare Montparnasse, two individuals, René Goine, known as Neneuil, and Henri Pared, known as "Nez Cassé" [Broken Nose] were arrested as they sought to claim some stolen merchandise they had previously deposited at the left-luggage office. Broken Nose tried, in vain, to swallow his baggage ticket, evidence of his guilt, but a police inspector fished it from his mouth. Broken Nose and Neneuil admitted their thefts. Then, their tongues having come loose, they "squealed" on one of their accomplices, Henri Fefeu, 26 years

old, known as "Pas-de-Chance": 20 Rue Pescaletti. And Pas-de-Chance was soon apprehended. The Pas-de-Chance of this petty crime and the Pas-de-Chance of *The White Book* are one and the same person.

In proportion as Cocteau's sexual appetite appeased itself by plunging into the *bas-fonds* of seaboard society, his opium consumption soared, to more than thirty pipes a day, a quantity which almost required the expertise of an Annamite boy. Cocteau's health had seemingly improved, however, lending credence to his theory that opium protects the addict from serious illness, like the cloves of garlic that peasants hang above their lintels to ward off the evil eye. But in September, 1931, as he was preparing to return to Paris for the fall season, this theory was suddenly and dramatically disproved. Cocteau came down with typhoid. The Bourdets had him transferred from the Hôtel de la Rade to a hospital. After a week of recoveries and relapses Cocteau survived. It took him only a few more days to find his tongue, and the monologue resumed. Bourdet paid him a visit every afternoon, to amuse and console the convalescent, but he could not get a word in edgewise and never returned home without some drawing chosen from among the dozens Cocteau nervously produced during his enforced leisure. "The doctor of the clinic, Jean Desbordes, and the Bourdets were my guardian angels," wrote Cocteau. He spent weeks recovering in the Villa Blanche, and when Édouard Bourdet left for Paris to attend the production of his latest play, Cocteau entertained Denise by reading Feydeau.

Desbordes meanwhile seemed to be going his separate way. He had become preoccupied with a woman considerably older than himself. Cocteau in turn discovered a younger and fresher consort in Marcel Khill, an Algerian boy whom he had been admiring on the beach. Khill's keeper proved to be an aged dandy with a far-flung reputation in North African homosexual circles and a member of Marshal Lyautey's entourage. His name might have been given him not by Christian parents but by some high-school humorist: Tranchant Lunel. Providentially, M. Lunel died that year, and Cocteau, when at last he returned to Paris, did so with a new lover.

Until the mid-thirties, when he moved into the Hôtel Castille on

Rue Cambon, Cocteau shared his flat on Rue Vignon with Marcel Khill. "There," he wrote, "I led the agoraphobic existence of the prisoner of Poitiers." His agoraphobia might have represented for most men the height of socializing. Fortified with a telephone, he managed to extend his intelligence network into every known salon and all the most promiscuous by-corners of the *beau monde*. Cocteau inhabited a sphere which pivoted about the theatre, *Vogue*, and a few nightclubs, but its four cardinal points were Marie-Laure de Noailles, Marie-Blanche de Polignac, Étienne de Beaumont, and Daisy Fellowes, an extravagantly beautiful, haughty woman born a Singer on her mother's side and a Decazes on her father's.

This society, concocted of French titles, high fashion, and lots of American money, waged incessant war against ennui. Its members were forbidden any very serious thoughts, and those who did possess some talent, such as Marie-Laure de Noailles, were gravely crippled by certain prejudices: one didn't publish one's writings or exhibit one's art, as though doing so were incongruous with one's station in life, an obscene form of social self-debasement. What was left to do but promote one's pleasure, complicate one's sentimental life, and conduct minute investigations into everybody else's? Was Madame X frigid? Everyone knew. Had Madame Y discovered her husband *en flagrant délit* with his gym instructor? Alert lovers straightaway offered to console her.

Cocteau found himself divorced for good from intellectual circles whose approbation he once sought at all costs. Their distrust of the well-born had now hardened into an ideology. Adopting this style or that would not allay their suspicions; they demanded *mea culpas* such as they required of themselves, and Cocteau's talent for guilt did not run along social lines. Even as communists and fascists paraded a hundred thousand strong during the bloody demonstrations of 1934, he was preoccupied with his latest effort at making Sophocles palatable: *The Infernal Machine*. The Manichean contest being waged in the streets escaped him. His world found its manifest destiny in its own pleasure, creating spectacles, setting fashions, appreciating the idiosyncrasies it could well afford, identifying universality with the grand manner. Except for fancy-dress balls at the British embassy, it held resolutely aloof from politics, engrossed as it was in governing its own domestic affairs. Cocteau wrote:

> That sojourn [referring to his convalescence in the Villa Blanche] was only the outline of a very high wave which would sweep us ahead, pell-mell, tragically and joyously, with the films of Marlene Dietrich, extravagant fashions, plays which we took turns reading to one another, and the thousand and one spells cast by the Rue Vignon where my room became the clasp of an extraordinary necklace of wave transmissions. Our gang really wasn't one. It grew more numerous by a gyratory phenomenon of molecular affinities, a kind of internal style. But it remained inaccessible to those who pulled strings in order to become part of it.

These alumni of Le Bœuf meeting at lunch and dinner at the Noailles' palace on Place des États-Unis, at the Bourdets' on Quai d'Orsay, at Daisy Fellowes' salon in Neuilly, at Étienne de Beaumont's Palace of the Uppercrust Muses (or on Sundays for musical soirées held by Marie-Blanche de Polignac) included Marie-Laure's intimate friend Igor Markevitch, that ever gregarious imp Max Jacob, Auric and his wife Nora, Jean Hugo and his mistress Frosca Münster, Marie-Louis Bousquet, Bébé Bérard, and René Crevel, each of whom added his grain of madness to the corporate ragout. They went to balls staged by the Beaumonts, by the Noailles, by Niky de Gunzburg, by Jean de Faucigny-Lucinge. And how did they go dressed? As characters from Madame de Ségur's seventeenth-century novels, or from Proust's *Remembrance of Things Past*. Their "internal style" must have looked like a telephone switchboard whose operator had gone berserk, connecting everybody with everybody else to disastrous effect, for all tongues wagged simultaneously. Once one was elected to their group, it took treason or suicide to escape. Like an amoeba, they enveloped their prey with doughy pseudopods. "*La Bande,* as we called this Comus crew of artists, drew closer and closer round us," wrote Diana Cooper, wife of the British ambassador, just after World War II, the upheavals and dispersions of which scarcely affected the band's adhesive inner lining.

Outsiders were inevitably struck by their collective charm and elegance. Inside, the air proved sticky. Cocteau may have thrived in this close pleasure dome, but he also suffered its penalties. Thus, for example, his alleged affair with a Russian princess who had followed her mother into exile after the Revolution, and grew up in Paris under reduced circumstances. Her marriage to an eminent couturier proved an unhappy one. In the course of it she apparently took up with Cocteau, who found her beauty, her title, and her sweet manner sufficient inducement to digress from his homosexual career. This liaison threw a number of women into jealous rages, and when it threatened to bear fruit, one woman who had always fancied herself the mate Cocteau would have chosen had he been given to heterosexual choices, prevailed upon the princess to abort the child. Overcome with anger, Cocteau confronted the princess' wanton *confidante* and, in public, administered her a resounding slap. She in turn avenged herself by burning the manuscript of *Les Enfants Terribles*, which Cocteau had previously given her in gratitude for her summer hospitality and her subventions. He consoled himself with the reflection that this world never intended a combination so preposterous as the scion of a French stockbroker and the offspring of Russian royalty.

Meanwhile Cocteau received doles from his mother and attended family gatherings at his brother Paul's apartment in the fashionable *seizième*. Mme. Georges Cocteau had become more pious than ever, supplementing daily mass with classes in religious instruction offered by a Dominican priest named Father Wébert who seemed to specialize in well-to-do ladies with homosexual kin. Years later, after his mother's death, Cocteau would tell an American interviewer, "I have never felt any connection with my family," but his work, much of it, seems a dark tribute to Mme. Cocteau. Furthermore, he depended on his family for money and, when the occasion arose, did not hesitate to use their political connections.

Fearful of being eclipsed by Jean Giraudoux, whose *Amphytrion 38* and *Intermezzo* had brought him wild acclaim, and by Gide, whose *Oedipus* had been performed by the Pitoëffs the same month *Blood of a Poet* was being shown at the Vieux-Colombier, Cocteau set about enlarging his original text for Stravinsky's oratorio *Oedi-*

pus Rex. This prompted one of Gide's more memorable witticisms: "An Oedipemic has broken out!" When in early 1933 the manuscript of *The Infernal Machine* had been put in presentable order, Cocteau showed it to the famous director Louis Jouvet, who was then in charge of a large theatre called La Comédie des Champs-Élysées. Jouvet agreed to produce the play but was soon made to regret his decision, for Cocteau's importunities annoyed him, and they frequently quarreled. In addition, Cocteau found himself at swords' points with Lanvin and Chanel, whose ideas for the costumes differed from his own. Above all, the great Rumanian actress Elvire Popesco had severe misgivings about the role of Jocasta, and it required all Jouvet's and Cocteau's combined powers of persuasion to win her consent. *La Machine Infernale* was not performed until April, 1934. By then Jouvet had decided to resign his directorship of the Comédie des Champs-Élysées. Cocteau's play therefore served as a kind of valedictory.

If Cocteau presented the Orpheus myth in the disguise of a young bohemian household, his *Machine Infernale* translated Oedipus, and Jocasta, into the smart set at play on an estate in the Midi. It is entirely appropriate that Cocteau should have dedicated his work to Charles and Marie-Laure de Noailles. Thebes is a travestied Hyères and Jocasta a composite of various wealthy, aging adventuresses so nonchalant about their children and so avidly interested in young gigolos that a son of theirs could, almost in the normal course of things, turn up at their side in bed and not be recognized until too late. Indeed, the scarf which appears from the outset as an omen of catastrophe and ultimately becomes Jocasta's noose calls to mind Isadora Duncan, whose neck had snapped when the end of her scarf caught in the spokes of her lover's sports car.

La Machine Infernale amounts to a period piece whose interest lies in its appurtenances. Whatever Cocteau lacked, his stagecraft and his ear for the accents of a certain milieu cannot be impugned. If Jocasta calls Tiresias "Zizi," that milieu freely distributed diminutives: to its members like pedigrees, to the High and Mighty like Alice's magic shrinking powder. "Youth and old age are not purebred," Cocteau once wrote, a judgment he turned against the blind prophet and even against Sophocles himself, on whose broad back

Cocteau danced a verbal tarantella in four parts, each part revolving about some piece of bravura, notably the Sphinx's soliloquy in Act II.

La Machine Infernale follows, broadly speaking, the lines of Sophocles' *Oedipus,* but each of its scenes is an intaglio of further borrowings. Act I, in which the ghost of Laius appears before two soldiers keeping night watch on the ramparts of Thebes, comes directly from *Hamlet.* Act II, in which the Sphinx confronts Oedipus in a double role, as an infatuated young woman and as Anubis the avenging Deity, bestowing upon him her favors the better to seal his fate, amounts to a variation of the Orpheus triangle: Orpheus, Eurydice, and Death. Act III—the nuptial night—corresponds exactly to Orpheus' plunge beyond the mirror. The maternity of death in *Orphée* (more explicitly developed in the film version), the mother's dual nature—a theme which haunts Cocteau's drama—shows through the dark mirror of reciprocal nightmares. While Jocasta dreams of a "gluey lump" which obviously represents the fetus, her son Oedipus dreams of Anubis, the Egyptian god of the dead. By now it had become a familiar device of Cocteau's to portray childhood fantasy as a play within the play, a fatal dream governing the apparent accidents of life. Bérard therefore designed the bedroom as a small stage, painted crimson, set within the larger one. The act ends on a Flaubertian note. Jocasta hears a drunk below singing a cruel ditty about women who marry men far younger than themselves, which recalls the scrofulous beggar whom the aging Emma Bovary hears, after her assignation with Léon, and again from her deathbed, singing a refrain about foolish young girls in love. Act IV survived intact from Cocteau's collaboration with Stravinsky.

All in all, *La Machine Infernale* has the personality of a master tinker's vehicle, composed of old spare parts ingeniously riveted together with gimmicks. Cocteau in later years made much of the paradox that he should have written *Antigone* before his Oedipus play, finding an elegant analogy of his method in the double pyramid of Dashur, where the Egyptian architects created a kind of temporal chain by using the height of one mausoleum as the apothem of a larger mausoleum enclosing it. But he worked rather more like the giants trying to scale Olympus by piling Ossa on Pelion; except his mounts were made not of stone but of cotton candy which kept dissolving beneath him, leaving him, with each new puff, higher and dryer.

Cocteau, ably abetted by Bérard, whose turquoise ramparts, crimson hangings, and free-flowing rock forms brought loud applause from the audience as soon as the curtain rose, earned critical acclaim from the conservative press. Once again he had broached but veered away from scandal, demonstrating masterfully that "the tact of audacity consists in knowing how far one can go too far." The reviewer from *Le Temps*, who admitted to having waited with bated breath for the nuptial scene, congratulated him on the artful euphemism by which he conveyed incest without violating the conventions of "good taste." The epilogue, in which Cocteau tips his hat to motherhood, was roundly appreciated. *Figaro* praised his style as follows: "That this relentlessly modern writing involves no disrespect testifies to Monsieur Jean Cocteau's art: his irony knows enough to make an about-face just as it threatens to plunge into farce. Moreover, he never misses the chance to bring off a piece of bravura in which he excels, constructing light edifices with words and consonants, like a magician drawing brilliant baubles out of his hat." *La Machine Infernale* had sixty-four performances, not enough to qualify it as a Boulevard success, yet too many to qualify it as an avant-garde fiasco.

Café society considered Cocteau its *poète maudit*, a kind of pet invalid whose fever chart became an integral part of his literary persona. It trotted him out at soirées like some infinitely eloquent poodle, or spoke of his latest "cure" in the hushed voices of initiates. When the English writer Rosamond Lehmann came to Paris in the early 1930s, the Princess de Polignac took her to a party where Cocteau was expected. "I had read him scarcely at all," she wrote. "I had heard that he was surpassingly brilliant, witty, original, sophisticated; also that he was an opium addict. The Princess added in that sort of low, uninflected, slack-jawed growl which served for voice . . . that at present he was in the throes of a cure, and might not be well enough to turn up." When at length she met him, it was on the verge of his departure. "He seized my hand, put his lips to it, and, still clasping it, declared (in French) that he was nothing but a poor invalid who no longer went out into society, but nevertheless he had come expressly to meet the author of *Poussière* and assure her of the sincere and profound admiration of a fellow poet. He stressed this word."

If Cocteau continued flitting about, opium did impair his ubiquity. The reputation for invalidism was gained at a price. He smoked as never before, sometimes falling into a narcotic slumber so deep he could not be awakened until opium was breathed into his lungs. Then, after days, he would suddenly come alive, frantic at the thought of being forgotten and quick to make his inevitable excuses. "I have a hospital at home," he wrote to Jouhandeau on New Year's Day, 1933. "My mother, on Rue d'Anjou, is suffering from pneumonia. I am playing nurse and nursing myself (all this transpiring within a kind of sentimental cyclone which has begun to subside a little)." His face had grown gaunt like an Oriental's, and opium had given him a yellow cast.

Increasingly he received at Rue Vignon, sitting on his bed like a Pharaoh in a smoky grotto suffused with red light, all his opium equipment near at hand. This was the posture and decor which served him for some years. It was thus he auditioned Jean-Pierre Aumont for the role of Oedipus in 1934. A few years later Peggy Guggenheim, making arrangements to exhibit his drawings at her new gallery in London, found him in the same position. "To speak to Cocteau," she wrote (he had by then moved to a hotel on the Rue Cambon) "one had to go to his hotel . . . and try talking to him while he lay in bed, smoking opium. The odor was extremely pleasant, though this seemed a rather odd way to be doing our business. One night he decided to invite me to dinner. He sat opposite a mirror, which was behind me, and so fascinated was he by himself that he could not keep his eyes off it."

Cocteau had become a kind of Chinese silhouette of Proust. He had Proust's invalidism, he had his grotto, he had in Marcel Khill an Agostinelli, he had a name whispered in hushed reverence or dismissed jokingly. All he lacked was a secret masterpeice. The comparison seems all the more apt on considering a series of reminiscences Cocteau wrote for the Saturday edition of *Figaro* in 1935,

Portraits-Souvenirs. It presents an image of pre-World War I France in some ways the reverse of *Remembrance of Things Past*. Whereas Proust strives for an impression of total recall, Cocteau hastens from great moment to great moment. In Proust, time gives three-dimensionality to figures. In Cocteau, it places them on a brilliantly lit stage where they are featured in hieratic poses at a theatrical remove which allows the nose to be seen but not the mole.

"History is composed of inexactitudes," wrote Cocteau, explaining his method. "It resembles Holbein's death's-head. When viewed from very near, it dissolves into its spots and brush strokes. One must place oneself at some distance, at a favorable angle to see the spots assemble and coordinate themselves; then the death's-head will appear. The details are of little importance. Only the masses, the volumes, the large format of a man or an act count." He enlarged the legend which he had created about his name into a full-blown method of history. Moreover, he believed himself. Having magnified the France of his youth into a golden age, he superimposed this image on the actors, actresses, boxers, music-hall singers, and fashion models who, more and more, comprised the bulk of his world. Cocteau arranged to blend their faces with those of de Max, Bernhardt, Polaire, Mistinguett, Madeleine Carlier. "1934–1935. A curtain is falling, another is rising," he wrote in *Portraits-Souvenirs*. "Life is dead, long live life! An age has died, an age I lived at its peak, unwillingly but with all my strength. My antennae inform me that a new age is beginning. I glimpse in it nobility and signs which make me hopeful. I am taking advantage of the short intermission to rise, to stretch, to turn about and survey the audience through my opera glasses."

In March, 1932, Gide had written to Cocteau thanking him for *The White Book*, which, except for a "few obscenities charmingly told," he condemned in his *Journal* as a futile melodrama. The letter merely recommends a vacation. "Why are we fooling around in this smoggy climate when Kuala Lumpurs await us?" While the ever-fidgety Gide was traveling far afield in the Belgian Congo and to Russia, Cocteau, rather like the esthetical hero of Huysmans' novel *Against the Grain*, satisfied himself with imaginary landscapes. He lacked not only Gide's considerable fortune, but his new-found concern with social injustice. Cocteau needed some more fitting pretext to leave France and one was suggested to him, apparently by Marcel Khill. The year 1936 was the sixtieth anniversary of Jules Verne's *Around the World in Eighty Days*, and Cocteau prevailed upon the director of *Paris-Soir* to subsidize a voyage commemorating Phileas Fogg's. In return, he agreed to write a series of articles.

On March 28 Cocteau and Khill set out, their itinerary dictated by Jules Verne's novel. From Rome they traveled to Brindisi, catching a steamer bound for Greece. After a few days in Athens they crossed the sea to Egypt by way of Rhodes, made short shrift of Alexandria, and continued to Cairo, where they remained for a week. Their next stop was Aden; there they boarded an English ship going to India. Their voyage across the Indian Ocean passed without incident, but the train voyage across the Indian peninsula from Bombay to Calcutta, in heat such as Cocteau had never experienced, nearly put an end to his frolic. Khill and he, much the worse for wear, caught a boat to Rangoon. With brief stopovers at Penang, Kuala Lumpur, Malacca, and Singapore, where they availed themselves of every opportunity to visit opium dens, the two, thin but euphoric, skirted the Malaysian peninsula. After visiting Hong Kong, Shanghai, and Tokyo, they crossed the Pacific on an American ship, the *Coolidge*. In the United States, Cocteau toured San Francisco, Hollywood, and New York, taking airplanes all the way so as to ensure his return before the eighty days had elapsed. On June 17 he was back in Paris.

All one can say with any certitude is that Cocteau visited the above places. His precious turn of mind, which seized only on baroque details (many of them apocryphal) made him a very bad reporter. "I admire Jules Verne for not even describing the diamond-studded nostrils of Miss Aouda," he wrote from Penang. "He describes an 'extraordinary voyage,' not what he sees. I should describe only the game of dominoes we played en route. . . . All in all, no great surprises. Never any disappointments. It's the way I imagined it would be, only better, more detailed, with depth and relief and shadows. . . . Our enterprise imprints on my mind not decors and faces but globes, maps, longitudes, latitudes, the revolving heavens." The collection of his reports—*Mon Premier Voyage*—reduces the world to a congeries of speechless ceremonies, self-quotations, improbable anecdotes, Conradian scenes, and one meeting written in the stars, the whole interlarded with descriptions of the sea reminiscent of Rimbaud's "Drunken Boat." It leaves the impression that Cocteau might as well have stayed home, for all he found abroad was himself, everywhere, quoting his Antigone in Malaysia and his Anubis in mid-Pacific. The voyage, his account of it, amounted to an adventure in self-promotion. "It was my purpose to colonize the unknown and to master its dialects," he declared. "At times I brought back dangerous objects which intrigued and enchanted, such as mandragora. They frightened some and helped others to live."

What was Cocteau's "unknown," however, but the ceremonial mask of it, some hidden vantage point we guess from the perverse mores, the drugged tempo, the *silence* it dictates? Cocteau was a master at suggesting depth by his elaborate system of bizarre cross-references. Dismissed by the French intelligentsia, he avenged himself by contriving to find in the Orient the world's better half, a civilization founded on Cocteauian principles, where ritual supersedes intellect and the wise stupor induced by opium supplants philosophy.

Perhaps Cocteau was, in the final analysis, a Taine stood on his head, for as Taine reduced the soul of England to some clear, known embodiment such as Samuel Johnson belching at dinner, Cocteau reduced the Orient to tics so imponderable or so improbable that they could be appreciated only by a sensibility as privileged as the author's. Thus the soul of India, he contended, lay in its abomination of farting. "A father lets wind while leaning over his son's cradle. His wife calls him a 'farter' and he must leave the village. Twenty years elapse. He wants to see his son again. He returns to the village incognito. He asks questions. His son has become a sturdy soldier in the Indian army. How proud he is! And there stand his son and his old wife at the threshold of her home. He forgets the past; he comes near. His wife recognizes him: 'Heavens,' she cries to her son, 'look, the farter has returned!' He flees and never again dares reappear." Japan, on the other hand, re-vealed itself to him in Kobe, where he observed a little "girl of the common people" drawing on the sidewalk the same ideal circle with which Hokusai signed his letters. "I should like to take this circle home with me," he wrote. "It opened . . . the secret of the Nippon soul."

The old man's fart and the young girl's chalk circle would have sat well in his curiosity shop on Rue Vignon, conversation pieces like the crystal cubes, the pipe-stem cage, the plaster face with waxen tears, the straw horses, the cardboard die, explaining them-selves through one another in a syllogism which operated very like his verbal *concetti*. The weightlessness of these objects, each com-memorating some inner occasion, and their ensemble presumably symbolizing a destiny, had a counterpart in Cocteau's social regis-ter, whose illusory bulk rivaled the Paris telephone directory. He amassed names chiefly to drop them, dropping them so familiarly, however, as to give the impression that there existed between him and various celebrities a kind of crazed empathy. Those meetings "written in the stars" constituted his public heaven, but often they answered no reality. *Paris-Soir* published Cocteau's version of his meeting with Charlie Chaplin aboard the *Karoa:*

> Two poets follow the straight line of their destiny. Suddenly it comes to pass that these two lines transect and the meeting forms a cross or, if you prefer, a star. My encounter with Charlie Chaplin remains the charming miracle of this voyage. So many people planned that meeting and tried to be its organizers. Each time an ob-stacle arose, and chance—which has another name in the language of poets—throws us together aboard an old Japanese freighter carrying merchandise on the China Sea between Hong Kong and Shanghai.

Cocteau was not one to leave chance to chance. His own best impresario, he had the steward deliver Chaplin a note suggesting they meet, but Chaplin, fearful of hoaxes, did not reply immedi-ately. After assuring himself at the purser's office that Cocteau was indeed among the passengers, he and Paulette Goddard went to Cocteau's cabin "leaping down the staircase four steps at a time." What ensued, as Cocteau describes it, was the incandescent union

of perfectly matched souls: "You can imagine the purity, the violence, the freshness of our extraordinary rendezvous, which we
owed solely to our horoscopes. I was touching the flesh and bone
of a myth. Passepartout (Khill) devoured with his eyes the idol of
his childhood. As for Chaplin he shook his white locks, removed his
spectacles, put them on again, grasped me by the shoulder, burst
out laughing, turned toward his companion, and said again and
again: 'Is it not marvelous? Is it not marvelous?' " During the following weeks, they became inseparable friends. Chaplin opened his
soul to Cocteau, unburdened himself of all his half-born projects,
of his inferiority complex, of quaint details about his own masterpieces, and so forth. "His enthusiastic flight toward me was, it
seems, unique," Cocteau proudly declared, "and he came to fear
this in a way. I then sensed that he was catching hold of himself
and folding in after having blossomed out."

Chaplin's version sheds some light on Cocteau's, demonstrating, if
nothing else, that the creation of legends is an art of omission. Midway through their first evening together, Chaplin realized that this
was not merely good conversation but The Conversation. Though
it proved more eloquent than other such Great Encounters, any sequel would have been anticlimactic. Chaplin and Cocteau exhausted
themselves that first night and, mainly to keep their charisma intact,
played hide-and-seek for the rest of the voyage, ducking through
saloon doors to escape one another, avoiding the main deck, and
feigning illness. "We had had more than a glut of each other,"
wrote Chaplin. "In the various stopping-off places we rarely saw
each other, unless for a brief how-do-you-do and farewell. But
when news broke that we were both sailing on the *President Coolidge* going back to the States, we became resigned, making no further attempts at enthusiasm."

Like Adrienne Monnier, Chaplin complained of migraines.

Cocteau wanted to be a French Chaplin, worshiped alike by the
elite and by the masses. Inside this mandarin there was a ragamuffin
screaming to be let out. Cocteau at forty-seven was an overgrown
Cocteau of sixteen, escaping from Dietz's boarding school to court
music-hall *mômes* in Montmartre. Increasingly he found himself

drawn to soulful, earnest, untutored children of the street; the more radically unliterary they were—like Khill and, somewhat later, Édouard Dermit—the more they appealed to him. It is doubtful that Cocteau possessed strongly paternal feelings. What he craved were pets, not children. At the end of his leash he wanted youth in some handsome, uncerebral incarnation. Advancing years made him the more desperate to be his ideal age. Thus his young men stayed twenty and came in simplified format: it was essential that they should be languid as he grew more hypertensive, and beautiful as he grew disturbingly gaunt. Cocteau never stopped behaving like the pampered child infatuated with luxury and with life in the raw. Whatever struck him as the reverse of himself seemed attractive: intellectuality or animal prowess, wealth or poverty, establishment or hoboism, the antiquity of a Sophocles or the youth of a boy scout. He was, above all, a perpetual have-not, leaning now toward one destiny, now toward some other, and usually toward both simultaneously. In the mid-thirties his preoccupation with youth and popularity obscured every other *raison d'être*. His company consisted of "his" actors, "his" singers, "his" boxer.

The growing discrepancy between Cocteau and his self-projections would have been burlesque if it were not tragic. He wrote a Prévert-like ballad called "Anna the Maid" for Marianne Oswald, a German singer who was one of the great early exponents of "existential" blues. For Arletty, who first came to the public's attention in Rip's Review of seminudes, Cocteau wrote a radio script called "The School for Widows" based on a story by Petronius. When Charles Trenet made his debut in 1937 he wore little wings designed by Cocteau.

It was inevitable that Edith Piaf should join this roster. "I admired Cocteau for a long time before meeting him," she wrote, "but I must say that the day mutual friends of ours introduced me to him I was at once dazzled and conquered. He spoke to me about songs with the extraordinary clarity which amazes his friends, however accustomed they may be to the fireworks display he mounts, and I was glad to learn that he liked the music hall. 'That's where one meets the true public, the public of football matches and boxing matches,' he said. 'We are no longer living in the age of ivory towers and snobs no longer count. Mr. Anybody is more interesting than they, but also more fastidious.' " For Piaf he wrote *Le Bel Indifférent*, a one-act play comparable to *La Voix Humaine* except that its heroine is not a bourgeoise but a poor girl living in a squalid room lit with reflections from street signs.

Cocteau's erotic fantasies made him an avid connoisseur of the music hall, but of the Bobino rather than the Folies-Bergère, for he needed the common touch. Like Lucien Daudet, Cocteau reconciled Petronius and the proletariat, whetting his pleasure with the idea of social self-debasement. By 1937 he was writing feature articles not for *Paris-Soir* but for *Ce Soir*, a Communist party daily whose director, having divorced himself from surrealism, could at last afford to recognize his affinity with Cocteau: Louis Aragon. Each sat on top of his proletarian heap.

Cocteau's appearance belied his affection for "Mr. Anybody." He was so thin, so made-up and effete as to look like a galvanized corpse staggering from one assignation to another. Cecil Beaton, whose room looked out upon Cocteau's in the Hôtel Castille (the two communicating by towel-semaphore), described him thus:

> I should like to make a catalogue of Jean's qualities and characteristics.
>
> Where to begin? His physical appearance: a fakir-thin body is held up by legs as thin as a sparrow's; yet curiously, he has flat feet. His hands seem so brittle you are afraid a sharp blow may crack them off. The fingers taper, can bend backwards. The nails are discolored and slightly dirty (a sign of the dope addict's *laisser aller*). As with most artists, the eyes communicate their owner's deepest secrets. As silent as Jean's mouth is talkative, the dilated pupils of his bulging fishy eyes, anguished and tortured, aghast and helpless, seem to be looking into another existence.

It was this extraordinary cross between a flamingo and a magpie who made the rounds of Montmartrian night spots in the company of Marcel Khill, pausing now at Suzy Solidor's cabaret, now at the Caprice Viennoise, where, through Khill, Cocteau met a Negro dancer named Al Brown. That meeting led to one of the more improbable adventures in Cocteau's checkered career.

Panama Al Brown was famous not as a dancer but as a formerly great boxer who had lost the bantam-weight championship of the world in 1934, two years before Cocteau met him, to a Spaniard named Balthazar Sangchili. That bout was staged in Valencia under sinister circumstances. Weary of the rigors of training, Brown threw a party on the eve of his match and spent the night in flamenco cabarets, staggering home at six a.m. quite drunk. Furthermore, he claimed that his own manager, in collusion with Sangchili's, had drugged him shortly before he entered the ring (in Cocteau's later publicity campaign for Al Brown the mickey is converted into "poison"). Sangchili won easily, and Brown, seemingly relieved at losing, began to dissipate himself with a vengeance. After two years of Parisian night life, at thirty-four and his body in bad repair, he had given up all thoughts of a comeback when Cocteau stepped into his life. Abruptly he found himself manipulated not only by a manager but by a Muse bent on restoring his championship. He had very little choice but to give up the dissolute life he loved, for Cocteau, once his mind fixed on some new role, performed it with manic energy. Picasso once expressed the hope that his paintings would some day cure toothaches. Cocteau was going to give a clamorous demonstration of the magical powers he arrogated to himself, the Poet, by raising a man from the grave.

Oddly enough, he succeeded, or at least he propped up Brown long enough for the boxer to regain his championship. Cocteau placed him in solitary confinement among the inmates of the Sainte-Anne lunatic asylum, where he spent a month abstaining from drugs and alcohol (possibly at Coco Chanel's expense: the beneficiaries of her generosity fed and cured their habits willy nilly); then Brown retired to a training camp in Aubigny, a village on the Cher. Smoking, drinking champagne during the afternoon and Bordeaux at meals, Brown nevertheless managed to recover his reflexes. Cocteau would drop by at frequent intervals to administer divine respiration. Their friendship was, as might be expected, the joke of French boxing circles. The *aficionados* did not take Cocteau's role seriously until the fall of 1937, when Brown scored a series of quick victories. Though advancing at the expense of opponents chosen for their ineptness, he did so with great style. Sports writers

were not long baptizing him the *enfant terrible*. His promoter was
able to arrange a return match with Sangchili in the Palais des
Sports, on March 4, 1938. Twenty thousand people attended, over-
wrought by the unusual publicity Brown had received and half-
expecting to see not another boxing match but a modern version of
Christ raising Lazarus. Cocteau did his utmost to depict the event in
this light, employing the same cant one finds in the preface to
Orphée and in *Opium*.

> The combat to which Jeff Dickson [the promoter] has invited
> us . . . goes strangely beyond the limits of a conventional match.
> Indeed, Al Brown, having left the ring and now climbed back into it,
> will find himself this evening opposite a personal enemy, a pugilist to
> whom he owes the loss of his title and his ruin. Al Brown was born
> the shadow of himself. The "black wonder," as journalists call him, is
> a frail being, thin, almost skinny, who has the nobility of an icon.
> When I met him, I guessed that he had died, poisoned at Valencia
> and his career cut short. It was his specter I saw skipping rope,
> knocking about Montmartre; it was his specter I decided to con-
> vince, against his will, to continue the work of Brown in flesh and
> blood. It meant overcoming the incredulity of the crowd and of
> sports fans, making them believe a poet untutored in this domain. But
> an Al Brown doesn't die like one of Catherine de' Medici's pages. His
> breeding gives him an almost plantlike resistance. His specter, his
> shade survives him. It is this shade I love, I respect, I am helping, I am
> lucky enough to see reach its goal.

The entertainment world came *en masse*. Raimu, Jean Gabin, and
Tino Rossi occupied ringside seats. Cocteau had cut short his vacation in Montargis. Flanked by Robert Toutain and the young Jean
Marais, he presided over the miracle as it unfolded round by round.
After the bout, a secretary of the Panamanian delegation entered
the ring to award Brown the Cross of Merit, Panama's highest
honor.

Al Brown did not live happily ever after. Cocteau published an
open letter in *Ce Soir*, advising him to quit while he was still ahead:
"Refuse to fight. Leave the ring. Travel across the world with a
stage routine that will show everyone the spectacle of your fragile

strength. A boxing match is nothing compared to the treasures of your awe-inspiring dance. . . . Try anything new. One surprise after another. A majestic tip of the hat."

But the boxer refused to observe a diplomacy which had served Cocteau himself in such good stead. He wanted one more fight, presumably to show that his victory had not been a fluke. On April 13 Brown fought Angelmann, again at the Palais des Sports. Cocteau, accompanied by Marais and a choir of Cocteauroons, again occupied the seat of honor. "His chin resting on two long pale hands with tapering fingers," observed one reporter, "Jean Cocteau followed the match with something approaching ecstasy. Occasionally the long, pale hands would join in brief and enthusiastic applause. One had the feeling that everything about Al Brown delighted the poet: his swings as well as his choreographic leaps." After his victory, Brown donned a tiny brown hat and left the ring followed by Cocteau, Marais, and a "choir of frenetic young men." He was now prepared to retire. Accordingly Cocteau found him a job at the Medrano Circus but, the very afternoon Brown was scheduled to perform, his dancing partners, Taylor and Muller, could not be roused from a drugged stupor. Cocteau volunteered to play, once again, Al Brown's impresario. He required only two hours to choreograph a "shadow-boxing dance," suggested by a scene from his own *Antigone*.[5]

The boxing world took Cocteau to task for what it considered irresponsible behavior. "If Monsieur Cocteau sees himself cutting a figure as some spiritual and muscular guide in the ups and downs of the black boxer, it must be granted that his imagination has run away with itself. What business is this of his anyhow?" Cocteau rejoined: "My advice was not an order and Brown doesn't take orders from anyone. I brought Al Brown back to the ring and, if he remains there, I shall be the first to applaud and to pay for my seat. My role as poet ends when reality begins."

---

5. Toward the end of the play one of Creon's guards accidentally drops his lance in front of Antigone. As he bends to pick it up, another guard grasps the opposite end; for an instant Antigone and Creon face one another on either side of this barrier, the lance symbolizing the rail in a courtroom. Cocteau simply translated the lance into a rope suggesting the boxing ring. Brown danced behind it, executing rhythmic leaps as the orchestra played jazz.

For Al Brown reality began as soon as his dance routine palled on the public. He traveled about Europe for six months shadow-boxing in the Amar Circus. Just before World War II he settled in Harlem but, unsuccessful at finding night-club engagements, returned to Panama. With what money remained from his championship purse, he opened a bar. It too failed. By 1950 he was, at forty-eight, back in Harlem, earning one dollar a round as a sparring partner, but working mostly as a dish washer. On Saturday nights he could often be seen at Small's Paradise on 123rd Street, wearing the only garment which had survived from his Parisian heyday: a smoking jacket he had bought in 1938 for the "Ball of the Little White Beds" in Montmartre.

One November day in 1950 he fell down on 42nd Street. At Bellevue Hospital he was found to be incurably consumptive. Mayor O'Dwyer secured him a room at the Seabright Clinic across the river from Manhattan. There he died. But impresarios pursued him beyond the grave. Three Negroes in a panel truck arrived at the clinic claiming to be relatives of the deceased. Astonishingly, they were given his corpse. For two nights they stood on the streets of Harlem collecting alms in the name of Alfonso Theophila Brown, whose remains lay aboard their truck in a white pine coffin.

Cocteau had been reprieved from an almost equally sordid end. His bills at the Hôtel Castille were paid by Coco Chanel, which permitted him to smoke so much that it was at times impossible to rouse him. Moreover, he would vanish for days on end, no one knew quite where. When Glenway Wescott visited Paris in 1937 after an absence of ten years, he called upon Cocteau at the Hôtel Castille only to discover that his friend had been incommunicado for some time. Inquiries got Wescott nowhere. He had all but given up hope when, strolling along a narrow street on the Left Bank, he spied in the window of a book store a printed notice that Cocteau would address a Boy Scout jamboree at the Sorbonne, in connection with his latest play *Oedipus Rex*.

Wescott found the amphitheatre crowded with boys in khaki knee pants. An aging ham-actor, his face stippled with red paint to simulate the bloody tears flowing from Oedipus' eyeless sockets, read from Cocteau's work. When the author himself minced on stage, he wore so much make-up as to have that livid, doll-like prettiness of the embalmed. Cocteau proceeded to assure his audience, above their shuffling feet and running noses, that the future of the world depended on them; it seemed a parody of some fascist youth rally.

"Do you realize," Cocteau sighed to a friend of his some years later, after being accosted by young autograph seekers in front of the Stock book store, "do you realize that I've had a starring role since the age of seventeen?—how exhausting, if only you knew. . . . And I have no choice but to play that role until the end!" Had he had the serenity, or the scruples, of a Valéry he might have phrased his complaint differently: "Who can tell me how, across existence, my person has kept itself whole, and what has borne me, inert, full of life and freighted with spirit, from one shore to the other of nothingness?"

Undone by opium and desperate to rescue himself from Cocteau's custodianship, Khill would suddenly turn upon his lover, administering such beatings that on one occasion Cocteau sustained a few cracked ribs. Like Radiguet and Desbordes before him, Khill reverted to heterosexuality, taking up with an actress. Like Desbordes, he would die during the war, the victim of a stray bullet fired by some German soldier who was unaware that France and Germany had the previous day signed an armistice. Shortly before the Sorbonne jamboree, Cocteau had met the handsome blond youth whom reporters observed at his side during Al Brown's boxing matches, Jean Marais. That meeting was mutually providential.

10

The Face of an Angel

Jean Marais was twenty-four when he met Cocteau, having been born the year Cocteau turned twenty-four, in 1913. The older man wanted a beautiful effigy of himself; the younger proved to be a character in search of an author.

Marais's father, a veterinarian, left for the Front as soon as war broke out and did not reappear until 1918. Mme. Marais was not altogether disconsolate at being left alone to rear her children in Cherbourg. Moreover, her beauty assured her the assiduous attention of drones excused from military service, "uncles" as Jean came to know them. The armistice marked for her a resumption of her conjugal misery. She resolved, after a year or so, to flee with her children. Accordingly, one of Jean's bogus uncles, the station master of the Saint-Lazare terminal in Paris, reserved a private club car for the family. M. Marais returned that night to an empty house ablaze with electric lights: his wife, who would visit her flair for theatrical entrances and exits upon her youngest son, had built a veritable bonfire to signal her liberation. For fear of reprisals from her husband, Mme. Marais adopted a pseudonym and settled in Le Vésinet just outside Paris, renting a millstone cottage surmounted by little turrets which looked like a composite of the witches' hideaways in Grimm's fairy tales.

Marais got what small education he had on the fly. A hysterical youth given to elaborate fibs, he was expelled from the best schools in France. In fact, he was the Dargelos of Cocteau's dreams, an insolent, untamable, excessively beautiful lad whose pranks had been suggested to him by the films he saw at every opportunity. In the Lycée Janson-de-Sailly, which was attended chiefly by the children of wealthy families, Marais distinguished himself as the hoodlum of his class, intimidating teachers with a revolver he was known to possess. At length his mother placed him in a parochial school, Saint Nicolas de Buzenval, where, always spoiling to outdo his classmates, he experienced a mystical seizure. By eighteen Jean Marais had demonstrated to everybody's satisfaction that he was singularly invulnerable to learning. His mind amounted to a temperament; meanwhile his face and his physique had organized themselves into the image of a Nordic god.

Awaiting the main chance, Marais supported himself by retouching identity photographs. On Sundays he would caddy at a Parisian golf course, despite eyes so severely myopic they could barely make out the fairway. Unable to afford acting lessons at the better-known schools, Marais enrolled in a tuition-free course offered by one Monsieur Paupelix, hoping thus to prepare himself for an audition at the State Conservatory. That he badly needed tutoring was sharply brought home to him by Dorival, director of the Théâtre Maubel, after Marais had auditioned by performing one scene from *Chatterton*. "My friend," Dorival observed, "you must go home and take care of yourself; you're hysterical."

He was, alas, rejected by the Conservatory, and the one movie audition that came of his relentless importunings proved to be a fiasco. Marais then prevailed upon his mother to pay for a course at Charles Dullin's academy, her one condition being that if he had not found a substantial role within one year he would admit his ineptitude and strive to earn an "honest" living. After a performance of *Julius Caesar* at the Dullin Academy, Marais was approached by students of Dullin's rival, Raymond Rouleau. They wanted to perform a new play in connection with the Paris Exposition of 1937, but found that they were short on male actors. The play represented Cocteau's latest, and last, squeeze of the Oedipus legend, *Oedipus the King*.

As always, Cocteau reserved the right to select his own interpreters. Like Jean-Pierre Aumont before him, Marais presented himself at Cocteau's opium parlor, now located in the Hôtel Castille.[1]

1. Gide no doubt envied Cocteau these interviews. Aumont recalls that when he auditioned for the role of nature boy in a pastoral film produced by Marc Allégret he was required to exhibit himself in the nude before a panel of judges including Gide and Philippe de Rothschild.

What he saw jarred his vision of the Great Man, for Cocteau, flanked by Marcel Khill and Al Brown like King Asmodeus and his henchmen, was wearing a filthy white woolen bathrobe riddled with cigarette holes and yellow with opium stains. The foulard round his neck was knotted so tightly that what little flesh he had folded over the material (an odd invariable in Cocteau's life, this sartorial self-strangulation: it has also been observed that his shirt cuffs were buttoned so tightly that his hands seemed drained of blood). "I felt intimidated, lost, declassed in this milieu given to strange forms of glory," wrote Marais, whose innocence was not in the least insincere.

After Cocteau waved his attendants out of the room, Marais became aware of something sizzling over a lamp and of a curious odor filling the room. Cocteau laid down his pipe and began to read from *Oedipus the King*, like a Siren hypnotizing her prey. Marais, to whom it did not occur that he was being wooed, marveled at Cocteau's consideration. "He treated the idiotic little boy I was as if he were the most cultivated of beings and sought my opinions like revelations." After one act Cocteau complained of feeling faint and invited Marais to come back in a week's time for the remaining installments. By then Cocteau had had the leisure to persuade himself that anyone with Marais's looks must be talented.[2] Three years before, Cocteau had given Jean-Pierre Aumont, at first sight, the role of Oedipus in *La Machine Infernale*. With equal promptitude he offered Marais the role of Oedipus in *Oedipus the King*, handing out his seemingly inexhaustible supply of Oedipi like valentines. The other actors in Rouleau's troupe revolted, however. Having imported Marais to play a secondary role, they found themselves corporately upstaged, and Cocteau was made to withdraw his nomination.

Resolved that Marais should become a star and convinced that he had the makings of a great actor, Cocteau cast him as Galahad in *The Knights of the Round Table*, a play written the previous winter during a vacation at the home of Igor Markevitch in Switzer-

2. Marais beheld himself far more modestly than his admirers: "I believe that my physical appearance when I was young mysteriously answered the vague and fugitive taste of an era and fixed it, crystallized it for a time."

land. That this play represented the end of Cocteau's "Hellenic" period in no way made it a new departure. Cocteau's Oedipus is no more Greek than his Artus is Arthurian. His characters are all cloaked in the same conceits; they breathe the same mock air, they commit the same cute extravagances and darling slips of the tongue, they find their lives organized about mirrors, masks, anesthetized stigmata, and bewitched abodes.

The familiar theme of illusion versus reality becomes so pronounced in *The Knights* as to require three schizophrenics playing both themselves and fraudulent selves, resulting in a double cast and a double drama. Cocteau created a fairy tale by inverting his image of Greek tragedy. The taboos which form the heart of myth, those desires so "real" they may come to light only in dreams, here become components of a false, a bewitched world. Thus the impersonated Guinevere is beset by Phaedralike desires for Lancelot's son Galahad, while the true Guinevere sits chastely at home. In other words, the characters behave immorally when *beside themselves*. It is Galahad's function, as *deus ex machina*, to set things aright. He comes onstage to the blare of Purcell's Trumpet Voluntary [3] (though one expects to hear Rossini's *William Tell* overture). By the time he leaves, hot on Merlin's trail, Camelot is free of the plague and its inhabitants have been reborn in a pure incarnation whose appearance is its reality.

Possibly *The Knights* should be understood in the light of Cocteau's addiction. He claimed that without quite realizing it he had written an account of his most recent cure. In that case, the bewitched or the dead would represent the "non-self" mimicking existence. But then addiction was an offshoot of Cocteau's sensibility, not the cause of it, and *The Knights* falls neatly into place within Cocteau's *œuvre*, as an installment of his recurrent nightmare: a nightmare characterized by some impossible love—precarious, yet safe so long as it occupies a closed space in a still world—which goes berserk as soon as the past and future make themselves manifest, as soon as that closed space is invaded and the world set in motion. Cocteau's plays nearly always begin with some mutation in the

3. The so-called Purcell Trumpet Voluntary is now attributed to one Jeremiah Clark.

order of things—a plague, some grievous injury, the outbreak or conclusion of an affair, a desecration, a message suddenly received from the underworld—and end, after a series of precipitate twists, with murder, suicide, or reincarnation. The family finds its cohesiveness threatened, it burrows into itself like a sick bird and dies convulsively. But *The Knights* is a shallow *tour de force* which did no one credit. "As for Jean Marais," wrote one critic, "he is beautiful. That much can be said for him, and no more."

Catapulted into notoriety, Marais was not lacking in humility. On the contrary, he understood that he would have to work tirelessly to acquire any stage presence whatever. Appropriated as he was, at twenty-four, by a luminous and vastly well-connected personality, he memorized the precepts drummed into him and closely observed the recommended models. The hectic, flamboyantly offhanded style so congenial to Cocteau—a style which exists for its own sake—inevitably became Marais's. Réjane was long since dead, but a few aging stage dragons still upheld the grand tradition, notably Yvonne de Bray, whom Marais met through Cocteau. When asked by his mentor, lover, and impresario what kind of role he would like to perform, his answer reflected his schooling: "the role of a young modern man with a high-strung temperament, who laughs, sobs, shouts, rolls on the floor; in short, a role set in some contemporary plot which could conceivably have been played by an old-time actor. For nothing interested me apart from the Yvonne de Bray style, the holy terror style of former days." Cocteau rewarded him with *Les Parents Terribles*.

Cocteau's life, despite its hallucinated irregularity, fell into a kind of pattern. Incapable of recoiling upon himself long enough to do any sustained work in Paris, he would move to the countryside whenever the urge came upon him, write convulsively, then return with a new play. Thus he and Marais, early in 1938, took up residence at the Hôtel de la Poste in Montargis, some sixty miles south of Paris and quite near Saint-Benoît-sur-Loire, that tiny hamlet distinguished by the presence of Max Jacob, whom the local ecclesiastics humored as if he were the village idiot, allowing him to live in their presbytery and to serve as sacristan in the abbey. Cocteau and Jacob repeatedly performed their famous duets for Marais's benefit.

"Their dialogue dazzled me," wrote Marais. "They reminisced about the heroic years, their war of letters, waged offensively against the bourgeois, defensively against the surrealists. Jacob cast my horoscope in great detail."

Limbering up for the work ahead, Cocteau improvised scatological couplets based on *The Misanthrope*, doing so with a kind of sustained frenzy often followed by periods of torpor during which he lay on his bed smoking opium. Marais learned, though reluctantly, how to prepare his lover's pipes and to blow opium into his lungs when he could not otherwise be awakened. Between fits, Cocteau made some effort to acquaint Marais with Western literature, urging upon him an incongruous syllabus of twenty titles which included Balzac's *Splendor and Misery of Courtesans*, Radiguet's *Count d'Orgel's Ball*, Madame de La Fayette's *La Princesse de Clèves*, and Richard Hughes' *A High Wind in Jamaica*. When at length the idea for his play reached full maturity, he required only eight days to write it down, working with such concentrated fury that his face, according to Marais, warped into a veritable Gorgon mask. "Work is a kind of torture for me, as is its aftermath; the void resumes and makes me fear that I shall never again be able to work."

Cocteau insisted that *Les Parents Terribles* was suggested to him by what he knew of Marais's relationship with his mother. "Their love and ferocious quarrels provided the basis of my play. People have seen in it all manner of scabrous things, that's quite possible, but I never intended them and never saw them. I was even stupefied at realizing how people must suppress neuroses—for how else could they imagine what they do about a simple situation involving a mother joined to her son by the umbilical cord?"

Such innocence on Cocteau's part, feigned or otherwise, lies at the root of his artistic credo. It accounts for the oddly deodorized atmosphere of plays and novels such as *Thomas, Les Enfants Terribles, Le Grand Écart, Les Parents Terribles*, in which the situation or predicament is but an instant that endures a lifetime between the pangs of birth and the throes of death. Between these two massive events Cocteau's characters behave in some predetermined way, performing blind, ritual antics at high speed, seemingly compelled to get the drama, and themselves, over with as quickly as possible. Cocteau plays his LPs at 78 R.P.M. so that even bassos sound like Donald Duck. The hysteria from which his characters corporately suffer is not psychological *but life itself, conceived as an instant.* Wasn't Cocteau fond of "demonstrating" existence by a flattened paper accordion he would pierce with a pin? Unfolded, the accordion reiterates that puncture in each of its folds, but the multiplicity is, he contended, an illusion. Given so drastic a *reductio*, the mind does not have time to afford itself; an instant, however, *is* time enough for a scream, a pose, a snapshot (indeed, the word for snapshot in French is *instantanée*).

Cocteau's characters are fully comprehensible only when understood as Épinal images incapable of ulterior motives, blindly self-identical—even at their slyest. Masks, unmasked they would be seen to wear the same mask. "Only the masses, the volumes, the large format of a man or of an act count." Cocteau beheld life at a temporal and spatial remove from which it appeared, essentially, a kind of visual legend. This comes clear in his *summa*, *Blood of a Poet*, but it accounts for the theatricality, the harassed rhythm of all his fiction. A bourgeois aphorist to his fingertips, Cocteau had a genius for flashes, for imaginative short-circuits which depend on some brilliant trope. His esthetic derives from that virtue, and suffers all its deficiencies. Cocteau's was a visual, a formalistic gift; yet, living against his grain, incapable of deductive thought, of portraying mass and organic development, he wanted at all costs to be known as "deep." His characters are born of an image and remain imprisoned in two dimensions: they are attentuated flickers, a kind of organized *mot d'esprit*. Only his "mothers" have any real bulk, but then, conferring as they do life and death, they are responsible for the infernal machine.

Les Parents Terribles pivots about a mother as *Les Enfants Terribles* pivots around a sister. The love of a sister for her brother had simply been translated into the passionate hold Yvonne tries to maintain over her son. In both works the hero finds another woman, and in both the sib rival does her utmost to foil his struggle for independence, driving the poor interloper out of the family nest. Finally one of the contestants commits suicide. It was Cocteau's intention to show, within a bourgeois setting, and using the "boulevard" formulae of a Bernstein, the wheedlings of some primitive matriarch making her last stand against the threat of exogamy. Next to Antigone, Death, Jocasta, the Statue, and Élisabeth (in *Les Enfants Terribles*), Yvonne takes her place in Cocteau's gallery of *monstres sacrés*. But *Les Parents Terribles*, precisely because its setting is, for once, so banal, and because Cocteau's language is comparatively unmannered, has the dramatic vitality lacking in his "Greek" plays. He succeeded in making his point, so well in fact that he tasted popular success for the first time and provoked, through greed for still greater success, his first authentic scandal.

The misfortunes dogging *Les Parents Terribles* constituted a boulevard play in the best tradition. Ironically, one of the protagonists in that play outside the play was none other than Henri Bernstein.

Cocteau preordained Marais for the son's role and Yvonne de Bray for that of the mother. Mlle. de Bray could not, apparently, wait to begin rehearsals, and staged the first one in an impromptu manner reminiscent of Bernhardt's attempted rape of Robert de Montesquiou. Less squeamish than the count, Marais was not provoked to the point of vomiting, but he barely refrained. "One day," he wrote, "in front of Cocteau, on his divan, she wanted to rehearse with me a bit of the play. 'I have it! Let's do the bed scene!' she exclaimed. I wanted to flee. I wanted to escape. I implored her to desist: I would prove inadequate! She stood firm. So did I. She threw out a line. I answered. I cried. I laughed. . . ." A few days later Mlle. de Bray began to act strangely. During a rehearsal at her apartment she would periodically vanish into the kitchen and return each time a bit giddier, until convulsed with laughter. The following day she failed to appear at the Théâtre des Ambassadeurs where *Les Parents Terribles*, a month or so later, would open the first of its two long runs. Cocteau and Alice Cocéa (the play's director) decided to fetch her, only to discover the shutters drawn and the door barricaded. The great actress' binge lasted some three days. She was replaced by Germaine Dermoz.

The second twist occurred some weeks after the opening. The villain of the piece was Henri Bernstein, whose career as a play-

wright had paved his way to important administrative positions in
the theatre world. Director of the Gymnase, he coveted the Théâtre des Ambassadeurs, a theatre owned by the prefecture of Paris
and occupied for the time being by Roger Capgras and Alice
Cocéa, whose lease could not be broken while *Les Parents Terribles* continued to run, barring some exceptional circumstance.
Bernstein was angling for that circumstance and Cocteau furnished
it. Capgras wanted to give free Thursday matinée performances of
The Misanthrope for students selected by the principals of various
lycées in Paris, a worthy idea at which Cocteau, however, took
offense, declaring that he did not wish to share the stage with anyone, least of all when young boys sat in the audience. "Didn't he
consider the schoolboy public his true public?" said Alice Cocéa.
"Morlière's competition didn't make him happy." Cocteau prevailed
upon Capgras to give Thursday matinee performances of *Les
Parents Terribles.*

Going out of his way to show schoolboys a play which Louis
Jouvet had rejected because it seemed too daring for adults may
simply have been one of those faultless maneuvers the masochist
cannot help making. More obviously, it reflected two highly neurotic emotions which governed Cocteau's life: his desire to remain
at all costs the foremost idol of French youth, and his shame
(mixed with bliss) at being acclaimed by a bourgeois public.

He got, at any rate, the whiplash he was asking for. As soon as it
became known that Cocteau had offered free chits to adolescent
boys so that they could watch an "incestuous" play, a shudder ran
through the municipal council, which was just recovering from a
similar scandal over Marcel Pagnol's *Topaze.* The French Right
had by now reduced itself to a vice squad viciously defending the
honor of the bourgeois family and assuming that any "perversion"
must have its roots to the left of center. A municipal councilor
named Fernand Brunerye specialized in licentious plays "threatening morality." It was he, supported by one Pierre Dailly, who
mounted the campaign against *Les Parents Terribles.* While disputes raged in the Municipal Council, Cocteau employed his energies writing open letters, one, for example, addressed to the student
body of France, which began: "My dear friends, I have always

worked for you. You have always fought for me. We are allies in a common cause." To the president of the Municipal Council, M. Le Provost de Launay, he explained his position at some length:

> I never offered a free showing of my play to schoolboys. I invited their masters to see it and to decide for themselves whether poor students from whom I receive daily requests for seats might not be able to take advantage of free admission.
>
> Accusations that it was all for publicity's sake are futile. The theatre is filled every night, and my artists are proud of the applause they receive.
>
> I could be entitled to the opinion that all my good strokes of luck I owe to the young. That would not be self-satisfaction but gratitude.
>
> If I have gone beyond certain limits, this affair has carried me beyond them and represents a threat to the freedom of the mind. It would be a serious matter if France were to become one of those countries which burn books and deport artists in the name of some false morality. It so happens that my play is a moral one. It could quite possibly have been the contrary. Even if that were so, I would defend it now with the same ardor.
>
> A play is an act. It is above being defined as a good act or a bad act. The centuries bear witness to that.

The Left refused to support Cocteau, not because of his Nietzschean remarks, but rather because he was Cocteau, a prominent member of the secret brotherhood of homosexuals which enjoys (especially in the realm of arts and letters) the power wielded in a former age by Jesuits, and a writer of politically irrelevant plays applauded chiefly by the very public that voted Right-Wing deputies into office. It therefore abstained, and the Council, by a vote of forty-seven to none, recommended that the Prefect of Paris give Capgras and Cocéa ten days to evacuate the Théâtre des Ambassadeurs. Alfred Willemetz, director of the Bouffes-Parisiens, offered the company asylum in his theatre. There, *Les Parents Terribles* continued its successful run. Shortly after the move it was announced that Henri Bernstein had been granted a fifteen-year lease to the Théâtre des Ambassadeurs.

Les Parents Terribles was revived in 1941 during the Occupation and, ironically, at Bernstein's former theatre, the Gymnase. This time it was closed by the Nazis, after French fascist militia laid siege to the theatre and hurled tear gas pellets onto the stage. By then Bernstein had lost not only his fifteen-year lease, but his country. In New York City, he engaged in literary polemics with André Maurois.

The success of *Les Parents Terribles* took the edge off Cocteau's hunger, but his was an insatiable appetite. He suffered, now as ever, the pains of anybody expecting universal approbation and love. His lifelong plea of innocence presented the inner facing of his extraordinary vanity, and it amounted, as often as not, to an accusation in disguise. He would take offense at indifference, interpreting it as a plot, a conspiracy of silence worse than outright calumny. Much as he inveighed against the anthropophagous world of Parisian letters, Cocteau was a city creature who liked feeling hemmed in and fought expertly in narrow places. Yet with whom did this latter-day Voltaire identify himself but with Jean-Jacques Rousseau?

The essay Cocteau wrote on Rousseau in 1938 is remarkable for its lack of self-awareness. Defending Rousseau against the Encyclopedists, he merely succeeded in condemning himself. The "speed," the intriguing, the writing of books as a means of sustaining one's social position for which Cocteau indicts Grimm could well have served as an indictment of Cocteau. Cocteau had set up a *trompe-l'œil* image of himself and ended by deceiving his own eye. "Rousseau committed the worst of imprudences: he made his entire life public, and he committed his life to his work." We are expected to accuse Cocteau of the same noble crime, but if ever a writer concealed his life, undressing a straw man bearing his name, that writer was Cocteau. He undressed himself more truly, however, in accusation than in defense, guilty as he was of the defects he ascribes to his enemies and innocent of the virtues belonging to his hero. When he says of Rousseau that "without his genius, he would doubtless have been a jack-of-all-trades" he tacitly vouchsafed himself Rousseau's saving grace.

More interesting than this essay in defense of Rousseau was the situation which provoked it. Cocteau found himself slighted by a whole generation of young *idéologues* coming into prominence. Malraux, Guilloux, Sartre, Beauvoir, Nizan weighed Cocteau on the scale of events and found him very light indeed. Imbued with philosophy and, like the surrealists before them, beset with all the scruples of the petty-bourgeois intellectual trying to maneuver his subtle equipment in a drastically simple world in which monolithic religions represented political reality, they found Cocteau—whose self-obsession made him immune to the larger issues of his age—an irrelevant figure. This slight might have been tolerable if not for Gide, whose conversion to communism, whose mission to Berlin on behalf of the Bulgarian Communist Georgi Dimitroff, and whose voyage to Russia in 1936 magnified his prestige in the eyes of French youth. Gide's defection from the Communist party following his return from Moscow stirred up a controversy of such violence that, compared to it, the *Les Parents Terribles* scandal seemed little more than a spirited game of croquet.

The Gide-Cocteau rivalry fastened onto young Claude Mauriac, who was courting the two simultaneously, not so much to play one against the other as to play both against his father. Wanting to be unlike François Mauriac, so desperately in fact as to associate with his literary enemies, Claude walked in his father's very footsteps. Forty years before, François Mauriac had been dazzled by Cocteau, then turned against him. Claude did likewise but left some fascinating notes in the process. He was capable of viewing Cocteau from a distance, unlike the epigones always to be found worming for recognition.

In May, 1939, one such epigone, Roger Lannes, drove Mauriac to Versailles, where Cocteau and Marais were sharing a room in the Hôtel Vatel, a quiet establishment for pensioned bourgeois who looked upon Cocteau and his friends as a squadron of noisy demons dispatched from hell. Their conversation—or Cocteau's monologue—took place in a cloud of opium smoke, which grew thicker as the evening wore on. Detective novels, cheap editions of Racine and Molière, and Cocteau's latest manuscripts lay strewn about the room—an airless, Cocteauian room uninfluenced by the soft countryside of the Île de France. Cocteau—his gray trousers half-unbuttoned, his belt hanging unbuckled, and his blue sweater a size too snug—paced to and fro, cackled, ground his teeth, mimicked people, read his latest manuscript, occasionally stretched his wiry frame onto a chaise longue, leapt up, punctuating his remarks with "*mon chéri*" and "don't you see?" and never slackening long enough for someone else to slip a word in edgewise. This filibuster lasted from six-thirty p.m. to one a.m. Mauriac's brilliant reconstruction of it gives a vivid sense of what was preying on Cocteau's mind but, more significantly, it conveys the form, the shape of discourse Cocteau practiced every day of his life:

> After the *maîtres* we have inevitably the *petits-maîtres:* monks aped by monkeys. The masters have genius, the same genius childhood possesses: Gide, now isn't he the old English lady who travels in a hat with a green veil to see the pyramids? Claudel? Isn't he really Baby Cadum? And Valéry's just a distracted schoolboy who raises his hand to leave the room. The true masters are *invisible.* That makes sense: nobody wants the fashions to change, everybody is used to the status quo. Today Rimbaud is *visible,* and it's my turn to be invisible. Do you know what the doctors mean by a "flesh wound"? The bullet that's clean and fast enough will pass through part of the body without leaving a trace: the flesh closes of itself. That's an image of my work: invisible, it's so clean and so fast. And that's to be expected. Ah! Rimbaud is not easily gotten off our backs! Look at the young poets of the moment. . . . Rimbaud is a chewing gum that sticks to all feet, and it won't come unstuck. But what he has meant to us! What other bondages he has delivered us from. . . . Thanks to him we meet images head-on without recourse to "like" and that's great. But the surrealists by their excesses ruined it all. Radiguet came and saved me from them. Without Radiguet I would have gone on looking for combinations more and more baroque, to writing three-word poems on postage stamps. . . . At the time that we met Radiguet, no one was writing simple stories or simple poems. As soon as he came a way was opened in the direction of purity. At last I understood that every mystery, all poetry, every miracle of the ineffable could be expressed, or better: suggested, without any contortions of the mind or the heart. Without Raymond Radiguet I never would have reached perfection. "L'Ange Heurtebise," for instance, is a very beautiful *object*, a poem without a blot. It is so pure, so beautiful that any thief who came with the intention of imitating

it would simply circle it and never find a flaw through which he could get in. Not to be imitated, a miracle like that simply isn't to be imitated! "L'Ange Heurtebise" is suspended between heaven and earth like a tremendous crystal-mint Lifesaver at the end of an invisible string. . . . But people are unable to *see* a thing like that. I'm *invisible*. . . . And all the same it's monstrous! Now Giraudoux doesn't know a thing about the supernatural and writes of fairies without ever having met one. Giraudoux is a poet for capitalists, he's a ten-cent store for poetry. And of Giraudoux they write (and they're serious and he allows it) "Giraudoux writes with blood!" But as for me, I'm always "that amiable clown." Me, Jean Cocteau, who have given myself body and soul to my work. Me, Jean Cocteau, who never hesitated to challenge Death itself to a duel! And I sit here waiting for the worst that Death has to offer after writing the last pages of my new *Potomak* where I take on death on its own terms, where I actually invoke Death—what I had to say was so pressing. And I am a bit worried, but it's for Jeannot's sake. But as for me, Jean Cocteau, what's the difference? The only value as far as I'm concerned is dedication to my message and *basta!* That's why I loathe a Voltaire or a Goethe so. . . . Nothing could be further from me! Gide once said of Goethe that perhaps someday it would be proven that Goethe was only a tin horn big as the column in the Place Vendôme. And people laugh at my exertions! It's never *my* blood that they discover, just Giraudoux's, and his impossible *Ondine* receives unanimous praise . . . I wrote to Jouvet about it. I said what's the use of lighting up that stupid palace from the inside when no light comes through his characters—they have all the transparency and life of stones. . . . But me, I'm a jester, oh yes. Marvelous! One day I asked Colette how it was she hadn't written anything you could exactly call a masterpiece in spite of her tremendous talent—she took me to a mirror and said, "Look at yourself. Now me, I want to enjoy life, to have beautiful legs and a healthy body. Now look at yourself. You haven't even kept anything comfortable to sit on!" She understood that I've become a mere pen from my devotion to writing and that my very blood has turned to ink. And Giraudoux, considered the ascetic of poetry, is not even *real!* It's marvelous . . . Giraudoux who doesn't even know what automatic writing is! Now without that you never have a masterpiece, not a real one with a voice that carries. Do you really believe that everything in *La Princesse de Clèves* or *Adolphe* was *planned?* What boredom, what sorrow, what coldness! But the unspeakable grace of these works which have every sign of being cold, sad, and boring proves that something divine has been at work, this mystery that not even the author himself fathoms and which makes him say more than he intends. That's how it is with my *Machine à Écrire*. That's how it is with my new *Potomak*. That's how it's been with everything I write.

This was Cocteau's "number." He parroted himself far better than the comics who were ridiculing him in their music-hall routines. Words, images, names, quotations, always the same ones, would come squirting out, like the ink of a squid, the instant he sensed danger or found himself before someone as yet unseduced. Nor could he ever stop talking, because there would always be some bright lad to impress and some brilliant contemporary threatening to eclipse him, if not Claude Mauriac and Giraudoux, then Radiguet and Breton, or Maurice Sachs and Gide.

But beneath tirades like the one above there lay a profound sense of loss. Cocteau's last summer in Piquey, sixteen years before, seems to have been one of those still points round which his life and his legend revolved obsessively. Did it not represent a moment of enormous security for him, aglitter with promises of literary pre-eminence? Radiguet had been a bulwark against Cocteau's past, he represented for Cocteau rebirth in a guiltless incarnation, and he stood as Cocteau's ally against the intelligentsia. When Radiguet died, Cocteau suddenly found himself hideously alone, fated to keep excusing himself, justifying himself, arriving at himself all over again. An *arriviste*, Cocteau must be considered that in the fullest sense, for the *arriviste* cannot, by definition, arrive, least of all while walking a treadmill to some mythical year zero in the past (*Potomak*, Diaghilev's challenge, Gide's *Paludes*, his meeting with Radiguet—depending on the circumstances).

This is what Sartre meant, no doubt, when he characterized Cocteau as a man who had spent his whole life seeking a tribunal simply to corrupt it. Cocteau stood accused of being Cocteau, a *bourgeois malgré lui*, and he racked his soul to prove the contrary. By 1940 he had perfected his plea, stacked the jury, bribed the magistrate, and planted his claque in the gallery. But, unconvinced by the acquittal, he kept on pleading. Cocteau had surrounded himself in self-protection with the "interpreters" of his legend. In February, 1939, he returned to Piquey, making a kind of pilgrimage to his ideal past. En route he wrote a short book called *The End of Potomak* which stands as another in his series of self-prefaces. His talk about invisibility, sleep writing, the poet's apprehension of his self, had by now amounted to a literature in its own right. Cocteau played The Poet, like one of his own heraldic personae. Yet the one person whom he never quite persuaded of his authenticity was Cocteau. Hence his compulsive tirades, his advocacy of Rousseau, his bitter outbursts against those intellectuals whom he could not seduce.

"It isn't uncommon," he wrote at the beginning of *The End of Potomak*, "for a man to become the captive of some zone in his city and to remain imprisoned there for life. Some spell binds him to the forms and fluids that emanate from it. In my case, the temple of the Madeleine forces me to radiate about its columns. From hotel to hotel, from flat to flat, I have been stumbling around for years within that geometrical shape which prolongs, like some baleful halo, the bulky, green-gabled church." At fifty, Cocteau set up house with Jean Marais in a seven-room flat on Place de la Madeleine, furnishing it with his bric-a-brac, with borrowed mattresses, fur covers donated by Yvonne de Bray, iron chairs stolen from the Tuileries, and tables bought at the Saint-Ouen flea market.

Cocteau considered the outbreak of war a resounding tribute to his prescience, for in 1913 he had written *Potomak*, and now in 1939 *The End of Potomak*. Actually, his works, including these two, are heedless of all but his own upheavals; they protract a few half-legendary instants of his life, repeated again and again, into something which achieved a semblance of history. In 1913 Cocteau may have been spoiling for the adventures that war held in store for him, but in 1939, after some thirty years of hopping about like a keyed-up mechanical soldier, he was relatively at peace with himself. Having temporarily given up opium for fear that Marais, who abominated drugs, would leave him, he partially recovered his health. He had a stage, and even a home of sorts, though it looked like a sevenfold enlargement of his one-room pads.

In August, 1939, this precarious structure had suddenly to be dismantled. Cocteau and Marais were vacationing in Saint-Tropez when France declared war on Germany. Marais left for the Front, and Cocteau, alone once more, decided to abandon their apartment on the Place de la Madeleine. Yvonne de Bray offered him lodging on her houseboat. After several weeks afloat, working at still another play, this one to be called *Les Monstres Sacrés*, he lived for a while in the Ritz, a few doors from Coco Chanel and at her expense. Then he took his scattered belongings to Christian Bérard's room in the Hôtel Beaujolais. There he lived throughout the *drôle de guerre*, the Phony War preluding France's catastrophic fall.

11 ❧❧

Occupational Hazards

Several million Frenchmen immediately answered the call to arms and hastened to the Front, where their generals, entertaining grotesque illusions about the strength of the eastern defenses, required them to loiter for months on end Marias, whose officers lacked means of transportation, donated his sports car and was named chauffeur. In this impromptu capacity he drove directly north. A large infantry camp had been set up at Montdidier, near Amiens. Here, and in Roye some ten miles distant, Marais spent eight months.

The discrepancy between the leisurely chaos of French forces and Hitler's minutely calibrated death machine makes the mind boggle. Not until Germany had finally struck could France appraise the extent of her self-deception; she would, furthermore, require a year of foreign occupation to see the difference between Naziism and Prussianism. Meanwhile Weygand and his general staff temporized, expecting the enemy of their dreams to bounce good-naturedly off the concrete ramparts which formed the Maginot Line. This allowed the French army time to fall into a bilious frame of mind and the civilians to grieve with impunity. Womanhood started crocheting *en masse*. Before long every *poilu* had his *marraine* (or godmother) sending him letters and sweaters to mitigate the ravages of waiting. Marais's proved to be Coco Chanel. Having made an offensive remark to Marais several years before, she now seized the opportunity to exonerate herself, and did so grandly. Lorries full of wine, cigarettes, Shetland pull-overs, and fur-lined leather jackets arrived in Montdidier. Marais's company desisted from persecuting him long enough to appreciate a windfall the likes of which they had never known in civilian life.

Marais found reason to appreciate Cocteau's far-flung network of wealthy dowagers, although their goodness did not always redound, as it had in Chanel's case, upon his comrades. While the infantry lived cramped in tents, their officers, determined to enjoy the fringe benefits of war, reconnoitered the countryside for elegant villas in which to billet themselves. One villa in particular seemed to capture their fancy: an exquisite Louis XIII château located outside Roye and called Tilleloy. Marais, still a chauffeur, was directed to drive there and demand lodging for his superiors. The chatelaine, attired in headgear such as Flemish women wore in the seventeenth century, fell into his arms crying "Jeannot!" and offered him the run of her estate. Mlle. Thérèse d'Hinnisdael had often received Cocteau and Marais at her family mansion, the Hôtel de Montmorency-Luxembourg on the Rue de Varennes, where stone *gisants* of her ancestors lay at the foot of an immense staircase. Her country villa having been demolished during World War I, she had had it reconstructed stone by stone, an enterprise which obviously discouraged her from entertaining the possibility of its being razed anew. Marais's officers were told to bivouac outside her gates. She declared a brief truce at Christmastime and even then had occasion to regret her leniency, as some British soldiers saw fit to express their gratitude by chanting the Marseillaise. "That revolutionary hymn, in my house?" she exclaimed, and would have driven the unwitting culprits from her house had not Cocteau intervened.

That Cocteau and Marais could commute between the Front and Paris—the one for parties at Tilleloy and the other to attend first nights on the Right Bank—gives some idea of the theatrical atmosphere reigning in France during this period. What restrictions there were had seemingly been invented to give the population at large a phony crisis by which to demonstrate their talent for circumventing restrictions. The *drôle de guerre*, as it came to be called, scarcely dampened the social season of 1939–1940. Thus, when *Les Monstres Sacrés* opened in February, 1940, at the Théâtre Michel, more people were heard to complain of the grippe than of the war. Cocteau went through his ritual fidgets backstage, while his entourage assumed characteristic poses in the audience:

Schiaparelli laden with rings, the incredibly obese Princess Violette Murat attired in baggy tweeds and teasing Colette, who answered her with an implacable eye, the dwarflike Marie-Louise Bousquet, "dressed like a Neapolitan fisherman in mourning," mustering the photographers for the benefit of *Harper's Bazaar* and leading Carmel Snow in tow: all this while the army, a few hundred miles away, played fort.

What Ernst Jünger observed of Cocteau, that he lived in a private hell but had made himself cozy there, could apply to the French as a whole. Marais's military career was disastrously typical. Having lost his post as company chauffeur, he found himself assigned to the bell tower of Roye where he was expected to scan the heavens for German aircraft. His commanding officer had obviously neglected to consult the medical report, and Marais, anxious to have a sinecure, was not about to reveal his myopia. For months he lived in splendid isolation some four hundred and fifty steps above the ground, surrounded by photographs of his friends and by demijohns filled with tinted water. To earn his keep, he would pretend to sight nonexistent aircraft, but he spent most of his time sun bathing and holding long-distance telephone conversations with Cocteau. Marais rigged a pulley with which he hauled up his food. Mlle. d'Hinnisdael joined him for tea daily, driving to the tower in her Cadillac and ascending the four hundred and fifty steps escorted by a Saint Bernard.

The Germans, alas, provided the last act to this *divertimento*. A squadron of their fighter planes suddenly descended upon Roye and circled about the tower, where Marais, hysterical with fear, was dancing like a Jansenist convulsionary in the cemetery of Saint-Médard. Only the tower—being a navigational axis for the Germans' raid—survived. Marais, when he finally descended, found little left of Roye. He rejoined his company. The French army had already begun a massive retreat, which stopped a month later at the foothills of the Pyrenees six hundred miles to the southwest. Marais was borne by this ebb tide to the forest near Auch; there he lived, briefly, at the hospitality of gypsies.

Meanwhile the exodus from Paris had carried Cocteau to Perpignan, only one hundred miles from Auch. News of the German advance had terrified Paris. After June 8, 1940, the civilian population stopped believing in miracles and the government made all due preparations to have itself relocated in Bordeaux, now firmly established as the Calvary of France's Third Republic. Boulevard Saint-Germain was crowded with peasant caravans. Herds of livestock, work horses, wagon-loads of poultry, and a flying phalanx of famished dogs descended on Paris from the east, north, and northeast, wave upon wave of them, leaving piles of dung in their wake. The few die-hards who had at first been appalled by this exodus joined it on June 11, when General Weygand declared Paris an open city. Millions converged upon the Gare d'Austerlitz or took to the roads, their bicycles and automobiles laden with everything portable.

"Beginning in the afternoon of the 11th," wrote one observer, "a dense, black pall of soot and smoke began to gather over Paris: a kind of apocalyptic cloud. When we left, the night was still choked with it, thickened and impenetrable. Our headlights lit up barely three yards and already, at the gates of Paris, on the roads, thousands of automobiles, transformed into weird junk wagons, stood bumper to bumper: mattresses on the roofs, bird cages, dogs, cribs, trunks, an uncomputable number of valises. . . . Impossible to move faster than ten miles an hour." The "apocalyptic cloud" came from the flaming stocks of oil and gas in seven river towns around Paris. Before long punctured tires, shards of furniture, packing paper, cardboard valises, excelsior, and broken umbrellas littered the roadside, soaking in rain which fell almost unremittingly throughout the month of June. From the air, Antoine de Saint-Exupéry saw the exodus as a "slowly flowing stream of black molasses."

When the Nazis entered Paris on June 14, goose-stepping round the Arc de Triomphe and down the Champs-Élysées, their parade went all but unwitnessed. Four-fifths of Paris, some three million people, had fled, including the keeper of the flame which burned beside the Unknown Soldier: he had waited till the last moment before extinguishing it. City archives had been bundled onto a barge which promptly sank near Roanne. Later the papers were brought to the surface and dried in a disused factory.

The hundreds upon thousands of refugees advanced confusedly toward Orléans, funneled across the bridges, and dispersed in every direction. More than half of the Île-de-France took flight. Cities and villages lying in the path of this human tornado were alternately emptied and bloated as their inhabitants moved out and outsiders moved in, pillaging with truly Gallic rapacity the shops and homes and schoolhouses. Within a few days, Chartres lost all but eight hundred of its twenty-three thousand inhabitants. Briare, a village of one hundred, suddenly became a city of twelve thousand. Parents gave up their children for temporary adoption en route. At the hospital of Orsay in Orléans five nurses, crazed with fear, administered fatal doses of morphine to the incurable and aged. Rumors of espionage and a fifth column were rife. Some mayors refused to leave their towns; most took to their heels, transporting, out of deference to the inviolable past, civil records dating back to the early nineteenth century. Fires in Orléans, started by the German bombardment, raged out of control, for the fire trucks had been commandeered by refugees. During an entire week Orléans, whose bridges loomed like life and death in the minds of people still north of the Loire, lacked electricity, gas, water, bread, money, and a mayor. Two hundred madmen who had escaped from the Semey asylum nearby wandered, many of them drunk and one woman stark naked, through the flaming city. Yet the most careful precautions had been taken that political prisoners in the Santé prison should not go free. They were herded into twenty-four paddy-wagons with almost nothing to eat and kept imprisoned there for eighteen hours, even during air strikes. The Third Republic clung to its native enemies as to a last shred of government.

In Bordeaux a bare quorum of the Senate conducted meetings in a cinema called the Capitole on Rue Judaïque while the Chamber of Deputies reconstituted its rump self in a grade school on the Cours Anatole France. Mandel, Minister of the Interior, saw to it that his new lodgings were redecorated at no small expense to the moribund republic, and Paul Reynaud, the premier, found time to confer with the Director of Public Sanitation about some faulty plumbing at military headquarters of the eighteenth district, where he was staying.

Most people counted themselves lucky if they had discovered a bed. Nearly a million people converged on Bordeaux: Belgians, Normans, Parisians, and the tattered remains of the French army. "*Tout Paris*, literally, was in Bordeaux," wrote Maurice Sachs, who had found employment with the French National Radio. "On the café terraces people spent their time shaking hands with one another. The anguish of the exodus gave way to the pleasure of surprise meetings. But I had found no place to stay and, since night broadcasts had resumed, I had to sleep by day." Every available hotel room was taken; hotel managers did a boom business letting armchairs in the lobbies. If nearly a million people remained in Bordeaux, fully twice that many spilled into villages throughout the Landes and occupied every resort along the coast between Arcachon and Saint-Sebastien.

On June 14 Weygand left general headquarters in Briare and arrived twelve hours later at the Bordeaux-Bastide railway station. Ten days later Reynaud offered his resignation. Pétain, his successor, broadcast an appeal to end all hostilities against an enemy "superior in number and in arms." The Phony War had now ended, and the civil war began.

"One imagines," wrote Sachs, "that the grave hours of a nation are lived by the public in an atmosphere of exceptional gravity. That is far from being the case. Everyone at every moment tends toward his norm: of comfort, of debauchery, of pleasure, or of quietude. Events outside us, however weighty they may be, penetrate us with the utmost difficulty." Perhaps it would have been inhuman to expect otherwise. In a world which had swung out of orbit, habits and addictions vouchsafed people a measure of sanity. Accordingly, Cocteau busied himself on the eve of his departure from Paris collecting jam pots in which to store several pounds of refined opium, without which a lengthy sojourn in the south of France would have been unthinkable. Actually, he had had no intention of leaving the Hôtel Beaujolais, but an acquaintance named Raoul Breton (the publisher of Trenet's songs), lured him away by describing the enchantments of his country estate near Perpignan. The trip south was more in the nature of a holiday from Cocteau's theatrical ventures than a flight from the marauder.

During the automobile ride Raoul Breton had ample time to explain that he did not own an estate. He did, however, have wealthy friends, and one, Doctor Nicolo, a bourgeois physician whose wife was heiress to a Dijon mustard fortune, admitted the refugees. Elated that the displacements of war should have brought him no less a celebrity than Cocteau, Nicolo extended his generosity to various young men who, once they learned of Cocteau's whereabouts, began to materialize by dribs and drabs. Marais donned what civilian garments he had on hand (the turquoise trousers he had worn in *Les Parents Terribles*, a stiff white shirt, and an opossum waistcoat Coco Chanel had sent to the Front), bade his adieux to the gypsy woman who would name him the father of her son nine months later, and hitched his way to Perpignan via Toulouse and Carcassonne. Roger Stéphane followed on his heels. Presently the place was alive with tattered druids whom Cocteau enrolled in costume parties beneath the complaisant nose of their host. It was a summer very like the previous one, and even less troubled, for Cocteau could take satisfaction in knowing that in Paris nobody had remained to connive behind his back. Like three million others, he was bound to wait until the storm subsided, for there was no gasoline available and such was the disrepair of France's railway system that those who risked a return north found it more excruciating than their recent exodus south.

Cocteau had long since completed another play, *La Machine à Écrire*, which certainly represents the nadir of his career as a dramatic author. He was now hard at work writing *Renaud et Armide* and the poems which comprise *Allegories*. Though not without formal beauty, his literary productions now seemed to lack everything else. Cocteau could turn verses more adeptly than any contemporary except Aragon. He had achieved the status of a great *précieux* very much in the tradition of seventeenth-century poets such as Théophile de Viau and Saint-Amant, but whatever his claims to the sacerdotal, to poetry as religious incantation, he no longer had energy enough to simulate it. From 1940 on, Cocteau would husband his life reiterating himself. The films he made of *Les Enfants Terribles*, of *Les Parents Terribles*, and of *Orphée* amount to a postponement of death, to a coda forestalling what he most feared: silence.

Before the summer of 1940 ended, Cocteau swung round the Mediterranean coast to Aix-en-Provence and Mas-la-Fourques where a group of friends, including the Aurics, had congregated at Jean Hugo's house. There they smoked their last reserves of opium. Cocteau spent some weeks in 1940 at the Clinique Lyautey, but the German Occupation would prove far more effective than any of his voluntary cures.

When Maurice Sachs returned to Paris in midsummer, he found a necropolis adorned with maleficent symbols, a city intact but depopulated:

> It was four in the afternoon. Sandbags formed zigzag obstacles at the gates of the capital, and down the main avenues nothing moved except an occasional stray dog pissing or a concierge scurrying along. We were anxious to make a tour of Paris. We saw a few people in the Latin Quarter, some girls sitting beside German officers on the terrace of the Capoulade, but on Rue de Rivoli, and Place de la Concorde, there was no one in view except German soldiers. What seemed most surprising at first glance were the huge red flags bearing swastikas which hung in the center of the city. It was a dead city, a rather beautiful spectacle in its way: the spectacle of a destroyed civilization. Nothing pathetic: just a dead city.

When Parisians returned in September and October, they had difficulty recognizing their new life, such was its drastically simplified appearance. A dream landscape prevailed. It was as if a whole community had been processed in some time machine rejuvenating it by fifty years. Its limits unaltered, the city had nonetheless stretched and contracted; for lack of automobiles, previously unseen vistas became visible, yet a combination of new factors—fear, uncertainty, the primacy of bargaining and bartering and improvising—converted the inhabitants into a tight, whispering, paranoid fraternity. Lights had gone dim, and silence, broken by the clickety-clack of wooden heels and by air-raid sirens, became a conspicuous element. All manner of antique and makeshift vehicles made their appearance. A few dozen hackney coaches dating to the *belle époque* plied the boulevards again. Great ladies, academicians, and even Cocteau made their rounds by bicycle. Children took to skates, and *clochards* were seen propelling themselves along on weird tinker-toy constructions.

In 1940 fashion called for hats bedecked with imitation flowers and birds; as life grew drabber, the Parisienne, taking infinite pains to defy *le boche*, wore millinery increasingly ornate. Pauperdom gave rise to Byzantine fantasies. A former queen of the sapphic set, Rachel Dorange, acquired an old coach which she drove through Paris wearing cowhide boots and a Havana homburg; at red lights she would ostentatiously light a long cigar. France, reduced as a nation to childhood, maneuvered now bravely, now pusillanimously within the humiliating circumstances imposed by the Nazis and, for the time being, dropped out of history.

In a way, the Occupation came as a relief to Cocteau, taking the edge off his hunger for celebrity. It offered him the same considerable advantages that sickness did. What alternative had he to staying at home? There was little to miss anyway, for the whole of Paris lay similarly bedridden. In the fall of 1940 he and Marais took up residence in a tiny flat Cocteau had recently bought at 36 Rue de Montpensier in the west wing of that stately quadrangle called the Palais-Royal. From his windows just above the inner arcade he could view gardens and galleries which had provided the stage for three hundred years of political connivance, fashion, gambling, philately, and whoredom. Here Mazarin had had secret assignations with Anne of Austria and Monsieur, Louis XIV's brother, had entertained young men. Under the arcades, Mme. de Montansier had in the eighteenth century operated the most fashionable brothel in Paris. At number 178, Charlotte Corday bought the knife that killed Marat. The Véfour, which became one of Cocteau's haunts, had been the favorite café of émigré nobles when they returned from exile after the Revolution. Above all, the Comédie-Française lay just down the street beyond the Galerie d'Orléans. If Cocteau had finally abandoned the Madeleine, he did so in favor of his spiritual home. Crimson velvet, like a swatch cut from the Comédie's curtain, covered the walls of his last *pied-à-terre* in Paris. He surrounded himself with a set of Delacroix's engravings for *Faust* which had once, reputedly, hung in Baudelaire's room. Colette lived next door, and mornings Bébé Bérard offered comic relief walking his Maltese pup through the gardens and provocatively crooking a hairy leg beneath Cocteau's window in the manner of eighteenth-century *Merveilleuses*.

Cocteau's problems with Vichy-France began in April, 1941. The catastrophic shake-up of French society had submerged the cream and brought to the surface sour scum in the shape of opportunists anxious to avenge themselves for years of obscurity. If a few gifted writers such as Drieu la Rochelle—then director of the *Nouvelle Revue Française*—or Céline supported the Vichy regime out of loathing for humankind in general, the hacks predicated their politics on some more specific vendetta. Thus, Cocteau found himself hated by Alain Laubreaux, a theatre critic who had earned dubious celebrity some years before in a trial in which he had been condemned for plagiarism (his father, a prison warden, had published under Alain Laubreaux's name a manuscript that a convict had been obliged to surrender). Before *La Machine à Écrire* opened at the Théâtre Hébertot, Laubreaux let it be known that he would scuttle the play in *Je suis partout*, a weekly which went collaborationist during the Occupation. Marais, in turn, promised to "smash his face in."

Eventually they both made good their threats. The day after the première German authorities ordered a halt to all future performances, though Hébertot had previously submitted the text to German censors and received their authorization. Hébertot therefore made loud representations, and two days later the play was permitted to resume. *Je suis partout* carried a scurrilous article in which Laubreaux, not content to tear apart the play and its cast, denounced —in true Vichyite style—Cocteau's sexual mores. Marais did not have to trouble seeking him out. An "impromptu" encounter was arranged by Hébertot, whose position in this quarrel defies understanding.

One stormy evening Marais and Cocteau were dining, as they often did, on black-market steak in a restaurant on the Boulevard des Batignolles when Marais received word that Hébertot wished to see him in a room on the second floor. A blackout having just been declared, Marais groped his way upstairs. In the room, no one spoke at first, and Marais could not identify the few people whose shapes he distinguished. A flash of lightning finally lit up Hébertot's bald head. Another person was introduced as Alain Laubreaux. Marais lost no time ascertaining that it was indeed Laubreaux, then spat in his face and struck him. The restaurateur, already twice imprisoned for serving black-market meat, implored them to settle their quarrel outside. Cocteau, fearful of violent gestures, did his utmost to dissuade Marais from fighting. As Marais prepared to step outside with Laubreaux, Cocteau asked him to stay, saying again and again, "Go home! You'll be shot! The Gestapo!"

But Marais would not be deterred. He disarmed Laubreaux of his walking stick and, with the rain coming down in torrents, administered such hearty blows that echoes of them resounded through Paris overnight, magnifying Marais's stature tenfold. "When Laubreaux grossly insulted Cocteau . . ." wrote Simone de Beauvoir in her diary, "Jean Marais went around and beat him up, which gave us great satisfaction." But, as Cocteau feared, Marais's increased stature made them both more visible to German authorities. They were obliged to hide for a while, and La Machine à Écrire closed on a more glorious note than it perhaps deserved.

This was not their last joust with Laubreaux. Being homosexual made them, ipso facto, enemies of the state, whose motto now read, "Work, Family, Nation." That triumvirate of virtues was promoted by flags, coins, bank notes, portraits of Pétain, parades, dedications, and endless apostrophes on national radio. French fascist youth, eager to make up for military defeat by bugling their virility at every opportunity, wore uniforms hardly distinguishable from the Nazis', developed their biceps at "work centers" in the forest, swaggered about under the ensign of Jacques Doriot's PPF (Parti Populaire Français), and all in all proved themselves to be such able henchmen that the Germans, during the first year of Occupation at least, could afford exquisite manners. "The family, always of signal anthropological importance in France, was spread to cover the whole population (excepting Jews, Communists, Gaullists, and

Freemasons) and Pétain was the Daddy of Them All. Father knew best, and his watchwords were Order, Obedience, Service, Faith." In the light of virtues sanctified by the fascist-bourgeois state, such a play as *Les Parents Terribles*, which hitherto had seemed merely offensive, was now considered seditious. When it had a revival in December, 1941, at the Gymnase, Laubreaux, still anxious to undo Cocteau, had no difficulty inciting young militiamen to make a shambles of the theatre.

These sanguinary youths made it their business to taunt Cocteau and Marais in public. A friend of Cocteau's, Lise Deharme, recalls one such incident. It took place in a little restaurant on the Rue des Pyramides where she was having dinner with Picasso and Dora Maar. Marais and his mother sat at another table. Presently a group of Doriotistes (PPF headquarters was located nearby) walked in. Catching sight of Marais, they began to jeer "fairy," suggesting that he no doubt slept with his mother. They were hoping for a pretext to disfigure him, but Lise Deharme prevailed upon Marais not to fight.

As for Cocteau, only once did he suffer physical harm, during a parade on the Champs-Élysées. A group of French youths attired in German uniforms came trooping down the avenue, while their flying phalanx ordered spectators to raise their arms in salute. When Cocteau, experiencing a fit of resistance, would not comply, they knocked him down, trampled him, and bloodied one eye. At the doctor's, he made light of his injury, calling it a *"compère-Doriot"* (a pun on *compère-loriot*, which means sty). That wound would stand him in good stead after the war, when the Incorruptibles set up an inquisition of their own.

The Germans at first behaved more correctly than their French surrogates. Indeed, their correctitude was part of Hitler's campaign to humiliate the defeated nation by other means than violence. The French had taken flight, "betrayed" by their leaders, "forsaken" by their allies, divided among themselves. Now the Germans would help them back to their feet. They provided gasoline to refugees returning by automobile. They hurriedly repaired the railroads. They offered seats to ladies on the Métro. They threw bars of chocolate from their trucks. Posters showing a Wehrmacht trooper feeding a hungry French child appeared all over France. Playing God, they compassionately offered the fallen race a malefactor—England—to alleviate it of its guilty burden. "I haven't seen the symptoms of real hatred in anyone yet," noted Simone de Beauvoir in her diary on July 1, 1940, "only a wave of panicky fear among the country villagers." That fear subsided into awe, and often servility, as the population of genteel, Aryan demiurges became more numerous. To promote the mystique of her ethnic superiority, Germany stationed her best-looking officers in Paris.

On December 28, 1940, the first of many *Avis*—notices printed in red ink—brought home the true nature of the enemy:

> Jacques Bonsergent, engineer, of Paris, having been condemned to death by a German Military Tribunal for an act of violence against a member of the German Armed Forces, was executed by shooting this morning.

By then the winter—one of the coldest in memory—had blighted what little sympathy Frenchmen may have felt for the "correct" interloper. Paris was allotted almost no fuel, with the result that people spent their days huddled by the stove, numb with cold, and at night crept between icy sheets wearing every available sweater. Paupers found asylum in the Métro or in libraries. This pain, suffered every winter of the war, was compounded by the lack of food. People stood on queues for hours to get their ration of meat and bread, knowing that the supply nearly always ran out before those at the tail end reached the counter. By 1943 the Parisian was entitled to about a pound and a quarter of meat per month and a few kilos of coarse barley bread. Families who lost their ration tickets suddenly saw the specter of starvation. "Now we are allowed one meat ticket a week," noted Lise Deharme. "The leaves on the chestnut trees look appetizing." Food became the obsessive subject of conversation. Parisians who had country cousins were well off at first (some three hundred thousand packages of food inundated the city every week), but the Germans, afraid that provisions intended for their army were being diverted into civilian stomachs, halted the flow. The black market therefore prospered, and city dwellers were obliged, at great risk and often with meager success, to forage clandestinely. Maurice Sachs, the confidence man *par excellence*, recalled one such expedition:

> The next day, furnished with two empty valises, Charles and I departed for Vendôme. We get off at the station before ours, discreetly lower our baggage from the train, thread our way beneath the nose of inspectors, race down pitch-black streets until we reach a bar where we park our valises. Then dinner at a shabby tavern. At nine we leave, we cross street after street, alleys and large thoroughfares. We reach a dead-end street. Charles knocks on the door as instructed; it opens. We find ourselves in the back room of a butcher who fills our valises and gets his fee, seventy francs [about four dollars] a kilo. We leave on tiptoe, stooping with the weight of our merchandise. We reach a private house where we are welcomed. A dismal country room with a crucifix, viny wallpaper, and old boxwood. "Let's open the valises," says Charles, "to air the meat"—and in so doing we witness the most appalling spectacle, like a cadaver freshly hacked up, Madame Bessarabe's trunk; my heart sank. . . . At four in the morning, we had to pick up and leave, and nothing had ever seemed quite so heavy as those thirty kilos of fresh meat. It remained to get them through the Gare d'Austerlitz, which is why I hired a porter . . . "You're in for a good tip if you don't go through customs," I whispered. "I'm carrying illegal merchandise."

Sachs was by no means exceptional. Multitudes spirited food out of the countryside, at prices which saw the French peasantry amass fortunes. Not infrequently the peasant arranged to fence his produce in Paris through a city cousin: watchmakers were selling sausage and dressmakers butter. One trafficker stuffed thirty-eight kilos of sugar and forty loaves of spice bread into his grand piano on Avenue de Clichy. The police dismantled a bed which they found to contain six large hams, eleven litres of gin, and another seven of *eau-de-vie*. In an empty mausoleum at the cemetery of Saint-Germain-en-Laye they discovered a vertiable *charcuterie*.

Nevertheless, Céline's contention that "the war of '39 was a windfall for thirty million French; there were ten million people to pity, no more" distorted a truth. Most city dwellers, unable to afford black-market goods or ethically averse to buying them, starved on noodles, thin gruel, and rutabagas. They spent, on the average, three-fourths of their income on inedible food. It was an era of the ersatz: soap made of lichen or mashed chestnuts, mayonnaise lacking eggs, coffee distilled from grains of eglantine, cigarettes containing the pulverized meat of Jerusalem artichokes, of wormwood, or of linden leaves in lieu of tobacco. It must be said that for every Parisian who played the game, ten refused. Germans, finding all eyes averted in the street, called Paris "the faceless city."

If these were chilly years for Cocteau, they were not unbearably lean ones. He and Marais had enough money to afford black-market food, but even so, Cocteau, like some Indian water diviner, always found at his fingertips, in whichever direction he extended his hand, a cornucopia. "Had dinner with Cocteau at the Cazanaves, who live in a factory," wrote Lise Deharme. "On arriving at the Chevaleret Métro station we find before us outworks, excavations, etc. . . . Suddenly we hear a few loud blasts from afar. Cocteau, with an unforgettable gesture, pointed toward the outworks in the direction of the detonation and said, sorrowfully, 'Come, let's return, our dinner has just been ruined.' . . . We had marvelous couscous, soft and pulpy like a sponge."

As with Paul Valéry, wealthy ladies found a *raison d'être* in the ministering to Cocteau's appetites. They gave him the fruits of the earth in exchange for some reflected light of his sun. Mme. Boudot-Lamotte and Marguerite Daney, to name just two women constantly hovering about him during the war, saw to it that Cocteau did not go hungry, Mme. Daney filling his stomach with milk and cheese she imported at will from her family's farms. Suddenly Cocteau struck up a friendship with Monsieur Vaudable, director of Maxim's, one of six restaurants (including the Tour d'Argent, Lapérouse, and Drouant) patronized by the German High Command and thus legally permitted to serve meat. The larder remained well-stocked at Marie-Louise Bousquet's flat, where on Thursdays people (including "nice" Germans such as Ernst Jünger) congregated as before the war. Cocteau cultivated the *nouveaux riches,* for with money even a gourmet could appease his appetite at little restaurants maintaining their stars against all odds. But if eating reasonably well was unpatriotic, then Picasso—who generally ate his fill at a place called Le Catalan on Rue des Grands Augustins—and Robert Desnos, who was killed by the Nazis in 1944, would have had to stand accused of unpatriotism.

Actually, Cocteau, whose chief interest in eating was to gulp it down indiscriminately, the quicker to resume his monologue, usually dined on macaroni in a bistro on the Rue de Montpensier, or in another called Les Capucines opposite the Molière fountain, where a little orchestra played the Marseillaise on the sly (for which infraction the Nazis deported its proprietor). Seemingly more concerned with his own career than with the scandal at large, Cocteau, like most people, accommodated himself to the new state. "I am absolutely astonished to see how little others are astonished at the most astonishing things," noted Lise Deharme in her journal, on July 19, 1942. "When one thinks that at this moment, at every moment, Jews are being tortured by maniacs. People get indignant, comment on it, but they aren't astonished. . . . This great wind of madness doesn't seem to ruffle anybody."

Cocteau's only fault was in having remained so disappointingly true to his nature. Not that he collaborated with the enemy. In that case it would have been improvident of him to correspond with a Jewish prisoner of war (Roger Stéphane), to attend the funeral of a Jewish painter (Soutine), and a wake in honor of a Jewish poet (Max Jacob). But, incapable as he was—for ambiguous reasons—of holding a grudge, he did not sufficiently behold the enemy as an enemy even at this time, when it was unprincipled to make peacetime distinctions between the "good" and the "bad" Germans, and arrantly naïve to believe that one could remain, as before, apolitical. That Cocteau failed to sense what categorical imperatives of shame and dignity the German Occupation called into play comes clear in Simone de Beauvoir's account of her first meeting with him, in the company of Sartre and Genet, at a bar on Rue Jacob:

> Cocteau looked just like the pictures of him, and his torrential flow of conversation made me dizzy. Like Picasso he dominated the conversation, but in his case words were his chosen medium, and he used them with acrobatic dexterity. Fascinated, I followed the movements of his lips and hands. Once or twice I thought he was going to trip

up; then—hoopla!—he recovered, the knot was neatly tied, and he would be off again, tracing a new series of complex and hypnotic arabesques in mid-air. He expressed his admiration of *No Exit* in several most gracefully turned compliments, and then began to recall his own early days in the theatre, and especially the production of *Orpheus*. It was at once apparent that he was absolutely absorbed in himself, but this narcissistic streak neither constricted his vision nor in any way cut him off from contact with other people: the interest he had shown in Sartre and the way he talked about Genet both offered ample proof of this. When the bar closed we walked down the Rue Bonaparte till we reached the quais. We were standing on a bridge, watching the Seine rippling beneath us like black watered silk, when the alert sounded. Pencil-thin searchlight beams swept the sky, and flares exploded. By now we had become used to these noisy apocalyptic displays, but tonight's seemed an especially fine one; and what good luck to find ourselves stranded near this deserted river, alone with Cocteau! When the antiaircraft fire died away, all was silent except for our footsteps—and the sound of his voice. He was saying that the Poet should hold aloof from his age, and remain indifferent to the follies of war and politics. "They just get in our way," he went on, "—the Germans, the Americans, the whole lot of them—just get in our way."

His view of Hitler was no doubt substantially the same as Marie-Louise Bousquet's. To a German officer present at her salon she ingenuously said, "Come now, admit that your Führer is a pain in the neck," only to see her *confidant* turn red, pick up his cap, and leave. The lights by which Cocteau and his circle judged things did not help them perceive the difference between impropriety and inhumanity, between an *emmerdeur* and a monster. It is as if the monstrous pertained to obscure people, to peasants and minor functionaires whose crimes comprise the *faits divers* page in daily tabloids. Boggled by appearances—by the Nazi uniform and display of power—Cocteau failed to recognize peasants and minor functionaries in disguise. Hitler's sheer celebrity mitigated his crime. Folly is the prerogative of a lord, and a lord is he who lords.

A combination of egoism and servility made many artists and writers vulnerable to the overtures of Goebbels' *Propagandastaffel*. They were given de luxe tours through Germany, unaware of being mocked like captive clowns, or aware of it too late. Thus the voyage made by Despiau, Derain, Vlaminck, Maillol, Van Dongen, Dunoyer de Segonzac, Othon Friesz, and Belmondo. Their impresario was the German sculptor Arno Brecker, an exponent of fascist monumentalism, who had frequented Montparnasse cafés and studied with Maillol before 1939. "It was that prick Arno Brecker who put us up to it," explained Vlaminck. "We all knew him from before the war; he had been Despiau's buddy. When he proposed that we visit Germany, to see what artists had been doing since Hitler, we listened gullibly; it was his idea and he had laid it, at first unavailingly, before Hitler, with whom he was on close terms since his wife used to read the Führer's fortune. Every time he brought up the subject, Hitler would say, 'Now is not the moment, later!' Finally he capitulated: 'To hell with you and your project, but since it means so much, see Goebbels and organize it.'" In Berlin, Derain and Vlaminck, totally indifferent to German art since Hitler, wanted to tour the city's bordellos, while Despiau seized every opportunity to fill his pockets with cigarettes. Back in Paris, the full force of their delinquency was brought home to them.

Cocteau's blunders were at once more venial and more foolish. If he never traveled abroad, he did attend the Franco-German Institute in Rue de Grenelle where Otto Abetz, the German ambassador to Paris, held receptions for visiting German dignitaries. If he was not the victim of Arno Brecker's persuasiveness, he was, still worse, an admirer of his sculpture. The cover of one issue of *Signal*, a Nazi organ published in French, showed Cocteau with his arm slung amicably round Brecker's shoulder. Somewhat later Cocteau made Brecker the subject of a dithyrambic article in which he looked forward to the day when "Brecker's statues would invade the Place de la Concorde." Unable to resist appearing on covers, no matter which ones, Cocteau was not a collaborator but a publicity-monger. In his eyes, Germany represented the latest fashion.

Ernst Jünger was plainly wrong when he observed, speaking of the Jouhandeaus, that "apart from venal subjects, Germanophilia declares itself especially in that segment of the population which still possesses some elemental force. It is an underground current which in Germany takes the form of Russophilia. The forces of order stand in its way: they [the forces of order] tend toward the Occident." Many homosexuals, more notably Jouhandeau and Montherlant than Cocteau, found themselves strongly attracted to the Nazis; this attraction, however, derived not from any "elemental force" but, on the contrary, from a feminine lack of it. Germany stood for power, and power for virility. In the lower regions of his self, Cocteau undoubtedly made some obscure equation between the monumental, the famous, and the masculine. He may not have written odes, like Montherlant, to a sinewy female runner, but he was moved by the spectacle of Brecker's muscle-bound statuary.

Above all, however, he wanted to be loved by the powers that be, in whatever realm they ruled. His attending functions sponsored by the Germans did not prevent him from courting Éluard, Picasso, Sartre (whose star was already in the ascendant), and whatever assailant past, present, or prospective he judged redoubtable enough to attempt seducing. "Never has our freedom been greater than under the German Occupation," wrote Sartre; ". . . since the Nazi poison filtered into our minds, every just thought was a victory; since the omnipotent police tried to force us into silence, every word became as precious as a declaration of principle; since we were at bay, our very gestures had the weight of vows." That freedom Cocteau did not know, under the Occupation, or ever. He was so much his own prisoner that everyone, the Germans and the French alike, seemed a warder, or a judge. "There is no longer a public, there are only judges," he wrote of the artist's predicament after the war; but had he not always viewed the public thus?

If Cocteau's self-involvement made him a political simpleton, it gave him on occasion the aplomb of simpletons. One incident graphically explains his wartime deportment. It occurred during the Battle of Paris, some few days before the city's liberation. The American army had advanced to within a dozen kilometers. German soldiers and their chief collaborators among the French had begun to flee eastward. The French fascist militia, determined to make a last stand, set up emplacements on roofs throughout Paris. A rain of crossfire chipped building façades and smashed windows. The streets were deserted but for guerrilla fighters darting in and out of doorways. Papers jettisoned from an upper story of PPF headquarters eddied up and down the Avenue de l'Opéra. Heedlessly, Cocteau and Marais left the Palais-Royal to keep a dinner appointment at José María Sert's establishment near the Place de la Concorde. On Rue Casanova, which bathed in portentous quiet, another pedestrian loomed ahead. As he came near a shot rang out from the roofs, and he fell, jerked himself upright, then collapsed, blood welling from a hole in his back. Cocteau and Marais took cover in a doorway, waited till their fear subsided, then continued to the Rue de Rivoli. At Sert's they were received by a liveried major-domo and dined at a giant tortoise shell which a South American church had given Sert in payment for one of his ghastly frescoes.

Cocteau's conversation that evening was brilliant.

Throughout his career Cocteau the writer took his cues from Cocteau the lover. He draped himself by turns on Radiguet, Desbordes, and Marais, producing treatises, novels, and plays suggested in large part by *their* imperatives. In them he discovered a means of regeneration, a kind of electrical charge which permitted him to lunge forward when his cells seemed dry. In 1937 he wrote *Les Parents Terribles* with Marais in mind, hoping to launch him on a boulevard career. In 1941 he wrote *Renaud et Armide* after the closing of *La Machine à Écrire* had convinced him that he and Marais would find no safe harbor outside state-subsidized theatres. This "verse tragedy," an antiquarian *tour de force* tailor-made for the Comédie, argued strongly in favor of Marais's election to that august body, whose director was now Jean-Louis Vaudoyer, a friend of Cocteau's from the time of Diaghilev's "heroic" years.[1]

Marais's brief tenure at the Comédie-Française proved to be a series of imbroglios. Having learned, the night before his audition, that a plot was afoot to reject him, he walked on stage wearing, in broad defiance of good taste, a parti-colored costume quickly sewn together for the occasion. Much to his surprise, the committee, swayed by Marie Bell, who had urged Marais to present himself in the first place, elected him. A week later, however, the influential

1. In 1911 Vaudoyer wrote the scenario of *The Spectre of the Rose*.

theatre magazine *Comœdia* described Marais as an interloper whose election had been rigged. Marais, angered by what he knew to be an inversion of the truth, wrote an open letter setting matters straight. Vaudoyer upbraided him for his rejoinder. Moreover, his colleagues, scornful of Marais (whose voice was so oddly without timbre as to be inaudible beyond the first rows), yet jealous of his celebrity, gave him a hazing which consisted of speaking their lines so rapidly that Marais was apt to forget his own. Unable to redress wrongs never formulated to his face, he found himself slyly persecuted as the self-infatuated upstart that Cocteau's eulogies led people to believe he must be. When, after very few weeks with the Comédie, Marais requested a leave of absence to fulfill contractual obligations, Vaudoyer advised him to resign, promising that he would automatically be accepted on reapplying. He was not.

Thus, *Renaud et Armide*, when at last it was produced in April, 1943, did not include the actor for whom it had been written. Cocteau later made amends by maneuvering him into the lead role of a film whose screenplay he had written, *The Eternal Return*. This anemic version of the Tristan and Isolde legend enjoyed such success in a country starved for entertainment that young females, swooning at the entrance to 36 Rue de Montpensier, and in the gardens behind, blockaded Marais in the Palais-Royal.

Renaud et Armide figures prominently in Cocteau's never-never period which began with *Knights of the Round Table* and sustained itself through 1945, the year he produced his play *The Two-Headed Eagle* and a film, *Beauty and the Beast*. It tells in remarkably adept Alexandrines the story of Renaud, a king of France who had led an argosy to some remote land governed by the fairy queen, Oriane. There he falls in love with Armide, an enchantress whose ring, which had been Orpheus', gives her the option of becoming a mere woman. For love of Renaud she forfeits the ring and, knowing that she will die on being kissed by him, consents to the fatal embrace so as to set her beloved free. Renaud returns to the throne he was prepared to abdicate. These few events are adorned with games of hide-and-seek, with spells, with a bout of madness in which Renaud mumbles about his mother like Oedipus, with incantations in the style of the Sphinx's soliloquy. "I made it my duty," wrote Cocteau, "not to give this work a façade answering its internal mechanism, its legendary complication. Its theme is the solitude of beings who guess one another sight unseen, and who don't succeed in uniting themselves once they have seen one another."

But when the play has ended, one is left with the queasy sensation that everything remains to be said, that its theme is still floating, unsupported by the armature of words and objects which have collapsed in a heap of bric-a-brac. Still, fairy tales, in which the Image embodies the thing itself, suited Cocteau's vision perfectly. Love is love and its consummation will be a beautiful face. In both *Renaud et Armide* and *Beauty and the Beast* a mask is turned inside out (the invisible becomes visible) which requires several hours of commotion. Both works begin with one appearance and end with another, as if "spiritual" beauty, declaring itself in some gallant forfeiture (Armide surrenders the ring endowing her with immortality, and the Beast the keys to his wealth) were striving for an appropriate physique. Many of Cocteau's works are predicated on Épinal images—the Lover, the Soldier, the Poet—which he develops through glittering ceremonies and flashy incantations; once that Image has materialized, it can do no more than behold itself, recognize its two dimensions, and freeze. Like Braque, who saw the stage as a façade and the actors as silhouettes, Cocteau created tragedies lacking one dimension, tragedies about masks ineligible for life full-round, tragedies circumscribed by the stage because they represent what might be called the tragedy of theatre. His characters are puppets playing life, achieving a semblance more beautiful than life itself, collapsing when the strings slacken. As the queen says to her assassin in *The Two-Headed Eagle:* "One must kill quickly and outdoors. One must assassinate quickly and be stoned by the crowd. Otherwise the drama falters, and everything that falters is frightful."

Renaud et Armide, and perhaps *Beauty and the Beast* as well, would have gained if staged as Punch-and-Judy shows. But there is good reason to believe that Cocteau, imbued as he was with the sovereign value of appearances, did not recognize his own values. The tragedy of theatre was his natural viewpoint for, wanting to be "another," he had condemned himself to pose; resenting his birth, he had created a literature of camouflage. "I have never had a beautiful face," he laments in *The Difficulty of Being* as if this were tantamount to the Fall.

Though imperfectly aware of himself, Cocteau was perfectly capable of recognizing in the work of Jean Genet what depths a fraternal imagination could sound. In 1942 a young friend of Genet's named Paul Quentin showed Cocteau a Genet poem which straightaway captured his interest. He asked to see more and was rewarded with the manuscript of *Our Lady of the Flowers*, which he spent the whole night reading. Apparently it did not please him, and he returned it to Quentin with a bouquet of faint compliments, but some residual feeling prompted him to want a second reading. It is impossible to know what door had meanwhile unlatched in Cocteau's brain, but he was soon pronouncing Genet the greatest writer of his age and repeating the Wildean repartees Genet produced at his trial.

"Cocteau spoke about a trial he had witnessed," noted Jünger on July 10, 1943. "A young man stood accused of having stolen books, among them a rare edition of Verlaine's poetry. The judge asked: 'Did you know the price of this book?' 'I didn't know the price,' he rejoined, 'but I did know its value.' Among these books one was by Cocteau. Another question: 'What would you say if you were robbed of one of your own books?' 'I should be very proud.'" His responses were bold indeed considering that a verdict of guilty for this his tenth offense would have meant life imprisonment in French Guiana. Cocteau sprang to his defense, writing a letter to the police court in the nineteenth *arrondissement*, a letter which declared that it would be criminal to deprive France of another Rimbaud. Cocteau's campaign was instrumental in bringing about Genet's acquittal.

There ensued between these wildly divergent personalities a brief affair. Cocteau found himself attracted, as in so many other cases, to the savage waif that Genet so resolutely was, while Genet had a greater aptitude for fidelity, a livelier interest in the merely picturesque, and less scorn of salon society than he affected. "In conversation as in his writing," wrote Simone de Beauvoir, "he was deliberately offhand, and asserted that he would never hesitate to rob or betray a friend; yet I never heard him speak ill of anyone, and he would not permit attacks on Cocteau in his presence." Their friendship lasted longer than their affair. Some years later, Genet, when asked by the magazine *Empreintes* to contribute an appreciation of Cocteau, wrote (in part) the following:

> . . . he knows what darkness, what undergrounds, what wilderness and near insanity Greece signifies. From *Opéra* to *Renaud et Armide*, these broken temples and columns we guess to be the visible form of a sorrow and despair which chose not to express themselves but to dissimulate themselves beneath a graceful appearance which they enrich. . . . That is the poet's tragedy. A thick layer of human humus, almost fetid, exhales puffs of heat which sometimes make us blush with shame. A sentence, a verse, the pure and almost innocent stroke of a drawing pen emits smoke between the interstices of words, at their intersection point: ill-smelling and heavy air which reveals some intense, underground life. Thus, the work of Jean Cocteau had the appearance of a light, aerial civilization suspended in the heart of ours. The poet's very person adds to it, thin, gnarled and silvery like olive trees.

He bestowed upon Cocteau the manuscript of *Our Lady of the Flowers*. And later he stole it back.

After nearly all of Paris had been liberated the Germans remained holed up in buildings round the Place de la Concorde and the Madeleine. In the early afternoon of August 21, 1944, three columns of Allied tank-supported infantry advanced westward from the Châtelet. The center column was to attack German headquarters at the Hôtel Meurice, while the other two concentrated on the Tuileries gardens and adjacent hotels still occupied by the enemy. After an hour of fighting the right and left columns converged at the Concorde, where they assaulted a group of German tanks. Having disabled the tanks, they confronted the Hôtel Crillon and the Naval Ministry. By mid-afternoon, Place de la Concorde appeared safe for de Gaulle's triumphant march down the Champs-Élysées. Tens of thousands, waving the tricolor, sobbing and screaming, massed along the imperial road. Cocteau, his secre-

tary Paul Morihien, and Marais watched the parade from a room on
the top floor of the Crillon, where a few hours earlier the war had
still raged. As de Gaulle's party approached, some fascist militiamen
hiding on the Crillon's roof opened fire. Their fire was immediately
answered by cannon below. Plaster came falling down, and one bullet, according to Marais, knocked Cocteau's cigarette from his
mouth. This was a foretaste of the Liberation.

The envy machine built into the heart of French society now
began whirring in reverse. "Purification" committees, largely devoted to the pet peeves of its members, were established. Céline
took refuge in Denmark, Drieu la Rochelle blew his brains out in
prison, Brassillach was executed. But many artists, writers, and
actors were brought before these *ad hoc* tribunals, humiliated, and
given severe penalties not because they had collaborated but because, for quite irrelevant reasons, their enemies wanted to draw
blood. Marais, whose periodic quarrels with the PPF sufficed to
give him an odor of purity, was told by the Union des Artistes to
arrest René Rocher, Cocteau's childhood friend, who had compromised himself badly; Marais refused on the grounds that his well-
known antipathy for Rocher, dating to before the war, would give
people the impression that he was merely slaking his thirst for vengeance. The Union then arrantly proposed that he blackmail several actors who had performed before the Nazis. Again he refused
and, to avoid further embarrassment, enlisted in the Leclerc division
fighting on the Rhine.

Meanwhile there was some talk of interrogating Cocteau, who
had enemies to spare, but his influential friends prevailed, one in
particular. When Louis Aragon returned from the Midi, where he
had played a key role organizing the Resistance, the first question
he asked of his close friend Lise Deharme was: "Who deserves
most to be whitewashed?" She named Cocteau.

Under the circumstances, his own behavior fell short of dignity.
He was busy manufacturing credos after the fact in order to dispel
the odor which now attached to him. ". . . when I got back to the
embassy," wrote Harold Nicolson in 1945, "there was Jean Cocteau waiting for me, looking like an aged cockatoo. He came up to
my room while I washed. He described how he had felt that he

owed it to his art not to join Aragon and others in open resistance. He explained how the *milices* had beaten him up and nearly knocked out his eye. Somehow it was not very dignified or encouraging."

Others were not so fortunate, especially if they happened to live in the provinces, where the Liberation often gave rise to bloody Jacqueries which saw houses burned, the throats of Vichy prefects slashed, and women who had slept with Germans shaved bald and driven through the streets like livestock. In Lyon three years after the Battle of Paris seven erstwhile members of the FFI, unhappy that Sacha Guitry had gotten off lightly (a brief sojourn in the Fresnes penitentiary), kidnaped him from his hotel room, stripped him naked, and made him stand all night long in a public square. By 1947 some thirty or forty thousand had been executed summarily, perhaps three times that number given prison sentences, and one hundred and twenty thousand functionaries and officers "purified."

During the confused interregnum which followed Paris' liberation, food and fuel were in shorter supply than ever. When the English writer Ronald Duncan dropped by the Palais-Royal to discuss the possibility of adopting the play, *L'Aigle à Deux Têtes* (*The Two-Headed Eagle*) that Cocteau had written in the fall of 1944 during a vacation in Brittany, he was taken aback by what he saw:

When the door opened I looked up to see a very handsome young man standing framed in it. He looked like a Greek statue—and knew it.

"Jean's expecting you," he said languidly; then he called "Jean, Jean, quick, look what we've got."

I couldn't think whether he referred to me, or, if not, what his last remark meant. But before I could fathom this, Cocteau came running out into the hall. I was shocked: he looked emaciated and raddled. He seemed oddly pleased to see me, demonstrably affectionate.

"Let me introduce you to Jean Marais. Isn't he beautiful?"

I glanced at the Apollo now standing posed on a white sheepskin rug and had to agree, but couldn't think how to say so. Then I noticed that Marais and Cocteau were regarding me with nothing less than a predatory glint in the eyes. I followed their look, then realized they were both focussing intently and silently on a carton of

Chesterfields which I'd picked out of my case at the hotel and forgotten I was carrying.

"Here," I said, handing them to Cocteau, who took them as reverently as if I had presented him with a wreath of laurel. He gave a packet to Marais. . . .

. . . I studied Cocteau. My first impression was confirmed. He looked wizened and this effect was heightened by the spruce and youthful style of his dress. My own casual diagnosis was that he was either suffering from yellow fever or jaundice.

"I suppose this is the result of your diet during the occupation?"

"No," he answered with clinical detachment. "You're looking at the effects of opium."

The retributive carnage was diluted, however, by a great wave of joy, and the lack of almost everything amounted to a token fee for the luxury of freedom. Liberation papers appeared everywhere like fireflies, people were voluble even by French standards, letting fly words and kisses which had been stanched for years. What Diana Cooper, wife of the British ambassador, called the "Comus band"—Bérard, Cocteau, Louise de Vilmorin, Cecil Beaton, Denise Bourdet, and the Aurics—revealed in one another's society and drew close about the British embassy, where Duff Cooper was the tactful shuttlecock in a game of battledore being waged by Churchill and de Gaulle. Cocteau held open house at the Véfour, and when sometimes the electricity failed it proved an easy matter to improvise elegant solutions: "I was learning for the first time in my life a little of the joy of power," wrote Diana Cooper. "It was amusing, when all the lights went out at a Palais-Royal restaurant where Bébé Bérard and Jean Cocteau were entertaining us, to send the car round to the embassy for twenty candelabra and priceless Price candles."

The positions formerly held by Vichyites were being distributed like booty. Cocteau was offered (or so he claimed) Jean-Louis Vaudoyer's directorship at the Comédie-Française. This seems doubtful, given Cocteau's soiled reputation: another decade would pass before the Comus band—Cocteau and Auric at any rate—passed into officialdom. Meanwhile, its members were writing, designing, composing under the pressure of ideas bottled since 1939.

"For five years I have been knotted up, paralyzed by a hostile, hating, dangerous atmosphere," wrote Cocteau in 1945. "My gift for improvising in public seemed utterly lost. Little by little I am recovering a kind of ease." Words, as Sartre put it, gained portentous weight during the war, but Cocteau was sufficiently the ham actor to play for the gallery, and the gallery had been under wraps during the Occupation. A film which he first conceived of in the summer of 1944, *Beauty and the Beast,* based on Perrault's fairy tale, would put him in public view once again. He worked at it as if Redemption itself were his reward.

It required six months to shoot *Beauty and the Beast.* Cocteau was by now thoroughly acquainted with the techniques of filmmaking for, since *Blood of a Poet,* he had apprenticed himself in various capacities to directors such as Marcel L'Herbier, Serge de Poligny, and Marcel Carné. In 1943, the year he saw the filming of *Eternal Return* in Nice, Cocteau wrote some dialogue for de Poligny's *Baron Fantôme,* in which he also performed a small role. In the course of these random efforts, Cocteau learned enough to undertake a full-length film of his own. In August, 1945, after a brief vacation in Arcachon, he led his technicians and cast to Rochecorbon, a small manor in the Loire valley, where they shot the sequences involving Beauty within the Beast's castle.

"A thing long dreamed of, imagined, seen on an invisible screen must, as of this morning, become solid, sculpted in space and in time," wrote Cocteau in his diary the morning work commenced. The lack of proper equipment, power failures, uncertain weather, the pressure exerted by his financial backers, and the maladies which beset his cast like a deferred toll of the recent Occupation taxed Cocteau's short supply of patience and his considerable gift for improvisation. He soon endeared himself to the crew, who called him "My general" (for Cocteau showed none of the aloofness they were no doubt accustomed to find in directors). This was his creation, and no aspect of it seemed demeaning. He helped build his own props, he toted equipment, he spent so much time in the glare of arc lamps that he finally contracted a form of eczema which deprived him of sleep during much of the filming. When at cross purposes with his technicians, who were apt to indulge the camera and make arty shots for their own sake, Cocteau tried to *persuade* them of his preference for what he called the "documentary style." Even Bérard, who designed the costumes, reproached him for his "dead angles," by which he meant the deadpan approach to bizarre images, a tendency to relate the extraordinary in an ordinary way, at a clip which seems fearful of slowing down, of lingering lest the tale lose its credibility.

Reviewing the film, Cocteau became aware of this. "With distance, I become aware that the film's rhythm is that of narrative. I narrate. It is as if, hidden behind each frame, I were saying: then such and such a thing happened. The characters don't appear to live, but to live a narrated life. Perhaps this was the proper thing to do with a story." This was equally how he *wrote;* in his fiction the characters always seem deployed from the outside by their own fatality; they *are* as semblances. Through the medium of film, Cocteau could behold his style as style, above and beyond its content and his purposeful canons. One has the feeling that here, by indirection, he broached the heart of his own esthetics, then became distracted.

What comes clear in Cocteau's diary is the harried joy he derived from working, day in and day out, at close quarters with people who formed a kind of private club dedicated to his self-fulfillment. It is as if he were driving them to muster for the Last Judgment; indeed, his diary reads like a debate between body and soul, the former withering in proportion as the latter comes into its own. Not a day seemed to pass without some sore declaring itself behind Marais's ear or on Cocteau's chest. The cast, to believe Cocteau, hobbled to salvation on fractured limbs and lanced boils, scratching itself and wheezing. "I behold myself in the mirror," he wrote. "It's appalling. I don't suffer in the least, though. The physical no longer counts. The work and its beauty must supplant it. It would be criminal of me to inflict my suffering and ugliness on the film. The authentic mirror is the screen, and in it I see my dream acquire physical life. I'm indifferent to the rest. Furthermore, I have tracheitis. I cough and this cough increases the pain of my open lesions. . . . If I were well, perhaps the film wouldn't be. I'm paying. I'm paying cash on the line."

Even pain formed part of a mythology. One wastes away in the service of art, one grows ugly as one's creation grows beautiful. Throughout his life Cocteau wavered between two images of himself: that of the genius whose works bubble freely from some hidden, inexhaustible source, and that of a monk sacrificing his flesh and blood to art. But the intimacy of a film company on location may have appealed to him the more strongly in that he lacked, in solitude, a sacerdotal sense of vocation. Contending with a budget, building props, weighing the relative virtues of Agfa and Kodak, keeping one eye anxiously cocked to the sky and the other to his actors' thermometers, obsessing himself with the hundred cogs any one of which could have doomed his apparatus, gave Cocteau a measure of relief. The doubting priest found faith performing a mass. "On the way to Saint-Maurice," he wrote in his diary of the film, "I felt happy, impelled by some kind of sprightliness. Nothing could be more beautiful than writing a poem with beings, faces, hands, lights, objects which one places wherever one's fancy dictates." But perhaps Cocteau came closer to hitting the mark when he said of himself, a few years later, in a radio interview with André Fraigneau:

> I sometimes wonder if my perpetual malaise doesn't derive from some incredible indifference to the things of this world, if my works are not a struggle to cling to objects which preoccupy other people, if my celebrated goodness is not a minute by minute effort to overcome my lack of contact with others.

The cause of his malaise was equally his remedy for it. Sartre's dictum, that one cannot be without playing at being, found, in Cocteau, its best-advertised embodiment.

The one illness that resisted his remedies was advancing age. Everything demonstrated to him that he was no longer young. Mme. Georges Cocteau had died in 1942 at a nursing home in Auteuil, after a period of dotage during which she recalled with presbyopic clarity the details of her youth and addressed her sons as young children. Cocteau drew somewhat closer to Paul, whose Loire estate he visited at frequent intervals while filming the first part of *Beauty and the Beast*. If he failed to see his own age, plus only eight years, written on his brother's face, photographs provided irrefutable evidence. "First major reportage on our work in *Monde Illustré*," he noted in his diary. "My photograph on the cover. One sees an old, sad-looking gentleman who's staring into space. It's me. I'll have to get used to it."

But getting used to it was no easy matter for someone who still viewed himself as a romantic energumen, who still wore capes and suede-leather jackets and turned up sleeves showing bright pink silk underneath, who liked to think of himself as truant in the eyes of the Establishment and congratulated Paul Léautaud (when they met on the street one June day in 1944) for having refused a prize which the Academy tried to confer upon him. Yet, as Léautaud observed, "his face, as so often happens, has become more interesting with age, more expressive than when he was young." Cocteau's new look featured thinning, whitening hair (which later on his *coiffeur* would bush into curls). The gawky, haunted countenance of the 1930s had now ripened into a face at once mellow and Mephistophelean. Cocteau was coming to resemble, strikingly, the man to whom he found himself compared throughout his life, Voltaire, except for his lips, which were pursed like an earnest granny's and incapable of a true rictus.

In 1946 Cocteau convalesced from his cinematic effort, first in the Swiss Alps, then at Louise de Vilmorin's villa outside Paris where he wrote most of *La Difficulté d'Être*, a series of Montaigne-like divagations on friends and friendship, on pain, on writing, on conversation, on haunted houses, on beauty, which sweep to the heart of minor issues but falsify the major ones: a dubbed soul is laid bare. As one critic has suggested, *paraître* was for Cocteau a more crucial verb than *être*. Appearance preoccupied him to the last, and there may be more of Cocteau in the postscript to a letter he sent Gide in 1945 than in the whole of *La Difficulté d'Être*. Having persuaded himself in the body of the letter that the acerbic judgments in Gide's journal only proved his affection, he wrote, "I should be very proud and happy if, one day, you were to add a note to that effect in your journal. For those who *believe* you and read only the letter of your remarks carry away a bad opinion of me. Maurice Sachs, the day of his 'death,' assured me that he had all along merely followed your example." Here he was soliciting, before Gide died, the one remark that would erase nearly half a center of aspersions.[2]

Though he still beheld himself as a young luminary, Cocteau, recognizing the inevitable, started to do what grownups do. They die, but before that they acquire property. Like all vagabonds, he dreamt of some fixed abode, and in 1946 he found one answering his dream. With Marais and Paul Morihien (who had meanwhile turned to book publishing), Cocteau purchased a charming house in Milly-la-Forêt, some thirty miles southwest of Paris. It, too, was not long in becoming an appearance, a kind of Cocteau museum where the Poet posed for photographs but rarely lived.

2. Publicly, he switched roles with Gide, as in *Maalesh* (1949): "Victims that we were of young mythomaniacs, we needed years to get together and rediscover our original tenderness. Gide would like to swallow his tongue. It's too late for that. But what does it matter? What doesn't come from the heart is worthless."

12

Santo-Sospir and Canonization

Cocteau bought a small historical monument. The villagers had always referred to his residence as La Maison du Bailli in reference to the bailiff who had built it five centuries before. Joan of Arc had reputedly slept there, but only portions of the original edifice remain. The house forms the impasse of a street round the corner from Milly's church, and it abuts a stream isolating it from the houses behind. Large bay windows lead from the salon into an extensive garden carved into oblongs like a medieval herbarium and adorned with espaliered pear trees. At one end of a patch of lawn opposite the main entrance stands the bust of a jinni looking rather sinister and displaced.

That bust, however, forebodes the interior, which, perhaps better than his literary texts, renders the atmosphere of Cocteau's imagination. Bulky settees and a Victorian divan are played against baubles such as a pair of gilded imitation fruit trees dating, apparently, to Regency Versailles. Bérard's large canvas of Oedipus and the Sphinx hangs amid the white, scalloped foliage of art-nouveau wallpaper. At the center of this main room and spiraling some eight feet into the air is the tusk of a narwhal which seems to command all the sinuous oddments littered throughout the house. There are rams' horns serving as lamp bases, tusks forming the legs of a footstool, spiny crustaceanlike knickknacks, there is a plaster cast of Cocteau's hands with those tendrillar fingers on which he prided himself, there are horns and horns lying to no particular effect, like jaundiced phalli, on polished table tops. The motif extends to the carved posts supporting a canopy above Cocteau's bed.

One becomes aware to what degree his taste and sensibilities lay rooted in the late nineteenth century. Genet was right in detecting smoke at the intersections of Cocteau's periods, but wrong to believe that it rose from some Hellenic underground. Its source was a fire built before the turn of the century, stoked variously by Barrès, Wilde, Beardsley, and Swinburne, and still crepitating behind Cocteau's tasseled exterior. Milly brings to mind Cocteau's description of a fifteenth-century court, Isabeau de Bavière's:

From the time she was fifteen, in 1385, and newly arrived from Germany, until the Treaty of Troyes in 1420, the reign of Elizabetha—the Queen's real name—elapsed in a series of ruinous masquerades. The harmless insanity of Charles VI abetted her passion for theatre. He loved to disguise himself. He and his friends would adorn themselves with feathers and sometimes catch fire on the torches. Costumes, decors, contraptions, balls, courts of love, religious masses abounded and led to fantastic orgies wherein everybody would give vent, beneath animal masks, to his vices. Women wore rams' horns, men cloven hooves and scorpion tails. The King's jesters sported donkey caps. These balls would commence with weird parades involving young men attired in women's robes twelve ells long, others nude but for a sleeve on their left arm and a skin-tight trouser on their right leg, still others dressed in Bohemian frocks which bore obscene limericks. They were followed by Isabeau, who would cast off her hennin, turn about, and curtsy at the door. Lastly, her ladies in waiting, who had just emerged from their baths of she-ass milk and from sweat-rooms where they covered their bodies with cupping glasses to lose weight.

This was written in 1952, but it reads like any number of lurid tales published a half century before, in Jean Lorrain's heyday. The private "drag" parties Cocteau staged at La Maison du Bailli assuredly never matched those revels of his imagination, for they lacked the Queen, the *Monstre Sacré*, the indispensable Mistress of Ceremonies. He atoned for her absence, however, by making her overwhelmingly present, under various guises, in his theatre. The image of innocent depravity, of emasculating flamboyance, of wanton motherhood which gave Bernhardt such prestige among esthetes during the *belle époque* survived, unchanged, all of the divagations in Cocteau's career. He could not write a play without reawakening the Bernhardtian syndrome. *The Two-Headed Eagle*, written in 1945, was no exception.

In a preface to that play, Cocteau summarized as follows his notion of theatrical selfhood:

> For some time now I have wondered why the drama has been degenerating, why the active theatre has been eclipsed by a theatre of words and scenery. I attribute this to the film-maker who, on the one hand, accustoms the public to seeing heroes interpreted by young actors, and, on the other hand, accustoms those youths to speaking softly and stirring as little as possible. The result is that the very foundations of theatrical convention have been shaken, and the *monstres sacrés* whose tics, whose resonant timbres, whose venerable *fauve*-like masks, whose powerful bosoms, whose personal legends counteracted the distance between audience and stage . . . have disappeared altogether.

The Queen in *The Two-Headed Eagle* would have been a perfect vehicle for Bernhardt's fiery demonstrations. Cocteau modeled her upon Empress Elizabeth of Austria, a renowned beauty whose assassination in 1898 at the hands of an Italian anarchist named Luigi Luccheni had far more dramatic repercussions than the death the next year of President Félix Faure in the arms of his concubine Mme. Steinheil. Elizabeth had cut a romantic figure, shocking court circles by her contempt for etiquette, her avowed partisanship of things Hungarian, and her love of horses. In later years she withdrew from public life, residing mainly at Achilloion, a palace she built in Corfu, traveling hither and thither like an uneasy shade, disconsolate at the death of her son, the suicide of her cousin Ludwig II, and the pall of doom hanging over the house of Habsburg. Like other equestrian monarchs (Elizabeth II of England being a notable example), she evinced no special interest in the arts.

The Queen of Cocteau's play does, however. By his own admission, she represents a cross between Elizabeth and Ludwig II of Bavaria. Like Ludwig, she loves poetry and suffers paranoid delusions which drive her from castle to castle in an effort to outwit her faceless assassin. That Cocteau should arrange for her to beckon, woo, and initiate the man whose sworn mission it was to kill her may demonstrate some understanding of his own persecuted mind, but only secondarily. He intended, by this affair, to rehearse the marriage between Jocasta and Oedipus. When Stanislas, the poet *cum* anarchist, leaps through a palace window, attired as a *montagnard* and his knee bloodied, the Queen is startled by his resemblance to her dead husband, Frederick. Later we learn that Frederick had been killed ten years before by another anarchist, attired in the same costume, whose knee was splattered with his victim's blood.

The symbolism could not be more obvious. Cocteau's dream of an incestuous union consummated in death is further borne out by the central image of a two-headed eagle. The whole play seems inspired by Cocteau's vocation for ecstatic self-martyrdom. It elaborates a symbiotic relationship in which the Poet gradually effaces himself as the Woman asserts her authority. Stanislas grows more contemplative as the Queen grows more active. In the end he proves himself the passionate victim of a vampire whose appetite for male blood persuades him of her sublimity, which is to say that in Cocteau's work the pure and the depraved only reinforce one another. His angels are really predatory birds with retractable beaks and claws, spiny bloodsuckers bloated with their "destiny." This highly ambiguous vision accounts for much of his imagery. Thus, the Queen is described as a Spanish Madonna from whom knives are radiating—an image which suggests that Cocteau never quite recovered from the post-Baudelairean pornography of his youth.

Neither, for that matter, had the surrealists recovered from it, and their literature is similarly rife with Salomes, vampires, virgin huntresses, immaculate assassins, and *belles dames sans merci*. It is as if a whole generation of writers, suffocating in the respectable *embonpoint* of Victorian motherhood, converted *en masse* to svelte, sterile divinities, with the result that, in the underground, Artemis supplanted Aphrodite as the embodiment of Eros.

Cocteau's nervous sytem followed the warp of art nouveau and decadent romanticism. He claims, in the preface to *The Two-Headed Eagle*, that his characters behave according to some "heraldic" psychology. What, however, distinguishes the heraldic from the "real"? Aren't fantasies, by their very nature, heraldic? If Cocteau wrote about *monstres sacrés* then he imagined *monstres sacrés:* a simple axiom with far-flung implications. His heroines—Antigone, the Queen, the Sphinx, the Princess—are intractable creatures whose "elegance of soul," as he puts it, finds expression in the unsexing of men. Their arsenal includes knives, horns, guns, horsewhips, poison, and spiny brooches. They themselves, when not clad in armor, are sculpted from various minerals, most of which figure in Cocteau's fantasy about Blanche of Castile:

> For us, Blanche of Castile is a myth, a symbol of strength and grace, a moving statue surmounted by a crown of iron. White from head to toes. With veils of marble and her torso carved of light marble, like a veil. A standing *gisante*. A block of transparency. Hard water. Crystal flowing, escorted by white froth. Blanche is the lady whom time has scoured of color. A kind of stone lily.

In *La Corrida du Premier Mai*, he imagines death in the shape of an equestrian statue called "The White Lady" outside the Madrid bull ring and fancies the bull, at whose feet a matador lies gored and ecstatic, her emissary: the homosexual triumvirate under yet another guise.[1] Above all, Cocteau's "She" is the icon who establishes the poet's vocation, the marble in whose cause he sheds his blood, the squeamish Dandy who wears long gloves to administer Death, the Priestess of Black Masses, the authority he enthrones, the unseduceable Mother *whom he strives to become*. The poet finds apotheosis in emasculation. At the end of *Blood of a Poet*, we see him resolved into the marble statue. At the end of *Orphée*, he is a marble head whose body has been appropriated by the Princess. At the end of *The Two-Headed Eagle*, he lies dead at the foot of a marble staircase: the Queen lies on top. How thin the line separating this extravaganza from Montesquiou's 1912 production of d'Annunzio's *Martyrdom of Saint Sebastian*.

Cocteau came clattering into old age aloft a wagon-load of Victorian fantasies, drawn by the wicked fairies of his youth, homebound for the French Academy.

---

1. The sado-masochistic identification of bull and woman becomes even more explicit in Cocteau's poem *Requiem:* "He [the matador] was loved by the lady / Beneath the gold and beneath the satin / His legs bright pink / The lady extended him her arms / Metamorphosed into horns . . ."

Milly did not terminate Cocteau's vagabondage. He lodged there on weekends, but it remained vacant for long periods while its absentee landlord superintended his interests elsewhere. The little star beneath his name required constant friction, for it was forever threatening to lose some of its glitter. Louise de Vilmorin recalls going to the movies one evening with Cocteau and Marais. Afterward Marais was besieged by adolescents who utterly failed to recognize his companion; Cocteau, standing on their periphery, looked woebegone. What publicity he did get did not always promote his career. In 1947 the *NRF* published Maurice Sachs' *Sabbat*, an autobiography whose savage thrusts drew more blood than all of Cocteau's anemic epigones could subsequently restore him. There were rebuttals to be made, interviews arranged, prefaces written, anthologies compiled, and literary soirées attended. Whenever someone, anyone, lifted an accusatory finger, he would come reeling back to Paris like a yoyo. The least invitation—provided his hostess had wealth or, in lieu of that, celebrated friends—sufficed to sway him from his attempts at living the serene life.

After the war he became a habitué of Florence Gould's salon on the Avenue Malakoff, where Paul Léautaud, an older habitué, was at leisure to train his beady eyes on him. "If Malraux was absent," he observed in 1946, "I found Cocteau, whom I had not hitherto seen at Mme. Gould's, though I presume he must know her well, as he refers to her as 'my little Florence.' . . . When I entered the salon, he immediately made for me and said, in front of the assembled guests, 'If I dared, I would kiss Léautaud,' and he dared, or almost, rubbing his face against mine. He thereupon proclaimed that, to his mind, the color best representing me is blue, and that the expression best characterizing me is 'elegance.' . . . Perhaps he means that, although attired very modestly, threadbare in fact, I have a way of appearing otherwise. As for Cocteau, who must earn piles of money from his plays, films, and books, he looked less elegant than one might expect. At lunch, I had to concede him my place next to Mme. Gould. I noticed that throughout the meal he rested his elbows on the table and dined thus. Mme. Gould wore a gown so low-cut that her breasts were perfectly visible, especially to me, since I was sitting opposite her. I brought this to her attention and whispered to Antonini at my side, 'She's doing it to make Cocteau hot.' "

Cocteau had heat to spare, and squandered most of it on literary politics. His life revolved about 36 Rue de Montpensier, which was usually buzzing with activity, more like the field tent of a campaigning general than the "exiguous cabin opening onto the Palais-Royal, hemmed by the sounds of footfalls" which Cocteau described. Footfalls could not be heard for the incessant ringing of the telephone, Cocteau's noisy conferences with his aides-de-camp, the endless parade of literary editors, film-makers, preface-seekers, autograph hounds, and sallow poets who talked their way past Madeleine, a maid whom Cocteau hired to say what his appetite for all ears prevented him from saying: no. Round the corner, he played the presiding deity at a combination art gallery–book store owned by Paul Morihien who had launched his short-lived publishing career on the strength of manuscripts given him by Genet, Sartre, and Cocteau.

Meanwhile Cocteau had begun in earnest the work of self-commentary and self-recapitulation which would occupy his dwindling years. Apart from a long poem, *Crucifixion*, a ballet entitled (predictably) *The Young Man and Death*, he devoted himself to the reissue and filming of previous works as if, for lack of fresh miracles by which to capture the public's attention, he were content to pun on stale ones (yet hadn't this always been his stratagem?—"Repeat the same thing, but each time with a different twist," he once advised a friend). In May, 1947, he collaborated with Roberto Rossellini and Anna Magnani in the filming of *La Voix Humaine*. No sooner had he completed a film version of *The Two-Headed Eagle* later that year (at the Château de Vizille) than the cameras started grinding out his screen play of *Les Parents Terribles*, in which Yvonne de Bray played the role she had foregone eleven years before. In 1949 he would produce what must stand as his cinematic chef-d'œuvre, *Orphée*. These productions were interlarded with two trips abroad in swift succession, one to New York late in 1948, and another to the Near East in February, 1949, with a theatrical company which staged some half-dozen plays, including *Les Parents Terribles*, *Les Monstres Sacrés*, and Sartre's *Huis Clos*.

The American trip coincided with the opening of *The Two-Headed Eagle* in New York. Cocteau performed his well-rehearsed stunts, created lots of hullabaloo, had himself shepherded about by Monroe Wheeler, Jean-Pierre Aumont, and the French consul, communed with familiar ghosts such as Maritain and Al Brown, then, after some three weeks, boarded an airplane on which he delivered himself of a hortatory farewell published under the title *Letter to the Americans*, in which he addresses a mythical people afraid, he claims, of dreaming and experimenting.

His voyage through Egypt, Palestine, and Turkey was more in the nature of a theatrical safari de luxe which lasted three months, time enough for him to afford leisurely dinners with beys and pashas, a tour of Luxor under the guidance of the great French Egyptologist Alexandre Varille, and pilgrimages to the Sphinx, with Cocteau staggering through his agenda thanks to vitamin shots. It must have been a spring more intriguing than his diary of it, *Maalesh*, in which, as in *Mon Premier Voyage*, Cocteau finds it incumbent upon himself to make deathless remarks, camouflaging the "trivial" with Images and Aphorisms spun from his all-purpose cant (dreamers, nondreamers, visibility and invisibility) as if fearful of being less than literary. But it was a spring edged with winter, a tour arranged under the most gloomy auspices. In January, 1949, Christian Bérard had dropped dead during a rehearsal of Molière's *Les Fourberies de Scapin*. The loss of his closest collaborator maimed Cocteau. And it reminded him, painfully, that his own past was growing apace.

Meanwhile another significant rupture had taken place in Cocteau's life. He and Jean Marais parted ways in 1947. The corporation they had formed to purchase their house in Milly was dissolved. Though remaining one another's closest friend, each found a different partner, Marais an American dancer and Cocteau a young man of Yugoslav-Italian origin named Édouard Dermithe, who accompanied him on the Middle Eastern tour.

Dermithe proved to be the last and least distinguished of Cocteau's dark-haired waifs. He was born in Trieste but was bred in the coal regions of northern France and at an early age followed his father into the pits. The immediate postwar years found him living intermittently in Paris as the protégé of Bernard Chêne, who figured, peripherally, in various literary and artistic circles. It would appear that Dermithe fancied himself a painter, but his greatest asset lay in his handsome face. His looks ultimately reprieved him from the mines, though the idea of living life as somebody's sumptuary creature did not straightaway occur to him. He sought useful employment, and accordingly Chêne introduced him to Raoul Leven, a saintly man who had always managed to improvise a livelihood as an art broker, a book dealer, or a steward of small avant-garde publishing houses such as the Éditions des Quatre-Chemins, where he first met Jean Cocteau in the late 1920s. Leven in turn recommended Dermithe to Cocteau. They met at Morihien's book store near the Palais-Royal.

Cocteau was immediately taken with Dermithe, whom he might have considered employing as his "secretary" if the young man had been somewhat more literate. Instead he proposed that Dermithe live at Milly, caring for the garden and grooming Marais's horses. Dermithe hesitated, for fear of losing his miner's pension, but was finally brought around. Having thus graduated from the coal pits to a cloistered garden, he soon made the great, Lawrentian leap from a garden to his master's house. Cocteau, determined to groom his new protégé into an artist and thoroughbred Frenchman, began by lopping off his final "he," then reduced "Dermit" to a pet known henceforth as "Doudou."

Making an actor of him proved a task to which Cocteau himself was not equal. Dermit played a minor role in the film *Orphée*, then a major one in the film of *Les Enfants Terribles*; in both cases Cocteau could do no better than cast him as himself: earnest, unsmiling, given to stiff, abrupt movements, and all but mute. He showed to good advantage, however, in underwear, and *Les Enfants Terribles* enjoyed enormous success, particularly among adolescents, who beheld their own disheveled bedrooms glorified and who believed that Cocteau's gnomic utterances lent prestige to their murky emotions. Attaching metaphysical significance to his work, Cocteau wrote to

an admiring friend that he "slaved over this small magic lantern.
. . . The fact that you like it proves to me that I have accomplished my mission, for nowadays few people understand the mysterious prestige inherent in the proportions and organization of the Void": a remark less arresting than its return address, the villa Santo-Sospir in Saint-Jean-Cap-Ferrat.

Midway through the filming of *Les Enfants Terribles* Cocteau discovered that he lacked funds to continue. Jean-Pierre Melville, the director, suggested that they approach a lady of no particular distinction but vastly rich and apparently anxious to cut a figure in the artistic world of Paris. Not only did the lady invest, she later invited Cocteau and company to spend a week recuperating from their labors at her villa on the Mediterranean, Santo-Sospir. It was thus that Cocteau fell into a triangular net which would deliver him, gaffed and half-dead, to his own mediocre temptations. Doudou and he remained at Santo-Sospir, as house guests of Mme. Francine Weisweiller, for the next decade. "What I am showing," he had written to Marcel Jouhandeau, referring to *Les Enfants Terribles*, "is limbo—the no man's land between life and death." On the threshold of *real* limbo, Cocteau failed to recognize it beneath its bamboo-railed terraces overlooking the Mediterranean and its suspended gardens flowering with hibiscus. The apparatus of luxury proved, as always, overwhelmingly attractive to him. Like the Beast, he wanted power to command any convenience with a snap of his fingers. And he acquired it.

Francine Weisweiller, née Worms, came of a well-to-do Jewish family who shuttled between Paris and São Paulo, where they had commercial interests. At seventeen she was married, and two years later left her husband, flouting her parents, who looked upon divorce with such orthodox horror that they temporarily disowned her. Set adrift, she began to smoke opium, earning her living as an *esthéticienne*, or beautician. In the meantime she was being courted by young Jewish millionaires. After massaging faces by day she would spend evenings with Guy de Rothschild or Alec Weisweiller. The latter lost no time proposing to her. When war broke out, the Wormses moved to São Paulo. Francine remained behind and married Alec Weisweiller under the so-called "laws of the

community," meaning that she became heiress to half of a vast fortune derived chiefly from Shell Oil.

By the late 1940s she began to weary of the rigorously closed
Jewish circles in which she moved. Behind her shy demeanor, she
apparently entertained notions of being destined for some career
more glamorous than the one that money had afforded her. She
wanted to figure in the world of *Tout Paris*, and Cocteau's advent
must have seemed providential. Francine Weisweiller found in Cocteau an impresario, and Cocteau found in her an adoring millionairess prepared to place her fortune at his disposal. Childishness and
mutual interest sustained the ménage, not, as most people assumed,
sex. Santo-Sospir proved to be a household no more passionate than
its mistress, a sentimental but rather cold woman who seemed content to live in adoration of her genius-in-residence. Milly lay fallow
while Cocteau organized, at the tip of a luxurious peninsula jutting
into the Mediterranean, one of the childish, introverted dens which
had always haunted his dreams.

As a gesture of thanksgiving, Cocteau set about decorating a
patch of wall above the fireplace with line drawings. Abhorring
voids (his pronouncements to the contrary), he let his crayon trail
into the white expanse until, four months later, every wall was tattooed with eyes, phallic squiggles, fishy profiles, geometric arabesques, Pre-Raphaelite hunters in medieval habit, figures reminiscent of Beardsley or Will Bradley, and of Plastic Man. Mme. Weisweiller was delighted to see her square salon transformed into an art-
nouveau aquarium cluttered with webs and tendrils and ephebic
swimmers. "For the past four months," wrote Cocteau to Élise
Jouhandeau in September, 1950, "I have been on ladders painting
the walls of a villa on the coast. Do not take offense at my silence.
It comes of my living day in and day out with people I love, with
whom I talk, of whom I ask advice; letter-writing seems vulgar by
comparison with this kind of exchange. I spent four days in Venice.
The Italian Catholic party feels that in *Orphée* I took unacceptable
liberties with regard to official dogma, which is rather odd considering that it has to do with a Greek myth. . . . Sides and Sides. I've
taken sides with myself. A free man is a veritable freak nowadays.
All of this amuses me for, as you know, I have become a kind of

Tibetan sage." By mid-1952 he had completed the ceilings and the front walk, thus enveloping himself and his playmates in reams of comic strip.

How did the "Tibetan sage" conduct his life? He rose earlier than in Paris, sleeping little and fitfully. At ten the telephone would begin to ring, and it would continue ringing throughout the day. Cocteau, a master at packaging conversations in three minutes and tying them with a curlicue, would answer the telephone himself and speak while balancing on one leg, like a flamingo. Mornings were devoted to drawing and to correspondence (in which he invariably complained of his latest ailments). By two p.m. Doudou had usually roused himself and would stumble half-asleep into the salon, where an earnest conference about the luncheon menu was in progress. Cocteau, attired in a soiled bathrobe and yellow foulard looped twice around his neck, would mix the cocktail *du jour*, using recipes he discovered in detective novels (which now constituted the bulk of his reading). After a meal of crustaceans, which he relished less for their meat than for the messy labor of cracking them open, he would, weather permitting, board the Weisweiller yacht *Orphée II* and cruise about the bay with Doudou and Francine, who listened appreciatively as he would mock the bourgeois tourists (on whom he conferred names like Madame Ordure and Madame Peau-de-Banane), inventing appropriate vignettes. Evenings Cocteau would write, in a small atelier adjoining the villa, or smoke opium *à trois*, retiring well before Doudou, who watched television, continued smoking, or read science fiction until the wee hours.

With minor variations, this summed up Cocteau's agenda at Santo-Sospir throughout the 1950s. As if striving, however, to blind himself to the banality of his life, he never failed to remind his correspondents that Francine and Doudou were at their easels or absorbed in books. His letters would invariably end with brief apocrypha such as "Francine and I still have fever. Doudou is painting, sleeping, and devouring volumes about China and India." The slighter his correspondent's acquaintance with Francine and Doudou, the freer he felt to convey their warm greetings and to report their bedside tables laden with an impressive syllabus. "Francine is painting. Doudou is painting. We love you. We miss you," he wrote to a virtual stranger, presenting himself as the spokesman of a holy trinity called alternatively *nous* or *on*, "we three" or "we one."

The vacuum separating Santo-Sospir and Cocteau's public image of it lay equally at the heart of his "friendship" with Picasso, whose rebuffs, however vicious, never proved equal to Cocteau's want of pride. Over the years Picasso, though amused by Cocteau's verbal invention, did not encourage his visits. The possibility of any fluent relationship was highly remote so long as Paul Éluard lived, for reasons which Françoise Gilot, Picasso's mistress during the late 1940s and early 1950s, explains at some length:

Occasionally when we were at Saint-Tropez visiting Paul Éluard and Dominique, we would run into Jean Cocteau. Usually he stayed with Madame Weisweiller. Sometimes as the four of us were sitting at the café Chez Sénéquié the Weisweiller yacht would cruise by, and Cocteau, seeing us there, would seek us out. Éluard had never liked Cocteau and would try to avoid him, but Cocteau generally wound up by pressing his hand into Paul's, whether Paul liked it or not. A little of Paul's coolness rubbed off on Pablo, and he was inclined to be rather short with Cocteau when Paul was around. Cocteau was always looking for reasons to come visit us, but since Paul disliked him so and Pablo was much more interested in Paul than he was in Cocteau, it wasn't until after Paul's death in November, 1952, that Cocteau began to make much headway. He knew he wasn't very welcome all by himself so he often made it a point to attach himself to a group that was coming for some specific purpose. Just before Pablo's big exhibitions in Milan and Rome, we were overrun with Italians of all kinds. One of them was Luciano Emmer, who wanted to make a film about Picasso. Cocteau knew Emmer because Emmer had made a film on Carpaccio for which Cocteau had written the script. Cocteau came along with that group, and since Italians are great talkers, he was in his element. . . . Cocteau got into the spirit of the occasion by inventing wild tales about a mythical Madame Favini, the widow of a rich shoe manufacturer from Milan. According to Cocteau, she was a great art collector and lived the most exciting and improbable adventures. He wrote me letters about her, which I read to Pablo and which amused him greatly. She listened

only to Schönberg and read only Rilke. She was so far left of left
that after Stalin died, she went on a hunger strike until her daughter
brought her back to her senses by squirting her with Fly-Tox.

It never occurred to those whose coat tails he rode that Cocteau
needed coat tails to ride, which sometimes placed his unwitting
vehicles in awkward positions. Such was the experience of James
Lord, an American writer who had already known Picasso for
quite some time when he first made Cocteau's acquaintance in
Villefranche. As yet ignorant of the thick undergrowth, thirty-five
years deep, entangling these separate trunks at their base, he found
it puzzling that Cocteau should immediately propose they pay Picasso an impromptu visit. Why impromptu, and why together?

His questions were answered, alas, as soon as they arrived at Picasso's villa, La Galloise. Picasso was guiding a Scandinavian photographer about his studio, and gracefully incorporated his two
callers. When the photographer, much to everyone's surprise, asked
whether he might have a large, beautiful drawing lying topmost on
a stack of other large, beautiful drawings, Picasso turned the request to mischievous account. He granted the photographer his
wish, then, turning to Cocteau, said, "Since I'm making handouts, I
must give you something as well, for old time's sake," whereupon
he disappeared into a back room and emerged bearing the shard of
a casserole. On it Picasso had sketched eyes and mouth, allowing
the casserole's handle to stand in lieu of a nose. "Here," he exclaimed, handing it to Cocteau, who could not have been more dis-
mayed had Picasso offered him a fresh turd. Seeing Cocteau's face
fall, he added a pinch of salt to the wound, assuring Cocteau that it
was signed on the inside surface. Indeed it was. On the return
voyage to Villefranche, Cocteau delivered a tirade recalling every
wanton act he had known Picasso to commit. Two days later,
when Lord paid Picasso another visit, this time alone, Picasso glowered at him in silence for a minute, then croaked, "Why did you
bring that whore to my house?"

After Éluard's death, however, Picasso—sufficiently the chest-
beater to understand and forgive Cocteau his trespasses—proved to
be far more amenable. His separation from Françoise Gilot augured
another bourgeois cycle in his life. Along with the new mistress

came a new dog and a new poet. Cocteau snatched from Éluard's grave the laurels he had surrendered three decades before.

If Cocteau belonged to no parties but his own, his own was the intersection point of everybody else's. A play he wrote in 1951, *Bacchus*, should be read as a rendition and apology of this predicament. The result is a hodgepodge whose language captures the spirit of Sartre's colloquial dialectics, and whose hero is a kind of existentialist in drag. Cocteau defends himself through Hans, a village idiot of remarkable beauty whom the citizens of a German hamlet, during the Reformation, have elected Bacchus, in accordance with pagan rites they still observe. As such he is omnipotent for one week. The Church has helped rig the election, fearing that if it were to abstain, or to reprove the festival, some Reformationist might seize power. Hans turns out to be not an idiot but a seer who has observed society behind his mask of idiocy; he now unmasks himself and strives to show the common people that their liberty is despised alike by the Reformation and by the Church, that the masquerade is a moment of truth and reality a masquerade. The people prefer not to see, and Hans suffers a martyr's death, impaled by an arrow as he exhorts the crowd.

Bacchus begs comparison with Sartre's *Flies*, by which it was no doubt inspired. Both revolve about the issue of human freedom, and if Sartre chose his spokesman in Orestes, the protégé of Athena, while Cocteau envisaged deliverance in the person of a reprobate god, a *daimon*, that comparison still holds. *The Flies*, however, derives from a body of thought, while *Bacchus* constantly excuses itself for lacking one. Sartre presents an issue, whereas Cocteau presents Cocteau.

Indeed, Hans stands as the inverted image of his author who is once again at work proving his innocence, this time before a Marxist-existentialist tribunal. Was Cocteau a wealthy bourgeois kept by an even wealthier bourgeoise? He translated himself into a common man. Was he a *précieux* who spent his intelligence on verbal finery, balancing the French language on one finger and twirling all its paradoxical effects like so many semblances of thought? His hero is a brilliant idiot badgered by the intelligentsia. Had Sachs' *Sabbat* brought to light his frigidity and emotional parasitism? Hans promotes love and fire for their own sakes. Had Cocteau's abstention from politics under the German occupation given him the stigma of moral cowardice? *Bacchus* condemns politics as a masquerade and suggests what Cocteau would declare openly, that ethics and acts are unrelated, morality belonging to some "invisible" order: "I call ethics a secret form of conduct, a discipline constructed and deployed according to the aptitudes of a man refusing the categorical imperative, an imperative which falsifies the mechanism of things. This private morality may seem the essence of immorality to those given to self-deception." Did Cocteau make a public spectacle of his invisibility? Did he write a lifetime of prefaces to the unwritten Work, and commentaries on the unlived Life? His *Bacchus* sanctifies this alterity, and proves him innocent. "The guilty man betrays himself. The innocent man escapes our definitions. . . . If the criminal expresses himself, we judge him for some act. If the innocent stirs, he engenders nothing but anarchy," says the cunning cardinal of the piece.

For all his talk of anarchy, Cocteau had never ceased to respect authority. In place of a vocation he had chosen its symptoms, martyrizing himself according to the tradition of *poètes maudits* without writing their poetry, provoking trials not so much to save his reputation as to sustain it, flagellating himself on the assumption that stigmata must be a sign of faith. He begged for friendship but ultimately respected only his prosecutors. Indeed, the symbiotic quarrels in which he and Gide engaged amounted to intimacy far surpassing Cocteau's intimacies, but now that Gide was gone and now that Cocteau himself had demonstrated his incorrigibility, prosecutors of some stature were few and far between. Thus Mauriac in attacking *Bacchus* performed an act of solidarity. As soon as one member of the Hellfire Club died, another assumed his role playing the game of a third, and doing so with hieratic expertise. If the helping hand grasped a knout, wasn't the "apotheosis of martyrdom," as he put it, precisely what Cocteau desired? Mauriac's open letter in the December 29, 1951, issue of *Figaro Littéraire* must have rejuvenated him by thirty years, for it is the kind of diatribe that instantly brings to mind Gide's open letter of June, 1919:

Getting down to essentials, Jean Desailly (Hans) is your spokesman. Do not try to deny it: you are speaking when he speaks. At times Desailly escapes his role and becomes Jean Cocteau-about-town, interpreting the Cocteau routine. *Bacchus* shows us Jean Cocteau in the light of Sartre, the same Cocteau whom we knew in 1910 lit by the waning light of Rostand but his eye already trained on Anna de Noailles. . . . Already Diaghilev, Satie, Picasso, Gide, Apollinaire, Max Jacob, and other major planets were drawing this wily satellite into their orbits.

Forty years have passed. We are now living the era of "God is dead." This idea is floating in the air and you have spent your life catching currents of air. Here's your chance, now or never—right? —to celebrate this death, and, more than that, settle your score with the boring, senile old Church which persists in wanting to scare us with tales of the other world, this Church which, long after we have left it, still manages to kill our joy. . . . Child Cocteau stamps his feet: "There is no hell! There is no hell!" There is no hell since there is no judgment; and there is no judgment since there is no God. Sartre is but the latest to prove it. . . . According to the newspaper Sartre was in the audience jubilating, while Cocteau bound his old Mother to the Marigny column and for three straight hours whipped her.

Before the fanfare had died away, Cocteau issued a new brief in self-defense, *Diary of an Unknown*, whose title speaks for itself. Here he grounds his innocence on a dime-store view of the physical universe, developing (thanks in large measure to his lay knowledge of medicine, his readings in science fiction, and his investigation of optical baubles such as the kaleidoscope) a cosmology in the spirit of Montaigne's *Apology of Raymond Sebond*, to wit: things, beheld from macrocosmically far or microcosmically near, are not what they seem to be. Vacuums are not empty, time and space are but points of view, and Cocteau's duplicity is a metaphysical phenomenon for which he cannot be held responsible. "I wonder," he asks, "if I could be otherwise than the way I am, and if my difficulty in being, if the faults which impede my career are not my very career, the regret of not having some other. A destiny I must shoulder like my physical self. Whence these fits of pessimism and optimism whose conjugation marks me. The systole and diastole of the universal rhythm." Cocteau is not what meets the eye; whatever he may be, it derives from a set of circumstances implicating the universe. Viewed in this light, his seeming faults assume their place within a larger perfection, and his neurasthenia reflects his transcendence.

Like *The Cock and the Harlequin, Diary of an Unknown* trails from asterisk to asterisk, but each paradox begs some point, each *pensée* conceals some inadmissible hurt, and even the asterisks form part of Cocteau's brief. Between them, like God poking a comminatory finger through stardust, he chastises his prodigal sons Maurice Sachs and Claude Mauriac.

In March, 1953, Cocteau was made an honorary citizen of Milly. "Both of you would have gotten a good laugh," he wrote to the Jouhandeaus, "seeing me, between the mayor of Milly and the minister, receive a bouquet from some little (or little more than) girl. I was named honorary citizen of the town: a marriage akin to the Doge's with the Adriatic sea." The immediate future held in store for Cocteau greater honors and weightier elections rigged with the help of Mme. Weisweiller: Mme. Weisweiller, whose generosity, as it proved, did not come free.

In exchange for winters and parts of every other season at Cap-Ferrat, for a chauffeured car, for de luxe progresses every year through Greece, Austria, Italy, or Spain, for the most minute solicitude with regard to all his material needs, Cocteau dedicated *Bacchus* to her, gave her recognition, and made her privy to the inner circle of Great Names which included his own. Like many religious converts, however, Mme. Weisweiller interpreted Glory the more strictly for seeing only its ritual face. Her fundamentalism took the form of exclusiveness. She was only too happy to receive Picasso, or to hobnob with celebrated residents of Cap-Ferrat such as Aly Khan and Somerset Maugham, but Cocteau found himself increasingly cut off from "lesser"—and frequently more devoted—friends who failed to meet his hostess' Rhadamanthine criteria. Others who would have been welcome (notably Marie-Laure de Noailles and the Aurics) preferred to see Cocteau *chez lui* in Paris or at Milly.

The demure Mme. Weisweiller found her tongue and when she did, let it wag with preposterous self-assurance. An acquaintance who chanced to meet her in Rome, a year or two after Cocteau had come to Santo-Sospir, discovered, much to his surprise, that she was "uttering opinions." Those opinions, lifted intact from Cocteau's conversation, grew inane at one remove from their source. Cocteau and Francine formed a couple, however. Mme. Weisweiller's anxiety to cut a figure sustained Cocteau's own *arrivisme*. It was difficult to know who was grooming whom for what, but, living in the lap of luxury, never perhaps had Cocteau felt more insecure, his Tibetan poses notwithstanding.

Even in the halcyon days of 1921 and 1922 he lacked the stamina to write a work of great breadth; now on the verge of extinction, his mind guttered out in letters, Gongoresque verse, sketches, and introductory blurbs for an extraordinary potpourri of books including *Arts and Sports*, *Greek Epitaphs*, *The Memoirs of Aga Khan*, *Nicole's Guide to Paris*, *Black-Out on the Flying Saucers*, *The Arabian Nights*, Ambrose Bierce's *The Devil's Dictionary*, and Gaston Criel's *Swing*. Like the bits of glass in a kaleidoscope, his few cant words could be shaken into prefaces of every description. His drawings reiterate *ad nauseum* a single profile. His poems, whatever their form, rely on the same tropes, rarely venturing beyond a conceit which sometimes works and sometimes does not. Cocteau was himself reduced to the bare nub of his own memorized techniques. Moreover, critics were proving less indulgent than ever. "I accuse you," wrote Jean-Pierre Resnay in *Combat*, "of having contributed more than your share to the public image of the poet as a man with a sandwich board, a trickster, a counterfeiter."

Cocteau was exhausted. "I have been very sick," he wrote to Marcel Jouhandeau from Cap-Ferrat in April, 1952. "Too much work and fits of weariness. I'm mending little by little on the coast and wonder if I shall have the strength to stage *Oedipus Rex*." It is understandable that his friends took these complaints in stride, for Cocteau had been complaining of obscure miseries since his youth yet seemed to thrive on them. While his face began to age drastically in the early 1950s, the transformation became him; he looked every bit the successful sexagenarian in Floridian retirement, deeply tanned and crowned with a whisk broom of white hair. But the attacks of angina which had first beset him after the war now came at more frequent intervals and inflicted greater pain. Furthermore, in 1953, while visiting Madrid for a performance of *Le Bel Indifférent*, he contracted uremia and nearly died of it. These were signs of a general systemic collapse.

One year later, at the beginning of July, 1954, he suffered a serious heart attack. "I was in a car riding up the Champs-Élysées with a friend when suddenly I was seized by some ghastly, superhuman pain which suffocated me. I just managed to make it home, where I writhed in agony." Cocteau was immediately transferred to Mme. Weisweiller's house on the Place des États-Unis. Her mansion became a veritable clinic run by France's outstanding cardiologists. When Cocteau had recovered enough to endure a voyage south, Santo-Sospir became his private solarium. Letters of good tiding arrived by the sack, and enemies honored his illness with a cease fire.

The sympathetic hush affected everyone except the invalid, who swiftly took advantage of it. By mid-August he was sufficiently himself to receive an interviewer from *Figaro Littéraire*, and expatiated in some detail on his physical life: "Heart attacks are treated with an antithrombic drug called Tromexane which prevents the blood from clotting. It's possible that the attendant modifications in one's circulatory rhythm will transform the whole organism and throw it out of kilter. Anyway, I'm unable to write, reading tires me, and I admire people who can loll about from morning till night. The only work I do is reading my mail and answering letters." X-rays like this one had always simulated revelations of the inner life. He created an atmosphere of mock intimacy with anatomy lessons.

The nearly fatal seizure seems, however, not to have given him any sudden perspective on matters of glory and selfhood. Like a child, he exploited it to voice long-standing grievances and to mend his Image, knowing full well that the adult world was bound to humor him. The bulk of the newspaper interview concerned Mauriac, whose open letter was, after two and one-half years, still preying on Cocteau's mind: "I have already answered Mauriac that I hate hatred. Hatred always emits deadly waves. I have never felt any for him and am happy to learn that he feels none toward me. Besides, affairs of friendship are so delicate that I consider it dangerous to discuss and finger them in public. It is natural that a quarrel should burst out, when it does, noisily. Less natural that this noise and display should attend the reconcilation. That is no one's business."

Bacchus, he went on to say, excited thirty-eight curtain calls when performed in Düsseldorf, "a citadel of German Catholicism"; its failure in Paris merely reflected the audience's ignorance of historical matters alluded to in the text. Having thus argued his greatness (buttressing the argument with nostalgic name-droppings such as "I was sad not to be at Picasso's side for the Fiesta de Vallauris"), he recited his inevitable *paternoster:* "We poets have within us things which want saying, but we are nothing but their vehicle, and when the vehicle is in disrepair . . . ," then resumed his fitful convalescence.

Illness has its prerogatives. In Cocteau's case, it made him eligible for official honors, as if a broken man, whatever his mores, were sufficiently sexless to merit social sanctification. Cocteau willingly played the prodigal son. Honors befell him, but not without his craving them. In fact, the conciliatory note he struck in his interview with the reporter from *Figaro Littéraire* may be considered the inaugural speech of his campaign to win a seat in the French Academy. Mauriac, after all, was one of the forty "immortals" whose votes he would, in accordance with electoral convention, solicit during the fall and winter of 1954–1955. To Paul Claudel, another member of the Academy, he announced his candidacy as follows: "Dear and magnificent friend, I have sent the fateful letter to G. Lecomte. It was my heartfelt duty to alert you (a somewhat crazy act). Your faithful Jean Cocteau." Claudel answered him in one line, "Of course, my dear Cocteau, you may count on my vote," but died before he could cast his vote. Cocteau, the man who professed to abhor all parties, told André Maurois that he could no longer stand erect without the aid of crutches, and Maurois rewarded this palinode with his sponsorship. As for the Fairy Godmother indispensable to the candidate for official honors, the role was played, with all the zest of self-fulfillment, by Francine Weisweiller.

With a sponsor such as Maurois, a hostess whose table left nothing to be desired, and a fund of conversation likely to amuse the economists, physicists, and *belles lettristes* who dined in sequence at the Weisweiller mansion on Place des États-Unis, Cocteau could not fail of election. Moreover, his ambivalent career made him the ideal candidate. He had enough avant-garde glamor so that the Academy could throw him as a sop to critics of its bourgeois tradition, yet he was not, by any means, unrepentantly bohemian. In considering Jean Cocteau, the Academy adhered to Cocteau's own motto: "The tact of audacity consists in knowing how far one can go too far." In electing him, it elected, beneath the occult trappings, one of its own: a *grand bourgeois* come home to roost. Early in 1955 the Belgian Royal Academy of Arts and Letters named Cocteau to the seat occupied first by Anna de Noailles, then by Colette, who had died in the summer of 1953. Taking courage from this precedent, the French Academy, two months later, gave Cocteau a seat hitherto warmed by a gentleman who proved mortal in his lifetime, Jérôme Tharaud. That seat once belonged to Edmond Rostand. Playing musical chairs, Cocteau came full circle, back to his original mentors, and back to himself.

One week after Cocteau's election, Mauriac, in *Figaro Littéraire*, publicly clasped the newest academician to his bosom: a scorpion's embrace formulated in the familiar "*tu*" but probing its victim's armor for fatal flaws.

He used to dance [Mauriac reminisced] in shafts of light emitted by others—a dance either wild or stately, with or without a balancing pole, from projector to projector. All the luminous threads of an era interwove their fires in him. Thus, we were persuaded that nothing he showed was his, and that sooner or later there would be nothing left on the nocturnal table but a moth with singed wings, its death throes observed by some child. Well, one by one the lanterns darkened and Jean Cocteau remained. His colors still adorn him, so they must have been his after all. I suppose that what attracted him to the Academy was the desire to have an ultraofficial certificate of durability. For he has never, appearances to the contrary, done anything by chance. He did not stumble into our Assembly dazed. He has had his eye fixed on the door for quite some time, waiting for it to open a crack so that he could slip in. He had to show the world, by his épée and his two-cornered hat, that the ephemerid was immortal.

Having stung him, Mauriac could then afford to apply balm, giving a Catholic appreciation of Cocteau's schizoid nature:

It is entirely to his credit that, a prisoner (as we all are) of his own nature, he nonetheless aspired to another Cocteau, he spent all his strength straining toward an ideal Cocteau whose unfinished portrait he would construct, feature by feature, before our very eyes.

Mauriac was right to formulate this portrait in the past imperfect. The French Academy may have congratulated Cocteau's ability to aspire, but what it did was consecrate his failure.

Cocteau's newest confidant and amanuensis Jean Denoël (who had previously played a similar role in Gide's life), organized a testimonial symposium—a *Festschrift*—in his honor. Seven months separated the election from the Epiphany, and they were filled with speeches. Cocteau labored at his own. "When do you get time to write?" he asked Jouhandeau. "Give me your secret—I can't seem to put my Academy speech together. You hit the mark in saying that I must prove to the 'others' that we can have what they have but they can't have what belongs to us." Cocteau was a master of the noncommittal commitment, but formulating this one taxed all his powers of ambiguity. He faced a problem far greater than the one Paul Valéry solved some decades before when, having to flatter his predecessor and *bête noire*, Anatole France, he did so without once mentioning his name. Cocteau was at odds not with his predecessor but with himself, not with the subject of his speech but with the speech. In delivering it, Cocteau would, *ipso facto*, become a member of the Academy, yet he wanted, in the same breath, to dissociate himself.

No wonder, then, that he gave his undivided attention to other matters, to the design of his academic épée, for example. Friends had formed a society to defray the cost of having it forged. The blade was manufactured by master swordsmiths in Toledo. Picasso executed various designs for the hilt which, in its final form, looked like a compact kit of Cocteauian symbols, the pommel forming a lyre, and the handle forged into a Greek profile, the haft sheathed in metal grating meant to represent the Palais-Royal, and the *coquille* bearing Cocteau's signature in the shape of a six-pointed star. This gaudy artifact was presented Cocteau on October 17, three days before his induction, at Mme. Weisweiller's mansion, and he responded in kind, with a few gaudy quatrains entitled "Thankful Acknowledgements to Friends Who Offered Me an Épée," in which allusions to Saint George and the Dragon verge on fond reminiscences of fellatio ("the angel whose mouth ejaculates a sword").

The induction ceremony eclipsed all of Cocteau's previous theatrical successes. Normally, anything connected with the French Academy induced smirks or polite yawns, but on October 19 people started queuing up for tickets at eleven a.m. and by late afternoon the line extended almost the length of Quai Conti. Twelve thousand people applied for seven hundred seats; on the black market, a ticket was selling at fifteen thousand francs, or about forty-five dollars. The galleries overflowed with fashionable writers, royalty, movie stars, models, and journalists invited by Cocteau. Newspapers gave it front-page billing. "The Enfant Terrible received beneath the Cupola," they announced, quoting the miraculous child himself: "I am an acrobat balancing himself on top of a pile of chairs."

The act unfolded without a slip. All mouths hushed as eight republican guards initiated a drum roll, like the drum roll accompanying Death's visitation in Cocteau's *Orphée*. He appeared in the Academician's official uniform, black with green facings, his sword at his side, and strode to the podium in step with the drumbeats, which ceased only when he rose to deliver his allocution. And what was the burden of his message? That he accepted, but in the name of *poètes maudits*, who, he failed to mention, never sought admission:

You are acquainted, Gentlemen, with the family whose members cannot boast or complain of belonging, for, far from being a privilege, it derives from a fatality which Verlaine dubbed malediction. A family of artists who, to avoid inciting the custodians of social order, to live with legal credentials, must add weights to their feet so as to remain moored on earth. In short, the members of this family, somewhat phantomatic and transparent, become artificially terrestrial in putting on deep-sea divers' boots, for otherwise they would rise in a flash to some indefinably mysterious surface. . . . It was a ghost's desire to share in the reign of living men which urged me toward you. . . . You know Paul Valéry's burst of wit after his election: "Now I shall have to let in the rabble." By rabble he meant the progeny of François Villon. I am sure, Gentlemen, that you are long-ing to redeem yourselves for having refused Balzac, and how can we correct this error without lending an ear to the race of sublime delinquents who allow France to amaze the world and who died in loneliness and poverty, some by their own hand, others in a hos-pital?

He was associating himself not with the brotherhood facing him, but with its absentees, the handful of glorious rejects such as Balzac and Baudelaire, the horde of nonapplicants living and dead in whose company he had never been allowed to sit for long. His words, however, could not immaterialize him. He now palpably stood for everything they despised, and he knew it. When volleys of applause followed his last word, was he perhaps thinking the expletive Daladier had been heard to utter beneath his breath on find-ing himself applauded by a hysterical crowd at Orly after his return from Munich: "Pricks!"? No one at Cocteau's side overheard any such tragic profanity. Queen Elizabeth of Belgium herself appeared at the reception held afterward on Place des États-Unis. In one fell swoop, Cocteau and his hostess had "arrived." "He who wins loses," Cocteau was fond of saying, and had dared say in his allocu-tion. But at the reception, noticing that a group of friends, includ-ing the Aurics, were looking at him askance, he went up to them and, as ever, pleaded innocent: "I only did it to make you laugh!"

Paul Léautaud, drawing upon the accumulated wisdom of his eighty-odd years, offered a jaundiced opinion of the ceremony, which he declined to attend:

Wednesday, 19 October, 6 a.m.—Perhaps the proverb holds true that wisdom comes with night-thoughts. This past night I have decided not to attend the academic reception for Jean Cocteau. It would do me in. Too much activity. And the difficulties I would have getting into the main hall, those steep stairs without a railing to grasp.

According to Jean Denoël, who telephoned me yesterday morning, the induction ceremony is highly fashionable. Many people asking for invitations; lots of them will remain on the sidewalk. He told me also that Cocteau made all necessary arrangements with building personnel to have me enter the inner courtyard through a private door. If memory serves me, that courtyard is out of bounds for the public, and on ceremonial days is lined with municipal guards in full dress. And am I about to exhibit myself there, me such an old man, so unsteady on my feet? And the sight of André Maurois, that manufacturer of cotton goods. Enough for the ethical side of it. There's also the physical angle, so to speak. I abhor whatever has to do with uniforms. The two-cornered hat, the black habit with green braid, the sword . . . This academic apotheosis of homosexuality, which really turns my stomach! . . . No, absolutely not! I'll stay at home. I'll read the speeches in a newspaper.

Thursday evening, October 20.—I bought *Le Monde* this evening, to read the academic allocutions, Cocteau's and Master André Maurois's. I write what I'm about to write because I'm sure it's just and true: both of them unreadable and lacking a scintilla of interest. Nothing alive. An exchange of preciosities. Makes me think of the *Précieuses Ridicules*.

What a good idea to have stayed at home, despite Cocteau's kind invitation.

Cocteau's election to the French Academy signified nothing and changed nothing. If he could persuade himself that tenure in this most official of bodies would somehow alleviate his insecurity, the insecure are apt to find comfort in the magic of officialdom. Honors and titles amounted in Cocteau's case to self-evasion, but had he not always adorned himself with the flashy appearances of erudition, and the symptoms of that divine malady from which he did not suffer, suffering because he did not? He would go on accruing diplomas in the hope that ultimately their sum would signify some poetic destiny, that he would "arrive." Yet weighting himself with academic braid and millinery only made him lighter in the esteem of those whom he truly respected. Because they refused to confer honor upon him, Cocteau sought it in every other shape and form.

In June, 1956 he returned to Oxford for that purpose. Twenty-six years before, he had gone there with Raymond Radiguet in deference, allegedly, to a dream; accompanied now by Francine Weisweiller and Doudou, he collected the fruits of not dreaming: an honorary doctorate of letters. "This red is very pretty," he declared, titillating the assembled dons. "It resembles the scarlet rugs of Isabeau de Bavière. And furthermore, it's far more esthetic than our French Academy uniforms. Am I happy? But of course, deliriously. I adore Oxford. People think I'm an iconoclast. I'm frightfully traditionalist." He was given a name and title to match his traditionalism, "Johannes Cocteau, Gallus poeta," but Johannes Cocteau would not be content until assured that among the poets of Gaul he was *primus inter pares*, and crowned accordingly by his own confreres.

In 1960 an election to name the "Prince of Poets" did in fact take place. It succeeded chiefly in bringing Cocteau and André Breton to verbal blows after a cold war which had endured for thirty years, and it illustrated, to the detriment of all concerned, the self-adulating hysteria of Parisian literary life.

This informal laureateship had been held for years by Paul Fort, an astonishingly prolific poet whose weekly meetings at the Closerie des Lilas had been an important locus of literary activity before World War I. In April, 1959, he died at an advanced age, and a literary review, *Nouvelles Littéraires*, arrogated to itself the responsibility of organizing an election to name his successor. Having polled several hundred poets, it conferred the title upon Jules Supervielle. The matter would no doubt have rested there if Supervielle had not died a fortnight after the election. An admirer of Cocteau's, one Philippe Mas who was known chiefly as the administrator of a poets' convention held yearly at Forges-les-Eaux, immediately staged another election, designing the ballot to suit his prejudices. The two hundred and forty-nine poets he telephoned (and most of the significant poets were not asked their opinion) could choose between Cocteau and anyone else. Not surprisingly, the majority chose Cocteau.

Mas then pronounced Cocteau Prince of Poets, bringing down

upon himself the wrath of the unconsulted who, led by Breton and
Jean Paulhan, formed a "committee of ten" to redress the wrong
they felt had been committed.[2] Paulhan wrote to Cocteau directly,
inviting him to dissociate himself from an election haphazard at best
and bigoted at worst, but Cocteau was reluctant to forfeit his title,
on the grounds that doing so would offend his electorate. "I have
received a letter from Paulhan," he wrote to Jouhandeau, "a letter
in which he expresses amazement that I should accept the title of
Prince when it was not given me according to Hoyle. Well, I am
grounding my claim on Paul Fort's, for before his death he had designated me his successor and went to Forges every year. My other
claims are (a) the fact that Supervielle's election met with everyone's approval though conducted by an ordinary review and (b)
the fact that the title reflects more the general demeanor of a long
career than any superiority over poets intent on proving their own,
etc. Would you give me your opinion in the matter? I am in a delicate position, for, in all humility, I should find it hard to annul the
vote of three hundred electors."

Whatever Jouhandeau's advice, Cocteau decided to abide by the
results of Mas's poll. Accordingly, Breton, whose interest in this
affair rose and fell in exact ratio to Cocteau's fluctuating pretentions, published a statement ferocious even by his standards. He
stirred up the muck of nearly half a century, doing himself no great
credit perhaps, but giving proof of his indissoluble grudge:

> It is generally known that, in view of Cocteau's clearly exaggerated
> claims to being a poet, poets like Aragon, Breton, Soupault, Tzara,
> Éluard, Péret, Desnos, Artaud, Prévert, and Char, in addition to
> younger men who have since observed a like diplomacy, decided
> around 1920 never to bother with him, never, under any circum-
> stances, to answer his gesticulations, however provoking they often
> were. Now that our silence can be said to have accomplished its end,
> it is not too late to break it.
>
> Everyone who knew Apollinaire heard him declare that it was
> Cocteau he portrayed (lyrically, of course) beneath the guise of
> *fapoite Paponnat*, *fapoite* being a contraction of *faux poète*, or coun-

2. The other eight were Gracq, Jouve, Mallet, Ponge, Soupault, Thomas, Ungaretti,
and André Pieyre de Mandiargues.

terfeit poet. Apollinaire specified that he meant by this "anti-poet." And the work clearly designates him as public enemy no. 1. Aragon, Breton, and Soupault will all testify to that effect.

Reverdy's opinion was in no way different and never wavered. Soupault can report statements he made on the subject before his death.

Why must Cocteau be considered the anti-poet?

Because in his writing the mechanics of the image—the image being that element by which poetic ability can be measured—always works backwards. . . .

He must be considered the anti-poet because his constitution is that of the arch impostor, the born con man. His trick has always been to pass off anticonformism as conformism, and vice versa. He was already doing this forty years ago, in connection with Radiguet. He merely repeated his sleight-of-mind, with still greater impudence, on being elected to the Academy.

We are concerned here with a title which has not hitherto been profaned. Had Edmond Rostand been elected Prince of Poets in 1912 (the year of Fort's election), his election would have been less grave than Cocteau's in 1960, for if Cocteau and Rostand are rhymers of the same stamp, Rostand never pretended to be otherwise. Should Cocteau win this reelection, his victory will have come about through machinations like those behind the farce of Forges-les-Eaux, machinations for which he is justly celebrated.

Breton thus buttressed himself against a Cocteau victory by disqualifying in advance any election Cocteau might win. Cocteau in turn prepared himself for defeat by dismissing any poet who would consent to usurp his throne. "Paulhan's poll," he wrote to a friend, "has no legitimacy. Any poet worthy of the name would never agree to take my place. Strange era, ours."

The new election, organized by the "committee of ten," provided for two ballots in case no one received a clear majority on the first. Early in October, at a noisy and populous convocation on the Terrasse Martini overlooking the Champs-Élysées, Jean Béarn announced the results of the first ballot: Saint-Jean Perse had polled 96 votes, Jean Cocteau 86, and André Breton 61. Philippe Mas, who was wearing a black ribbon round his neck for the occasion, then rose to announce the results of a counterelection he had held to ratify the original choice of Cocteau. Of the nearly 1300 questioned, 1174, he said, approved Cocteau's laureateship. These statistics were greeted with shouts of "Down with poets! Death to poets!" which provoked a wild Donnybrook. The proceedings lost what little dignity remained when Maurice Lemaître, director of a small publication called *La poésie nouvelle* declared that the five thousand subscribers to his review had elected one Isador Isou god and emperor of poets. M. Isou acknowledged his title in person, and appointed M. Lemaître his viceroy. Little wonder that these high jinks inspired Breton and company to resume a silence they regretted having broken. The final ballot never took place, but if Saint-Jean Perse was cheated of certain victory he received ample compensation for it when, in November, the Nobel Committee awarded him the literature prize. For Cocteau the committee reserved no consolation trophy.

It is axiomatic that the greater one's material presence the more one stands to lose, the greater one's power the more beholden one has become to the source of power (barring heroism). Always fearful of asserting himself in issues of great moment, Cocteau was now more discreet than ever. He had come to deserve Mallarmé's epitaph on Edgar Allan Poe's tomb: "Into Himself Eternity has transformed him." Substitute *arrivisme* for the word eternity and the same static effect would be achieved, though immanently rather than transcendentally. Cocteau's "arrival" had merely brought him full circle, back to himself in minuscule, the prisoner of adults whom he wished to please, talking as if his life depended on it, anxious to shine brightest in the poetic heavens, and wanting certificates of his magnitude. Indeed, he was apt to portray himself now as the *primum mobile* of all avant-gardes, past and present, literary and cinematic, which prompted one critic to accuse him of being "a madman who thinks he is Jean Cocteau." Being Jean Cocteau, at any rate, was a full-time occupation. It required him to address conventions, to appear among the great, to broadcast his voice, to rival Picasso at ceramics and Matisse at chapel art, to quote himself as if he were a literary tradition in his own right, to exhaust himself performing public acts of piety likely to memorialize his name.

In the guide to the Saint-Pierre Chapel in Villefranche, which he had spent much of 1956 and part of 1957 decorating, Cocteau offered his patented self-apology: "Anticonformist conformism is in fashion. The avant-garde has become the classicism of the twentieth century. All the right wings now have the virtue of leftism. . . . A free man owes it to himself to perform an act worthy of underlining the astonishing attitude of Raymond Radiguet who first discovered that the avant-garde, not tradition, must be opposed: an attitude which I have made my rule of life. Entering the French Academy was an anti-intellectual act calculated to illustrate this attitude. I then had to bolster this act with some work. Decoarting a chapel struck me as being the ideal solution." In 1925 Cocteau had spent his summer writing the *Letter to Jacques Maritain*. Now, some thirty years later, he painted a chapel, sandwiching any number of small impieties between clamorous conversions.

But he was never sufficiently free to hazard an opinion in some truly consequential matter. Sooner than risk estranging part of his audience, he would shift to anodyne topics of conversation. Sooner than suffer the discomforts of any weighty commitment, he would plead ignorance of the cause at stake. Hence his silence during the Hungarian Revolution of 1956. When James Lord published an open letter to Picasso in *Combat* exhorting the painter to break ranks with the Communist party, Cocteau, offended that *his* silence had not been conspicuous enough to inspire an open letter, fearful that it might, and apt to confuse himself with Picasso anyway, managed to take the American's criticism personally. He wrote Lord an unsolicited reply which bears out André Breton's contention that Cocteau's native habitat was behind-the-scenes:

My dear James,
   You know how I abhor showdowns and those clumsy stains which even cleaning fluid of soul cannot subsequently remove. Your letter to Picasso hurt me deeply. These are things to be thrashed out in private, never in public, for such things are quite beyond the public's comprehension. Why stage the bloody *corridas* they like watching just to spice their mediocre existences? Let this error fade with time, it is unworthy of us. I met you through Picasso and you have consistently shown that what you like in me is the straight and somewhat naïve line incapable of following the intelligentsia's zigzags. The last

thing I want is a tiff, but neither should I like to see myself the victim of my weakness for being argued out of my own point of view.
When Picasso read your letter, he felt as though a weapon were
brandished at him by a comrade who had free run of his house. But I
mustn't go on needling this fresh wound lest I prove unworthy of
your confidence.

P.S. A simple soul who knows nothing about us, Madeleine,[3] *cried*
on reading your letter in the newspaper.

Cocteau took cover behind simplicity whenever it proved convenient, and denounced mind in favor of "heart" whenever his own
lost courage in its sophisticated maze. Under duress, he defended
himself with the rocklike clichés of his bourgeois brethren.

There was always Mme. Weisweiller's lap, thankfully, and into it
he curled. "We're striving for a desert-isle style of life," he had
written to a friend in 1952. Alas, he had stranded himself with
companions unequipped to keep his mind alert. The verbal assaults
of a critic such as André Parinaud may have provoked in Cocteau
spasms of intercostal neuralgia, but perhaps, inadmissibly, he
needed neuralgia to feel awake. Indeed, his work suffered to the extent that Cap-Ferrat did become a desert isle. Cut off from the rest
of the world, Cocteau gave vent to his passion for self-résumé. On
the occasion of his seventieth year, he filmed his "testament." The
Testament d'Orphée, shot at the villa Santo-Sospir in 1959, takes as
its frame of reference Cocteau's previous works; *The Infernal
Machine* and *Orpheus*, rehearsing, with less art than sheer introver-
sion, the theme of visibility and invisibility. "This film shall be far
more austere than *Blood of a Poet*," wrote Cocteau to Milorad in
January, 1959. "The film opens with a kind of abstract farce, à la
Goldoni, on time and space. That sequence plunges me into a series
of obscure intrigues from which Cégèste saves me. . . . It is a kind
of Bach fugue with Godsent, or Devilsent charm." Telling his
legend had become such a familiar exercise for Cocteau that the
Testament simulates, at twice remove from reality, the undigested
reality of home movies.

As for his later verse and prose, they have a patina sixty years

3. Madeleine, it will be remembered, was Cocteau's maid and factotum, a kind of
female Leporello.

old. Senescence restored in Cocteau the subversive melodrama of his youth; he became once again the young esthete of 1900, finding artificial paradise in Spain and Venice, conjugating the lurid and the mystical, fabricating object-poems in the symbolist style, involuting his syntax with a vengeance, worshiping the *ange du bizarre* whatever its epiphany, but above all the poetry of Góngora and the architecture of Gaudi. His poem "Gondola of the Dead," in which the gondola is compared to a scorpion whose tail is poised to strike itself, gives a vivid idea of his late, mannered style. It runs, in part, as follows:

Debout Lord Byron et Wagner
Et toutes leurs belles mortes
Le menton sur les diamants les narines
Palpitantes l'œil
Frappé jusqu'au velours
Par ton poing Eros et la gifle
D'innombrables pigeons qui marchent
Les mains dans le dos sur le marbre
De long en large et soudain rejoignent
Dans un ouragan de soie
Les aptères réfugiés
Sur les corniches

. . . . . .

Belles dames adriatiques
Vénus qui des nacres vint
Ira-t-elle mettre à vos doigts
(Du sommeil elles sont les algues)
Doge votre profonde bague?

Byron and Wagner lording it
Among all their dead beauties
Chins resting on diamonds nostrils
Palpitating eyes
Dazed unto their velvet
By your fist Eros and the slap
Of countless pigeons walking
Hands behind their backs on the marble
To and fro and brusquely joining

> In a gale of silk
> Their apterous kin roosting
> In stone asylum
> On the cornices
>
> . . . . . .
> Lovely pearls of the Adriatic
> Will Venus who sprang from nacred shells
> Place upon your fingers
> (Which are the seaweed of sleep)
> Doge your mysterious ring?

Cocteau was not fated to die in the sumptuous sloth of Santo-Sospir, however. Mme. Weisweiller grew weary of life on a desert isle before he did. After some ten years of relative seclusion with Cocteau she wanted a man instead of a divinity and found him in the shape of an aging playboy, who had once seemed destined for a brilliant diplomatic career but fell victim to alcohol and now supported himself by writing detective novels. Perhaps he saw in Francine Weisweiller his chance to repeal years of wasted obscurity, for, thanks to her association with Cocteau, she had become a celebrated personality. In any case, he and Cocteau—both of them formidable perorators—could not tolerate one another; Cocteau, after a succession of quarrels and sordid delations, found himself evicted from Santo-Sospir. He remained in Villefranche a while, then brought his shattered self to Jean Marais's charming villa in Marnes-la-Coquette outside Paris where he spent the spring of 1960 mending. It is sadly typical that Cocteau, having freshly suffered humiliation at the hands of a shrew, should have begged her friendship. Jean Marais telephoned Mme. Weisweiller on his behalf. She answered his representations with a cold voice.

Cocteau settled for good in Milly-la-Forêt, escaping the wave of boredom which periodically curled over him with sojourns in Paris and voyages abroad, to Sweden in 1960, to Spain in 1961, to Poland in 1962. His health was ruined. In 1959 he had suffered another rather slight heart attack but, ignoring it, he continued to work feverishly. There seemed no end to his prefaces, to his radio interviews, to his letters (never more than one page long and meandering about all four margins as if reluctant to admit the existence of a reverse side). But even as he puttered, Cocteau was trying to put together a kind of last-ditch epic, or "saga" as he called it. "I dare not yet answer you," he wrote to Élise Jouhandeau in 1962, "and here is why. When I was ill with intestinal flu, I had to write, lying on my back, a long saga entitled provisionally *Requiem*. Now that I have recovered, my hieroglyphs are totally illegible. Deciphering them is the task now absorbing me, and I have no idea how long it will take."

The provisional title stuck, and Cocteau finally deciphered his hieroglyphs, but *Requiem* did not bring him apotheosis. It seems more a digression than an epic, despite its length, its division into cantos (called "periods"), its Dantesque itinerary from a private hell (inhabited by the chimerae of Greek antiquity) to Heaven by way of Spain, his childhood in Maisons-Laffitte, the Middle Ages, the rocks of Easter Island. Like *The Cape of Good Hope*, it seems to be a brief poem stretched to indecent lengths, sustaining itself, for lack of any real armature, with wizardly word plays, switching from Alexandrines to octosyllabic lines and back again as if to catch its second and third wind, heaping image upon image, and resting on homages to da Vinci and Manolete. Cocteau rummaged his mind for the accumulated names, places, aphorisms, and metaphors of a lifetime, and even came up with an epitaph: "Without having lived I die." *Requiem* was appropriately titled. It represented Cocteau's last résumé, and he knew it well:

> Oh you, dark Lord whose dwelling-place I am
> . . . . . .
> Answer me, are you there?
> And just as I was hoping my death had half died
> You kindle with the sun the pyre on which I die

In April, 1963, Cocteau suffered a massive coronary, yet somehow survived to write another hundred letters. This time, however, he felt spent in every fiber of his body. Doped on sedatives and antibiotics, he wrote to Marcel Jouhandeau: "I'm trying to climb back up a slippery slope, and I'm having trouble doing it." In July he moved to Jean Marais's house, where an oxygen tank stood at his bedside. Letters came pouring in, as well as recorded get-well messages from the great and the celebrated. Even those less well-disposed toward Cocteau felt stirrings of sympathy. The sympathy subsided, however, when Cocteau proved so slow in dying. Robert Craft wrote in his diary:

A journalist calls asking Igor Stravinsky to record a get-well message to Cocteau, as Braque and Picasso have already done. I.S. refuses, however, and so firmly that parts of the telephone fly off as he cradles the receiver. Then at lunch, with all ears to him, he says that *"Cocteau ne peut pas mourir sans faire réclame"* (Cocteau can't die without making publicity out of it). Though part of this remark is to be taken merely as a sign of reversion to type—as I.S. became more Russian in Russia, so in Paris he always returns to that between-the-wars society which lived for the clever remark—there is nevertheless a change of feeling. Only two weeks ago, the news of Cocteau's heart attack (or the thought of the subtraction and the narrowing circle) deeply upset him. Then, when a few days ago he heard that Cocteau had begun to recover, little signs of annoyance began to appear, as though, having already written off an account, he disliked reopening the books.

Cocteau himself was duped by his signs of recovery, for in September, ignoring Marais's plea to remain, he moved back to his house in Milly, confident that the worst was over, though deeply depressed at not being able to recover his strength. "I am surrounded by doctors who have torn me from death without bringing me back to life," he grieved to his old friend, Louis Gautier-Vignal. Confined to bed much of the day, he worked at his last (still unpublished) book of memoirs, *Le Passé Défini* (*The Historical Past*) and received visits from his closest friends. He lived to celebrate his seventy-fourth birthday.

It was now Mme. Weisweiller's turn to make amends. She arrived in Milly the second week of October, hoping for a reconciliation. "You bring death with you," exclaimed Cocteau on seeing her.

At eight o'clock on the morning of Friday, October 11, French National Radio announced the death of Edith Piaf. Only one year before she had married a handsome, strapping coiffeur half her age and seemed about to begin life afresh when her health failed. In an effort to get well she settled in the Midi, but, sensing the imminence of death, returned to Paris. Throughout the morning of the 11th, reporters scurried about Paris collecting and recording eulogies. At noon, radio listeners heard Cocteau's voice pronounce the following words of praise:

> Edith Piaf dies consumed by a fire that brings her just glory. I have never known a being less frugal of soul than she; she not only spent her soul, she squandered it, she threw its gold out windows. It was my luck to offer her her first stage role, in 1940. She read the monologue of *Le Bel Indifférent*. She had recently telephoned me to say that she wanted to revive it in October. Like everyone who lives on courage, she did not envisage death and on several occasions even conquered it. At least we have salvaged her voice, that great, black-velvet voice magnifying whatever it sings. But if I retain her great voice, alas, I have lost in her a great friend.

At the very hour these words were being transmitted, Louis Aragon called Milly wanting an article about Piaf for his literary weekly, *Les Lettres Françaises*. Dermit explained that Cocteau was too feeble to speak on the telephone, but Cocteau rose to answer anyway, and, as he did, he felt sharp pains in his chest, signaling an attack of pulmonary edema. As the congestion grew swiftly worse, blood-tinged foam came bubbling out of his mouth and nose, staining the counterpane, and he began to choke. There was no oxygen tent on hand as there had been in Marais's house. By the time he could be transported downstairs, his rattle filled the house. At one o'clock in the afternoon, Cocteau was pronounced dead.

The following Monday, October 14, mourners began to stream into Milly. Those with official credentials were met at the door of the Maison du Bailli by an elderly servant who escorted them to the salon, which had been converted into a mortuary chamber. Cocteau's last letters lay unopened on an end table; next to them stood a photograph of the deceased, held in a lyre-shaped frame, and next to the photograph a tear-off calendar stilled at October 11. Perfume floated in the air. The shutters remained closed and Cocteau's embalmed corpse lay enveloped in semidarkness. For once, and for all, his face was serene. For once, the long, gesticulating hands in which he had taken such pride were still, folded across his breast. The spirit had flown, leaving behind a dead body adorned with all the trappings of archrespectability: about its neck the red collar signifying commandership in the Legion of Honor, at its side the Academic sword, at its feet a two-cornered hat. Roses and gladiolas lay piled against the coffin, spilling onto the floor and disguising an icon of Our Lady. Roses inundated the native balm and belladonna of Milly; a huge bouquet, sent by Maurice Chevalier, lay at the entrance to the town hall. It carried the dedication, "To the One and Only."

Cocteau's last request, that he be buried in his own garden, was for practical reasons denied. The funeral took place on a luminously clear October day. Ushers, wearing white gloves ("as if they were about to appear in one of Cocteau's films," observed one reporter), channeled the large crowd toward Milly's church, where an honor guard of firemen had aligned itself before the portal. Three administrative officers of the French Academy led the procession. They were followed by nine more academicians, including René Clair, André Maurois, Marcel Pagnol, Jean Paulhan, and Jean Rostand. The family came next, after Immortality—but a family ecumenical enough to include Jean Marais, Francine Weisweiller, Georges Auric, Serge Lifar, and Picasso's son Paolo. A motley throng of prefects and government ministers brought up the rear. Had Cocteau lived to stage his own funeral, he would surely have cast it and marshaled its acts more flamboyantly. The notable absentees would have been subpoenaed from all quarters of the globe. Indeed, there were those who half expected him to leap out of the wings and bark stage directions with that resonant, nasal voice of his, persuading the celebrants to do his bidding with fond diminutives and *chéris*. "I'm amazed," wrote Mauriac, "that he could do something as natural, as simple, as undevised as dying."

At Cocteau's request, red instead of black figured as the official color in the Office for the Dead. A member of the Saint-Eustache choir intoned the Credo, whereupon the funeral procession slowly wended its way across Milly to the chapel Cocteau had decorated, the Chapel of Saint Blaise des Simples. There, in a cemetery redolent of gentian and sweet mint, his coffin was lowered into the earth, with a lyre of red roses.

Bibliography

I. The Jacques Doucet literary library contains Cocteau's correspondence with André Gide, Albert Gleizes, Edmond Jaloux, Marcel and Élise Jouhandeau, Paul Léautaud, Francis Picabia, and Tristan Tzara. Unless a published source is specifically mentioned in the notes, it may be assumed that all letters quoted are in manuscript.

Quotations from Cocteau's published works will refer to the following editions (each title preceded by an initial used in the notes):

B *Bacchus.* (NRF, 1952)

BB *La Belle et la Bête. Journal d'un film.* (Monaco: Éditions du Rocher, 1958)

CBE *Le Cap de Bonne Espérance.* (Geneva: Marguerat, vol. III in *Œuvres Complètes,* 1947)

CN *La Comtesse de Noailles. Oui et Non.* (Paris: Librairie Académique Perrin, 1963)

CO *Cordon Ombilical.* (Paris, 1962)

DD *La Difficulté d'Être.* (Monaco: Éditions du Rocher, 1965)

DGS *Discours du Grand Sommeil.* (Geneva: Marguerat, *Œuvres Complètes,* vol. IV, 1947)

ET *Les Enfants Terribles.* (Geneva: Marguerat, *Œuvres Complètes,* vol. I, 1946)

FP *La Fin du Potomak.* (Geneva: Marguerat, *Œuvres Complètes,* vol. II, 1947)

GE *Le Grand Écart.* (See ET)

JI *Journal d'un Inconnu.* (Paris: Grasset, 1953)

LB *Le Livre Blanc.* Quotations in the text will refer to the English translation, *The White Paper.* (New York: The Macauley Company, 1958)

MJO *Le Mystère de Jean l'Oiseleur.* (Paris: Champion, 1952)

ML *Mystère Laïc.* (in *Essai de Critique Indirecte,* Paris: Grasset, 1932)

O *Opium.* (Paris: Club Français du Livre, 1957)

OP   *Opéra*. (Geneva: Marguerat, *Œuvres Complètes*, vol. IV, 1947)
OR   *Orphée. Film*. (Paris: André Bonne, 1961)
P   *Le Potomak*. (See FP)
PC   *Poésie Critique*, 2 vols. Contains *inter alias, Démarche d'un poète, Lettre à Jacques Maritain, Lettre aux Américains, Discours de Réception à l'Académie Royale de Belgique, Discours de Réception à l'Académie Française, Le Discours d'Oxford, Discours sur la Poésie, Le Secret Professionnel, D'un Ordre Considéré comme une Anarchie, Jean-Jacques Rousseau*. (Paris: Gallimard, 1959–1960)
PS   *Portraits-Souvenirs*. (Paris: Grasset, 1953)
PV   *Mon Premier Voyage*. (Geneva: Marguerat, *Œuvres Complètes*, vol. II, 1947)
RF   *Reines de la France*. (Paris: Grasset, 1952)
RO   *Le Rappel à l'Ordre*. (Paris: Stock, 1948), contains *Le Coq et l'Arlequin* and *Carte Blanche*.
SP   *Le Sang d'un Poète*. (Monaco: Éditions du Rocher, 1957)
T   *Théâtre*. (Paris: Grasset, 1957), 2 vols.
TI   *Thomas l'Imposteur*. (Geneva: Marguerat, *Œuvres Complètes*, vol. I, 1946)

The Marguerat edition of Cocteau's works, *Les Œuvres Complètes*, published in ten uniform volumes between 1946 and 1950, is far from complete. Bibliographies of Cocteau's *œuvre*, established in 1955 and 1959 respectively, may be found in Crosland's *Jean Cocteau* and in J. J. Kihm's *Cocteau*. In addition, Kihm's book contains a record of all tapes (up to 1960) made by Cocteau for French National Radio and available in the *Phonothèque* of the Radiodiffusion Télévision Française.

II. The following is a selective bibliography limited to books and articles which proved most useful in the preparation of the present biography. Where it is not clear from the title of a memoir what era it covers, an asterisk denotes pre-World War I, and a cross the interbellum period.

Adéma, Marcel. *Guillaume Apollinaire* (Paris, 1952)
Amouroux, Henri. *La Vie des Français sous l'Occupation* (Paris, 1965)
Antoine, André. *Antoine, Père et Fils* (Paris, 1962)
Arbellot, Simon. *La Fin du Boulevard* (Paris, 1964)
Arnaud, Lucien. *Charles Dullin* (Paris, 1952)
*Astruc, Gabriel. *Le Pavillon des Fantômes* (Paris, 1929)

Beaton, Cecil. *The Wandering Years, 1922–1939* (Boston, 1961)

*Bibesco, Marthe. (A) *La Duchesse de Guermantes. Laure de Sade, Comtesse de Chevigné* (Paris, 1951)

*———. (B) "Jean Cocteau et Son Étoile," *Revue Générale Belge,* December, 1963

Boissière, J. Galtier. *Mon Journal pendant l'Occupation* (Paris, 1944)

Borgal, Clément. *Jacques Copeau* (Paris, 1960)

Bourdet, Denise. (A) *Édouard Bourdet et Ses Amis* (Paris, 1945)

———. (B) "Jean Cocteau," an interview in *Pris sur le Vif* (Paris, 1957)

Brinnin, John Malcolm. *The Third Rose. A Biography of Gertrude Stein* (Boston, 1959)

Buckle, Richard. *In Search of Diaghilev* (New York, 1956)

†Cendrars, Blaise. *Trop C'est Trop* (Paris, 1957)

Chalupt, René. "Quelques Souvenirs sur Erik Satie," *La Revue Musicale,* June, 1952

Chaplin, Charles. *My Autobiography* (New York, 1964)

*Charles, Jacques. "*Caf' Conc*" (Paris, 1966)

Cladel, Judith. *Rodin* (Paris, 1950)

Cocéa, Alice. *Mes Amours que J'Ai Tant Aimés* (Paris, 1958)

*Colette. (A) *Mes Apprentissages* (Paris, 1936)

†———. (B) *Le Fanal Bleu* (Paris, 1949)

†———. (C) *En Pays Connu* (Paris, 1950)

†Cooper, Diana. *Trumpets from the Steep* (New York, 1960)

*Corpechot, Lucien. *Souvenirs d'un Journaliste.* Vol. III (Paris, 1937)

Craft, Robert. (A) *Conversations with Igor Stravinsky* (New York, 1959)

———. (B) *Expositions and Developments* (New York, 1962)

———. (C) *Dialogues and a Diary* (New York, 1963)

———. (D) *Themes and Episodes* (New York, 1962)

*Crespelle, J. P. *Montparnasse Vivant* (Paris, 1962)

Crosland, Margaret. *Jean Cocteau. A Biography* (New York, 1956)

*Daudet, Léon. (A) *Souvenirs* (Paris, 1920)

———. (B) *Quand Vivait Mon Père* (Paris, 1940)

*Daudet, Lucien. *Dans l'Ombre de l'Impératrice Eugénie* (Paris, 1935)

Deharme, Lise. *Les Années Perdues; Journal 1939–1949* (Paris, 1961)

Desbordes, Jean. *J'Adore* (Paris, 1928)

†Desnos, Youki. *Les Confidences de Youki* (Paris, 1957)

†Dolin, Anton. *Ballet Go Round* (London, 1938)

†Duke, Vernon. *Passport to Paris* (Boston, 1955)

*Dussane, Béatrix. *Dieux des Planches* (Paris, 1964)

Ehrlich, Blake. *Resistance. France 1940–1945* (Boston, 1965)

Everling-Picabia, Germaine. "C'Était Hier: Dada . . ." in *Les Œuvres Libres* (no. 109, June, 1955)

†Faÿ, Bernard. *Les Précieux* (Paris, 1966)

Fifield, William. "Interview with Cocteau" in *Paris Review* (Summer–Fall, 1964)

*Fouquières, Comte André de. *Mon Paris et Ses Parisiens*. 4 vols. (Paris, 1953–1956)

Fraigneau, André. (A) *Entretiens Autour du Cinématographe* (Paris, 1951)

———. (B) *Cocteau par Lui-même* (Paris, 1961)

———. (C) *Entretiens avec André Fraigneau* (Paris, 1951)

*Garros, Roland. *Mémoires* (Paris, 1966)

*Germain, André. (A) *Portraits Parisiens* (Paris, 1918)

†———. (B) "Un Demi-Siècle de Souvenirs" in *Adam International Review* (no. 300, 1965)

Ghéon, Henri. "La Danse de Sophocles," review which appeared in the *Nouvelle Revue Française*, September, 1912

Gide, André. (A) *Journal* (Paris, *Pléiade* edition, 1941)

———. (B) *Les Faux-Monnayeurs* (Paris, 1926)

———. (C) "Lettre Ouverte à Jean Cocteau," in the *Nouvelle Revue Française*, June 1, 1919

Gilot, Françoise. *Life with Picasso* (New York, 1964)

Gilson, René. *Jean Cocteau* (Paris, 1964—in Le Cinéma d'Aujourd'hui series)

Goesch, Keith. *Radiguet* (Paris, 1955)

†Goudeket, Maurice. *La Douceur de Vieillir* (Paris, 1966)

Grigoriev, Serge. *The Diaghilev Ballet* (London, 1953)

*Guitry, Sacha. *Si J'Ai Bonne Mémoire . . .* (Paris, 1952)

*Gramont, Élizabeth de. *Mémoires*. 4 vols. (Paris, 1928)

Guggenheim, Peggy. *Confessions of an Art Addict* (New York, 1960)

*Hahn, Reynaldo. *Notes. Journal d'un Musicien* (Paris, 1933)

†Hamnet, Nina. *Laughing Torso* (New York, 1932)

Hort, Jean. *La Vie Héroïque des Pitoëff* (Geneva, 1966)

Hugo, Valentine. (A) "Le Socrate que J'Ai Connu" in *La Revue Musicale*, June, 1952

———. (B) "Il y a Trente Ans" in *La Parisienne*, December, 1953

Jacob, Max. (A) *Lettres de Max Jacob à Jean Cocteau, 1919–1944* (Paris, 1949)

———. (B) *Correspondance 1921–1924* (Paris, 1955)

Jouhandeau, Élise. (A) *Joies et Douleurs d'une Belle Excentrique* (Paris, 1952)

———. (B) *Le Spleen Empanaché* (Paris, 1960)

———. (C) *Une Liane de Roses* (Paris, 1964)

Jullian, Philippe. *Robert de Montesquiou* (Paris, 1965)

Jünger, Ernst. *Journal de Guerre et d'Occupation*, 2 vols. (Paris, 1953)

Kahnweiler, Daniel-Henri. *Entretiens avec François Crémieux* (Paris, 1961)

*Karsavina, Tamara. *Theatre Street* (London, 1961)

*Kiem, Albert. *Le Demi-Siècle* (Paris, 1950)

Kihm, Jean-Jacques. *Cocteau* (Paris, 1960)

Kyrou, Ado. *Luis Buñuel* (New York, 1963)

Lannes, Roger. *Jean Cocteau* (Paris, 1945, in the "Poètes d'Aujourd'hui" series)

Lanoux, Armand. *Paris in the 'Twenties* (New York, 1960)

Léautaud, Paul. *Journal Littéraire* (Paris, 1954)

Lieven, Prince Peter. *The Birth of the Ballets Russes* (London, 1936)

Lifar, Serge. *Serge de Diaghilev* (Monaco, 1954)

Macdougall, Allan. *Isadora* (New York, 1960)

Marais, Jean. *Mes Quatre Vérités* (Paris, 1957)

Mariano, Nicky, *Forty Years with Bernard Berenson* (New York, 1966)

Markevitch, Igor. *Point d'Orgue. Entretiens avec Claude Rostand* (Paris, 1959)

†Martin du Gard, Maurice. *Les Mémorables*, 2 vols. (Paris, 1957–1960)

†Maurois, André. *Choses Nues* (Paris, 1963)

Mauriac, Claude. (A) *Jean Cocteau ou la Vérité du Mensonge* (Paris, 1945)

———. (B) *Conversations with André Gide* (New York, 1966)

Mauriac, François. (A) *Mémoires Intérieurs* (Paris, 1959)

———. (B) *Nouveaux Mémoires Intérieurs* (Paris, 1965)

Milhaud, Darius. (A) *Entretiens avec Claude Rostand* (Paris, 1952)

———. (B) *Notes sans Musique* (Paris, 1963)

Mistinguett. *Toute ma Vie*, 2 vols. (Paris, 1954)

†Monnier, Adrienne. *Rue de l'Odéon* (Paris, 1960)

Morand, Paul. *Journal d'un Attaché d'Ambassade, 1916–1917* (Paris, 1949)

Myers, Rollo. *Erik Satie* (London, 1948)

Nadeau, Maurice. *Histoire du Surréalisme* (Paris, 1945)

Nicolson, Harold. *Diaries and Letters. The War Years, 1939–1945* (New York, 1967)

†Oberlé, Jean. *La Vie d'Artiste* (Paris, 1956)

Ouellette, Fernand. *Edgard Varèse* (Paris, 1966)

Oxenhandler, Neal. *Scandal and Parade* (Rutgers, 1957)

Painter, George. *Marcel Proust*, 2 vols. (London, 1966)

Peeters, Georges. *Les Monstres Sacrés du Ring* (Paris, 1959)

Penrose, Roland. *Picasso* (New York, 1958)

Perreux, Gabriel. *La Vie Quotidienne des Civils en France pendant la Grande Guerre* (Paris, 1966)

Piaf, Edith. *Au Bal de la Chance* (Paris, 1958)

Pillaudin, Roger. *Jean Cocteau Tourne Son Dernier Film* (Paris, 1960)

*Polignac, Princesse Edmond de. "Mémoires" in *Horizon* (London, August, 1945)

*Porché, Simone. *Sous de Nouveaux Soleils* (Paris, 1957)

* †Porel, Jacques. *Fils de Réjane*, 2 vols. (Paris, 1951–1952)

Poulenc, Francis. *Moi et Mes Amis* (Geneva, 1963)

Ray, Man. *Self-Portrait* (London, 1963)

Rivière, Jacques. *Marcel Proust et Jacques Rivière. Correspondance, 1914–1922* (Paris, 1956)

†Rose, Sir Francis. *Saying Life* (London, 1961)

*Rostand, Maurice. *Confessions d'un Demi-Siècle* (Paris, 1948)

†Sachs, Maurice. (A) *Le Sabbat* (Paris, 1946)

†———. (B) *Au Temps du Bœuf sur le Toit* (Paris, 1948)

†———. (C) *La Décade de l'Illusion* (Paris, 1950)

†———. (D) *La Chasse à Courre* (Paris, 1945)

Sanouillet, Michel. (A) *Picabia* (Paris, 1964)

———. (B) *Dada à Paris* (Paris, 1965)

———. (C) *Francis Picabia et 391*, vol. 2 (Paris, 1966)

Sert, Misia. *Misia and the Muses* (New York, 1953)

*Shattuck, Roger. *The Banquet Years* (New York, 1958)

Siohan, Robert. *Stravinsky* (Paris, 1959)

Stéphane, Roger. *Jean Cocteau* (Paris, 1964, *hors commerce*)

Stravinsky, Igor. *An Autobiography* (New York, 1962)

Thomson, Virgil. *Virgil Thomson* (New York, 1966)

Tintori, Giampiero. *Igor Stravinsky* (Paris, 1966)

* †Warnod, André. *Fils de Montmartre* (Paris, 1955)

Wescott, Glenway. *Good-bye Wisconsin* (New York, 1928)

White, Eric Walter. *Stravinsky* (Berkeley, 1966)

Willy (Henri Gauthier-Villars). *Souvenirs* (Paris, 1925)

Notes

Chapter 1: *L'Enfance Terrible*

PAGE

6. "*fils d'une famille bourgeoise* . . ." P, p. 123
10. "Childhood has its odors . . ." PS, p. 62
12. "If I close my eyes . . ." PS, p. 105
12. "An intelligent student . . ." Georgel catalogue, p. 11
13. "Disciplinary reasons . . ." PS, p. 123
13. "At an age . . ." P, p. 147
14. "Only now . . ." PS, p. 145
14. "The theatre used to fill my dreams . . ." PS, p. 40
15. "They visited the machine room . . ." Adrian, *Histoire des Cirques Parisiens*, p. 53
17. "After two hours . . ." Léon Daudet (A), p. 206
19. "We climbed Rue Lepic . . ." Keim, p. 151
19. "Noctambulism was at its height . . ." Astruc, p. 167
21. "Cocteau and his friend . . ." Mistinguett, I, p. 83
24. "Life interests me . . ." in Bibl. de l'Arsenal dossier
24. "A gamin, a goose . . ." in de Max, *Mémoires*, Paris, 1918
27. "He would advance . . ." Dussane, p. 190
30. "Since I was marveling . . ." de Max, *Mémoires*
31. "It must be a dream . . ." DD, p. 200

Chapter 2: *A l'Ombre des Jeunes Gens en Fleur*

33. "He had something . . ." PS, p. 170
34. "Voluble, white, and melting . . ." Colette (A), p. 73
34. "We Semites . . ." Willy, p. 79
38. "Let us not be deceived. . . ." *Decadence*, New York, 1921, pp. 188 ff.
36. "She was large . . ." PS, pp. 171 ff.
37. "A death mask . . ." PS, p. 178
38. "Cocteau was very different . . ." Rostand, p. 122
40. "Watch out . . ." Painter, II, p. 229
41. "Cocteau and I . . ." Rostand, p. 36
44. "Had I been a poet . . ." PS, p. 194
45. "What I fear for him . . ." Painter, II, p. 176
46. "He made a triumphal entry . . ." Bibesco (B), p. 45
47. "I was imprudent enough . . ." Simone Porché, p. 209
48. "When I saw Blanche at Dieppe. . . ." Gramont, II, pp. 139 ff.
48. "When I come to speak about. . . ." Ghéon, *NRF*, September, 1912
50. "She was just leaving some lecture . . ." PS, p. 208
52. "She always had resplendent eyes . . ." CN, p. 198
52. "She was performing . . ." PS, p. 213
53. "As a child . . ." Corpechot, p. 119
53. "The countess stuffed her ears . . ." CN, p. 21

PAGE

53. "Madame de Noailles is an Oriental princess . . ." Corpechot, p. 114
54. "It would be eleven o'clock. . . ." CN, p. 206
54. "She straightaway gave vent . . ." CN, p. 121
55. "In the evening . . ." CN, p. 205
56. "I admit that as soon as I felt . . ." PS, p. 211
56. "I have written this night . . ." Corpechot, p. 118
57. "M. Jean Cocteau seems to me . . ." Ghéon, NRF, September, 1912
60. " 'Simplify your handwriting'. This remark . . ." CN, p. 97
60. "How many times did I hear myself reproached . . ." CN, p. 96

Chapter 3: Saints and Maenads

62. "Mais je ne tiens pas . . ." Jullian, p. 46
62. "Dandyism appears especially . . ." NRF (Pléiade), p. 900
63. "Dandyism is above all . . ." NRF, p. 899
66. "Unimpeachable sources . . ." Jullian, p. 285
66. "I shall be delighted . . ." Jullian, p. 282
67. "Cocteau was imitating everyone . . ." Gramont, II, p. 239
70. "I owe him many treasures . . ." PS, p. 187
71. "a handsome boy, curled and pomaded . . ." Painter, II, pp. 228 ff.
71. "It is understood that Jean . . ." Lucien Daudet, p. 160
72. "I was beginning to lose my nerve . . ." PS, p. 199
72. "Lucien Daudet, Mauriac, and I . . ." PS, p. 205
73. "I, who am not and shall doubtless . . ." Hahn, p. 137
74. "Among Cocteau's letters . . ." Rostand, p. 169
74. "When we had coaxed him . . ." DD, p. 109
76. "Marcel, why at least . . ." PC, II, p. 123
76. "He supplemented his epistle . . ." O, p. 178
77. "Swann is a gigantic miniature . . ." Painter, II, p. 201
78. "This young man staged . . ." Ibid., pp. 160 ff.
79. "sculptured by the air . . ." Art Nouveau, ed. Selz and Constantine, New York, 1959, p. 62
79. "Unending acclamations . . ." Macdougall, p. 87.
79. "The school of the ballet today . . ." Ibid, p. 102
82. "there was not a middle-class home . . ." Lieven, p. 126
83. "The red curtain rose on spectacles . . ." Lifar, p. 197
83. "The success of the ballets is based . . .' Lieven, p. 99
84. "I am: 1. A charlatan full of brio . . ." Tintori, p. 37
84. "did not know the meaning of economy . . ." Figaro Littéraire, November, 1953
85. "Diaghilev was not a creative genius . . ." Lieven, p. 32
86. "What did he desire? . . ." Lifar, p. 194
87. "Like a mischievous fox terrier . . ." Karsavina, p. 239
88. "I want the virgin! . . ." Morand, p. 79
89. "In the name of everything you hold dear . . ." Buckle, p. 95
89. "Diaghilev was doubtful . . ." Grigoriev, p. 66
89. "There was once a young man . . ." L'Art Décoratif de Léon Bakst, Paris, 1913
90. "Nijinsky was brooding as usual . . ." DD, p. 50
91. "Beginning around 1912 . . ." RO, p. 47
91. "The orchestra played unheard . . ." Lifar, pp. 252 ff.
92. "My true friendship with Stravinsky . . ." RO, p. 53
92. "His conversation was a highly . . ." Craft, (C) p. 45
93. "It was in a way the first draft . . ." RO, p. 53
93. "It was for me a period . . ." Ibid., p. 53
94. "Cocteau was very brilliant . . ." Craft (C), p. 113
94. "One night at the theatre . . ." P, p. 122

PAGE

94. "The Eugène, the first Eugène . . ." Ibid., p. 47
95. "The arc lamps and the mercury tubes . . ." ibid., p. 116
95. "I tried to surprise . . ." Ibid., p. 119
96. "Potomak's role is to be . . ." P, p. 118
96. "I had swiftly ascended . . ." Ibid., p. 15
96. "I didn't inherit a ship . . ." Ibid., p. 107
97. "The greatest literary masterpieces . . ." Ibid., p. 17
97. "For a long time . . ." Rimbaud, *Oeuvres*, Garnier, 1960, p. 228
97. "Discover what the public . . ." P, p. 39

Chapter 4: War Theatre

100. "I took no pleasure . . ." Gide, *Journal*, I, 473
101. "There are some people . . ." Morand, p. 85
102. "Rendezvous with Jean Cocteau . . ." *Revue Générale Belge*, December, 1963, p. 51
104. "From afar . . ." Sert, p. 137
105. "I am undergoing. . . ." Ibid., pp. 201 ff.
106. "An artist friend . . ." *Le Mot*, March 13, 1915
106. "Schönberg is knocking . . ." *Le Mot*, February 27, 1915
109. "One night . . ." Faÿ, p. 34
110. "Well the angel . . ." DGS, p. 25
112. "a feminine landscape . . ." TI, p. 151
113. "Listen, you're not about . . ." Stéphane, p. 99
114. "Had he been an authentic marine . . ." TI, p. 161
115. "I am distressed . . ." Gide (A), I, p. 516
116. "Oh, my child . . ." Porel, II, p. 6
116. "It is impossible . . ." Morand, p. 33
117. "To think, all my Julys . . ." Ibid., p. 273
118. "Somebody must have stepped . . ." Ibid., p. 295
119. "I much prefer clowns . . ." Ibid., p. 79
119. "Cocteau has periods . . ." Ibid., p. 246
120. "Imagine, wasting . . ." Ibid., p. 266
124. "I'm suffering too much . . ." *Revue Musicale*, June, 1952, p. 144
126. "We borrowed it from . . ." Astruc, p. 113
126. "We were simultaneously . . ." RO, p. 55
127. "Satie is an angel . . ." Sert, p. 142
130. "Dear friend, excuse me..." *Les Heures de Milly-la-Forêt*, Paris, 1956 (catalogue of the Cocteau-Satie-Six festival), item 31.
130. "Dear friend, I received the manuscript . . ." Ibid.
130. "Don't be anxious . . ." Ibid., item 13

Chapter 5: Arts and Craft

135. "He was a handsome little guy . . ." Crespelle, p. 20
135. "it felt like a triumph . . ." Penrose, p. 195
136. "My poor Eva . . ." Penrose, p. 189
136. "The plaster frieze . . ." Review *Du* (Zurich), October, 1961
139. "In Montparnasse, I kept my Right Bank costumes. . . ." PC, II, p. 257
139. "The Rotonde was our mall. . . ." PC, II, p. 256
140. "If I close my eyes . . ." PC, II, p. 258
142. "a spark in the comet's tail . . ." Lifar, p. 267
142. "If only you knew how sad . . ." Penrose, p. 191
143. "It's settled . . ." Ibid.
143. "When Picasso showed us . . ." RO, p. 55
144. "I have worked at . . ." *Les Heures de Milly-la-Forêt*, item 19

PAGE

146. "We walked by moonlight . . ." RO, p. 286
147. "Instead of the sunshine . . ." Stravinsky, p. 67
147. "Their rivalry centered . . ." Lifar, p. 267
147. "I composed a background . . ." RO, p. 58
148. "In Rome, I saw nothing of Rome . . ." ML, p. 60
152. "Full house yesterday . . ." Morand, *Journal*, p. 243
153. "Sir and dear friend . . ." Shattuck, p. 153
154. "One doesn't know whether to admire . . ." Gide (A), I, p. 688
158. "I dined on this rainy Sunday . . ." Morand, p. 84
159. "Many things that grew up quickly . . ." RO, p. 86
161. "I came across him during a reception . . ." Milhaud (B), p. 101
163. "I was flattered . . ." *Revue Musicale*, June 1952, p. 44
164. "Of Six there are only five . . ." P. Rosenfeld, *Musical Chronicle* (1917–23), N.Y. 1923 (September, 1921, Chronicle)
164. "Those who tell me . . ." Review *391*, No. 17, p. 3
165. "which seemed to grind up . . ." Milhaud (B), p. 103
166. "The music hall, the circus . . ." RO, p. 30
167. "I admire the harlequins. . . ." RO, p. 13
168. "Theatre corrupts everyone . . ." RO, p. 41
168. "I consider *The Rite of Spring* . . ." RO, p. 41
169. "White paper, ink . . ." DD, p. 19
169. "When I read a book . . ." DD, p. 203
170. "I congratulate myself . . ." O, p. 283

Chapter 6: The Angels Come of Age

171. "He was handsome . . ." Monnier, p. 99
171. "The house I live in . . ." Nadeau, p. 321
172. "All schools . . ." Valéry, *Oeuvres* (Pléiade, 1957) I, p. 720
173. "I concede a little affection . . ." Nadeau, p. 45
174. "Jacques Vaché's swift journey . . ." *Pas Perdus*, Paris, 1924
175. "He adored poetry . . ." Monnier, p. 102
177. "Agreed, we have resolved . . ." Sanouillet (B), p. 84
178. "An entire generation's idea . . ." Garaudy, R. *L'Itinéraire d'Aragon*, Paris, 1961, p. 26
179. "I would have become . . ." Sanouillet, p. 449
179. "I've just been strongly moved . . ." Ibid., p. 450
182. "In Paris, nothing afoot . . ." Ibid., p. 454
183. "I see him browsing . . ." DD, p. 181
184. "The morning of Armistice . . ." DD, p. 179
184. "My dear André . . ." Adéma, p. 253
184. "His little room . . ." DD, p. 180
185. "I elaborate . . ." CBE, p. 22
186. "Listen to me . . ." Ibid., p. 42
187. "Jean began to declaim . . ." Fay, p. 270
188. "He was such a spoiled child . . ." Monnier, p. 104
190. "Dear Madame, Happy New Year . . ." *Les Heures de Milly-la-Forêt*, item 21
191. "I need to live sprawled . . ." Sanouillet (A), p. 19
193. "Jean Cocteau is in everybody's . . ." Sanouillet, p. 485
194. "Picabia, who is . . ." Everling, p. 151 (quoting Pierre de Massot)
194. "Cocteau enters . . ." Ibid.
194. "Cocteau's face lit up . . ." Ibid., p. 153
195. "You know my candor . . ." Sanouillet (C), p. 192
197. "The word 'cacodylate' has not . . ." Everling, p. 172
197. "You have no idea how alert . . ." Sanouillet, p. 441
201. "I have read, I have reread . . ." *Figaro*, October 19, 1963

Notes
PAGE

202. "I am profoundly grateful . . ." Rivière, p. 268
202. "Beneath this rubric, I propose . . ." RO, p. 79
206. "Poets must bring . . ." T, I, p. 4
206. "Phono One: The bride . . ." Ibid., I, p. 13
208. "The secret of Theatre . . ." Ibid., I, p. 6
209. "I got assistance . . ." Milhaud (B), p. 106
211. "I'll arrange dinner for you . . ." Maurice Martin du Gard, I, p. 169
214. "who engaged in hostile banter . . ." Painter, II, pp. 344 ff.
215. "Those New Year's Eve galas . . ." Cendrars, p. 137
216. "When she stood up . . ." Sachs (C), p. 170
217. "It was the warehouse of gay . . ." Sachs (B), p. 91
217. "Cocteau had me sit down . . ." Fraigneau, p. 13
218. "Cocteau, wearing a hat . . ." Sachs (B), p. 91
219. "My relations with Gide . . ." PC, II, p. 189

Chapter 7: An Illusion of Paradise

220. "From the first . . ." DD, p. 33
222. "Max was marvelous . . ." Gilot, p. 79
223. "He liked above all the idea . . ." Goesch, page ix
224. "How many times I sat . . ." Ibid., p. 14
225. "Radiguet used to read our works . . ." DD, p. 26
229. "The accursed-angel attitude . . ." RO, p. 190
229. "Poetry in its raw state . . ." Ibid., p. 218
231. "Living is a horizontal fall . . ." O, p. 31
232. "The next day I related my dream . . ." ML, p. 70
233. "I am a lie . . ." OP, p. 152, "Le Paquet Rouge"
233. "I staked my fortune . . ." RO, p. 247
234. "J.C.: Is it the person . . ." Valentine Hugo (B), p. 1683
234. "A disorderly man . . ." Le diable au corps (Livre de Poche, 1964), p. 185
235. "My last memory . . ." Goesch, p. 54
235. "Listen to something . . ." preface to Le Bal du Comte d'Orgel (Paris, 1924)
236. "I appeal to your reason . . ." Jacob (B), p. 262
237. "I wanted to attain . . ." MJO, p. 10

Chapter 8: The Versatile Inferno

240. "As for the inseparable friends . . ." Kahnweiler, Juan Gris (London, 1947), p. 29
241. "Everything leads one to believe . . ." Breton, Manifesto du Surréalisme, (NRF, 1963), p. 76
241. "The house I live in . . ." Nadeau, p. 321
242. "the crystal paperweight . . ." P, p. 17
242. "There is in man . . ." O, p. 31
242. "In opium, euphoria leads . . ." Ibid., p. 10
243. "One memory strikes me . . ." Ibid., p. 122
244. "Yes, my dear Jacques . . ." PC, II, p. 27
245. "Confronted with this man's ease . . ." Ibid., p. 41
245. "If He counts us . . ." Ibid., p. 48
245. "Paris tears me apart . . ." Ibid., p. 27
246. "Nothing fascinates me more . . ." Ibid., p. 42
248. "When I think about it calmly . . ." Sachs (A), p. 127
249. "He was a boy of great stature . . ." Wescott, The Grandmothers (New York 1950), p. 125
251. "A little half-moon . . ." from "The Sailors" in Good-bye Wisconsin
253. "furnished with fake . . ." Francis Rose, p. 72

PAGE

254. "a cabbage reeling . . ." Ibid., p. 75
255. "Mother remained . . ." Ibid., p. 76
256. "The reason for Barbette's success . . ." In volume 9 (Edition Marguerat), p. 261
257. "I was living . . ." CO, p. 25
258. "Cocteau mimed the roles . . ." Arnaud, p. 59
260. "Give me music . . ." Kochno in *Le Ballet* (Paris, 1954), p. 258
262. "I feel bruised . . ." Mariano, p. 176
263. "Marcel Herrand having decided . . ." O, p. 153
264. "A living room . . ." T, I, p. 125
264. "Ladies and gentlemen, this prologue . . ." Ibid., p. 126
265. "What does the marble . . ." Ibid., p. 156
266. "Art is born of coitus . . ." O, p. 142
267. "Supplanting the object . . ." Siohan, p. 101
267. "It was already true . . ." Nadeau, p. 205
268. "The first person to arrive . . ." White, pp. 62 ff.
269. "a medium not dead . . ." Stravinsky, p. 125
269. "I wished to leave the play . . ." Craft (C), p. 4
269. "I thought that I could not do better . . ." Stravinsky, p. 125
270. "What is purely Cocteau's . . ." Craft (C), p. 5
271. "I ask myself . . ." Lifar, p. 309
272. "It may have seemed to Ernst . . ." Ibid., p. 307
274. "Working with him . . ." Markevitch, p. 84
275. "Dima, we Parisians . . ." Duke, p. 196
277. "Yes, Bernard . . ." Faÿ, p. 281
278. "My very dear Bernard . . ." Ibid., p. 282
279. "Be assured that primitive man . . ." Interview with Rouzaud (Marguerat, vol. 9), p. 363
279. "I am an example . . ." Ibid., p. 350
280. "Bernard, say whatever you like . . ." Faÿ, p. 284
280. "Jean has received . . ." in *Empreintes*, Cocteau issue, Nos. 7–8, 1950
282. "Too many and too limiting . . ." LB, p. 6
282. "What futile fluster . . ." Gide (H). I, p. 942
282. "For Passavant, the work of art . . ." Gide (B), p. 98
284. "Singular beings . . ." ET, p. 235
285. "Servants of an inflexible law . . ." Ibid., p. 236
286. "An unesthetic act . . ." O, p. 280
286. "I couldn't describe it . . ." DD, p. 114

Chapter 9: Self-Impersonations

289. "She withdraws . . ." Kyrou, p. 145
293. "At that time . . ." *Paris Review*, Summer–Fall 1964
294. "We admired . . ." Fraigneau (A), p. 69
301. "At the Vieux-Colombier . . ." SP, preface
302. "At Hyères, with the Noailles . . ." Gide (A), I, p. 963
305. "The doctor of the clinic . . ." PS, p. 140
307. "That sojourn . . ." Bourdet (A), preface
307. "*La Bande*, as we called . . ." Cooper, pp. 232 ff.
308. "I have never felt any connection . . ." *Paris Review*, Summer–Fall, 1964
311. "That this relentlessly . . ." *Figaro*, April 13, 1934
311. "I had read him scarcely at all. . . ." Review *Adam 300*, 1965, p. 139
312. "To speak to Cocteau . . ." Guggenheim, p. 48
313. "History is composed of inexactitudes . . ." PS, p. 229
313. "A curtain is falling . . ." Ibid., p. 15
313. "a few obscenities . . ." Gide (A), I, p. 942

PAGE

313. "Why are we fooling around . . ." In *Empreintes*, Nos. 7–8, 1950
314. "I admire Jules Verne . . ." PV, p. 226
315. "It was my purpose . . ." Ibid., p. 149
315. "A father lets wind . . ." Ibid., p. 243
316. "Two poets follow . . ." Ibid., p. 279
316. "leaping down the staircase . . ." Ibid., p. 280
317. "You can imagine . . ." Ibid.
317. "We had more than a glut . . ." Chaplin, p. 418
318. "I admired Cocteau for a long time . . ." Piaf, p. 165
319. "I should like to make a catalogue . . ." Beaton, p. 280
321. "The combat to which Jeff Dickson . . ." Peeters, *Les Monstres Sacrés du Ring*, "Panama Al Brown"
321. "Refuse to fight . . ." Ibid.
322. "His chin resting . . ." Ibid.
322. "If Monsieur Cocteau sees himself . . ." Ibid.
322. "My advice was not . . ." Ibid.
324. "Do you realize . . ." Goudeket, p. 210

Chapter 10: The Face of an Angel

327. "I felt intimidated, lost . . ." Marais, p. 44
327. "He treated the idiotic little boy . . ." Ibid., p. 45
327. "I believe that my physical . . ." Ibid., p. 51
329. "the role of a young modern man . . ." Marais, p. 54
330. "Their dialogue dazzled me . . ." Ibid., p. 56
330. "Their love and ferocious quarrels . . ." Ibid., p. 54
332. " 'I have it! . . . .' " Ibid., p. 61
333. "Didn't he consider . . ." Cocéa; p. 122
334. "I never offered. . . ." Ibid.
335. "Rousseau committed the worst . . ." PC, I, p. 282
337. "After the *maîtres* . . ." Claude Mauriac (B), pp. 60 ff.
340. "It isn't uncommon . . ." FP, p. 167

Chapter 11: Occupational Hazards

345. "Beginning in the afternoon . . ." Sachs (D), p. 22
347. "*Tout Paris*, literally . . ." Ibid., p. 26
347. "One imagines . . ." Ibid., p. 30
349. "It was four in the afternoon . . ." Ibid., p. 38
352. "When Laubreaux grossly insulted . . ." Beauvoir, p. 385
354. "I haven't seen the symptoms . . ." Ibid., p. 361
354. "Jacques Bonsergent . . ." Ibid., p. 376
354. "Now we are allowed . . ." Deharme, pp. 77 ff.
355. "The next day . . ." Sachs (D), p. 162
356. "Had dinner with Cocteau . . ." Deharme, entry for December 2, 1942
357. "I am absolutely astonished . . ." Ibid., 19 July, 1942
357. "Cocteau looked just like . . ." Beauvoir, p. 462
359. "It was that prick . . ." Crespelle, p. 218
359. "apart from venal subjects . . ." Jünger, entry for August 21, 1943
362. "I made it my duty . . ." Fraigneau (C), p. 151
364. "Cocteau spoke about a trial . . ." Jünger, entry for July 20, 1943
364. "In conversation as in his writing . . ." Beauvoir, p. 459
365. "he knows that darkness . . ." in *Empreintes*, Nos. 7–8, 1950
366. "When I got back to the embassy . . ." Nicolson, p. 440
367. "When the door opened . . ." in *Adam 300*, pp. 164 ff.
368. "I was learning for the first time . . ." Cooper, D., p. 235

PAGE

369. "A thing long dreamed of . . ." BB, p. 22
370. "With distance I become aware . . ." Ibid., p. 77
370. "I behold myself . . ." Ibid., p. 133
371. "On the way to Saint-Maurice . . ." Ibid., p. 158
371. "I sometimes wonder . . ." Fraigneau (A), p. 22
372. "First major reportage . . ." BB., p. 60
372. "his face, as so often happens . . ." Léautaud; *Journal*, XV, p. 359

Chapter 12: Santo-Sospir and Canonization

375. "From the time she was fifteen . . ." RF, p. 28
378. "For us, Blanche . . ." Ibid., p. 21
379. "If Malraux was absent . . ." Léautaud; *Journal*, XVII, p. 65
386. "Occasionally when we were . . ." Gilot, p. 302
389. "I call ethics . . ." JI, p. 15
389. "The guilty man . . ." B, p. 133
390. "Getting down to essentials . . ." P. H. Simon, *Mauriac par Lui-même* (Paris, 1963), p. 175
390. "I wonder if I could be . . ." JI, pp. 36 ff.
393. "Heart attacks are treated . . ." *Figaro Littéraire*, August 28, 1954
395. "He used to dance . . ." Ibid., March 12, 1955
397. "You are acquainted . . ." PC, II, p. 140
398. "Perhaps the proverb holds true . . ." Léautaud; *Journal*, XVIII, p. 281
401. "It is generally known . . ." *Figaro Littéraire*, September 24, 1960
404. "Anticonformist conformism . . ." *La Chapelle Saint Pierre* (Monaco, 1957), p. 1
405. "This film shall be far more austere . . ." *Adam 300*, p. 161
409. "A journalist calls asking . . ." Craft (D), p. 244
410. "Edith Piaf dies consumed . . ." *Figaro*, October 19, 1963
411. "I'm amazed . . ." Ibid.

Index